The Outlaws

Jason Vail

The Outlaws

THE OUTLAWS

Copyright 2014, by Jason Vail

All rights reserved, including the right to reproduce this book or portions thereof in any form.

A Hawk Publishing book.

Cover illustration copyright Danielsbphoto/dreamstime.com.

Cover design and maps by Ashley Barber

ISBN-13: 978-1503051379
ISBN-10: 1503051374

Hawk Publishing
Tallahassee, FL 32312

ALSO BY JASON VAIL

Stephen Attebrook Mysteries

The Wayward Apprentice
Baynard's List
The Dreadful Penance
The Girl in the Ice

Lone Star Rising Series

Lone Star Rising: Voyage of the Wasp
Lone Star Rising: T.S. Wasp and the Heart of Texas

Martial Arts

Medieival and Renaissance Dagger Combat

The Outlaws

The Outlaws

The Outlaws

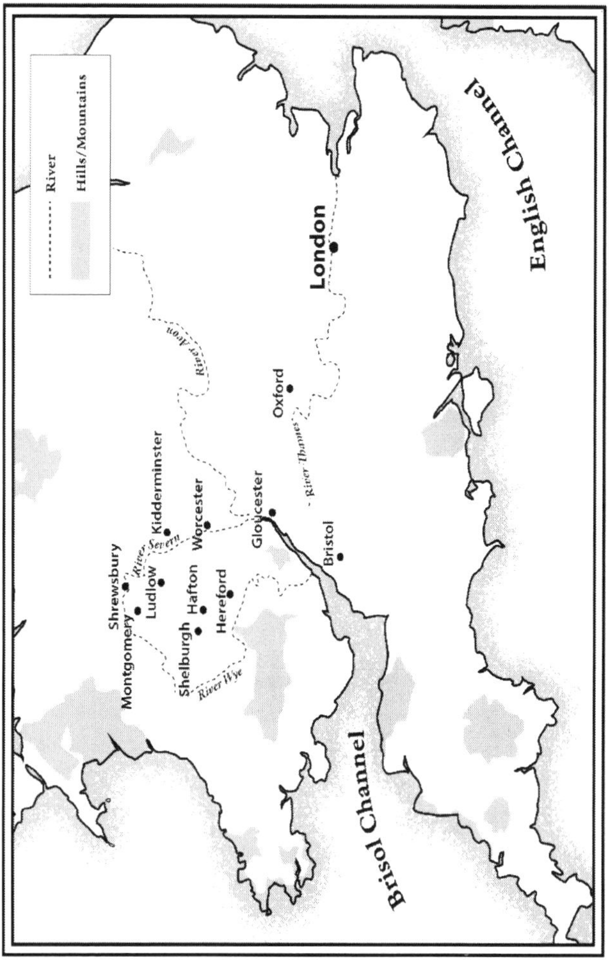

River
Hills/Mountains
London
English Channel
Brisol Channel
River Avon
Oxford
River Thames
Gloucester
Bristol
Worcester
Kidderminster
River Severn
Shrewsbury
Montgomery
Ludlow
Hafton
Hereford
Shelburgh
River Wye

The Outlaws

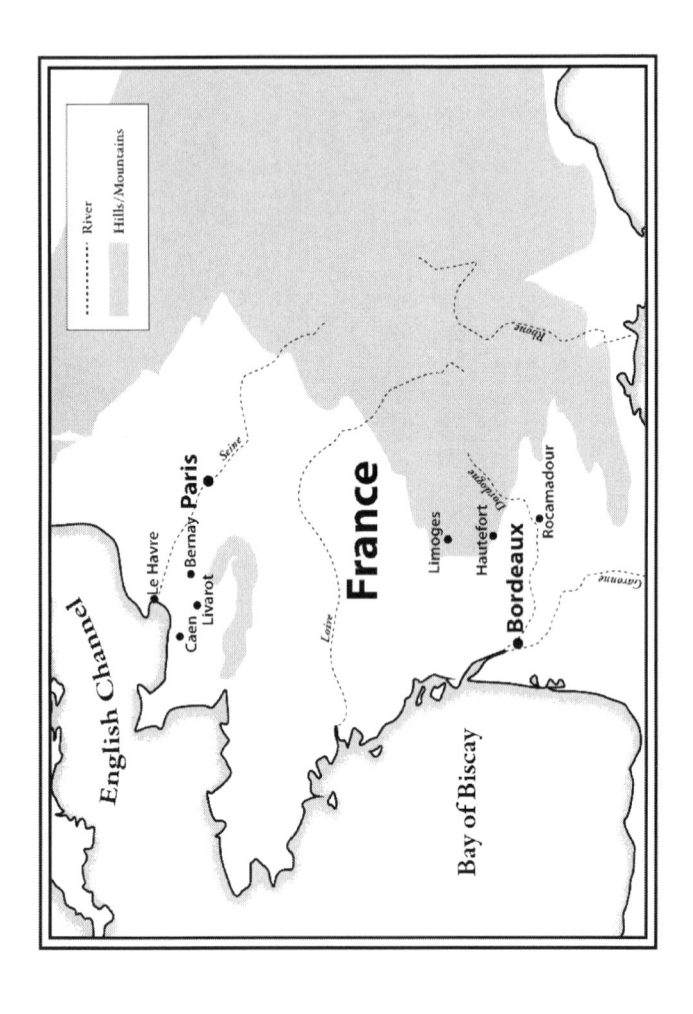

PART 1
1173-1175

The Outlaws

CHAPTER 1

Shelburgh village, England
October 1173

Matilda Attebrook awoke from the nightmare naked in the yard.

She wasn't aware at first that she was naked or that she was in the yard. She opened her eyes to find her arms locked around her knees, shivering from more than the cold air of the pre-dawn.

A child's voice sounded behind her: "Ma, what's the matter?"

Matilda's head snapped around. Her oldest son Robert, a skinny boy of ten, stood in the doorway of the house, clutching a blanket around his shoulders. Only then did it register where she was.

She shot up straight and glanced toward the lane, which was almost invisible through fog and gloom, giving the yard and the house the aspect of being apart from the world. Tendrils of fog slithered along the ground. It was acceptable to be naked in bed; most people slept that way. It was another thing to roam the garden with your bottom showing.

"Mum?" Robert asked when he got no immediate answer.

"Nothing. It's nothing."

"You sure?"

"Thought I heard something. In the cabbage."

Robert craned his head toward the garden where the late cabbage was hiding behind a palisade of tall grass and a little wicker fence, which was meant to keep out the pigs. There was little enough to eat that the notion of some creature, whether two- or four-legged, stealing the cabbage was a matter of serious concern. As man of the house while his father was away, its safety was his responsibility. "I don't hear anything."

"Neither do I," she said, marching past him into the house. "Now."

The Outlaws

Matilda took her undershift and dress from the peg by the bed and put them on. It was too early to be up, but it was no use going back to bed. The twins, Alice and Agnes, watched her from the bed with eyes as round as the moon, while their brother Brian slept on beside them.

"Lie back down," Matilda ordered the girls and they sank beneath the blanket.

Robert, meanwhile, was fumbling his way back across the house's single room to his pallet. He barked his shin on an unseen bench and said, "Shit."

"Mind your tongue," Matilda snapped, although she felt some sympathy and wondered how she had made it with her eyes closed around the hearth, the single trestle table, the two benches and their few stools, which besides the bed and her loom were the only furniture they had.

"Sorry," Robert said.

"It's Sunday. You shouldn't curse."

"Right, Mum," Robert said, perhaps hoping she might mistake the appearance of obedience for its substance. No doubt when he ran with that gang of rough housers from the village they cursed to their hearts' content, as long as none of their elders could hear them.

"And not you," she said. The pigs were rustling behind the board fence separating the bier from the rest of the house. The sow had heard the commotion and she was snuffling at the gate. There were acorns in the wood and she was anxious to be at them.

"Not me what?"

"Not you. Can't have you laying about all day. Might as well let the pig out. Just make sure she doesn't decide to have the garden for breakfast. And fetch some water."

"Oh, Mum," he said. "Just a little longer. The sun's not up yet."

"Get going." She knew the injustice of the order. Sunday was a lay-in-bed-late day, but she didn't want him watching her. She had to have some time yet. He was canny, that boy, and he might guess what she was feeling.

Robert threw on his shirt and renavigated around the household obstacles, bare feet crunching on the rushes. He paused near the doorway, silhouetted by silver fog, a stick caricature of a man, as if he was thinking of making one final plea for normalcy. But he seemed to think better of it. Taking the switch by the bier gate, he ushered the sow and her precious little brood out of the house, and plodded into the soup, which had begun to glow with the dawn. A shouted "Ho! Ho! Get on, you, get on," told her some of the piglets had made a break for the cabbages. Then the back gate clapped shut and she knew the garden was safe for the morning.

Matilda sank onto a bench and rested her head in her hands. The despair was almost more than she could stand without crying out. It wasn't right she should feel this way. There was no reason to. It was silly. Foolish. Weak. But she couldn't help it. She always worried when Harold was away. Something bad could happen to him: an accident, a sudden illness, a bully with a knife at a tavern. Not that any of these things couldn't occur in the village. They could. His absence just magnified the possibility. If anything happened to him, there was her weaving and what she could bring in working for others standing between the family and starvation. She learned what starving was like when she had been a slave in Wales and it wasn't a pretty way to die.

Harold had been gone a week now, which was a very long time for him to be away. He made their living by doing odd jobs as a carpenter, but in reality at anything anyone would pay for. A man named Alecoc had hired him and others in the area to help put up a barn. It didn't take a week for all those men to throw up a simple barn. He should be back by now.

She imagined him laying over somewhere drinking up all the money he had made. But other men might do that; not him.

"It's nonsense," she said to herself. "Just nonsense."

Robert came back from the brook, lugging the pail. She could see him pause in the yard, his outline fudged by the fog.

The Outlaws

He put the pail down and rubbed his thighs. When he reached the doorway, she saw he had spilled a good deal of the water on his legs and feet, which were muddy from dirt in the yard. He put the pail down by the hearth.

"I told you, always wear your boots in this weather," she said. "You'll catch your death."

"But they always get wet. "ou know how I hate wet shoes."

Matilda fumbled in the dark by the plank where she laid out her pots and trenchers. She tossed him a rag. "Well, dry yourself with this. Can't afford to have you sick. Your father doesn't bring in enough as it is."

Robert gave her a sharp look, as though he expected her to bring up the prospect of more work. She and Harold had argued over this very thing just before he left: that Robert was getting big enough to hire out rather than provide sporadic help as he did now. Harold had maintained he was too small yet; give him another year.

Robert finished drying and cleaning himself. He put down the rag and asked, "Shouldn't we light the fire?"

Matilda raised her head with great effort to look at him. "I suppose so."

She made to push away from the table and take care of the chore herself, but he beat her to it. He removed the clay cover from the embers on the hearth, which sat on an earthen bank held up by boards, and added dry leaves to get the fire started. Presently there was a little flame crackling. A driblet of smoke curled toward the hole in the roof and the room began to feel warmer inside.

"I'm hungry," Robert said.

"You're always hungry, mouse," Matilda said.

"I am not a mouse anymore. I am a fox." Robert smiled. It was like the dawn itself. He had his father's face and dark blond hair with its strands of gold and that same sweet smile. She forgave so much for that smile, both in his father and him. More than she should. Robert spent too much time with that layabout uncle of his, Nicholas, shooting arrows, wrestling and practice fighting with sticks rather than working. Harold defended this play. "Small men need to know how to fight more than big men," he said. Matilda did not approve of fighting. If she didn't find some kind of craft for Robert, who displayed no talent for carpentry and even smaller interest, he could end up a soldier, which made her shudder. Most soldiers were just brigands drawing pay. Or he'd be a ditch digger or a hedge cutter, and poorer than they were now. What decent girl would want such a poor man? She was determined that none of this would happen.

"If you were a true fox, I would have to send you out to find your own breakfast," she said.

His smiled broadened, and took on a trace of slyness. "I am a true fox and I will just hunt here." Then said: "I can spell fox. F-O-X."

Matilda was startled.

"And I can spell my name," and he did so. "And I can write them too." He got down on the floor, spread the rushes to expose the dirt beneath and made the letters with a finger.

They were just marks in the dirt to Matilda, who could not read. Her father had not thought girls needed to read, although he had seen that her brothers had been lettered. She said, "Who taught you that?"

"The vicar. Yesterday. While you were out ditching."

"Hmm. I had no idea. And I thought you were supposed to be trimming hedges." She nodded, pleased and thrilled. The vicar already had taught him all the letters and how to make them, but she had not realized Robert had gone beyond that. "And I suppose you expect a reward for this feat, Master Fox?"

"Breakfast will do."

"Will it, then?" She could not resist the smile that tugged at her lips. Matilda felt less depressed at Harold's absence. Robert often had this effect on her, as on other people. She opened the bread box. To her horror, a fat mouse stared up at her. Furious, she swatted at the mouse, which hopped out of the box with amazing speed, plopped onto the ground and

The Outlaws

scurried through a gap in the wattle wall of the house. "God's blood," she blurted, forgetting what she had said about not cursing, "how did he get in there?"

The mouse had chewed a sizable hole in the loaf. She tore off the part on which it had been dining and threw it into the bier, where the pig would find it later. She gave half the loaf to Robert, whose eyes widened with surprise and greed. He never got a half loaf all to himself. Then he glanced at Alice and Agnes, the four-year-olds, who were sitting up in bed, their yellow hair in tangled halos about their heads, blue eyes watching the half loaf in Robert's hands. Reluctantly, Robert started to break off pieces for the twins.

"No, fox, it's yours," Matilda said. "Best go easy on it, though. It's got to last you the day."

"Why?" Robert asked.

"Because I'm sending you to Alecoc's. I want you to check on your father."

Robert looked relieved. A journey to Alecoc's was not work. It was an adventure. "Now? I'll miss church."

Matilda nodded. "Yes."

Robert smiled. He hated church and always fidgeted and made noise in the back with the other children which embarrassed Matilda when others called attention to it.

"And put your boots on and take your cloak," Matilda said, as he started for the door. "It looks like it might rain today."

"Right, Mum."

Alecoc's was an hour away on foot, across the river and through the forest in the land of the Mortimers.

Robert paused at the foot of the wooden bridge over the river. The toll-taker, who occupied a booth at the village side, was not on duty today, this being Sunday. Robert sat in the booth for a moment, pretending to be the toll-taker. It was an unsatisfactory occupation until two imaginary knights came up and asked for passage, which he refused no matter how much money they offered him. When they wanted to fight, he turned his walking stick into a sword, launching terrible blows from one guard and then another, and sent the imaginary knights scurrying on their way. A movement caught the corner of his eye. The hayward and his wife and four children had come out of their house down the road and the daughters were pointing at him and laughing. The hayward's wife had a disapproving look on her face, but she always looked like that at everyone. Robert stuck his tongue out at her. Later in church, she was certain to tell his mother he had been disrespectful, but he didn't care. He was on an adventure and he was not going to let anything spoil it. Besides, he would say he stuck his tongue out at the girls, not the wife.

When the hayward and his brood had gone up the road, Robert gathered a handful of stones from the river bank and, pausing at the middle of the bridge, cast one stone after another into the black current. Robert loved the river. It wasn't much of a river; a boy could throw a stone across from one bank to the other with room to spare and almost everywhere you could wade across. In fact, one favorite pastime was for gangs of boys to have a battle by flinging stones at each other across it. The river was dark and mysterious, though, a wonder that so much water could come from somewhere high in Wales and run all the way to the sea. Robert wished he could go to the sea.

Robert heard horses approaching behind him just before he reached the footpath beyond the bridge. Their hooves boomed on the wooden planks of the bridge. There were two, ridden to Robert's surprise by boys a couple of years older than he was. They were both carrying crossbows; must be going hunting. Robert recognized the boys as squires from the castle. One was the earl's bastard son, Eustace, who had just returned in disgrace from the abbey school where he had been sent to become a priest and had somehow failed. Eustace had a big bruise on his cheek from where the earl had hit him two days ago. The other was a boy named Reginald le Bec. Eustace gave Robert a stony glance and then rode past.

The Outlaws

Reginald, however, cut at Robert with his whip. It happened so fast that Robert didn't have time to duck. The blow landed on his shoulder and was so painful that he could not stifle a yelp. Reginald laughed as his horse carried him out of range. Eustace did not even turn around to see what had happened.

Robert found a stone and almost threw it at Reginald, who was still laughing as he and Eustace drew off. But, hefting the stone, Robert thought better of it. Those two boys could chase him down on their horses and when they caught him, they'd beat him up. He was too small yet to fight even one of them alone. So he stood at the edge of the road, fuming, hating being small and weak, his shoulder smarting. He pulled back his collar to check the damage. He had a nasty weal but was not cut.

When the riders had gone round the nearest bend, Robert found the footpath and turned in. The path skirted the river for half a hundred yards, and then some fields before it turned into the forest. The forest was dark despite the fact all the trees were bare, and as always, frightening. There were supposed to be wolves still in these woods and even bears. Wolves had never attacked anyone he knew, but once at the Leominster fair, he had heard about a girl near his age being killed and dragged away and eaten. Robert looked around, ready for the wolves. He wished now that he had brought his bow. He had been so excited about the prospect of the adventure that he had rushed away without it.

Although Robert was thinner than many of the boys his age, he was quick and he made good time. In a quarter hour, he had reached the fork in the path: left led north toward Knighton; right angled southeast to Alecoc's.

Shortly after Robert started down the right fork, he saw the ravens. There must have been a dozen perched in the bare branches ahead, an unholy looking congregation. The sight of them made him shiver with anxiety. Robert had been well educated about forest spirits, and he thought this might be a gathering of them. People said they fed on souls as well as flesh. It was bad luck at best to walk under such a flock. To avoid them, he left the path and cut through the wood to the right, intending to circle around and pick up the path beyond them.

The wind changed, with a faint rattle of branches. Robert caught the sour, gut-curling scent of rotting meat.

Glancing back through a wicket of branches, he saw the feet.

Booted in brown leather, they lay in the path beneath the ravens.

The boots and feet were attached to patched, dull brown hose. The boots looked like any man's boots, but the patches on the brown hose caused Robert's heart to beat faster and his mouth to go dry.

He forgot about the ravens. They weren't interested in him.

When he emerged onto the path, he saw the rest of the body. A fat raven sat on its chest, flapping away to a low branch at his appearance.

The dead man was his father.

His head had been almost cut off.

The ravens had been eating his eyes.

Robert sank to his hands and knees beside the body. He reached out to his father's face with trembling hands. But he could not touch him. So he settled for straightening father's collar, stiff and crinkly with black dried blood, as if somehow that might give father comfort. He crouched on his heels as the trembling grew into great waves of shudders. His mouth fell open. He wanted to scream, but he could not more than grunt; nor could he cry. He just rocked back and forth, clutching his knees, stomach clenched, mouth contorted.

Unimpressed by Robert's grief, one of the ravens decided it was safe enough to descend again. The fat black bird landed so close that Robert could almost touch it. It cocked its head and regarded him as if to say, don't you dare bother me, boy.

Robert snatched his walking stick and held it as if to strike the arrogant bird. "Who did this!" he screamed. "Who did this!"

The Outlaws

The big raven did not answer. It jumped into the air and flapped to a low branch.

Robert clambered to his feet, swaying.

"Who did this?" Robert whispered to the forest. But it did not answer either.

Robert sank crossed-legged on the path, head in his hands. He remained there for a long time, eyes closed, hoping when he opened them the world would have turned back to the way it was.

A rustling in the branches brought Robert back to the world. He looked round and saw that the ravens were growing restless.

He took a deep breath, then another and then a third.

He emptied his sack, which he spread across his father's ravaged face and then covered him with his cloak. There was no way the ravens could peck through these.

"You can't have him," Robert said to the ravens in the trees. "He belongs to us."

He waved his walking stick, jumping to strike the ravens in the lower branches, and the flock scattered. He threw the half-loaf and cheese as far as he could. Let them eat bread and not men.

Then he ran back to the village to tell his mother.

CHAPTER 2

Shelburgh
October 1173

"The steward's here," Eadwin said, approaching Matilda wearing a worried expression. "He wants to see you."

Matilda rested her tankard on her lap and scanned the throng assembled in the village churchyard for Harold's wake. The yard was choked with people. The yard was often crowded and festive after mass, but this day was exceptional. Harold had been popular in the village and just about everybody in Shelburgh who could walk and some who couldn't were here. "Where?" she said.

"By the gate," Eadwin, who had been one of Harold's closest friends, said. "There."

Matilda nodded. Earl Roger ruled here, but the steward ran things, both in the castle and in the village. For him to seek out someone like her so far down the social ladder was odd in the extreme.

She put her tankard on the folding chair and walked around the fresh mound of earth to the gate.

People saw her coming and, judging by their expressions, they knew something was up. They fell silent at her approach and drew out of her way, until she stood before a tall man whose face had the sagging look of a wax figure left too long near the fire. Richard d'Evry's rheumy eyes fell on her, drinking in the way she looked.

Then those eyes flicked beyond her to the crowd in the yard, where the nearest spectators were watching them with the looks seen by bettors at a bear-baiting.

"You asked for me, your honor?" Matilda asked.

He nodded his large head and smiled. "I wanted a word with you. Walk with me, will you?"

He turned away, and she didn't have a choice but to follow. Even though the family was free, unlike most people in the village, they still had to answer to him for the five acres they rented in the village fields.

The Outlaws

They crossed the commons and reached the road heading toward the river. "I wanted to discuss," he said, "your situation."

"Our rents are paid for this quarter," she said. She had been with Harold when he made the October payment two weeks ago, the day before he left for Alecoc's. There were witnesses: she struggled to remember who else had been there.

"And next quarter? What are you going to do with two half grown boys who can't bring in a half penny a day between them?"

Matilda experienced a moment of relief that Richard was concerned about the future and not the past. "I can weave and sew."

"Perhaps, but it won't bring in enough. It hasn't up to now."

"I'll manage," Matilda said with more certainty than she felt. She had a box of pennies buried in the dirt under the bed, and she'd raid it when she had to. But eventually, she knew, it would run out. When they couldn't make their rent, the steward was certain to expel them. Born in Ireland of Danish parents, she had no family in this country to fall back on, other than Harold's good-for-nothing brother, Nicholas, who was a poacher and some-time fletcher when he bothered to put aside his ale cup, and could not be counted on to help. They'd be just another group of beggars wandering from village to village, and starving in the woods. She'd been so consumed by grief during the past week that she'd given no thought to any of this. But the bubble of fear that normally was not very far away began to boil.

"Bravely said, but you have your children to think about. I thought I might offer you an opportunity."

"What opportunity?"

"Respite for your children. Peace of mind."

She regarded him, unable to speak. The black thought of what he was about to propose blossomed in her mind and clamped down her tongue.

"You have only to grant me ... certain liberties. And in exchange, I will see that your wants are satisfied and your children protected."

Her heart pounded in her ears so that the noise of the wake receded. She had the urge to shout "NO!" in his face. But she had to answer carefully. He was a powerful man who could make life difficult, even impossible, if offended. "I am flattered that your honor thought me worthy of such attention, but I am not able to think about such things now."

"Ah, your grief. It must be overwhelming."

"It will be a long time before I can forget," she said, thinking not of Harold's face but how he smelled when they brought back his body.

"It was a terrible thing, a tragedy." He stopped walking and faced her. "You will think about it, though?"

"Your generosity is more than an ordinary person should expect."

"A pretty answer," he said, signaling to a young man on a horse on the other side of the commons. The young man spurred his horse forward, leading another. "Enjoy your wake."

"What did Richard want?" the alewife asked as if she didn't care when in fact it was obvious she cared very much.

"He wants to fuck me." Matilda put down the tankard and stared over her shoulder to the churchyard, where the wake was still going on despite her absence. She thought about going back, but she was feeling a little drunk on free ale, and she didn't want to face any questions. Questions like this one, which she had answered more honestly than was prudent.

"Most men do, you know. Now that Harold's gone, I suppose they'll be lined up clear to my house."

"It's a curse," Matilda said. "I wish I was ugly. That's all men've wanted since I had my first period. That's why I was stolen in the first place." Ever since she was a child, people

The Outlaws

had told her how beautiful she was. For some, it was the color of her hair, yellow as ripening wheat. For others, it was her eyes, pale blue as the sky. For some it was her breasts; for yet others her hips, wide and inviting. She didn't feel beautiful, though. She thought her nose was crooked, her freckles off-putting, and her ears stuck out too much. And by this time, she had borne four children. Yet she had retained her shape. She was grateful for that. But it was such a burden, and had brought more trouble than benefit.

"Well, that actually turned out all right, didn't it? You'd not have found Harold otherwise."

"No," Matilda said. "I wouldn't." That had been just over eleven years ago. Harold had been a soldier then. He and his best friends Eadwin and Grelli the huntsman had been in King Henry's army, and found her chained to a post in a Welsh farmyard. He had put his cloak around her and had been kind even though the Welsh had left her covered in shit and smelling like a privy. She had loved him ever since.

"Well," the alewife said, "some women don't see it as a curse."

"I don't feel right doing it for money." Screwing anybody for any reason would be an infidelity to Harold. Matilda fixed an eye on the alewife, all two of her. "You don't do it for money."

"Ah, no. That's true. I've Aelgifa for that trade." Aelgifa was the village whore. The alewife grinned. "But she'll make room if you change your mind."

"Bitch."

The alewife threw back her head and laughed, and Matilda laughed with her.

"I don't know what I'm going to do," Matilda said.

"I expect one thing you're not going to do is give it to Richard."

"No. I won't."

"You didn't tell him that, though."

"No."

"You can't put him off forever."

"I don't want to hurt his feelings."

"I've thought you many things, Matilda, but not tender-hearted."

They shared another laugh.

"You could get married again," the alewife said. "That might solve your Richard problem."

Matilda didn't answer right away, and when she did, she said, "I've got to find work for Robert. Real work. Not just ditching and hedging and chasing crows and breaking clods. Work that pays."

The alewife looked thoughtful. She leaned on her elbows. "It's a long shot, but I know someone you might see."

"Who?"

"That wool merchant who comes through every summer, Jean of Gloucester."

"He wants to sleep with me too?"

"I'm sure he does, now that I think about it. But his clerk, that fellow named Jack or Jacques or something."

"Jacques. His name's Jacques. He's French."

"Whatever. He said something to Aelgifa about them losing a stable boy who can manage pack horses. Robert knows how to do that, doesn't he?"

"It's been months since they were here. They've probably got someone now."

"But they don't."

"What are you talking about?"

"Jacques sent Aelgifa a letter. It was in the letter. It came yesterday. The fool is smitten, but this is what she gets for letting him have it free."

"No," Matilda sputtered in disbelief. The thought of anyone receiving a letter in the village was mind-boggling, let alone a letter for Aelgifa. And more amazing still: it had come yesterday and she was just now hearing about it.

"So all you have to do is get to Gloucester."

"Gloucester." Matilda was dismayed. "That's a long way away." She had no idea how far, except that it was somewhere off to the south.

The Outlaws

There was shouting from the churchyard. Matilda turned to see a pair of boys had squared off with singlesticks. These were used for play, but the boys were hitting at each other as hard as they could, egged on by the crowd. The combatants collided at grips and fell over the stone fence about the yard, where they rolled to their feet and continued. The revelers spilled into the commons to watch.

She spotted Robert on the edge of the crowd watching the fight. Harold's younger brother, Nicholas, stood next to him. Nicholas looked so much like his brother that Robert could be mistaken for his son. But where Harold had been sunny, Nicholas was morose. He drank more than he should and was given to fighting. Over her objections — and with Harold's approval — he had taught Robert the singlestick, as well as how to wrestle and fletch an arrow, which was his normal trade when he wasn't off somewhere in someone's army. She feared Nicholas' influence on the boy.

Matilda put down her tankard and crossed the commons to them. Everyone was so focused on the battle that no one noticed her coming, and Robert was not aware of her until she put a hand on his shoulder.

"I haven't done anything," he said.

"Not yet," Matilda said. "Come away." She drew in a deep breath, trying to clear her head of the ale and dispel thoughts of Gloucester. It would mean breaking up the family if it came to pass, because once Robert went to Gloucester he'd be gone for good.

Then she remembered that the family was already broken.

She would have cried if there weren't people who would see.

Gloucester
October 1173

Matilda stepped up to the shop window on Saint John's Lane, hoping deep in her heart that this was just a fool's errand.

A young man with black hair looked up from a writing desk in the far corner where he was scribbling something when he became aware she was standing there. "Yes?"

"Are you Jacques?" Matilda said.

The young man frowned. He wiped ink from his fingers with a rag. "I am."

"I have a letter for you."

Jacques looked surprised. "You do?"

"From a mutual friend. We were coming here and she asked me to deliver it."

"She?" Apprehension dawned, due to the fact that Jacques didn't write many letters to women in distant places. Jacques hurried around the desk.

Matilda held out the letter. Jacques snatched the folded parchment and cut the seal with his knife. He read the letter with the wide-eyed eagerness of a starving man having just been given a meal, turning his back just enough to prevent Matilda from reading it. He needn't have bothered. She knew the letter almost by heart, because she'd been there when Aelgifa had dictated it to the vicar at her suggestion. Not that Aelgifa had needed much prodding once the suggestion of making a reply had been put to her with the dividend that delivery was free. She seemed to like Jacques.

"Master Jean wouldn't happen to be here, would he?" Matilda asked.

Jacques turned back. "He might be. Why?"

"I just thought to say hello."

"He knows you?"

"Of course. He comes through Shelburgh every summer." Well, the last part was true, at any rate.

Jacques tapped the letter on his fingertips, thinking. "All right. A moment, then."

"Oh," Matilda said, hating to have to say the words, "Aelgifa said you mentioned you had lost your stable boy. Is it true?"

Jacques paused in the doorway. "Yes."

The Outlaws

"Have you replaced him?" she asked, trying as hard as she could to make the question sound off hand.

The effort must not have been successful, because Jacques glanced over the counter at Robert, whose attention was absorbed by a party of mummers who were just then trooping by.

"Not yet." He went out.

Jacques returned followed by a man about thirty carrying a roll of woolen fabric, which he stacked on top of a dozen others occupying shelves along the far wall. He turned to Matilda and regarded her with cool eyes. He wasn't what anyone would call handsome, but then neither was he repulsive, just ordinary: ordinary black hair, ordinary high forehead, ordinary pale face. The only disordinary thing about him was a goatee that might have worn better on an aristocrat rather than a middling prosperous wool merchant. Jacques said, "She wanted to see you."

Even with the goatee, Matilda recognized him as Jean the wool merchant. He said in an accent that was foreign and not Norman, "I'm sorry, I don't remember your name."

"Matilda Attebrook."

"Jacques says you know me."

"I know of you."

Jean nodded. "He must have heard wrong."

"I think he might have been carried away with his message."

"Perhaps. I heard you had delivered a letter. Normally, he is quite reliable." Jean rested his hands on the counter. "He says you asked about the stable boy."

"I did."

"For him?" Jean glanced at Robert, who had lost sight of the mummers and was now watching a cart holding a bear in a cage.

"He's a hard worker. He knows horses."

"He's rather small."

"He's big enough."

"Horses are large creatures, especially to such a small boy."

"He's been around them all his life."

"Being around them doesn't mean he knows anything about the work."

"If he doesn't work out, you can send him back."

"And what if I am in Chester and find him lacking?"

"By the end of the week you'll know."

Jean stroked his goatee. "I don't know."

"Then try him now. He will make an acceptable groom."

"I think I will." He beckoned them to enter the shop and led them through the house to the rear garden, where a small stable sat beside a gate to a back alley. Two of the three stalls were occupied. "Tack the roan."

Robert looked at Matilda and licked his lips in uncertainty. Although he had some experience with plow horses, he had next to none saddling riding horses: his exposure to a riding horse had been the practice the vicar had allowed on his nag before they had set out. She nodded encouragement, although now she was certain she had made a mistake coming here and that her wish for failure would be fulfilled, bringing embarrassment with it.

After some hesitation, Robert rummaged for currying brushes and a hoof pick. He led the roan out and tethered the halter to a ring by the door. Then with deft strokes he brushed her down. Matilda had a few tense moments when he struggled to lift the roan's hooves to pick them clean; but Robert managed the task without the horse falling on him or planting a hoof on a foot.

He found the saddle pad and laid it across the horse's back high on the withers. Matilda's hands twitched, since they wanted to readjust it as she thought the vicar had instructed. But she remainded still. The saddle came next, and because the top of Robert's head did not quite reach the height of the horse's back, there was a moment when Matilda thought he might fling it in the air to get it in place, which she was sure

The Outlaws

would not be satisfactory. But somehow, Robert managed to settle the saddle without a jar.

Then, for Matilda, came the most excruciating part: the bridle and bit. Bridles always seemed to her to be such a messy, inscrutable tangle, yet Robert sorted it out, and slid the bit into the horse's mouth without incident or a shriek from his mother, who worried about a loss of fingers. Horses have a nasty bite.

Jean said, without giving any indication whether Robert had passed the test, "You can untack her and put her up."

The two of them stood around until Robert had finished. Then Jean led them back through the house to the shop. He said, "Well, at least it's not his first time."

"No, it isn't," Matilda said.

Jean stared at the floor. "There was a post script to me in Jacques's letter."

Matilda looked at him, dumbfounded. She knew nothing about a post script.

"It seems you just lost your husband and you need to find a place for your boy."

Matilda nodded. The ground — and her bargaining position — seemed to settle beneath her feet. What could have possessed Aelgifa to say such a thing: unless it had been the alewife, who thought she was doing Matilda a favor?

"I am a charitable man, but charity is one thing. Business is another."

"I understand that," Matilda managed to say, dismay mingling with relief that she had failed. She would find something for Robert closer to home after all. "I'm sorry to bother you."

"Sorry? Hmmm. I will take him on. Wages will be a quarter penny a day, and room and board. He can't be worth more than that, raw and unlearned as he is."

"All right, but only for the first three months, then a half penny thereafter, if he proves himself, and a full penny a year from now." Matilda snapped her mouth shut, appalled that she had made such a reckless demand. Well, he could tell her goodbye and she would be happy with that.

Jean put his hands on his hips. "You walked all the way from Shelburgh — how many days, three? Four? To drive so hard a bargain?"

"He will give you good service. If he doesn't, send him home."

To her shock, Jean nodded. He called through the door, "Jacques! We've got our new stable boy! Show him the room in the loft."

Jacques came through the door and put a hand on Robert's shoulder.

"Can I say goodbye — outside, if you don't mind?" Matilda asked.

"Certainly," Jean said.

Matilda took Robert's hand and led him into the street. She bent down so their faces were close and said, "Work hard. Save every farthing. Deliver it all home when you come in the summer. We're depending on you."

Robert's lips quivered.

She said, "You won't fail us, will you, Robert?"

A tear leaked out of a corner of an eye and dribbled across his cheek. Matilda wiped it away with her fingers. She put her fingertips to her lips and tasted the salt.

"I won't," Robert said.

She straightened up. "Good boy. Now, there you go."

Robert rubbed his eyes and stepped into the shop.

Matilda turned her back on the shop and headed down the street, finding no consolation in success.

CHAPTER 3

Shelburgh castle
June 1175

The day Eustace FitzWalter first thought about killing his sister the plan came to him at breakfast. He was wary of the plan at first. It seemed too simple. Simple, but not easy. There had to be a flaw. He thought about it for a week, examining the idea from every side for defects and traps. But in the end, he was convinced he could do it, if he wanted to, without being caught, without anyone even suspecting it was murder.

On the day Eustace at last decided to act, he crossed the bailey to the chapel, a little free-standing stone building next to the hall. It was Sunday, but mid-afternoon, so the place should be deserted.

He opened the door and slipped in. The main room was small, capable of holding about fifteen or twenty people at a time. It was cool and dim inside and smelled damp.

Eustace crossed to the scriptorium at the back, where the chaplain who also served as the manor's chief clerk did his writing and kept the manor's most important documents. The door was open and he could hear voices.

He looked in and found his friend Reginald le Bec and two other squires about his age, fourteen. They were holding a boy about two years younger than they were: A skinny boy dressed in a peasant's gray shirt and brown hose. The boy's blond hair hung across his face, straw entwined in the long uncombed strands. Eustace recognized him when he looked up. The sight of the boy so took Eustace by surprise that for a moment he thought he was drowning. A kaleidoscope of memories cascaded through his head: the forest in autumn, gray and dark; a sense of deep desperation at having angered his father the earl for being sent home in disgrace from the abbey school; Grelli the huntsman's shocked face. With an effort he pushed the memories away. Now Eustace remembered that the boy, whose name was Robert, had been sent away to Gloucester to work for a wool merchant named

Jean of Calais, who was here now to bid on the manor's wool clip. Robert must have come with Jean.

"What's he doing here?" Eustace asked.

"We found him getting into the chaplain's books," Reginald said. "Look at this." He handed Eustace a wooden writing tablet, its surface coated with wax in which letters had been scratched with a bone stylus. When Eustace had been student at the abbey, he had had one just like it.

Eustace peered at the scratchings.

"What's it say?" Reginald asked.

"It's in Latin," Eustace said, looking up. "He's been copying something in Latin."

"Waste of time for the likes of him," Reginald spat. "What's he going to do with Latin, for God's sake? Cows don't speak Latin."

Eustace nodded in agreement. He shook the tablet. "Where did you get this?"

"It belongs to my master's wife." Robert glared at him. "She's teaching me to read and write and cypher as well. I'm going to be a clerk."

"You have no business learning to read," Eustace snapped.

"I am free. I can do what I like."

Eustace could not let this defiance go unanswered, since it had occurred in front of the other boys, so he leaned the tablet against the wall and stamped on it, breaking it in two.

"You'll pay for that," Robert snarled.

Eustace's eyes narrowed at this further defiance. This boy must be stupid. He said, "Don't be silly. I can do what I like with people like you, and there's nothing you can do about it. Like this." Eustace stepped forward and hit Robert in the stomach with his fist.

Robert grunted and sagged.

Eustace hit him again.

Reginald and the other boys let Robert go and he collapsed. Eustace kicked Robert a few times in the kidneys, while Robert curled into a ball, using his arms to protect his

The Outlaws

head. Despite the severity of the blows, Robert had yet to make a sound. Eustace paused to catch his breath.

Eustace could have continued the beating, if he had wanted to. Not that he got much pleasure out of it. Unlike Reginald, causing others pain gave Eustace no special satisfaction. Doing so was an exercise of power, and it was from power that respect grew. When he showed the others his power, the other boys became more manageable, which is what satisfied Eustace.

Then Eustace heard the latch on the chapel door rattle. Someone who didn't know the secret of the latch was having trouble getting in. It sometimes stuck and refused to open unless you knew the trick to it. Eustace said, "She's here. Not a sound out of anyone, understand? And keep him quiet."

"Right." Reginald grinned. He squatted down and whispered in Robert's ear, "Not a sound out of you, hear? Or I'll cut your throat."

Robert nodded.

"Can I have a piece of her when you're done?" one of the other boys asked.

Eustace grabbed the boy by the shirt and whispered, "If you so much as peep or show your head in there, I'll have your guts on the ground."

A year ago, such a threat would have been laughed at, but not now. Eustace had grown fast and he was now as tall and strong as the other boy, who was a year older. Moreover, Eustace's fighting skill had improved to the point that he was taken seriously as an opponent. When the squires fought with singlesticks, Eustace now gave beatings more often than he took them.

The other boy pushed Eustace away. He hissed, "All right. But next time I want a piece."

"Sure, next time," Eustace sneered and went out. Not on your life, he thought.

He stepped back into the chapel and shut the door to the chaplain's scriptorium. It all depended now on Bruette. Had she come to surrender, or just to tell him off, as a couple of the maids had done when he tried to seduce them, unimpressed with his status as the earl's bastard? Eustace didn't know, and the anticipation was painful.

He lifted the latch and pulled open the door. Bruette stood there, hands behind her back, a little smile on her face. She was no beauty: short and thin but with large breasts, wary dark eyes, a large nose, and a receding chin. Those breasts were her vocation; she was his baby sister's wet nurse. Eustace couldn't wait until he had a look at her breasts.

"Good day," Eustace said, afraid that his voice might fail him.

"Good day, my lord," she replied.

Eustace overlooked the mocking. She'd pay later, anyway. Instead, palms sweating, he thought about those large breasts.

She stepped up to him and took off her cap.

Her breasts brushed his chest. Good, he thought, as he pushed the door closed. He didn't need to talk. He cupped one of her breasts with both hands. He could feel her nipple tighten under his palm. He squeezed the nipple with his fingers; he might be young and not too experienced, but he knew how to do it right.

She moaned and took his hands in her's and pressed them to her. It amazed him how pillow-like breasts were. He bent and kissed her on the lips. She opened her mouth and her tongue brushed his lips, the first time he had ever kissed a woman like this. He nearly came right then. She sucked until he gave her his tongue, and he almost came again. He couldn't stand it.

They sank to the ground, the fragrant scent of her hair mingling with the sour aroma of old rushes beneath them.

Behind, he thought he heard tittering from beyond the door to the scriptorium. He wanted to laugh. Being watched made it more exciting. He would have to be careful it wasn't over too soon.

Robert heard voices in the other room: Eustace's and a girl's. Then it was quiet, except for the stealthy breathing of

The Outlaws

the three squires crowded around the door. One of them had eased it open and they were peering through the crack. Robert watched them from his position on the floor a short distance away, wondering what was going on.

The girl moaned.

So, Robert thought, Eustace is screwing a servant girl and the others get to watch.

With the squires' full attention on developments in the chapel, Robert thought about escape. If he didn't use this chance to get away, Eustace might come back when he was finished with the girl and resume the beating.

Robert looked around for a way out. The windows in the scriptorium were larger than those in the chapel, and consisted of squares about two feet on a side, more than enough, with the shutters open, to admit sufficient light to work by even on a cloudy day. And big enough for a boy Robert's size to squeeze through. The problem was, they were higher up than a man's head, too high to reach by jumping. But there was a desk covered with parchments under one of the windows that might allow Robert to reach it.

He raised himself, gathering his feet under him.

Then like a shot, he was up on the desk, slipping on parchments, scattering scrolls, and diving head first out the window.

It was a long hard fall to the ground, far enough to break a neck, but Robert's forearms cushioned the impact and he rolled to his feet. No one had called out, nor did there seem to be any pursuit.

But as he stood up, a strong hand grasped his collar and his feet left the ground.

"What are you doing?" a gravely voice said.

Robert squirmed. He saw that his captor was Grelli the huntsman, a tall lean man with a large head.

"Nothing," Robert said.

Grelli put him down but did not remove the hand from Robert's collar. "People don't go jumping out of chapel windows if they're up to nothing. Is this something I should tell your mother about? Or the steward?"

The prospect of Robert's mother or the steward being drawn into this was terrifying, even if he had done nothing wrong. He said in a rush, "I was reading the chaplain's books. Eustace and some of his friends came in. They beat me. I jumped out the window to escape from them. Eustace is in there right now, screwing some girl while the others watch."

When Robert finished, he looked anxiously at Grelli. He was aware that the story, though true, was probably too outlandish to be believed. But he had not been able to think up a satisfactory lie.

However, the story's effect on Grelli was unexpected. For a moment, Robert saw an odd expression ripple across the older man's rough-hewn face; it might have been fear, it might have been something else. Grelli's lips closed in a grim line. He pushed Robert away. "Get on, now. And stay out of trouble."

When they were done, they stood and repaired the damage to their clothes. Eustace picked the straw from her dress and hair. He had heard Blanche, his father's wife, say once in an argument with father that feigned friendship and kindness could reap benefits greater than to those of bribes and threats and at less cost.

"When can we be together again?" Eustace asked. He was still a bit overwhelmed by what had just happened.

She smiled at him. "Why not tonight?"

Eustace was taken aback. He hadn't expected things to move so smoothly. He guessed that once a girl made up her mind that she liked you, surrender was complete. The hard part was overcoming the initial resistance. "How?"

"When everyone is asleep, come to me in the solar. I'm at the south end. I have a room all to myself."

"I'll come!"

The Outlaws

"Good-bye, then," she said. She kissed his cheek and went out into the yard.

As Eustace shut the chapel door, Reginald and the other squires spilled burst in from the scriptorium, giggling and making rude comments.

"Quiet!" Eustace snarled. "She might hear! I have one more shot at her and I don't want you to ruin it."

The tittering dwindled but did not cease, even as the group emerged into the yard.

In his moment of triumph, Eustace had forgotten about the Attebrook boy.

Lying in bed with Bruette's head on his chest, Eustace felt drained. He had had her three times within the last hour. His loins ached and he felt as though he could sink through the goose feather mattress.

While he waited for her to fall asleep, he played with her hair, which he had found to be as erotic a feature as her breasts. It was long and thick and brown. She took pride in her hair. It was well combed, clean, and perfumed. She had driven him wild by rubbing a thick rope of it over his naked chest, groin and legs.

After a time, Bruette's breathing settled into a regular rhythm and soon she began to snore, a delicate low purr.

Eustace lay there a long time, reluctant to get up. The feather mattress sucked him downward. He had not slept on a feather mattress since he had lived with his mother; that had been more than seven years ago. He slept on a hard cot in the barracks with the castle guard and the other squires. And it was cold in the room. But he was going to have to rise if he intended to finish what he had started.

The baby, which shared the room with Bruette, stirred in her cradle.

Eustace listened to the sounds of the hateful child's breathing, trying to work up his nerve. Now that he was on the brink, he was afraid to act.

Despite his anxiety, he began to get drowsy. He lingered in that twilight world between waking and sleeping and almost let himself be seduced by the comfort of that feather bed and the warmth of the woman beside him.

But then he realized his whole life depended on what he did in the next few moments. He snapped awake, fear coursing through him.

He sat up in bed. He drew off the blanket so as not to disturb Bruette. The night air was cold against his naked skin. Goose pimples erupted on his back and legs. He stepped out of bed. The wood floor was hard and prickled his feet. Bruette stirred but did not awaken.

Panting with trepidation, Eustace crossed the short distance to the cradle and gazed down at this threat to his future.

She was so tiny, this baby: no longer than his forearm. She had a round wrinkled face that everyone said was so pretty, but Eustace thought she was the ugliest creature he had ever seen. How he hated her. Eustace had been the earl's only living child, the old man's posterity. All the other children delivered by the earl's previous wives and mistresses had been born dead, or had died as infants. Blanche, the present wife, had been barren for six years. Then this baby had been born.

In the near total darkness, the baby was just a dim form. She lay on her back, her little fists balled up by her ears, the heiress to the earldom. She was the one thing that stood between Eustace and his father's honor. For bastards could inherit. He had learned that at the abbey school. It was rare, but it happened. The great King William had been a bastard and look how far he had gone. Boldness and cunning, that's what it took.

Eustace knew he had the cunning: he had escaped from imprisonment at the abbey school and reached this moment. But did he have the boldness? Standing over the little form, he still wasn't sure.

The Outlaws

The child stirred. She made little smacking noises with her lips. Eustace became afraid she would wake up and ruin everything. It was now or never. Should I do it? he asked himself. Should I really?

Then, without further thought, as if some strange power had taken control of his body, Eustace clamped fingers over the baby's nose, careful not to leave a mark on the tender skin, and put the other hand over her mouth. The baby began to struggle, but was so swaddled that she didn't make much noise.

Eustace almost withdrew his hands from the baby's satin face. But if he did, she would cry out. It was too late to stop now. Pressing with more determination, he looked over his shoulder at Bruette for any sign of awakening, casting about for an excuse in case she sat up.

But the wet nurse did not awaken.

After a short time, the baby's struggles ceased. Eustace held her a while longer, then withdrew his hands.

Panting, Eustace covered his mouth with one hand, as if to stifle a groan. His whole body shook with reaction.

After several anxious glances at Bruette, Eustace leaned over and put his cheek just above the little open mouth. He could feel no tickle of breath. The hateful little thing was dead. People would think she had died in the night. Babies often died in the night for no apparent reason. That was the key, that was what the devil had whispered in his ear.

He let out a long, ragged breath, appalled at what he had done. But he had gotten what he wanted. He was Earl Roger's only living child again. Bastard or not, that counted for a lot.

He got dressed and tip-toed down to the hall.

PART 2

1179-1180

The Outlaws

CHAPTER 1

Gloucester
March 1179

Being chief and groom, assistant clerk, and general counter help, didn't give Robert much free time during the day for his new letter writing business. He wrote at night either at the Frightened Swan despite the clamor, or in the loft. But today he had a letter due a customer who would be by at sundown and he hadn't even started copying over from his wax tablet. Robert rushed through mucking the stalls during the late morning and stole into the loft. He was halfway done copying the letter to parchment when the ink bottle went dry.

He looked out a loft window while worrying what to do. He made his own ink, but there was no time for that now. There was ink nearby, but he would have to steal it. If he took a little, it wouldn't be missed, and he'd make up the loss with the next batch he made for himself.

He heard Jean's wife, Emily, call from the back of the house that dinner was ready. Today was Jacques's turn to mind the counter during dinner, a chore he resented. He had argued that Robert should have this task since he was the junior member of the household. But Master Jean had decided they would alternate days.

Robert went through the yard and entered the kitchen, a plan forming in his mind. He took a roll and an apple from the table, slipped them in his pouch and strolled through the house to the shop.

Jacques glanced at him from the counter. "What are you doing here? I heard the dinner call."

Robert rubbed his stomach. "Not feeling well. I'm not sure I should eat."

"You don't mind if I go then?"

Robert sank onto a stool and grimaced as if he had the grippe, but not missing the flicker of satisfaction at his

The Outlaws

suffering that crossed Jacques's face. Robert said, "Go right ahead."

When Jacques went out, Robert sat at the writing table. He lifted the lid to the compartment where spare quills, parchment, and ink were kept. He unstoppered one of the clay ink bottles and began to pour a driblet into his own. A thump in the house to the rear, sounding as if someone was approaching, gave him a start and he spilled some of the ink on the parchments. He wiped up as much as he could.

He lifted the folded parchment that had taken the brunt of the spill, thinking that perhaps the best thing was just to dispose of it, when he noticed that the parchment was not, in fact, a blank sheet, but a letter, with a wax seal and a name scrawled on it in a cramped but neat hand.

His name.

Robert's heart pounded as he recognized the vicar's handwriting and seal despite the fact it had been broken, a simple rose with a bent stem. He had got one letter years ago bearing it. It had been from his mother.

He unfolded the letter and began to read.

The letter said:

> Matilda Attebrook of Shelburgh village, to her beloved son Robert, Greetings:

> February last your Uncle Nicholas was caught in the earl's forest with a hart. That was crime enough but he compounded it by fighting over the beast with the idiot boy Dudda and killed him. Now he is to hang, when the earl returns, which should come after the Feast of the Annunciation of the Virgin. I am sorry to tell you this. Otherwise all is well here, although the winter was hard. I hope all is well with you. Your mother.

Robert read the letter again, mouthing the words, as he often had to do, with a sense of shocked disbelief. He had to close his eyes to think, to absorb it.

Today was March 22. The Feast of the Annunciation was three days away.

When he next became aware, he was at the threshold to the hall. The remainder of the household was there — Master Jean, Emily, their young daughter Cicely, the laundress, the maid, the two cooks. And Jacques.

"What is it, Robert?" Jean asked.

"He," Robert sputtered, so angry that he could barely speak, "had my letter!"

"Your letter?" Jean glanced at Jacques, who had begun to redden.

"It came yesterday," Jacques said. "I put it away and forgot about it. I was busy."

"Not too busy to read it!" Robert thundered.

"What are you talking about?" Jacques asked, speaking with forced calm.

"The seal was broken."

"That's nonsense. You were in the writing desk?" Jacques asked, in what seemed an effort to change the subject. As chief clerk, the desk was his domain, and he spoke as if to imply that Robert had no business being there.

"You opened my letter and read it, and then put it away so I couldn't find it," Robert said.

Jacques threw down his napkin and stood up. "I did no such thing."

Nothing more might have occurred except a further exchange of words, except Jacques said, "I'll not put up with such accusations from the likes of you." He pushed Robert out of the way and started to leave the hall.

Robert struck his shoulder against the door jam. It was bad enough that Jacques had hidden the letter out of sheer spite — a letter with such important word about his uncle. But then Jacques manhandled him as if he was just a beggar in the way on the street. What remained of Robert's temper vanished. He cursed and punched Jacques in the side of the head.

The punch drove Jacques against the wall. In a flash they were exchanging blows in the doorway.

The Outlaws

Jean tried to step between them but failed to stop the fight, and nearly got hit with a wild swing. Jean and one of the cooks dragged them apart.

"I will not have anyone behave this way in my house!" Jean shouted. "Least of all servants!"

He snatched up a stave kept by the fireplace. Masters kept such staves handy for disciplining servants and apprentices. Robert had never seen Jean so much as touch the stave before. But now Jean had released his grip on Jacques's neck and stepped around the clerk toward him, the stave raised.

Robert readied himself for the blow. By law, even defending against such a blow would be counted as an attack on his master, which would be punished, but he was beyond caring.

Then Cicely, who had picked up the letter from the floor, handed it to Emily.

"Wait, Jean," Emily said, staring at the letter. She gave it to Jean, who scanned it.

"This doesn't change anything," Jean snapped. "He has broken the peace of my house. He has to go." He turned back to Robert. "Get your things together and get out."

He held out the letter. Robert snatched it and rushed out of the hall.

Behind him he heard Emily say, "That was unnecessary."

Jean replied, "What was I to do? Beat him?"

"Yes, then it would have been over and quickly forgotten. . . ."

But more than the words, Robert took with him the memory of the sneering smirk of triumph of Jacques's face.

Shelburgh
March 1179

Robert reached Shelburgh just before sundown.

He paused on the bridge across the brook that marked the village's east end and looked to the thatched roofs along the road ahead. Despite the reason he had come, Robert was glad to be home.

Tom, one of the village's two tollmen, saw him and waved from his shelter at the far end of the bridge. It was not a big bridge for it was not a big brook, although here it was almost as wide as the River Lugg, which it met a dozen yards away. It was just a little wooden span thrown across what had been a ford so that people didn't have to get their feet wet when they crossed and the lord could charge a toll for the convenience.

Robert waved back and came across.

"Come for the hanging, have you?" Tom asked.

He nodded. "I haven't missed it, have I?"

"No. The earl just got back yesterday. He needs time to unpack and get settled before he indulges in a good hanging."

"What happened? The killing, I mean."

"Depends on who you talk to. Nick claims Dudda started it, but hardly anyone believes him. That sharp tongue of his has started more fights than anyone can count."

"What do you think?"

"I've had my differences with Nick, same as everybody else. Doesn't matter, anyway. He's to hang for the deer, not for Dudda."

"It's getting a little late for you to be out here, isn't it?"

"I was thinking about knocking off. Walk with you?"

Robert nodded.

Tom stood up and gathered his crutches. He had lost a leg years ago in one of the wars with the Welsh; shot through the calf, it had gone gangrenous and had to be amputated above the knee. Toll collecting was the only work he could do now.

Robert picked up Tom's dinner pail and the pillow he sat on. "I'll carry those for you."

"Thanks, lad," Tom said. "Always dropping that stuff, you know. Got to get the wife to make me a satchel, but she's always too busy."

They walked up the road to Tom's house. Robert held the gate for him while he passed through.

The Outlaws

The village alehouse was next door, and there were four men and two women sitting at the table in the yard. "Look who's here!" called out one of the men, whose name was Tondbert the tanner, at the sight of Robert. Tondbert tugged on an imaginary noose about his neck and stuck out his tongue. "We'll be having some fun soon!"

"Too bad it's not you, asshole!" Robert called back.

Tondbert rose as if to make more of this, but the woman at his side, his wife Mildgyth, grasped his forearm and pulled him back to his seat. "Your time will come!" Tondbert replied. "You're as much trouble as that useless uncle of yours!"

"He's worth twice what you are!"

"In a pig's eye, you little shit!"

"Fuck you!"

This was too much. Tondbert broke free from the woman's grasp and ran out the gate toward Robert, who watched him come, measuring the distance.

As Tondbert closed, he reached out for Robert's collar with his left hand while he raised his right to strike.

Robert ignored the left hand and lunged with a straight left punch of his own. The combined force of the punch and Tondbert's momentum knocked him off his feet. He landed on his back, out cold.

"That'll teach you to swing wild, you idiot," Robert said.

"I'll appeal you for that!" Mildgyth shouted.

"Appeal till you're out of breath!" Robert said, turning away. "Won't do you any good." He'd be gone before the next manor court and he didn't think he'd be back, so Mildgyth could charge him with an affray all she liked. Nothing would come of it.

He went back to the lane leading westward from the bridge, keeping an eye out behind in case Tondbert got up and wanted to continue the discussion, or his friends wanted to continue it for him. But Tondbert's friends gathered around him and helped him up with a good deal of muttering, pointing of fingers in Robert's direction, and a bit of fist shaking.

The house was the fourth on the left and the last on the lane, which petered out into a footpath that disappeared into the forest.

The older twin Alice, who was weeding in the garden, spotted Robert first, and called out, "Robert's here!"

The rest of his family — Matilda, Agnes the other twin, and Brian — came out of the house and surrounded Robert as he passed through the gate.

"Just in time for supper," Matilda said. She had to stand on her tip toes to kiss his cheek now. She made a face at the fuzz on his cheeks and chin. "You don't think you need to shave?"

"Barbers cost money," Robert said as he removed his woolen cap and put his bow and arrow case by the door. "What's for supper?"

"Sit down, and you'll see."

It saddened Robert to see what was on the table: the same drab fare as always in the spring when the family was at the end of its supplies, dried peas and beans boiled together into a thick soup, dried apples, barley bread, and cider. He felt guilty about how much better he had eaten at Jean's house.

After Matilda set out and filled the bowls, she sat down beside him. "What's the matter, not hungry?"

Robert picked up his spoon and dipped it in the soup. He could already imagine its flat taste. "Oh, no. I'm starving. D'we have any salt?"

"No, we're out," Matilda said, in that dismissive tone she used when they lacked something.

Robert got up from the table.

"What are you doing?" Matilda said.

"A moment, Mum." He retrieved a leather pouch from his satchel and sat down again. "Thought you might be needing some extra."

Matilda examined Robert with narrowed eyes, trying to gauge if this was some kind of tease. She poured the salt into a

The Outlaws

bowl, which she then gave to Brian. "Careful. Don't spill any. Take care of your sisters, too. And make sure your fingers are clean before you dip. That's a good boy." She took back the bowl and put a couple of pinches of salt in her own soup before handing the bowl to Robert.

"Now," she said, "tell me how things have been with you."

Robert thought about lying, but said, "I've lost my job."

Matilda looked alarmed. "How?"

"Got in a fight with Jacques. The master didn't like it."

"He discharged you over a fight?"

"It was at dinner. In the hall. Don't worry. I'll find something else. With Uncle Nick gone, I suppose I'll start looking right away."

"Quite so," Matilda said, somewhat relieved. After Harold had died and Robert went away, Matilda had allowed Nicholas to move in, as much to discourage the steward as to give charity. She had written to Robert about her surprise when Nicholas, who had never been inclined to display industry, had managed to make a contribution to their support by making bows and arrows. He was very good at it, and although he didn't work much, he fetched high prices. He gave half to Matilda and drank up the rest.

At the mention of Nicholas' name, Alice and Agnes fidgeted in their seats. Robert could tell they were bursting with something to say. Matilda glared at them and they looked at their laps. Robert asked, "What happened with Uncle Nick?"

Agnes blurted: "He's in gaol."

"At the castle," Alice added.

"For poaching," Agnes said. "And murder!"

"He killed a deer in the south wood," said Alice.

"A week before the feast of St. Mathias," said Agnes in an imitation of a whisper.

"Yes," said Agnes. "He poached all through the winter."

"We had lots of meat," said Alice. "And mother made the most delicious pie, and smoked the rest."

50

"But it's all gone now," said Agnes.

"It was good," said Alice, looking sad at the memory.

"And this murder?" Robert asked. Nicholas was a temperamental and argumentative man. He had often argued with people in the village when he was drunk, and sometimes got into fights. But he had never killed anyone.

Alice said, "He killed Dudda."

Robert nodded. "That's what Mum said in her letter." He remembered Dudda well. He was a massive hulking fellow, the son of the village's richest man, an enterprising villein named Godbold who had acquired a lot of land through crafty business deals and hard work. Dudda, however, was slow in the head, and unable to manage a holding. He got by on charity and odd jobs. He was always taking things that belonged to other people without asking first, and he had a temper when told what to do.

"With an ax!" Agnes said. "Chopped him in the forehead right between the eyes."

"Over the game," Alice said.

"They were poaching together," said Agnes.

"And they couldn't agree on how to divide the prize," Alice said. "Nicholas shot it and Dudda was there only to help carry it back, but he demanded a full half for the work, and Nicholas refused him. There was a fight."

"They say he will hang," Agnes said.

"Now that the earl is back," Alice said.

"Have you ever seen anyone hang?" Agnes asked Robert.

"At Gloucester, yes," he said. "They hang somebody there every couple of months. It's not a pretty sight."

Alice shuddered. "I wouldn't want to watch."

"I would," Agnes said. "Amanda said I could go with her." Sulkiness crept into her tone and her eyes slipped sidelong to Matilda, who was frowning. "But Mama said we aren't allowed to go even if we wanted to."

"But someone from the family has to be there," Robert said. "To claim the body. Otherwise, they'll just throw him into a hole in the ground, like planting a turnip."

The Outlaws

Matilda looked out the door and nodded. Robert understood then why she had written. He was to be the sole witness. Matilda would not go, nor allow the children to watch. She had disapproved of Nicholas, had never liked him, in fact, and might have driven him out if he hadn't been his father's younger brother to whom she felt some obligation.

"I suppose I'll have to dig the grave myself this time," Robert said. He remembered having to stand as head of the family at his father's burial six years ago. He had been ten years old then; too young for grave digging. His mother had given him two pennies out of her hoard to pay the grave diggers, and he had stood by during the morning to watch them dig.

"No," Matilda said. "I'll give you money for the grave diggers, and shroud him, too. Just don't expect me or the children to watch him hang."

She got up and began to clear the table of the empty bowls, which she dropped into a bucket and handed to Brian, whose job it was to wash up. But she could not conceal from Robert the haunted look that played upon her face. Then he guessed why she could not watch Nicholas hang. It wasn't because she disliked him, but because he reminded her too much of Robert's father. They had looked so alike they could have been twins, although they couldn't have been more different in temperament.

"I'll have to go see him," Robert said.

Matilda nodded. Although she had tried to discourage it, Robert and Nicholas had been close. Nicholas had taught him how to fight, and to make a decent bow and arrows. She said, "I'll give you a loaf to take tomorrow. They don't feed the prisoners, you know. He'd have starved already if we hadn't been feeding him."

"Starving them saves the trouble of a hanging," Robert said.

The gaol was on the ground floor of the barracks, which sat on the southeast side of the bailey. A man-at-arms of the castle garrison unlocked the gaol's door and held it open for Robert, eyeing the black interior with a bored expression and a nose wrinkling at the stench. The door shut and the lock clicked behind Robert. The interior so stank of urine, feces and rotting straw that Robert wanted to gag. The single window was a tiny one in the door a hand-width's wide, so the interior was dark. When Robert's eyes adjusted to the dim light, he made out two figures sitting on the ground, each secured to posts in the wall by a leash of chain fastened to a neck ring. Sitting was all they could do. The leash wasn't long enough for the prisoners to lie down or to stand upright.

"Hello, Uncle Nick," Robert said.

"Robert, boy." Nicholas glared up at him. "So good of you to come all the way from Gloucester for the hanging."

"Mother sent a loaf and a bit of cheese and butter."

"You the delivery boy today, are you? A hard woman, your mother. Who'd have thought there was any kindness lurking in her heart. Well, don't just stand there picking your nose, let's have it over."

Robert squatted and unwrapped the bread and cheese. Nicholas broke off bits of bread, swabbed them in the butter and stuffed them in his mouth. This close to Nicholas, Robert was able to get a better look at him. Nicholas had been a handsome man once, but hard living had made him gaunt and weather-beaten. Robert smoothed lanky strands out of Nicholas's face and was shocked to see the gaping sores and unhealed, pussy wounds on his face. Nicholas had also lost his front teeth.

"What happened to your teeth?" he asked.

Nicholas swallowed a wad of bread and said, "Foresters knocked them out. They had to have their fun before they got me back here. Hanging me isn't enough, I suppose, although I can't but wonder why anyone would want to go to such trouble over Dudda."

The Outlaws

"Who's he?" Robert asked about the other prisoner, who was watching Nicholas eat. Nicholas broke the loaf in half and tossed it to the other man.

The man answered for himself. "My name is Adam."

"He's a clerk," Nicholas snorted. Nicholas held clerks in contempt. "His crime is more interesting than mine."

"Oh?" Robert said.

The clerk looked embarrassed.

Nicholas chuckled, exposing the gaps left by the missing teeth. He said, "He made a poem for Lady Blanche."

"Why is that a crime?" Robert asked, puzzled. As the earl's wife, it probably wasn't unusual for people in the earl's court to write her poems.

"It was a love poem."

"So?"

Nicholas cackled. Adam looked more embarrassed. Nicholas said, "The earl caught him singing it to her — in her bedroom. While they were both naked!" Nicholas slapped his thigh and rocked back and forth. "Now he gets to hang because he couldn't keep his dick in his drawers!"

"My dick was in my drawers," Adam said. "It was just a poem. And we were not naked."

Nicholas cackled. He didn't believe Adam. Evidently nobody else had either, which was why he was here chained to a wall.

Robert felt sorry for him. "Leave him alone."

"Why should I?" Nicholas snapped. "You sound like a damned priest."

Robert stood up to go. Nicholas caught his ankle. "Wait," Nicholas said. "There's something you need to know."

"What?"

Nicholas motioned him to bend down. Robert squatted beside him. Nicholas whispered, "Godbold's going to bring suit against your mother for Dudda's death after I'm gone. He's going to demand forty shillings in death geld."

"Forty shillings!" Robert was appalled. "I've known cows that cost more!"

"So've I. That bastard wasn't worth tuppence, if you ask me, but no one's going to object. Anyway, I think the earl will grant the petition, even if she had nothing to do with it. The damned steward d'Evry's held a grudge against your Mum ever since your dad died and he's got the earl's ear. 'Sides, neither of them give a damn about the murder. The earl gets his cut of the fine. You know that."

"Where's Mum going to get forty shillings?" Robert thought aloud. Despite all the help he'd given the family, he couldn't imagine that she had forty shillings buried under the floor. She would have to sell all she had — the bed, the loom, the tools which she had accumulated for Brian so he could be a carpenter like their father. Even that wouldn't cover the debt. He had a terrible thought: she might even be imprisoned if she could not pay, or given to Godbold — she and his brother and sisters.

"I know a way you can get it." Nicholas' voice dropped into a lower register. His eyes grew crafty. Robert shivered. He had seen that look before: it was Nicholas' plotting look. Robert almost wished he had not come for the hanging.

"How, rob someone on the highway?" Robert asked.

"Too dangerous. You can get it from him." Nicholas pointed to Adam.

Adam nodded.

"Where are you going to get forty shillings?"

Adam said, "My family holds a manor in Norfolk. If you get me out of here, they'll pay you for your trouble. I swear."

Nicholas rubbed his thighs. "And you'll fetch me too, of course, won't you boy? You wouldn't leave your dear uncle behind, now, would you?"

CHAPTER 2

Shelburgh
March 1179

They still had their heads together when the man-at-arms interrupted them with a loud knock and a growl as he unlocked the door. "You've been in there long enough. Time's up."

Robert stood up. Nicholas put his head in his hands. Adam twiddled a piece of straw.

The soldier grinned. "Won't be long before you can count the hours left on two hands, lads."

"I didn't think you could count that high," Nicholas snapped, looking up.

"Keep it up," the soldier said, "and you'll take no teeth at all with you at the scaffold."

Nicholas was about to respond, but Robert cut him off before he could say something he might regret. "I'll see you tomorrow, Uncle Nick."

"Have your mother send a soup. Her bread's hard to chew."

"I'll tell her you said so."

"You do that."

As they emerged into the bailey, Robert gave the soldier a quarter penny for his trouble. The soldier was surprised at the generosity. "Too bad you have to be kin to that piece of shit," he growled.

The casualness of the insults saddened Robert. Nicholas wasn't a likeable fellow, but he didn't deserve to be treated as he had. "If you could see him shoot, you wouldn't talk like that. He can knock an apple off a post at thirty yards, and he's a great wrestler. And he was a good soldier. Served the king in the French wars."

"Don't matter now, though, do it? Won't save him from the hangman." The guard looked toward the hall. "The earl said this morning that they're to dangle day after tomorrow, when he gets back from Shrewsbury. You sticking around for it?"

"No," Robert said. "I think not."

Robert walked back to the village, mulling over how he could get the prisoners out. Halfway there, he sat down on a fallen tree to think. Because they were older and thought they knew better, both Nicholas and Adam had been full of instructions, but none of them had been that useful. Nicholas had never been inside the castle before and had a hazy idea how it was laid out or run. Adam, who had lived there, had not paid much attention to things that Robert knew were important: such as how many watchmen were awake during the night and where they could be found. Rather than argue with them, Robert had nodded and smiled and pretended to be willing to do as he was told.

Gazing back at the motte through the branches, he saw he had three main challenges. First he had to get into the cell without a key. Then he had to get them free from the chains. And finally, he had to get them over the wall without being seen by the watchman. He wondered if the watch was run the same as at Gloucester castle, which could get lax in peacetime.

As the plan formed in his head, Robert felt better. He could do this. It would work because no one was expecting it, and nobody would know he was involved.

If he didn't get the forty shillings, his family would be ruined.

The next afternoon, Robert gathered a few things, which he put in his satchel — a loaf of bread, some goat cheese, a few dried apples and plums.

"You're leaving?" Matilda asked, alarmed.

"Soon, yes."

"You said you'd stay."

The Outlaws

"I'll stay long enough to do what must be done." He didn't want to tell her what he was going to do. She would raise all sorts of objections if he did.

Matilda looked relieved.

"The hanging's tomorrow," he said.

"Yes, I heard that," she said. She surprised him by looking sad. He had thought she hated Nicholas and here she seemed to feel sorry for him. She added, "I've yet to speak to Eadwin, though."

Eadwin, the village reeve? Ah, for Nicholas' grave. He said, "I'll do the digging myself. No sense spending the money."

"You're sure? I don't mind."

"It's all right, Mum. Really." No sense in wasting money on a grave that wouldn't be needed.

Then he kissed her and went up to the castle.

It was not a grand castle, as castles went, nothing to compare to the stone eminence at Gloucester. It was small and cramped and consisted of an earthen rampart capped by a wooden wall which had recently been repaired so that large swaths of gray planks were punctuated by the bright yellow of new wood. The walls surrounded a little bailey that was as packed with buildings as a town. Their gray thatched roofs projected above the wall, and Robert had merely to close his eyes to see them in his memory: the great timber hall, long and tall and dignified; stables, barracks, dovecot, kennels, pig sty, kitchen, smithy, wood and pottery shops, laundry and garden, as well as shacks for some of the servants who were privileged enough not to sleep on the floor of the hall. The entrance to the bailey was guarded by two wooden gate towers which were ancient and gray, and which sagged a bit at the corners like a pair of old soldiers ready for retirement. At the far end, presiding over the whole, was the tall mound on which sat a square wooden tower, squat with the top story wider than the one below it under a peaked room from which flew the red and green FitzWalter pennant.

The gate stood open. There was no guard in view; and if he remembered right, there frequently wasn't. People were able to go in and out most of the time uninspected and unchallenged in peacetime.

Dinner had finished long ago, but the kitchen was swarming with servants, some cleaning up after the mid-day meal, others preparing supper.

Edging behind the shacks which stood at the base of the earthen rampart, he made his way to the stable and barn. After a few brief minutes of searching, he found a shovel and an iron pry bar. Robert climbed into the loft with them. Unless there were young lovers in need of a secluded spot, he could remain undetected here through the rest of the day. Robert burrowed into a pile of straw and settled down to wait.

Robert woke up in the dark, heart pounding with anxiety that he had slept too long. But he calmed down when he peered through cracks in the walls and saw, from the position of the shadows and the full moon, that it was about midnight.

Robert dug the shovel and pry bar out of the hay, and climbed down from the loft.

He found the bailey silent, the air filled with muted cricket song from the forest outside the walls. A slight breeze carried the sweet stench of garbage from the cesspit at the base of the motte. The smell was strong enough to penetrate the sharp odor of fresh manure here by the barn. He paused at the door, watching the walls. No one moved up there. A faint light leaked from a shuttered upper window in the left-hand gate tower: that had to be the watchman warming himself by the brazier.

Keeping to the edges of the shacks and in the shadows, he made his way to the barracks. He went around behind to the corner where he reckoned the gaol to be.

He knocked on the wall a few times. An answering knock told him this was the right place.

59

The Outlaws

He put down the pry bar and, glancing over his shoulder at the rampart, he began to dig.

The soil, though packed and hard, was rootless. Within half an hour, he had a hole dug under the wall that was wide enough to slip through.

Robert wormed through the hole.

"Damned glad to see you, boy," Nicholas growled. "I thought you'd changed your mind."

"And spoil your big surprise?"

"Not so loud," Nicholas said. "Some of the boys are light sleepers."

Robert glanced at the ceiling. Above them, the castle garrison and squires slumbered — at least he hoped so.

Robert worked with the pry bar at the steel pin driven into the post securing Nicholas' chain. It was a rusty pin. It took both Robert and Nicholas on the bar to get it free.

Then Robert started on Adam's chain, which came free with a loud screech. They listened for movement overhead. There was just was the creaking of timbers.

"All right," Robert said, kneeling at the mouth of the hole. "Let's go."

He squirmed through, half expecting to be met on the other side, but the yard was as empty and as quiet as he had left it. Even the dogs were silent. After the others were through, Robert threw the tools into the hole and pushed in the pile of dirt he had created in the digging, hoping that the hole would not be spotted until they were far away.

Nicholas and Adam would have scrambled onto the rampart in their eagerness to get over the wall behind the barn, but Robert grabbed their sleeves and forced them to lie in the shadow of the building, while he scanned the wall walk left and right. Watchmen could get pretty lazy, and often patrolled the walls once after they changed shifts, which occurred every two hours.

"I think it's clear," Robert said. He stood up.

"About damned time," Nicholas hissed. "I'm about to piss my drawers."

"Go ahead. It'll warm you."

They clambered up the grassy slope of the rampart, where a dirt path beside the timber wall marked the guard's walk.

"You first," Robert said to Adam.

Adam swallowed and hesitated, then with resolution that seemed odd in someone so willowy and slight, he slipped over the wall. Robert dangled him by the hand so that the fall was not so far, then let him go. Adam tumbled down the outside embankment to the bottom of the ditch.

As Robert turned to help Nicholas, who sat straddling the wall, there was a shout from the gate towers that made Robert's legs go watery. "Hey, you! What're you doing?"

"Shit," Nicholas said. "Nothing ever goes right."

Robert offered Nicholas his hand. Nicholas batted it away. "Best you not tarry, boy," he growled, and disappeared over the wall.

Robert hung on the wall for a moment — but it was a moment too long. Just as he released his grip, a beefy hand caught his sleeve and held him dangling in space.

It was the soldier who had let him into the gaol the other day.

The soldier recognized him too. He laughed, and said, "Got you, you little runt," as he began to haul Robert back to the top of the wall as if he was just a large fish.

Robert reached behind his back with his free hand, drew his dagger, and sliced the soldier across the hand.

The soldier cried out and jerked the wounded hand away.

Robert flashed the dagger to cut the other hand, and the soldier let go.

Robert fell to the embankment and tumbled backward into the ditch. He fetched up at the bottom of the ditch with the wind knocked out of him and a twinge in his knee. But there wasn't time to think about that now.

All three fugitives jumped to their feet without a word and scrambled up the far side of the ditch to the open ground around the castle. The forest, which seemed to press in most times, seemed far away now.

61

The Outlaws

As they pelted for the shelter of the wood, Robert heard a sound he dreaded: the snap of a bowstring followed by the hiss of an arrow passing over his right shoulder. Another thumped into the ground by his feet.

Then Nicholas grunted and fell to his hands and knees.

Robert turned, and to his horror saw an arrow sticking out of Nicholas' lower back. The arrow had gone clean through; the narrow bodkin warhead, meant for piercing mail, stuck out of Nicholas' groin.

Frantic, Robert grasped Nicholas' collar and pulled him to his feet.

Nicholas tried to push him away. "Leave off, boy," Nicholas panted. "I'm done."

Adam tugged Robert's arm. "You can't help him now. You've done your best."

But Robert could not give up. He threw Nicholas across his back, and stumbled toward the trees as more arrows hissed about them.

According to Robert's plan, by morning when the escape was discovered they were to be twenty miles away and safe from capture. But that plan was in tatters now.

In the distance, Robert heard the frenzied howling of boar hounds. Bred for fighting wild boars, they could tear a man apart when they caught him.

"Ah," Nicholas whispered in Robert's ear, "I could use a drink. Just a bit of ale. My mother made the best ale, did you know that? No, you wouldn't. She died before you were born. Sweet ale, the best in the village. Wish I had some now."

"We're almost to the brook," Robert gasped. "You'll have to settle for water."

"I've had to settle for less all my life, why should anything change now?" Nicholas breathed.

When they reached the brook, Robert paused to rest. He was so spent that he was unsure he could go on. He laid Nicholas on the ground.

Adam flopped down. "I heard dogs," he said, panic in his voice.

"So did I," Robert replied, trying to sound calm.

"We're done for. We can't outrun dogs." Adam began to cry.

"We're not done for yet." But he had no idea what to do. His mind felt frozen.

Robert offered Nicholas a palm full of water to buy some time to force his head to work. Nicholas did not move. Robert touched his hand; it was limp and clammy. Robert put a finger under Nicholas' nose. Nicholas was not breathing.

Robert wiped his mouth with a trembling hand. He wanted to scream. He'd killed Nicholas and got himself outlawed — that is if he was lucky enough to survive.

"At least he died a free man," Robert murmured to himself.

"What?" Adam said.

"Nothing. He's dead."

"Oh. A pity."

Robert pulled Adam to his feet. "Come on. We better go."

They splashed into the brook and headed downstream, leaving Nicholas on the bank where he had died.

When Robert didn't come home that evening, Matilda began to worry. There was no reason she could think of why he had not come back.

No good reason.

Matilda put the children to bed but did not go herself. Instead, too anxious to sleep, she put a few sticks on the fire and sat at the table. For a while, she stared into the flames, hands clenching and unclenching, her stomach knotting. Worry was her constant companion even when times were good. You never knew when good times might turn to bad, and they always did. That fool boy.

The Outlaws

After a while, she got out a piece of embroidery she was doing for Lady Blanche, thinking that work would divert her thoughts from the dark paths they wished to tread. But she succeeded in sticking herself in the thumb.

At some point during the night, fatigue overwhelmed her and she fell asleep at the table with her head on the crook of her arm.

The sound of horses in the lane outside jerked her awake. Nobody ever rode horses in the lane in the middle of the night. That was alarming enough, but then they broke the gate and came into the yard. She almost opened the door to see who was there, but an instinct stopped her. She waited for the booming knock and the deep-voiced call to open up. Then she counted to five before she pulled the door open.

A squire from the castle stood in the doorway. Matilda recognized him as the earl's bastard, the one called Eustace. His black hair was in disarray as if he had just gotten out of bed. His handsome face was hard.

"What is it?" Matilda asked, a reasonable question under the circumstances. Soldiers didn't come banging on villager's doors in the middle of the night. And they had no more right to invade the house of a free cotter than they did the manor house of a lord.

But Eustace was upset about something, and in no mood to respect anyone's rights. He pushed her aside and entered the house followed by four men-at-arms.

"You," Eustace said to one of the men. "Check the loft. You and you the bier. And you, look over the garden. They may be hiding among the weeds."

The soldiers investigated the house and yard. It wasn't hard to do. There were no places to hide.

Then they went outside to the front yard to confer.

Matilda listened at the door to the conversation and to her horror had her fears confirmed: Robert had broken Nicholas out of the castle gaol but Nicholas had been killed as they ran.

She couldn't imagine how he had managed it, but he must have: the proof was standing in her yard right now. That stupid boy. How could he have let Nicholas talk him into such madness! But then Robert had always admired his lazy sot of an uncle.

The soldiers were considering the possibility that the fugitives might come back here. "I don't think they've been here yet," Eustace was saying. "She seemed truly surprised to see us. But there's a good chance they might turn up. I'll leave you two here just in case. The rest of us will head up the brook."

Matilda glanced behind her at Robert's things. He had bundled all his goods and food for travel and left his bow and arrows with the bundle beside the door, which the soldiers had overlooked. He never traveled without the bow. He did mean to come back, she was certain, and when he did they would catch him.

The children had awakened at the commotion, and had spent the search huddled in the corner where she had put them.

She took several deep breaths to calm herself. Then she hissed, "Brian!"

"What, Mum?"

She handed him the bundle of Robert's things. "Take these and put them in the bushes by the bridge. Hide them well from view on the bank. Quickly now." She knew he would understand that she meant the plank bridge over the brook just behind the house, not the timber bridge on the road.

Brian ran out the back door, which Matilda shut behind him, just as two soldiers came in the front. They didn't notice that Brian was gone, and settled at the table. "What have you got to drink?" one of them asked.

"Only cider."

They made faces. They were hoping for ale. "All right. We'll have that."

The Outlaws

While she poured from the clay jug, the soldier who had asked for a drink said, "Everybody back in bed. And keep quiet, or you're in for it. Understand?"

The twins crawled into bed when Matilda confirmed the order with a nod.

At that moment, Brian came in through the back door. The hem of his shirt, which hung to his knees, was damp, and his his calves were wet with dew and plastered with bits of grass.

"The devil!" the soldier said, startled. "What have you been up to?"

"Had to take a pee," said Brian. A tall gangly twelve, he had a habit of talking back to his elders that no amount of scolding or claps on the ears could tame, and he did not seem intimidated by the soldiers. The way he spoke was so in keeping with his normal way that Matilda almost laughed out loud.

"Well, get your ass into bed and be quiet," the soldier grumped.

Matilda also sat on the edge of the bed, and clasped her cloak around her. Brian climbed in beside her under the blanket after wiping his feet on a rag. They locked eyes for a moment and Brian dipped his head: he had accomplished his mission. Matilda let out a breath.

For a moment, she thought that was all she could do. Then she thought about the fire. She put a few more sticks on it. The interior of the house grew warm. The soldiers sat at the table and finished their cider. They stared into the fire with bored eyes. One of them began to nod with sleep. He wasn't used to being up in the middle of the night.

Dawn was a suggestion in the east when Robert reached the house, the light faint and gray, but enough to reveal streams of fog trailing among the trees.

Both he and Adam were soaked and shivering. It had taken most of the night to work their way down the brook, which curved around the village on the west and south. Several times patrols had passed them by, including one with dogs. They had avoided detection by sinking beneath the frigid water and holding their breaths until the patrol passed by.

For the last hour, however, they had seen no one. Off in the distance, he heard the voices of men calling to each other on both sides of the brook and once or twice the baying of the hounds. But no one passed close.

Robert crept up the bank to the fence around the house. The fence was made of woven sticks. As he got close in order to see better through the gaps in the sticks, Adam tugged at his leg.

"Look," Adam whispered.

Robert saw he was pointing to a bundle lying in the grass near the bridge: his cloak, a bag of food, a blanket and his bow case and arrows. He wondered what on earth they were doing there.

Then he noticed the house. It was a little early for people to be up. Yet a thick stream of smoke curled from the hole in the roof. Orange light peeped from cracks around the back door, which meant that a fire was burning on the hearth. And someone had let the pigs out. He heard the sow snorting in the garden and the rustling of the piglets as they rooted in the cabbage and the colewort. The wind was blowing from their direction or they would have smelled Robert and Adam and have come over to say hello. The sow never missed an opportunity to get Robert to scratch her back.

And his mother would never have let the pigs into the garden.

"What is it?" Adam asked through chattering teeth.

"The house isn't safe."

Adam looked dismayed. "I need that fire."

"Well, you can't have it," Robert said as he collected the bundle.

"What will we do?" Adam asked, turning round and clasping his knees, shivering.

The Outlaws

"Hold up in the forest until nightfall and then try to slip away by the river, I guess. They'll probably have people posted on the roads, but they can't watch everywhere."

Adam put his head in his shivering hands. While Robert drew the bow stave from its canvas case and strung it, Adam rocked back and forth. "I can't do it," he moaned. "I can't."

"Keep your voice down!" Robert hissed. "There are soldiers in the house."

But voices carry in a fog, and this time was no exception.

The back door to the house opened and a man looked out. He was indeed a soldier. "There they are!" the soldier shouted and pointed. He ran across the yard toward them, drawing his sword.

Robert hauled Adam to his feet by the collar and pushed him ahead across the plank bridge.

On the far side, Robert stooped and heaved the little bridge into the water. That should slow up foot pursuit for a few moments.

Then he clambered up the bank.

At that instant, their luck seemed to run out. Three horsemen were passing in the lane and wheeled into the yard at the soldier's call. Seeing Robert mounting the bank, they spurred their horses. One animal baulked at the back fence, but two jumped it.

Robert paused at the top of the bank, nocked an arrow, and loosed one at the riders. The arrow struck the man in the thigh, penetrating the leg, the saddle and the horse's side, pinning the man's leg to his mount. He grunted and clutched the shaft.

The second rider did not even look back or pause in his charge. His animal sent up plumes of spray as it crossed the brook. The rider lashed his beast, intent on reaching Robert before the boy could nock another arrow.

Guts churning, Robert drew to the corner of his mouth, tried to steady his shaking hands, and loosed the arrow just as the second rider cleared the brook and started up the bank not six feet from him.

The arrow caught the rider just below the jaw and went clear through the man's neck, flying cross the brook and sticking into the far bank.

The man remained in the saddle long enough for the horse to storm by Robert, who was so stunned at what he had just done that he didn't have the presence of mind to jump out of the way and was almost trampled. Then the knight fell to the ground like a sack of grain, landing on his back with a pronounced bounce, and didn't move.

Robert went weak in the knees at the enormity of what he had just done.

He had just killed Ralph, the master of squires, and one of the lesser FitzWalters, a cousin or something to the earl.

Robert didn't have time to contemplate this. There were still a mounted squire and two soldiers across the brook shouting that they'd found the escapees and calling for help. But seeing the wounded and the dead, they made no attempt to cross the stream. They knew he would shoot them down if they tried.

"Hurry! Look what I've got!" Adam called behind him.

Adam had caught the horse. With a horse, they might escape after all.

There was one more thing Robert had to do.

He turned back and shot across the brook at the squire's horse. The arrow hit the beast in the neck. It reared, then turned in panic in an uncontrollable circle.

Robert hated to kill the horse, but he had to make sure the squire, whom he recognized as Reginald le Bec, couldn't follow them.

When he turned back, Adam had already mounted. The animal was restive at the new, strange rider, but Adam showed that he knew how to ride.

Adam yielded a stirrup so that Robert could climb up behind him.

Then Adam turned the horse to the south, and they rode hard away.

CHAPTER 3

Shelburgh castle
March 1179

Eustace was tired and hungry by dawn, and when the night's work produced only the body of the poacher, he abandoned the search to get breakfast. He had just put up his horse and was crossing to the bailey, when one of the hired knights galloped through the gate and skidded to a halt before the hall. The knight slipped off his horse, but rather than rushing into the hall, he tarried at the door.

"What's going on?" Eustace asked when he came up.

"Ralph's dead," the knight said. "The Attebrook boy killed him."

"What?" Eustace found that too incredible to believe.

"Shot him through the neck. He hit Jermain, too."

"Two men!" Eustace marveled, still too shocked to be angry. "And they've not been found yet?"

"They stole Ralph's horse. They're miles away by now."

No wonder the knight was afraid to go in. This was disastrous. FitzWalter would be furious. Ralph had been a cousin and a childhood friend. They had known each other all their lives. No one liked to be near when FitzWalter lost his temper. He was liable to do anything.

"Will you tell him?" the knight asked. "I can't."

Eustace didn't want to be the deliverer of this news any more than the knight. But if it came from him, perhaps FitzWalter would be less inclined to lash out at those around him. "All right."

"Dear God, thanks. I owe you."

"Don't think about it. Tell me more about how it happened."

Eustace went into the hall, sticking close to the walls for all the trestle tables that had been set up for breakfast, yet with the entire garrison out searching for the fugitives, there were few people here. Coming around behind the head table, he knelt beside the earl.

You were supposed to wait for the earl to notice you before speaking. But this was urgent business, so Eustace said, "My lord, I have terrible news."

FitzWalter wiped his mouth with his napkin. He had a small mouth for such a large man, beneath eyes as cold as a hawk's. "What is it?"

Eustace decided there was no use trying to soften the blow. "My lord, they have killed Ralph!"

"They, they? You mean . . . ?"

"The Attebrook boy, the one who went off to Gloucester. Crossing the brook south of the village. Ralph charged him and was shot through the neck. Clean through, I'm told. He also shot Jermain in the leg."

"A clerk has killed Ralph?" FitzWalter's voice was icy.

Eustace was prepared to leap back when the thunderstorm broke. He wanted to be out of reach if FitzWalter's rage turned murderous. He had not been prepared for this icy, controlled response. It was scarier than a tantrum.

FitzWalter stood up. He said in a tight voice, "Where is Ralph now?"

Not knowing the answer, Eustace said, "Where he fell, I imagine, my lord. The messenger just arrived with word."

FitzWalter brushed by him, stalking toward the door and calling for a horse.

By the time FitzWalter and Eustace got to the Attebrook house, every knight, soldier, and man pressed into the search for the fugitives had collected in the yard or the surrounding lane. Among and behind them, almost the entire population of the village had gathered, too.

Ralph's body had been carried back across the brook and laid on the grass of the embankment. FitzWalter got off his horse by the body. Ralph's wounds were as the messenger

The Outlaws

described. The arrow had gone clean through Ralph's neck and had severed his spine. There was a lot blood on his face and in his hair. Someone had pulled the bloody arrow from the bank. The man gave it to FitzWalter who looked at it in amazement.

Eustace was surprised to see that there were tears in FitzWalter's eyes, which he wiped away with his gloved fingertips. FitzWalter bent down to touch the dead man's face. "My dear Ralph," he murmured. "Such a shame."

FitzWalter closed Ralph's eyes and stood up.

Some of the men had removed Jermain from his horse and laid him on the bank not far from Ralph's body. The arrow still pinned him to the saddle. Matilda Attebrook straightened up from tending to Jermain, who looked in a bad way. He waved at the earl.

FitzWalter examined the wound. FitzWalter had been in battle against the Welsh and had seen such things before, so he knew what do. "Get a pair of sheep shears, cut off the arrow head and pull the arrow out. That's the only way to deal with this."

"We have shears in the house," Matilda volunteered.

FitzWalter did not look at her.

"Get them," Eustace said.

Matilda ran to the house and returned with the shears.

After Matilda had fetched them, FitzWalter directed four men to hold Jermain down. "He'll need a strap to bite on," FitzWalter said to Eustace.

One of the men unbuckled his belt "Bite down on this," he murmured.

Jermain nodded. He had seen arrows extracted before and knew what was coming.

The man-at-arms with the shears snapped off the head and drew out the shaft. Jermain bit down on the belt so hard that Eustace thought he must break a tooth. The shaft slid out, bright with blood. More blood seeped from the hole, but there was little of it.

The man who removed the arrow patted Jermain on the shoulder. "You'll be right as rain in a month."

"Ruined my damned saddle," Jermain said.

"We'll get it washed off."

FitzWalter lost interest now that the arrow was out. He stalked to the yard, where a pig was running loose in the lane beyond the house, having made a bid for freedom at the gap in the fence created by the horses. A skinny boy who Eustace remembered was Robert's younger brother Brian pursued the animal, trying to guide it back by yelling and waving a switch. Chickens scattered at FitzWalter's approach. Matilda stood by the door, wiping her hands on her apron. Two girls about ten years old peered from a window, their foreheads and eyes visible. The knights and squires fanned out behind FitzWalter, trampling the garden.

"She must have hidden them," FitzWalter said.

It was dangerous to contradict the earl, but Eustace was afraid of how he might react when he learned that Eustace had been responsible for searching the house. Yet he was bound to hear of it eventually.

"I had the house searched myself, my lord," Eustace murmured.

"Did you now?" FitzWalter's voice dripped with menace that made Eustace's knees weak.

"Yes, m'lord. The loft, even the bier."

"Not hiding under the straw, eh?" FitzWalter said. He glanced through an open window. His brows rose in astonishment for against the far wall was a real bed with carved posts. "Did you think to look under that?"

"Yes, m'lord, or course," Eustace lied. No one had thought to look under there. It also occurred to him that the bed was big enough that at least one man could have been concealed under the covers. It had been full of children at the time, and they had not bothered to pull the blankets back.

"Hmm," FitzWalter grunted. "Yet they were here." He turned away from the house. "Burn it."

"The house, m'lord?"

73

The Outlaws

"Are you deaf?"

"Well, m'lord, we own it." Eustace wasn't sure that was true. He didn't keep up with such things. But they could own it now, and squeeze some small profit from the rent. The house was ten years old, by the look of the timbers, and had another ten years more.

FitzWalter shot him a fiery glance at him. "Do we? Can't burn our own things, can we. What do we do then?"

"Turn them out, m'lord. Set them to the road."

FitzWalter smiled. To make beggars of the family, compelling them to wander from village to village existing on what charity they could eek, was almost a death sentence. He liked that suggestion, but he said, "That's not enough."

"What more should we do, m'lord?" Eustace asked, relieved that FitzWalter did not seem inclined to blame him for Ralph's death.

"Whip the boy."

"Of course," Eustace said. He shouted at two of the men-at-arms, "Off with his shirt! Then you two each hold one of his arms. We haven't a scaffold, so you'll have to play the part. And you, find a whip!"

While the two men-at-arms caught Brian and stripped off his shirt, the third soldier searched the house and emerged with a length of rope. "Should I send to the castle for a proper whip, m'lord?" he asked.

"That will do," FitzWalter said.

"How many?" Eustace said.

"Twenty," FitzWalter said. Twenty lashes was a hard sentence for anyone.

Eustace spotted the soldier that Robert Attebrook had cut the previous night, his hand wrapped in a bloody rag. "Let Horsa do the honors. He has a score to settle as well."

FitzWalter nodded. The man-at-arms with the rope handed it to Horsa, who accepted it with odd reluctance, eyes going to the crowd of villagers in the lane. Eustace had not expected this; then he wondered if Horsa was afraid of how the villagers might react. One of the married castle guards, he lived with his own family in the village. The Attebrooks, apart from Nicholas, were a popular family. For a moment, Eustace wondered if there would be trouble, but he dismissed the thought as soon as it came. The opinions of village people didn't matter.

"Twenty, my m'lord?" Horsa asked.

"That is my judgment," FitzWalter said.

Horsa nodded, his face now an unreadable mask. He tied knots along the length of the rope. He braced himself, took a few practice swings, then brought the rope down hard on Brian's back.

Brian screamed even though the blow had not broken the skin. Matilda looked away. The girls in the window began to bawl.

"Stop that damned caterwauling," the earl snapped without looking around.

Eustace stepped over to the window and slapped his hand on the sill. "Quiet, or I'll have your tongues pulled out," he said.

The two girls shot back from the window and covered their mouths, eyes wide with fear.

"That's better." Eustace turned around, arms folded.

Red streaks soon covered Brian's back and became seeping cuts. Brian jerked and cried at every blow.

A murmur of discontent arose from the lane, where the villagers were crowded together. There was also a great deal of shifting about and many angry expressions. No one had the courage to utter more than a murmur, though, for everyone knew how terrible was the earl's temper. Yet it was a mark of their disagreement that people even went this far.

Eustace strode to the fence and shouted, "Get back to work! Quit your dallying here, or I'll have the lash applied to you as well!"

This was no false threat, so most people began to melt away toward the village, but some in the crowd appeared ready to defy the order to disperse, for they tarried in the lane

The Outlaws

until friends or relatives tugged at their arms. In a few minutes, the lane was empty.

By this time, Brian had received his twenty. The men-at-arms holding his arms released him and he collapsed.

Matilda ran to him and held him up by the shoulders. "Be strong, Brian. You must be strong."

FitzWalter had turned back to the house now that the whipping was over. He peered in again, noting the bed and the loom.

"Those are our goods," Matilda said. "We should be entitled to sell them before we go."

"Whatever you own belongs to me," FitzWalter said.

Matilda's breast heaved at this. "You won't turn us out without even so much as a blanket!"

"Give her a blanket," FitzWalter said.

Matilda asked, "And what about Nicholas? Who will bury him?"

"We'll find a hole somewhere for him," FitzWalter said.

But Matilda persisted. "Whatever he may have done in life, he deserves a Christian burial."

FitzWalter shrugged. "I don't see why. The only time he ever went to church was to piss in it."

He crossed to his horse and mounted. "Drive the animals up to the castle," he said to Eustace. "That's a good pig. We'll have her for dinner one day. And get rid of them."

"At once, my lord," Eustace said. Perhaps he had escaped retribution after all — and better yet, FitzWalter had taken his advice and had given him responsibility. This was the first time that FitzWalter had ever relied on him for anything. It was a heady experience.

Eustace went into the house and chased the two girls out. He pulled a blanket from the bed and tossed it out a window. The knights and men-at-arms ushered the family into the lane.

Just before Eustace stepped into the yard, his eyes fell on a quiver of arrows leaning in the corner. Good arrows were expensive. He caught up the quiver and went out.

"Leave a man here to keep watch," he called to the knights. "The vermin will strip the place bare once our backs are turned if we give them the chance."

Then he climbed on his horse and rode out of the yard.

CHAPTER 4

March of Wales
March 1179

Matilda plodded along in a daze. But she had to think. She had to form a plan. Yet her mind refused to function. Panic lay close by, foiling every attempt at thought.

One of the soldiers, a fellow named Tad who lived in a house round the corner of the lane, touched her shoulder. They had gone far enough down the road that the village was out of sight and he felt safe about extending sympathy.

"Matilda," he said, "let me have him. You've a long way to go yet, and you've got to save your strength."

She looked at Tad as he put Brian on his back. "Where are we going to go, Tad? What are we going to do?" It seemed a simple question, but she was surprised by how frightened she sounded. She didn't want to seem frightened to the children.

"There's places," Tad said, setting off.

"What places?"

"I don't know. There's lots of manors hereabout where you could find work. You might have to give yourself up, though," he added, knowing how proud the Attebrooks were of the fact that they were free. People often gave themselves up as serfs in hard times, just to find a place, a roof, and regular meals. It wasn't so bad a life. Here in the March people had so few rights anyway that it hardly mattered whether you were serf or free. Even Tad was a serf, though he came from a family that was much better off than the Attebrooks.

"I guess I might have to," Matilda said.

They walked on a bit, then Tad said, "You know, I've a cousin in Hafton. She might put you up for a few days. Until you get sorted out."

"Do you think so?"

Tad chuckled. "Well, she isn't the most charitable sort, but she owes me a favor."

"I don't want to be a burden."

"Hafton's not a bad place, though it's small and out of the way. I hear the lord's found iron there and is opening up a mine. The boy could work in the mine."

"He doesn't know anything about mining."

"Neither does anybody else around here. But he does know how to hammer a straight nail. Mines need carpenters."

"I don't know," Matilda said. She didn't know anything about mines except they were underground, all dark and wet and dangerous. She didn't want that kind of life for Brian. She wanted him to be a craftsman like his father, but better off.

"You can't afford to turn your nose up."

"I know."

They reached a point about a mile from Shelburgh where a pile of white-painted stones beside the road indicated the end of the village's lands. This was not the end of the honor, however, for it extended another mile to the ford of the south branch of the River Lugg and beyond to the other side.

Tad set Brian on his feet. The boy tottered and sank to the ground, face vacant as if he had no idea where he was or what was going on.

"Well," Tad said, "this is as far as we go. You're on your own now. I'm supposed to warn you about turning back, but you already know not to do that."

"I'll never see Shelburgh again," Matilda said with more regret than she expected. It had been home for seventeen years, and although not the best place in the world, she had grown used to it, so it was hard imagining living anywhere else.

"It's a shame," Tad said. "Well, remember my cousin. Griffa's her name."

"Thanks, Tad."

"Don't mention it." He turned away and said to the other two soldiers who were hired men and had no connection to the village, "Don't you go saying anything about this, you hear?"

The Outlaws

"We didn't see nothing. It was a nice walk in the country," one of them said.

Matilda watched them until they reached a bend in the road and the forest swallowed them up.

It was some time before Matilda pulled Brian to his feet. "Come on, we can't sit here all day, much as we'd like to. Girls! Quit your playing! Time to go!"

"Coming, Mama!" Alice called from the edge of the wood, where she and Agnes had been collecting dandelion bulbs. In better times, this was a game they relished, but they had played it half-heartedly, glancing at Matilda and whispering to each other.

They set off eastward, away from Shelburgh. It occurred to Matilda that she had not asked Tad for directions to Hafton. He had assumed that she knew where it was, but she had never been farther from Shelburgh than the ford of the Lugg, and had no idea how to get there. She knew it lay to the east along the river somewhere a couple of hours away, but that was it. Not knowing the way, it would be easy to take a wrong turn or miss the right one. On another day, such a mistake would entail mere inconvenience, but with Brian and two girls soon calling for food, it would be a disaster.

A mile on they came to Combe, where the road crossed the south branch of the Lugg. A fortified manor house stood here, a holding of a FitzWalter retainer, and a few houses, to watch over the ford and to take advantage of the fertile ground that lay to the north on the flat between the streams.

Matilda had planned to ask directions at Combe, but it looked as though the entire population of the village was out in the fields on either side of the road, where several plow teams of oxen had begun the spring plowing, while other teams of people spread straw mixed with manure upon the ground ahead of the plows so it could be driven into the soil and so increase the crop's yield. Beyond the lane separating the ordinary people's houses from the manor house, there was a woman tending her garden behind a fence draped with washing. Matilda paused there and would have called out but for the disdainful look thrown her way. She could not afford pride, yet her tongue caught in her throat at that look and would not speak.

The ford was just beyond the hamlet. The banks here were steep and the road ran down a small cut to the stream. A peddler was resting on the opposite embankment, which had not been cleared and was covered in dark forest coming into leaf. He was a wealthy peddler because he had a hand cart for his goods. Most peddlers carried everything they had for sale on their backs in packs so great that people marveled they could even get them off the ground, let alone carry them about the country.

"Come on, girls," Matilda said at the edge of the stream. "Off with your shoes."

Brian took the moment when her attention was on the twins to sit down.

"You, too," Matilda said to him. "I'm not carrying you across."

Brian nodded, and fumbled with the knots of his laces.

Matilda waded across the stream, holding up her skirts to keep them from the wet. It was knee deep in the middle, and the stones on the bottom wanted to cut her feet.

"It's cold!" Agnes complained as she and Alice crossed over, pausing to peer at the fish that sped between their legs.

"What's the matter with him?" the peddler asked as Brian hobbled through the ford. When Brian sank into the grass an arm's length away, the peddler regarded him. "Ah, you've been run out, have you? What for?"

Matilda did not want to answer that, but she nodded. "Nothing."

"Nothing! People don't get run out of their homes for nothing."

"It wasn't anything I did, or any of the children."

"Someone you know, then, obviously."

The Outlaws

"My oldest boy. He broke his uncle out of the earl's gaol. Killed one of the earl's knights."

The peddler looked astonished. "And all the earl did was run you out? You're lucky."

"That wasn't all," Matilda said.

"I see that." He glanced up the road to the hamlet. "Why, you're such criminals I shouldn't even been seen talking to you."

It was the kind of statement that gave offense, but the peddler said it with a smile. He dug into the cart and removed some dried beef and several apples. "I'll bet they even sent you off without breakfast."

"Thanks," Matilda said as he handed her the beef and apples. The girls chewed so fast on the fare that she said, "Slow down, or you'll choke."

Even Brian perked up at the meal.

"What are you going to do now?" the peddler asked.

"A friend told us to go to Hafton. Have you heard of it?"

"I might have." He waved to the east. "I think it's over there."

"How do we get there?"

"You don't know? Ah. If you help get my little cart across this massive *fluvium*, I might deign to assist you in that regard."

"The massive what?"

"This flood here. My cart has a dislike for water and often gets stuck in the middle of it."

"That's not a very helpful cart."

"No, but it's the only one I have. Would you mind, really, giving me some assistance?"

Matilda swallowed the last of her apple. "My pleasure."

"I know it's not, but you shall be well rewarded and you can take pleasure in that."

Matilda almost missed the road to Hafton. It was no more than a cart track through the forest that was so overgrown at the mouth with grass that anyone not knowing it was there could well bypass it. Had the peddler not warned her to watch for a stand of blue-eyed mary at the base of a pine tree, she would have missed it.

Alice wanted to tarry and pick the blue blossoms, but Matilda grasped her by the collar. "It's getting late and I have no idea how far we have to go yet."

It was, in the end, about a mile more, for as they crossed a rise topped with trees, the village lay before them in the low ground strung out along the track. Beyond them the manor house rested behind an embankment and palisade with a cluster of timber buildings dominated by a small stone tower. And above them, were more fields and then the stream, which was marked by a line of willows in the distance.

The children wanted to rest at the top of the rise, but Matilda was anxious to be there so she could make arrangements for the future, even if it was the next few days. "No resting. We're almost there. And it's downhill. You could almost fall into it."

"Mama!" Agnes said, not convinced.

"Help your brother," Matilda said.

The girls each took one of Brian's arms over a shoulder and they plodded down the hill, appearing more tired than if they had just completed a march of twenty miles or more.

There were some women and children at the edge of the village under an oak taking a break from plowing and mulching.

"I'm looking for a woman named Griffa!" Matilda called to them. "Can you tell me how to find her?"

The group stirred and heads turned toward one of the women, whose mousy brown hair had come undone from her cap. She had a face marred by smallpox scars and a pug nose that would have looked handsome on a pig but did nothing for her. The woman stood up. "I'm Griffa. What do you want?"

"Tad said that you might allow us to stay at your house for a few days."

The Outlaws

Griffa grunted. She cocked a hand on her hip and took a deep drink from a leather cup. "Tad's pretty free with my charity. Who're you?"

"Matilda Attebrook. This is my son Brian and my daughters Alice and Agnes."

"Attebrook, I've heard that name."

"You may have known my husband, Harold. He was a carpenter. He got about quite a bit."

"Ah, the one who was murdered. That's been a few years."

"Yes."

"A pity, that. Never found out who was responsible, have they?"

"The earl don't care about people like us," one of the other women muttered. "We could all drop over dead as far as he's concerned."

"But then who would tend the fields for him, eh?" Griffa asked.

"Not us, thank God," said the woman who had spoken out against the earl. "We've a decent lord, at least."

Griffa looked off into the sky as if considering her options. "A few days, is it? I suppose that won't cost much. You'll have to work, though, and the children too."

In the field, the men around the plow who had been resting climbed to their feet. One of them removed the feed bags hanging from the ears of the oxen. A boy held a bucket under the oxen's noses to give them a drink. The women under the tree stood up, and bent for their baskets of mulch.

"You can start now," one of the women said. "There's still hours left in the day, and lots yet to do."

Griffa looked askance at Brian as the women headed out to the field, for he had sunk down under the oak as the others had dispersed. She notice his blood-soaked shirt.

"What happened to him?" she demanded.

After Matilda told the story of what had happened that morning, Griffa gaped in astonishment and stroked her chin. "Unbelievable. Girls!" she called out to the women who were already before the plow throwing down mulch. "You must hear this!"

No one made a point of commenting about Brian's failure to join them in the work after that.

News of crime and murder has a way of getting around fast, and when people quit work at the end of the day, many came to Griffa's house to hear the story, for such things arrived often second, third, or fourth hand. It was a great novelty to be able to interrogate one of the witnesses.

In consequence, it took Matilda a considerable time to get through her bowl of pea soup, moldy dried cherries, and sour bread and butter, which were rather flavorless owing to a lack of salt. But neither she nor the children uttered a single complaint, for they were glad even to have that. And if she had to pay for the meal by having to repeat the story over and over without losing her patience, well, that had to be done.

Her good manners paid off, however, because neighbors brought over poultices, various salves, and bushels of advice for how to deal with such dreadful injuries as Brian had suffered, which everyone agreed was unfair, and someone even gave him a new shirt, new that is to him, though the wool had thinned, the elbows were patched, and the hems frayed.

With all the poultices, salves, and the puttering attention of the neighbors, particularly the elderly women, Brian avoided infection, and by the end of the week was up and around enough that Griffa put him to housework, which was often neglected while she and her husband were in the fields. Brian did not much like doing women's work, such as changing the rushes, sweeping up, or washing pots, but he

The Outlaws

looked forward even less to the hard work that went on in the fields with plowing, ditching, and trimming, so few complaints were heard from him. At least he was not required to watch Griffa's daughters, who were too young yet to work. That duty fell to Griffa's mother, who was so old that she had few teeth or hair and required a cane to get around.

He tried to draw the line at laundry, as well. During the plowing and planting and harvesting months, laundry fell on a Sunday even though you weren't supposed to work on Sundays. Glad to have the extra hands about the house, Griffa decreed on Friday that Matilda was responsible for laundry. Matilda thought this meant Griffa's laundry, but it turned out to be that of at least four other houses, who brought their washing over in wheelbarrows, which they left in Griffa's yard.

"You can at least help me get all this down to the river," Matilda said to Brian, who was leaning on his broom, a piece of straw in his mouth.

"My back hurts," Brian said.

"It will hurt more if you don't help," Matilda said.

Brian moped about, dragging his feet and radiating discontent, but he took the handles of one wheelbarrow after Matilda had separated the woolens, which they hung over the fence, from the linens. She took up the handles of another and off they went.

A road led toward the river, where it crossed by a ford, and part way there, a narrow track worn deep into the ground by the passage of hundreds if not thousands of wheelbarrows branched off before the ford to a spot up upstream.

Matilda reached the clearing on the bank where washing was done well ahead of Brian, who halted many times for rest.

He looked a little pale, although he made no complaint, so she took pity on him after all and sent him back to the house with instructions to get started on the woolens which had to be brushed and beaten, while she returned for the last two barrows. It would have been easier to put all the linens in a single barrow, but then they'd have got mixed up, which would anger the owners who were likely to get the wrong laundry.

At Shelburgh, the linens had been washed in tubs with lye, but Hafton was too small and poor for tubs or lye. There was a board and a paddle in the grass for beating the dirt out of the cloth. There was also a tub of sorts, formed from a circle of stones at the edge of the stream to keep the clothing from washing away. Matilda dumped a load into the circle, took off her shoes, and began to tread upon them. This was easier than beating the dirt out by hand.

When she was on the third barrow, she heard voices on the other side of the stream. Two horsemen came into view beyond the screen of willow on the opposite bank. They paused, and she could see them peering at her, one of the men pointing. "That's her," he said.

The other man brought his horse to the edge of the bank. He was so well dressed, in a bright red tunic with sleeves open at the shoulders to allow him to take his arms out of them, a green undertunic, and an embroidered blue hat, that he had to be the lord. Matilda expected hostility or suspicion but instead his expression was one of stunned amazement, as if he could not believe what he saw. He recovered, however, and smiled. He was quite handsome despite the fact that a square jaw made his face seem broad and rather heavy, framed by light brown hair.

"You're our visitor, I take it," the man said. He spoke with an accent that differed from that spoken by people around here, which meant that he had come from some other part of England. Even Earl Roger spoke Herefordshire when he bothered to talk English at all, which was very seldom.

"I see I've been betrayed," Matilda said. She stopped treading and held her hem above the water.

The other fellow, still behind the willows, called out, "This is Lord William! Address him properly!"

"Easy, Baldwin," William de Hafton said. "She is new here and doesn't know who we are yet." To Matilda he said, "It's hard to hide in such a little place." He glanced up across

The Outlaws

the stream where one of the plow teams had got in trouble. The plow had tipped onto its side and the men around it were struggling to right it. "Will you be staying long?"

"That depends on when Griffa's hospitality runs out, m'lord."

"Well, you have a small reservoir there. I'm surprised you've lasted this long."

"As soon as my son is well, we'll be going." Matilda wondered with some alarm whether Griffa already resented the strain they put on her household. People were so poor that they had little to spare for charity. "We don't want to be a burden."

"I'm told you can do embroidery."

"You are remarkably well informed, m'lord." If he knew that, then he knew the full story of why she was here. Matilda braced herself for an order to get off the manor.

"It is my business to know what goes on around here. I need a seamstress up at the house. You can stay on doing that, if you're interested."

For a moment, Matilda was speechless, unwilling to credit what she had just heard. They weren't to be run out?

"I have three children." Matilda worried that he might withdraw the offer when he found out that she came with four mouths to feed rather than just one. But then, he must already know that.

"They're old enough to work, aren't they?"

"My boy is twelve, the girls are ten."

"Good. When you finish up here, come to the house and we'll get you settled. Good day to you."

William waved and turned away. As he and Baldwin rode off toward the ford, she heard Baldwin say just before they went out of earshot: "Sir! Have you lost your wits? If Earl Roger ever learns that you've given her sanctuary, he will not be pleased!"

William laughed. "Roger can stick it up his ass for all I care."

CHAPTER 5

Shelburgh
April 1179

The house seemed normal. Smoke dribbled from the vent at the top of the roof, rising into a darkening sky where the thin smile of a crescent moon hung in the west. The light from the fire glowed through cracks in the shutters and the door. But something was wrong, something was off.

Robert could not put his finger on what it was at first. Then he noticed that the back gate was ajar. There was pile of rubbish outside the back door which should have been thrown into the latrine pit. And the plank bridge over the brook still lay in the stream where he had thrown it during the escape. His mother would never have tolerated any of this.

He heard voices from the house raised in argument, a woman's and a man's where there should be no man.

The back door flew open and a woman stalked across to the woodpile, shouting at the man that he was a lazy, good for nothing drunk. A boy of about four came out after the woman, pulled down his drawers, and began to urinate against the wall by the door. The woman shouted at him too as she returned to the house with an armload of wood. The boy yanked up his drawers and scampered for the latrine at the back of the yard.

Robert knew everyone in the village, but he had never seen these people.

There were strangers living in his house.

He sat with his back to a tree, filled with despair. He had not given any thought to what Earl Roger might do, but he should have. He had wanted to help and instead he had brought down disaster.

He awoke before dawn, back still against the tree. It would be light soon. He couldn't stay here. He would be seen. Yet if he slipped away, which was the prudent thing, he would not know what happened to his family.

The forest was thick with fog. It would not last long but as long as it did, there was something he might do. He rose, and circled around west of his house, crossing the brook just out of sight of it. He approached the village proper, which lay strung along the road. Short of the back gardens, the forest ended in a narrow strip of land filled with high grass where people let their sheep and cows graze. He crossed the strip on hands and knees to the back fence of one of the gardens.

He was considering whether to hop the fence and knock on the back door of the house when Old Tom stumped out to the latrine by the woodpile. Tom stood over the pit, steadying himself on a post, and pulled down his drawers.

Robert threw a stone at him and hissed, "Tom!"

Tom glanced in his direction. Robert raised up and waved. Tom's mouth dropped. He finished his business retied his drawers

"What the hell are you doing here?" Tom growled. "Have you lost your mind?" He looked around to see if anyone else was about. So far, the neighbors' back gardens were empty.

"Where's my Mum?"

"You've come back for that, have you? Idiot. You were safe away."

"I have to know."

"She's gone."

"Where?"

"Run off, of course. You don't think the earl could stand to look at them after what you done? They're lucky to be alive."

"I didn't mean to do it."

"Yeah, nobody ever really intends to do murder. It just sort of happens. Like bad luck. Get out of here before someone sees you. If anybody comes out, I'll have to call out. If I don't, I'll be whipped just like your brother and driven out, if not hanged. Besides, I wouldn't mind a bit of that reward."

"Reward?"

The Outlaws

"Yeah, the earl's put of a price on your head — two pounds. Who'd have thought you'd be worth that much. But then it's not about you, is it? It's about the earl's pride and the harm you did to it by killing his cousin."

"If you're not going to shout, tell me quick then. Where did they go?"

"Like I have some idea! They've just gone."

Tom's wife stuck her head out the door. "What's keeping you?"

"Thought I saw a rabbit in the garden!" Tom called back. While rabbits outside the garden belonged to the lord, people were allowed to catch them within their gardens. In consequence, there was often a plague of rabbits in the village, as a well-thrown stone could bring one down long enough to catch it.

"Don't be too long!"

"I won't!" Tom leaned on the pole. "You never heard this from me. Nobody else knows but me and Tad. He told them to head for Hafton. He has a cousin there who owes him a favor. They probably stayed there a few days. You can find out where they went from there."

"Thanks, Tom."

"Fuck that. Just get your ass out of here before I'm tempted to seek that reward."

CHAPTER 6

Hafton
April 1179

"Oh, my lord," said Eleanor the steward's wife when they were all seated for dinner and those whose turn it was to serve were setting down the soup. "A letter came today."

She removed the letter from her drooping sleeve and handed it across her husband Baldwin to William.

Giselle, as lady of the house sat on her William's right, the place her mother occupied when she was alive, leaned forward at the announcement, for it was unusual that Eleanor should intercept one of William's letters. Her father paid no attention to Eleanor's expression, but Giselle spotted a hint of slyness on Eleanor's face as she extended the letter.

William's spoon stopped on the way to his mouth and returned to its bowl. "A letter? Excellent!"

William was from Kent just above Cambridge. People traveling to and from London had often stopped at his father's house if they could not find accommodations in the town, and he had grown up hearing the news of the world. Hafton, however, was about as far off the beaten track as you could get in England, so he would have had no idea what was going on if he hadn't cultivated correspondents. It was expensive receiving letters, but he took great pleasure whenever one arrived, even though it cost for delivery.

William flipped the letter over. "I don't recognize the seal. Is the messenger still here?"

"He's gone, my lord," Eleanor said. "He said he could not tarry."

That sly smile appeared again, and vanished.

"That's odd," William said.

He broke the seal and opened the letter. A frown appeared, which deepened as he read.

"It's from Humbert de Grasse," William said, looking up at Giselle.

The Outlaws

"Humbert de Grasse!" Giselle said. She had met Humbert at the Ludlow fair last autumn. She recalled him as a man no taller than herself of about twenty-five with a flat piggish face and a reputation of getting drunk with his friends and pinching the breasts and bottoms of serving girls. He was a second son who lived at sufferance on one of his father's manors, a situation that he made known to her was far too constricting and which would not last long, as he was a man of talent with friends at court.

There was only one reason why Humbert would write to her father out of the blue, and William confirmed it. "He's made a proposal for your hand."

"He has?" Giselle asked, as if the matter was of no importance.

"It seems he has come into his full inheritance," William said. "What is that, eight manors?" He shook his head at the thought. A man with eight manors could count himself a baron.

"He had a brother," Giselle said. "What happened to him? And his father?"

"They died," Baldwin said. "Their ship sank on the way to France."

"How would you know that?" Giselle asked.

"I heard when I went up to Ludlow last month," Baldwin said.

"And you didn't say anything?" William asked.

"I forgot about it, m'lord. It didn't seem important."

"Well, it's important now, isn't it," William said, resting the letter beside his soup bowl. "What are we going to do about it?"

"Nothing," Giselle said.

"This is the third proposal this year," William said. "The richest one yet."

"I don't care how rich he is. I wouldn't marry that little pig if he was king of England."

"Giselle, you are almost fourteen. We need to start thinking about finding you a husband. In a few years, people will begin calling you an old maid."

"I'd rather be a nun than married to the likes of him." Then she added the *coup de grace*. "Mother would not have approved of him." She didn't invoke Mother very often, but this situation seemed to call for it.

"I suppose she wouldn't," William said with a sad smile.

"So," Giselle said, "we shall have no more talk of Humbert de Grasse, shall we?"

"That damned girl!" Eleanor raged when she and Baldwin were alone in their room above the hall.

"Quiet down!" Baldwin said, alarmed at the volume of her rage. "People will hear! The walls are thin!"

Eleanor shuddered as she struggled to contain her anger and disappointment. But Baldwin was right. It would not do for anyone to know how disappointed she was that William had allowed that stupid strip of a girl to manipulate him. Not if she wished to succeed in her plans.

"I was sure that William would agree to this match," Baldwin said in a whisper, taking his own advice.

"I knew it would fail," Eleanor said in a lower tone, but not in a whisper. "I warned you." She had, of course, done nothing of the kind. She had been all for writing to de Grasse to suggest that William would welcome a proposal when Baldwin had brought the news of his inheritance. She had been certain that the prospect of marrying the girl to such wealth would be too much for William to resist. Eleanor had not counted on how strong a hold sentimentality had over William. Giselle was his only child, his sons having died as infants, and she so took after his dead wife, with her pale skin, black hair, and swan-like beauty, that he was a slave to his emotions. "I should have foreseen it," Eleanor fumed.

"Ah, well," Baldwin said as he pulled off his boots and wriggled his toes. "She'll have to go eventually. Be patient."

The Outlaws

"I am tired of being patient. She should have been fostered long ago. Then I'd not have to worry about her interference." It was the custom of the gentry to send their children to the households of others so that they could be educated. The usual practice was to send children off when they the age of eight or nine. But so far, Giselle had managed to avoid even this.

"Fostered . . ." Eleanor muttered to herself. "Of course. That's it!" If she could separate William and Giselle, it would be easier to convince William to marry off the girl to someone far away; distance would diminish the power of her protests. Meanwhile, Eleanor could rule as lady of the manor in substance if not in name.

She swung around to Baldwin who was now stark naked and covering himself with the blankets, which he smoothed around his legs. "You shall put that idea into William's mind. She needs to be fostered. She has resisted that step far too long."

"I shall?"

"He listens to you. You are the steward."

"I suppose I can give it a try."

"Do not merely try. Succeed, for my sake."

"Of course, dear. Now blow out that candle and come to bed. We haven't played our game in a long time."

The next morning was the monthly manor court.

Giselle had no role to play, but she often sat at the end of the high table where William presided, pretending to work on a piece of embroidery while she listened to the problems the villagers brought up and how William resolved them. Most such problems were mundane, but they were vital to life in the village, and she enjoyed hearing about them, dreaming of the day when she might be the one making the decisions. Today was no different than any other court: there was a question of a fine for someone sent to work in another's place but who performed inadequately; the plowing over the balk separating one villager's strip from another in what the victim presented as a deliberate attempt to appropriate land that wasn't his; a fine for a village boy who wanted to marry outside the manor; a request to commute labor services because of illness; a claim for battery arising from a fight over a broken jug of ale that had been the main scandal before Matilda Attebrook's arrival; and the request to build a new house to replace one that was falling down.

It took most of the morning to resolve these pressing questions because none could be addressed without a lot of talking by those involved. It was dinner time before William was done, and the household servants chafed around the edges of the crowd, waiting for it to clear so they could set up the tables.

At the end of court, William usually got up and stretched his legs, but today, Baldwin grasped his forearm and they had a conversation with their heads together. They were just far enough away that Giselle could not hear what was being said over the babble of the crowd, which often used a manor court as a holiday and a chance to gossip. But the way that William threw a glance or two in Giselle's direction made her worried that they were talking about her. She could not guess what this might be about, but she had the feeling that it would not be good.

After Baldwin departed, William remained in his chair, hands clasped over his stomach, lips pursed in thought.

After a considerable time, he rose and came over to Giselle. "Walk with me," he said.

William spoke in a distracted way, but the tone was ominous nonetheless. Giselle put down her embroidery and followed her father into the yard.

William walked through the gate with Giselle a step behind, hands behind his back and that distracted look still on his face, as if he was not sure how to bring up whatever was on his mind.

They walked this way until they reached the churchyard, where William turned in and stopped before the monument

The Outlaws

marking the grave of his wife, Hanelore, and the smaller stones beside it for the graves of the two sons who had died as infants.

This had Giselle worried, for he had never led her to Mother's grave before. She suspected that father had changed his mind about de Grasse's marriage proposal. She thought she would rather die than marry such an oaf.

"All right," William said at last. "You don't have to marry that de Grasse fellow. But you'll be fourteen this summer, and it's time we start looking."

Giselle contained a sigh of relief at this reprieve, although the prospect of having to marry a stranger picked out by her father without her having any say in the matter still felt like punishment, even if such things were commonplace.

"Do you have someone in mind?" she asked.

"Not yet. But England isn't so small a country that there aren't quite a few eligible fellows to choose from. Some of them you might even like." He put his hand on top of Hanelore's monument as if drawing strength from it. "In the meantime, we also must think about your education."

That announcement sent almost as much of a chill through Giselle as the prospect of a marriage proposal. She knew what it meant. "You're going to send me away."

"It's for your own good," William said. "Your mother would have taken matters in hand much earlier than this, so that you are properly brought up. I've been too sentimental, keeping you close, and your education has suffered for it." William stroked her hair. He looked as sad as Giselle felt. "You look so like your mother. It's as if she had never gone. But it's time."

"Have you decided where I shall go?"

"I was thinking my brother's house."

Giselle was appalled not so much at the possibility of having to live with an uncle she had never met, for at least he would not be a total stranger, but William's elder brother lived on the family manor in Kent. It was so far away it might as well have been in France. Yet this was not something she could argue against. Nothing she could say would change William's mind. Giselle had known, of course, that such a day would come, but she had held out hope that it wouldn't, somehow. "When?" she managed to say.

"I shall write to him straightaway."

That brought some relief. It would take time for letters to travel back and forth between Kent.

"Can I stay at least until the harvest?" Giselle asked. The harvest was one of the most festive and happy times on the manor. She didn't want to miss that.

"Until the Ludlow fair," William said. "I'll take you over afterward."

So, Giselle thought as they turned away from Hanelore's grave, she had until September. Then she would have to leave Hafton. How she loved it here, and how she hated to leave it.

CHAPTER 7

Hafton manor
April 1179

Eleanor paused in the doorway to Giselle's room, her pinched face even more pinched as it labored with a thought that had to mean no good.

Matilda, who was seated on the window seat for the morning light mending one of the lord's tunics beside Giselle, pretended not to see Eleanor, wishing they had closed the door. In the short time that Matilda had lived on the manor, she had learned it was best to be invisible when Eleanor was about, when she had that flinty look. It always meant some unpleasant task which if not performed to her exacting views could result in a beating.

"We are shorthanded," Eleanor said in that stiff way of hers. "I need help carrying water."

"Ah," Giselle said, not looking up from her embroidery, "it is Saturday, isn't it."

Saturday was bathing day for the lord. This entailed his total immersion in warm water, which was heated at great effort and with lots of firewood in a kettle in the yard and then carried in buckets to the tub which took up part of the chapel. Matilda had never heard of bathing in a chapel, but it was the one place to put the tub that afforded any privacy and did not require carting the water up stairs. Lords often bathed on Saturdays, when they also enjoyed a shave. More often was considered eccentric if not unhealthy. Other people, which is to say just about everybody else, made do with a rag, a washbasin, and cold water, and in the winter some went months without even this, except for a scrubbing of the face and hands.

"What's happened to Burghard or Osgar?" Giselle asked, peering rather too intently at the stitching she had just put in. Burghard and Osgar, father and son, were the two grooms who did most of the heavy work around the house.

"They have taken a quarter of grain to the mill," Eleanor said.

"A bath," Matilda murmured.

"Have you ever had one?" Giselle asked.

"When I was a girl. Three times a week."

"Good Lord! Who bathes three times a week!" Giselle said.

"We did."

"I can't believe that."

"Well, my family did. We are Danes. The Irish of course never bathe. You should see their feet in summer — many go barefoot and never wash them, even before they go to bed." Matilda remembered her father remarking on this and how important it was to be clean and tidy. The Danes of Dublin were, in fact, renowned for their cleanliness.

"You're Danish?"

Matilda nodded. "I was born in Dublin."

"Danes live in Dublin? I had no idea."

"Some do. Traders and merchants."

"I said," Eleanor intoned again from the doorway, a frown beginning to cloud her face, "I need a hand carrying water."

"I suppose she means you," Giselle whispered.

"I suppose she does," Matilda said.

"Her hands are much too delicate for carrying buckets," Giselle said. "Besides, I wish her to finish father's tunic before dinner."

Eleanor did an admirable job of confining a twitch to a small corner of her mouth. "She came to us looking like a woman used to hard work. Those don't look like the hands of a seamstress to me. Besides, there's no one else, and the lord will be back soon." William had gone across the river to inspect the mines again.

Matilda sensed a confrontation building. She didn't want to be caught up in the struggle between them. Matilda stood up. "Coming, mistress."

The Outlaws

As she left the room, she couldn't miss the pout of frustration on Giselle's lips.

Matilda, two boys from the kitchen, and her daughters Alice and Agnes had just dumped the last buckets of water into the tub when William entered the chapel. In the flurry of activity that followed as the servants scuttled out and he disrobed, Giselle caught Matilda's arm before Eleanor could think of something else for her to do, and led her back upstairs to the window seat, where the unmended tunic still awaited. Giselle seemed in good humor, not the least put out that she had been balked at keeping Matilda at her side.

The next hour passed in light conversation, before they heard the sounds of William coming up the stairs.

"At last," Giselle said, putting down her embroidery. "My turn. Why don't you join me?"

"I don't know," Matilda said. While it wasn't unusual for people to share a bath, she wasn't sure that sharing one with Giselle was acceptable.

"Come. I need someone to wash my hair."

"Your maid can't do that?"

"She is too rough." Giselle leaned forward: "She takes her lessons from Eleanor! Come on, you cannot refuse me. I command it." Giselle stood up and pulled Matilda to her feet.

When put that way, of course Giselle could not be refused.

The chapel was a small timber building beside the hall. Its windows were kept open in good weather such as they were having today, which explained the abundance of sparrows' nests in the rafters that the chaplain had not got around to clearing out, but owing to the fact that it was now Giselle's turn in the tub, the chaplain pulled the shutters closed and scurried out with a "Good day to you, my lady."

Matilda and Giselle stood in the rectangle of light cast by the open door until Giselle's maid, Athelhild, brought in a cake of brown soap, a pair of candles, a jug of ale, and two clay cups. She put those down on a plank laid upon two trestles, and undressed Giselle. Matilda had to fend for herself in that chore.

It was chilly in the dark. Giselle wasted no time once she was naked in climbing into the tub. Athelhild went out and shut the door.

"Hurry," Giselle said. "It's still warm."

If there had been a step, someone had taken it away, so Matilda had to clamber in. She settled down to her chin, sitting cross-legged; the two of them could just fit in the tub this way. It *was* still warm. It felt wonderful.

Giselle stood up, soaped herself, and sat down as soon as she could.

"Don't forget your feet," Matilda said.

"I'm not standing up again, not until I have the aid of a towel." Giselle raised a foot above the water and dangled it over the side. She grinned. "You wash it. You're my maid now."

"I'm not your maid. I'm just a house servant. Do house servants ordinarily wash feet?"

"You are my maid if you want to be."

At first, Matilda thought the girl was joking, but Giselle's gaze was level and true. "You mean that?"

"I do. Until I leave, anyway. And with father's permission, you might be able to come with me. I'm going to need two maids where I'm going. People will think me a poor relation if I have only one. It would shame father for his brother to know how we just scuff out a living in these hills. I'm sure father will see the sense in that."

"I don't know anything about being a maid."

"It's easy. Just keep quiet and do what you're told. Watch Athelhild. She'll show you what to do."

"I have my children to think of. I can't leave them here. Aren't maids unmarried women?"

"Usually. I could call you a body servant, I suppose. It amounts to the same thing. Are you looking for excuses to say no?"

The Outlaws

It was an excellent offer and Matilda could not think of any good reason to turn it down. "All right, I'll do it."

"Good, now wash that foot."

They had almost finished the jug of ale between them, and were quite relaxed when Athelhild returned with an armful of towels, gowns, and underclothes. She laid out a green embroidered gown on the plank and held out the two others, a blue one with silver embroidery not much different than the one she wore or that lay on the plank, and a plain brown one.

"Which is it?" Athelhild asked.

Matilda wasn't sure what she meant by this, but Giselle pointed to the blue gown. "That one."

Athelhild smiled. "Good then. She's decided to join us."

"Less work for you," Giselle said.

"That's what I'm hoping for."

"I must wear that?" Matilda said, startled.

"Well, it was my mother's," Giselle said, as she accepted a towel and climbed out of the tub to dry herself off, "so it might not fit, but you're smaller than she was so I don't see where there's likely to be a problem."

"Your father won't object?"

"I don't see why," Giselle said, as Athelhild helped her into her underclothes.

"All my clothes are hand-me-downs from our dear lady," Athelhild said. "Besides, Lord William picked it out himself."

"Lord William!"

"He thought you would look well in it. The blue matches your eyes."

"It does," Giselle said.

"He knows then?" Matilda asked. She climbed out of the tub and dried herself with a towel.

"Of course, he knows," Giselle said. "I couldn't take you on without his permission." Her nose wrinkled. "I'm just a girl. I can't decide things for myself."

Having seen how Giselle got her way over de Grasse, Matilda wasn't sure about that. She fingered the gown, which Athelhild draped on the plank.

"Hurry up," Athelhild said. "We've got to dry and braid my lady's hair! Come on, now! It will be dinner time soon."

The women emerged from the chapel as Burghard and Osgar were putting up the two other tables in the hall for dinner. With ten people on the household staff, plus children, three tables were all they needed for everyone.

On an ordinary day, their appearance would have gone unremarked, but today was different. Everyone stopped and stared.

"Good heavens! Who's that?" muttered Stigand, Burghard's father who was so blind that he could see only shapes and colors. "We've a lady visiting?"

"No, dad," Burghard's wife said in his ear. "It's only Matilda."

"The new girl? What's she doing dressed like our lady?"

"I don't know."

Whatever questions anyone had about that were answered when Athelhild took Matilda by the arm and guided her to a place beside her nearest to the high table.

Matilda sat down, nervous at all the eyes on her, fretful that she might spill food on the pretty gown.

She glanced at those at the high table as Giselle took her place to her father's right. Baldwin was lustful, leering even more than he usually did. William was thoughtful but no less interested.

Eleanor, on the other hand, could not conceal her hostility.

Matilda wondered what Eleanor had to be angry about. It wasn't until one of the servants put a soup bowl and a loaf of bread in front of her and Athelhild that it occurred to Matilda that Giselle had used her as a pawn in the struggle of wills between her and the steward's wife.

105

The Outlaws

CHAPTER 8

Hafton
April 1179

Robert had never been to Hafton before, so he didn't know quite what to expect. The track he had been told to take led north from the road up a hill. He walked the horse until he reached a point just short of the crest, where he dismounted and tied the horse to the branch of a tree. He walked on foot to the top of the hill to see what lay beyond without, he hoped, being seen himself.

He was glad he'd taken this precaution, for the slope below had been cleared and and was dotted with sheep. A shepherd's hut lay some distance to the right. The shepherd was visible sitting on a bench with his back to a wall of the hut.

People were plowing and harrowing a field further down where the land bottomed out. Beyond them lay the village, the houses strung out on the track and between them and a line of trees that had to mark the river was the manor house within an earthen embankment and palisade.

Robert considered what to do. He couldn't just ride in there. Strangers at any time attracted a lot of attention, and he wanted as little of that as he could get. A horseman as poor as he who had no business with a horse, would excite even more notice.

After puzzling over the problem for some time, he returned to the horse and rode back down the hill, then circled west into a patch of forest. The forest ended at another field. The village sat across the field.

He sat down to wait for sundown. His stomach growled. He hadn't eaten for two days now and he was hungry. He hoped they'd at least feed him before he got on his way.

Toward sundown, the people working in the fields went home for supper. When Robert thought the fields were clear and he was less likely to be seen, he crossed the field, careful to keep to a furrow separating one field from another so as

The Outlaws

not to trample the area set aside for growing things. It was a great trespass to cross anyone's planted field.

He came out at the north end by the last house. No one called out, so he felt safe. He had no idea which of the two dozen or so houses that made up the village belonged to Tad's cousin. He would have to ask for directions. He dreaded having to do that, but there seemed to be no other way.

The best bet was the village priest or vicar. It wasn't hard to figure out where to find him. The church was the only stone building hereabout except for a small stone tower within the manor house's palisade which he had seen from the top of the hill. He was about to head for that when a boy emerged from the nearest house carrying a pail which, from the easy way he carried it, had to be empty.

The boy stopped when he spotted Robert. "Who're you?"

"Nobody," Robert said.

"What are you doing here?"

"I'm looking for someone named Griffa."

"What for?"

"Her cousin Tad asked me to deliver a message."

"About what?"

"It's a family matter."

"Huh." The boy came through the gate. "Third house from the end. On the right." He gestured toward the south.

"Thanks."

"Try not to get lost." The boy turned away toward the open space before the church where the village well must stand.

Robert managed to find the third house from the end without too much trouble. He pushed the gate open and went up to the door. He could hear voices within: two children arguing about something, almost drowning out the voices of a man and woman in a conversation of their own. The sound made him smile, it was so much like coming home, even if this wasn't home. He knocked on the door. The voices of the adults stopped, although the children continued their dispute.

The door opened. A stout woman with a pock-marked face and the stubbiest nose he had ever seen stood in the doorway.

"What do you want?" she asked.

"I'm looking for my mother. Her name's Matilda Attebrook."

The woman grabbed him by the shirt and jerked him inside. "Boys! Look what we have here! A murderer, in the flesh!"

Robert realized that he had made a big mistake. He tried to break free of the woman's grasp, but she swept his feet from under him with the skill of an accomplished wrestler, and kneeled on his chest.

"Don't think you can get away," the woman said, shaking a fist before his nose. "I've laid flat bigger men than you."

The woman flipped him on his stomach as the man she had been talking with and a boy almost Robert's age pulled on his arms so he could neither resist nor escape. Then they bent his arms behind his back and tied his wrists and elbows with lengths of old cloth.

"Go fetch the steward," the woman said. "Tell him we've caught Matilda's murderous whelp."

"Right, ma!" the boy exclaimed and raced out into the evening.

Now that Robert was trussed, neither the man nor the woman seemed much concerned that he might escape even though they had not thought to bind his feet. They both retreated to a bench where a pot of ale waited on the table nearby. They filled drinking bowls while the three children Robert had heard arguing scuttled over to investigate his saddlebag.

"Get out of there!" Robert snapped.

"Best keep your temper, boy," the woman said after a long pull at her drinking bowl. "You're in no position to tell anybody to do anything."

"That belongs to my mother," he said.

"Do it now?"

109

The Outlaws

By this time the children had managed to untie the bindings securing the flap. One reached inside but the older sister snatched at the bag.

"You two," the woman said, "stop that fuss. Let's see what we've got here, what has our little outlaw so concerned." She knelt by the bag. "Ooh, that's heavy! What you got in here?"

"None of your business."

But it was too late to frustrate the woman's curiosity, for she had put her hand in the bag, a look of astonishment sweeping over her face. The hand came out with a cloth sack which the woman carried to table with obvious effort and let it fall with the unmistakable clank of coins.

"Good God, I think he's got the whole damn royal treasury in here!"

The man and the woman bent over the bag. It took longer than normal to get its strings untied because they kept getting in each other's way. But at last they had it open and spilled the contents on the table: a wave of silver pennies.

"How much you got here?" the woman asked Robert.

"Forty shillings."

"Where'd the devil you get forty shillings?"

"He stole it, that's where," the man said.

"If that's so, there'll be a reward for its return, just like there is for him," the woman said.

"You don't care you might set off Matilda?" the man asked.

"What do I care what she thinks?"

"She's gone to live in the big house. The young lady has taken to her, you know that."

"Pssshhh! Just another maid, that's all she is. Come on Teddy, think of how rich we'll be with not one but two rewards!"

Teddy did not have a chance to respond to this, for a muscular man in high leather boots, a blue tunic trimmed with white that hung to below his knees, and a blue embroidered cap filled the doorway. He had light brown hair, a broad nose, and a square jaw. The lines around his eyes and mouth suggested that he smiled a lot, but he was not smiling now.

Teddy and the woman shot to their feet as he entered the house.

"My lord!" they exclaimed at once.

"That's him, Griffa?" the lord asked the woman.

"Came knocking at our door just moments ago," the woman Griffa said, "as if it was the most natural thing to do and he had nothing to fear. Our first thought was to send for you, sir."

The lord glanced at the money on the table. Even he, who had to be used to seeing large sums in hard coin, looked surprised. "What's this?"

"The fruits of this ruffian's outlaw ways," Griffa said. "He said there's forty shillings in there."

"Forty shillings! You brought this?" the lord asked Robert.

"It belongs to my mother. I came to deliver it to her."

"You were away and you came back? Not a very prudent thing to do. How did you get it?"

"I delivered someone safely home."

The lord appeared to be about to ask whom that might have been, but something checked the impulse. "An expensive task, by the look of it. All right, Teddy." He scooped the spilled coin back into the bag, which he cradled on his arm. "Bring him along. We'll have to put him up in the barn."

"You could put him up with the pigs, m'lord," Teddy volunteered while he hauled Robert to his feet.

"That would be unfair to the pigs. Besides, one might eat him before we have a chance to give him over to Earl Roger."

"I don't think the earl will mind much."

"Probably not. But he might give the pig indigestion, so it's the barn, not the sty."

The lord marched out into the dark with Teddy pushing Robert so hard that he stumbled over the doorstep and almost fell on his face.

The Outlaws

"You're enjoying this far more than you should," Robert said.

"So what? There isn't much to do around here, and nobody will mind if you've got a bruise or two, except for that mother of yours. And as Griffa says, she don't count for much."

"I see you've not had much to do with my mother."

Teddy gave Robert another shove as they passed the church. "Don't think you'll get anywhere with me with threats."

"Stop that!" the lord called from ahead. "I want him in the barn with all his teeth in his head!"

"Coming, sir!" Teddy called back. He tugged Robert along. "Watch out for them ruts. They can make for nasty falls in the dark. They sure can. Won't be my fault if something happens."

This time Robert could not avoid a fall as he tripped in a rut.

Teddy kicked him in the ribs. "Get up. I'm tired of hauling you to your feet."

Robert lay there a moment, savoring the sensation that the cloth bonds, never tied that well, had loosened. His heart beat fast. Here was a chance, if he played it right. "A moment. I've twisted my ankle."

"Damn your ankle!"

"What's going on there?" the lord called back out of the dark.

"Nothing, lord! The fool boy's tripped, that's all!"

Robert struggled to his knees as the bonds on his wrist came so loose that the rags just hung like old washing. Teddy lost patience and grasped Robert's shoulder to lift him up, and was surprised when Robert stood on his own, his hands free, and rammed the heel of a hand into Teddy's chin. Teddy was made of stuff that was harder than he looked and he stumbled backward without falling as Robert had expected.

"You little shit," Teddy said, and reached for Robert's collar while raising a fist he planned to smash into Robert's face.

But Robert could run when he had to and before Teddy's fingers could find the collar he had turned about and raced up the lane.

Here again Teddy proved to be made of harder stuff than he looked: he pounded after Robert so close that Robert feared a diving tackle would bring him down. Before such a thought could occur to Teddy, Robert swerved left and vaulted the stone fence surrounding the church. He heard Teddy clear the fence with a grunt, but dared not spare a look backward as he jumped one headstone, swerved around others, nearly tripped on an unseen one in the dark, and dodged and danced away for more.

He reached the church doors a few strides ahead of Teddy. He flung the door open, filled with relief that it was neither barred nor locked, and dashed into the church. It was darker inside than up a cow's ass, and he had no idea what lay ahead to snare his feet and foil his escape, for he would not be safe until he reached the alter at the far end.

But reach it he did, vaulting the barrier, and cried, "Sanctuary!" just as Teddy blundered into him from behind with an impact that nearly knocked him away from the altar and the only salvation left to him.

Teddy picked himself off the ground, cursing fast so that the words were almost unintelligible. He was attempting to pry Robert free from the altar when the lord asked from the church door, "Did he get to the altar?"

"No, m'lord," Teddy gasped, as the struggle continued.

"I did!" Robert cried.

"Hold a moment there, boys." There was the snick of flint on steel. A flame flared in a bowl of tinder by the candle rack. The lord lighted one of the candles from the rack and held it up to illuminate the nave. "Leave off, Teddy. He's made it."

"No one has to know," Teddy said.

The Outlaws

"I'll know. Come away from there."

Teddy's hands fell away from Robert and he retreated down the nave to the lord and his candle. "Don't think you're getting away."

"Fuck you, too," Robert said.

The lord handed Teddy the candle. He said, "That was well done. Stay here and keep an eye on him while I rouse Wulfric. The boy'll have to be watched."

Robert spent a hard night. If he got any sleep at all, it was when he lay on the altar, for Wulfric had set up a watch at the door where one of the villagers sat on a stool to keep an eye on him in case he let go of the altar, when he could be seized. The watchman burned candles throughout the night, and the air stank with tallow. The altar was a small thing, half his length, and he felt by the morning that he had known stones that were more comfortable.

Toward dawn the watchman fell asleep, and began to snore so that he roused some of the sparrows nesting in the rafters. Even then, Robert dared not venture away from the altar, as the sound of voices and the calling of cocks announced the start of the new day.

The vicar came in to stare at him as the sun topped the trees, followed by barefoot boys and girls, who gaped at the criminal from the doorway. Their pushing and shoving woke the watchman. He grunted and snorted and blew his nose on a sleeve, then declared, "Away with you, away with you! Unless you've any stones you'd care to aim at this vile murderer!" But then he remembered they were in the church and sent them packing.

"Isn't it time for breakfast?" Robert asked the watchman. "Shouldn't you be going?"

"You'd like that, wouldn't you? Think you can get away? You wouldn't get far, and then we'd get to see you dance!"

"Well, I was thinking you might fetch me something."

"Fat chance that." There was some commotion outside the door, and the gangly reeve, Wulfric, appeared on the walk with two other men. "Ah," the watchmen said, standing and giving a great stretch, "my relief."

He went out and shut the door. Robert pulled himself up so he could see out one of the narrow windows. There was a fresh watchman sitting on the stone fence eating an apple. Robert checked out a window on the other side of the church. A villager was sitting with his back to an elm tree. He waved at Robert. "Thanks for getting me out of plowing!" the fellow called.

"My pleasure!" Robert called back.

He dropped down and went back to the altar, where he sat with his back to it. He felt as low as he had ever felt in his life, lower even than that day he had discovered his father murdered in the woods. He saw no way of getting himself out of this jam. He couldn't outrun a whole village. They'd have horses and dogs and he'd be caught. He hated to think what would happen if Earl Roger got hold of him. He had heard stories about how people were tortured in the castle: some hung by their thumbs, some by their hair, some by hooks dug into their shoulders, some laid in boxes with stones piled upon them, some with their heads forced in a box and smoke pumped about them so they couldn't breathe. People said that was worse than having your head dunked in a bucket. Mostly these stories were told about the days before he was born when King Stephen and the Empress Matilda fought over the throne. He had no idea if any of it was true or if the present earl indulged himself this way, though people said he did. This was worrisome. Because if the earl didn't, he had good reason to revive some of these gruesome pastimes. Nothing to look forward to.

There was the sound of footsteps on the path beyond the door. Robert leaped to his feet and grasped the altar, prepared again to defend his claim to sanctuary. The door creaked and opened, admitting fresh yellow sunlight. Two girls stood there. Even with the light behind them, Robert could see that

115

one of them was stunning. She had an oval face, delicate features, and large dark eyes. Coal black hair cascaded from beneath her headscarf, coiled in braids that fell down her back. She came across the nave, followed by the other girl, who was pretty, but not as arresting as the darkhaired girl.

The dark-haired girl stopped before him. "So that's what one looks like," she said to her companion. "How ordinary."

"That's *what* looks like?" Robert asked.

"A murderer. You are a murderer, aren't you?"

"I don't think so." He couldn't very well confess to what he had done, even though there was no secret about it.

"Well, I'm sure the crown justice will have something to say about that."

"Crown justice?"

"Yes."

"What's he got to do with anything?"

"Everything, of course. When the sheriff gets here, he'll throw you in a pit and wait for the justice to show up so he can conduct your trial and send you to the rope."

"You're not handing me over to the earl?"

"Of course not. He has no jurisdiction to deal with murderers."

"Glad to hear that." He noticed that the other girl had a basket under her arm, and he had become aware of the smell of bread, not fresh-baked, but new enough, and of a cheese. "What's in there?" he asked, indicating the basket.

"Oh, yes. Your mother sends you breakfast. We have to keep your strength up so you will live to see the crown justice."

"She said that?"

"No, but she sent the breakfast."

"She's here then, my mother?"

"She couldn't send you breakfast if she wasn't here."

"But she wasn't in the house I went to last night."

"She lives with me now."

"And who are you, exactly?"

"I am Giselle de Hafton."

"*De* Hafton? I suppose that was your father last night, that lord."

"You should take a more respectful tone when you're speaking of my father."

"Since I'm going to hang eventually, I'm not sure I care to."

"And I will expect a more respectful tone when you are speaking to me, as well."

"Oh —" Robert almost said "piss off," but caught himself. Giselle had not yet extended that basket.

"Oh, what?"

"Oh, nothing. Can I have the basket now before I drop dead of hunger?"

"I suppose. Athelhild? Would you mind?"

The other girl, Athelhild, set the basket on the ground at her feet. It was too far away for Robert to reach it without letting go of the altar.

"Give it a little push," he said.

"No," Giselle said. "You come get it. Afraid that I'll wrestle you to the ground? I could, you know. If I wanted to."

"The devil you could." Keeping his eyes on Giselle and Athelhild for any signs of an intention to pounce, he edged away from the altar. When the two girls remained umoving, he snatched up the basket and vaulted to the top of the altar. He opened the basket. His eyes confirmed what his nose had foretold: there was bread and cheese, and a sausage besides. He took a bite out of the sausage. "You know, it seems to me that as long as I have the altar, you're not handing me over to anyone."

"You'll surrender. Hunger will drive you to it. That's what Wulfric said."

"Did he? Seems to me that you shouldn't be feeding me, then, should you."

Guilt appeared on Giselle's face.

"Don't worry," Robert said. "I won't tell anyone."

"You better not, especially as this was a gift of your mother."

The Outlaws

"She couldn't come herself?"

"She's angry with you. She was in a mood to crack your head. So I came in her place."

Robert finished the sausage and broke off a piece of cheese. "Send her my thanks — and my love."

"I think she'd rather hear an apology for the ruin you've done. Now, give me back that basket. We have to be going."

Giselle and Athelhild turned around and left.

"Is there anything else I can get you, sir?" the servant asked. He stepped back from the trestle table he had carried in from the hall and set up in William's chamber. The room had no table of its own, just the bed, a chair, a pair of stools, a rug on the floor that Hanelore had treasured, and a pair of chests for storing things, mostly clothes. So the sight of the table was odd indeed.

"No, that will be all," William said.

"This is quite unusual, sir," Baldwin said from the doorway. "Are you sure you aren't ill?" It was clear that William intended to do some sort of work in the privacy of his chamber.

"I'm fine, Baldwin. Now go away."

"Very good, sir," Baldwin said, although from the tone he didn't think this was very good at all. He hated being left out of anything, or rather, his wife hated it on her own and his behalf.

William smiled at the thought of Eleanor badgering Baldwin for the secret. With Teddy in the know and likely to have blabbed every detail of last night's business, it wouldn't take long for her to guess what he was up to. Yet he did not feel comfortable doing what he was about to do in full view of everyone.

William went to his clothing chest, which sat in a corner, and fetched the cloth bag with the money he had taken from the boy Robert. He dragged a stool to the table and emptied the bag on the top. He had no immediate idea how many pennies there were in forty shillings, and he had to puzzle out the number by counting on his fingers: four-hundred-eighty. An ordinary laboring man could work a year at the going wage of a penny a day and not earn that much money. It was more in hard money than even he kept around the manor at any one time, and though Hafton was not a rich manor, William was proud of what he was worth.

He counted out the hord by making small piles of twelve pence each. It took a long time to count it all, but by the time he was done there were forty piles of one shilling each. Not a penny short.

A boy like Robert — or most men for that matter — had no conceivable business with this much money. Few had so much at once: moneylenders, rich merchants, the holders of vast lands perhaps, for most people's wealth was tied up in the lands and goods they possessed. Theft seemed the plausible answer. Yet stealing such a sum, and getting away, was so difficult that even the thought of theft became farfetched as he contemplated the problem.

Maybe the boy had been telling the truth, although William suspected he had not told all of it.

William scooped the money back in the bag, which he returned to the chest. He locked the chest with a stout padlock, and went down to the yard.

The church's windows were above Robert's head and he had to chin himself on the sill if he wanted to see out. This was too tiring to do for any length of time, but he found that with some struggle, he could climb up and stand on the sill, and even sit down, although the seat was narrow and precarious. Still, the view, such as it was of the common, the village well, rows of houses, and the field to the south, was more diverting than the plastered stone of the interior.

He was on a window sill when the door creaked open. Startled and alarmed, he leaped off, rolling with the impact, and dashed for the altar.

The Outlaws

He needn't have bothered, for the intruder, whom Robert recognized as Lord William, took a few unhurried steps into the nave.

"Admiring the view?" William asked.

"The window could be bigger," Robert said. "It's dreary in here. You could use a few paintings on the walls. I saw a church in Gloucester like that, with painted walls. Scenes from the Gospels."

"I'm afraid that if I knocked out larger windows, the walls would fall down."

"It's an old church."

"Some people say it was here even before the village. But what do they know?"

By this time, William had sauntered to within ten feet. Robert watched him, on the lookout for some trick, although it seemed unlikely that William would try something by himself. That was not the style of lords. They had underlings do the dirty work. William's hand came out from beneath his cloak. He held an apple. He tossed the apple to Robert.

"I thought you were trying to starve me out," Robert said.

"Who told you that?"

"No one."

"No one, indeed. Well, anyway, whether I starve you out depends on what I decide to do with you."

"I've heard you've summoned the sheriff."

"I have. He should be here any day. Then you'll have the choice of surrender or exile."

"Exile." Robert had not thought of that as a possibility. The idea was chilling. He could not imagine living in a foreign country where everything was strange. "Exile to where?"

"I have no idea. Somewhere out of the country." William scuffed the ground. "I wanted to ask you again about the money. Where did you get it?"

Robert rolled the apple in his palms. "The word was, Dudda's father was going to sue my mother for the death and that the case was fixed. There was another prisoner in gaol with my uncle. He comes from a good family in Norfolk. He offered to give me enough to pay mother's fine if I got him out as well."

"And the family paid you?"

"They did."

"And you came back with the money. Despite the danger."

"I did."

"So the money belongs to your mother."

"It does. Were you thinking of keeping it yourself?"

"You are an impertinent boy."

"I've nothing to lose by it now."

"But you do. You have your future to lose."

"How's that?"

"Because I may feel inclined to help you."

"Why would you do that?"

William was quiet for a time. "None of your business."

He backed away and went out.

"Your lord father would like to see you," Burghard said from the doorway to Giselle's chamber. "Her too."

Giselle glanced at Matilda. They put down their sewing on the window seat. "Where is he?"

"In his chamber."

That was odd. William never spoke to people in his chamber. Only Baldwin or his valet ever went in there. He had locked himself in this morning for a long time, too, which was unusual, and then had gone to the church. Giselle almost asked Burghard what William wanted, but she checked her tongue. Something was up and it did no good to question Burghard about it, other than to excite more curiosity about something that may best be kept quiet.

"Come along, Matilda," Giselle said, sweeping by Burghard.

Father's door was a few steps away, and it was open. Giselle and Matilda went in. Father was standing by a window looking down at the yard. "Close the door," he said.

The Outlaws

He turned from the window and gestured at a cloth bag on the bed. "That's yours, Matilda. Go ahead, you can open it."

Matilda hesitated, then strode to the bedside. She opened the bag and gasped. "What's this?"

"Your son had it. He was bringing it to you."

"He better not think that this makes amends."

"That was not his intention." William explained where the money had come from and why.

"How much is here?"

"Forty shillings, to the penny."

Even Giselle was astounded. It was a fortune. She felt a moment of alarm. With that much money, Matilda could leave and seek a life elsewhere.

"You best not tell anyone you have it," William said. He went on, looking out the window again. "When the sheriff comes, the boy will be offered the choice of surrender or exile. If he chooses exile, he will be escorted to a Channel port and put on a ship for the continent. He will arrive there with no prospects and no money. But there is another problem. By this time, Roger FitzWalter will have heard that the boy has been made prisoner here and has claimed sanctuary. He will expect the boy to choose exile."

"What are you saying?" Matilda asked.

"Exiles on their way to their port of embarkation are outside the law. People can harm them with impunity. If I were Roger, I'd have the boy killed on the road before he can reach his assigned port."

Matilda looked anguished. As angry as she had been with Robert, she could not endure the thought of his death. "What can I do?"

"Nothing, yourself. But there is something I can do." When Matilda did not reply, he went on, "I have a brother-in-law in Normandy. I can give your son a letter of introduction to him. That will give him a place and perhaps some prospects, assuming that he does not ruin them with his rudeness."

"But what good will that do if he is killed on the way?"

"The earl will not be able to harm him if somehow Robert manages to slip away in the night."

Giselle grasped where her father was heading. "Burghard and Osgar! If they are on watch tonight, they can be depended on to fall asleep."

"Or at least they can be trusted to say they did," William said.

There was no time to waste in writing the letter, since the deed had to be done tonight. There was no telling when the sheriff or one of his deputies would show up and spoil everything. Since William could read but not write and Giselle, at her mother's urging, could do both, she had to write the letter if they were to keep the secret of what they were about to do to as small a circle as possible.

The chaplain, like many of his kind, doubled as the manor clerk. For this purpose he had a small room to himself built off the chapel where he kept a chair, table, slanted writing desk, and shelves for documents and letters. The place smelled of ink, soot, the faint rancid aroma of tallow, and must.

Giselle slipped into the chapel and crossed to the door to that little office. She listened there for a moment. Hearing no activity, she went inside. She found a fresh sheet of parchment, the ink pot, and a quill. She set the parchment on the writing desk, and dipped the quill in the pot. Giselle's mind had been filled with phrases for the letter, but now that the pen hovered over the parchment, her mind was empty. Her hand shook, and her breath came faster than normal. Once she put down a single letter, she would be complicit in murder. Until then, it was all just talk.

Giselle was locked in indecision when the door opened behind her. Her head jerked around to see who it was. It turned out to be the chaplain, Evrart, but she was sure that she had guilt written on her face.

The Outlaws

"My lady," Evrart asked, "what are you doing here?"

"I am writing a letter, obviously."

"Can I not help you?" Evrart edged forward and looked over her shoulder.

"It is a personal letter."

"Ah."

"Yes. To someone I met at Ludlow."

Evrart smiled. "It wouldn't be a possible suitor, would it?"

"Father says it's time I was married. I'd like to have some say in who that might be."

"And you have someone in mind?"

"I'd rather not discuss it, if you don't mind."

"Of course. These matters of the heart are most delicate. Does your father know this person?"

"Please don't tell him. I'd like to be the one to bring it up. You'll keep my secret, won't you, Evrart?" Of course, Evrart could not be trusted to keep confession confidential, let alone secrets on which one's life depended, which was why Giselle was writing this letter and not him. Before the end of the day, everyone in the manor would know that Giselle had written to a man. She was embarrassed that she had not thought to say she was writing a poem, but the choice of the lie could not be helped now.

"Certainly, my lady." The chaplain backed to the doorway. "If you should need anything, however, I am always willing to help."

"You are most kind."

Quite a few moments passed before she got her thoughts in order. Her hand stopped quivering, and she began to write.

Eleanor spotted the chaplain seated at the hearth nursing a cup of ale. Evrart should be found puttering over his accounts, or something, rather than seated before the fire, or at least acting as if he had something productive to do, since William despised idleness. Then William came down the stairs and descended to the yard. He could not have missed Evrart, but he pretended not to notice.

Eleanor's senses tingled. Something odd was going on. She didn't like it when things went on about the manor that she didn't know about. She sank to a bench beside Evrart. "Are you well?"

"I'm fine, mistress," the chaplain replied.

"Have you no work to do, then?"

"I've plenty of work, but no place to do it."

"I don't follow."

"Lady Giselle has ousted me from my writing chamber."

"That is strange. Why would she do that?"

"I doubt she wanted to practice her alphabet, mistress."

"Evrart, do not get sharp with me."

"Sorry, mistress, but our lady said I am not supposed to tell."

This was the wrong thing to say to Eleanor. She would pry out whatever little secret Evrart possessed even if she had to sit on his head to do it. "Well, you can tell me."

Evrart looked away. "She was writing a letter."

"To whom?"

"I do not know. She said some man. She made it sound as though it involved a question of romance."

"That's hard to believe." Before Eleanor could inquire more about this letter, Matilda Attebrook emerged from the pantry with a large basket under one arm. A round loaf of fresh bread projected from the basket. She met Giselle at the door. They conferred in quick whispers and then went out. They had to be going to the church to feed the murderer. Yet it was odd that Giselle would go now. She had already been there to see the spectacle, and had no good reason for going again. It was probably nothing, but Eleanor did not feel inclined to take that chance. She wondered if the writing of that letter, without Evrart's help, was connected with any of this.

"Evrart," she asked, "would you mind following Giselle and that Attebrook woman?"

The Outlaws

"Why?"

"They are up to something. I'd like to know what it is."

Evrart put his cup on the ground and stood up. "I suppose I can."

"Be careful that you aren't noticed. I think they're going to the church to see that boy. I have a bad feeling about it."

"I shall be careful, madam."

"You should be able to listen to what they have to say at one of the windows."

Robert was sitting cross legged on the altar when the door opened yet again. The church was getting more traffic now that he was in residence than it did at any other time than Sunday. He was about to say that he should charge these visitors for admission, since he couldn't imagine what they might want other than to satisfy their curiosity as several others had done that morning in addition to Lord Willam. But the words stuck in his throat.

"You get down from there this instant!" Matilda barked at the sight of him. "Have you no decency?"

Robert hopped down. Since it was his mother and that lord's daughter he felt no need to stay within arm's reach of the altar. "Sorry, Mum."

His mother did not seem to take this apology seriously, for she marched down the nave, and gave him such a slap that he reeled back against the altar and almost fell.

"That's for what you've done!" Matilda stood over him. "What were you thinking!"

"Lord William didn't tell you?"

Matilda fumed. "He told me. It doesn't excuse anything. You'd have broken out that useless uncle of yours without the incentive of money. And we'd still be in the same straights. You have no idea what they did to your brother! Whipped him within an inch of his life! He's lucky not to have died."

Robert nursed the cheek where the blow had landed, considering a reply. He had seen his mother in rages before, and it was best to let them pass without comment, which tended to make the storms worse even when he was in the right. Now, he had no defense, so silence was the best choice.

But his tongue didn't listen to reason. "It seemed like the right thing to do."

"Did you not once consider what would happen to us after?" Matilda jabbed a finger at Robert's head. "What have you got up there, cheese?"

"I just didn't feel it was right to let him hang."

"He deserved to hang. He was guilty."

"You can't just let family hang."

"So the rest of us have to pay so you can feel good about yourself? You owed us a duty, more than that good-for-nothing."

"So you came here to beat me?" he asked.

"It's less than you deserve."

Matilda started pacing, her lips pressed together.

Giselle had been standing by, watching all this with surprise, as if she had not expected any of it. She grasped Matilda's arm and removed the basket hanging from the older woman's shoulder. She held it out to Robert. "Don't eat all of it at once. It's got to last you some time."

Robert, who was hungry again, opened the basket. Much of its contents was obscured by a large round loaf of black bread. He smelled apples and onions lurking down there somewhere, and a whiff of dry cheese. "What do you mean it's got to last me some time?"

"Because you're going away," Matilda said.

"I know. That's what Lord William said. I'm to be exiled as soon as the sheriff comes."

"No," Matilda said, "you're leaving tonight." She held out a leather bag. "Your traveling money."

Robert accepted the bag. "What do you mean I'm leaving tonight?"

"Right after dark the guard will change. If you slip out a window, neither of them will see you."

"Is this some kind of trick?"

127

The Outlaws

Giselle said, "It's no trick. If you wait to elect exile from the sheriff, Earl Roger will have you killed on the road. This is your only chance."

"So I'm just to run off?"

"Not quite. There is a condition," Giselle said. She handed Robert the folded parchment. "You're to leave England and seek out my uncle's house in Normandy. This is a letter of introduction from my father to my uncle, asking him to take you in. You must under no circumstances allow anyone but my uncle to see this. We've put no seal on this letter so that if you are caught we will say it is forged. But take this token so that my uncle will know the letter is genuine." She held up a ring with a green stone. "It belonged to my mother. Uncle Helmo will recognize it."

Robert looked to Matilda for confirmation. She nodded.

"So it is exile then."

"I am afraid so," Matilda said. And she began to cry.

CHAPTER 9

Hafton
April 1179

A rolling bank of gray cloud crept in at suppertime, bringing early darkness. Lightning flashed within its folds, and the servants hastened to close all the shutters before the rain came. Had it not been for the covered walkway connecting the kitchen and the hall, those doing the evening's service would have got drenched, and as it was there were complaints every time someone opened the doorway and the wind whipped rain into the hall, spattering those within reach and chilling everyone else.

People went to bed after William's retirement as the tables were being taken down. On most nights, he would remain by the fire and there would be talk, storytelling, and laughter, but not tonight.

After Athelhild and Matilda had put Giselle to bed, Matilda lay on her pallet on the floor, listening to the twins breathing over the drumming of the rain. She was too worried to sleep, and after an hour or so, she rose and went down to the hall.

The central fire was still burning, someone having fed it a log before retiring to his own pallet, and its orange glow reached up into the rafters and threw shadows of the people under their blankets onto the walls.

Matilda settled on a bench before the fire, glad for its warmth, for although it was spring, the storm had brought cold along with the wet.

She sat that way for hours, unable to sleep, rocking in her worry, running through her mind all the terrible things that might happen, praying that they would not. But most of all, she was sad that Robert was going away. She would never see him again.

Somehow she managed to doze off, for some time in the night a hand prodded her shoulder. At first Matilda thought it might be one of the twins needing something or Athelhild

The Outlaws

summoning her to return to her proper place, but it proved to be Burghard, wrinkles on his kindly face and big nose amplified by the glow of the fire.

Burghard was drenched, proof that he had been out in the rain and not hiding under a blanket after all. He nodded, which was enough for Matilda to know that Robert had, indeed, got away, and as he withdrew with Osgar to a corner to lay down their pallets, Matilda reflected that the bad weather helped with the deception.

There was no reason to remain here now, so she climbed the stairs to Giselle's chamber.

At the top of the stair, she bumped into someone, which gave her a fright. For an irrational moment she thought it might be Baldwin, the steward, but it was Lord William.

He leaned close and whispered in her ear, "It is done?"

Matilda nodded.

She expected him then to get out of her way, but he blocked her passage. His fingers brushed her cheek.

"I'm no good at wooing," he said. "I hardly know what to say or what to do."

"And yet you managed with Hanelore," Matilda said. Giselle had told her how theirs had been a love match, the marriage taking place over her father's objections because at the time William had been a landless knight in the company of King Henry.

"I don't know how that happened. It seems a miracle."

"She was a lucky woman."

The hand fell away. "Yet she died before her time."

"I'm sorry."

"I want you in my bed. I am sorry to be so blunt."

"You have only to order it, my lord. We both know that."

"I would ask rather than order. I would rather you came because you want to."

"And if I refuse?"

"You will still have my protection. Nothing will change."

It could have been a lie, yet Matilda believed him. There were worse men, after all, and she had been so long without a man.

"I will come," she said.

William nodded. He took her hand and led her down the hallway to his chamber.

CHAPTER 10

Hafton
April 1179

There was no hiding the fact the next morning that Matilda spent the night in William's chamber. His valet found them in bed when he went to attend to the lord's morning toilet and get him dressed, and it wasn't long before everyone on the manor knew.

On any ordinary day this would have been prime gossip, but it was overshadowed by the discovery that Robert had disappeared. With a great deal of shouting and random recrimination, William ordered an immediate inquiry which failed to establish when he had run away, as all the watchers swore they had been awake throughout the night.

As the last watcher gave his testimony and the crowd in the hall — everyone in the village, for work had been suspended for the day in view of the weight of the matter — broke into a babble of conjecture. William gave no indication of his feelings, apart from an occasional glance at Matilda and Giselle, who were seated on a bench by the door since they had no part in the inquiry. Without a word to them or anyone else, William climbed the stairs to the chambers above the hall.

Few others marked William's mood, except for Eleanor off to the side by a far wall. She whispered to Baldwin, "He knows who did it!"

"I say, how could he?"

"Because he's responsible. It must have been either Burghard or Osgar."

Baldwin blinked. "That is farfetched, and you better not speak of this aloud. It is a dangerous accusation, especially without proof."

"Look at how she seems so unconcerned, sewing away like nothing has happened."

"I'm sure she's concealing her relief," Baldwin said. "It would be any mother's natural reaction."

"She's doing altogether too good a job of it. Guilt is written all over her face."

"Do you think she had anything to do with it, then?"

"And his rage is feigned," Eleanor went on as if Baldwin had not spoken.

"It seemed genuine enough."

"And look at how he looked at her."

"Well, everybody does that, after all," Baldwin said. "If I had a penny for every time a man looked at that woman, I'd be as rich as the king."

"He seeks her approval."

"I cannot believe that. Our sort doesn't need the approval of such people."

"You must admit that the coincidence is odd."

"Coincidences are not proof."

"But what of yesterday? The chaplain overheard them. It was plotting, I'm sure now that's what it was."

"As I recall the conversation, he didn't hear much, some shouting and murmuring is all. Nothing anyone would put any stock in."

"In which the words Normandy and Helmo were said. Why say such things to a boy like that if they had no plan to send him there? Recall now that Giselle wrote a letter yesterday! A letter, for God's sake! It had to be to her uncle on William's behest. Who else could write such a letter without us hearing about it?"

Baldwin looked uncomfortable. "Even so, what can we do? Nothing."

"The law has been flouted. Don't you feel some obligation?"

"I think it is better to be prudent than righteous. Since when did you become such a partisan of the law, anyway?"

"I don't like her. I've never liked her. She's trouble."

"Trouble for a man's cock," Baldwin said.

"Exactly. And you know where that can lead. And has led in this case — to the suspension of good judgment. Who

The Outlaws

knows what damage she might do if she is allowed to remain here."

"Well, she won't be here come autumn."

"If you think that, you're an idiot."

"Hmm," Baldwin muttered, reconsidering, oblivious to the insult. "Yes, you could be right about that. She won't be going with Giselle now."

"Quite right." Eleanor's eyes narrowed. "That whore will lie with any man for whatever advantage she can wring from it. We must act to protect our lord from further harm. Who knows what she will demand next?"

"Why do I not believe that is your chief concern?"

"Whatever you think is my chief concern, keep it to yourself."

CHAPTER 11

Shelburgh castle
April 1179

Eleanor spent two days considering what to do next. She could not just traipse off to Shelburgh. She had no reason to go there, and such a visit would provoke questions. Then she recalled the chaplain remarking that a group of Benedictines had founded a priory at the edges of the Radnor Forest to the west of Shelburgh. By his account, it was just a collection of rude huts, but it was not so unusual for people to make gifts to such places to ensure the success of the enterprise and for the sake of their souls, so Eleanor announced that she wished to contribute to the little priory, and like that, a journey was arranged for her. What a coincidence that Shelburgh lay along the route she must take to get there.

It took perhaps an hour to reach Shelburgh, and when they entered the yard before the village church, Eleanor had the sudden need for a privy and some refreshment. She sent the alewife's boy after the bailiff's wife, but instead of the wife, a messenger from the castle came and announced that Lady Blanche, FitzWalter's wife, required her attendance.

Eleanor had not expected to find either FitzWalter or his wife in residence, since such wealthy people rarely stayed a long time at any one of their properties, and moved among them. But she was pleased with this news, and with the invitation.

Lady Blanche received Eleanor in the hall. Blanche was a coolly beautiful woman in her mid-twenties. She had black appraising eyes that matched her hair and an insincere smile. She was from a branch of the de Clares, a powerful family centered around Gloucester, and she was proud of that connection.

Ordinarily, a woman from that sort of family could be counted on to look down on people like Eleanor, whose father had been a mere knight, but Blanche was gracious.

The Outlaws

Blanche greeted Eleanor pleasantly, seated her on a cushioned chair, and made sure she had a full cup of wine.

Blanche even smiled, but the smile did not extend to those black eyes. There was something reptilian about them, and Eleanor felt nervous in her presence.

"Tell me what has been happening in Hafton," Blanche said. "We hear there have been . . . events."

"Yes, my lady, there have. I feel constrained not to speak about them."

"There have been . . . visitors."

"You know about the Attebrooks then, my lady?"

"Of course. It is impossible to keep such a thing secret."

"Then you know that my lord has given her shelter."

"Yes."

"And you are offended, my lady?"

"We are not happy. But my lord knows that there is nothing he can do about that. There is, however, the business of her boy. The word is he came there."

"Yes, my lady."

"But he did not stay."

"No, my lady. The village people tried to arrest him but he took sanctuary in the village church. He managed to slip away in the night."

"How does one manage that when it is under watch? It was under watch, wasn't it?"

"It was supposed to be."

"But you suspect not."

"My lady, you must realize that I am torn when asked to speak of this thing."

"How so?"

"I owe my lord loyalty. Yet there is also my duty to the king."

"Ah, the king. Because of the felony. But how could your loyalty be torn between those two obligations?"

Eleanor swallowed, her nervousness rising. "There are some in Hafton who believe that my lord had a hand in the boy's escape."

"Good Lord, you can't be serious."

"That suspicion has been on a number of lips."

"Why would William do such a thing?"

"He has taken up with Matilda Attebrook. It happened at exactly the time the boy escaped."

"And you suspect that William acted to obtain her favor? That's hard to believe."

"It is not I who suspect that, my lady. I believe my lord is above reproach. Yet I fear for him. The woman has a baleful influence."

"I can understand your concern. We know the woman very well. She bewitched more than one man hereabout."

"I don't know what is to be done about her. I wish there was some way to convince my lord to put her aside, but I do not know how to bring that about."

"It is a thorny problem. You shall have to think hard on it."

"I shall, my lady."

Shelburgh castle
May 1179

"It is a grave insult that cannot go unpunished," Blanche said after supper on the evening of Earl Roger's return from Winchester.

FitzWalter had held his temper throughout most of the report, but now he could not contain himself. He slammed a fist on the table, causing his wine cup to leap into the air. It landed on its side, spilling its contents, which spread across the table in a maroon wave.

Eustace slid his chair back to avoid getting wet when the spill reached the edge of the table and cascaded to the floor. Servants rushed forward with cloths to swab up the mess.

"I'll have his head for this!" FitzWalter thundered, and many within the range of his voice cringed, for when FitzWalter called for someone's head, he usually got it. Some in the hall, however, did not cringe. Though the object of his

The Outlaws

wrath was a much poorer neighbor, he was a knight and a member of the gentry. It could mean war, though a small one, but war nonetheless, and these men were bored. They had not had a decent war in a long time.

"He deserves to lose it," Blanche said, "but you can't just attack him."

"Why not?" FitzWalter asked, drawing back.

Undeterred by the earl's furious expression, Blanche went on just as coolly, "Because he holds his lands from the king. An attack on him might be seen as unprovoked, no matter what story we put out, and thus an attack on the king himself."

"Right," FitzWalter said, reining himself in a notch. "There is that." King Henry was well known to guard his prerogatives, and he did not like his lords fighting one another. An attack on Hafton could result in a loss of some of the rents owed to the king. He would not stand for that.

"We need to be more clever," Blanche said.

"I suppose you have an idea?"

"We must accuse William, of course."

"But that means going to law. The next assize isn't for months." Aiding a fugitive murderer was an offense against the crown and therefore had to be tried by one of the crown justices, who traveled about England holding courts called assizes. FitzWalter righted his cup, which a servant filled. FitzWalter waved dismissively. "It will take years. He'll only have to pay a fine."

"There is an opportunity here as well."

"What sort of opportunity?

"You have always wanted to recover Hafton. This may present a chance to do so."

FitzWalter grumped, not yet accepting this notion, attractive as it was. Once William's honor had been part of his own. In 1147, FitzWalter succeeded to the earldom after his father died when his horse stumbled on a rock while crossing a stream. The then-earl hit his head on a stone and drowned in the fall. Partly out of thanks for his good fortune at succeeding to the honor so much sooner than anticipated and partly because it was expected of him, FitzWalter had pledged to go on crusade. To raise money, he had sold Hafton. The buyer had died without heirs and the manor had escheated to the king, who gave it to William as a reward for loyal service. FitzWalter had always regretted selling Hafton and had always wanted it back.

"I don't follow," FitzWalter said. He ran a finger around the edge of the cup. "What do you mean?"

"We accuse William in front of all his friends, in a manner that is as insulting as possible, and challenge him to single combat in Ralph's name. William is the proud sort who cannot abide any suggestion of dishonor. He will agree. I'm sure of it."

"Henry will not abide even that," FitzWalter growled. "What if we lose?"

"At best *you* will have to pay a fine."

FitzWalter grunted, indicating his distaste for fines.

Blanche said, "But it may not come to that."

"You are full of ideas tonight."

"With William gone, that leaves only an unmarried girl to inherit the tenancy."

"A wardship," FitzWalter said. Widows and orphans became the wards of the crown, which sold the rights to manage them and their estates until they remarried or came of age, or married in the case of orphaned girls.

"Yes," Blanche said. "Once we have the wardship, all sorts of opportunities become available."

"But that will cost money."

"Which can be repaid from the profits of Hafton. He has opened a mine there, after all. Surely there is money in that."

Eustace had listened to this exchange without making any contribution to see where Blanche was headed. Now he asked, "Who will be our champion?"

"Why not you?" Blanche asked.

"Me?" Eustace replied, alarmed at the prospect, although he tried not to show it.

The Outlaws

"Certainly," Blanche said. "You did well in the tournaments last year in France."

"A tournament is a game," Eustace said, "not a fight to the death."

"You have nothing to fear from William," Blanche purred. "He's forty if a day, and hasn't fought seriously for what, fifteen years? He's out of practice and you're in your prime."

Eustace heard the insult in her words and tone, insinuating that he might be afraid.

Before he could say anything, however, FitzWalter said, "I think Eustace is up to the task."

"When do you propose we do this?" Eustace asked. Now that FitzWalter had accepted Blanche's idea, there would be no arguing his way out of it.

"I think the Ludlow fair," Blanche said. Ludlow held its annual fair in September on the day of the Nativity of the Virgin, when most manors had completed the harvest. "William always attends it. Everyone of any consequence in the area will be there."

September, Eustace mused to himself. It seemed a long way off. Something might happen between now and then that saved him. He didn't know what, but he would think of something.

CHAPTER 12

On the River Charentonne
Near Bernay, France
July 1179

Robert Attebrook awoke to the sound of shouting.

Shouting in the camp was not unusual. Officers shouted at the men, the men shouted at each other, the camp followers screamed and fought. But there was something shrill and desperate that raised the hair on the back of the neck.

While Robert pulled on his socks and boots, a tent-mate stuck his head in. He looked terrified. "The French are coming! Hundreds of them!"

At first the words sounded like nothing more than fuzzy babble. His former employer, Jean the wool merchant, was from Calais in northeastern France, and spoke that dialect at home, which Robert had picked up. But the speech of Calais was different than that spoken in this part of France and Robert had to struggle to understand it.

"Oh, dear God!" wheezed Robert's other tent-mate, Ordicorus. "What are we going to do?" Ordicorus was a white-haired clerk with a patrician's thin face, arrogant eyes, and a manner to match. Their lord, Giselle's Uncle Helmo of Fervaques, had made Odicorus come along to keep accounts of the loot they expected to take. Robert was supposed to be his assistant when there was no fighting.

"I think we ought to go out and see what's happening before we get too worked up," Robert said, trying to sound calm. He gathered up his bow and arrows and his sword and went out of the tent with Ordicorus bumping against his back.

The camp was in a tumult. People were running every which way. Knights and men-at-arms were pulling on their mail shirts in frenzied haste. Officers shouted and waved their arms, while they armed themselves. A loose horse galloped through the tents, knocking people over or forcing them to dive out of the way. A stolen cow pegged outside a tent munched on a pile of looted hay as if nothing was the matter.

The Outlaws

Then the man who had stolen the cow dashed up, yanked out the peg and pulled the animal toward the River Charentonne behind the encampment. Three whores ran past followed by a boy of about six, heading for the river too.

Robert could see the cause of all the excitement in the hazy distance: a large column of French horsemen was approaching at an easy trot in a mowed hay field beyond the camp. As he watched, the column spread out into a line, erect lances giving it the appearance of hedge. They stopped for a moment about two-hundred yards away to dress their line. The shouting of the French officers was audible even across that distance.

"Holy Mother of Christ!" Robert said. He guessed there must be at least at least a hundred knights out there. That was a lot of fighting men. Helmo's Norman war band had eighty men altogether, fifteen of whom were knights or men-at-arms. The rest were archers, like Robert, or peasant spearmen. No wonder everyone was running around. They were all going to be slaughtered.

He turned around to speak to Ordicorus, but the clerk had already gathered up the skirts of his habit and dashed toward the river.

During the summer of 1179 there was unrest along the border between France and Normandy. Louis, the French king, did not want a war, but the local lords had grievances against their neighbors across the border, and they ignored Louis' desire not to provoke the Normans. Raids took place on the frontier. Norman villages burned.

One of those villages belonged to a friend of Helmo's. The friend asked for his assistance. In June, Helmo kissed his wife goodbye and marched out with three knights, four men-at-arms, fifteen peasant archers, and two clerks, Odaricus and Robert, who had arrived with his letter only a week earlier.

The French raids had been mounted from the castle at Lieurey. The Normans decided to take the castle and tear it down to punish the lord who held it and to burn its village. But taking castles was a difficult, expensive, and often time-consuming business. The little army lacked the manpower to take it by storm or siege, and so had determined to rely on trickery. The bulk of the army, about two-hundred men, would demonstrate inside French territory, burning villages and looting, to draw the enemy's main force away from its base at Lieurey. When the enemy's army had gone a sufficient distance, a picked force of fifty knights would make its way secretly to the objective by a circuitous route and launch a surprise night assault on the expectation that the castle would be lightly defended and no one there would anticipate such a bold move. Helmo's following was assigned to the decoy group.

Once across the border, the decoy army split into threes, the better to harry the countryside. Most soldiers enjoyed harrying more than they did fighting. It paid better and was less dangerous.

The French battle line started toward the Norman camp at a walk, and then at a trot. Robert gaped at the incoming horsemen. They seemed relentless, irresistible. He would be knocked over and trampled if he was lucky and impaled if he wasn't.

A knight pushed him hard from behind. "Get in line, you idiot!" the knight screamed, as he fumbled with trembling hands to tie the chin strap of his helmet. "Don't just stand there!"

By this time most of the Norman infantry had crossed the river to what they hoped was safety. The river here was deeper than elsewhere along its length, where it could be waded, and a number were floundering and a few had already drowned. The bodies of the dead drifted downstream looking like so many bags of laundry.

None of the Norman knights and men-at-arms had fled, and about forty spearmen and five archers remained. Officers

The Outlaws

bawled at them to form ranks in a semi-circle with its ends anchored on the riverbank and there was chaos while everyone hurried to comply, but somehow, with much shouting and pushing, out of the swirl, the mob formed into a curved line.

Behind the line, there was a small knot of archers who hadn't swum the river cowering by a pair of wagons beside the bank. Robert stood with them, supposing they had been placed there for some purpose.

Helmo called to them, "String your bows, boys. There may be work for you to do here."

Just as the Normans finished forming up, the French knights trotted into the camp. They made their way through the tents toward the shield wall by the bank, pulling down a tent here and there, and flushing a few hidden stragglers, whom they speared like wild pigs. They stopped about thirty yards from the Normans, their horses stomping and snorting in a terrifying way, looking large enough to pound their way through the line by themselves.

The leader of the French called out, "Who's in command here?"

"I am," Helmo answered.

"I call on you to surrender," the French knight said.

"Who are you?"

"My name is Abelard."

"Well, Abelard, what rights will you give us if we do?"

"The right to be ransomed," Abelard said.

"We will give up what we have taken and retire in good order."

"No. You have caused much damage here. My home is burned and people are dead on my manor, and the situation is the same for those with me. Reparations must be made."

"Then let us talk about a sum to settle your damages," Helmo said. "We will give hostages for its payment."

"No. We'll have the lot of you and you will pay whatever we say."

"What about the infantry?"

Abelard was startled at the question. He had not expected it. "What about them?"

"If you have me and mine for ransom, we will have quarter for the infantry, and your promise that they can go to the border unmolested."

Abelard tapped his thigh with a short corded leather whip. He was growing impatient. "I don't think so."

"Let me consult with my friends."

The Frenchman waved a hand in assent. Helmo huddled with the other two lords in the war band. Robert was near enough to hear what they said to each other. None of the lords wanted to lose infantry needlessly. The peasants provided the labor that enriched them. It was senseless to throw away the lives of workers if it could be avoided. "We could hold them, if we had the archers," Helmo said.

"But we don't. Most of them are gone," one of the lords said, waving at the far shore.

"Not all of them. Go across the river and collect as many as you can. See if you can find a way into the flanks of the French while we hold them here. That may drive them away. If we surrender now, they could kill us out of spite when Serlo takes Lieurey."

The two other lords nodded. They agreed this was all they could do. One of the lords jumped down the bank and, despite wearing full armor, swam the river to the other side, where he shouted for the men hiding there to gather around him.

"I see I have my answer." Abelard stood in his stirrups and looked across the river.

"Yes," Helmo said. "You have it."

"May God have mercy on you then," Abelard spat. "We won't."

The French knights got off their horses and tethered the animals among the Normans' tents. Then, holding their lances overhand like spears, they reformed a line and advanced with a shout.

The Outlaws

The French war cry almost made Robert's knees tremble. He had never been so frightened. He could see that the other archers, none of whom had armor, were just as scared. They were all aware that their situation was desperate.

One of the archers looked at the river and asked, "Can any of you swim?" He had to shout to make himself heard because the noise of even this tiny battle was deafening: a maddening crescendo of rattling and hammering and clanging of arms striking shields and the ringing of swords on swords mingled with the shouts and screams of men.

"No," said another, "can you?"

None of them could, except for Robert. Had they been able to swim, they would have crossed the river long ago.

The lord who had swum the river swam back across and clambered up the bank. He looked disgusted. He shouted in Helmo's ear, "It's no use. They're all gone."

"Then let us hope the French decide to show us quarter after all." Helmo turned back to the fighting.

The archers, who could not shoot at the enemy because their own men were in the way, edged toward the bank. They looked ready to take their chances in the river even though it meant many of them would drown in the attempt. Robert thought about what Helmo had said. If he could get these archers across the river, they could shoot at the French, which might make all the difference. He wondered how to make it happen, and then the idea came to him. The barrels of wine in the wagons were each secured by single strand of rope that snaked all round them. He handed his bow to one of the others, climbed on one wagon, cut the ends of the rope loose and tugged it free. "Get that other rope, there," he pointed toward the other wagon.

A couple of archers, mystified at his objective but willing to try anything, leaped to the other wagon and brought out the rope used to secure the barrels.

By knotting the two lengths together, Robert had a single strand long enough to reach across the river.

As he tied one end to a tree root that protruded from the bank, he told them his plan, which was met with more than a little enthusiasm, since it meant putting the river between them and the French. Shucking his sword belt and arrow bag, Robert jumped in and swam across the river, holding the rope in his teeth. The archers shouted encouragement, while keeping an eye on the fight that raged behind them for a sign of a breakthrough by the French.

When Robert reached the far side, he tied the other end to another root.

He had hardly got the end knotted around the root when all five archers jumped into the river and started pulling themselves across in a hurry to get away. None of them brought Robert's bow and arrows and sword, although they were not so panicked that they forgot their own, which they held above their heads.

Robert wasn't about to abandon his property, if there was a chance he could get it back. The bow was the best he had ever made, with fine horn ends and a good string, and the sword, which he had taken from a prisoner, was worth five pounds at least. So Robert swam back, reaching the battle side as the last archer left it.

To his amazement, the Norman line still held. He had expected the French knights to cut through the peasant infantry. But he could see that the peasants, facing certain death, were fighting like demons.

As Robert buckled on his sword belt, he found that his clever idea proved to be the undoing of the Norman war band. One of the spearmen in the second line, which engaged the French over the shoulders of the knights in front of them, spotted the archers struggling across the river on the rope. He nudged a friend, who saw them too. In an instant, those two had abandoned the line and run for the rope. Before Robert could blink an eye, the entire second rank and the wings were rushing toward him, men leaping into the water and fighting for a grasp of the rope.

147

The Outlaws

The Norman knights and men-at-arms held their ground, however, which allowed the French to surge around the broken the line, engulfing them in the center. The Norman knights and men-at-arms fell back into a circle and fought on, except for two Norman sergeants who were cut out of the formation and who stood back-to-back, swinging their swords in great circles against the enemy who surrounded them.

Seeing the French hacking at the backs of the peasant infantry, enraged Robert. He couldn't stand to watch without doing something. He climbed onto one of the wagons by the bank and nocked an arrow. He shot one Frenchman in the chest, and then shot another in the side. A third ran toward the wagon and tried to climb up before he could nock a third arrow. Robert kicked him in the face. The French who had been attacking the infantry turned their shields toward him to avoid his next arrow. Lacking a good target, Robert shot at the back one of the Frenchmen menacing the two Norman men-at-arms who had been cut off from the rest of the party. The wounded man gave a shout and clawed at the arrow in his back. This so alarmed the French that the two knights were able to break out and back toward the wagon. One of them made it; the other suffered a sword cut on the leg and went down.

Robert recognized the sergeant who had reached his wagon perch as Hugh Fontaine, one of two hired men-at-arms in Helmo's service whom everyone called Hugh le Gros because he was short and stout.

Robert jumped down from the wagon and tugged Hugh's shoulder. "We should go now!"

Hugh glanced at the struggling mass at the rope. "I can't swim!"

Robert shoved his bow and arrow bag into Hugh's hands. "Hold these and your breath."

Then he grasped a fold of Hugh's chain mail shirt and jumped into the river just as French knights rounded both sides of the wagon.

The spot where they landed was only waist deep, but the bottom dropped away. Within two steps it was over Robert's head.

Hugh had the sense not to struggle and went stiff as a board, eyes closed tight and holding his breath as water washed over his face.

It was a hard swim across the river, holding Hugh's head up, with a sword and a bagful of arrows tangling in his legs, but Robert made it somehow. One foot touched the mud near the opposite side and he steadied Hugh on his feet. The French across the way shouted insults at them. Robert retrieved his bow, nocked a sopping arrow and drew as if to shoot. The French mocked him. Two or three threw rocks, which splashed short. They turned away in disgust.

Meanwhile, several Frenchmen had reached the root that held the rope and cut it so that the strand curved downstream with the current, carrying clusters of struggling men. Dismayed, Robert watched them glide past where he stood safe by the bank. He reached out with the bow toward several who went by, but none came close enough to grasp it.

All the common soldiers who had not jumped into the river had been killed. The French knights who had slaughtered them lost interest once they were dead. The corpses had nothing of value worth looting.

The Norman knights and men-at-arms fought on, surrounded by a pack of Frenchmen for a short time, but soon they were overwhelmed, and most of them were killed.

"Look," Hugh said, taking off his helmet in the shallows, "they have taken Helmo." They could see there were at least five Norman survivors across the river. Helmo was one of them. He tottered in the grip of two French knights, who had begun to tear off his armor. There was blood on his face from a head wound, but he was alive. The French had not carried out their threat to kill everyone. Live knights were worth more than dead ones, after all, and the urge to profit had overcome the desire for revenge.

"Thank God for that," Robert said.

149

The Outlaws

Robert climbed up the bank and offered Hugh a hand. "We better get out of here before they find a way across," Hugh panted. "They don't have to go far for that."

Robert said, "I suppose we have to go back and tell Petronilla." She was Helmo's wife.

"I wish there was a way to avoid that," Hugh said.

CHAPTER 13

Normandy
July 1179

"I'll do the talking," Hugh said, as he and Robert entered Fervaques' marketplace. Ahead lay the village church. The road next to it ran west to the castle, which lay on the other side of a large stream. They were almost there. "She won't want to hear from you. You're just an archer."

"Right," Robert said, looking forward to a real bed and a decent meal. "I don't matter."

"Exactly. Well, you know what I mean. She's a lady after all. What are they looking at?"

An inn and tavern sat at the corner, well situated to attract the attention of any travelers who might happen by this small patch of Normandy and business on market days. People had come out into the street and were staring at them, cups in hand. It was not allowed to carry your cup into the street in Fervaques, partly because of the lord's dislike of public drunkenness but also because the proprietor feared he might not see his cups again. Next door was a draper's shop, its timbers painted a pleasant light blue, and the owner and his journeymen were leaning out the windows to get a look at them. Eyes followed Robert and Hugh as they passed out of the marketplace, but nobody said anything, lending an air of unnatural quiet to the atmosphere.

"You'd think we were a funeral," Robert said.

"Maybe we are," Hugh said. He had worried ever since they had got away how they would deliver the word of Helmo's capture to Petronilla. Hugh kept saying that she had a furious temper, although Robert had not seen many signs of it, perhaps because she had not been much in Fervaques during the last few months.

It was a relief to pass out of view of the watchers, although a few followed them as far as the corner of Castle Street.

The Outlaws

A wooden bridge crossed the stream to the castle's main entrance, where Helmo was building a new gate tower. It was about ten feet high at the moment and covered with scaffolding. Two men were walking the treadmill for a crane beside it, lifting a pallet of stone that had been shaped by the masons at the foot of the tower. One of the men on the treadmill spotted them just before they reached the bridge. He nudged his companion, and they whispered and smirked.

"I don't think we're that funny looking," Hugh said as they came up to the gate, which stood open. After the violent events along the border, one might have expected it to be closed as a precaution against a sudden assault, but both the castle and village seemed to be carrying on business as if it was a normal day.

"Well, you do look funny without your horse," Robert said.

"Perhaps I should ride you!"

"Now that they would find truly funny."

Any hopes they might have had of passing though the gate and into the comfort and safety of the bailey were dashed when one of the gate wards emerged from his nook and barred the way with his spear.

"Sorry, boys," the ward said. He was one of the older men, over fifty, and had been left behind to guard the castle. "I can't let you in."

"What do you mean you can't let us in?" Hugh said, astonished. "Out of the way."

He pushed the point of the spear aside, but the ward stepped back and re-leveled the spear. "I got orders. I'm not to let you in."

"Orders?" Hugh asked. "From whom?"

"From our lady, of course. Who did you think?"

"Come on, we're tired and hungry. We haven't had a decent meal since the day before yesterday."

The ward looked apologetic. "If it was up to me, I'd have no problem with you. But our lady heard what you done, and she's furious enough to dangle you at the end of a rope."

"Heard what we did?" Robert asked.

"Ordicorus got here yesterday. He told us about the battle, and how you ran and deserted the lord."

"We were cut off!" Robert protested. "We didn't have any choice! It was that or be slaughtered."

"That's not how Ordicorus tells it."

"That rat bastard," Robert fumed. "He was one of the first to run away."

"He isn't a fighting man after all," the ward said. He spat into the dirt. "Man like that is bound to run away. Anyway, the lady believes him. You best get out of here while you still can, before someone alerts her that you're here."

Hugh lay on his back, hands behind his head, looking up at the purple dusk above the trees, as the scent of roasted rabbit dissipated on the whisper of a breeze. "All I ever wanted was to sit on my front steps at a time like this, a cup of wine in my hand, and look across my vineyards. I'll never have that now. I might as well hang myself, or something."

Hugh was the fourth son in a large Gascon family, and when he came of age, his father had kicked him out without bothering to find a good marriage for him.

Robert kicked dirt on the cook fire. He thought about having his own manor. He saw his mother, the twins, and Brian sitting before a great hearth in the dead of winter with the wind howling around stone walls, yet they were safe and warm and had all they wanted to eat. It was an impossible dream for someone like him, of course. He said, "We have to move."

Hugh propped himself on an elbow. He glanced at the dying fire. "What for? Why did you put it out?"

"We can't sleep here. It's a beacon to whoever owned the rabbits, and the gamekeepers might care enough about them to make trouble."

"You make it sound like you've done this before," Hugh said, climbing to his feet.

The Outlaws

"Not I. I'm a law-abiding fellow."

"Don't tell lies. I've seen you in action. Desperate rabbit poachers are not to be trusted."

"As you shared in the spoils, I doubt the gamekeeper is liable to distinguish between the two of us. And since you are the sergeant, you'll hang first. Rank has its privileges, after all."

"If it has its privileges, why did you get the bigger rabbit?"

"It was just big-boned. It didn't have any more meat on him than yours."

"I take issue with that."

"My God, you're starting to sound like a cleric, always disputing this issue and that, like it made any difference."

"Now you really are getting insulting," Hugh said, as they moved away from the remains of the fire.

They stumbled through the darkening forest a few hundred yards until they reached a small stream.

"This will do," Robert said, settling down at the base of an oak. He wished he had a cloak or a blanket, but at least it was summer and the nights weren't that cold.

He thought about the problem of manors again. While the possibility of him obtaining one was so remote that it wasn't worth dreaming about, Hugh might still manage it, with luck and patronage. Robert might be able to ride upward with Hugh. Meanwhile, there was the problem of how to feed themselves and find work. He said, "In the autumn, don't they usually have tournaments? I heard some of the boys talking about it before we left."

"What? So?"

"If you fight, you might take a prize, enough to buy a manor. Some horses are worth a whole manor.

"I doubt I'll take any prizes," Hugh said. "Besides, they only allow knights to take prizes. I'm not a knight.

"You just tell them you are a knight. No one will know."

Hugh looked doubtful. "That's not very knightly."

"Do you think that the high-born are honest when they stand to gain by lies? How old are you?"

"I still don't like it."

Robert bushed aside Hugh's doubt and went on, enthused by his plan, "Then maybe you'll come to some lord's attention and he'll take us on."

"Us?"

"Of course, us."

"How am I going to fight? No horse, no shield, no lance, just some rusty mail and a sword."

"Don't towns have wrestling matches on market days? We do that in England."

"Yes," Hugh said. "Sometimes."

"Livarot is only fifteen miles from here. When's its market day?"

"I don't know."

"Well, it's the closest town. Tomorrow we'll go there."

"How is wrestling for a pig or a brace of chickens going to get me a horse and arms?"

"When you get the pig, you don't eat it. You sell it."

Hugh snorted. "Pigs aren't worth that much. Certainly nothing close to a good horse."

"Well, how many pigs does it take to equal a horse?"

"That's a crazy question."

Robert smiled in the dark. "Maybe not so crazy."

Hugh spat. "What do you know about the cost of a pig? The last time the steward bought one, it cost three sous."

Three sous in French money was the equal of three shillings. That was as much as his father might have earned in a good month, or maybe two. He sensed that it would take quite a few pigs to buy a horse. "Oh."

"Right, oh!" Hugh said with satisfaction. "A decent war horse can cost twenty livres."

"Oh," Robert said again, startled. Twenty livres — twenty pounds in English money — was so vast a sum he could not imagine it.

"So there," Hugh said.

Robert was silent for a while as he worked out the sums in his head. He couldn't do that, so he cleared leaves from a spot and did his figuring in the dirt as best he could, given the

The Outlaws

near dark. At three shillings a pig, it would take more than a hundred-thirty to buy a horse worth twenty pounds. And they would need other things as well: a lance, a shield, a saddle, and bridle, all of which would add to the amounts they needed. Clearly trading in pigs was not enough. There had to be another way. He asked, "Are you a betting man?"

"What do you mean?"

"I mean, do you bet on things, horse races, dice, cards? That sort of thing."

"What man doesn't?"

"They bet on wrestling matches too, you know."

"So?" Hugh said. "We don't have any money to bet with."

"We can get money."

"How?"

"In Livarot, from a moneylender."

"You can't just walk up and ask for money. At least, we can't. We're strangers."

"We can if we put up security."

"Like what, your bow and arrows?"

"We won't get enough to make the betting worth while."

Hugh sat up. "What are you suggesting?"

"How much do you think we could get for your mail?"

"I'm not hocking my mail," Hugh snapped, horrified. "What are you risking?"

"I'm doing the wrestling. You couldn't wrestle a boiled cabbage. This is how business is done: one man puts up the money, the other does the work, and they both share the risks and the profits."

"Business," Hugh said, as if the word meant something dirty. "My people do not do business."

Robert realized he had made a mistake. The gentry looked down on business people as lower than peasants. Yet when the circumstances suited them, they were as tight with a penny and as quick to do a deal as anyone. "Do you want that manor or don't you?"

"Well, yes."

So do I, a small voice dared to whisper in Robert's head. He said: "Then you're going to have to lower yourself and take some risks." Robert lay back down. "Me, I'm betting I don't get my arms broken. That happens, you know, now and then. That's got to be worth something."

Livarot was a pleasant little walled town, hugging the east side of a placid river that seemed to lie motionless under a hazy sky.

The air was hot and sticky, and they were both dying of thirst by the time they crossed the timber bridge to the town's north gate. The shade beneath the gate tower was a welcome relief, and the stones radiated cool dampness and smelled of moss.

The single guard in his niche surveyed them without rising from his stool. He was not much impressed with the rabbit Robert had shot on the way, but he agreed to take it for the entry toll.

As the guard tossed it on a table in the guardroom next door, Robert asked, "Are there any moneylenders here?"

The guard snorted. "What would you want with a moneylender?"

"Money," Robert said. "What does anyone want with a moneylender?"

"You think they'll lend you anything? I've known beggars who were better off than you."

"No, I'm going to rob one."

"You go ahead. I like to watch hangings. Did you steal that mail?" The guard nodded toward the rolled up mail shirt under Hugh's arm.

"It's his," Robert said, "and don't make him mad. He's got a short temper and he's a demon with a sword. He killed half a dozen men in battle last week."

"Six men! Fat chance. If it was true you wouldn't be walking. He hardly looks a demon, and you don't look old enough to get hard for a woman!" The guard roared.

The Outlaws

"We lost the battle," Robert said.

The guard chewed his lip. It seemed to help him think. "Soldiers, are you, down on your luck?" he asked, with some sympathy.

"And out of work."

"Our lord's not hiring. But you can get a free meal at the castle."

"Thanks. We'll remember that."

"You'll find the moneylenders in the lane of the goldsmiths. Far side of the parish church. Best of luck. Poor bastards." His laughter followed them up the lane.

They found the goldsmiths' street without much trouble. It was a narrow alley connecting two bigger ones just around the corner from the church. A series of inquiries directed them to a shop with its shutters folded down to make counters. They could see three bearded men and a boy making gold jewelry. It was intricate work requiring the use of fascinating small hammers and other odd tools. The oldest man noticed them watching and came over to the window. "Can I help you?" he asked in a tone that was polite enough but suggested that he thought he was wasting his time.

"We understand you lend money," Robert said.

"I will need security," the man said.

Robert reached for the mail shirt. Hugh clung to the shirt. Robert said, "Which would you rather give him? The shirt or the sword?"

"What about your sword?"

"If you expect to share in what we make, you'll have to share the risk."

Hugh released the shirt, but he didn't look happy about it. "I'll keep the sword."

"Good." Robert spread the shirt out on the counter. "Will this do?"

The jeweler fingered a fringe of the shirt. "It's rusty."

"We've had to sleep in the woods."

"Rust makes it worth less."

"Take a good look at it!" Hugh said. "There's not a rent in any of the links. It just needs a little cleaning."

The goldsmith shrugged. "You should have cleaned it before you brought it to me. I will give you twenty deniers on it."

"Twenty!" Hugh exploded. "It's worth sixty."

"Twenty-five."

"If we don't pay you back, you'll still make more than thirty on it if you have to sell, " Robert said.

The goldsmith sniffed. "But when I sell it, I won't get thirty. Weapons dealing is not my business. I will have to sell to someone who deals in such merchandise. He will get the thirty and will demand less from me. I cannot go higher than thirty."

Hugh was unhappy with this offer, but before he could reject it, Robert said, feeling light-headed for dealing in such an extraordinary amount of money, "Done."

They agreed on terms of interest and the repayment date.

The goldsmith went round to the door and let them in the shop. Then he guided them to the rooms at the rear, where he offered them ale and a seat at a table while he disappeared into rooms further back. He returned with a small wooden chest which he set on the table. They waited while he counted out three and a half livres in silver pennies, each of which was no bigger round than the nail on Robert's first finger. When the jeweler was finished, he saw that they had nothing in which to carry the money, so he scooped the pile of coins into a leather bag. He said, "When you make repayment, return the bag. Otherwise, it will cost you two deniers."

"Thank you," Robert said. He picked up the bag, which was heavy, but that was right since it contained a small fortune, and fortunes should be heavy. He handed it to Hugh, who nearly dropped it, and they went out into the street.

"What now?" Hugh asked.

"Let's get something to eat."

"Now that's an idea," Hugh said with relish.

159

The Outlaws

They spent the afternoon at an inn, making up for the lack of decent food over the last few days. That night, at Hugh's insistence and over Robert's objections at the expense, they slept in a bed with a real goose down mattress.

After breakfast, Robert said, "We need to get you a bath and some new clothes."

Hugh perked up. He cocked an eyebrow. "No bath or clothes for you?"

Robert shook his head. "We're spending too much as it is. If we don't win back every penny, you won't see your mail shirt again."

"And I thought you were so confident."

"I am. I just think we should be careful."

"But you'll spend on clothes for me."

"If you're going to wager a lot, you should look prosperous. Otherwise, no one will take your bets."

"I agree," Hugh said. "I deserve to look prosperous."

The bath, which should have taken no more than an hour, consumed most of the morning. Robert waited and fretted in the street, which turned out to be a profitable interlude, since passers-by who saw him sitting cross-legged by the door thought he was a beggar and dropped a total of three pence in his lap.

The visit to the tailor made Hugh less than happy. To get what he wanted would have taken a week to make, and the wrestling matches were scheduled for that afternoon. So Hugh, after some argument, had to settle for a second hand shirt, hose, hat and cloak. This put a dent of almost shilling in their savings. Hugh didn't seem to notice, but Robert felt the loss like a stab in the kidney.

When the tailor bundled Hugh's old things to throw them out, Robert collected them.

"What are you saving those rags for?" Hugh protested.

"Because when we travel, the poorer you look the less likely you'll be robbed."

"I never thought of that."

"Well, you should. We'll be carrying around a lot of money and there's only the two of us to protect it."

They arrived at the marketplace half an hour before the start of the matches. At a corner, next to the parish church, a ring of hay bales and benches had been set up. The match organizer, the town bailiff, lolled in his high chair nearby, while beneath him an under-bailiff collected the entry fees of those who wanted to enter the contest. The prize, a lean and black-haired sow, was tethered to one leg of the chair, and surveyed the proceedings with a majestic air.

"Skinny pig," Hugh sniffed. "Not much of a prize."

"Remember, we're not wrestling for the pig," Robert said. "Bet heavily on me each match, especially toward the end when it looks like I'm losing."

Hugh made a face. "I know how to bet."

Robert left him and paid the entry fee out of his takings from the street. Then he sat on the ground nearby and waited for the matches to start.

A pair of heralds wound through the stalls of the vendors, whose wares were spread out on blankets on the ground, announcing the start of the matches, and a crowd began gathering around the bales. The jostling, the spilled ale and afternoon drunkenness, the calls of the sausage and bun sellers and alewives, the boys racing underfoot and squeezing between the men at the edge of the ring for a better view, the shouting and pushing all reminded Robert of market days in Gloucester, even though he had trouble following what a lot of the people said. For a moment he missed Gloucester and wished he was back home instead of in this foreign place among strangers. The way things were, it was unlikely that he would ever get home again.

The bailiff climbed down from his chair, and took up his referee's staff. The under-bailiff whispered in his ear, and he called out the names of the first contestants. Two strong-looking farm boys stepped forward from a place close by Robert and entered the ring.

The Outlaws

When the wrestlers got set, a murmur arose from the crowd as the betting began. Robert looked about for Hugh, but couldn't spot him. Now that it had come time to carry out the plan, doubt and anxiety bubbled in his stomach. Many of the other contestants standing near him were larger and stronger than he was. Everything depended on whether he could win. He wasn't as sure of success as he had been.

The first match went on for a long time as the wrestlers played at their grips, then the shorter man snatched his opponent's leg and threw him, to be declared the winner.

The bailiff called out the names of the next contestants.

He had to repeat one of them several times. It sounded to Robert like "Rober' de la Attehbruukeh!" and at first he didn't realize it was his turn.

He shucked his shirt and stepped over the hay bale barrier into the ring.

By his fourth match, Robert was exhausted. He had a lump the size of a small egg under one eye where he had been kneed, a wrenched shoulder that twanged now and would hurt even worse in the morning, and he ached in all sorts of places. He wished he could quit.

When the bailiff called the final match, Robert scanned the crowd for Hugh, whose round shaven head made him stand out from the towns people and village folk. But Hugh was nowhere in sight. Robert wondered how successful his betting had been.

His opponent for the final match was a hulking mason's apprentice named Emil who stood a full head taller and had chiseled shoulders from carrying stone. There were doors in many a house not tall or wide enough for a man like him, and his fists looked as though they could carve granite by themselves. Robert had grown to just above middle height, and he was not as big as this giant. Robert regarded him with dread. His desire for the pig and the money she represented diminished the more he measured Emil, who seemed to grow in size as he strutted about the ring, playing to the crowd. Robert had the urge to run away, but it was too late for that now. The mob wouldn't let him go if he tried.

Emil had many friends, and those who weren't his friends howled for him against Robert, who was a stranger. The hooting was so loud that Robert's head felt about to split apart. A dirt clod hit him in the side of the head, then another struck his shoulder, just the first of a pelting volley from Emil's friends, mixed with bits of bread and apple cores. When the bailiff's deputies moved in to calm the worst rowdies down so the event could go on, a shoving match broke out that came close to erupting into a fight, but cooler heads among the bystanders pointed out that if arrested the boys would miss their champion trounce another opponent. Emil had broken the arm of the man in his last match, and his friends were hoping to see more of the same.

The wrestlers squared off and the bailiff shouted, "Wrestle!"

Robert and Emil circled in the ring, sizing each other up. Robert had marked him as a possible finalist early on, as much from his size as from his ferocity. So he had watched Emil to see what he might be up against. Emil was a pouncer. His technique consisted of a sudden rush and a grab. Once he had hold of an opponent, the man was doomed. Emil's great strength enabled him to secure a lock or a choke, or smash the man to the ground, and the fights had quickly ended either in unconsciousness or with wrenched or broken limbs.

The rush came after a few preliminary swipes with one of those mallet-like fists. Robert ducked, sidestepped, and punched Emil in the ribs as he went past. He might as well have hit a stone wall for all the good it seemed to do. Emil turned and laughed. The spectators howled.

On the second rush, Emil showed that he was not stupid. Anticipating the defensive sidestep, he waited until he had Robert maneuvered so near the edge of the ring that there was but one way to go, which Emil had blocked.

The Outlaws

At the last moment, Robert saw his danger. Upon the rush, he grabbed Emil's forearms and dropped backward, planted his feet in Emil's stomach, and propelled the larger man over his head. Emil landed with a thud that Robert felt through the ground, but the impact hurt the mason no more than the punch had done. Emil still had an iron grasp on one of Robert's arms, but somehow, Robert managed to yank the arm free. Emil's fingers left livid red marks on his skin. As Emil swung around to face Robert on hands and knees, Robert kicked him in the side of the head.

The blow snapped Emil's head to the side but did not seem to bother him any more than a little slap. Perhaps Emil's head was made of stone as well, like his ribs.

Emil snarled, not happy now, and charged from his crouched position. Robert rolled out of the way, but Emil grasped an ankle and pulled Robert toward him, triumph on his face, batting aside a kick by Robert's free foot.

Robert's situation was desperate, so he tried a desperate measure. He aimed a finger at one of Emil's eyes, but Emil turned his head just in time. Emil used the moment to jump forward and secure a headlock. He squeezed so hard that Robert thought his head would pop. Robert saw stars and began to choke. The lack of air brought on a sense of panic. He would be unconscious in a few heartbeats.

Lying there about to give up, he noticed Hugh's face at the far back of the crowd. Hugh looked frantic. Waving his fist, he was shouting something lost in the uproar.

Robert had the sudden thought: Oh, God, he's bet all the money.

Robert had to get free somehow or they were ruined.

He turned his head to relieve the pressure and managed to gulp a breath. Then Emil tightened his grip and cut off his wind again.

Robert knew a trick that might get him out of this fix. He wormed a hand around Emil's shoulder to his neck and thrust with a finger into the soft hollow of the throat above the breast bone. Emil gagged and turned his head away to avoid the finger. Robert kept up the pressure and Emil let go.

That gave Robert an opportunity to slip out of the headlock.

Both were gasping for breath as they climbed to their feet and faced each other.

Robert noticed that a curious silence had fallen. It was the silence of surprise. No one had expected him to break free. They had thought he was finished. None of Emil's earlier opponents had succeeded in escaping from his grip.

For a moment, Robert thought: I might win this thing. Then Emil began stalking him.

But Emil was tired now and wasn't as quick to close as he had been and it was easier to avoid him.

The crowd took Emil's fatigue for caution, and screamed insults. A few critics threw trash at him.

Emil liked his popularity, and the howls drove him mad. With a snarl, he bent to sweep Robert's legs from under him. Robert jumped just in time. He landed as Emil pivoted, presenting his back.

This was Robert's opportunity. He snaked an arm around Emil's neck from behind to choke him with a forearm, and wrapped his legs around Emil's waist.

But Emil knew tricks of his own. He was so strong that he managed to struggle to his feet with Robert on his back. Then Emil reached over his head, grasped Robert by the hair, and pulled him over a shoulder.

Robert landed hard on his back, the wind knocked out of him.

Emil sat on his chest and with those two massive hands began to choke him again.

Robert struggled, but could not get free. He tried to bend back one of Emil's fingers but couldn't manage it. Those fingers were as strong as bands of iron. Robert opened his mouth, but not a puff of air went in or out. It hurt! He became afraid that Emil intended to kill him. Would no one stop this? Couldn't they see that he was finished?

The Outlaws

In moments, even the fright evaporated and he lost consciousness.

CHAPTER 14

Livarot, Normandy
July 1179

Robert awakened to find a pair of drunken mason's apprentices urinating on his face. They were laughing so hard that their aim was bad and they got themselves wet, too.

The few spectators who remained nearby thought this was good fun, and almost fell off their hay bales in laughter. One man spewed his ale.

Robert didn't think it was so amusing. He staggered to his feet and reeled over to the bailiff's chair, where he had left his sword and bow and arrows in a deputy's hands. He unsheathed the sword before the deputy could stop him and turned on the apprentices. Tittering, daring Robert to hit them, they avoided his cuts, dancing backward and pelting him with handfuls of dirt, which stuck to his wet skin and hair as he reeled about. People laughed harder, if that were possible. The laughter made Robert's rage balloon. He had not intended to hurt anybody; he had just wanted to frighten the boys into shutting up. But he had made things worse, and he found himself so furious that now he wanted to hit someone very hard.

But the deputy was an older man who saw that things had gone beyond amusement and that he had potential murder on his hands. He called over his shoulder for help.

Help came running, and Robert was surrounded by six deputy bailiffs, armed with clubs. Although a good man with a club could disarm a swordsman, none of the bailiffs seemed eager to try it, despite the fact they had Robert out numbered.

The crowd in their corner of the marketplace grew quiet, waiting to see what would happen. A fight with weapons was always more exciting than a wrestling match.

"He's disturbing the peace!" one of the apprentices called. "Arrest him!"

"He tried to kill us!" the other shouted.

The Outlaws

"Put down the sword," the senior deputy ordered Robert, paying no attention to the apprentices.

Robert realized to his dismay that he had succeeded in making a fool of himself, and that he was now in serious trouble. Drawing a sword on someone was a serious offense. He'd probably be arrested, beaten, and thrown in some nasty pit and left to rot. It seemed so unfair, too, since he was the one wronged.

Just then, Hugh pushed through the ring of spectators and stepped to Robert's side. "I will take responsibility for him. He is my man." There was a tone of command in his voice that Robert had never heard before that established Hugh meant to be obeyed. Although the clothes they had bought that morning were just this side of shabby, they were good enough to lend credence and weight to his suggestion that he was a knight and therefore a man of some substance. Hugh said, "Leave him alone. You can see he has been sorely used."

Hugh dropped a handful of pennies into the senior deputy's hand and took the sword from Robert. "Let's get you a hot bath and a meal," he said. "You've done enough work for today."

The senior deputy, glad to see that a bad situation had been calmed without anyone getting hurt or him having to do anything, tossed a coin to each of the other bailffs and slipped the remainder in his purse . "All right, then."

"Aren't you going to arrest him?" cried one of the apprentices. "He almost killed me."

"If you'd lost your head, nobody would have missed it," the deputy replied. "Now disperse, all of you. The fun's over."

Hugh led Robert down a side street away from the marketplace. When they were away from the crowd a smile replaced his grim expression. "Feel this," Hugh said. He handed Robert the leather money bag, which hung under this cloak. It was swollen with silver pennies and so heavy that Robert, not expecting the weight, almost dropped it. "I'd have gotten to you sooner," Hugh said, "but a certain burgess was slow to part with his wager."

Robert was incredulous. "You mean you won? You bet on him?" He felt a bit betrayed.

Hugh shrugged. "On how long you'd last. There was a linen merchant in the crowd who bet me you wouldn't last two turns of the sand clock. You gave me a fright, though, when he had you down the first time. I thought you were done for, and the clock hadn't been turned once then."

Robert noticed that they had reached the lane of the goldsmiths. In moments they came to the shop of the smith who had lent them the money.

The goldsmith's nose wrinkled when he came to the counter and saw Robert. "What happened, boy?" he asked. "Fall into a cesspit?"

"Sorry, no."

Hugh said, "A couple of mason's apprentices treated him roughly."

"Well, they're known to do that here. They're a nasty lot, always knocking people down in the streets. Stand back, won't you? You're pretty foul."

"We've come to redeem the shirt," Hugh said, plunking the leather purse on the counter.

"So soon?" The goldsmith asked, startled. "All right. You," indicating Hugh, "come on in the back. You," squinting at Robert, "stay there."

Robert loitered in the street while Hugh was occupied with the moneylender, thinking about the bath Hugh had promised him. He had never had a hot bath in his life. Settling chin deep into a kettle of hot water seemed odd, as if you were a carrot, but people paid good money to do it and came away praising the experience.

Hugh emerged from the shop, wearing a big smile. "We have eighteen shillings and eight pence." He handed Robert a leather bag heavy with coins. "Here's your share."

"There's half here?"

The Outlaws

Hugh sniffed, offended. "Want to count it? You think I'd cheat you?"

"You made so much," Robert marveled. Why, with nine shillings, he could buy a horse. An old sway-backed nag, perhaps, but still a horse. He wouldn't have to walk any more. He'd be almost like a lord. Girls would pay attention to him if he had fine clothes and a horse.

Hugh shrugged. "It's not hard when you're as good as I am."

"What's a bath cost, anyway?"

Hugh blinked. "You don't want to eat first?" Food was the first thing he thought of in the morning and the last thing at night.

"Don't they feed you at the bathhouse?"

"They do. And fill your cup at every opportunity. But I thought you were worried about expenses."

"Damn the expense. Let's go, before you grow roots."

By September, they had earned enough for two cheap horses, a ten-year-old gelding, not quite a warhorse but trained as one, and a mare for Robert, along with tack for both, a pair of shields, and a couple of lances. Robert was glad for the mare and the fact they had more than enough to eat. For the first time in his life, he put on some weight, despite the constant wrestling matches and the fact that Hugh now forced him to practice sword and lance play every day, since Hugh had to stay sharp and had no one else to beat on. Hugh started calling him *le Grossette*, the little fat one. Robert didn't mind. He almost forgot about being homesick.

CHAPTER 15

Ludlow
September 1179

The Ludlow autumn fair was so well attended that when Earl Roger FitzWalter arrived late with his assembly of knights, squires, clerks, clerics, cooks and servants, and their women, all the inns were taken. That left no choice but to camp in the tent village that had grown up at the north end of the castle meadow, which lay by the rivulet of the River Corve. This crowding was a symptom of the fair's burgeoning popularity, which was growing like the town itself. FitzWalter could remember the days during the civil war when Ludlow was nothing more than a stone keep with a few huts in the shadow of the castle gatehouse. Today the town sprawled along the ridge above the meadow and down its slopes, behind its wooden palisade, with an impressive stone church and a busy marketplace. More than a thousand people must live here now.

FitzWalter envied the Lacys for their possession of a town. Having a town was worth a dozen manors. A town could make you rich. Although an earl, FitzWalter was a lesser one than the other families in the March such as the Mortimers or the de Clares. All he held besides his title were four English manors southwest of Ludlow, six in the south of England, and four that he had seized in Wales and held at great expense, because they had to be fortified, and stone castles cost more than a thousand pounds just to build, not to mention the cost of upkeep. He would gladly trade his Welsh manors for a good small town with a market he could tax and burgesses from whom he could squeeze high rents. Hardly a day went by when he did not chafe about his expenses or mull ways to get more money.

Shortly after they arrived and raised FitzWalter's banner to announce his presence, a messenger came down from the castle with an invitation for supper.

The Outlaws

Hugh de Lacy wasn't in residence yet. His return from Ireland, where he spent most of his time as justicar and lord of Meath and Dublin, had been delayed by rough seas and storms. So it fell to Lacy's wife Sybil to host the feast that marked the night before the fair. This event drew in the notables from the surrounding region because it was a good time for them to get together and exchange news and transact business: the rentals or sales of lands, the arranging of marriages, and so on. And the Lacys' table was always well stocked and the wine excellent.

After supper the men went outside to the bailey, where servants had taken the benches from the hall and several ale kegs had been set up so the men could continue drinking.

FitzWalter and Eustace wandered through the crowd after dinner, chatting here and there with friends and acquaintances. They came upon William de Hafton talking with some townsmen and merchants. FitzWalter was about to pass by, but then William pulled a brownish rock out of his pouch and showed it to the others. FitzWalter's curiosity was piqued. Why would anyone be so interested in a lump of dull stone?

"What's that?" FitzWalter asked.

"Iron," said one of the townsmen. "William has opened a mine on his land."

FitzWalter had heard of this mine, but it had never registered as being of any importance. To FitzWalter, legitimate wealth derived from the land, or the stuff that could be grown on land, not what might be dug up under it — and in rents, and plunder. Nevertheless, he was interested in anything that might bring a profit. He asked, "What's a mine worth?"

"It depends on what kind of ore that's in the ground, how much there is and how pure it is," William said. He gave FitzWalter the rock. "Especially how pure. The more iron in the ore, the more people will pay for it because they get more metal out of it."

FitzWalter fingered the rock. It looked like just any other rock. "And this is good ore, you say?"

"The smelters in Gloucester tell me that the rocks in this vein have almost two-thirds their weight in iron," William said.

"What do you care about this?" FitzWalter asked the townsman who had spoken up.

"William is looking for loans. He needs cash to develop the mine."

"How much profit do you think you can get from this mine?" FitzWalter asked.

"Twenty pounds a year," William said.

Twenty pounds! FitzWalter regarded the estimate as exaggeration to impress the townsmen to get them to loan the money that William needed to get this venture going. Yet if it was true, the mine itself was worth more than Hafton. FitzWalter tossed the rock back to William. "That's hard to believe."

"It's true."

"Good luck to you," FitzWalter said, and turned away. He had heard enough and didn't want to spoil the afternoon any more than he had done by spending time with William.

On the ride down the hill to camp that evening, FitzWalter listened to the news that Blanche had gathered from the women. He had found all his wives to be useful in this way. Women often learned things from other women that he did not from the men.

Despite FitzWalter's interest in Blanche's news, his mind wandered back to the conversation with William and the mine. Then something she said caught his attention. "Repeat that," he ordered.

Blanche said, "I was saying that Richard Beaumont, you know him, the earl of Leicester's youngest son, offered for Giselle de Hafton's hand."

FitzWalter was flabbergasted. It was astonishing news that the Earl of Leicester would offer to marry a son to William's child. It was such a poor bargain for Leicester. William was

The Outlaws

not important, despite his connection with King Henry, just a household knight given a small reward. Yet such a marriage would be significant from FitzWalter's perspective. If the marriage took place William would be attached to one of the leading families of the country. "Why would he do that?"

"Richard is the third son. The match gives him an honor, since William has no male child to inherit. So he'll get land, little though it is. And Richard fancies the girl. I understand there was quite an argument about it between father and son over whether an offer would be made. The earl was opposed to it initially, but he's an old man, and Richard is his last and youngest child, and the favorite. The boy's always gotten everything he wanted except an inheritance. And he fancies the girl."

FitzWalter nodded. Giselle, now fourteen, was of marriageable age, and quite beautiful. "But William's so damned healthy. He'll live for years. They won't have anything to live on."

"The earl offered the gift of a manor for them to live on until she inherits."

FitzWalter shook his head in wonderment. The things people will do. "What was William's answer?"

"He said he would think about it."

Now FitzWalter was shocked. "The man's addled. What in God's name could have come over him? What an opportunity!"

"It seems that the girl has second thoughts. She isn't sure she wants Richard, apparently."

FitzWalter was acquainted with this Richard. He recalled an ordinary enough fellow, although a bit blustery and given to grand pronouncements. Richard's main passion was fighting dogs. Yet FitzWalter could not imagine what qualms Giselle might have about him or why they would even matter. "Girls like her can't afford to be so choosy." He shook his head. "What a match that would be."

Then he had another thought. "We can't afford to move against William now. He might call on Leicester for support. And Leicester is closer to the Lacys than we are."

Blanche nodded. "Quite right."

"Shit," FitzWalter said.

"William might reject the offer, though."

"The devil you say."

"He's already rejected one this year."

"No!"

"Yes. From the de Grasse family."

"But why?"

"The girl didn't like the boy."

"That girl is too spoiled for her own good," he said with disgust.

Blanche was quiet for a time. She said, "I think she likes Eustace, though."

"Really." FitzWalter wondered what was the point of that.

"Yes. I saw them talking. They spoke for a long time. He made her laugh and I saw how raptly she watched his face. I know how strongly you want to provide him with a place of his own."

This suggestion seemed altogether too friendly toward Eustace. FitzWalter was aware that Blanche tolerated rather than liked Eustace, but then one was not expected to like children. "Yes, he does need a place, doesn't he."

"Perhaps arranging for Eustace to inherit Hafton would be better revenge," she said.

This idea appealed to FitzWalter. It would solve two problems at once. But he had to act to forestall any arrangement with Leicester.

Shortly after daybreak the following morning, he visited William's tent. Negotiations of this kind often were conducted by emissaries to avoid potential embarrassment to the principles should they fail, but FitzWalter thought he could be more persuasive in person.

William was sitting on a folding chair before his tent having breakfast. He ordered a second chair brought out for

The Outlaws

FitzWalter, who accepted the offer of bread, cheese and watered wine.

They chatted for a few minutes before FitzWalter broached his subject. "My son has developed a powerful attachment to your girl," he said.

William nodded. "He is a fine boy, a credit to your house."

"If she fancies him enough, I thought we might explore the possibility of a union between our families. We aren't the Beaumonts, but my family has a good heritage and I'm a man of some stature."

"It may make sense to reunite the estates," William said.

William was asking if FitzWalter meant to make Eustace his heir. FitzWalter hedged. "I may yet have more children. My wife is young still."

William twisted his napkin. "Will there be provision for the couple during my lifetime?"

"I will give Eustace a manor. There will also be a gift to you of twenty pounds." The gift of the manor would be illusory. FitzWalter intended to construct the grant so that he retained control. The cash portion would be placed in William's hands rather than those of the groom. It was a bribe, pure and simple. FitzWalter was used to getting what he wanted and he expected this proposal to be hard to resist, since William was starved for cash.

"That's a very generous provision."

FitzWalter suppressed a smile. He felt he had the man. "He's a good son, and I wish him well in the world."

"An important matter like this deserves careful thought," William said. "Shall we talk again in a few days?"

"Certainly. These things should not be rushed."

"Yes, that's so."

CHAPTER 16

Ludlow
September 1179

On the evening before the last day of the fair, Eustace went to the bear baiting. He had heard that after the bear had finished the dogs, it would fight a man. He wanted to see that. He hoped the bear would kill the man.

The scene of the baiting was at a big crossroads at the east end of town where High Street, Old Street, Galdeford Road, and Corve Street all came together that the locals called the Bull Ring.

Eustace came down Corve Street to the selected spot in the company of a half dozen knights. They paid three pennies each to get beyond the rope — the price so high because a man would fight tonight — and pushed through the crowd to the open space at the center.

The bear was a big brown bruin. He was shackled by a rear leg to a post driven into the ground in the center of the open space. Lying there with his head on his forepaws, he looked like a tired dog who'd rather have his ears scratched. In the firelight from the torches surrounding the ring, Eustace could see that this was an old bear; grey fur fringed its mouth.

At the sound of yapping dogs, heads turned in the crowd as the dog handlers with the dogs on leashes made their way through the crowd. As they approached, the bear's head came up and he sniffed the air. The pace of betting increased.

When the dogs reached the edge of the ring, the bear's owner stepped forward and swatted the animal across the rump with a quarterstaff. The bear jumped to his feet and whirled on the man with astonishing speed. The owner leaped backward with inches between him and the swipe of the bear's massive paw. The crowd laughed at the near miss, which the owner had intended. It made the bear look more vicious than it was. The owner waved his hat in the air, acknowledging the laughter.

The Outlaws

He spotted William across the ring, who was watching the spectacle with crossed arms and a solemn face. Beside him stood FitzWalter, who wore a smile. It was hard to tell whether FitzWalter was smiling at what had just happened or at something he and William were talking about.

He imagined they were talking about his proposed marriage to Giselle.

Eustace had no enthusiasm for the idea. But he saw no way to refuse, now FitzWalter had set his mind on it.

He also saw weaknesses to the plan that seemed to have eluded FitzWalter and Blanche. Neither seemed quite able to apprehend that William might hate them with equal measure, yet be reluctant to refuse to FitzWalter's face. Moreover, even if William was disposed to accept, it was clear that sealing the deal turned on Eustace's ability to charm that silly girl. Eustace had confidence in his charm, but he was not such a fool that he knew he could not fail. Success with women was never certain. The few times he had been in Giselle's company she had been cold even when he had tried his charming best. He understood that she had a great deal of influence over her father in this matter, and Eustace was convinced that she would reject him. There was also the possibility that William would reject the match. Marrying a daughter to someone's bastard was a poor proposition from William's perspective, after all, no matter how much FitzWalter sought to sweeten the deal. Eustace certainly wouldn't agree to it if he was in William's position. But whatever drove the decision, FitzWalter would blame Eustace rather than the hopelessness of the scheme or himself.

Eustace feared FitzWalter's anger more than anything.

The dogs barked and strained at their leashes.

William pulled from his spot at the rope a moment before the dogs' release and pushed his way out of the crowd. A plan leaped into Eustace's mind at that instant. There was something he could to get out of this mess. It wasn't easy or tidy, and entailed a great deal of risk. But it was the only thing he could think of that would bring FitzWalter what he wanted.

Eustace caught up with William just before Corve Gate, but remained a dozen paces behind. Even though it was after sundown and the gate should have been closed, it was open in honor of the bear baiting up the street, where the roars of the crowd reverberated between the houses. He let William pass through first. William exchanged good evenings with the gate warden. Eustace gritted his teeth at that. The warden might remember William's passage from that simple courtesy. Eustace himself strode through with his head down, pretending to ignore the warden, praying that he would be forgotten.

Beyond the ditch, a footpath headed toward the meadow north of the castle. William turned there. Eustace hurried to catch up with him. William heard him coming and turned to see who it was.

"Ah!" Eustace said, "my lord, no interest in the contest?"

"No. Those fights are fixed. There's no sport in that."

"Fixed, you say?"

"The bear always wins. It's easier to get dogs than it is bears, so the owner won't hazard the bear."

"I'm glad I didn't stay then."

"No interest?"

"It amuses me enough, but I'm feeling poorly. An upset stomach. Something rancid I ate, I think."

They walked on in silence for some time as the path curved into the meadow away from the houses that lay along Linney Lane. Ahead, bonfires burned among the tents where people were up long past their normal bedtimes. The hum of conversation overlaid with someone playing a lute and a group of people singing wafted across the field. Eustace recognized the song: The Maid from Canterbury. It had many verses, some of them very bawdy like the ones about how the maid had seduced the Archbishop.

The Outlaws

As they neared a large oak that stood alone in the field, Eustace let William get a step ahead. He drew his dagger. William half turned as if to say something. Eustace grasped him around the head and drove the dagger into his side. William grunted. Eustace stabbed him again. William began to struggle, and as Eustace stabbed a third time William caught his arm. Eustace had not expected this much resistance. Petrified that William might disarm him and cry out, he yanked his arm free and drove the dagger into William's throat. William made choking sounds. He sank to his knees as the dagger, still in Eustace's hand, slid out of his neck. Then William collapsed onto his back, legs folded under him in an awkward, unnatural way. He gasped a few more times, slower and slower, until he was still. It was a terrible way to die, and Eustace wished there had been some other way to do this, but it was the only thing he could think of.

Eustace dragged the body off the path into the tall grass beside it, hoping that it would not be found until the morning. He cut William's purse, and emptied the contents into his hand, fumbling the silver pennies, which he stuffed into his own purse, fearful that someone would come along. He dropped William's purse on the dead man's chest so that when the body was found people would think that the motive for the killing was robbery.

He was about to leave when he noticed the clasp to William's cloak. It looked to be made of silver in the form of a cross with a polished blue stone. No self-respecting thief would leave such a jewel behind. Eustace cut it free.

Glancing backward now and then, he slipped back to his tent.

He sat on his cot, shivering and breathing so hard that the valet sleeping on the other side of the tent woke up. "Are you ill, my lord?" the valet asked.

"I'm fine. Go back to sleep."

Eustace wished he could do the same, not that he was likely to even if he lay down now. But he had one thing left to do. He fumbled in the arrow bag beside the cot for an arrow.

He waited until the valet's breathing indicated he had fallen asleep.

Then he tip-toed out into the night.

CHAPTER 17

Ludlow
September 1179

The normal rules governing bedtime were suspended during fairs, and having no curfew outside the town, people in the tent village stayed up late. With father in the town, Giselle had taken advantage and accepted an invitation from the daughter of a knight from Stanton Lacy. The girls had a tent of their own and had played dice — a thing normally forbidden to women of their class — and backgammon and chattered away while a hired minstrel played and sang until nearly midnight. They had all felt so wicked.

So she slept later than usual. The sun was above the line of trees along Linney Lane by the time Giselle emerged from the tent, wondering what wonderful things she would do today. This was the last day of the fair and she had to make the most of it.

Cook was preparing breakfast at the small table they had brought with them, his long face longer than usual. Athelhild, who had risen earlier although she had been with Giselle, also was quiet, glancing at the town with a concerned look. Athelhild bent to ask Osgar something. Osgar, squatting by the fire with his father Burghard, shook his head.

"What's the matter?" Giselle asked.

"Your father didn't return last night," Athelhild said.

"He isn't here?"

"No. No one knows where he is. The last anyone saw him he was at the bear baiting."

It was very odd that William would go anywhere without any of his people knowing about it. Perhaps he had tarried at one of the whorehouses in town. Giselle had never known him to do that, and with Matilda now in the house that seemed unlikely. But it was the only thing she could think of, repellant as the thought was, and she rejected it.

Off toward the town there was shouting and a crowd began to gather not far from a large oak tree whose limbs were so massive that the lower ones touched the ground. A party of men separated from the crowd and ran toward the tent village. They made their way to the de Hafton camp and stopped before the fire. They removed their caps and stood awkwardly as if none of them quite knew what to say. One of them asked Giselle, "Are you Sir William's daughter?"

"I am," Giselle replied with a mounting sense of unease.

"You need to come right away."

"What is it?"

"It's your father. Someone's killed him."

The crowd parted for Giselle. They were quiet now, and she was conscious of the sweeping sound her skirts made upon the grass and the call of a robin in the oak tree. The path people made for her led up to a crumpled thing lying in the grass which looked more like a pile of discarded laundry than a man. But it had been a man once.

Giselle knelt by the body, so chilled by shock that she wasn't sure she could breathe, let alone cry. There were several hundred sets of eyes on her now. It was not the time for that sort of weakness.

The finders must have discovered William on his stomach, for his legs were crossed at the ankles, and his hair lay across his face. Giselle smooth the strands away. His eyes were open as if he was looking into the distance, and there was a great gash on his neck where his throat had been cut. The slash was so deep and savage that his windpipe was visible, and there was a lot of blood soaking his clothing and the ground where he lay. An arrow showed above William's right shoulder, pressed down by the weight of his body. Giselle struggled to turn William to get a look at the wound, but she could not manage alone. When helping hands turned William on his side, she saw the arrow had penetrated his back just below the right shoulder blade. She released William's shoulder and he settled on his back again.

The Outlaws

One man held out an empty purse. "Was this your father's, my lady?"

Giselle nodded, not yet trusting herself to speak. She noticed that the silver clasp William always wore on his cloak, a gift from her mother, was gone too. A coin dropped by the killer glistened in the grass by William's head.

"A robbery," the man said. "It was pure robbery and murder!"

The respectful quiet that had prevailed vanished in a wave of condemnation, for no one tolerated robbery or murder. They were the worst crimes anyone could commit, worse even than rape.

Giselle heard the tumult as if it was far away. She felt disconnected from it, from the indignation, from the whole world itself. She stood as though upon the edge of a great chasm, one foot poised in space over the brink. Just moments ago, her life had been solid, certain. Now, in a heartbeat, it had unraveled so profoundly that it would never be whole and complete again. What was she going to do?

Osgar took her arm in a manner that was tender yet insistent, and more familiar than she should allow. His whole face was contorted with grief, tears streaming down his cheeks and falling onto his chest, tears she could not yet shed.

"My lady," he managed to say after several false starts, "come away. This isn't a fit sight for you. Let us take care of him. He'll be all right."

Although how William would ever again be all right she could not fathom.

"No," she said. "I shall go with him. Please have someone fetch something we can use to carry him back."

She waited there in the field, feeling more alone than she had ever thought it possible to feel, until poles and a blanket were found to make a stretcher.

Before they could go, however, they had to wait for the undersheriff, the local coroner being too indisposed by drink to perform his duties, to conduct the initial inquiry into the death.

It wasn't long before the undersheriff appeared, a big young man named Gilbert of the Braz de Fer family, minor tenants of the FitzWalters, and three deputies. Braz de Fer examined the body, then broke off the arrow head and drew out the arrow himself. "Well, it's pretty clear what happened. Someone lay in wait and shot the gentleman in the back and then slit his throat while he lay wounded."

He showed the shaft to the assembly and asked, "Has anyone seen this work before?"

An arrow shaft might appear indistinguishable from another, but there were subtle differences of style and workmanship, such as in the trimming and binding of the fletching and the form of the head. This shaft also had three rings painted on the wood just ahead of the fletching, marks of ownership in red, yellow and red. It was not uncommon to paint the shaft bright colors so that it could be found in the forest if a shot went wild.

A man dressed in a brown wool shirt and gray stockings spoke up. "I have."

"Who are you?" Braz de Fer asked.

"Hugh of How Chapel."

"What can you tell us?"

"There was a man from Shelburgh who made arrows like this. He peddled them at the Ludlow and Hereford markets now and then. I have a few myself."

"Do you remember his name?"

"It was Nicholas . . . Nicholas Attebrook."

Braz de Fer spotted Eustace at the edge of the crowd. "I remember that name. The poacher who died escaping the earl's gaol."

Eustace nodded. "The one whose nephew tried to get him out, and went outlaw afterwards."

"Right. I don't recall his name."

"Robert, also Attebrook. He had been a clerk or something like that in Gloucester, or so I'm told. He's a desperate fellow. He killed my cousin."

The Outlaws

"Yes, I remember it now. Bad business." Braz de Fer nodded. "He's not the one you've put two pounds on, is he?"

"The very one."

"This was cold work. A man like him could have done this," Braz de Fer said, tapping the arrow shaft against a palm. "Fairs are good places to find men with money. Like a flock of sheep to a wolf."

"It could be anyone in Shropshire," Hugh of How Chapel said. "Many have arrows like that."

"Could be," Braz de Fer said. "What provisions have you made to take care of your father's body?" he asked Giselle.

Giselle shook her head. She hadn't thought that far ahead yet.

Eustace spoke before she could answer. "We'll take care of it. We're neighbors."

"What a stroke of luck," FitzWalter said over the rim of his wine cup.

Blanche, seated beside him outside their tent, looked pleased. She crossed her legs at the ankles and leaned over to smooth a scuff on her boot. "Eustace is right. Now it's just a matter of securing the wardship. You can take what you like out of Hafton then, with no one to complain."

"Wardships are one thing," FitzWalter said, "but we need to take the long view." He shook a finger at Eustace. "I'll have you married to that little bitch before next spring. Then that shitty piece of dirt comes back into my honor."

"That is as it should be, my lord," Eustace murmured. In his haste to rid himself of one problem, he had not thought of the possibility that FitzWalter would want to marry him to the girl after having secured the wardship. But he should have foreseen it. He seethed that FitzWalter would force him into such a low and unprofitable marriage. It showed what contempt FitzWalter had for him.

Well, he thought, if it came to that, there were many ways to rid yourself of an unwanted wife.

CHAPTER 18

Ludlow
September 1179

No one thought of dinner after the finding of William's body. Osgar and Burghard went to find a wagon for hire to take the body home, and were gone for most of the day. Athelhild went up to the town to buy linen for the shroud. Cook asked Giselle if she wanted something to eat, but she declined and remained on a stool by the pallet where they had laid her father while the servants ate scraps.

Athelhild returned in midafternoon with a roll of linen, and then there was a long search for a needle and thread, since no one had thought to bring any, and they had to borrow them from a neighbor.

At last when these few preparations had been made, Athelhild knelt beside Giselle. "We must undress him first."

Giselle rose. "I can't do it. I can't touch him."

"I understand. I'll take care of it. You go."

Giselle nodded, at once relieved and ashamed. It was her responsibility to prepare her father for burial, to wash him, to dress him, and to sew up his shroud.

She took her stool and sat by the cook fire, rocking with her arms clasped about her knees. The fire had died down since the morning, but toward the end of the day, cook began to feed it so that everyone could have supper. Giselle wished he would just leave the ashes alone. But people had to eat. Life had to go on. It was so unfair.

She had not been there long before Athelhild emerged from the tent. "You need to see this."

"What?" Giselle asked.

"Something that's not right."

"Nothing that's happened this day has been right."

Athelhild shook her shoulder. "Come on. You must."

"Very well."

The Outlaws

Giselle went into the tent. It was shocking to see her father lying naked on the pallet. "What in God's name must I see?"

Athelhild knelt by the body and pointed to William's back. "There. See? That little slit."

The mark where the arrow had struck beneath the shoulderblade was plain, but lower down, where Athelhild pointed, was a small slit.

"What is it?" Giselle asked.

"It looks like a dagger wound."

"So?"

"So, whoever killed our lord not only shot him with an arrow, but stabbed him in the back as well."

"So?"

"So it makes no sense. Think about it. It was dark last night. No self respecting robber would shoot someone in the back in the dark. The chances of missing are too great. And why shoot him in the back and then stab him there?"

"I don't follow."

"Whoever killed him likely stabbed him first, then pushed the arrow in to make it look like he'd been shot. Doesn't it seem odd to you that that very arrow is one that could be linked with you-know-who?"

"With Robert Attebrook?"

"Exactly. To divert suspicion. This was not an ordinary robbery."

"I cannot believe any of this."

"It is supposition, but it is the only thing that makes sense."

"But why?"

"I don't know. But we may find out in time. We must keep our eyes open, and be watchful. Now, you go, I'll finish here."

The next morning Roger FitzWalter sent men over to the de Hafton tents to help pack up for the return home.

Athelhild tried to send them away with an indignant, "We can take care of ourselves, thank you very much."

But the FitzWalter men could not be sent off, and when Athelhild appealed to Giselle, she said, "What does it matter? Let them help. We'll be on the road more quickly."

"It is none of their business, mistress!" Athelhild protested.

Giselle was in no mood to argue. She waved a hand, and the packing went on so that by an hour after dawn, the packhorses were loaded and the body laid in the rented wagon. The FitzWalter men guided the train over to the FitzWalter encampment, where a similar train was just as ready to depart.

Lady Blanche had a wagon to herself, and she called to Giselle: "Come ride with me, dear! I need the company!"

Athelhild hissed in Giselle's ear, "What is going on?"

"I could use the company as well." Giselle had no great appetite for a journey in the back of a wagon, even if it had its own canvass awning to shade passengers from the sun. But the invitation offered the chance of a diversion, and conversation might fill the great void in her heart.

"This isn't right," Athelhild said as Giselle climbed into the wagon.

"What isn't right, dear?" Blanche asked.

"Nothing, my lady," Athelhild replied.

The road to Hafton and Shelburgh was no worse than any other in England, which is to say, it was one jolting rut and stone after another all the way.

At a stop to conduct necessary business, Giselle emerged from the bushes to the roadside, where some of the men were still urinating in the grass, to see Osgar and Athelhild with their heads together. There was something furtive in the way they conducted themselves, so Giselle went over to find out what was going on.

"What are you up to?" Giselle asked them.

The Outlaws

"The FitzWalters mean to accompany us all the way to Hafton," Athelhild said.

"Nonsense," Giselle said. "Why would they want to do that?"

"They plan to stay for the burying," Athelhild spat. "As if they really cared about him."

"But I thought father was in the process of patching things up."

"You don't really believe that."

Giselle blinked. "It is a friendly gesture on their part. I cannot reject it."

"Friendly gesture or not, we have to warn Matilda."

Giselle could see the sense in that. There was no telling what might happen if the FitzWalter people came across her: nothing good, that was certain. "How will we do that?"

"Send Osgar on ahead," Athelhild said.

"All right. Do that."

Giselle turned away. Athelhild grasped her by the shoulders. "Come to your senses! Can't you smell the danger here? We aren't safe among these people."

"I don't know what you mean." Giselle pushed Athelhild's hands away. She stumbled back a few steps, then fled to Blanche's wagon.

Athelhild's warning weighed on Giselle's mind for some time after that, but Blanche and her maids were friendly and warm to her and before long she had forgotten about it, glad to be relieved of any worry.

At last the train crossed the ford north of the house, and the old stone tower, square and solid beside the house itself, came into view. They rounded the embankment, and Giselle perceived that FitzWalter meant to enter the yard. She called out, "I would like my father laid in the village church!"

FitzWalter reined up and came back to the women's wagon. "Not in your chapel?"

"No, my lord," Giselle said, climbing out of the wagon. "He would want to be buried beside my mother, who is buried in the churchyard with my brothers."

"Very well," FitzWalter said, not sounding very interested. "Do what you must."

"Thank you, my lord," she replied, although as she turned away she wondered why she'd felt it necessary to have his permission to do anything on her own land.

Giselle followed the cart carrying her father's body into the village, while the FitzWalter entourage entered the yard.

When the cart stopped, the crowd closed in around it, everyone staring at the shrouded corpse. More than a few had begun weeping, and many reached over the rails to touch the linen covering the body.

Wulfric came to Giselle's side. "A sad day, mistress."

She nodded.

"I'll have Sebbi make a coffin for him. It isn't right to lay him in the ground like some pauper."

"Thank you, Wulfric."

"Osfrid! Hereric!" Wulfric said to two men behind him. "Fetch a plank so we can get our lord into the church. We can't lug him around like a sack of grain."

Proper coffins took some time to make, but Sebbi and his sons, despite having little experience with building coffins, threw one together in just over an hour that looked as though it had taken a whole day, so that William could be laid out before the altar rather than on the bare ground, like most people.

All the people in the village tried to pack into the church at once, and since it was a small church, there wasn't room enough for everyone. As on Sundays, the overflow stood at the doors and beneath the windows, but this wasn't a Sunday and now everyone wanted a chance inside. The press was so intense that those in the front row were nearly pushed into the altar or even the coffin itself — Giselle was saved from this

The Outlaws

indignity by Wulfric's rough hand on her shoulder. With a great deal of shouting and jostling, Wulfric forced people to form a line that shuffled through so that everyone got their look.

By this time, it was almost sundown and the supper hour, and stomachs were growling all around. Before long, everyone had their chance and only Wulfric and Giselle remained in the church, which had filled with dust churned up by all the feet.

"You staying, mistress?" Wulfric asked from the doorway.

"I shall. Please see that I'm not disturbed."

"Will you be wanting anything to eat, though?"

"Not tonight."

"I'll leave you to it, then." He shut the door.

Giselle stood over the coffin for some time before she settled to her knees and began to pray.

Sometime during the night, the door creaked open. Giselle was about to warn off the intruder when she heard in Matilda's voice, "Giselle? Are you still here?"

"I am."

"Do you mind?"

"No. Come in."

Matilda groped her way to the back of the nave. Giselle felt her hand on her arm and they clasped hands. Matilda sank beside her. Giselle felt her reach out into the coffin to touch what remained of William.

"He's really dead," Matilda said, leaning back on her heels.

"It seems impossible," Giselle said.

"It always seems impossible until it happens. He was a good man."

"What will I do now?"

"You will go on. That's what we women do. The hardest lot always falls to us. No matter what, you will endure."

"I don't want to!" And now the tears came. Giselle's shoulders wracked as she sobbed. "I want everything to be as it was!"

Matilda put an arm around her. "You must and you will."

CHAPTER 19

Hafton
September 1179

Giselle awoke to the sensation of fingers brushing her forehead. Matilda was leaning over her. Dawn had arrived, the church windows filled with gray light.

"I have to go," Matilda said.

Giselle sat up. "I'll walk you home."

Matilda smiled. "Such as it is for now."

"Where have they put you?" Giselle asked, as Matilda helped her up. "I was afraid you might have fled."

"And miss the burial? You're not the only one who cared for him." Then Matilda added, "Or would care for him."

Giselle was not sure what that meant, but did not pursue it as they had left the church and she was overcome with the surrealness of the morning. There was fog so thick outside that the houses on the other side of the street were mere suggestions. A few early risers could be seen here and there, apparitions that seemed to drift along, all sound muffled. No one noticed them as they came out of the gate, crossed the road, and went down a footpath leading to the west.

"I will be glad when the FitzWalters are gone," Giselle said.

"As will I. I suppose you will have to go to your uncle's now."

"*We* shall have to go."

"We shall see."

"You won't come?" Giselle stopped on the path, astonished at Matilda's reluctance.

"You may change your mind about it in time." They had reached a small house that had been the home of a widow who had recently died. It had lain empty since then. Matilda turned in the gate.

"What are you talking about?" Giselle grasped Matilda's arm. "Tell me!"

"Now is not the time. Go home. Get ready for your father's funeral."

The remainder of the day went by in such a swirl of events that later Giselle could barely recall them. Breakfast in the hall was a noisy, chaotic affair, the place full to the brim with the FitzWalter entourage, many of whom had to sit on the floor for a lack of tables. Afterward, everyone dressed in their best, and trooped down to the church, where the entire population of the village waited outside for Giselle and his lordship to enter first. The village priest said the mass over the open coffin. FitzWalter looked bored; Blanche seemed distracted by something and kept picking at her gown; Eustace stood stony faced; Eleanor was more smug than Giselle had seen her in a long time; and Baldwin kept shuffling his feet and refused to meet Giselle's eye whenever she looked at him.

After the priest sprinkled the body with holy water, said the Lord's Prayer, and gave the Absolutions, Sebbi and his sons nailed on the lid of the coffin, and he, Wulfric, and four others lifted the box and carried it out into the churchyard. Everyone else who could grabbed a candle from the rack and followed them, but the wind, which was rising beneath a gray sky, snuffed them out before they reached the grave site beside Hanelore's stone.

Someone handed the priest a wooden shovel, and he dug a cross in the ground, then handed the shovel to the villagers who were being paid to dig the grave proper, and they set to work.

The passing of the shovel to the gravediggers signaled the end of the ceremony, at least as far as Earl Roger was concerned. He left without a word, followed by his wife, Eustace, Baldwin, and Eleanor. Four of FitzWalter's knights remained in the churchyard, however, sitting on the stone wall apart from everyone else.

Athelhild eyed the knights. "Something's not right."

195

The Outlaws

"I'm sorry?" Giselle said.

"I said, something's not right."

"I don't understand."

"I just feel that something's wrong."

"What could it be?" Giselle asked.

"I don't know. We must keep our eyes and ears open. We cannot trust these people."

"I am so tired. I wish they were gone."

The wind stirred the grass, carried off a few hats, tugged at the cloaks of the small number who wore them and the clothes of everyone else. The sky had grown darker, dropping tendrils toward the ground. The grave was half dug and it would rain soon.

"It's all right if you want to go," Giselle said to the villagers. "No sense in getting wet and falling sick."

People were reluctant to depart at first, but more and more trickled off home so that by the time the two grave diggers had completed their work, only Giselle, Athelhild, Wulfric, and Sebbi the carpenter remained at the graveside, not counting the knights.

"That's deep enough," Wulfric said to the grave diggers. He and Sebbi pulled them out of the hole.

The four men lowered the coffin on ropes. Giselle threw the first spadeful of dirt on the coffin, where it struck with a hollow sound. Then the two gravediggers began shoveling dirt into the hole in earnest, eager to beat the rain. It seemed to take no time at all to fill up the hole, far less than it had taken to make it.

"Well, that's that," Sebbi said. "Begging your pardon, mistress."

"No need to beg my pardon," Giselle said. "You best get on home yourselves before you get wet." A few raindrops had begun to fall, leaving pockmarks on the bare earthen mound before them. She pulled up her hood and turned toward the gate.

"Why are you still here?" Giselle asked the knights as they rose at her approach.

"For your protection," one of them said.

"I hardly need protection here on my own land," she said.

"A lady like you can't be seen walking about without an escort," the knight said as they all fell in about her and Athelhild. "It isn't seemly."

He said this with a smirk that seemed out of keeping with a protective impulse.

Someone must have been on lookout at the manor house, for as they crossed the bridge and entered the yard, Eustace was there waiting for them.

Behind him, it seemed that the entire FitzWalter party and all their horses were in the yard, saddled and ready to go. Blanche's maids had already climbed into the wagon, and Blanche herself stood beside it, eyes on Giselle.

"You're leaving?" Giselle asked Eustace.

Eustace did not answer. He gestured to Athelhild. "Take her to the house."

Two knights grasped Athelhild's arms and marched her toward the manor house. She looked appalled, but did not resist or speak.

"What are you doing?" Giselle cried and tried to follow, but Eustace clasped her shoulder.

"Your things are already packed and loaded."

"What are you talking about?"

"A young girl like you cannot be left unprotected. My father will take care you come to no harm."

This sounded so like what one of the knights had said outside the churchyard that Giselle had the panicked feeling this had all been planned since Ludlow. "I'm not going anywhere. This is my home. I'm staying here."

Eustace pushed her into the arms of one of the knights. "There's no time to argue. We must get going before the rain turns the road to mire."

The Outlaws

He gestured toward the wagon, and the knight dragged her there. He forced her aboard. Blanche climbed up behind her.

"Why am I not allowed my maid?" Giselle asked. "Where is Athelhild?"

"We are told she is difficult and quarrelsome," Blanche said, settling on her cushion. "We will find you another maid. One more suitable."

"She is my maid. I want her."

Blanche fixed her with a cold glare. She slapped Giselle hard. "You will do what you are told henceforth, without complaint. You have been spoiled altogether too much for your own good."

Servants dropped the canvas cover so that it prevented anyone from seeing the passengers, and the wagon jerked toward the gate.

CHAPTER 20

Hafton
September 1189

Earl Roger's party had just got beyond the last house in the village before a boy came running up the path to the abandoned hut where Matilda and her children had taken shelter with word that he had gone.

Alice and Agnes threw down the wool and spindle they had been working with. Alice began kicking dirt on the fire.

"What are you doing?" Matilda asked, looking up from some embroidery.

"You're not thinking we should spend another night in this place?" Agnes asked.

"It's not that bad," Matilda said.

"How can you say that?" Alice asked, finishing with the fire. "The roof leaks and it has holes in the walls. Birds could fly in at any time. Who knows what lives in the thatch!"

"You two have got spoiled living in the manor," Matilda said. Even so, she stood up and put the embroidery in a satchel with what remained of their food. She had no desire to remain here any longer than necessary than the girls did. The place smelled of rot. "All right. Brian, fetch the blankets."

They came around the bend and approached the manor house.

As they got near, Wulfric came through the gate, his face more grim than it had been at William's funeral.

"You better not go in," Wulfric said when he reached Matilda.

"What's the matter?" she asked.

"Earl Roger has taken Giselle away. He means to have her wardship. He's left his bastard boy in charge."

"Eustace?" Matilda was appalled, thinking of her danger rather than the terrible thing that had befallen Giselle.

The Outlaws

Wulfric nodded, looking back to the manor house to see if anyone had spotted them. He urged them down the road to the village. When they had rounded the bend and were out of sight, he said, "You best make yourselves scarce. Eustace asked after you. He wants to talk to you about your son. He knows the boy was here and he thinks you know where he went."

"I'm sure he intends more than that," Matilda said, remembering the whipping delivered to Brian. There surely would be more of that to come, and perhaps not just to him.

"We're just to go now? Like this?" Alice asked. "What about the —"

Matilda put a hand over Alice's mouth, knowing she was going to ask after the money. Matilda had buried it in a corner of the barn one night where she was sure that no one would look for it, just as she had buried her small hord under the bed at Shelburgh, where it still remained. If they went away now, all they had was Matilda's satchel with the remainder of the cheese, a quarter loaf of bread, a few apples, and their blankets. She'd held out not a single penny.

"Wulfric's right," Matilda said. "We can't stay." From the looks on the children's faces, they were as frightened of the prospect of falling into the hands of a FitzWalter as she was.

They arrived at Wulfric's house, right by the church. "Wait here," he said.

He hurried into the house while they waited alone in the street, the wind whipping around them and the scent of rain metallic in the air.

Wulfric came out with two loaves of bread, a whole cheese, and a sack of onions. "It's all we can spare."

"Thank you," Matilda said.

"If you're caught, tell no one about this. Promise?"

"I promise. I have one last favor to ask."

"All right," Wulfric said.

"Can you ask Osgar to meet me? I'll be waiting in the wood beyond the top of the hill.

Wulfric nodded. "I suppose I could." He went back into the house.

"What will we do now?" Agnes asked.

"Where will we go?" Alice asked.

"Far from here. Come on, girls, Brian. Pick up your feet."

It was night before Osgar dared to come again. But he had no trouble finding Matilda, since she was waiting in the same spot where they had talked earlier at the edge of the wood.

Osgar handed her a cloth bag that smelled of earth. "Careful on the road with that," he said. "I've never seen so much hard money at once, and I daresay, no one else has either."

"Thank you, Osgar," Matilda said, opening the sack. "You can't know how grateful I am."

Ogar grinned crookedly. "Oh, I think I can imagine."

She handed him a handful of silver pennies, a lot of compensation for this night's work. "For your trouble."

"Why, thank *you*," Osgar said, astonished at her generosity.

"I'll never forget this," Matilda said. "Not that we'll ever see each other again."

"I suppose we won't."

"No. Girls! Brian! On your feet. Time to go."

201

CHAPTER 21

Lagny-sur-Marne
October 1179

"If you drink any more of that," Robert said, "you won't be able to walk a straight line. And we need you sober."

Hugh regarded the contents of his cup. "Please do not imply that I cannot hold my wine. It is not fitting for the squire to criticize the knight." He belched and sipped again. "It's not a bad wine, you know, though I'm sure I could do better once I have my vineyard."

"Well, you're not exactly a knight, and I'm not exactly a squire. So I'll say what I like."

"You're the one who said we must do our utmost to maintain appearances." Hugh squinted off across the field. They were sitting under an oak where a tavern keeper from the town had set up a temporary establishment complete with tables, benches, and barrels upon barrels of wine, separated from the hubbub of the fair by ropes stretched from posts pounded into the ground. Outside the rope, merchants hawking everything imaginable had set up stalls, and beyond this market could be seen the tops of the tents of those, gentry and nobility alike, who had established camps in what had been a pasture. They, like Robert and Hugh, had come for the tournament. "So let me remind you, as my squire you must address me in a deferential manner."

"If you ever hope to have that vineyard, you better lay off now." Robert finished his ale, and put the cup in a barrel reserved for used cups standing by the gap in the rope fence that served as the entrance. He picked up the wool sack that contained their mail shirts and hung the helmets, which were connected by a thong, from one shoulder and his own shield from the other. "Come on. Time to sign up."

Hugh gulped the last of his wine and tossed his cup toward the barrel. The cup struck the lip and bounced out onto the ground. He slung his own shield from one shoulder.

"I suppose we can't put it off any longer," Hugh said as they stepped outside the rope and dodged a vendor who bore a tray of honeyed apples suspended from straps on his shoulders. The tray was almost as big as a door, and Robert marveled at how the vendor was able to hold it up without spilling any of the apples with all the people flowing around him.

"No, we can't. Not if you want that vineyard."

"The Flemings, you said," Hugh mused. "It must be the Flemings."

"The word is they are taking on men. They say the English team have two-hundred men."

"We'll have to fight the English then. I don't think I'll like that."

"What does it matter?"

"Well, they are our countrymen, after all. Yours anyway. And as a Gascon, I do feel some affinity for them, owing to the fact we share a king. But Flemings? We have no more in common with them than Moscovites. Besides, what if they find out and bear a grudge?"

"I doubt anyone will ever know or care. Anyway, the Flemings are set to fight the English first, and they're short-handed. They don't want to be outnumbered. Hurry, before they fill up with Germans. There are more Germans around than flies on horse shit."

Despite the urging to hurry, Hugh halted to watch actors staging a play from the backs of a large wagon. Robert tugged him away from that only to lose him again at a bear chained to a post. Nearby his keeper was already taking bets for the noon bear-baiting as the challenger dogs howled at the tops of their lungs from their pens. Honey sellers with little coated buns on trays which dangled from their necks by straps like the man with apples hovered around them, creating a clamor with demands they buy something. As Robert broke them away from these distractions, they stumbled over a dice game going on a blanket, to be interrupted by a pair of boys who raced through pursued by a man with the points on his shoes so

The Outlaws

long that they struck the ground like whips as he dashed after them. They pressed through a mock sword fight between another set of actors who kept hitting themselves on the head or falling down, and passed a preacher on a box shouting something about the end of the world, the crowd in front making way for a rich nobleman accompanied by a bishop identifiable by his white robes and flat red hat and gloves. A pair of whores called to them as they stumbled by, or rather Hugh stumbled when Robert yanked on his coat to save him from sin and distraction.

"They're over there," Robert said.

"Right," Hugh said, leaving the whores to their fate and swerving toward the Flemish standard hanging from its pole.

A crowd of knights and men-at-arms were clustered about the standard and the tent beside it, tending to their gear and horses or drinking wine from bowls and cups that servants refreshed without being asked.

Hugh stopped a half dozen paces away. "I'm not sure about this."

"What?"

"This was a mad idea. The chances of taking a prize are small."

"How are we supposed to pay back the money-lender?" The summer had been good to them, but not good enough. Hugh had reckoned that they presented such a sad picture that no lord would take them on as hired men. Yet they had come to Lagny-sur-Marne on the chance that fortune might favor them. But to convince any of the teams to allow them to join required a proper war horse, and those were expensive. They had borrowed the money for the horse.

"We should never have bought the horse. It was a mistake."

"It's too late for second thoughts now."

"We should just sell it."

"And how will we pay the interest?"

"Wrestling?"

"I'm done with that. We agreed. I'm tired of getting hurt."

"You don't think you'll get hurt out there?" Hugh waved toward the field beyond the tents where the tournament would take place.

"My job's to keep you out of trouble, not to fight. Come on. We can do this. If we take nothing, all you lose is the horse." They had pledged the horse as collateral for the loan. It had seemed like a grand plan when they had first conceived it: enter the tournament, snatch a prize. Even a small one could make them rich.

"I suppose."

Although Robert thought he might have to prod Hugh further, Hugh stepped up to the Flemings lounging about the tent. "Gentlemen," he said, "Good day to you all. I understand that you are looking to fill your ranks to fight the English tomorrow."

One of their number lowered his cup. "With the likes of you?"

Hugh bowed. "I may be down on my luck, due to the wars in the spring, but I can fight as well as any man."

"If you fall off your horse, you're on your own."

"I do not expect anything more."

The knight called over his shoulder. "My lord! There's a pair of paupers here who want to join us!"

The lord turned out to be Philip, the count of Flanders himself, of black hair, scowling eyes, drooping moustache, and silver spurs, who parted the flaps of the tent without the help of a servant. He peered at Hugh and Robert with the same expression as one might reserve for a spot of shit on a boot.

"Can they speak French?" Philip asked.

"That one can," the Flemish knight said. "I don't know about the other one."

"Who are you, sir?" Philip asked Hugh.

"Hugh Fontaine, of Gascony."

"And that child?"

"Robert. My squire."

"You can afford a squire?"

The Outlaws

"As I was telling your man here, we had a bit of bad luck this year."

"Why can't God bring me Germans?" Philip asked. "At least they fight like lions."

"But they'll be able to follow orders," the knight said. "The Germans?" He shrugged. "They can't speak properly, most of them."

Philip nodded. "All right. Gerard is short-handed. Send them to him."

Hugh and Robert reported to Gerard the following morning after dawn. Gerard was a spare man shorter than Hugh with a sour expression that did not improve at the sight of them, as his gaze lingered on their horses.

"You're going to ride that?" Gerard asked, indicating Robert's horse, the rouncy.

"He won't be fighting," Hugh said.

"What's he supposed to do, hold your hand?"

"Give me his weapons if I lose mine."

"And pull your ass out of a tight spot, right?"

"Well, there is that."

"I suppose somebody has to be your nursemaid. Nobody else will. Well, don't wander off. We'll be taking the field soon. Here." Gerard handed them yellow ribbons and turned away.

There wasn't anything for them to do now but wait.

Flemish servants moved through the assembled knights bearing trays with bread, cheese, and cups of wine. Some of the knights drank more than one cup, a few tossing them back so hastily that wine dribbled down their chins and threatened to splash onto their mail shirts if their squires and personal servants had not been there to wipe up the spills.

Finally, Philip emerged from his tent. He was armored the same as everyone else and it would have been hard to tell him apart from the others in the Flemish contingent were he not so tall and for the yellow ribbon tied around his helmet.

Everyone else had a yellow ribbon tied around their right arms.

The marshal behind Philip shouted, "Mount up and form up!"

The Flemings, who now numbered close to two-hundred men, were so spread out that not everyone heard the order, but echoes of it passed through the assembly as the leaders of the *conrois*, groups of ten men, heard their neighbors relaying it.

A great deal of shouting and confusion erupted. Robert held Hugh's horse so he could mount, handed him their lances, then mounted himself.

Out of the chaos order asserted itself, as Philip took the lead and the contingent began to file through the tents in a column of twos, horses stamping and jostling as men waited their turn to join the parade.

The column, more than four-hundred yards long, cleared the tent city and picked up a trot as its head entered the vast field to the north of the Marne. Spaced across the field were fenced enclosures, the lists, which were places of safety where combat was not allowed to occur.

Robert struggled to keep his lance erect and at the proper angle once the mare broke into a trot to keep up with the horse in front of them, aware that he did not belong here and feeling that everyone's eyes were on him. Any moment now, he expected to hear someone shout, "Imposter!"

He glanced at Hugh, but the Gascon's eyes were fixed straight ahead, his mouth a tight line, and Robert realized that Hugh was afraid.

"That makes two of us," Robert muttered to himself. He wished he had never thought up this insane scheme. When they were sitting around the fire in their forest camps over the summer savoring their prospects for the future, he had not appreciated the enormity of what they were about to do. This was a game, like a wrestling match to be sure, but all the weapons carried by those about him were real and sharp, as were those of their adversaries, the English and Norman

The Outlaws

contingent, which he could see in the distance just now drawing into line. Soon they would be put to use with the same vigor as in a real battle. But it was too late to back out now. "We only need one. We only need one."

"What's that?" Hugh asked.

"I said, we only need one."

Hugh smiled. "Then we are done."

"Right."

"We gang up on one, drag him from his horse, and make for the nearest list. I like that plan."

The column was well out in the field by now. Philip and his bodyguard halted, but the head of the column kept going. Robert and Hugh passed by Philip. He seemed relaxed, joking with the men about him, handing back a wine skin given to him by a retainer, and spitting into the grass.

The column halted to commands of "Turn to the shield!" and "Open order!" which meant a left turn, converting the column into a line of battle with Philip at its center, and more jostling as each rider made sure that at least three feet separated them from the men on either side. The men checked the space by extending their arms so their fingers touched, while the officers rode up and down before the line ensuring that it was even.

In this evolution, Robert found himself in the first rank with Hugh behind him. Hugh said nothing about this, but Gerard noticed. "You two! What the devil are you doing! Change places! Jesus Christ on the Cross! Hurry up there! We're fucking about to start!"

This required Robert to bring his horse forward so she could turn around, while Hugh backed his. Robert slipped through the line, hoping that he did not appear clumsy even in this simple maneuver, for ten men in the *conroi*, not to mention those on either side of it, were watching him.

A distant trumpet called from the English line, to be answered by a closer one from the Flemings. The English lion banner, visible as a red-and-yellow smudge far across the field, waved back and forth, also answered by enthusiastic display of the Flemish colors.

Hugh turned in the saddle. "Remember, stick close. Keep the enemy away from me."

Yet although Robert thought things would begin in moments, there was a lull while heralds rode out to a spot between the lines for some sort of conference.

One of the men beside Robert asked, "What's your name, boy?"

"Robert."

"Robert," he said in the guttural Flemish accent. "I'm Baltin. You're not a Gascon."

"I might be," Robert said, grasping the nasal bar to settle his helmet, wishing he had tightened the chin strap.

"Gerard says your knight is from Gascony, but you don't sound like it."

"How would you know? You've never been there."

Baltin made a face at the man on the other side of Robert. "He thinks he's tough."

The other man pushed Robert's chin up with the butt of his lance. "We have to fight with babies, now," he said. "Big talking babies."

They both laughed.

"Just one word of advice from people who really know what they're doing," Baltin said. "Don't piss your drawers. It ruins the saddle."

"Takes forever to get the stink out," the other man said. "If you're lucky."

The heralds finished their conference and cantered back to their respective lines.

"Ever been in a battle, boy?" Baltin asked.

"Once," Robert said. "This past summer."

"Really?" Baltin regarded Robert as if he didn't believe the claim, but the line of his mouth softened.

"We fought on foot, though."

"This will be different. Best way to capture a prize is to unseat your man in the charge. After the charge, we'll all break

The Outlaws

up into a melee, where it's pretty much every man for himself, unless you stick with a group, and harder. Watch out for the dog robbers."

"Dog robbers?"

"Packs of infantry. They roam the melee pulling men off their horses. We don't have any, but the English do, the bastards." Baltin said this as if he regarded having dog robbers as cheating.

The heralds reached their lines. Trumpets blared to the left and right. "Forward!" came the call from the left, where Philip had taken his place, echoed by the *conroi* leaders. The line started forward at the walk.

The only sounds were the clinking of mail against the saddle pommels, the creaking of leather, and the swish as the horses moved through the grass. To the right, an officer shouted, "Keep the line!" Otherwise, no one spoke. Hugh glanced back, but he said nothing and returned his gaze to the enemy, which had also set out toward them at a walk, the hedge of their lances undulating with the folds in the ground.

After they had gone about two hundred yards, the trumpet blared again. Hugh and the other men urged their horses into a trot. Robert was a little slow in keeping up with this. He fell behind and had to canter to catch up. Baltin's mouth drooped as he regained his place, but said nothing.

It seemed they had traveled no distance at all before the trumpet clamored again, and the line burst into a canter.

He had been paying so much attention to Baltin and Hugh that he had not looked at the enemy, but now, Robert saw them. They were barreling forward at a frightful speed, huge and terrible, the points of their lances glinting in the sun. The thunder of hooves drummed out all noise, all thought, all mercy, even all hope. Gaping at them in the last moments before the collision as the lances came down all at once, everything that Robert had practiced, all that Hugh had shared with him, flew out of his head. He wanted to turn and run away, wanted to flee with every fiber of his body, but he was even more afraid of what the others would think if he turned away.

The world shrank in those last seconds. For Robert all was dark and dim, except the enemy coming at the gap between Hugh and man on his right. The enemy knight had a shield painted blue with a red cross and a yellow bird in the upper right corner, and a helmet with a face cover so Robert could see no expression except for the man's mouth, which was twisted into a snarl. The knight was big and strong, and frightening.

The time for reflection, the time for doubt, the time for worry, passed away, and with it, a little of himself, so that it was like someone else sitting on the horse, someone else fumbling with the shield while trying not to lose the reins, a stranger straining to keep the lance, which had grown so heavy, steady at the enemy's face.

Robert just had time to think, dear God in Heaven —

And then the two lines came together.

The knight on Robert's right front was unable to deflect the spear aimed at his belly from his unprotected right side. The point went clear through his body and emerged out his back. The force of the impact lifted him clean out of the saddle and he hung in the air for a moment before he disappeared from view. It all happened in a blink of an eye: he was there and then he was gone.

Robert had no time to spare for horror or pity. The enemy knight with the blue shield drove his point at Hugh, who deflected the thrust by swinging his kite shield over his pommel. The shaft of the lance broke with a sharp crack and jolt that drove him against the cantle, and the enemy flashed past Robert, ducking Robert's point, which had aimed too high. The man behind the first enemy aimed his lance at Robert's face. He barely had time to raise his own shield while pulling his lance low in the hope it would strike under the other's shield. The impact almost tore the shield from Robert's arm and he thought the arm had broken. The impact of his own point shattered his lance shaft with a thunderous

The Outlaws

snap. And then the two lines passed through each other, and the horses were wheeling, the men drawing their swords for the melee.

Robert strained to stay with Hugh, pulling hard on the reins, leaning right as the mare pivoted left, taking the turn in the wrong lead so she was in danger of falling. Another enemy wearing a red ribbon on his arm charged at Hugh from the right. Robert clouted the knight on the head with the stub of his lance, but the enemy knight caught himself before he fell out of the saddle. Then the melee carried him away.

There was nothing left of the neat lines of horsemen. All about Robert, men hacked at each other with swords and axes in a seething mass. One knight caught another by the mailed sleeve and dragged him off his horse, which stepped on the fallen man's chest. The clatter of steel on steel and wooden shields drowned out even the shouts of those nearest to him, and a choking fog of dust reduced his field of view to only a dozen feet.

Robert struggled to stay near Hugh, who was standing in his stirrups and pounding left and right at anyone who came near him. A blow struck Robert on the head from behind. It felt as though he had been hit by a cudgel and silver stars raced across his field of vision. By a miracle, he did not fall, and without looking slashed backward with his sword. It struck an object that he did not see, and he spurred the mare to keep up with Hugh, who had slid between two knights exchanging blows with axes. Robert pushed between them, ducking under his shield as they swayed apart and then came back together when he passed.

Two of the enemy now closed on Hugh, one on either side. Hugh threw blows at both antagonists, but he might as well have been hacking wood for all the effect they seemed to have. And the enemy's blows were telling as they landed on Hugh's shoulders and arms.

Robert was about to charge into the man on Hugh's right when someone grasped Robert's mail shirt and then snaked an arm around his neck. Robert wrapped one arm over the other man's, trapping it on his shoulder, and pressed down as hard as he could as he dug his right spur into the mare's side. She shied from the pain, dodging to the left, and the enemy knight fell from his horse.

Here at last was an opportunity, but what to take — the man or his mount?

During the moment of indecision, another English knight came to the fallen man's aid. The savior trotted by the mare's head, grasped the bridle, and kept going. The unexpected tug turned the mare's head around so swiftly that she could not keep her feet, and she toppled onto her side.

Robert had a glimpse of several infantrymen armed with hooked bills and wearing kettle helmets watching him fall, as he kicked loose from the stirrups and slid away so that he would not land under the mare and be trapped.

He landed hard on his back. The horse's rump thudded into the ground half a foot away with an impact that shook the ground. The horse struggled to its feet. The English knight regained his grip on the bridle, and both knight and mare disappeared into the press.

Robert stood up and struggled to catch his breath, shocked and dismayed that he had lost the mare, but more worried at the moment about what had become of Hugh, who was nowhere in sight.

The rump of a warhorse slammed into Robert from behind. The impact swung him around so that he faced the group of infantry who had watched him fall. One of the infantry pointed at him and said something to his companions, but although they were close enough that Robert should have heard him, the words were drowned out by the commotion. The infantry closed in.

He fled. Shield over his head, Robert pushed his way toward one of the lists, which he spotted about fifty yards away. He was almost there when three more English infantrymen appeared out of nowhere and cut him off. There was but one place of safety left, a line of trees just visible through the dust. Robert ran toward the trees.

The Outlaws

He reached the tree line and paused to catch his breath, casting about to see what had become of the pursuing infantry. He couldn't see any of them, but that did not mean they were not still on his trail. Robert ducked through the trees, hoping they would conceal him, and that this ordeal would come to an end. He had no intention of coming out until the battle was over.

The tree line turned out to conceal a stream. Across the narrow water stood a party of five red-ribboned horsemen and one blue-ribboned man, all in the best and brightest armor. The blue-ribboned man was tied to his horse, a prisoner.

"We have company, William," said one of the English knights, who wore a red surcoat decorated with golden English lions. He couldn't be more than ten years older than Robert but he was very rich — only the rich could afford such a vibrant red. He was handsome too: tall and strong-limbed, with reddish blond hair and a freckled complexion.

"So we have, Henry," said the one addressed as William. "But he's alone." This man was shorter and stockier than the rich blond knight named Henry, but Robert couldn't see much of his face except a strong chin and stern mouth, for he had kept on his helmet and coif.

The blond knight relaxed. "He's no threat then." He dismounted and knelt by the stream, then paused and said to Robert with elaborate courtesy, "I trust you won't mind if we share the stream."

"It isn't my stream," Robert said. "Go right ahead."

While the blond knight drank, the one called William regarded Robert as though he was a piece of meat on a platter and William was trying to decide whether to eat or not. The look made Robert uncomfortable, so he did not approach the stream even though he wanted a drink. He waited to see what might happen.

A smile signaled that William had reached a decision. He unsheathed his sword and jumped across the stream.

"William!" Henry called, put out. "What the devil are you doing?"

"I fancy that sword," William said.

"For God's sake, he's a boy. He isn't worth the effort."

"That's why it shouldn't take but a moment."

Henry shook his head and said to one of his companions, "The man's incurable."

Robert couldn't believe this was happening. This fellow William wanted to fight and take everything he had, even if it was a second hand helmet, second hand mail, a battered and well used shield, and his sword, the only decent thing he owned. It seemed unfair, even if prize-taking was the point of tournaments.

He knew he ought to turn and run. William looked like a formidable opponent. Beneath William's square face and rather large nose was a muscular body, broad shoulders giving way to thick arms and wrists. William twirled his sword in circles as he approached.

William cut at Robert's head. The blow seemed to move at once in slow motion and with blazing speed. Robert just got his shield up in time.

Robert backed away. This made William impatient. He called over his shoulder, "No wonder he cowers in the wood. He has no stomach for fighting."

"Then finish it quickly," Henry said. "There are better quarry elsewhere."

William launched a succession of blows, feinting low to the legs and then striking high, one of them glancing off Robert's helmet. The force was stunning and drove Robert to his knees. But the pain made him angry, and he cut at William's legs.

William dodged out of the way with a laugh. "You couldn't cut grass!" he cried. But rather than move in to finish Robert off, he waited for Robert to get to his feet.

Henry nodded in resignation, and sat down on a fallen tree to watch.

The Outlaws

Robert stood up, panting. The anger had not abated. He would not be taken. Not now. Not ever. He would die first.

With a snarl, he raised his sword and thrust over the top of William's shield. William parried the blow, and just avoided its swift follow up, a cut to the legs.

William stood back out of range and regarded Robert speculatively for a moment. Then with a nod, they began fighting in earnest, jockeying for position, feinting, dodging, cutting, butting shields in an effort to force the other's aside, trading blow for blow in the intricate dance of swordplay.

It wasn't long before the initial heat of anger had been spent, and Robert settled down to fight with his head rather than his heart. He realized that he could not win a duel with William if it went on very long. William was older and stronger, and had far more experience. He was a very cold fighter who moved with measured skill and who did not fail to take advantage of Robert's mistakes. It wasn't long before Robert grew exhausted, his shield arm was numb from the shock of repeated impacts on the thin wood, and his arms, legs and shoulders. Robert knew he was losing. He had to do something desperate — and unexpected.

He let his shield drop, exposing his head. William accepted the invitation, throwing two blows in a row, which Robert ducked without returning them.

Then, when William was in mid-strike again at Robert's head, he ran forward, shield out.

They struck, shield to shield, and the force of the impact, as Robert drove forward, threw William backward. He lost his footing and toppled into the stream.

Water closed over William's head. When he sat up, he spat blood from a cut on the inside of his mouth. "Damn you!"

But as he tried to rise, Robert held him down with a foot planted on William's shield.

"Ho!" Henry called with a laugh — although he was the only one of this group who dared to laugh at William; the others looked stunned.

Robert put his point to William's face. "Do you yield?" he panted.

William pushed the point away. "Yield? This puppy, this piece of shit wants to know if I yield!"

"Well," Henry said, "he does appear to have you at a disadvantage."

William grasped Robert's blade. "No, I will not yield. Henry, for God's sake, don't just sit there."

"Oh, all right, if we must, although it isn't sporting." Henry got to his feet. "Come on, let's go save William's reputation."

As the four other Englishmen splashed into the stream, Robert kicked William's hand free of the sword. Robert backed up.

He was set to turn and run when the French prisoner intervened. Somehow during the fight when the others were distracted, the Frenchman had worked himself free of his leather bindings. He snatched up a lance stuck butt first in the ground and spurred the horse at the men about to surround Robert.

The English scattered, while the Frenchman whirled the lance around his head two-handed, raining blows with the head and butt.

With a shout, the Frenchman jumped across the stream and joined Robert.

"I don't know about you, boy," the Frenchman said, "but I've had enough of this. Can you run?"

"I can when I have to," gasped Robert, although he was so spent he wasn't sure he could even stand upright much less take a single step.

"Then run for all you're worth. I'll buy you a moment to get some distance. But only a moment."

Robert bolted. A splendid warhorse with an expensive saddle was in his way, reins tied to a tree limb. Robert hacked through the limb with his sword and snatched the reins. At least he might have a horse to replace the one he had lost.

The Outlaws

Robert was staggering before he had gone a hundred yards into the field. He turned and saw that he had no pursuit, except for the Frenchman. He looked at the captured horse with amusement as he trotted up.

"What's so funny?" Robert asked.

"You, boy."

Robert drew himself up. It felt like he was being insulted, but the Frenchman wasn't being nasty about it.

"You don't really know, do you," the Frenchman said.

"Know what?" Robert asked.

"What you've done."

Robert shook his head.

"Boy, you just knocked down William Marshal, and in the bargain have stolen his horse. That whelp with him was Henry, the Young King." The Frenchman tugged his black beard. "It's a good thing not too many people saw what happened."

Robert's mouth fell open. He knew who Henry was, of course, eldest son of the great Henry Plantagenet and who had been made nominal king of England, though one without any real power people said, by his father Henry II. Robert had never heard of William Marshal.

"Oh," Robert said. "He'll want the horse back, I suppose."

"Don't be silly. The horse is yours, fortunes of war and all that. William should be yours by rights too, but you've lost him, unfortunately. Still, you've denied him a rich prize and that's worth something."

"What rich prize?"

"Me."

"Oh," Robert said again.

"You don't know who I am?"

"No, I'm afraid not."

"Well, I'm really just a nobody," the Frenchman said with false modesty. "Just a poet and song-maker. My name is Bertran de Born of Hautefort in Perigord, sometime friend of Marshal and the Young King, but today their enemy." Bertran pivoted in the saddle, looking around the field. "I think it is wise to retire before some roving band of dogs snatches us up and we lose the benefits of your bravery. Shall we go?"

"All right."

Bertran spurred toward the tent city. Then he reined in and looked back at Robert, who was following on foot. "You really should ride that thing, you know."

"Oh, yes, I guess I should." Robert mounted and caught up with Bertran.

"That's better," Bertran said. "You cut a fine figure on a horse, boy. I like that."

Robert wasn't so sure about that, but he was unwilling to discourage the opinion.

When they reached the tents, Robert realized that Bertran was more than a mere poet. He was a rich lord. His blue and red tent sat in the middle of like colored tents, and it was filled with brocaded and embroidered cushions. Servants rushed up to remove Bertran's mail and bring him spiced wine.

"Fighting is thirsty work," Bertran said, giving Robert the first cup with his own hands.

"Yes, it is, m'lord," Robert said. He gulped down the wine.

"You haven't told me your name."

"Robert."

"Robert. That's all?"

"Robert Attebrook."

"Attebrook . . ." Bertran said the name several times. Being a Frenchman, his pronunciation was off. "It is English, is it not? What does it mean?"

"By the stream, or the people by the stream."

"Ah." Bertran's expression changed. Robert realized that he had just confessed his humble origins. "Well, Robert Attebrook, you have done me a great service today — and saved me a good deal of trouble."

Bertran produced a purse, which he pressed into Robert's hands. "Please take this as my expression of thanks."

The Outlaws

Robert was surprised, both at the gesture and at the weight of the purse. "I did nothing. You freed yourself."

"You made it possible. Will you stay for dinner?"

"I can't. I have to see after a friend."

"Well, let me give you one more thing to see you on your way." He summoned a servant to fetch a basket, which he handed to Robert. "If you ever find yourself in Perigord and you need a place to rest, feel free to call on me."

"Thank you, m'lord." Robert led his prize away to search for Hugh.

CHAPTER 22

**Lagny-sur-Marne
October 1179**

The battle had ended by the time Robert reached the Flemish camp, and the knights were shedding their armor and talking about their successes on the field, while their captured knights sat about on hay bales looking battered and disgusted.

Robert spotted Gerard "Have you seen Hugh?"

"The Gascon? Over there." Gerard pointed through the crowd to a tent. He looked startled at the horse Robert had in tow, but said nothing.

"Thanks."

Robert pushed his way through and found Hugh seated on a folding chair, head in his hands. Hugh had no mail, no shield, no sword, and none of the gear piled nearby looked like his.

Hugh looked up and said, "What happened to you? You were supposed to watch my back!"

"I lost my horse. After I fell, I lost sight of you. What happened?"

"I was taken," Hugh said.

"So you've lost everything."

Hugh dropped his head in his hands. His shoulders shook. But when he raised his head again, although his eyes were reddened, they held no tears. He nodded. "I've got bruises all over, and nothing to show for it. We have to get out of here. When the moneylender learns what happened, he will have us arrested for debt."

"Maybe not. I captured a horse."

"You did not!"

"Come see."

Robert led Hugh outside. Hugh stared dumfounded at Marshal's stallion. "How did you manage that?"

"He was just walking around loose," Robert said.

"That is quite a horse," Hugh said, patting the animal's head then running a hand over the saddle and the rich pad

The Outlaws

beneath it. "This is a rich man's horse. It must be worth a lot of money." A greedy expression stole across his face. "We should just go, leave now."

"Without making repayment?"

"We either have to sell the horse or give him up. I don't want to do that."

"No."

"What do you mean, no?"

"What I said. No."

"I'm the knight. I decide what we do."

"That's not how we've been working things. Besides, you're not really a knight yet."

Hugh glanced around, aware that things had gotten quiet and all the nearby faces were turned their way. His voice quavered as he said, "I am so a knight."

"All right, you're a knight then, but I'm not your squire. I am my own man."

"That!" Hugh shouted, pointing at Robert's mail shirt and helmet. "That belongs to me! And that! I paid for them."

"With our money, but you can have them back just the same." Robert tossed his helmet at Hugh's feet, undid his belt, and pulled the mail shirt over his head. He threw the shirt on the helmet, and the shield on top of the pile.

"And the horse?" Hugh said.

"You didn't win him. I did. If you want him, you can have him when I'm dead."

Hugh's eyes dropped to the sword in Robert's hand. His mouth worked, but he said nothing. His eyes were full of pain and loss, and Robert didn't understand why: desperation and wounded pride, perhaps. But whatever lay within had just destroyed their friendship, and he was sorry about that.

"I hope you find that manor, Hugh," Robert said.

He led the horse out of the circle of watching men.

Merlun, France
October 1179

Bertran de Born reclined in his canvas chair outside the inn, and flipped little sticks into the River Seine, watching the current carry them off toward the wooden bridge to the island in the middle of the river. The spot was pleasant and shaded, and the day was warm. Bertran had awakened in a black mood and had stayed in bed until almost noon. At supper he had far too much wine, and now he was drunk. He had thought that getting drunk would make him feel better, but he was wrong. It had made him feel worse.

He was in a bad mood because of Richard, son of old Henry the true king and brother of Young Henry, the king of England in name if not in substance. Richard had shown up toward the end of the tournament, and they had quarreled. Normally, Bertran got on well with Richard, who could be very affable, with his zest for life and his love of a good song and a good story. But Bertran had made a mistake. He had heard that Richard, ruler of Aquitaine while his mother Eleanor was imprisoned at Salisbury, intended to impose a new tax. The levy was fixed at five livres per knight's fee, to be paid half now, and half in the spring. It was a huge sum and would fall most grievously on landowners like Bertran, who held one castle and its village. There were many such small gentry in Limousin, and none were happy at the prospect of the levy. He asked Richard about the tax, expecting him to disown it, but Richard, rather curtly, had affirmed it. When Bertran said he and others like him could not pay, Richard had snapped that he would do as he was told. Richard might as well have slapped him in the face. It had always been this way when Richard wanted something and others protested — he beat down the opposition. There had been many such edicts issuing from his chancellery these days. Bertran and his friends were tired of them. The answer to unfair taxes was war; not tomorrow, perhaps not this year or even the next. But Bertran would see to it they had a war. It

The Outlaws

would take some doing, for many landowners in Limousin were afraid of Richard. But somehow Bertran would bring it about.

He heard footsteps behind, and out of the corner of his eye detected his chamberlain. Bertran ignored him and poured himself another cup of wine from the pitcher on the little table beside him. When the chamberlain saw that Bertran didn't want to notice him, he would go away.

But the chamberlain did not go away.

"What do you want?" Bertran said.

"There is a boy to see you."

"Who is it?"

"The young fellow from Lagny, my lord."

At first Bertran wasn't sure whom he meant. Then he remembered. "The one with the English name?"

"Yes, m'lord."

Bertran was a little put off by this news. He was grateful for having been saved from Marshal; owing his horse and arms to Marshal would have cost him more than Richard wanted to steal. But he thought he had paid his debt. His offer of aid had been just courtesy, and he hadn't expected the boy to come with his hand out so soon. He considered having the boy sent away, but Bertran had been raised to be courteous and he could not escape the habit. "All right. Let him come."

"Yes, m'lord."

The figure that emerged from the rear of the inn took him by surprise. He wore a peasant's broad brimmed straw hat and a peasant's brown woolen shirt and hose. But he also wore a sword and a long dagger, which he carried with the ease of one used to their weight.

There was no other chair nearby, so Bertran motioned to the bench beside the table. "Please, Robert, welcome. Sit. Have you eaten? I'll have something fetched."

Robert sank onto the bench. He sat stiffly, distressed about something.

"Well," Bertran said, "at least have some wine."

"That will be fine, m'lord."

Bertran filled a bowl that sat beside the pitcher. He asked, "Where is your master?"

Robert shuffled his feet. "Well, he wasn't exactly my master. But I've lost him."

Bertran felt sorry. "He died, then."

"No. We had a falling out."

"That happens, sometimes." Bertran thought about Richard as he spoke.

"I wish it hadn't happened."

"So do I. Comradeship should be forever, but for some reason it isn't. It's sad that we're so imperfect, we men." He hesitated. Then his charitable impulse took over. "Is there anything I can do for you?"

"I need a lord. I will give you Marshal's horse and my oath if you take me as a man-at-arms — with the possibility of knighthood in the offing. I regret I do not still have the saddle. I had to sell it to pay off a debt."

Bertran was so stunned at this that for moments he couldn't think of anything to say. "Boy, don't you have any idea what that horse is worth?"

"Enough to buy a manor, I suspect."

Bertran chuckled. "Marshal owns nothing but his arms and his horses, but he owns the best. Why are you asking this?"

"I can always win another horse. A place in society has to be given, if I am to amount to anything."

Bertran chewed on a lip. What he had just heard took a moment to sink in. If the horse was his, he could return him to Marshal. Marshal could be on the other side in the war that would come, but it was always wise to keep on good terms with those whose help you may need. And there was no guarantee Bertran and his friends would win. He'd need friends in the other camp if that happened.

"Why are you dressed like a peasant?" Bertran said.

"We divided our things in the falling out. He got the armor, I got the horse."

The Outlaws

Bertran laughed. "I'd have liked to have seen that bargain made."

"I can read and write, too, if that's any use to you."

Bertran nodded, surprised at this fact, since most men were illiterate, even high up in the nobility. A plan began forming in his mind of how he could use this boy.

He leaned forward and spoke in a low voice so he was sure it would not carry. "I am going to start a war." Seeing Robert's startled expression, he said, "Not right away. Perhaps not even for a few years yet. It will take some intrigue and persuasion, and I need men who can carry messages, who can keep secrets, who can spy out things and report them truly, and who will keep their bond no matter the hardship. Can you do that? Will you do that? For me?"

Robert blinked. Whatever he had been expecting, this wasn't it. "I think so."

Bertran sat back, satisfied. "Then will you enter my service, Robert Attebrook, squire, and have me for your lord?"

"I . . . I will."

Bertran held out his hands. Robert looked at them, puzzled. Bertran said, "You put your hands together."

When Robert had done so, Bertran cupped them in his own and began his part of the oath, aware that a savage joy and sudden purpose which had not been there before had displaced his black mood.

CHAPTER 23

London
March 1180

Matilda awoke before dawn with a nagging backache. She welcomed the backache. It meant that the baby would be born soon. She was so round and heavy with her pregnancy now that she had trouble moving. She lay on her pallet, waiting for the pain to ease. Around her in the loft of Odo's tavern, the Red Lion, she heard the soft breathing of her children, and at the far end the snores of those who had remained overnight.

This high above the ground the stink of the Fleet River, which ran beside the tavern, was not so sharp, just a lingering suggestion of shit and garbage.

The river was the tavern's bane. Odo's wife Margery had told her that on warm summer days the smell was so intense that people had to hold scented rags before their noses like people living around a tannery, although this information had come with the advice that she would get used to it. The river was one of the reasons the tavern did such poor business despite its location on Holborn Street a mere three-hundred yards outside the city. Matilda had yet to experience the river's full force, but it was bad enough.

One of the overnight guests rose and knelt over the chamber pot. Taverns were not supposed to take overnight guests, but Odo paid the bailiffs not to notice.

Matilda had been lucky to find work here when they reached London. The streets were full of unemployed country women seeking positions, and competition for work had been fierce. She wouldn't have gotten the job if she hadn't been a witness to the argument that led to the last serving girl's departure, and had offered to take the woman's place. That Odo got the labor of three — Matilda and the twins, who were eleven now and could do an adult's work — for the price of one had helped clinch the deal.

Brian coughed and sat up. He swept his fingers through tangled hair. He had found work on the new cathedral going

The Outlaws

up at Ludgate. He got up and put on his coat and shoes, fumbling on one foot then the other. He collected his tool box and the bag of bread and cheese Matilda had set aside the evening before as his breakfast and dinner. Then he thumped down the steep wooden stairs to work.

Matilda got up and followed him to the hall.

She removed the ceramic cover from the fire on the hearth and added straw from the floor to the embers. Then she went into the yard carrying a brand from the hearth, which she used to light the fire under the great kettle. Margery intended to brew a batch of ale today and she liked to get an early start.

Odo and Margery came down stairs. Odo was shorter than Matilda, but broad and strong. Not a hair grew on the top of his skull, which was speckled with brown spots too large to be called freckles and about which he was very sensitive. Mentioning them was a good way to start a fight. He was quick with his stubby fingers but not at meaningful work; he liked to play them over the women who worked in the house, as Matilda had discovered her first day on the job, when he put his arms around her, gave her breast a squeeze, and licked her ear, while Margery looked away. He had let her alone, though, when he found out she was pregnant. But once she had the baby, she was sure he would be at her again.

Odo liked to strut around giving orders, but Margery, a creature as slender as a broom handle, did most of the actual work. Odo rarely bent his back at anything, although he was good at manly conversation and making sure tankards were full.

With a fire flickering under the kettle, she returned to the house and began preparing breakfast. This was one of the tavern's busy times, for much of their custom came from the neighborhood men who stopped to eat on the way to work or who came by at dinner time. Alice and Agnes appeared to help her. Matilda sent Agnes to fetch eggs from the hen house which lay behind the shack that Odo called a stable.

She forgot about Agnes as people began to come downstairs. It was time to throw open the doors, and the morning's regular customers, already waiting there in the street, filed in and found places at the tables set up in the hall. The usual crowd started a game of dice on the hard packed floor at the rear. They liked to be served quickly.

At a spare moment, she realized that Agnes had not returned from the hen house. Matilda glanced out the window, wondering where Agnes was. At first she was put out at the delay, but something outside seemed wrong. Margery was hunched over the fire, arms crossed and a hard look on her face. The groom that Odo employed to care for guests' animals was coming across the yard, wearing a guilty look. He and Margery exchanged glances. The groom shook his head. Margery's mouth turned down and she stirred the mash. Odo was nowhere to be seen.

With a sense of foreboding, Matilda went into the yard and crossed to the stable. Margery started to follow but turned back. The door was open a crack. Matilda pushed it open another inch or two so she could slip inside.

She saw Agnes lying on a pile of straw. Her skirt was thrown up above her waist and her linen underpants had been torn off. Odo lay between Agnes's legs in the act of trying to force his penis into her. He was having some trouble. The girl grimaced with each unsuccessful probe. She saw Matilda and closed her eyes.

Odo was absorbed in his work and had no idea that Matilda had come in. She took a pitchfork from the wall and drove the wooden tines into Odo's naked backside as hard as she could. He shouted in pain and rolled over. Agnes rolled in the opposite direction and ran behind her mother.

"You bastard!" Matilda snarled.

"She wanted it!" he retorted. "She's been taunting me for weeks, the little flirt."

"Liar!" yelled Agnes. "Mother, he tried to rape me!"

"Nobody could want a pussbag like you," Matilda said.

The Outlaws

"She offered herself. I have a witness." He waved a hand, and Matilda spared a glance behind her. The groom stood in the doorway. "Tell her, Adam."

Adam the groom, who had turned around and followed Matilda, looked at the ground, but said, "It's as he said. She came in, smiled, showed a bit of her leg."

Agnes cried, "He's a liar, mother. He asked me to help him with a hen that had gotten loose, and when I came in, he," she pointed at Odo, "was waiting. I didn't, I never —"

"You don't have to explain yourself to me, child. I believe you," Matilda said. "And so will the bailiff, when he sees this gap toothed fart of a man."

Odo climbed to his feet and attempted to restore some dignity to his appearance, pulling up and re-tying his hose. He began to sidle close. Matilda backed through the doorway into the yard.

Odo realized that they had an audience. Someone in the tavern had spotted the confrontation. People were leaning out the windows to watch. Under their eyes, Odo became more aggressive. "Insolent bitch!" he cried, and then moved quicker than Matilda ever anticipated. With a quick sweep of his hand he knocked the pitchfork aside and clouted her on the side of the head. "I'll not take that from you, you shit-mouthed turd."

The blow drove Matilda to her knees. Grabbing her by the hair, Odo pulled her across the yard, through the gate and pitched her into the street. The girls both followed, afraid that he would beat her, but powerless to prevent it.

"And don't think you can come back, either!" Odo cried.

"I want my property then!" she shouted back, relieved that she had avoided a beating.

"What property?" Odo sneered, glancing at the crowd that had begun to gather at a confrontation that promised to be diverting. "You came to me with nothing, and you leave with nothing."

"I'll have the sheriff on you, you bastard."

"Have him on then, whore."

"Then I will, thief, and you'll answer for it!" she said and turned away. She could see that she couldn't get him to back down before a crowd. He was the kind of man who had to strut and preen before spectators.

The onlookers turned away, too, now that there would be no fight.

Matilda watched the crowd disperse, wondering what to do. She stood there a long time, looking up and down the street, alternating between rage and despair.

A window on the upper floor where Odo had his solar opened, and Margery tossed a large bundle into the street and waved before ducking back inside. Matilda didn't know whether to curse her or thank her. She had known something terrible was happening in the stables but had been unwilling to do anything about it because she was afraid of Odo. Yet she was willing to defy him by returning at least some of their things.

Alice fetched the bundle. They opened it to find a few bits of stray clothing that Margery had snatched up in haste; at least they would have cloaks to keep warm. Their remaining money wasn't here, of course; it was buried by the back fence.

Matilda and the girls went down Holborn Street, turned right onto Snore Hylie, and stopped outside Newgate to wait for Brian. They could not enter the city because they lacked the half penny for the entrance toll.

The gate was a narrow cut in the city's eighteen-foot high wall. It was wide enough to admit one cart or two men riding abreast. This early in the morning, there was a press to enter, the crowd spreading out in a fan shape with its nape at the gate.

There was nothing to do but squat on a door stoop and hope that a bailiff would not run them off as unlicensed beggars. Matilda had an excruciating back ache and it was a pleasure to sit down. She was hungry, because the fight at the tavern had occurred before she had got breakfast, but she made no complaint, nor did the girls. They were all used to being hungry.

The Outlaws

About two hours before noon she felt a sudden cramp. She grimaced at the pain, and it soon subsided. About half an hour later, she had another cramp, followed soon by another.

She felt a warm wetness between her legs, as if she had urinated. But this wasn't urine. She sighed, knowing what it was. The girls hadn't noticed anything and she said nothing and continued to wait.

In mid-afternoon, when the pains came less than a quarter hour apart, she said to the girls, "Help me up."

After they pulled her to her feet, she said, "Come on," and waddled off down the lane known as La Ballie, which ended at Smithfield about a hundred-fifty yards away, the broad open field where the city held the Friday horse fair and young men played ball, shot arrows, and practiced at arms, and where the sheriff conducted public hangings in a grove on the west side.

Houses, packed close together, stood on either side of the lane, the ones on the right backing up against the city's ditch and wall. Just beyond Vyteries Lane, there was an alley used to reach a stable at the rear of one of the houses. Matilda entered the alley and spread her cloak on the ground behind a wood pile out of sight of passers by. Then she hitched up her skirts and sat on the cloak.

"Is the baby coming, momma?" Agnes asked.

"Yes, dear. It's time."

The girls looked worried.

"Shouldn't we go for the midwife?" asked Alice. They had arranged for one, a woman named Eldrida, who lived on Fleet Street, the road leading to Westminster.

"Girl, with what would we pay her now? Come on. You can do this. It's about time you learned, anyway. You'll be doing this yourself one day. All you have to do is catch the baby when it comes out." There was, of course, more to it than that, but Matilda would have to handle that part by herself.

"I don't care," Alice said, "I'm going." She got up and ran down the alley.

"Don't leave me!" Matilda cried out. "Don't leave me."

Alice stopped at the head of the alley, then came back, looking scared. "I won't Momma."

Matilda breathed hard to get control of herself. Then she said, "Here, tear a pair of strips from your undergown. We'll need them later."

"What for?" asked Agnes.

"Never mind. You'll see. And have your cloak ready. We'll need something to wrap the baby in."

"Does it hurt?"

"A little. Not much."

"How much longer?"

"Any time now. The pains are coming fast."

And hard, too. When the next one arrived, she bore down with it, uttering a low guttural growl in the back of her throat. She pushed harder, for she wanted to force the baby out quickly.

After a while of this, Alice said, "I see something. It's the head."

Matilda was relieved. At least the baby wasn't coming out breach. A breach birth baby could get hung up and kill them both. "You're sure it's the head?" she gasped.

"It has hair," said Agnes.

Matilda smiled. "What color?"

"Wet and dark."

Matilda pulled her skirt up above her waist so she could see. Indeed, the top of the head was there, an oblong ball covered in wet dark fuzz. Then she had a contraction and the baby's head disappeared.

"What's happening, momma?" Agnes cried, alarmed.

"Don't worry. It's all right."

She had another contraction and this time the baby's head reappeared. With another couple of contractions, it had emerged completely, and she could see its face. She reached down to touch it. Its skin was warm. She said, "All right, hold its head."

The Outlaws

"I've got it, Momma," said Alice, cupping her hands underneath.

"Here come the shoulders." Matilda had to force herself to sound much calmer than she felt. Having to instruct the girls somehow made it easier. "Support them, too, but don't pull. Let the baby come out by itself."

Once the shoulders emerged, the rest of the baby seemed to squirt out of her, like a cake of soap from wet hands. Its skin was a slate blue. As Agnes lay it on the cloak at Matilda's feet, it began to cry without prompting, a thin but lusty wail. The bluish birth tinge vanished, replaced by healthy crimson. It was a boy.

The baby urinated on both girls, who made noises of disgust.

Using strips Agnes had torn from her stockings, Matilda tied one piece on the cord near the child's belly button and the other a few inches away. Then she bit the cord in two, getting her chin and fingers bloody.

"Wrap it up," she said.

"Are we done now?"

"No, there's more. Comfort it, will you?"

Agnes swaddled the baby in her cloak and talked to him in a low sing-song voice. It grew quiet.

About a quarter hour later, Matilda delivered the afterbirth. She felt it coming and was able to drop it in the dirt so she didn't soil her cloak. After a few minutes rest, she buried the afterbirth in a shallow hole.

She straightened up, and took the baby from Agnes. It was a heavy child. She waddled toward the street. "Let's go. I think we'll wait by Newgate."

Brian would not appear until sundown, which was still several hours away. So they returned to their post on the door stoop.

The baby slept on Matilda's lap. She was glad it did not fuss because she had slipped into the darkest, deepest depression she had ever experienced, and might have thrown it down right there if it had made the slightest demand for attention. Her body ached in every bone, in every pore, and although she did not sob, tears streamed down her cheeks from closed eyes. The girls tried to comfort her but she pushed them away, so they clung to each other in alarm and said nothing.

She wiped her face, rose and set off down Watling Street. "Where are you going?" Alice asked.

"Never you mind. Stay here and wait for Brian," she said. "I'll be back soon."

When she had gone perhaps fifty yards she turned back to make sure that neither was following. They hadn't. They squatted by the same stoop that had been their station throughout the day, holding hands and watching her with anxious, fear-filled faces. How she loved them. They were such beautiful children. I am doing this for them, she told herself.

She crossed the bridge over the Fleet River. Odo's tavern lay on the right at the mouth of Goldinelane, which ran north parallel to the little river, and she was afraid she would be recognized. But no one called out.

Just beyond was the lane called Sholond, which ran south toward Fleet Street. Ahead on the left was the entrance to the Dominican Friary, which was her objective. There was a porter at the gate house, of course, so she passed further on to Smalebriggelane, which formed the southern border to the friary's garden. At the end of the lane, by the Fleet, there was a hole in the wall. The girls, who had told her about the hole, had used it along with some of the neighborhood boys to get into the garden and raid the monks' pear trees.

Matilda slipped through the hole and sank to her knees, scanning for the presence of other people. Seeing none, she crossed the garden to the gate in the wall leading to the friary buildings. She dared not enter there, for fear of discovery. But if she left the child here, it was certain to be discovered in the

The Outlaws

morning, when the monks entered the garden to do their chores.

She put the baby down. It had been a good baby, sleeping throughout the trip.

It opened its eyes and stirred as she turned away, thrashing small arms and legs against the restraint of Agnes' cloak. A fat round cheek brushed the edge of the cloak and the baby turned its head, mouth searching for the breast that wasn't there. It's hungry, she thought.

She left it there and started back across the garden. Someone will find it and have mercy.

She was thirty paces away when it began to cry. The high tiny lament cut her in two. All right, she thought. I'll feed you first.

So she went back and picked it up. Her breasts had begun to leak, her milk coming sooner than it had with the others, and the baby seemed to smell it, ceasing to cry and turning its head toward the source.

Matilda uncovered a breast and brought the child to it. It sought the nipple and began to suck — so hard that she winced. She felt him draw life out of her and she sank down against the garden wall.

Agnes ran ahead of the others and found her at sundown, sitting by the corner of Sholond and Smalebriggelane. The baby was asleep in her arms.

"Momma, what are you doing?"

"Resting."

"Where were you going? What were you going to do?"

"Nothing."

"Will you come back now?"

"Why? To what?"

"We have a place! Meurig has agreed to take us in!" Meurig, a Welshman, was Brian's master. He had a house in the city by St. Mary Magdalen church off the west fish market. "Alice and I got through the city gate without paying the toll.

The guard tried to stop us but we ran too fast. And we found Brian at the cathedral. And we told him what had happened. And Brian and Meurig and a half dozen of the other men with hammers went by the tavern and made Odo give over all our belongings! They threatened to beat him if he didn't."

"They did that?"

"Yes, I was there, I saw it. And Brian even recovered our money from where you had hidden it."

"Oh, God."

"Let me help you up. We must go. It'll be dark before we get back and cold. Can't you feel the cold? I'm already chilled to the bone." As she must be without her cloak. "Can you walk?" Agnes bent and took the baby from Matilda and held her hand while she climbed to her feet.

"I can walk."

"You won't have to go far. They're not far away. I ran on before. They followed with the cart."

They started back toward Holborn Street. It was almost dark by the time they got there.

"Have you given our brother a name yet?" Agnes asked.

Matilda paused for a moment. "I think I'll call him Harold." Why she had named the child after her long dead husband rather than his father, she could not explain.

Agnes nodded. "I miss Dad."

"So do I, child."

They turned the corner onto Holborn and headed toward the city.

PART 3

1180-1181

CHAPTER 1

Hereford
June 1180

When Giselle and Eustace emerged from the cathedral, the crowd outside fell silent for a moment, then shouted thunderously. Walking in a daze of disbelief that she was now a wife, Giselle stumbled on a flagstone and might have fallen if Eustace had not caught her arm. He whispered, "Careful. Do not embarrass me. Remember our conversation last night."

Last night Giselle had made one last plea to Earl Roger not to be forced into this marriage, nothing more than a frightened "Please don't make me!" FitzWalter had snorted and waved a hand at Eustace. "She needs another, I see," he had said. "She's almost more trouble than she's worth." Then he went upstairs while four housemaids held Giselle across a table as Reginald le Bec applied the cane to her back and legs. Eustace had knelt by her head and said, "It will stop when you agree to do as you're told. Why do you make things so difficult?" Giselle had always expected to be brave in the face of adversity, but beatings have a way of changing people's minds in a way that she had not anticipated. She felt dirty and small and unworthy, glad that her father had not lived to see what had become of her and how useless she was.

"I won't," she murmured.

"That's good. Now smile and pretend to be happy. I know that's difficult, given the circumstances. I shall try to do the same."

Earl Roger and Bishop Henry, who was being carried on a litter because of a broken leg, came up behind them. Eustace tugged Giselle aside to let them pass. Together, the two magnates led the crowd to the corner of the yard where tables and benches had been set up in the open air for the wedding feast.

Many of the tables were laid out beneath a huge oak under limbs as thick as a man was tall. Giselle was thankful for

The Outlaws

the shade it provided, because the sun was hot. Eustace and Giselle sat on the earl's right and the bishop on his left, with Lady Blanche beyond, and the other important guests arranged in descending order of their social status. Hundreds of lesser people milled about, competing for places to sit. There weren't enough tables to accommodate everyone who came, and many sat on the ground. Smoke from the cooking fires lingered over the scene, delivering the aromas of roasting pork, lamb, beef and a dozen other scents she could not identify. Despite herself, Giselle was hungry.

Eustace was at the height of his form. Giselle had never seen him so charming and gracious, although he did not bother to speak to her. She kept her eyes down and her hands in her lap and tried not to look unhappy.

The meal proceeded in a multitude of courses: twenty-five cows and as many pigs had been slaughtered and prepared in a variety of ways — some roasted, some baked, some cut into pies and stews. Dishes of mackerel, herring, haddock and eel, accompanied by butter and cheese and pies of peas and leeks and beans — spiced with sugar, pepper, cloves, cinnamon, saffron and other things she could not identify — marched across the table before her. Oysters followed to the acclaim of the crowd, for they were popular and rare so far from the sea. Roasted ducks, swans and pigeons also made their appearance, to disappear under the knives and fingers of the hungry mob. Wine barrels were rolled out and uncapped, young and sweet and sharp, replacing the bride's ale in a great show of extravagance — for everyone was expected to buy a cup to drink to the bride, to whom the proceeds went as a wedding gift.

The noise generated by the crowd was so intense that people at the head table had to shout to make conversation, and the wash drowned out the songs of the jongleurs strutting about among the tables so that Giselle only saw their mouths moving and fingers plucking in the din.

When the food had been consumed down to the last bit of gristle and crust, the serious drinking got underway, with casks of wine and ale set up on saw horses so that the thirsty guests could serve themselves if they were too impatient to wait for servants to attend them.

At this time, the bishop excused himself. The church had taken the view that people drank too much at wedding feasts and wakes. The bishop, who had to adhere to the official line, did not want to see what might happen so as to avoid the need to rebuke FitzWalter for the excesses that were sure to occur this afternoon. Better to turn a blind eye.

Giselle took his departure as a signal that she was free to go, too. No one expected the bride from a gentle family to take part in the drinking. As she took her leave of Eustace and FitzWalter, Blanche also stood. Together they returned on foot to the earl's townhouse on Brode Street.

Giselle climbed the stairs to her room, where she changed from her wedding dress to a simple linen gown with a pleated skirt and sleeves. It had a high waistline that concealed her figure. The effect was modest and virginal. She did not bother to check herself in the mirror before going downstairs to the other women. How she looked didn't matter any more.

Blanche and the other women were sitting on the steps with their sewing. A half dozen children of various ages — the offspring of Blanche's attendants — were playing ball in the stable yard. On another day, Giselle might have wanted to join the game, but the glare sent her way by Blanche, who would not approve, and her own despair kept her rooted to the steps.

At the approach of sundown, guests of the wedding party began appearing along the road on the way to their lodgings. Giselle watched them pass by from a window overlooking the street. She searched for Eustace's tall form in the gloom but did not see him. He would be here soon to claim his marriage rights.

She had no idea what to do now. The thought of having to lie with him made her quail. In the past few weeks, she had put these thoughts out of her mind, hoping for inspiration on how to avoid him, but none had come and she had no plan.

The Outlaws

She went into her chamber, closed the door, and sat in the dark for a few moments, trying to collect her thoughts. There was no bar on the door, no lock, just a simple iron latch. There was no large piece of furniture that she could move in front of the door to prevent its opening. She could almost hear his footfalls on the boards outside.

She snatched up the cloak thrown across her bed and went downstairs.

Blanche intercepted her at the doorstep. "My dear, where are you going?" she asked. She and the other women had been about to come up to gown Giselle so that she was dressed to receive her husband.

"To church," Giselle blurted.

"At this hour? Whatever for?"

"To light a candle for my father."

Blanche looked exasperated and took Giselle's arm. "Can't you do that later?"

Giselle pulled away and threw the cloak about her shoulders. "No."

"But he'll be here any moment."

"I won't be long." She ran down the steps to the yard and passed through the gate into Broad Street.

The falling night brought a chill with it and the scent of approaching rain. Hood up, Giselle was able to move through the streets, which were still filled with homeward bound party guests, without being noticed. Because of the feast, the curfew had been suspended.

Her first impulse was to seek refuge in the cathedral. But the cathedral grounds were walled, with access only through the gates, which would be shut by now. There was another church across the street to the right. But that would be an obvious place to look for her. She turned north, crossing Behynder Lane, and passed through the narrow alley that led to Eigne Street. At the head of the alley stood All Saint's Church, which she remembered seeing on her arrival in town several days before.

Its door was closed. Giselle tried the latch. It was unlocked. The hinges shrieked as she opened the door. She paused, waiting to hear voices calling, but there were none. She went in. The interior was cold and musty. She groped her way to the altar at the back and sat down on the hard-packed dirt floor.

She wrapped the folds of her cloak about her legs and rested her head on her upraised knees.

The cry of hinges awakened her and she jerked up in fright.

The door had opened. Two cloaked figures, one tall and the other short, stood in the dim gray rectangle. The tall figure paused by the trestle at the door. There was the snick-snick of flint and steel, and the yellow glow of a torch.

"There you are," Eustace said. "Your candle has gone out."

"It was only a small candle."

"I had begun to think you weren't coming back. Blanche is at her wits end."

"Then she will have to gather them as best she can."

"And she has been so good to you, I thought, the way she has taken you under her wing." He shrugged, a grin spreading across his handsome face. He put the torch in a niche by the trestle. "You should be more grateful."

Giselle's eyes flicked to his companion. She saw it was a woman, her face half-concealed by the hood of her cloak.

The woman pulled back her hood to reveal a pretty round-cheeked face set in a disdainful expression. The face was powdered, the hair escaping her wimple a light blond. She was dressed like an aristocrat, with a fur-lined cloak. A pleated linen skirt showed through the gap in the cloak, gathered at the waist by an embroidered belt. Finely tooled slippers covered her feet.

"I have forgotten my manners," Eustace said. "This is Aelfwyn. But then I think you already know each other."

The Outlaws

"We do," Giselle said.

Aelfwyn made a shallow reverence, mocking in its brevity. She was the daughter of a wealthy tenant farmer who worked a hide of land at Hafton.

"I admire your taste in gowns," Giselle said.

"Hafton prospers under the hand of our lord," Aelfwyn said.

"Were you intending to stay the night here, then?" Eustace asked Giselle.

"No."

"You're embarrassing me. I told you not to do that."

"I am sorry," Giselle said without contrition.

He held out a hand. "It's time to go. For your sake, I will pretend I knew this is where you intended to come. My father will not be so angry with you then."

Giselle wondered if he would beat her in front of Aelfwyn. She got to her feet.

"Good girl," Eustace said.

Aelfwyn laughed.

Giselle slapped her.

Aelfwyn put a hand to her face. "Eustace!"

Eustace laughed.

Aelfwyn stamped her foot. "Damn you," she said. She struck back at Giselle, who ducked the blow.

Eustace laughed harder, amused by the possibility that they might fight. But he was unwilling to let the fight proceed, and he stepped between them.

"How dare you bring your whore to my wedding," Giselle spat.

Eustace shrugged. "You have nothing to say in the matter."

Giselle's anger swamped her fear of him. "I'm not going back. I'll enter a convent before I lie with you."

Eustace's smile disappeared. He took the torch from its niche and reached for her. Backing away from him as he advanced, she retreated until her shoulder touched the cold stone of a wall. Eustace reached behind her head and drew out a length of her hair. He held the torch close, passing the ends of the long black braid through the flame. The hair crackled, curled, and stank.

"If you don't come with me and do what I say, I will burn it all off."

"You wouldn't dare," she spat.

"Well, probably not now. Not until I get you back home." He tossed the torch spinning into a corner, then turned back and slapped her on the cheek. It was a stunning blow with the heel of the palm, more powerful than a mere punch would be. Giselle's head rocked and she sagged to her knees. Eustace grasped a handful of her gown. Strong enough to lift her off the ground with one hand, he threw her over his shoulder and went out of the church.

Eustace carried Giselle into the house and deposited her in front of an angry FitzWalter and a distressed Blanche. "Make her ready," Eustace ordered the servants standing behind the earl, and went past them into the hall, where his friends were waiting. He plopped onto a chair and called for a flagon of wine.

The ladies' maids bustled Giselle upstairs to the bridal bedchamber, where they stripped off her gown, dressed her in white linen bedclothes and unbraided and combed her hair. The burnt strands evoked some sharp looks, but no questions. They all knew about Eustace's temper and were afraid to ask her what had happened. Giselle ignored them anyway, her eyes shut tight.

When they were done, they lifted her into bed. One of the maids scattered rose petals on the bed and floor, while another went downstairs to summon the groom.

Eustace came up followed by his closest friends, wine cups in all hands and bawdy jokes on their lips, trailed by a trio of minstrels with pipes and lute singing lewd songs. Earl FitzWalter, wearing an absurd-looking garland that rested askew on his salt-and-pepper head, brought up the rear. The

The Outlaws

garland had been Eustace's but he had bestowed it on his father on the stairway and FitzWalter for some reason had not taken it off, despite the injury it did to his dignity. Eustace's friends removed his clothes and helped him into a night shirt. FitzWalter returned the garland, which Eustace removed from his head with a laugh and spun to one of his friends. Giselle sat on the bed with her back to these proceedings. Reginald le Bec offered her a drink, which she refused with a shake of her head.

"It will dull the pain," le Bec said.

"Go away."

"Well, don't worry," le Bec said into her ear. "It will be over in a minute. He never lasts long."

Eustace threw a shoe at le Bec, who dodged out of the way. The shoe bounced off Giselle's shoulder. She flinched but did not look around. "You don't have permission to talk to my wife," Eustace bellowed.

"She's not properly a wife yet," le Bec said.

"Well, I'm about to make her one, now get out."

But nobody took the order seriously, for it was the local custom among the gentry that consummation of the marriage had to be witnessed, the failure of consummation being a major reason for annulment. Le Bec moved over to the window sill and crossed his arms. Earl Roger leaned against the door frame. Blanche and the other women gathered at the foot of the bed. Only the minstrels left. FitzWalter shut the door behind them.

Eustace pulled Giselle to him and forced her on her back. Then he drew her nightshirt up over her breasts and paused to look at her. His stare made her skin crawl. She lay rigid, her legs crossed at the ankles, and put her hands over her breasts. Eustace pulled them off. When she put them back, he slapped her.

"Spread your legs," he said. When she did not comply, he leaned close and said, "If you don't I'll have le Bec and the others hold you down. Do you want that?"

"Let it be so." She glared at him and, finding a last drop of courage she did not know she had, slapped him as hard as she could. The impact rocked his head back and he roared, surprised at its force and that she had dared to hit him. For a moment she was certain he would beat her again. But instead, he called for Reginald, Alexander, Quinton and Gerald to hold her arms and legs.

When the men had pried her legs apart, Eustace knelt between them, continuing to stare at her body. His eyes seemed to lick her from collarbone to ankles. She wondered how he could find her body so fascinating. It was such an ordinary body, small breasted, narrow-waisted and narrow-hipped, thin arms and legs. She had heard the other ladies referring to her as boney. "Won't be good for bearing children," one of the ladies had said.

Eustace had his penis in hand. It had grown to an astonishing size. She closed her eyes and waited for him to have it done, praying, as le Bec had said in jest, that it would be concluded soon.

When he put himself to her, at first he could not enter: she was dry and unready. But one of the young men poured oil from a lamp on her for lubrication and that helped a bit. After several thrusts, Eustace penetrated all the way and settled his body upon her, his face against her neck. The pain was sharp at first but faded, and his breath was warm and ticklish and repulsive. His thrusts began slow and even, but grew more quick and violent, so hard and bruising that she thought he would lift her from the feather mattress. She kept her eyes closed and tried to imagine being somewhere else. This is not happening to me, she repeated to herself over and over.

Presently, Eustace had his climax and he climbed off the bed. What should have been a moment for jovial congratulations was muted and somber. Eustace's friends went out, silenced by the look on Eustace's face if they ever had any intention of speaking, while the maids changed the soiled bed sheets. Then they left too. Eustace saw them to the

The Outlaws

door. FitzWalter paused at the threshold. "She's not properly broken, I see. Well, you have some work yet to do."

Eustace shut the door and leaned against it. Giselle sat up in bed, trembling at the thought that he intended to sleep here, repelled by the prospect of having to spend the night with him beside her.

"Are you going to hit me again?" she asked.

"No. I'm too tired now."

There was a faint rap on the door. Eustace opened it. Aelfwyn peered through the crack. Eustace took her hand.

"Sleep well," he said to Giselle and went out.

Giselle bounded to the door and latched it. There was no lock, so Eustace could come back whenever he liked and she could not stop him. But the latch gave her a small symbolic comfort. Then she found a rag and wiped the oil, Eustace's fluids and her blood from her thighs. She thought: If I have a baby in me I will find a way to kill it.

CHAPTER 2

Hafton
June 1180

Giselle heard the singing and the banging of the drum even before they reached the crest of the hill south of Hafton. It was far away yet, just a suggestion that might have been dismissed as imagination. But the wind changed and it came again.

For the first time in months, her spirits rose. She sat straighter in the saddle. Her eyes came off the horse's neck, where they had remained during almost the entire journey from Hereford. She leaned forward; the horse took this as a signal to pick up the pace, and she had to rein the mare back so as not to give herself away.

At the front of the column, Eustace looked back at her, and she dropped her eyes. No good showing him that she was feeling better.

Then they topped the crest, and there was Hafton before her in its little valley by the river — gray thatched roofs among the birch and elm, the regular patterns of wattle fences enclosing back gardens, and the old square tower at the manor house.

In the south field, a line of men swung scythes to the beat of the tune and the drum, carving a path through the grass, while other men, women and children collected the cuttings and bound them into bundles which they leaned against each other to dry. Almost the entire village was there, a hundred people at least — men, women, and children, most working, but the younger ones playing.

As Eustace drew near, people stopped what they were doing and stared, hands over their eyes against the glare of the sun for a moment. They could see it was his company and no one stopped work any longer than it took to be sure of this.

Giselle noticed that many people seemed thin, as if they were not getting enough to eat. Almost everyone she could see was barefoot. While it was not unusual for people to go

The Outlaws

barefoot in the summer to save shoe leather, there were always a few proud ones who wore boots throughout the year to show off their prosperity.

She almost said something about this, but Eustace tugged her bridle and led them forward to Baldwin, who had walked to the roadway from his folding chair under the big oak. His legs seemed more bowed than she remembered, and the wart under his left ear seemed to have grown.

"My lord, my lady," Baldwin said. "Welcome home."

Eustace settled into her father's high-backed chair by the hearth and propped his feet on a stool. A maid rushed to take off his boots and another to serve him wine. Aelfwyn took a seat beside him in another chair, its back not quite so high, and looked at Giselle, daring her to make a scene, while another maid hurried up bearing a tray with a pitcher and a cup for drinking and a bowl and towel for washing. Whatever need there had been to maintain appearances upon their arrival no longer seemed to apply.

"Thank you, my dear," Aelfwyn said to the maid as she dabbed her face with the towel. She sipped from her cup and leaned back as if this was her house and not Giselle's.

Giselle had been about to let things lie and retire to her room, but the sight of Aelfwyn reclining in the chair that should be hers and that simpering thank you made her temper flare. She didn't care a whit if Aelfwyn was Eustace's chief bed pony, but being shoved aside in her own house, the place where she grew up, in front of people she had known all her life, was more than she could stand, even if it meant another caning. She threw her gloves on the floor. The maid who had accompanied her, Eanfled, reached for her arm to restrain her, but was too late. Giselle marched over to Aelfwyn, and batted the cup from her hand. Wine sprayed on Aelfwyn and she leaped to her feet.

"Get your harpy out of my house," Giselle snapped to Eustace.

Eustace regarded Giselle over the rim of his cup. He looked irritated. "Reggie," he said to Reginald le Bec, "take my wife to her chamber."

"Of course, my lord," le Bec said. He sounded irritated too.

Giselle almost burst into tears. She had thought of marriage to Eustace might bring a little more freedom. And Aelfwyn had provoked this tantrum. Deliberately. Giselle could see the gloating in her eyes.

Le Bec rose from his bench and took her arm. "Come on."

He directed her toward the stairs.

Giselle halted there. "Thank you, Reginald, I know my way."

Le Bec hesitated and looked to Eustace for direction.

Eustace waved a hand, signifying that le Bec had done enough. Le Bec returned to his place by the fire.

"Good evening, husband," Giselle said.

"I hope you sleep well," Eustace said.

As Giselle climbed, Aelfwyn settled onto Eustace's lap.

Eustace remained at Hafton for three days. Giselle spent the entire time in her room, even for meals, which Eanfled delivered on a tray.

Eustace came about midnight on the second evening. He rattled the latch, and when he found it wasn't locked, he entered the room and halted a step or two inside the door. He stood there for a few moments while Giselle pretended to be asleep. Then he went away without a word or any explanation.

On the morning of the third day, she awoke to the clamor of voices and the thumping of many feet moving about. The commotion made its way downstairs and then outside to the yard. Giselle cracked her door and checked the hallway. Seeing and hearing no one, not even a maid, she tip-toed across to the room opposite hers, which had been given to le Bec. She cracked that door. No one was inside and it was bare. Le Bec's

The Outlaws

trunk was gone and there was no sign he had ever slept here. Giselle crossed to the windows, which overlooked the yard and peeked out to see what was going on. Eustace and le Bec had their horses saddled. Aelfwyn was with them, looking a peeved at something. They were leaving.

It took several moments for this to sink it. They were leaving — and leaving her behind!

Giselle stumbled out to the head of the stairway, where she could see down to the hall. It was empty, the front door standing open. Baldwin could be heard talking from the stairs outside.

Then le Bec entered. Giselle wanted to run at the sight of him. He must have come back to fetch her. She had not been forgotten after all. The horror of that thought froze her feet to the floor. He crossed the hall and mounted the stairs.

"It's about time you got up," le Bec said.

"What's going on?" Giselle managed to ask, glad that her voice sounded far more calm and reserved than she felt.

"We're going to Harleigh," le Bec said. "He likes it better there." Harleigh was another of the FitzWalter manors a few miles south of Hafton. Earl Roger had given it over to Eustace to manage.

Le Bec brushed by her and went into the lord's chamber, where Eustace and Aelfwyn had slept. He emerged with a mirror and a comb. He noticed Giselle staring at the comb and mirror with some amazement.

"She sent me back for a fucking comb," he said. "I'm not her fucking servant."

"She'll make you one if you let her."

"Like hell." Le Bec went by, descended the stairs, and went out.

Eustace called for them to move out.

Giselle slipped down to the door, careful not to let herself be seen through it. She peered around the jam. Eustace was just passing through the gate with Aelfwyn at his side, followed by his mounted retinue, such as it was, le Bec, two men-at-arms on loan from the earl, and most of the servants.

Within a minute, they had gone, and a hush settled on the yard. It was a warm summer morning, the sun was out, the sky was blue, and the air was full of hope and all sorts of possibilities.

Giselle drew a breath and let it out.

They were gone. *He* was gone.

She was free — as free as she was ever likely to be in this marriage.

And she was at home.

Eleanor and Baldwin came in from the yard where they had gone with what remained of the household staff to see off Eustace.

"Mary!" Eleanor barked to one of the two maids who had stayed behind. "The hearth needs cleaning out. And you —" Eanfled "— the floor needs sweeping."

Mary dashed for the bucket and shovel in a corner, and Eanfled, a resigned look on her face, crossed the hall in search of a broom.

"I require them to help me dress," Giselle said.

Eleanor turned as if she had just now become aware of Giselle's presence. "I say, you are dressed."

"You shall address me properly," Giselle said.

Eleanor hesitated. "Of course, my lady. Your pardon."

Giselle reached the foot of the stairs. "Girls! Come!"

Mary and Eanfled put down neither shovel nor broom. They glanced at Eleanor, who nodded, before they followed.

Giselle climbed to her chamber and began to go through her trunks. Since her arrival, she had worn the same simple brown woolen gown. But she wanted something more than that now. The FitzWalters had not lavished her with fine clothes or playthings, just enough to keep her from being an embarrassment at social gatherings, which meant she had had a wardrobe of second quality material. That had changed when the earl obtained the right to wed her to Eustace. She had been given over to tailors, and two week's worth of

The Outlaws

furious dress-making had resulted in a modest but fine wardrobe suitable for the wife of a member of the lower gentry. She had two elaborate silk gowns for formal occasions and half a dozen each of linen petticoats and heavier, embroidered surcoats to go over them. She had another half dozen simple gowns that varied in color and in the length of their sleeves. She chose one of the simple gowns, a high-necked red one with long sleeves that almost dragged on the floor if she let her arms fall to her sides. It was impractical for hard work on the manor, but that was one reason she chose it — ladies weren't supposed to do hard physical work; people worked for them.

After indicating her choice, she held out her arms so the maids could remove her clothes and then she let them dress her in the red gown. She wished there was a mirror to look at the effect, but her father had not had one. Eustace had made off with the sole one within miles.

Then she sat down so the maids could comb and braid her long black hair, which they coiled in a great bundle at the back of her neck. Now that she was married, she couldn't let her hair hang loose. Then the maids covered her hair with a tasteful round hat and white linen headdress.

She finished by selecting a gold pendant in the form of a cross on a delicate gold chain. Blanche had given it to her as a wedding gift and so she despised it, even though it was very valuable. But wearing it now would make a nice point.

The transformation complete, she swept out of the room and went down to the hall.

Eleanor was not in sight, but Baldwin was seated at the table working on documents with Evrart. He looked at her sourly when she told him to come along, and for an instant she thought he would refuse. It occurred to her that a man in his prime would not find it easy taking orders from a fifteen-year-old girl, but she was the lady of the house now and he had no choice. With an irritated, "We'll finish later," to the clerk, Baldwin rose the trailed her out the door to the yard.

They started with the undercroft: the timber house sat on top of a stone foundation that provided a storage area beneath the floor of the hall. It was filled with barrels and boxes and various tools, all neatly stowed. Marks had been chalked on the sides of the barrels and boxes to indicate what they contained — wine, ale, nails, candles, drums of wax for candle making, butter, lard, hides of leather bound in rolls, salt, cinnamon, dried beans, bolts of linen, spools of wool, bars of iron, and a host of other sundries. There was a cart and a ladder as well.

After that she toured the barn and granary, the dovecot and kennel, the chicken coop, the stables, the pigsty, the forge, and the kitchen and storehouse. All the buildings were in good repair and several had been painted in bright blues and yellows.

The last thing she looked at was the garden. It was a smaller version of the vast vegetable garden outside the walls to the west: bursting with spinach, cabbages, leeks and onions, radishes, beans, peas, and carrots, all in their neat rows with hardly a weed in sight. The broad beans and cabbage were ready for harvesting, but the rest would not be for a month or two. Strolling through the rows at the edge of the herb garden, where the fragrance of marjoram and fennel was in the air, she flushed a pair of rabbits which dashed off in zig-zags, pursued by the boy assigned to tend the garden.

Everything was neat, tidy, and prosperous looking. She had nothing to complain about.

The bell rang for dinner, so Giselle returned to the hall, where a second table had been set up and the places laid with cloths, spoons, and wooden trenchers. She settled into father's high-backed chair with its feather pillow. Eleanor took her seat at her side and was about to clap in order to get the servants moving with the service, but Giselle beat her to it, and earned a sour look for her audacity.

Dinner was good, though not sumptuous. There were no raisins, imported from Portugal, or figs made into luscious puddings, or any of the marvelous sauces of garlic and

The Outlaws

mustard and vinegar that the earl's cook was so skilled at preparing. But it was plentiful and satisfying: a mussel soup which was very salty, followed a vegetable pie, and baked doves glazed with a honey gravy, with lots of white bread, and a sweet bun covered in honey to top things off — quite a bit for the assistant cook and his helper to put together by themselves. Giselle, who had skipped breakfast in her haste to make her inspection, was hungry and had to restrain herself from tearing in an unladylike way into each steaming dish, in stuffing herself unceremoniously with bread so that her cheeks bulged, or in mopping her trencher to get that last bit of sauce.

She wiped off her knife, returned it to its little scabbard in her pouch, and leaned back in the chair for a moment to recover. She remained there, while Burghard and Osgar took down the second table. The ladies of a house often spent the hour or two after dinner in conversation in the hall or in sedentary chores like sewing and embroidery, but Giselle wasn't having any of that. She was too eager to see the rest of Hafton. Giselle caught Osgar just before he went out and asked him to saddle a horse for her.

The best part was not having to ask anyone's permission.

As Giselle approached the wide spot by the church occupied by the village well, she heard the clamor of voices and smelled the musty odor of sheep and the pungent aroma of dung and fresh hay. A fold had been set up in the commons, and it was full of sheep, their wool so thick and ready for shearing that they looked like barrels with legs.

Giselle tied her horse to a fence post. She looked around, shielding her eyes from the sun, which was so hot that she had begun to sweat in her heavy gown. She wanted to talk to someone, to find out the village news and catch up on nine months of lost gossip. There were at least half a dozen villagers lounging in the shade of the trees lining the commons, but no one came up to her or called a greeting. They were at pains to pretend not to see her.

Behind her there was the unmistakable snicker of sheeps' hooves on the road. She turned to see a flock of about twenty jogging into the common, a boy leading them with the help of a dog. Wulfric Ploughman, the village reeve, was strolling along at the rear, a long staff on his shoulder.

As the boy led the sheep into the pen, she awaited Wulfric, bouncing up and down on her toes and unable to contain a grin. It was good to see old Wulfric, steady as a rock Wulfric. She could remember sitting on his knees after church as a child, weaving necklaces of grass with his daughter Elwy, who was the same age as she was. At least Wulfric didn't avoid her. He stopped at her side, spat on the road, and leaned on his staff. "Good afternoon, my lady."

Wulfric towered over her. He was so tall that he always seemed to slump over to bring his head closer to people when he was talking. He didn't have to get down on a knee as he had once had to do, but it almost felt like it. Like many of the village people, he seemed thinner and went barefoot; his cheeks were sunken and there were great circles under his eyes. "Are you well, Wulfric?" she asked.

"Well, enough," he grunted. "Considering."

"Considering what?"

He shuffled his feet, looked into the distance over the trees, and was some time in answering. Then he said, "There was a few died this winter and it's been hard waiting for the harvest."

"What did they die of?"

Again, there was a long pause. "The hunger."

Alarmed, Giselle asked, "There's been a famine?"

"Yea." Wulfruc stroked his beard and spat again. "One of my granddaughters died of it."

"Oh, dear. Which one?"

"Amanda."

Giselle remembered a fat little baby in a basket, a plaid coverlet across her middle, little fists waving, and a gurgling

The Outlaws

smile. She recalled the birth because the baby had come at the same time that Attebrook boy had gone to France. "I'm so sorry."

"Nothing you could do. Elwy's milk dried up."

Poor Elwy. What a tragedy to lose a child. It struck her as odd, though, that there could have been a famine. The harvest last year had been good, same as at Shelburgh. Same as everywhere. The summers were long and the autumns warm, and the talk all round was how bountiful the harvests were. No one should be starving. "His lordship did nothing?"

Wulfric shuffled his feet. "He's the one what brought it on. Took over three eighths of the harvest and taxed every man, free and unfree, ten pence besides. There were a lot who couldn't pay, so he took over their lands for the demesne."

Giselle was stunned — half the harvest taken. With that much grain confiscated it was no wonder people were hungry. They were probably fighting with the chickens in the dirt for the scattered grains that were left. She remembered that she hadn't seen a single pig in the village when she had ridden through. It had been odd, all those empty sties and not a single sow on the road or at the edges of the woods, rooting around with an entourage of piglets. She hadn't marked it at the time, but now she understood. They'd all been eaten. Now she thought of it, she hadn't seen a single goat either.

"Wulfric," she said aghast.

Wulfric sighed. "We thought it would just be hard times until the earl found you a husband. Now you're one of them. It'll never end." He looked frightened. "I shouldn't have said that. It's not my place. You won't let on that I've told, will you? That Eustace, he'll set le Bec on me."

Giselle pressed her lips together. "I'd have found out anyway." It was true. The signs were all there, the shabby clothes, the lean and hungry faces, people shoeless, the absence of goats and pigs, gardens well tended, demesne land less so. She had been too wrapped in her own misery before to see signs.

"Yeah, well, you won't let on?"

She grasped his forearm, hurt that he thought she would betray him. "Wulfric! How long have I known you!"

The anxiety eased on his face. "Ah, missy, you're cut from the same cloth as your dad. But it's too bad there's nothing you can do, being just a wife."

CHAPTER 3

Hafton
June 1180

It was still dark when Giselle woke up the next day. The night was so short this time of year that she felt she had not gotten any sleep at all. The smell of smoke from the kitchen and the sound of voices coming through the open window reminded her that people were already up and working.

She threw off the blanket and rose to wash her face at the basin by the window. Angry shouting and cries of pain from the kitchen interrupted this ritual, but when she looked out a window with a dripping face to see what had caused it, no one was in sight in the yard except Osgar, who was on his way to the stables and seemed unconcerned at the hubbub.

Giselle patted her face dry with the skirt of her nightgown, since Eanfled had forgotten to set out a towel the night before. The wind shifted, bringing the aroma of the sheep in the fold which had been erected beyond the palisade. The sharp odor of manure was enough to make a person gag, but it reminded her that shearing was supposed to start today, and shearing was one of the best times of the year, after the harvest.

She was about to call for Eanfled to help her get dressed when the maid stumped in, rubbing sleep from her eyes and carrying a candle. As Eanfled put the candle down on the table by the basin, the wind blew it out. "Damn," Eanfled said.

"No matter," Giselle said. "We've no need to waste candles this time of day." The sky had lightened to a dull gray. The sun would be up in half an hour. She turned to rummage in her trunk.

Eanfled emptied the basin out the window, and Giselle heard Eleanor shouting at her from below in the yard.

"Sorry, m'lady," Eanfled called, flinching at the rebuke, and put the basin back down on the table with a hasty thump.

"It's all right. Don't pay any attention to her," Giselle said.

"Of course, m'lady," Eanfled said without conviction. "Will you wear the blue or the red today?"

"The blue."

"Very good."

"Let's hurry. Don't bother with my hair. I'll just tie it up. There aren't any men around today worth impressing."

Eanfled grinned. "Right."

When she descended into the yard, Giselle gathered up her skirts against the dew that still clung to the few clumps of grass that survived the coming and going, and marched across to the kitchen, a round wooden building beside the house. The sun was almost up and there was pink light at the tops of the clouds.

The kitchen had huge shutters all around it that were folded down to let out the heat from the cooking fires. The assistant cook, a pot bellied man who had not been here last summer, and his sole helper were hard at work. The boy was ladling dried green beans and peas from barrels into a big kettle over the fire. He had a bruise on his cheek and had been crying. The cook was occupied cutting up leeks. As Giselle came through the door, the cook scraped the leeks from his board into the pot and turned to line big baking pans with dough from an enormous wad in a tub.

"Good morning," Giselle said.

"Morning, m'lady," the cook and his boy responded.

Just then Eleanor emerged from the pantry at the rear. The corners of her mouth plunged downward. She nodded and snapped, "G'morning. My lady."

"Making meat pies for dinner?" Giselle asked the cook.

The cook swiped at a strand of lank black hair that had fallen across his face. "Yes, m'lady."

"How many have you planned?" Giselle asked.

The cook's eyes flicked to Eleanor. "I'll have five going shortly."

The Outlaws

Five, Giselle mulled. The trays were big: almost a foot across. More than enough for the household. "That's more than we need."

"We are sending three to Harleigh," Eleanor said.

"His lordship likes my pies," the cook said.

"They must be fine pies," Giselle said.

She strolled through the kitchen, inspecting the contents of the barrels beside the tables. There were the three of beans and peas and one of offal and entrails, which was meant for the meat pies. She tapped the one with the entrails. "Where did this come from?"

"We've slaughtered an old ewe," the cook said.

The carcass was not in view, but it would be hanging on one of the hooks under the eaves out of sight. It should have been on a spit or cut in pieces and boiling in a pot. "We won't be having that today, I take it."

"Lady Eleanor says we will slow roast it for tomorrow."

It irked Giselle to hear Eleanor addressed as a lady. But she did not correct the cook.

"You've a lot of dough there," Giselle said. "It's not all for bread, is it?" The dough for pies had to be made with less yeast so it wouldn't rise as much as for bread.

The cook's lips curled with disgust. "The boy made too much. I'll turn what we don't use into biscuits."

Giselle fingered her lip in thought. "There must be enough for twenty pies."

"Yes," cook said.

"Well, then," Giselle said. "We'll just make twenty pies."

"Twenty!" Eleanor snapped.

"Yes," Giselle said. "Twenty."

The cook wrung his hands. "We'll have to kill another sheep. The expense!"

"Have it done," Giselle said trying to make her voice sound haughty and commanding. "You," she pointed to the cook's boy. "Find a ewe and butcher her, if you please." When the boy hesitated, she added, "Right now."

It was pleasant to see the stunned expressions on the faces of the cook and the boy, and to have the boy hurry to obey.

"Twenty pies is a waste," Eleanor said. "What are we going to do with twenty pies?"

"We shall feed the laborers," Giselle said. "They deserve a meal for their work."

"My lord left specific instructions. I've already arranged for bread and ale."

She had, had she? The only sign of activity at the ovens was baking rolls for breakfast and loaves for dinner and supper, enough for the household. So Eleanor was going to feed the laborers old bread. They would be sure to like that.

"Then they will be pleased to get the pies as well," Giselle said. "Don't just stand there, master cook. Get the mutton you have cut up and boiling. It's the quickest way to prepare it. I want the lot ready by dinner time."

"We can't eat two sheep quickly enough to prevent them from spoiling," Eleanor sputtered.

"Give half to the laborers," Giselle said from the doorway. "We'll keep a quarter and send the rest to his lordship. I'm sure he'd sooner have mutton and gravy than meat pies."

Giselle crossed the yard to the chapel, satisfied with the way she had handled Eleanor. Firmness, that was the way.

She caught Evrart the chaplain in the writing office whittling a stick. He should have been preparing to perform Prime, the first service of the day. He put the stick aside and stood up.

"Don't let me interrupt you," she said.

"Is something troubling you, my child?" he asked.

"I want to see the accounts and the records of the manor court."

Evrart looked troubled and a little frightened. "There is no need," he said. "They are all proper and in hand."

263

The Outlaws

"I'll decide if there's a need, and I've already decided," she said.

The chaplain fumbled beneath his robes for a large iron key on a chain. The manor's records were kept in a big trunk secured with an iron lock. Evrart opened the lid, which squeaked.

"Needs a bit of oil," he murmured. He stepped back, folded his hands, and made no effort to do anything further.

Giselle had expected him to be more helpful than this. She was a bit puzzled why he seemed so cool and evasive.

The trunk was full of rolled vellum sheets, each tied with a blue ribbon. "Which one has the most recent accounts, covering since last Michaelmas?" she asked.

"That one," the chaplain pointed to the topmost roll.

"And the manor court?"

"The one beneath it."

Giselle set them both on the table side by side, undid the ribbons, and set candlesticks on the ends to hold them open against their natural tendency to curl. The entries were in Latin, like just about everything in the world that was written down, except for correspondence. It was unusual for a girl to be taught Latin, but Evrart's predecessor has schooled her enough that she could understand what she saw.

She would have liked to have the chaplain's help in deciphering the rolls, but he seemed tense. "You can go," she said.

"At your service, m'lady," Evrart murmured and slid backward out the door, which he closed behind him.

"At my service indeed," Giselle muttered.

Settling on a stool, she leaned over to study the accounts roll. Entries were all a-jumble, receipts were intermingled with expenses one after another. The single aid to telling them apart was the fact that amounts for income were in one column and payouts in a parallel one. As she scanned the entries, her mouth moving as she struggled to decipher the handwriting, patterns began to emerge. The number of fines had increased. From the look of things, there had been an outbreak of carnality: more than twenty fines for sex offenses in December alone, more than she could remember having occurred in two years of hanging around the fringes of the manor court. Also in December, there were two enormous tallages, general levies on the people, coming just two weeks apart, with a running account of how they were paid, almost all in grain. She nodded at the timing of it. Eustace had waited until all the threshing was done. People threshed their own grain with more enthusiasm than they did their lord's.

She cross referenced the fines against the entries on the roll of the manor court just to be sure she wasn't misreading things, but the entries were there, along with dozens upon dozens of other fines: for fighting and housebreaking, and at least four fines for house hire after Eustace had rebuilt them following fires which had taken them all in the space of a week. It was odd that four houses should burn down all within a week. Only houses that had been paid for had burned, too. There was account after account of someone having lost land to the demesne. Wulfric had been right after all.

Back into the accounts roll, she found that rents had gone up in the spring for everything, as well as fines for use of the forest. And references to other extraordinary fines popped up: for wool, for fish, for fodder. Fines like these were special ones levied for special expenses of the manor. Eustace must have been buying all sorts of things.

The strange thing, though, as she scanned the record, was that there was no sign of the purchases. She wondered about that. After chewing her lip, she rummaged through the chaplain's things for a waxed tablet and stylus.

She began adding up all the income noted in the roll, which was written in Roman numbers, intending to match them to the expenses. The work was hard and absorbing. It seeme that she had hardly got started when Eanfled knocked on the door to announce dinner time — Giselle couldn't remember having heard the bell.

The Outlaws

"I'll eat here," Giselle said, and Eanfled had returned with a pitcher of ale and a platter of steaming meat pie, mutton with gravy, and bread. With a pang of guilt, Giselle realized that she had not made sure that the cook and Eleanor had complied with her orders on feeding the laborers. Those two needed watching. The maid stood around gazing at the rolls on the table, but soon grew bored and left.

She worked through the afternoon. With the sun a couple hours from setting, she heard the supper bell this time, and went back to the house, bearing the scrolls with her. She had a feeling she shouldn't leave them lying around.

After supper, she retired to her chamber, where she unfurled the scrolls by the window and went back to work.

She hadn't finished when the sun set, so she lighted a couple of candles and kept on.

It was hard to tell how much time had passed since sundown. Perhaps an hour, for the moon, in its fifth night as a growing crescent, had set. But she had finished her figuring. It had taken so long because she had added the numbers four times to make sure she had not been mistaken. Her head and back ached, and her vision had grown blurry. She stood and stretched. The air coming in through the window was cool and fresh and still smelled of sheep. The crickets were singing beyond the palisade. She heard a woman, who should have been asleep, laugh in the distance.

She blew out the candles and stood at the window for a long time, thinking about what she had found. The manor had taken in enormous amounts of money from the mine and from fines and other exactions. But there had been no corresponding spike in expenditures. So where had all that money gone?

CHAPTER 4

Hafton
June 1180

It was the second Thursday of the month, manor court day. Giselle remained in her seat after breakfast as the few servants left cleared off the table and removed the cloth. Villagers began trickling in. Giselle remembered manor courts as loud and boisterous. Even if no one had any business before the court, it meant they had hour or two devoted to the session off work, and that was always a reason for celebration. But the groups gathering in the hall was sullen and quiet.

"You should retire to your chamber," Eleanor said.

"Why?"

"Baldwin has been given authority to act in his lordship's absence."

"I am his wife. It is my duty to preside in his absence."

"Our lord has made his wishes known. Baldwin shall preside. He knows our lord's wishes in these matters."

"He has not made is wishes known to me."

"You know you are to do as you're told."

"Not by you. You have no warrant to instruct me in anything."

"You will retire, if you know what's good for you. Shall I send a messenger to Harleigh?"

Giselle could not believe what she was hearing, but she knew that Eleanor was serious, from the smug turn of her mouth. "You'd enjoy seeing me beaten, wouldn't you."

"How my lord chooses to exert his authority is his business."

"Tell me one thing. Where do all the fines go? They don't benefit the manor."

"Where they go is none of your concern."

"I am the wife! This is my manor. Everything that happens here is my concern."

"Not anymore."

The Outlaws

"If you don't leave on your own accord, I shall have you carried," Baldwin said with uncommon authority. "That would be most undignified. I'm sure you should like at least to preserve appearances even among . . . these people."

Giselle stood up. She had no choice. Open rebellion would mean another beating, and she could not face that.

She had to pass Burghard and Osgar to reach the stairs. "Wait a few moments, and then follow," she whispered.

Burghard nodded. Osgar pretended not to hear.

Giselle went upstairs as Evrart called the first case.

She went to her father's chamber, where she had moved her things after Eustace's departure. It had been meant to indicate that she intended to take responsibility for the manor in his absence, but now she realized it was an empty gesture.

She heard footsteps in the hallway, and Burghard and Osgar entered.

"We're sorry, my lady. It shouldn't be this way," Burghard said, twisting his wool cap in his fists.

"It ain't right," Osgar said.

"I am a prisoner in my own home," she said.

Both men nodded.

"I shall at least know what's going on, even if I can't do anything about it. The manor is being stripped."

Burghard hesitated. "It is, m'lady."

"Where is the money going? And the grain?"

"Earl Roger is taking it," Burghard said.

"All?" Giselle was astonished.

"Most of it," Osgar said.

"Practically everything," Burghard said. "He leaves even little for our lord to live on. It is a matter of some contention between them. But our lord has no ability to refuse."

"I could feel sorry for him, but I don't."

"No need to feel sorry at all," Osgar said. "He's keeping two sets of accounts."

"*Two* sets?"

"Hush!" Burghard stepped to the door to look into the hallway. "Don't speak of this!"

"One for his father and one for him," Osgar said.

"Osgar!" Burghard hissed. "This is too dangerous to speak of!"

"He's cheating the earl?" Giselle asked.

Their heads nodded in unison, Osgar's with more vitality. "We're not supposed to know. Nor are you. So don't let on."

"But I saw the accounts yesterday!"

"Only the ones people are allowed to see."

"What's happened to the surplus?"

"That Eustace keeps for himself? What's in money is kept in a strong box. Normally, it's chained to the bed." Osgar pointed to a worn spot on one of the bed posts. "When he's gone it's in Baldwin's chamber."

"And the grain?"

"We have a new barn in the forest by the mine for what hasn't yet been sold."

Giselle waited four days before she dared to go see this new barn. One might suppose that since she was the lady of the manor, she could go anywhere she pleased at any time she liked. But she had the sense now to know this wasn't true, that she was under observation at all times, and that whatever she did would find its way back to Baldwin and Eleanor, and then to Eustace. She regretted pressing Evrart to see the manor accounts. God knew the price she might have to pay for that bit of curiosity when Eustace returned, although at least so far she had managed to avoid a lecture or a public humiliation from Baldwin about it. In the night, she imagined Eustace riding straight here after receiving Baldwin's alarm, and the prospect caused her to spend a great deal of time pacing in the darkness of the bedchamber. But Eustace did not come.

She hit upon the notion of taking rides about the manor as if inspecting how all the work was going. Neither Eleanor

The Outlaws

nor Baldwin objected to her rides as long as she didn't interfere by giving instructions to anyone.

The good thing about these rides was that she was able to make them alone. Eanfled, who had been stepped on by a horse as a child, viewed riding one with the same horror as she would an order to muck out the garden, and Mary, the other maid, had never been on a horse. Giselle's initial impulse was to ride up to the barn once people had grown accustomed to seeing her riding about so that they would not think anything of it. Yet when she went up the road to the mine, it occurred to her that she had no idea where this secret barn was. A cart track veered into the forest just short of the mine. She supposed the barn lay at the end of it. But she was afraid to ride down there in daylight, and as she steeled herself to do so, two miners came down the track from the mine and asked if they could be of service. Being seen broke her nerve.

It took the first day to make a complete inspection of the manor, so she had to come up with some other plan to explain why she was riding about, especially if that meant going places out of common view. The sight of Osgar practicing with a crossbow behind the stable during some idle time gave her an inspiration: she would go hunting. She could not do this alone, however. While no one might comment on her riding about in sight of everyone in the village, she couldn't dare to enter the forest without an escort. She had heard of noblewomen hunting on their own, but that was not done here in the March, which was still wild country often filled with desperate men. She did not want to enlist anyone in this plan, but there seemed no alternative.

The next day was Sunday, and she could not justify riding about then. She chafed until Monday morning after breakfast, when she had Osgar saddle two horses, and fetch crossbows and bolts for the both of them.

That first day they did go hunting. Giselle had not been hunting for so long that she forgot how much she enjoyed it. They flushed a red deer stag west of the river, and chased it for several miles through the forest, the wind in her face and branches snatching at her hair, leaping ditches and fallen logs even though she bent so far over that her face was buried in the horse's mane, before the deer stopped from exhaustion. Her shot went over its shoulder, but Osgar's took it in the chest. It ran on for another hundred yards before it bled out and died. They brought the carcass back over the rump of his horse, and Osgar lied and said she had killed it.

The third morning they took the south road up the hill on the way that led to the main road. At the crest, they veered left, up slope, and continued for some time to the top of the hill and then down the other side, weaving through trees that grew so close to each other than she could see no more than ten feet ahead.

Giselle had played as a child all over this hill and its dips and hollows. She turned north and after half an hour, they reached the river, where they paused to water the horses.

"Tell me," Giselle asked, "where exactly is this secret barn?"

"Barn?" Osgar answered with some alarm. "You want to know where the barn is?"

"Show me."

"I never go there. I've no business there."

"If we sit here arguing about it, the sun will go down, and I'll still not know where it is."

"Why do you want to know, mistress?"

"I want to see it for myself."

"What will you do then? Tell the earl?"

"What good would that do? Eustace will just make some excuse. He's clever that way."

"He may be clever, but the earl's bound to see through being cheated."

"Why don't you tell him and rid us of my husband?"

"Because I like being alive." He squinted at her as they climbed the opposite bank. "That's what this has all been about, all this riding around? Finding the barn?"

"I knew you were clever."

271

The Outlaws

"I'm good for things other than scraping shit off horses' hooves. If only someone would give me a chance. Not that I'll ever get a chance here. Baldwin hates me." He did not add that his family were serfs and bound to the manor, so he could not leave. "I don't like being a part of this plot."

"What makes you think I've got a plot going? I'm just a wee girl, too small and weak for plots."

"Small I'll give you, but not the weak part."

"If I was strong, I'd never have married Eustace."

"We heard what they did to break you. No one could have resisted that."

"I wish that was true."

"Brian told me getting whipped is the worst thing in the world."

"Brian?"

"Matilda's son. You remember him. The carpenter's apprentice."

"Of course," Giselle murmured, embarrassed that the connection had slipped her mind.

She spotted movement. Giselle stood in her stirrups and aimed at a squirrel, which had paused on top of a stump to inspect an oak nut it had found in the leave litter. The crossbow twanged and the bolt knocked the squirrel off the stump.

"I doubt we'll be lucky enough to find another deer, so I suppose that will have to do," she said. "Now, about that barn."

They found the barn on flat ground below the mine. It sat in a cleared space with oaks, elms, and beeches pressing in close and towering over a thatched roof. It was small for a barn, squat and long rather than tall.

Giselle tied her horse to a tree, and slipped to the edge of the clearing. Osgar joined her behind an oak. She listened for sounds of anyone about, but heard the rustling of the wind in the trees.

"Seems deserted," she said. They were on the back side of the barn, for there was no door, nor even windows, on the two sides she could see, just the usual timber frame filled with plaster-covered wattle.

"There's supposed to be a guard," Osgar said.

"Now you tell me?"

"I didn't think we'd be getting this close. You only said you wanted a look. You have that."

"I don't see any guard."

"He may be asleep, or taking a piss in the woods."

"Who are these guards? Nobody from the village, surely."

"No. From the mine. Anybody would rather guard a barn than go down in a mine. I would, if it was me."

Giselle nodded. Most of the people working the mine were Welsh, and not from the village. They had their own little camp of huts and shanties along the track leading up to the mine, and they seldom mingled. The wind shifted and brought the stench of privies. They were close, then.

"Have you seen enough?" Osgar asked. "Now you know where it is."

"I suppose so."

She rose and they crept back to the horses.

The hard part of the plan was getting out of the manor house at night in a way that would not cast suspicion upon her.

At sundown on Wednesday, Giselle collected her things in a wicker basket, and went to the pantry. She put a cheese and several apples and plums on top to cover them.

Eleanor spotted her coming out of the pantry. It was unusual enough for Giselle to go there in the evening, but to come out with a basket and head for the door was strange indeed. "Where are you going?"

"It is the anniversary of my mother's death," Giselle said. "I'm going to the church."

The Outlaws

Eleanor frowned. "But I didn't think that was until Friday." Everybody in the manor remembered the date of Hanelore's death. Giselle's father had always spent the night in the church to commemorate it.

"But she fell sick on the eighteenth." Hanelore had taken ill several days before her death, but Giselle now wasn't sure how many. She had been ten at the time. However, Eleanor and Baldwin had not been employed here then, so she was free to lie about it.

"I see. Well, then." Eleanor did not seem convinced, but Giselle did not wait for her to think of some other reason to protest. She went down the front stairs and made for the gate as fast as she could without arousing further suspicion.

When Giselle reached the churchyard, she paused at her parents' graves. No stone marked where William lay. If you didn't know he had been buried here you'd never be able to tell. Eustace had no interest in incurring the expense of a marker even though she had asked for it. She put her hand on Hanelore's stone. "Give me strength, Mother."

She wondered if Mother would approve what she was about to do. She listened as if the wind on the grass might provide an answer. But she heard nothing.

She went into the church.

Giselle waited an hour after full dark before she left the church.

A half moon hung low the southeast. It was still except for the humming of crickets.

She went back down the road and passed the manor house. In times of danger, there was a watch on the wall, but now there should be none since it was the middle of summer and Welsh raids came in the autumn after the barns were filled with the harvest. Still, Giselle felt as though dozens of eyes were watching as she took the track to the river.

The gurgle of the stream reached her ears and the trees, which grew thick along the banks, closed in so that she moved in gray-dappled darkness, and the aroma of water filled the air.

She removed her boots at the ford, and waded across. On the opposite bank, she dried her feet on her skirt before putting her boots back on. She took it as a good omen that she sat on a suitable stick. She collected the stick and continued onward.

The ground rose toward the hills and the trees fell away as she entered a broad field that had been sown with rye last year, but this year lay fallow, filled with tall grass that had not yet been cut for hay. The track wound through the field to the black cloak of trees that covered the hills ahead. Somewhere within that cloak lay the mine and the secret barn. A rabbit broke from the grass and dashed across the track, disappearing on the other side. Something swooped on it from above — an owl seeking its dinner. But the owl was disappointed. It flapped great wings to take flight from the grass, its talons empty, silhouetted against a swath of stars as it passed close above Giselle's head.

I wish I could fly like you, she thought.

She reached the place where the track entered the wood and darkness closed about her again.

It was so dark beneath the trees that she almost missed the fork to the right that led to the barn.

Giselle cringed at the faint grinding of pebbles beneath her feet. She didn't expect a watch upon the road, but she did not want to blunder into him if he turned out to be there.

The wind shifted and this time brought the stink of privies. She was getting close.

Then the forest opened up before her, a tapestry of grays, whites, and deep blacks, like a drawing in charcoal. The barn, low and squat with its peaked roof, sat there in the clearing.

She hugged the margin, alert for any sign of a night guard, but all was quiet. Nothing moved.

She dashed to one corner and pressed her back to the wall, feeling dizzy and more frightened than she had ever

The Outlaws

been. It was mad, this thing she planned to do. She knew it, and that she should back away. Eustace would kill her if he found out she was responsible. But hatred of him and the sense that she could deprive him of something he wanted obliterated her doubts.

Giselle put the basket down, and removed the underwear and flask of oil she had stolen the day before. She wrapped the underwear around the stick and poured the oil on the underwear. Then she arranged straw taken from the barn in a pile, and crouched over it with the flint and steel. She struck sparks into the pile. The sparks flared and went out. Frustrated and fearful of the noise, she struck harder and faster. Finally, one of the sparks kindled in the straw. She bent over it and blew upon them. The ember almost went out, but caught at last, and in moments she had enough of a flame. She held the oil-soaked underwear to the flame. The garment caught fire and blared into a torch that lit up the area around her.

Giselle held the torch to the thatch above her head. It was dry and the ends of the thatch glowed and burst into flame. She moved along the side of the barn to the far corner, lighting the eaves, and continued around the back, ready at any moment to throw down the torch and run for the forest.

But there was no shout of alarm, no sign that anyone was about.

With a pang of guilt that almost stayed her hand, she wondered if the night guard was *inside* the barn. If so, he might be burned to death. She hadn't thought of that possibility. It was too late now to stop, for flames were coursing up the thatch roof, illuminating the dark.

Halfway along the rear of the barn, her nerve failed at last. She thrust the torch into the thatch, and ran for the forest.

She circled back through the trees to the track. She was almost there when the barn door opened and a figure emerged and ran up toward the mine. By this time, the barn's roof had blossomed into a terrible pyre, flames reaching a hundred feet in the air, lighting up the area as if in daylight.

As she reached the fork, there was shouting at the mine. She ran as fast as she could toward the ford, heedless of the noise in her haste to get away.

CHAPTER 5

Hafton
August 1180

Someone rapped on the door to Giselle's chamber. She flinched, afraid that it might be Eustace again, but he wouldn't have bothered to knock.

Since the fire, she had retreated to her chamber and rarely went out. She could not bear to look people in the face after what she had done and what had transpired as a result.

The satisfaction of revenge had dissipated upon Eustace's return, replaced by guilt and shame. He had initiated an inquiry which was short and brutal. All the miners and villagers where interrogated, many harshly. When no evidence surfaced as to those responsible, he had hanged the watchman, a boy of twelve, and expelled his family. Then he had forced everyone in the manor, villagers and miners alike, to rebuilt the barn. He imposed even greater fines and rents to make up for the loss.

Even though Giselle's behavior on that night had been unusual, Eustace had not suspected she might be responsible. And when the beatings and questioning began, and the hanging took place, she had remained silent, paralyzed by fear. She knew that if his eyes turned to her and he put her to questioning, it would not take long for her to confess. He would kill her then, she was sure of it.

"Come!" Giselle called when the pounding on the door did not cease.

Eanfled stuck her head in. "M'lady, we've a visitor asking for his lordship."

A visitor! Oh, God, another person to see her humiliation. "Have Eleanor take care of him."

"She's in the village collecting eggs."

"What about Baldwin?"

"He's with my lord."

"And where are they?"

"Gone to the mine for the day."

"Well, what about Aelfwyn?"

"Still asleep," Eanfled sniffed.

That wasn't surprising. Aelfwyn liked to sleep until breakfast, which was at least an hour away. Giselle lifted the wad of raw wool which she had been carding from her lap, put it in the wicker basket at her feet, and stood up. She wasn't going to be able to avoid seeing the visitor after all. "Very well, I'm coming."

She paused at the master bedchamber. Giselle heard a creak as Aelfwyn turned over in bed. There was a thump as bare feet hit the floorboards. Aelfwyn was getting up. In moments, she would call for a maid. Hearing the same alert as Giselle, Eanfled hurried downstairs, not wanting to be the one who had to answer the summons. Aelfwyn was demanding and had a bad temper after she had just awakened.

Giselle descended the stairs to the hall. The visitor turned toward her. He was an old man, beyond sixty, his hair a dense bush of thick gray. A thicket of gray beard masked his face. He was a big man with broad shoulders and thick arms. His shirt and hose were wool, threadbare and patched in spots, instead of linen, the blue and red color dulled with age and hard use. He carried a sword on a worn leather belt. Giselle crossed the room to him.

"I am Giselle," she said. "Welcome to Hafton manor."

The old man measured her with cool gray eyes, eyes that seemed rather familiar. "So, you are the wife."

Giselle was startled by his directness. "I have that . . . singular honor."

The old man grunted. "How old are you, child?"

"Fifteen."

"Are you ill?"

"No."

"You look a bit thin. Don't they feed you enough here? Any chance you're pregnant yet?"

"Goodness, no!"

"Too bad. Diotte would like to be a grandmother."

279

The Outlaws

Giselle's forehead wrinkled in puzzled astonishment. Who was this man? And who was Diotte? What gave him leave to be so familiar with her?

She was thinking about things to say to put him in his place when he chuckled, showing good strong teeth. "He hasn't spoken of us then. I thought not. We're an embarrassment to him these days. I am Warain, Eustace's grandfather. Diotte's his mother. I've come for him."

Giselle was startled to learn that Eustace had a grandfather and this was the first time she had heard mention of a mother. But this made them family — her family now. Poor relations, by the look of them. Well, that was no reason for her to be rude. She managed to say, "He's at the mine across the river. I'll have him fetched for you. Won't you sit down and have a drink? We'll be having breakfast soon, if you're hungry."

"No, thank you. I must see him right away."

"I'll take you, then. Eanfled, please have Osgar saddle my mare."

On the way, they had a chance to talk, mostly about little things, and Giselle found him to be friendly once you got beyond his gruffness. He had a farm at a bend in the River Avon south of Warwick, a small place that in theory was a knight's fee, but poor. The land had been in the family for over a hundred years, since before the time of the first King William. The original honor had been larger. Over the intervening century, the family had sold off parcels to pay debts. He lived no better than any tenant farmer now.

When the cart track up the hill from the river broke into the clearing at the mine, they found Eustace with one foot on top of a pile of stones, talking to the head miner, finger jabbing for emphasis of some point. Baldwin stooped, picked up a rock, weighed it in his hand, then heaved it into the woods. The head miner shouted to one of the mine boys to retrieve the rock. At the sight of Warain, Eustace came toward them.

"You're a long way from home, Grandfather," Eustace said.

"And my backside knows it, boy."

Eustace mouth turned down. He did not like being called a boy, now that he was a knight and held two manors. But he surprised Giselle, who expected a sharp retort. He said, "It's Mother, isn't it."

Warain nodded his head. "She's dying."

As soon as they returned to the house, preparations were made for a departure that afternoon. Horses were saddled and packs prepared for the packhorses, food and clothes gathered, and weapons oiled and laid out.

Warain watched the proceedings with Giselle from a seat on the steps, where he drank wine from a wooden bowl she had brought out for him.

It was apparent from the preparations that Eustace planned to accompany the old man without her. "You're not going?" Warain asked Giselle.

Giselle looked at the ground. "I'm sure he doesn't want me to."

"Hmmmph," Warain grunted. He heaved himself to his feet and crossed the yard to the spot where Eustace and le Bec were tightening girths and checking bridles.

"She says she isn't going," Warain said to Eustace.

"She'll just be in the way," Eustace said.

"Your mother said I was to bring her along, if she'll come."

Eustace's lips tightened, but he marched across the yard and stopped before Giselle. "You're invited if you want to come," he said in a tone that suggested she should refuse.

"She's dying. Of course I will come."

Eustace looked over her head to Eleanor, who was standing at the top of the steps. "Get her things ready. She's coming, too."

The Outlaws

Warain's house lay at the northern edge of its village, big and careworn, with rot on the corner posts and patches on the plaster walls, an old house ready to be torn down and replaced.

A cook with a stained apron across her round belly and flour on her forearms came out of the house when they rode into the yard.

Eustace jumped off his horse. "Gretta!" he cried and embraced her.

Gretta tapped him on the head with a spoon as she drew back. "Look how tall you've gotten. And who's that beauty with you — your wife? We heard you had got married."

Eustace's grin withered. "Yes, that's her." He went by Gretta into the house.

Warain reached for Giselle to help her down. He had no trouble lifting her from the saddle. "Child," Warain said, when he had set her down, "I've known chickens heavier than you. Gretta! We need to fatten this girl up! She's not big enough to bear children!"

"She's barely a woman yet," Gretta said, putting a fat arm around Giselle's shoulders. "Next year's a good time for her to start having babies."

Giselle smiled politely, a little shocked that a house servant would be so familiar not only with her but with Eustace, who disliked familiarity from anyone, and let Gretta lead her inside. When they entered the house, they found Eustace waiting at the foot of the stairs at the other side of the hall. He asked Gretta, "Is she awake?"

"Yes, I just left her."

Eustace pounded up the stairs. "Don't tire her out!" Gretta called after him.

Giselle followed more slowly. She stood in the doorway, afraid to enter. Eustace sat on his mother's bed with one of her hands in both of his. Diotte's arm was a stick; her face withered and sunken. It was clear she had been a beautiful woman once. She had long silken brown hair, soft eyes, and a small nose that turned upward at the end.

"Mama," Eustace said. He glared at Giselle and she backed out of the doorway and closed the door.

Giselle could hear them talking through the door.

"Why did you send her away?" Diotte asked. "That's your new wife, isn't it? I so want to meet her before I die."

"Mama —" Eustace began to cry. "I don't want you to die."

Giselle had not thought Eustace capable of caring for anyone, and despite all the pain and humiliation she had suffered, she felt sorry for him.

"I'm ready to go. I'm tired of the hurt," Diotte said.

Later, Eustace came downstairs to get something to eat. Giselle slipped upstairs while he washed up and went into Diotte's room. It might be the only opportunity she had to pay her respects. Giselle thought she might be asleep, and was about to withdraw when Diotte said, "Come in and sit down."

Giselle settled on a stool by the bed. Diotte turned her head to look at her; even that slight movement seemed made at great effort. "What is your name?" Diotte asked.

"Giselle."

"You are a pretty thing. I was a pretty thing once, too. It was my misfortune. Why does he dislike you?"

"He doesn't really want me. He married me to please his father so that the earl could obtain my inheritance."

Diotte sighed. "That sounds like Roger."

Giselle crossed her arms and hugged her knees. "They beat me until I consented."

Diotte chuckled. "I went willingly. But I wasn't lucky enough to become a wife. Not enough money for Roger, you see. You're lucky in that."

"I wouldn't call it luck."

Diotte grimaced. Giselle leaned forward and put a palm on the older woman's forehead. It was hot. A rag lay beside a

The Outlaws

wooden bowl on the bedside table. She dipped the rag in the water, wrung it out and daubed Diotte's forehead.

"Fever's not the problem child, it's the pain — it's in my bones." She pointed to a clay vial on the windowsill. "That. Get that, please."

Giselle brought over the vial. Diotte needed help to hold it steady at her lips to drink.

Diotte made a distressed face. "There isn't enough. I'll need more."

Giselle sniffed the vial. "What does it do?"

"It dulls the pain."

"I'll get more, but where do I go?"

"There's an old woman in the village. Take the last lane before the mill. Her house is the last on the left. Her name is Gerda. Tell her you've come from me. You won't have to pay then."

"I'll go right away."

Giselle met Eustace at the door. He was bearing a tray with a bowl of soup, a quarter loaf of bread, and cheese. "Wait," he said to her. He put the tray down and grasped her hand, forcing her to surrender the vial. "What were you doing with this?"

"Going for more. It's empty."

"Go downstairs. I'll do it."

"She's in pain now."

Eustace put his hand on her neck. His touch was gentle, but he way he stroked with his thumb told her he was not far from strangling her. "Do what I say."

Giselle backed out of the room as he shut the door.

Gerda was sitting on a bench beside her front door watching the sun go down when Eustace reined his horse to a halt at her gate. He tied the reins to a fence post and crossed the yard. They say she had been the most beautiful girl for miles around, too — until Diotte was born. She was over seventy now, he reckoned and showed every year.

"I remember you," she said. "The earl's bastard. I hit you with a rock once." Eustace had lived in the village from the time the earl cast off his mother, when he was three, until he was six and the earl came and took him away. The village children had sometimes taunted her from the lane. She kept a bucket of stones of her own for such moments, and had a good arm.

"I think I still have the lump on the head," Eustace said.

"At least you didn't cry. What do you want?"

"My mother needs more of your potion." He gave her the clay vial.

"Poor thing." Gerda went into the house. Eustace did not follow. It was dark and stank of clammy, nasty things.

Gerda emerged with the vial. "I made this one stronger than before. Tell her no more than two spoonfuls at a time. More could kill her."

"I'll tell her."

"Be certain she understands. The last I saw her, she was in terrible pain. She may be tempted to take too much because of it."

"I'll give it to her myself."

"Good idea. Keep it out of her reach." Gerda sat back down on the bench. The sun had set and the sky was red and orange in the west, the colors fading fast.

Eustace gripped the vial but did not turn away.

"Is there something else?" Gerda asked.

"Yes."

"A love potion, perhaps? For your new wife?"

Eustace snorted. "You know about her?"

"Warain is bursting at the prospect of little Eustaces."

"No. I need something altogether different."

Gerda waited for him to go on.

"My wife carries a child," he lied.

"My congratulations. Does your grandfather know?"

"It is another man's. It seems that she was not a virgin when we married."

The Outlaws

She rubbed her chin. "Well, well. Old Gerda can help you there. She's helped many a lassie with that problem."

She went back in the house and returned with another clay vial. "This is an extract of hyssop, the fleur-de-lis — that pretty little blue flower over there. Put no more than a spoonful into a cup of beer or wine. That should be enough to cause her to expel the child. More at one time and you risk killing her. Like the poppy, the hyssop can be deadly if not used carefully."

"How much is here?"

"Enough to end three or four pregnancies. You may need more than one dose, you see. You have to try again if the first dose fails."

"One spoonful it is," he said.

He stood up and deposited a leather purse on the bench. It clinked with the sound of money.

"Get yourself a new gown. You look like a witch."

Gerda cackled, displaying the three teeth she had left. She liked his little joke. "Oh, I will, your honor. I will."

It was dark by the time Eustace returned to the house, and everyone there had settled into bed, the remains of the coals covered with clay tops and the windows shuttered.

Eustace trudged up the stairs and entered Diotte's room.

"Do you have it?" she asked.

"Yes, Mama."

"Give it to me!"

He pulled out the cork, wondering what to use for a spoon to measure the dose. Her hand, gnarled as a hawk's foot, grasped his forearm. "Hurry," she whispered. He couldn't stand to see her in such pain. Her suffering was like a knife in his belly.

He put the bottle on the table. "It's here, Mama. By the bed."

She turned to search for it. "Where?"

"On the table." He held the candle so she could see.

He backed toward the door. It wasn't murder if she drank it herself, and it wasn't suicide if she had no idea that to drink the whole meant death, so she could find a measure of peace at last and go to God and be buried in consecrated ground, untarnished by sin. I will bear the sin, he thought.

Her hand closed on the bottle as he went out and shut the door.

Giselle found him in the early morning, asleep at the top of the stairs, leaning against a post. There were tear stains on his face.

"Eustace," she said, shaking his shoulder. "Go to bed."

He sat up and rubbed his eyes. In the moment before he looked at her and realized who had awakened him, there was a terrible sadness in his eyes. Then his expression hardened and he pushed her away. "Leave me alone."

He stumbled downstairs. She heard the door bang as he went into the yard. She watched from a window as he went to the well to wash his face in the bucket left on its stone rim.

Giselle knocked on the closed door to Diotte's room. There was no answer. She opened the door and tiptoed across to the bed. Her toe kicked a small object lying on the floor, sending it careening off a baseboard. Giselle started at the unexpected racket, fearful that she might wake Diotte, but the old woman did not stir. She lay on her back, her mouth open. There was something alarming in her slack-jawed expression. Giselle put the back of her hand on Diotte's forehead. It was cold, and she was not breathing.

After a moment, Giselle went downstairs to tell the others.

CHAPTER 6

Shelburgh castle
Autumn and Winter 1180

In mid-September, FitzWalter summoned Eustace to Shelburgh to account for the income from Harleigh and Hafton in preparation for the annual trip to Winchester at the end of the month, when FitzWalter in turn would account for his holdings to the Exchequer. Eustace preferred to leave Giselle behind, as usual, but FitzWalter made a special point of requiring her to come.

While they were there, Blanche, who was six-months pregnant, went into early labor and bore a son. Astonishingly, the baby was born alive, but lived less than a day. FitzWalter had him baptized as John.

Afterward, FitzWalter was withdrawn and angry. He did not say a word to Blanche, even when she had tried to apologize for the baby. She left for her favorite manor near Gloucester, where she had grown up.

The Yule season, normally a festive time at Shelburgh, passed with muted celebrations without Lady Blanche, who knew how to make parties lively. FitzWalter drank too much, brooded, and beat two servants. He wrote a will, which he kept a secret, and fought with Eustace over Aelfwyn, who had come with them. "You spend more time with your whore than your wife!" FitzWalter shouted at him.

"What does it matter to you?" Eustace shouted back. "I brought you Hafton back!"

FitzWalter knocked him down. Although he was thirty-five years older and Eustace was taller, FitzWalter could still beat him in a fight. He stood over a stunned and furious Eustace. "You may be the only child I ever have who lived. I'll not see the end of my name because you can't stand her."

"You could have done better by me than her."

"You're lucky you got as much." FitzWalter spun away and left Eustace on the floor.

When Giselle tried to help Eustace to his feet, he pushed her away so that she almost fell into the hearth. The hem of her gown caught fire but le Bec cut the flaming skirt away and saved her from a bad burn.

Eustace threw her a blanket. "Cover yourself. You are indecent," he said, and stalked out to the snow-covered courtyard.

The next morning, Eustace came to Giselle's room while she was still in bed. She thought he wanted to lie with her, but he sat on the edge of the bed and made no attempt to pull down the covers.

"I want you to do a favor for me," he said.

"Why should I, when you treat your dogs better?"

For a moment, she thought he would hit her. But he said, "I will trade a favor for a favor."

"I am expensive."

"The way you dress I would never have known it. I've seen farm girls who dress better than you."

"Yes, you're fucking one right now."

He laughed. "What do you want?"

"I want to be mistress of Hafton. In truth as well as in name."

"So you can order Aelfwyn and Eleanor around?"

"Just so."

"I'll give you Eleanor, but not Aelfwyn."

"Then it would be better for us all if she lived at Harleigh. You like it better there, anyway."

He thought about that. "All right. Here's what I want. I want you to find out what Roger's will says."

Giselle laughed. "Why — afraid he's disinherited you?" No, she thought, that can't be right. She had an inspiration. "Of course — whether he's made you an heir at all?"

He gave her a nasty look confirming her suspicions. She went on, "Why don't you get Aelfwyn to do that for you? All she has to do is fuck the clerk. He'll give her whatever she wants."

The Outlaws

"The clerk can't be bribed, even with that. He's incorruptible. And Aelfwyn can't read."

"Then why not do it yourself?"

"You read Latin well enough and you'll attract less notice than I will."

"What if I'm caught? Roger will know you put me up to it."

"I'll take the risk."

Giselle thought hard about it. What did she have to lose, really? "All right. I'll do it. But you must find a way to keep the clerk out of the writing office."

Although the notion of sneaking into the writing office while the clerk was distracted seemed easy as Giselle lay in her bed, the actual execution proved to be more difficult.

The writing office had been in a little room off the chapel, but when FitzWalter built the stone wall around the bailey, it moved to a tower on the first floor. It was a quiet, isolated room, and its three narrow windows overlooking the field to the south of the castle provided adequate light and pleasant views. Above it was an apartment given over to the deputy castellan and his family.

The difficulty lay in the fact that Giselle had no reason to go there. She could not gain access without someone seeing her and wondering what she was up to.

Giselle pondered this problem for a day, and then spent several more becoming acquainted with the deputy's wife, Clarimond, and her children, two small boys and a baby girl. Mere acquaintance did not give her any reason to visit the apartment, but then the baby fell ill. Illnesses in babies was a matter of great concern, for many of them did not recover. Giselle obtained a flask of goat's milk and a basket of dried fruit, and crossed the bailey to the tower when the clerk was in the hall. Eustace watched her go and set about his part.

Clarimond was surprised and grateful for the attention, and it was almost an hour before Giselle could descend the stair to the first floor.

There the stair paused at a landing which was walled off from the writing office, creating a tight compartment with a door. Giselle tried the latch. It lifted and the door swung open. There was thumping above her head. Giselle looked up to see one of Clarimond's sons, the four-year-old, peering down at her. She put her finger to her lips. The boy turned away and she heard him running across the room. She waited a moment, but Clarimond did not come to investigate.

Giselle took a deep breath and stuck her head in the chamber. No one was there. A broad table with a slanted writing platform sat under the windows. There was was a series of honeycombed cabinets around the walls containing rolled up documents. She was appalled at the sight of so many parchments and vellums, none with any indication of what they were about. It would take hours to find the will, even if it was here. She doubted that Eustace could keep the clerk occupied while she conducted a search.

She shut the door.

The movement of a shadow caught her eye. She looked up, thinking that Clarimond's son had returned to the top of the stairs, but it was Clarimond herself. Clarimond smiled and descended to Giselle.

"You're looking for the will, aren't you?" Clarimond asked.

"Why would you think that?"

"Everyone knows how much your husband wants to succeed the earl. He's been in knots ever since the earl rewrote his will."

Giselle did not answer.

"He won't, you know."

"How would I know that?"

"You wouldn't, but I do."

"You know what's in the will? I can't believe that."

The Outlaws

Clarimond shrugged. "I heard Earl Roger tell the clerk what to put in it. I heard them through the floor. He was drunk and talked more loudly than he should have. You know how he is when he gets drunk."

"I know he gets mean."

"Our earl? Mean? I don't know what you're talking about."

"Why are you taunting me like this, if Eustace will never be earl?"

"You will have power, eventually."

"What are you talking about?"

"The earl provided that if you have sons, your eldest will inherit the honor. If there are no sons, the honor goes to Fulbert de Membri."

"Who is that?"

"A nephew. The best of an otherwise bad lot, I understand. I've never met him. He's never come here and we don't get about much. I hope that you remember this favor when your son succeeds. He will require the guidance of his elders, who will be in the position to favor those who have helped them."

"I shall remember. Thank you."

Clarimond turned away and climbed the stairs, where the baby had begun crying again.

Giselle went down to the bailey.

Eustace absorbed Giselle's report with a face that grew ever more sour. "You're making this up," he said.

"You can believe it or not."

"You believe it?"

"I don't know what to think."

Eustace was quiet for a while. "He hates me because of Mother."

"Why? It's not as though she was a common girl."

"You don't know the half. She left him. He never got over it. He hates it when people don't do what he wants. Women just don't *leave* him. He discards them."

"So punishing you is his revenge?"

"It's always been about punishing Mother. That's why he took me away. To hurt her. Because she loved me."

"I'm so sorry." Giselle was surprised that she meant this.

"I'll never be earl. His final punishment."

"You couldn't really have expected it, could you?"

"I thought there was hope. Foolish me."

She saw now that this was the one thing that he wanted most, perhaps the only thing that mattered. "No matter what you do, you can never please him, can you."

Eustace put down his cup and grasped her wrist. He drew her to her feet. "I can give him the heir of the blood that he wants. Perhaps he'll feel better then."

He led her toward the stairs and their bedchamber.

CHAPTER 7

Hafton
March 1181

Eustace packed Aelfwyn off to Harleigh as he promised, and gave Giselle a free hand, more or less, at Hafton, although she found her discretion limited by the need to remit to Earl FitzWalter as much of the fines and produce that could be squeezed from the villagers. She had not considered the possibility that this bargain would make her complicit in their suffering, and now that she was, she did not know what to do about it. She'd had vague thoughts about softening the regime, but when she presided over the manor court under Eustace's gaze, and imposed the same burdensome fines however reluctantly, the look of disappointment on people's faces was almost more than she could bear.

Eustace for his part spent every day at Hafton, and every night he performed his husbandly duties. Giselle had never taken pleasure in this, and it was clear that Eustace did not either. It was something that had to be done, but thankfully it was over in moments, without fuss or bother, like having to swallow an unpleasant tonic.

After the first month, Eustace went to Harleigh. He was gone a week. After that, he alternated a week at Hafton and a week at Harleigh. Giselle was glad for the respite. Eustace's spirits seemed to improve as well. He didn't snap at her as much when he was there, if he paid any attention to her at all.

Eustace returned from Harleigh on a day when low clouds rolled in from the west, and the air smelled like rain. He came through the door to the hall looking more grumpy than usual, and his eyes were red-rimmed, his nose raw, and he sneezed twice before he even said good day. His face, when he pretended to kiss her cheek, seemed to radiate heat.

"You have a fever," she said, feigning concern, for she had the thought that perhaps he might die from it. Wouldn't that be good fortune? And hated herself for thinking such a thing, although the notion of the freedom it might bring lingered in the back of her mind. "Get to bed right this instant."

She took his arm and towed him upstairs to the master bedchamber. He seemed to like the attention, but then he always liked being the center of attention.

As the maids undressed him and tucked him under the sheets, he croaked, "Get packed. We're leaving in the morning."

"We're not going anywhere until this fever breaks. You're not fit to ride across the bailey."

"It's nothing. I got here from Harleigh, didn't I? I'll be fine tomorrow. Go get packed."

She stood back, fists on her hips. "Where are we going?"

"None of your business. Just get ready."

Put off that he would not tell her, nonetheless she went to her room with Eanfled to pack. Disobedience was not a possibility. Even though she had a free hand at Hafton, as he had promised, it was not that free. She still had to obey direct orders.

"Will you be taking anyone with you?" Eanfled asked.

"Just you, I suppose." Giselle looked toward the door, which stood open a crack. She said in a lower voice, "I don't trust any of the others."

"It's a good thing," Eanfled sniffed. "I suppose I should pack too."

"Yes."

Eanfled went out and Giselle finished packing her trunk. It was hard to decide what to take because she had no idea where she was going.

When Eanfled came back, Giselle was sitting at her window, looking at the field beyond the wall. Low gray clouds were drifting in. She said without turning, "It will rain soon. Traveling will be dreadful if we really go tomorrow."

"M'lady," Eanfled said, "you need to hear this."

The Outlaws

Giselle turned from the window to see that Osgar stood beside Eanfled. They both looked upset.

"What is it?" Giselle asked.

"My lady," Osgar said. He had his cap in his hands, twisting it out of shape.

"Go on, Osgar."

"My lady . . ."

Eanfled poked him in the ribs. "Out with it!"

"All right," Osgar said. "When I was at Harleigh, I heard our lord talking with Aelfwyn about her child."

"What about it?" This was the first that Giselle had heard about any child by Aelfwyn.

"God's breath, Osgar! Where's your tongue when you really need it?" Eanfled blurted. "You're to be sent to a convent until Aelfwyn births her brat. Then our lord will force you to claim it as yours."

Osgar nodded to confirm this.

"To claim it as mine?" Giselle asked.

"Yes," Osgar said.

"That's absurd." Giselle shook her head, refusing to believe it.

"He'll find a way to make you bend," Eanfled said. "You know it."

Giselle leaned her hands against the window sill. The promise that Eustace had made at Shelburgh had expired now that he no longer had a use for her. She had the terrifying thought that he might even lock her up somewhere, claiming that she had gone mad.

"If I agree, Aelfwyn's child and not mine will inherit Hafton," she said, thinking aloud.

"That's true," Eanfled said, and sat on the bed with her chin in the palm of her hand.

It began to rain the next morning as the servants brought down Giselle's trunk and she followed in riding clothes. Eustace watched the rain fall from the doorway until a gust of wind left him wet. He closed the door, his face drawn and pale. He passed Giselle without a word or a look, and climbed the stairs to the master's chamber. Eleanor rushed after him, asking over and over, "My lord, are you all right?"

"You won't be going anywhere now," Baldwin said, settling on a chair by the hearth. He motioned one of the servants to put more wood on the fire.

"A pity," Giselle said. "I so like journeys in the rain. All that good mud, the slipping about, and falling down."

Baldwin looked at her under sagging brows, but didn't respond. He had accommodated himself to the bargain Giselle had made with Eustace better than Eleanor, who had fled to her room for a week when it was explained to her. Since then, they had stayed out of each other's way and pretended the other wasn't there. Baldwin, though, was Giselle's minder when Eustace was away, and though the leash she had to contend with was long, it was there nonetheless.

There wasn't anything to do now with the rain, not anything Giselle cared to do, at any rate. The prospect of leaving and not knowing where she was going left her too anxious for the usual activities, carding wool, sewing, playing games, telling stories, or reading. Wherever it was had to be some kind of imprisonment.

She considered trying to pry it out of Baldwin. He knew, of course. Every so often, she caught his eyes on her. He looked away as soon as she noticed, but could not keep a faint smile from his lips. She doubted that he would tell her, however. It was some place she was sure to dislike, and he did not want to soften the shock of it by revealing the truth.

Giselle looked up in the direction of the master bedchamber, thinking that Eleanor might know as well. Eleanor would be unable to restrain her impulse to gloat, and would spill the secret. But then Eustace, and certainly Baldwin, would anticipate that, so she probably had not been told yet.

The Outlaws

What did it matter, anyway? She couldn't escape whatever fate Eustace had planned for her. She was just a wife, and powerless. She had no friends to ask for help, not that anyone would give it in a dispute between a husband and a wife of their class. She had to try to make the best of it.

The messenger arrived in the late afternoon. The arrival of strangers to such an out-of-the-way place as Hafton was unusual enough, but a messenger was extraordinary. He stood dripping just inside the doorway while a servant tried to relieve him of his cloak. He declined the courtesy, saying, "Thank you, but I don't plan to stay."

The messenger's hand came out of a waxed pouch with a folded piece of parchment that was unmistakably a letter. Baldwin told a servant to fetch the letter. As the steward, it was his responsibility to read all letters first before passing them on to the lord, but the messenger refused to put the parchment in the servant's hand.

"I am to deliver this into the hands of the Lady Giselle," he said. "Is she here?"

"I am." Giselle stood up, astonished at this announcement. No one had ever sent her a letter before and she could not imagine who might do so now.

Baldwin was astounded as well, and his mouth worked to make a protest or mount a question, but Giselle preempted whatever thoughts he might have by hurrying across the hall.

The messenger handed her the letter with a slight bow.

"Are you sure you won't stay?" Giselle asked. "Supper is not far off."

"No, I must reach Knighton before dark."

"Well, have some ale to see you on your way." Giselle waved to one of the maids to fetch a pitcher and cup. As the messenger drank, she remembered an important detail about letters.

"How much are you owed?" she asked, since letters were supposed to be paid for by the recipient.

"Nothing," the messenger said, handing back the cup. "It's paid for. Good day to you, my lady."

"Such as it is, thank you. The same to you. Safe journey."

The messenger bowed and went out into the rain.

Giselle settled into her chair across the fire from Baldwin, conscious of his eyes on her and his fingers working as if to grasp an invisible object, no doubt the letter, as she broke the seal and opened it.

It was written in English in the neat, clear hand of a professional letter writer, and read:

To Giselle de Hafton, from Matilda Attebrook, Greetings. I hope this letter finds you well, although I must confess, we do not hold out hope that your situation is to your satisfaction after the events of last year. I write to let you know that we are all right, but more importantly to deliver a piece of news that I hope will provide you some comfort. After we were forced out of Hafton, I discovered that I was with child by your father. I have delivered a boy. He is strong and in good health. I thought you would like to know that you are not the last of your father's blood, and that you have a brother, even if he comes from me and is a bastard. If by some chance you should ever make it to London, you can find us at the Red Lion. It is an inn on Holborn Street beside the River Fleet. I hope this finds you well. Your servant.

Giselle folded the letter on her lap and stared into the fire. She had a brother, a half-brother and a bastard, but he was still a brother. She could not believe it. Yet here was the proof. Bastards did not have rights unless the family acknowledged them and made allowances. She wondered what her father would do. It didn't matter. What counted now was what she would do.

The Outlaws

She lay the letter upon the fire and watched it burn. Baldwin almost reached for it.

"Who was it from, my lady?" he asked, unhappy that he was unable to rescue the letter.

"If I said Lady Blanche would you be so nosy?"

"Oh. Was it?"

"Perhaps it was. You shall just have to wonder."

Lady Blanche was as possible a prospect as one could imagine, although a distant one, but the suggestion would have to tide Baldwin and Eleanor over. But when Eustace got well, he would want to know too, and Giselle wouldn't be able to resist telling him.

Yet that might not matter.

For an idea, a mad, reckless idea, formed in her mind.

There was a way out, after all.

The good thing about fevers was that people didn't get over them right away. Once they took hold, it could often take more than a week to recover, supposing that the victim was lucky enough not to die in the interim. And Giselle had the feeling that Eustace was not likely to die. So she might have that long, but the sooner she acted, the better her chances of success.

First she needed money. Because neither Eustace nor Baldwin allowed her any, she had to steal it.

No one had any use for money on the manor, and any money thereabout was either buried under someone's floor, or in the manor's strong box. Giselle doubted that it had been moved back to the master's chamber, but to be certain she slipped into on the pretense of showing concern for Eustace, not that he needed it, for with Eleanor and two of the maids, there was enough concern floating about in the chamber to choke an ox. She lingered at the bedside, even deigning to touch his forehead, finding it blazing hot, long enough to determine that the strong box was not chained to its usual bedpost. That meant it was still in the chamber across the corridor that Baldwin and Eleanor shared.

She lifted the latch to their door once and found it locked.

Locks could be picked, but she had no expertise in that craft, so it would take time as she fumbled about, exposing her to the chance of discovery if anyone happened by.

There was one other way into the room. It had a window on the back side of the house overlooking the strip of ground between the house and the surrounding embankment.

Beneath that window was the thatched roof of a shed that ran the length of the house and sheltered the back door to the undercroft. Unfortunately, the roof reached as high was the floor of the hall, a good story below Baldwin's window. To get to that window, she'd need a ladder. Fortunately, no good manor house was without a ladder: there was one stored in the undercroft beneath the hall.

She went to her chamber and packed a saddlebag with a spare gown and stockings, her extra comb, a French romance that had belonged to Athelhild, a book of Latin poems by Ovid that she had never finished reading, and a few other odds and ends that had not found their way into her trunk. There were things in the trunk she wished she had, but it was down in the hall, and she couldn't get to them without provoking more questions from Baldwin, who would be suspicious at any unusual activity.

She dropped the saddlebag onto the roof of the shed, beneath her window. It landed with a thud that made her cringe, then slid down the thatch and landed in a puddle. Lord, everything would be soaking and the books might be ruined!

Giselle hurried down to the hall. Her cloak lay across her trunk by the front door. She put on the cloak, concealing the fact that she also took up her father's dagger.

"Where are you going in this wet, my lady?" Baldwin asked.

301

The Outlaws

Giselle had an excuse prepared against just such a question. "Oh, to check on supper. I've a desire for something warm rather than leftovers. And our lord needs a broth."

Baldwin nodded, eyes returning to the fire. "Very good. A warm supper would be welcome on a day like this."

Giselle rushed down the wooden stairs outside, careful not to fall, as leather soles often slipped in the wet, and a tumble on the steep stairs could be painful. No one was about in the bailey, as she hoped, since no one liked to be out in the rain if they could help it.

She ran around the back of the house, retrieved the saddlebags from the puddle, and tossed them over the wall.

Heart pounding, she glanced up at the windows high above her head. They were shut against the rain, but she imagined someone throwing one open and spotting her standing where she had no business standing.

The rain prickled her face, and she wanted nothing more than to return to the relative comfort of the hall, but her wishes could not turn things back the way they used to be. She had to do the awful thing that was in her mind.

She went back around the house to the stable.

She saddled her favorite horse, a mare named Jenny who was more affectionate than most people.

She patted the horse on the nose, and fed Jenny a handful of grain. She said, "Sorry, m'lady, to take you out in this wet." Jenny nuzzled her shoulder as if to say she didn't mind. Giselle smiled and drew her cloak around her again, as she peeked out the stable door. The house was closed and quiet; all the shutters were up on the kitchen and the only signs of life from either place was the smoke leaking out of the holes in the roofs.

"Time to go, Jenny," she murmured. "Not a sound, now, understand?"

She ran across the bailey, leading the horse, and passed through the gate.

The smart thing now was to keep going, but she retrieved the saddle bags, and tied the mare to a stone at the lip of the ditch.

Then she went back in the bailey.

She dragged the ladder and a shovel from the undercroft, leaned the ladder against the awning, and climbed up. The awning was steeper that she expected and she had to grasp the thatch with her fingers and toes to prevent sliding off, and there was the danger that the cross bars supporting the thatch would not bear her weight. There was a lot of creaking and sagging, but they held. She pulled the ladder up with her with a great deal of struggle.

Finally, she managed to plant the foot of the ladder beneath the window of Baldwin's chamber. She lashed it to the thatch with her belt.

Then she climbed to the window.

It was barred, of course, but Giselle was able to worm father's dagger through the joint in the panels and push up the bar. The shutters swung open. She clambered over the sill into the room.

It was dark inside, except for the gray light from the late afternoon sky, which threw a rectangle on the floor. Like all chambers, it was sparsely furnished, the main furniture the bed, two chairs, a wardrobe, a pair of trunks stacked on top of each other indicating they were not being used, and a table by the window supporting a wash basin. There was no sign of the money box.

Giselle looked under the bed, but saw a single shoe.

Someone paused at the door, and she nearly died from fright, but the footsteps continued down the corridor.

The other possibility was inside the wardrobe. She pulled the doors open. She expected to find a tidy array, since Eleanor was so adamant about order, but instead found a heap of clothing at the bottom. Giselle burrowed into the clothing, and her hands met a hard object. She grasped it, and pulled out the money box. She put the clothing back in the wardrobe and shut the doors.

The Outlaws

The box was padlocked. Eustace had one key; she had no idea where he kept it. Baldwin had the other, which he wore on a chain round his neck with a medallion of Saint Mary. If she was going to get into the box, she would need to smash it open. She couldn't do that here, of course. It would make too much noise, so she staggered to the window. Even though it was not that big — perhaps a foot long by half a foot tall — it was so heavy that she struggled to lift it to the sill. She climbed out around it, and went down the ladder.

Unbuckling the ladder from the thatch without losing the box was a challenge that she failed, as the ladder slipped from her fingers and toppled to the ground.

She cradled the box in her lap, aghast at the utter failure of her plan. She was now trapped on the awning with no way to get down. She inched down to the lip and stared at the ground. The distance between the awning and the dirt had not seemed so far when she stood upon the ground, but from this vantage point it seemed an impossible distance. She imagined breaking a leg and lying there in the puddle for hours before someone finally found her.

There was nothing for it but to jump. So she dropped the box. It made a terrific splash in the puddle that surely must have alerted everyone within miles. But no window opened to enable an investigation of the sound.

Then she followed.

She landed by the box and fell over into the puddle, getting as soaked as if in a bath, grateful that nothing had broken and she could still walk. She rose, clammy and wretched, hefted the box and the shovel, and lumbered out of the bailey.

Time was critical. While Baldwin was not the most attentive of persons, he was sure to have noticed her long absence. It did not take that much time to visit the kitchen, after all. She heaved the box onto the saddle. Giselle have expected Jenny to shy away, but the mare continued cropping grass as if nothing was happening. Good old Jennie. What a dear.

She mounted, balancing the box on the pommel of the saddle. It would be awkward riding this way. Giselle would not be able to go fast, which she needed to do, until she got rid of the box.

Well, she would have to make do. She urged the horse forward into the woods, which lay like a dark wall ahead.

She did not dare ride through the village, and instead went east and up the hill, through the woods, before turning south when she felt confident that she could not be seen. She came out of the woods at the crest of the hill overlooking the village from the south across that long open field. There was a small stone hut used by the village shepherds here. It was unoccupied this time of year. She dragged the box into the hut, where it was dry, if not warm.

She put the box on the dirt floor, breathing hard from the exertion. She had intended to take what she needed, not the entire box, hoping that the theft would not be missed. But she had not thought things through, nor contemplated the enormity of what she had just done, and the repercussions it would have, for she was not the only person who might pay for the loss of the box.

"Forgive me," she said, "Please forgive me. I'm so sorry."

She struck the box with the shovel. It took several blows before two of the wooden panels on its top broke. Giselle pulled up the broken panels and scooped out handfuls of pennies, which she put in a sack. Then she dragged the box to a corner of the hut, where she buried it. She hoped no one would be able to tell she had been here.

Teeth chattering, she changed into the old clothes she had brought. The dry wool and old linen felt good against her skin. Her boots were soaked and cold, but she had no replacements for them so they went back on her feet.

The Outlaws

She returned to the horse outside, where the rain had subsided to a misty drizzle. It was almost dark, and she could barely make out the village from here. But she could see it behind closed eyes, every roof and tree and rutted path. The vision made her cry.

With a groan, Giselle pulled herself into the saddle and rode over the crest of the hill.

PART 4

1183

CHAPTER 1

Limoges, Limousin
February 1183

When Robert Attebrook rode into Limoges with word that Duke Richard Plantagenet was one day's march away at the head of an army bent on attacking his elder brother, Young Henry dismissed the warning as rumormongering. Nobody thought it possible for Richard to assemble an army and march down so quickly from Poitou after their falling out.

"Did you see this army?" Henry had sneered when Bertran de Born brought Robert to make his report to the Young King.

"I saw their advance party, your grace," Robert said. "Their cavalry screen prevented me from getting close enough."

"You merely saw the advance party? And I suppose you traded gossip in some tavern, and they told you what they were about."

"We took a prisoner."

"Where is this prisoner? I should like to speak to him."

"He died of his wounds."

"That's inconvenient. What do you think, William?" Henry had asked, turning to Marshal beside him at the supper table.

Marshal had the good sense to look troubled. "I think we should make sure the gates are secure tonight, and to double the watch. It couldn't hurt to call out the town militia as well."

Now it was Henry's turn to look anxious. "We'll leave them as they are. If they are under arms, there might be trouble." Henry had brought his own army to Limoges. It was composed of landless knights, and men-at-arms, almost all mercenaries eager to profit from war. So far there had been no battles nor any opportunities for looting, so they had taken out their avarice on the townspeople, who had not had the grace to endure their predations without complaint.

Knowing there was some reason for this decision, Marshal did not argue with him.

Richard did not show up the following day, but instead the day after, having tarried to break a siege of a fortified church by some of Henry's mercenaries in which a few of Richard's supporters had taken refuge. Before breakfast, the watch sent word to the citadel, and by the time Henry and Marshal, trailed by their retinues, climbed the city wall for a look, Richard's army was in battle line just out of bow shot.

Marshal's mouth was moving as he counted the number of men in Richard's array. Marshal said to Henry, "I make it five hundred horse and a thousand foot."

Henry nodded, worried, even though his force outnumbered Richard's. He said to Bertran, "Just as your man reported."

"Robert's usually right about such things," Bertran murmured.

"What is he thinking?" Henry sputtered. "He hasn't enough men to attack a whole city!"

"Richard never does anything without a plan," Marshal said.

"Whatever he has in mind, why couldn't he at least wait till after breakfast?" Young Henry asked, his voice plaintive. "Richard never has had any manners."

Bertran's war, which he had schemed so hard to provoke, came about because of Young Henry's wounded pride.

This was not, in fact, the first such war among the brothers of the great King Henry, the second of his name. His sons were a quarrelsome lot. Where other brothers might come to blows, these boys often relied on their armies rather than their fists.

Young Henry's present complaint stemmed from the fact that their father, Henry the true king, had given Richard Poitou and Aquitaine to rule with his own hand, while young Henry, nominally king of England and duke of Normandy, in

The Outlaws

fact ruled nothing but his own household — and even then he had to depend on his father for an allowance. Richard had aggravated Young Henry by building a castle on the Young King's lands in Anjou. At a family gathering on New Year's Day, the elder Henry forced Richard to give up the castle and demanded that Richard swear allegiance to the Young King. Richard refused to swear and stormed away from court. The older Henry, who should have known better from the bitter experience with Thomas Beckett, muttered too into his wine bowl that someone ought to curb Richard's pride, which the older son took as a signal, with more than a little prodding from Bertran, that he had permission go to war against his younger brother. So at Bertran's urging, Young Henry hastened to Limousin in Aquitaine, where he provoked the barons, who didn't need much prodding because they hated Richard's heavy hand and their resentments had been well stoked for the last few years.

The ranks of Richard's army parted, and a party of men bound with ropes was led out in view of those watching from the town.

"What could this be?" Henry wondered.

"The men taken yesterday, I expect," Marshal said, for a pair of survivors of the disaster had managed to escape and bring word of it to Limoges.

"Oh, yes. Them. Do you think Richard expects me to ransom them?" Henry asked in an incredulous tone.

Marshal glanced around with concern in his eyes. Most of the men about Young Henry were loyal retainers, bound by oaths of service, but further away along the wall and on the street below were mostly hired men. "That's what we usually do for prisoners," he said uneasily as if he had a foreboding about what Richard intended.

"You don't seriously expect me to waste money on that?" Henry asked.

"It would be the prudent thing," Marshal said.

Henry scoffed.

It became apparent that Richard did not have profit in mind for the prisoners, as they were forced to kneel and men with axes and swords began cutting off their heads. Pleas for mercy floated across the intervening two-hundred yards, but were snuffed out.

"Well, that's that," Henry said, almost relieved. It was easier for him to lose a few rented soldiers than to part with silver. "Thank goodness he didn't make an offer for them. I'd have been in a pickle then."

Marshal looked grim. "That's that all right."

Robert caught Bertran's expression as he turned away from the spectacle in the field. He was dismayed. He murmured, "Henry, Henry," but said nothing more and composed himself so that the Young King could not read his feelings. Henry did not like people who disagreed with him. They did not last long in his court.

Richard's soldiers collected the heads and tossed them in a cart. A party of knights escorted the cart across the field to the city ditch. The cart stopped at the lip of the ditch, and the cart drivers tipped the heads into the ditch.

Henry regarded the tumble of heads with distaste. "Not a pretty sight, I must say."

"No," Marshal said.

"I wonder why he did that?" Henry mused.

Marshal looked at Henry for a moment in disbelief. "I haven't any idea," he said.

Marshal turned to Bertran. "Richard deserves a reply."

"Of course, my lord," Bertran said. "How would you like it phrased."

"Something with steel in it."

"Very good. Robert, my good man, the lord marshal wishes to send his regards to Duke Richard. See if you can kill one of those knights."

Robert took Bertran's words literally, although later he realized that Bertran meant that he should have the thing done by someone lower down on the social scale. In his

The Outlaws

incomprehension, he took a bow and arrows from a nearby archer, drew, and loosed at one of the knights on his horse across the ditch. The enemy knight was so close that he could hardly miss. The arrow struck the knight low in the stomach, and stuck there. The knight's grunt and the way he bent over at the impact suggested to everyone along the wall that the bodkin head had penetrated both his mail shirt and the padded jacket beneath it, and a cheer rent the air.

"Well done!" Henry cried. "Well done, I say!"

"A fair trade," Marshal said. "One knight for forty common men."

The carts and the remaining knights withdrew across the field. When they reached Richard's army, its front ranks turned about, and the army began to file off the field.

"Look how we've sent him running," Henry said. "He doesn't dare to attack after all."

"I rather suspect he has something else in mind," Marshal said.

"Do you now? You're always worrying. We've nothing to fear from Richard."

"He's got something planned. I'd like to know what it is."

"Well, I leave that matter to you. I'm going to breakfast." Henry turned toward the stair and descended to the street.

Most of the entourage followed him, but Marshal stayed and he grasped Bertran's arm, a signal for him to remain as well.

They watched the last of Richard's army leave the field.

"What do you want, William?" Bertran asked.

"I want you to find out what's in Richard's mind."

"How do you expect me to do that?"

Marshal glanced at Robert. It was the first time that Marshal had looked at Robert. Whenever Robert was around, he pretended that Robert wasn't there. "You'll find a way."

Then he followed the last of Henry's retinue to the street.

CHAPTER 2

Limoges, Limousin
February 1183

Later in the day, Robert was in the castle yard working at one of the practice posts with a wooden sword and shield. It was a good place to avoid de Born, who spent his afternoons flattering Henry, pursuing women, and engaging in miscellaneous intrigues. Robert whacked the post and worried about what Bertran would require him to do.

A party of knights emerged from one of the barracks against the castle wall. There was no mistaking William Marshal's bulky muscular figure in the lead. Robert watched the group approach with dismay, for Robert had been avoiding Marshal too. He would rather face the lash than the man's contempt.

Marshal ordered some of his men to work at the posts and others to break into pairs for practice fighting. As the knights began their work, Marshal circulated among the men giving instruction and comment.

Then Marshal stopped by Robert.

"Care to practice with me?" Marshal said with studied casualness.

Robert tried to read the man, but Marshal's face was cold and aloof. "Drilling or sparring?"

"Sparring."

"All right," Robert said. Asked in front of the others, who had paused what they were doing to watch, Robert did not feel he could refuse.

Marshal smiled, but there was no humor or warmth in it. "Good."

They squared off with wooden swords. Marshal's attack was furious and unrelenting. Within the span of seconds, Robert had been struck three times — on the head, the right arm and the knee — any one such blow would have killed him had Marshal been armed with a real sword. Robert had to back away to avoid further rough treatment, but Marshal

The Outlaws

pursued him and landed two more stunning thumps on Robert's helmet, knocking the rim over his eyes so he could not see for a few vital seconds. He back peddled enough to evade Marshal's follow up at his legs, then pivoted to the right as Marshal came on. It was Marshal's single mistake, for Robert managed to swat him hard on the crown of the helmet with the scalp-parting strike. But that was the extent of Robert's victory, because when Marshal recovered he beat Robert mercilessly.

At last, Robert stumbled as he dodged and fell and did not get up. He signaled with his hand that he had had enough.

Marshal squatted by Robert, leaning on his wooden sword and breathing hard. His expression now was not as cold, but it was still not friendly.

"You underestimated me before," Robert said.

"Yes, but not now."

"I never underestimated you."

"You were wise." Marshal added, "You have said nothing about our . . . previous encounter?"

"There was no reason to."

Marshal nodded. He stood up and walked away.

CHAPTER 3

**Limoges, Limousin
February 1183**

"How did you get that bruise?" de Born asked after supper that evening.

Robert shrugged. He hadn't seen the bruise himself, owing to a shortage of mirrors, but from the looks he had been getting in the hall before and during supper, it must be something. It smarted enough, although he had no memory of being hit there.

De Born asked, "Marshal, wasn't it?"

"Yes."

"Damn his pride," de Born fumed. "Damn pride in general."

Robert maintained a diplomatic silence. De Born had pride enough himself for a dozen nobles, and was as prickly as a hedgehog at even little offenses.

"Doesn't he realize I need you in one piece?" de Born asked. "If you're spoiled, it may prompt questions. We can't afford questions if this is going to work."

"And what would that be?" Robert asked, although he already had an inkling of the answer.

"You heard us this morning. We need to know what Richard is planning."

"And you volunteered me."

"I did," de Born beamed. "You are just the man for this mission."

"You want me to sneak into Richard's camp."

De Born's smile faded a little. "Yes. That's right."

"Right," Robert said without enthusiasm.

De Born raced on, "You won't mind, will you? Slip in, gather a few tidbits of gossip, and slip out. That's all there is to it. Good, then. That's settled. Henry will be so pleased. You'll leave tonight. I've had it all arranged."

The Outlaws

The clanging of city's church bells for Compline faded with the last of the daylight as de Born and his men gathered at the water gate to see Robert off. Richard's army, though not large, had blocked all the roads and the only safe way out of Limoges was on the river.

They stood in a little knot in the midst of a swirl of activity as watermen loaded five boats standing at the wharf with barrels and trunks and boxes and sacks. A few other knots of people — families evacuating the city and enamel merchants spiriting out their inventory — stood here and there in the throng, talking in low voices. When the boats had been loaded, the passengers and crew began boarding.

Marshal pushed through the crowd. "They told me I'd find you here," he said to de Born.

He looked with astonishment at Robert, who was dressed in a battered wide-brimmed straw hat, a brown wool coat that was a bit too large and frayed and patched, a soiled linen shirt which was frayed, and russet hose that were rolled down to just above the knees where they were kept up by leather thongs that served as garters. His gray cloak was rolled into a bundle and hung from his shoulder by a leather strap.

"What's this?" Marshal asked. "You look like a peasant."

Although the old, patched fabrics were comfortable and familiar, for they were the kind he had worn most of his life, Robert felt awkward in them at Marshal's disdain. Robert had concealed his precise origins even from de Born, who probably suspected but didn't seem to care very much, but Marshal knew them, for he had been born in England and could tell by Robert's accent. Robert was afraid that Marshal would make those origins known and destroy his hopes of rising in the world. Masquerading as a peasant was so unlike anything most gentry would do that it could reinforce Marshal's hostile opinion.

De Born smiled. "You and his grace wish to know what's in Richard's mind. This is how we'll find out."

Marshal grunted with distaste. "A dirty business, I see."

"Regrettably so," de Born said.

"It's time," said Alphonso, de Born's youngest son who had just turned fifteen. He handed Robert a stained wool satchel that contained enough food for three days.

"Go with God, my boy," de Born said. He embraced Robert and kissed his cheek.

Robert crossed the wharf and jumped into the back of a boat. He waved at his friends whom he could just make out in the twilight. They waved back.

Marshal watched, unmoving.

CHAPTER 4

Outskirts of Limoges
February 1183

Robert fell in behind a line of grain carts coming up from Bordeaux at the outskirts of the enemy camp. He hoped that the guards on the road would take him for part of the procession. But when he reached the checkpoint, one of the soldiers pulled him out of line.

"Where do you think you're going?" the soldier demanded.

"In there."

"You're not one of them." The soldier nodded toward the head of the procession, where one of the drivers was looking back at them.

So, Robert thought, they had asked the head carter about him after all. "All right. So I'm not. So what?"

The soldier's wrinkled his nose. "You're not from around here. Where are you from?"

Robert's French made him stand out as much here as in the north, and there was no point in hiding it. "England," he said. "Had a bit of trouble back home."

"Looks like you had some trouble here, too."

Ah, the bruise. Robert had hoped that the day and a half it had taken him to walk from the Vienne would have given it time to fade. "A person was rude to me on the road."

"Spoke with his fists, eh?"

"He thought I should show him the contents of my purse, not that there's anything in it."

"Is there?" the soldier asked.

"I've saved a couple deniers."

"Let's see."

Robert hadn't counted on having to pay a bribe to get into the camp. But it wasn't unusual for soldiers to shake down the peasantry when they got the chance. He upended the purse and two deniers tumbled into his hand. It was a lot of money for a peasant: the equivalent of two days' wages. He allowed them to slip to the ground, but made no effort to recover them.

The soldier eyed them for a moment, then stooped to pick them up. He held the coins in his fist. "You lost something."

"And you've found it."

The soldier flipped one of the coins to his companion and closed his fist around the other. The soldier said: "We don't want trouble here."

"Neither do I. I could use a job." Robert's plan was to slip into the camp and see if he could find work, which would enable him to hang around. Armies always needed strong backs for chores that the soldiers didn't wanted to do.

"The quartermaster's over there." The soldier pointed to a tall green and yellow tent just visible in the distance at the center of the camp. "Go see him."

"Can I say you recommend me?"

The guard smiled. "If you like. Just don't use my name."

"I probably couldn't pronounce it anyway."

Robert did not proceed to the quartermaster's tent. Instead, he wandered through the camp to get a sense of things. It covered three or four acres and appeared to be the usual hodgepodge of tents lying in a series of circles: in the centers were the large conicals belonging to a major lord and about each one were those of his followers. Knights and squires had tents to themselves, but the infantry and laborers slept in the open, even though the weather was still cold. Large numbers of infantry and their women, looking dirty and unkept, were huddled around their fire pits, trying to keep warm. None of them seemed very happy. A good number were sick, and Robert saw a woman shrouding the corpse of a man, while his friends sat around on logs and the bare ground, complaining about a fever sweeping the camp.

The entire camp was ringed by a line of stakes driven into the ground. The stakes wouldn't stop determined infantry, but

The Outlaws

cavalry could not get through, discouraging raids by enemy horse, which was their purpose. On the south side of camp, near the big paddock for the horses, men were pulling up stakes and moving them out a considerable distance.

Robert asked one of the men what was going on

He spat and replied, "Damned if I know. No one tells me a thing."

Robert nodded and moved off. De Born thought that spying involved little more than moping around a few days eavesdropping on the gossip. Robert had expected that was about what this job would involve, since secrets shot through a camp like a bad disease. But he began to worry that he might have to start asking questions, which could attract notice.

On the other side of the road, parties of carpenters were hard at work. Robert paused to watch, gnawing on a dried apple. Many of them were building ladders, but a large group was nailing together an odd shack-like structure. It was long, about as wide as the average road, and mounted on wheels. It took Robert a moment before he realized, with a start, that it was a ram.

Richard was preparing to assault the town.

And he was expecting reinforcements, if the expansion of the horse paddock was any indication.

One of the carpenters working on the ram stopped nearby, where an ale barrel had been set up.

"How long does it take to build one of those things?" Robert asked him.

"We'll be done in three or four days, I expect," the carpenter said.

"Will we attack then?" Robert said.

The carpenter looked at him. "I'll not be attacking anything except a good meal."

"I wouldn't mind one of those."

"Your lord not feeding you well?"

"He's a skin flint."

"They all are." The carpenter put the leather tankard on the top of the barrel and returned to his work.

Robert wandered away, struggling with how he was going to learn how many were coming, who they were, when they would arrive, and when Richard would strike.

Richard wanted his attack to be a surprise. He was counting on his brother being lax and unprepared.

Young Henry would want to know this.

But more important, Marshal, the real war leader of the Young King's party, would need to know.

If Robert could bring back information as valuable as this, perhaps Marshal might accept him, even respect him.

Close held secrets of this kind dwelled in two places Robert could think of: the minds of the leaders and the chancellery. It was unlikely that Duke Richard or any of his confidants would share secrets with Robert or that he would chance to hear any by accident. But the chancellery was another matter. That was the place letters were written and received, and if anyone was coming to help Richard, he would be preceded by letters.

So all Robert had to do was get into the chancellery and steal the letters.

It was mad, of course. No one guarded chancelleries. Although the secrets in chancelleries might be worth the gold in any treasury, no one considered that anyone would try to steal them. But they were in the center of things, someone was always around, and there was never a chance to get in and do a burglar's work. This was even more the case with a traveling chancellery such as this, which was housed in a black tent a few steps away from Duke Richard's own towering red and gold one. Guards were everywhere, and the chancellor and his clerks slept in the tent with their vellum treasures.

Robert watched the comings and goings in the black tent for almost a full day before making his move.

The Outlaws

The staff in the chancellery was small for a person so lofty as a duke: less than a dozen men. It wasn't long before he had all their names and a sense of where each of them stood in the hierarchy.

He decided to approach an Italian named Giuseppe, who appeared to be the chancellor's chief clerk. He was an older man, tonsured as a priest, with a kindly face and a bulbous belly out of keeping with the scrawniness of his arms and legs.

"Yes, yes, what do you want?" Giuseppe turned rheumy eyes at Robert as he stood at the entrance to the tent. "I've seen you standing there all day. We have no alms here."

"I wondered if, perhaps, you might be able to take me on," Robert stammered in his most modest, unassuming and respectful voice.

"Take you on? As what? A woodcutter?" Giuseppe laughed at his own witticism. "We have no need of woodcutters here."

"I can read and write."

Giuseppe looked him over from head to toe. "I find that hard to believe."

At that moment, the chancellor himself appeared at the flap which divided the tent in half. William Longchamp had an aspect that could put fear into children and came close to putting it into Robert, who was used to formidable men: beak-nosed and sallow, sunken gray eyes that regarded the world with hatred and suspicion, a wispy fringe of dull brown hair sticking out like so much straw from beneath a squashed cap, and a stooped posture that was so bad he was almost a hunchback. He regarded Robert with unconcealed animosity and asked: "What is this?"

"He asks us to take him on," Giuseppe in a voice that suggested he was still amazed at the request.

"Send him away."

"He says he can read and write. We are short handed, after all, my lord."

"Humfph. Let me see your hands."

Robert turned his palms toward Longchamp and spread his fingers. Longchamp bent close to examine them. He paid particular attention to Robert's second finger on his right hand, where he had a small chafed spot, almost a callous, from copying over messages de Born had dictated for him to take to other Aquitainian lords.

"I'll be damned," Longchamp said, straightening up. "You don't do much writing, but you do some."

"Yes, m'lord," Robert said.

"Have you references?"

"Not exactly."

"No?"

"I had to leave my last master in a bit of a hurry."

"Why?"

"I owed a man money. He threatened to cut off my hands if I didn't pay."

"Why did you owe him money?"

"I had a bad day at dice."

"And you've been wandering ever since? I hope you've learned your lesson."

"Oh, I have, m'lord," Robert said with all the sincerity he could muster. "I would like nothing better than a chance to prove myself."

Longchamp turned to Giuseppe. "See what his hand looks like," and he swept back into the other half of the tent.

Giuseppe found a wax copying tablet, the kind used for giving writing lessons. He passed it along with a bronze stylus and an old letter to Robert. "Let me see a few lines."

Robert sat cross-legged on the ground with the tablet in his lap. He copied the letter, which proved to be a copy that the duke had sent to the master of Bordeaux calling on him to send more grain. When he had filled up the tablet, he handed it back to Giuseppe, who rubbed the bridge of his nose and held the tablet out to arm's length.

Guiseppe saw Robert's odd look and said, "My eyes are not what they used to be."

"Is it all right, sir?"

The Outlaws

"I've seen better."

"Oh," Robert said, worried.

Longchamp came back. "Is he finished yet?

Giuseppe passed him the tablet.

"This is awful," Longchamp said.

Robert picked up his satchel, certain he was about to be dismissed.

"How are you with horses?" Longchamp asked.

"I was a groom before I was a clerk. I managed my master's string when he went on buying trips even after I was clerk — well assistant clerk, actually."

"What did your master do?"

"He was a wool merchant."

"You're a failure as a clerk. But you'll do for a groom. I need one. See to him, Giuseppe."

"Yes, m'lord," Giuseppe said with a faint smile. When the flap had fallen on the divide to the tent, he leaned forward and whispered to Robert: "It really wasn't that bad. We may make a clerk out of you in time."

CHAPTER 5

Duke Richard's camp outside Limoges
February 1183

A courier arrived on a lathered horse. Robert could tell he must have important messages because he was a knight and had an escort of six men-at-arms. Ordinary messengers were often lowly men like Robert who operated by themselves. The courier slipped from his horse, tossed Robert the reins, and entered the chancellor's tent while the men-at-arms dismounted and stood around waiting for him.

Robert didn't know what was expected of him regarding the horse, so he also waited outside the tent to see what would happen next. He had come to appreciate that you could learn a lot just from keeping your eyes and ears open.

"Come a long way, have you?" he asked the nearest man-at-arms.

"From the king," the man replied.

"Which king would that be? There are so many."

"Our king, idiot. The only one that counts. Where you from?"

"The March in England. And you?"

The man nodded, and went on in English with an accent Robert did not recognize. "I'm from Devon. I hate speaking French. That asshole won't speak to us in anything but, though he knows how well enough."

"I take it he's not your lord."

"And thank God for that. He's a demanding little priss."

"Aren't you worried that he'll hear you?"

"He's probably so deep in a wine cup by now that he hasn't the ability to attend anything else."

"Any word on what the king's going to do next?"

The man-at-arms' eyes narrowed. "We aren't supposed to talk about that."

"I just wondered when he'd be arriving is all." It was a shot in the dark.

The Outlaws

The man-at-arms put his face so close to Robert's that their noses nearly touched and confirmed the suspicion. "Nobody's supposed to know about that, hear? And you best not repeat it."

"Well, I hear things, is all. You know, owing to my position."

"Best you pretend not to."

"Of course.

One of the clerks working for Longchamp parted the tent flap. "His lordship wants to see you," he said to Robert.

"Lord William?" Robert asked, thinking he meant Longchamp.

"No, his other lordship." He dropped the flap, not bothering to wait for Robert.

"Hold this, will you?" Robert handed the horses reins to the man-at-arms and entered the tent.

The courier was seated on a folding chair with a brass wine cup balanced on a knee. "He'll want water and corn. No oats, understand? He can't abide oats."

"He?" Robert asked.

"My horse, you idiot." The courier waved fingers at Robert. "On with you."

"Of course, sir."

Robert backed out of the tent and retrieved the horse.

"So you play dice, do you?" Giuseppe asked Robert after supper.

"I used to," Robert said. Many apprentices of his acquaintance in Gloucester had been fond of dice games, of which there were many. But every penny had been so dear then that he had not dared to play because to lose would have incurred his mother's wrath. Anyway, dicing required no skill. It was like throwing money to the wind.

"Ah, well, we have a nightly game. I thought you might like to join it." He glanced toward the tent divider. "I can count on your discretion, of course."

"I wouldn't mind watching."

Giuseppe grinned as if he suspected shaky resolve. "Come along, then."

Giuseppe led him to a maroon and gold tent near the fence of stakes. It was crowded and stuffy inside from an iron brazier smoldering in the center, but the warmth was welcome, given the bitterness of the evening.

Three games were already going, each within its own circle of players. Giuseppe joined one of the groups and was greeted as an old friend. Robert stood over them to watch.

Robert saw they were playing the French version of hazard, which used two dice rather than three as in the Spanish game.

He knew the rules as well as anyone. The caster, the person throwing the dice, selected a number between five and nine, which was called the main. If the caster rolled the main, he won, or nicked. If he threw a two or three, he lost, or threw out. If he rolled an eleven or twelve, whether he won or lost depended on the main. With a main of five or nine, he threw out with an eleven or twelve. With a main of six or eight, he threw out with an eleven, but nicked with a twelve. With a main of seven, he nicked at eleven but threw out at twelve. If the caster threw any other number, it became the chance. If a chance was in play, the caster continued to roll until he either threw the main or the chance; he won if he rolled the chance and lost if he rolled the main. Spectators bet against each other on whether the caster would nick or throw out. It wasn't a complicated game, but sometimes it was hard to keep track of things when people were drunk, which they often were.

Giuseppe lost his very first bet, when he laid down a full pence on whether the caster, a man-at-arms from Carcassonne, would nick on the chance. He threw the main of five on the third cast.

His next bets were equally, if not more, lavish: two pence here, five pence there, for these games were high stakes. He did not always lose, but the trend was against him, and about

The Outlaws

two hours in, after darkness had fallen and the curfew had been called, he had reached the bottom of his purse.

Giuseppe tapped his upturned purse into the palm of his hand as if surprised to find it empty. The top of his head and ears were red from all the ale he had been drinking. He asked, "Would any of you care to spot me a sou?"

"No," one of the players said.

Giuseppe looked distressed.

Robert caught Giuseppe's eye. He motioned toward the tent flap and went out.

"What is it, my boy?" Giuseppe asked when they were outside.

"I can spot you five denier."

"Oh, my, could you? That would be much appreciated."

Robert handed over five pennies from the secret purse that de Born had given him for expenses. "Try not to lose it."

"Ah, never fear. My luck always turns. I sense now is the time."

Now was not the time, however. Guiseppe lost every penny.

"I'll pay you back when we are paid," Guiseppe said as they walked back toward the chancellery tent. He did not seem the least unhappy at the fact he had lost so much money. "Never fear."

"I hope I last that long."

"What do you mean?"

"I don't think Longchamp likes me much. I fear I won't hold my position very long."

"Oh, never you mind. He's like that way with everyone. He has the disposition of an old prune."

"He seems more like a vulture to me."

Giuseppe chuckled. "Vulture. That's good."

"Well, perhaps I should consider other employment anyway. I hear the Old King's coming. When he gets here, there will be more opportunities."

"Who told you that?"

"Everyone seems to know."

"People talk more than is good for them."

"Is it supposed to be a secret?"

"It was."

"I don't see what's to be gained."

"Duke Richard is afraid that if word reaches his brother, Young Henry will run away."

"Why would he do that?"

"Because the Old King is bringing five thousand men — eight-hundred of them knights! We'll show Young Henry what's what when they get here, that's for sure. Don't you repeat any of this."

"I won't. You can count on me."

God bless drunks and gamblers, Robert thought.

The next morning after breakfast, Robert walked out of the camp. There was always so much coming and going at the gates at that time of day that no one paid him any mind. He went south about three-and-a-half miles to a point where the River Vienne bent from northeast to west and another, smaller river ran into it. There had been a wooden bridge near this place but it had been burned while Robert was in the enemy camp, to deny Richard the opposite bank. Robert swam across upstream from the remains of the bridge. Four women washing clothes on the south bank regarded him with alarm and backed away as he waded out of the water. Even a smile and wave did not allay their suspicions since it was not normal for grown people to swim in rivers let alone cross them that way. These were strange times, though, when anything could be expected, none of it good.

Then he walked up the trail along the bank until he reached Limoges.

The Outlaws

CHAPTER 6

Limoges, Limousin
March 1183

The door to the guard room at the water gate opened. One of the gate wardens entered, followed by Alphonso de Born.

"You know him?" the guard asked.

"He may not look like much, but he's a reputable fellow."

"If you say so."

"Don't worry. I'll see that he doesn't get into any trouble."

Robert rose from the bench where the guards had put him and threatened to take cudgels to him if he strayed even to the piss pot. Alphonso clapped him on the shoulder as they reached the street. "We thought you'd been killed. Even Marshal's stopped asking about you."

"We need to see your father straightaway."

"What is it?"

"The Old King will be here in less than a week with a big army. Meanwhile, Richard's building a ram and scaling ladders."

"You don't think they are going to assault the town?"

"I will let Marshal and your father decide what it means."

Bertran de Born was waiting for Robert at the castle's main gate, a sign that he was more than eager to hear what Robert might have to say.

"He's supposed to be at Chinon," de Born said when Robert finished his report. "How do you know this?"

"A man who reads Richard's letters told me."

"It must be true then. People will lie to a man's face but less often in their letters." De Born sighed as they crossed the bailey to the donjon. "It's the end of our little game, I'm afraid."

"How so?"

"Oh, the Old King will forgive Young Henry in the end and make peace — with him at least. Not with the rest of us. He'll blame us for his son's decisions and we'll pay dearly."

"There's no chance?"

De Born shook his head. "Richard will talk the king into picking off the rebels. We'll fall one at a time, like ripe fruit, and there's nothing we can do about it."

"Can't we make an army without Young Henry? We could join and fight."

"We've no money to pay the mercenaries. And alone we aren't strong enough against six thousand, which is what our enemies will put into the field if your report is accurate, and without Young Henry's support, our people won't have the heart to fight," de Born said with some bitterness. "When the prince finally deserts us, they'll run for their holes, hoping to make the best deal for themselves as they can."

"You really don't think he'll leave us!"

"My boy, Young Henry is a charming companion and a dear friend, but as changeable as the wind."

"You bet everything on him."

"I bet everything on him against Richard, and on the fact I could keep him on a leash. They have enough anger at each other to sustain them both. But against his father?" He shrugged. "He's never been able to stand up to his father."

"Then why not submit and seek forgiveness yourself?"

De Born shot him a hard look. "I'm sick of bending my knee to Richard. He never appreciates his friends. He measures his regard by how much he can squeeze out of people."

They reached the wooden stair that led to the first floor of the donjon, where Marshal awaited to be alarmed and disappointed.

De Born eyed the doorway above as if he had second thoughts about going in and delivering the news. "Well, you might as well come up and get some supper."

The Outlaws

Marshal appeared at window above their heads. "Damn it all, boy!" Marshal shouted. "Where the devil have you been? Get up here and give your report."

De Born stroked his nose and grinned. "I think William is upset. We better hurry."

The Old King did not storm the city. Instead, he appeared at the base of the city wall the morning after his arrival and demanded a conversation with his son.

Robert climbed to the wall at the tail of Young Henry's entourage, and stared down at England's real king. Robert had never been close to any king before, let alone England's real king, who was so close Robert could have hit him with a rock. He was everything Robert had heard about him: of middle height, but well muscled, with a barrel chest and thick arms. His red hair had lost some of its luster with the onset of age, for he must be fifty years old by now, his freckled face lined about the eyes and along his mouth.

"Welcome to Limoges, your grace," Young Henry called down.

"What are you doing, meddling in Richard's affairs like this, inciting his vassals to rebellion?" the Old King demanded.

"I am doing no more than your will!"

"My will? Good God, what are you talking about?"

"At New Year's — don't you remember?"

"Remember, what is there to remember? A warm fire, lots of drink and good songs, and a knockdown family argument. A perfectly normal family gathering, that's what I recall."

"An argument, yes. He is supposed to be my vassal. You said so yourself. You called on him to swear an oath to me — and he refused! He refused! And you did nothing to enforce my rights, for he owed me an oath for that damned castle he built on my land. And besides, I am the elder brother, with the right to rule over him. Then he stomps out, and you demanded that someone curb his damnable pride. And if anything needs doing in this world, it's that. Who else has a better right but me?"

The Old King looked stunned for a moment. His mouth opened and shut, and he muttered, "I don't remember it that way. Anyway, I say many things. They shouldn't all be taken literally."

"That's how I remember it. So you should just go home and let us work this out between ourselves."

"I can't do that. I can't have you quarreling this way. Philip will take advantage of the distraction. We are weak enough along the borders as it is."

"Philip can go to hell and take all of France with him."

"I'm sure that's where he's headed, but before he gets there, he can do an awful lot of damage. So there will be no fighting between you. You'll both make up and make peace."

"And my oath?"

"There will be no oath," the Old King said.

"Then there will be no peace."

"Henry, march out and surrender the town. I won't warn you again."

Before Young Henry could reply, a crossbow bolt shot from the battlements to the right and struck the Old King's horse. The horse reared in pain, and would have thrown the king if one of the knights beside him hadn't grasped it by the bridle. The king slipped off the horse and the knights gathered around him in a protective circle, lifting up their shields in case another bolt followed the first.

"Who shot?" Young Henry cried and stormed along the wall walk toward the source. "Who shot?"

A group of townsmen, armed and armored, stood across the way, glaring at him with undisguised hostility, unimpressed with his kingship. They did not let him pass, and Henry, after a moment exchanging glares, went back to where he had started.

"It seems the townspeople want to keep their rebellion," Robert said to de Born as the Old King's party withdrew.

The Outlaws

"More heart than I expected. Nobility doesn't command the respect it once did," de Born said.

"I suppose they'll attack now."

De Born crossed his arms, making way for Young Henry and Marshal, who descended into the town. "He's said that before to the boys — that he's given his last warning. He always gives them another. He indulges them too much. As long as Young Henry remains here, the town is safe. God help people when he leaves."

The Old King came back twice to ask for his sons to make up and the town to surrender. Each time he got the same answer, a bolt from a crossbow.

After the last attempt, deserters who came in the night told the watch that the Old King had given the order to storm the town.

"It's a bluff," de Born said when he heard this. "He wants to make Young Henry run."

If it was a bluff, it worked. Young Henry called out his army during the third watch of the night, crossed the Vienne, and headed south.

CHAPTER 7

Limousin
June 1183

As the advance guard of what remained of the army cleared the forest of Singes a mile or so from Rocamadour, Young Henry slid from his horse and stumbled into the wood. Coming in from a scout ahead, Robert saw Marshal follow him. Others, including a pair of Henry's valets, attempted to do so as well, but Marshal stopped them with a harsh word.

Marshal emerged from the undergrowth as Robert rode up and dismounted. He regarded Robert for a long moment with a measuring glare, making up his mind about some crucial question of Robert's character. Whatever debate raged in his mind, Marshal did not linger over it. He asked in a low voice for Robert to fetch rags, an extra pair of linen underwear and hose from the king's trunk, and a flask of wine. "Be quick," Marshal said, "and say nothing to anyone, do you hear?"

Mystified, Robert collected the specified items from the baggage train and returned.

He found Henry sitting on the ground, naked from the waist down. His legs were spattered with blood and feces.

"Help me clean him up," Marshal said.

The two of them working together used the rags and the Young King's soiled hose to wipe him clean and then dressed him in the fresh clothing.

They threw the dirtied objects away and Robert kicked leaves over them.

"Did you bring the flask?" Marshal asked.

"Yes." Robert produced it and Marshal turned to Henry.

Marshal said, "Here, drink this."

"I'll not keep it down," Young Henry muttered.

"Try anyway."

Henry allowed himself to be persuaded, but he threw up.

"Henry," Marshal asked, "can you ride?"

The Outlaws

Young Henry nodded. "We best be going now before someone notices how unnaturally long this toilet has taken." Henry leaned on Robert, who was alarmed at how warm his hand felt. "Help me to the edge of the wood, will you, boy?"

"Certainly, your grace."

"That's a good lad."

When they reached the edge of the road, Henry disengaged himself, walked stiffly to his horse and mounted.

Marshal paused beside him. "What's wrong?" Robert asked.

"Just the grippe, I hope," Marshal said in a low voice, but that word grippe covered a multitude of disorders from the fatal to the mild stomach ache. "If not that, then perhaps dysentery."

"Dysentery!"

"I said, keep your voice down."

"Yes, sir."

"I don't want anyone else to know how sick he is. If the mercenaries find out, they'll pillage the wagons before you can blink your eyes once, and be off into the woods before you blink twice. Now, let's attend our king before he falls out of the saddle and all hell breaks loose."

Young Henry surprised de Born by refusing to quit the war after fleeing from Limoges. This is not to say that the Young King prosecuted the hostilities with any vigor. In fact, he did his best to avoid battle, and the army spent the spring wandering about Limousin and Perigord, growing smaller everyday as it became clear there would be no fighting, or even any raiding. The mercenaries depended on both to make a profit, and without either they had little incentive to remain. A few hundred hung on now, hoping for some change of fortune, their appetite for plunder unslaked by the church or monastery that fell across the army's path, the most lucrative being the shrine at Rocamadour. Disgusted at pillage of

Rocamadour and Henry's refusal to accept responsibility for it, de Born went home.

"You stay here and keep an eye on things," he told Robert. "Bring me word of the end. I don't imagine that it will be much longer before things fall apart and Henry makes amends with his father. Then we will have to face the Old King the best we can."

The village of Gluges, its roofs visible through a screen of trees, lay at the foot of tall, chalky cliffs. Robert waited for the army at the bridge over the Dordogne south of the village. He had been ordered to ride ahead and ensure that the bridge was free and passage could be had. But sitting here, he reckoned the day's work was not done, since the road leading out of the river valley appeared to climb through a cut ahead that could be a spot for an ambush. Marshal came up to Robert and halted. For a few moments, he examined the ground ahead.

"I plan to stop for the night at Martel," Marshal said. "Ride ahead and find lodgings for the king. A place where he can be comfortable for several days, not some flea-bitten inn."

"Yes, sir."

It was about three or four miles to Martel, but a good bit of it was uphill through the rocky cut, and Robert's horse was tired by the time they reached it. It had been a long day and he must have ridden thirty miles to the army's fifteen.

Martel was not much bigger than Gluges, although its location on a major crossroads made it a stopping point for travelers so that it had more than its share of inns. Robert stuck his head in each one even though Marshal had ruled them out just be sure none would do in case the occupants of one of the private houses couldn't be persuaded to surrender their home for the duration of their stay. He had learned in their travels that people disliked giving up their houses even if well paid for it, because the tenants often left things a wreck.

The smith's house seemed the best candidate. It was large, having four stories above a shop and adjacent forge. It

The Outlaws

smelled of fresh paint, the timbers black and the plaster between them a dazzling white.

Robert dismounted and entered the forge, where the smith was hammering a glowing slat of iron held with tongs by an apprentice. He had never spent much time watching smiths at work. He had imagined them pounding away at the obstinate iron, since iron was so hard, but this smith tapped at the piece with a massive hammer as if coaxing it to take a new shape rather than commanding it.

The smith stopped tapping and motioned to the apprentice, who dunked the iron strip into a pan of water, sending up a gust of steam.

The smith looked Robert over, his expression guarded. It couldn't have been that unusual for an armed and armored man to put in an appearance at the forge. The countryside was crawling with soldiers of one sort or another. While many merchants might get the short end from soldiers, smiths tended to be an exception. "How can I help you?"

"King Henry is coming and wishes a soft bed. We would like to hire your house."

The smith pulled his beard while he considered the request. "Very well," he said, "one sou a day."

"One sou per day is too much," Robert said. A knight was lucky to be paid one sou a day. Two deniers, and not a pence higher."

The smith snorted. "Have you just fallen from the sky? Have you no idea of what inconvenience this will put me to? I'll have to move out and rent rooms for my family. Two deniers won't cover my own costs, let alone yield the small profit to which I am entitled. It is an insult. Ten deniers. I can come down no further. These are difficult times. A man cannot make a living in such chaos."

"The king has great expenses," Robert said. "I will come to three."

Negotiations went back and forth until they finally agreed on five sou.

Then the smith demanded payment in advance for three days.

Robert thought this seemed unfair to spring it at the end. But the smith was obstinant. Robert emptied his purse into his palm. He had seventeen deniers left of the money that de Born had given him on the day he left the army. He counted out fifteen. "Here's for three days."

"Will the king be arriving soon?"

"Within the hour, I'd expect."

The smith wiped his hands on his apron. "Well, then, I must inform my family. And we must hurry to make ready for him."

Robert met Marshal and Young Henry at the edge of Martel and led the way to the smith's house.

The household staff helped Henry from his horse and took him inside the house and up the stairs to the master bedchamber. There was no disguising his haggard appearance and sunken eyes from the army any longer.

Once the servants had Young Henry in the house, Marshal shouted for orders to make camp here, in front of the smith's house, and everyone got to work untacking their riding horses and removing packs from the pack animals to get at the tents.

Robert, who had no pack horse and no tent, put his horse in the trap line forming on a side lane, and took his saddle and blankets to the nearest overhanging eave, where he expected to spend the night. He had been sleeping in the open for weeks now, but it wasn't too bad when it didn't rain.

Marshal came by the spot he had chosen. "How much did it cost?"

"Did what cost, my lord?"

"Henry's bed."

"Fifteen deniers for three days."

"A bit steep for that fleabag. Fucking merchants, always trying to gouge people."

The Outlaws

The smith was a craftsman, not a merchant, but Robert did not correct Marshal. "I already paid him."

"Did you, now? The whole lot?"

Robert shrugged and nodded.

"That's a lot of money for someone like you to carry around."

"My master gave it to me. For my expenses."

Marshal looked toward the marketplace, where tents were going up, crowded next to each other so that people could barely move between them. He said, "We can't afford to repay you. Not now anyway. We're rather low on money."

Robert had known that the Young King's finances were shaky, but hadn't thought it was so bad that he couldn't afford fifteen deniers.

"Well, that's that, I suppose." Robert would never see that fifteen deniers again.

Marshal glanced at the saddle lying against the wall of the house. He prodded it with a toe. "Bring that into the house. You can sleep in the hall."

It was a casual way to be invited to join Henry's household, and a great privilege, even if things were falling apart. "Thank you, sir."

"I wonder what that smith has in his pantry, eh? By the way, you didn't happen to notice if he had any daughters about, did you?"

"I expect that every daughter in the village has been moved to the next county by this time."

"They would do that, wouldn't they."

"Along with their livestock and anything of value."

The vomiting subsided during the night, but the diarrhea continued. The household physician bled Young Henry, but it did no good. Henry could not rise from the bed even to use the chamber pot without help, and he refused food and drink, except for wine laced with herbs.

On the third day, Henry croaked, "Get me a clerk."

This request occasioned quite a bit of running about, for neither the chancellor nor the two clerks could be found. Eventually, a soldier located the chancellor at a farmhouse outside the village, where he had got drunk on the farmer's wine.

"How may I serve you, my lord?" the chancellor asked Young Henry when he reached the king's sickbed.

"Take a letter to my father."

"Of course, my lord." The chancellor had a writing box and a folding table fetched, not without some grumbling out of the king's earshot about the missing clerks. He sat on a stool, his pen poised. He looked at the king, who now appeared to have fallen asleep. "What shall we say, my lord?"

Henry opened his eyes. "Tell him that I have reached my end. That I wish to see him before I go. That I want to ask his forgiveness for all the wrongs I have done him."

"That's it, sire?"

"Make it sound good."

"Of course."

Old King Henry did not come himself. Fearing a trick, he sent two emissaries instead.

Count Rotrou of Perche and Bishop Bertran of Agen brought a ring the old king had inherited from his grandfather, King Henry I, so there could be no mistake about who had sent them.

Marshal conducted the count and the bishop into Young Henry's chamber, where they stood just inside the doorway, speechless at the sight of the young king, who was now as gaunt as a skeleton.

Marshal shut the door, leaving the emissaries to their business and stood outside it as if on guard. Most of the servants wavered under his glare and decided that the best course was retreat to the hall below, so in a short time Marshal and a few of Henry's most loyal retainers occupied the hallway.

The Outlaws

Robert, at the margins of this small group, could hear the murmur of voices behind the wall as the emissaries talked with the Young Henry. After a considerable time, they emerged wearing grim faces and bearing a rolled up letter which Young Henry had dictated for his father.

"It's the end, isn't it," Rotrou said to Marshal. "He's dying."

"It seems so, my lord," Marshal replied.

"A pity," Rotrou said. "That leaves Richard the heir."

"I suppose it does."

"What will you do now?"

"What one does with heirs. Make amends."

"He has a temper. He may not forgive you."

"I know about his temper. He will understand that I was only doing my duty."

"I hope so. Good luck to you."

Rotrou and the bishop went downstairs. Marshal returned to the bedchamber. Robert had a glimpse of Henry, golden hair lank upon the pillow, sunken cheeked, open mouth before Marshal shut the door.

The count and the bishop were enjoying a cup of wine by the hearth while they talked more about what Young Henry's death would mean for the kingdom. Robert would have liked to listen to that conversation, for he suspected de Born would be interested in their speculations. But they were surrounded by their own courtiers who regarded him with suspicion. Before one of them could send him away, he went out to the marketplace.

Over the last few days, the army had dwindled in size so that there were less than half as many tents in the marketplace as when they had arrived.

He leaned against a post beside the forge, and wondered if he should leave as well.

He was still there when Marshal came out of the house.

Marshal regarded the few soldiers who remained with disgust. "By sundown only the household will be left."

The next day, Young Henry ordered the servants to spread ashes on the floor beside the bed. When they had done so, he crawled out of bed and had the servants dress him in a hair shirt, and then lay him upon the ashes. A priest came and delivered the last rites.

The Young King lay there for several hours without moving, except for the slight rise and fall of his chest, while the people closest to him gathered in the room.

Henry died without anyone in the hot, crowded room even detecting the precise moment.

A squire beside Robert noticed first. He crept across the floor on hands and knees. Many of those in the chamber leaned forward, their mouths open at the squire's temerity, for in less trying times it was an offense for him to approach the royal person without being summoned.

"I think he's dead," the groom said.

William Marshal looked up from his place by the window. He bowed his head and a tear rolled down his nose and hung from the tip. It fell off when he raised his head again. "We're all fucked now."

Robert went into the hall to put on his armor. Marshal found him struggling into his mail coat.

"Let me help you with that," Marshal said.

"My lord, I can do it myself. I've had to often enough."

"It goes quicker with help." Marshal began tying the leather thongs that held the byrnie together at the back.

"Thank you."

Marshal handed Robert his sword belt. "Running off, too, are you?"

"I am going to my master. He'll want to know what's happened."

"Yes, I suppose he would. He loved that fool man, too. If you must leave now, let's find you a loaf to take with you."

The Outlaws

"That's unnecessary. I'll be in Hautefort in time for breakfast."

"Fifty miles? You'll have to ride through the night."

"I know the way."

"A moment before you go. Come with me."

Marshal went out of the house and down to the trap line. He had a half dozen horses himself tied up there, three of them stallions. He untied a bay with a white face and stockings and handed the rope to Robert. "He's yours, for your service to the Young King. I admit, he needs to be trained. He can be ridden but he isn't used to things flying by his head yet. But if you work with him, he will come round and give you good service, I think."

"My lord, this is . . ."

Marshal stopped Robert with a raised hand. "It's just a horse. They come and go. I'll find another to replace him soon enough. Now go with God, and keep your eyes open on the road, especially behind you."

CHAPTER 8

Hautefort castle, Perigord
August 1183

The advance guard of the king's army arrived at mid-morning. They sat on their horses a hundred yards away from the main gate as if unconcerned about the archers and crossbowmen on the castle walls, except for the leader and two sergeants, who rode up and demanded to speak to Bertran de Born.

De Born had been summoned by the watch at the guard's appearance and he was among those looking down on the leader. He leaned over the wall so he could be seen.

"Hello, Joce," de Born said. "You're looking well."

"My compliments to you," Joce de Munchency said. "You've got yourself in a bit of a mess, haven't you?"

De Born shrugged. "You throw the dice, sometimes you nick out."

"An expensive wager." De Munchency stirred in his saddle. "I'm supposed to tell you that the king demands your surrender."

"Let him come here himself and ask for it."

"Oh, he's coming." De Munchency glanced over his shoulder toward the northeast. "He'll be along soon. I am also supposed to tell you that your lands are forfeit, but if you surrender, you can have your life."

"That is kind of Henry."

"Our king is wise and merciful. Besides, I think he likes your singing. What do you say?"

"You know what I'll say."

De Munchency sighed. "Lands that have been lost can be regained, in time."

"But not honor."

"You won't be the first person who has accepted exile. There's no dishonor in that."

"There is if I desert my friends."

The Outlaws

"But they've all deserted you already. You're the last hold out. Makes you special, I suppose."

"That's why the king is coming himself to seal my humiliation?"

"No, he's angry because you put Young Henry up to that sad business, not to mention all the others. He's coming because of that."

De Born did not reply to this, since it was true, although he didn't want to admit it to de Munchency.

"You can't resist, you know. This place will fall in the end." Hautefort was a small castle, covering about an acre and a half, with walls three times the height of a man, towers every thirty yards and at each corner in addition to the towers at the gate, and a squat donjon. Its best feature was its location, at the eastern end of a ridge. The only flat land was on the west side, where the main gate was located, and all of that open space was within range of the archers on the walls. It was strong but every castle could be taken with the right amount of determination.

"I shall do what I must." De Born motioned to the men beside him. They lowered large baskets over the wall by rope. "I am sure you're hungry and thirsty after your long journey, and I'll not send you away starving."

When de Munchensy's men-at-arms pulled the covers from the baskets, they found bread, meat, cheese, and good wine.

De Munchensy smiled at the gesture, which was meant not so much as a courtesy but to say that the castle was well provisioned and could withstand a long siege. He waved as he rode back to the woods.

De Munchensy left pickets in the woods at the end of the ridge, and retired with the advance guard to Saint-Agnan, a village about a mile to the west of the castle.

It wasn't long before a suspicious dust cloud became visible to the north, the direction of Limoges, where according to rumor the king had remained while Richard did all the rampaging necessary to bring the rebellion to a close.

With the main gate under watch, de Born sent Robert and two sergeants out a sally port to observe the arrival of the king's army so he would have some idea of the size of the threat.

Robert went north through broad fields. Copses of trees too big to be cut down dotted the fields here and there, but they gave little concealment. There was a tree line thick with the foliage of summer, marking a small, but steep-sided stream in the center of the valley. He made for that and worked his way along until he was about a hundred yards from the ford where the road from Limoges passed through the stream. From this vantage point, hidden in the wood along the stream, they could see both the ford and the tower of Saint-Agnan's church, which was visible to the south upon gently rising ground. He had the horses concealed in the stream itself, and sat down to wait.

It was two hours by the sun before the army appeared. There was some confusion at the ford as men stopped to fill their water bottles, and a great deal of shouting from the officers at this lack of discipline. Eventually, they got things sorted out, however, and the army marched down the road to Saint-Agnan.

Robert counted the ranks of men, marking on the ground with a stick so that he wouldn't forget or get confused about the count. When the wagon train appeared, which had to be the end of the army, he slipped back to where the others were waiting with the horses.

Neither of the men who had come with him had much appetite for this adventure. Glad that they had remained out of sight, they received Robert with anxious faces.

"Can we go now?" one of them asked.

"How many are there?" asked the second man.

"I make it about two-hundred knights and men-at-arms, and about a thousand foot," Robert said.

The Outlaws

"We're fucking doomed," said the first man to speak. "There's not even forty of us."

"Forty have held out before against a thousand," Robert said, trying to sound confident.

"How the hell would you know that? You're just a child."

"I'm twenty!"

"Right, and how many battles have you been in? The king's so pissed that he's certain not to give us terms," the second man said.

"He'll cut off our heads," the other man said, remembering what Richard had done with his prisoners in the spring. "Like at Limoges."

"Those were common men," Robert said.

"No, they were men not worth ransoming. Like us. Like you — when the castle falls."

King Henry went into camp at Saint-Agnan, and then made no move for four days.

On the fifth day, after breakfast, the watch on the walls reported movement in the forest. When Robert reached the wall, the movement proved not to be a change in the enemy pickets, but what looked like the entire army drawing into battle line at the edge of the distant wood.

Some of the archers, village men who had not run away with their families, nocked arrows and would have loosed if de Born hadn't ordered them not to waste their arrows. "You'll have better targets when they get close."

"We don't want them to get close," one of the archers said.

De Born heard, although he was not meant to. "I don't want them to get close either. But they will, and there's nothing we can do to stop that. Yet make no mistake, we will stop them from getting over the wall. Stout walls and stout hearts, boys! We've got both! They haven't enough men to starve us out, and we'll send them off with bloody noses!"

"More than bloody noses!" Alphonso said.

"Indeed, boy," de Born replied. "More than bloody noses. Now, I want you and Robert in the south tower. Get yourself a bow and use it well. Stay off the wall walk."

"But, Father —"

"No arguments. Now go."

Alphonso looked petulant at the order, for it meant that he was to keep out of the real fighting, but de Born's face was hard. He shouldered his shield and stalked to the tower.

De Born caught Robert's arm. "Keep him out of it. If they get over, hold out in the tower. You should be able to surrender and escape with your lives, even if the fortress falls. I'm counting on you to keep him safe."

"I'll do my best, m'lord."

"See that you do."

King Henry's army surged across the open ground at an easy walk, shields of blue, red, yellow, purple, and green held aloft in expectation of a volley from the battlements. Select parties of knights carried scaling ladders, eight as far as the defenders could see, with archers following, while men labored in front of the whole with broad shields called pavices for archers to hide behind. The mass halted about a fifty yards from the walls, though the pavices continued closer. Officers shouted for the archers to draw and loose.

The enemy volley arched high in the air and came plunging down on the defenders from above. There was nothing Robert and Alphonso could do but shelter under their shields. The four village archers with them at the top of the tower had no such protection and they all crowded together against Robert and Alphonso as arrows thudded into the shields or struck all around sounding like hail.

"Anyone hit?" Robert asked.

He was answered by shaking heads. He said, "Then up! Let's get off a few of our own before they shoot again."

The village archers stood and drew, while Robert and Alphonso found bows of their own.

The Outlaws

As Robert drew his arrow, he had a clear view of the ground before the gate. The knights carrying the ladders were already at the ditch beneath the wall. He got off one shot, which flew over the heads of the ladder parties before the enemy archers loosed another volley.

He crouched against the wall, trying to make himself as small as possible, not bothering with his own shield, which three of the archers had taken up.

After that volley, everyone was on their feet without being told what to do.

The ladder parties had planted the feet of their ladders in the turf of the ditch and had already begun the long climb to the top of the wall. Robert shot one of them on the nearest ladder in the leg, and the knight jumped off and rolled to the bottom of the ditch.

Now that the enemy was climbing, there could be no thought to shelter even though arrows fell all about. Two of the villagers were hit, and staggered down the stairs, while Robert and the others now shot as fast as they could nock.

One of the wounded villagers stuck his head through the passage to the lower floor. "Robert! The south wall!"

"What?"

"They're coming at the south wall!"

For a moment, Robert wasn't sure what the man meant. Then he scuttled across the top of the tower and looked out over the south side of the castle, which overlooked the village on the slopes below.

To his horror, he saw another party of the enemy just now clambering up the slope to the foot of the wall bearing four ladders. There must be at least a hundred men down there, and no man defended that portion of the wall. All were on the west, facing what they thought was the main attack. But Robert realized that this was a diversion. The real threat came from the south.

"Alphonso!" Robert shouted. "Tell your father they're coming at the south wall!"

He threw down the bow, grabbed his shield, and jumped through the hole to the floor below. He had a glimpse in the dim light of the frightened faces of the wounded villagers as he raced out to the wall walk.

Piles of stones as big as Robert's head had been placed at intervals along the wall, more as a precaution than in any expectation that they might be needed. Robert picked up a stone and leaned out to see the ladder parties just then planting the feet of their ladders in the grass. Although the ground was steep here, the ladders had been fitted with metal spikes on the ends so they would hold. Robert threw his stone at the leader of the line of knights waiting for the ladder to be put up. His attack was so unexpected that the man looked up in surprise. The stone struck him in the face. He went down, his head a gruesome ruin.

Robert had no time to entertain a sense of satisfaction at this small victory. He continued to fling stones upon these attackers as fast as he could, while shouting for help. But his voice was lost in the clamor of the battle. The enemy began to climb, shields overhead, deflecting the stones. Robert managed to knock one knight off a ladder and to break the arm of a second despite the shield.

A pole with a Y end had been laid against the parapet along with the stones. Robert took this up and pushed against one ladder and then another, toppling them despite the weight of the men upon them.

One ladder remained, but Robert did not get to it in time. He reached it just as a big man reached the top of the parapet. This knight had gray eyes visible behind the nasal guard of his helmet, the rest of his face concealed behind a flap of mail. Robert recognized the standard on his shield, which hung from his neck on a thick leather strap. It belonged to Duke Richard.

The duke grasped the lip of the wall to hold the ladder firm so that Robert could not push the ladder away from the wall. Robert beat the duke's hands with the pole and, when he let go, Robert unbalanced the ladder to the side with a motion

The Outlaws

not unlike that employed when rowing a boat. The ladder was heavy, loaded with men, and did not move for one long sickening moment, while Robert strained and grunted and his pole bent into a U shape. But at last the ladder toppled over. The duke disappeared from view. There were shouts below.

In the meantime, the enemy had reset one of the ladders Robert had knocked over, and the enemy was already at the top of the wall.

An enemy knight climbed over the wall onto the walk and swung his shield off his back. Another knight climbed up behind him, then another. At that moment Alphonso emerged from the tower and rushed at the enemy, sword over his head.

Robert drew his sword and went to help Alphonso, although he had left his shield near where Alphonso now traded cuts with two of the enemy while the third man faced him.

Robert's opponent advanced, hiding behind his shield. Robert felt naked without a shield, but it was too late to worry about that now. He grasped the pommel of his sword with his left hand and raised the weapon to the Ox guard, hands by his left ear, point toward the enemy.

The enemy knight rushed at him, pushing out his shield, in an effort to get past Robert's point, where he would be helpless.

Robert stepped to the left as much as he could in the narrow space and cut two-handed at the man's head from the side. The blow rang off the man's helmet, but the impact was solid enough to knock him silly. He staggered on a step and fell off the wall into the baily.

The two knights facing Alphonso had no inkling what had happened to their companion, so intent were they in overwhelming the boy, who could not cut back for the furious blows landing on him.

Robert stabbed one of them in the leg, then clouted him on the neck. The knight's coif prevented him from losing his head, but the blow drove him to his knees, and Robert kicked him onto his face.

The remaining enemy knight turned to half face Robert and Alphonso, and for a moment they all paused, breathing hard.

Then four sergeants came through the tower from the west wall to provide assistance. Outnumbered, the enemy knight said, "Will you give quarter?"

"Certainly," Robert said.

The knight handed Robert his sword, while one of the sergeants helped the wounded man to his feet and relieved him of his sword.

The other sergeants looked over the wall at the enemy.

"What's happening?" Robert asked

"They've given up. We've won."

For now, Robert thought.

De Born's men had captured eight of the enemy and driven off the rest. The man whom Robert had knocked off the wall died from the fall. Robert stared down into the dead knight's face. He was much older than Robert, with white strands in his black beard. The quality of his equipment was poor. The sleeves of his padded jacket were stained and frayed; his helmet was dented in several spots. He had a missing front tooth. Robert wondered what his name was, but his friends did not volunteer it, and he did not ask.

After the king's army withdrew to the forest, de Born allowed the captives to leave, bearing their dead upon their shields.

When the gates were closed again, de Born summoned Alphonso and Robert to explain why Alphonso had not remained in the tower. He listened to the explanation with a frown, but when they were done, de Born clapped Alphonso on the shoulder. "You did well."

Alphonso grinned. "I had them handled before Robert butted in."

"I've no doubt of that," de Born said with a smile, although nobody believed this, not even Alphonso. "I'm

The Outlaws

hungry. There's nothing like fighting to give a man an appetite. Let's go see about some dinner."

"Do you think they'll try again?" Robert asked.

"They might. We'll have to keep an eye out."

After the failed escalade, King Henry took a different course. He began to build a wooden siege tower at the edge of the forest. Construction required a full week. When the tower was finished, it rose thirty-five feet, a full ten feet above the walls of the castle. Its timbered sides were covered with hides to ward off any pitch or oil the defendants might try to apply to it. Archers at the top would be able to shoot down on de Born's wall, sweeping it clean of any defenders. The floor beneath had a wooden drawbridge that would be lowered to the parapet when the tower, which rested on great wooden wheels, was pushed close, enabling an attacking force to rush across and seize a foothold.

When the siege tower was finished, the king had it pushed to within forty feet of the ditch. All that remained was to fill in the ditch so that it could be brought to the base of the wall.

De Born went to the top of the gate tower and gazed across to the siege tower, where Duke Richard stood, enjoying the view.

"Will you give terms?" de Born asked.

"Had enough, have you?" Richard called back.

"I am weary of fighting."

"You had your chance. There will be no terms."

De Born was quiet for a moment. "I will come out after dinner. A man shouldn't have surrender on an empty stomach."

"Fair enough," Richard replied, unwilling or unable to prevent his thin lips, a gift from his French mother Eleanor, from curling into a triumphant smile.

During dinner, de Born made arrangements for Alphonso to escape through the sally port, since the king had not brought enough men to surround the castle. Alphonso did not want to leave, but de Born told him, "You will go. I don't trust Richard's mercy. When my head comes off, yours is likely to be close behind. You and your brother are to take care of your sisters, understand? No argument."

Alphonso cried at this order, while de Born offered escape to the remainder of the garrison. The village archers and hired men-at-arms took him up on the offer, but the five knights and Robert refused to go.

After dinner de Born retired to his chamber, emerging a couple of hours later with his black hair curled, and wearing his finest clothes, a ring on every finger.

When de Born reached the main gate, the entire population of the castle about him, he paused. "There is something I forgot to do. You two," he motioned to Robert and Alphonso, who had not yet departed. "On your knees."

Robert knelt with Alphonso at his side, uncertain what to expect at this unusual order.

"You both fought well," de Born said. Raising his voice to all he added, "You all fought well, and I am proud of everyone of you. But you two," he continued, addressing Robert and Alphonso, "deserve special merit. Our enemies deceived us by hiding in the houses of the village and thought to take us unaware while we were preoccupied at the gate. You two singlehandedly prevented that. So, in my last act as the lord of Hautefort, I make you both knights."

De Born clapped Robert and Alphonso on the sides of their heads. They looked at him, slack mouthed, not believing what had just happened. He said, "That's it. We're done. You can get up now. Alphonso, get the hell out of here. And you who are going with him, get moving."

De Born waited a quarter hour to give Alphonso a head start on his escape. Then he said, "All right. Open the gate. Let's go say hello to the king."

At word of the impending surrender, the enemy army sat down in the field, while King Henry and Duke Richard retired

The Outlaws

to a tent at the edge of the wood to await de Born's appearance in greater comfort than bare grass afforded.

De Born and the others had to descend into the ditch, since the wooden bridge across it had been taken down, and when they climbed out, enemy knights surrounded them.

Robert was surprised that William Marshal was with them.

"I'll have your weapons, gentlemen," Marshal said, as the other knights took the swords and daggers of de Born's companions.

"Nice day for a surrender, don't you think, William?" De Born said.

"No day is a good day for a surrender. And this day will probably end in an execution."

"Ah, well. Would you be the one to do the honors? I know your hands won't shake at the prospect of separating my head from my body. Quick. That's how I like my executions, especially when I'm the one being executed."

"There are so many volunteers for that I'm not sure I will be favored. If you would?" Marshal gestured toward the siege tower. "Please come over here while we summon the king."

Over here, meant the bottom floor of the siege tower, where the captives were made to sit on the floor.

After a considerable time, Henry and Richard came up on horseback. They dismounted at the foot of the siege tower, and climbed the ladder to the bottom floor.

De Born and his men came to their knees. "Good afternoon, your grace," de Born said.

Henry grunted and began pacing in front of the kneeling men. Richard sat down on a barrel of crossbow bolts.

Henry stopped pacing and stood over de Born. His massive shoulders hunched with tension, and his long muscled arms and powerful hands flexed. His reddish blond hair needed a combing. His gray eyes were dull, and his ruddy freckled complexion was pale and drawn. He wore expensive mail, the double meshed variety that would stop an arrow, and which had mail mittens and leggings so that the king was protected from collar to toes.

"My lord," de Born said, "may I present my retainers. I ask that you deal leniently with them. What they did, they did out of love for me."

Henry glanced at the others without interest. Richard, however, noticed them and a spark of recognition lit his eyes at the sight of Robert, whose stomach trembled.

"Bertran," Henry said, "you used to boast that you never used but half your wit. Now you will need more than you ever possessed to explain yourself here."

"That's true, my lord," de Born said. "I have said so, and it was true."

"What have you to say for yourself now?"

"Not a thing."

"It appears that your wit has finally failed you."

"Yes, my lord. My wit failed on the day I learned that your son, the Young King, had died."

Henry turned away, his face pained at the mention of his oldest son, whom he had dearly loved. He knew that young Henry had loved de Born. He went to a wall and peered out an arrow slit. He had heard the story of Young Henry's death, and in his mind's eye, he saw his son lying on a hardwood floor and a bed of ashes, followed by other visions: the boy as a newborn, as a child of seven with his first pony, when he broke his arm falling from an apple tree at ten, the time he nearly drowned while swimming in the Thames at Oxford, on his wedding day, at last New Year's they had their quarrel, on the wall at Limoges when he had shown real defiance for the first time. Henry had held such memories at bay, but the cascade of recollections caught him by surprise and was more than he could stand. He sank to the floor and cried for the first time since he had received the news of the death of his beloved son.

Everyone thought for a moment he had fainted, and a servant was summoned with a bowl of water to wash his face. Henry leaned his head back and let the man wipe his face with

The Outlaws

cool water. It felt good. But he was king, after all, and he had things to do and he could not indulge himself in this way for too long.

So he pushed himself to his feet and confronted de Born again. He said, "Sir Bertran, you had good right and reason to forget your wits for my son. He loved you better than any man in the world." Better than he loved me, Henry thought bitterly. Not that I didn't give him reason. I gave him position but no power; I made him king in name but not in substance. While his brothers Geoffrey and Richard were a duke and a count with real powers over lands and peoples, that boy had only his immediate entourage and his crown, a useless circlet that in the end brought him no happiness. It was a crown of humiliation, not of kingship. He fought against me to make it real, to erase the humiliation of his impotence. But I had to treat him so. I could not trust him — he was good boy, but so feckless, so heedless, so wasteful of everything given to him. How could not I think that he would not waste England? A kingdom must be nurtured like a field, the power and the wealth derived from it coaxed and cajoled from its bosom. The boy never understood that, he never listened when I tried to teach him. What was I to do?

Yet now, facing the reality of irreversible loss, Henry was overwhelmed with the sense that he could have done better. Unlike his mother, the Empress Matilda, who had fought a long and bitter war with King Stephen over the succession to the throne that tore England apart because she could not admit to herself that she was wrong, Henry was aware of his capacity to make mistakes. He had made plenty in his long life, and had tried to learn from every one.

So now it was time to atone for his mistake with Young Henry. Here was the last thing he could do for that beautiful, proud, rebellious, fractious boy. He sighed and said, "For your love of him, Bertran, I will give you your life, your lands and . . . and all that you have and hold."

Richard's head jerked around at this pronouncement. Henry knew that, like him, Richard had been pulled two ways over the problem of de Born. Like his older brother, he had liked de Born. But de Born, with his nettlesome songs and his urge to provoke rebellion, could be infuriating. And Richard was not as quick to forget an anger as his father. He had wanted de Born's head. To Richard's mind, rebels should be shown no mercy, and in a royal breath their victory here was pushed aside. But to Henry's relief, Richard said nothing.

"Thank you, my lord," Bertran said, bowing his head, withholding the smile of relief that threatened to spread across his face.

Henry shuffled out of the tower. He waved a hand behind him at de Born without turning his head. "I will have five hundred marks sent to you for your damage."

The king got perhaps thirty yards from the siege tower when a figure stepped out of the ranks of his army and called to him.

"My lord king," the young man said. "I beg your indulgence."

Henry blinked. He turned to Richard. "Who is that?"

"Eustace, son of Roger FitzWalter, on the wrong side of the bed," Richard said.

"What is it?" Henry said to Eustace.

Eustace came forward and made his submission. Then he rose and said, "That man is an outlaw against the king's peace in England and against my father. He has committed murder. I would have justice against him, by your leave."

Henry turned to follow the direction of Eustace's finger.

It pointed at Robert Attebrook.

CHAPTER 9

Hautefort castle, Perigord
August 1183

"You accuse him?" Henry asked, buying time so he could think. His head felt thick, full of sadness. Young FitzWalter's words almost sank into the mush without leaving an impression. He did not want to deal with it now. He didn't want to deal with anything now. He just wanted to go to a dark place and lie down and not think about anything. But FitzWalter's accusation hung in the air, a palpable thing, full of menace.

"I do," Eustace said. "I accuse him of the murder of a knight in my father's service, Ralph, our cousin, and a man-at-arms, Jermain. He was one of our villeins at the time," Eustace added.

"So." Murder was a serious business. Henry turned to the young man in question, seeing him for the first time.

The young man, who couldn't be yet twenty, burst out, "I was never any man's villein. We were always free!"

"I did not ask you to speak," Henry snapped. He was beginning to warm to the matter. His head lifted and his shoulders straightened. His nostrils flared as he breathed. At the transformation, the boy looked frightened. Henry almost smiled at the fear he inspired.

"Your grace," de Born said, "he came to me a free man, of low estate it is true, but by his excellent service I have made him a knight. He fights well and bravely. He and my son alone held off the duke's own assault."

"It's true, your grace," a knight several ranks back in the king's army shouted. "He's the one who knocked Osbert off the wall and killed him."

"That is a lot of work for any man," Henry said. He glared at the boy, who did not shrink but returned the gaze, hands behind his back. Henry found himself beginning to like him. Henry liked capable men. But he checked the impulse. He could not allow himself the feeling. He had a case to decide. It presented knotty problems, legal and political. There was the question of how to try the boy, foremost whether as a villein or as a knight. If he was a villein, he had no rights to trial before the king; villeins found justice in their lord's manor court, where this boy would get none. On the political side, he had to placate the FitzWalters. He needed their help in men and money for his wars, help they grudgingly gave, like all the English barons. On the other hand, he could not afford to let them become too independent, because a powerful independent nobility undermined royal power; so curbing the independence of the barons had been one of his central objectives.

Before he could say anything, Marshal said, "Your grace, may I speak?"

"What is it, William?"

"I know him."

"Eustace?"

"No, the boy. Robert. I don't believe he ever was a villein, even if he was born in a low estate. He participated in a tournament last summer and took a prize."

"Really?"

"My horse."

"How did he manage that?" This surprised Henry, since he had never known Marshal ever to lose at a tournament.

"There was a set to at a stream. He made off with it in the melee. But as a point of honor, he and his lord returned the horse. And he gave Young Henry good service, especially at the end. And he fights well."

That the boy had served Young Henry well weighed in his favor. And for Marshal to say that a man fought with skill was indeed rare praise. "He is a knight, then?" Henry asked de Born.

"In my service," de Born said.

As far as Henry was concerned, this settled the matter of the boy's estate. Henry asked Robert, "Did you kill those two men?"

The Outlaws

The boy stiffened. Then he said, "I know one died outright. I don't know about the second. But I admit I shot them both."

Henry welcomed the confession. It showed the boy's courage and honor. And it left Henry having to decide on a punishment.

"I will award the FitzWalters compensation. Twenty pounds sterling."

It was an enormous sum, enough to buy a knight's fee. Its very size was harsh because if the boy could not pay, he could be handed over to the FitzWalters in satisfaction of the debt. He waited to see what would happen next, expecting de Born to offer the fine.

But de Born and Robert exchanged glances. Robert held up a hand. De Born smiled sadly.

"May I have a few moments, your grace?" Robert said.

Henry frowned, a bit surprised at the request. "What for?"

"To collect the fine."

Henry nodded, curious about what had passed between de Born and Robert.

The boy entered the castle and emerged a short time later riding a fine stallion.

Robert dismounted and handed Henry the reins. "Will this do, your grace?"

Henry appraised the horse. It was not just any animal, but fit for a warhorse. "How did you get him?"

"A gift."

"From whom? It is as expensive a gift as I have seen in a long time."

"I'd rather not say, your grace."

"Well, suit yourself. It doesn't matter." Henry passed the reins to Eustace, who did not look the least bit satisfied at having such a fortune deposited in his hands.

"I declare that the debt is satisfied," Henry said, glad that the matter had ended so well. "Your outlawry is removed. I'll have my clerk draw up the pardon."

He turned away, at last free to indulge his grief. He remounted his horse, and went down hill to camp.

The king's army departed and the quiet of summer returned to Hautefort. The siege tower was dismantled and the timber given to the villagers to help rebuild houses that had been damaged during the fighting.

In September, after the harvest was in, Robert asked de Born for permission to leave.

"Where will you go?" de Born asked.

"Home. To England."

"You're not happy here?"

"Very happy. But I must see to my family."

"Well, you cannot leave here on foot. That won't do." So de Born gave Robert two horses, both sturdy palfreys.

The next day de Born walked Robert to the gate. Before the younger man mounted, he gave Robert a final gift, a purse containing five livres.

Robert was astonished. "My lord, this is too much."

De Bord shrugged. He took pride in his impetuous generosity "Off with you. God be with you."

"And you, my lord."

The Outlaws

PART 5

1184

The Outlaws

CHAPTER 1

Gloucester
January 1184

By the time Robert reached Gloucester, it had begun to snow. Beautiful if observed from the comfort of a warm house, it compounded the misery of the thirty mile ride from Bristol and the preceding awful crossing from Cherbourg.

Robert paused at the head of Saint Johns Lane, reluctant to go any further. He shivered in the saddle. The palfrey's head drooped and turned to look at him, as if asking whether they were through for the day.

"Almost," Robert said, patting her on the neck. "We're almost home." Jean the wool merchant's shop lay up the street, just out of view owing to the slight bend ahead.

At last, he summoned his courage and continued down the lane to Jean's shop. He wasn't certain why he had come straight here rather than finding an inn. He had no home left anywhere in the world other than this place, which, given the manner of his leaving it, he had no right to call home. But it still felt like home. The shop was shuttered, as were all the shops on the street, since it was cold and dark and past supper.

He paused before the door. Then he rapped, remembering that it was hard to hear callers from the back of the house.

After a considerable time, the door cracked open and a face appeared in the interval between door and jam. It was Jean himself. He said, "Can I help you, sir?" Then he stopped, mouth open in surprise as he recognized Robert. "I'll be damned. I'll be righteously damned. I never expected to see you again. And look at you."

"Evening, sir," Robert said. "I thought I should apologize for the way we parted."

Jean regarded him. "There is no need. It was long ago and I'm over it. I heard you were outlawed. Is it safe for you to be here?"

"The king pardoned me."

Jean was astonished. "The king himself?"

"I ran into Eustace FitzWalter. He accused me before the king, and the king heard the case."

Jean shook his head at such an unlikely thing. "Absolved or not, you better stay away from Shelburgh, and Hafton, too. The FitzWalters are a vengeful bunch."

"Why Hafton?"

"It belongs to the FitzWalters now. Roger married his bastard to William's daughter after his murder." He smiled. "Not a good marriage, apparently."

"Oh?" Robert suffered a pang — of what he was not sure — at the idea that Giselle had married Eustace. The news that the marriage had not been happy did not make the pang go away.

"She ran away. Nobody knows where. It caused a great scandal at the time. But most people have forgotten about it now."

Robert could understand why there had been a scandal. Gentry women did not abandon their marriages and disappear. The pang became a gnaw. But he had a greater concern. "Mother's not still there, is she?"

Jean shook his head. "No. She left long before."

Robert was at once relieved and worried: relieved that she was not vulnerable to FitzWalter vengeance and worried about where she was. "What happened to her — do you know?"

"Enough standing here in the wet. I'm not even in the snow and I'm freezing. Where are you staying?"

"I don't know yet."

"You might as well stay here."

"I'd like that."

"Well, take care of your horses and hurry inside. I'd like to hear your story almost as much as I'm sure you'd like to hear mine."

CHAPTER 2

London
February 1184

Robert spotted the sign of the Red Lion Inn, a red lion with a yellow mane curled up on a wine barrel. It was where Jean said it would be: just this side of the Fleet River. He'd have urged the palfrey into a trot if there hadn't been so many people and carts in the way.

As he drew nearer, a disturbance erupted. People were ducking and shouting and pointing. It took a moment to realize what was going on. A pack of small boys was pelting pedestrians with cinders from the remains of a house that had burned down. At first Robert thought it must be urchins, but then he saw that they were too well dressed for that: just neighborhood boys having a prank.

He was easing across the street, hoping to pass out of missile range, when the boys scattered. A young woman burst out of the yard around the burned house and dashed after one of the boys, a small blond lad covered in soot.

The boy was quick for a child his size; he couldn't be any more than four or five. But the woman was quicker. He fell to the ground under her determined grip. She hauled him to his feet by the scruff of the neck and clouted him a good one on his behind with the flat of her hand.

The woman was administering a methodical spanking as Robert drew up. He thought she seemed familiar. Then she glanced at him and he saw her full face.

She frowned. The boy prepared to use the distraction to escape. But the woman twisted his ear and snapped, "Stay where you are!"

The woman put her hands on her hips and asked, "What are you doing here?"

Robert wasn't sure whether to be dismayed or pleased. She was the last person he expected to see in London, dressed as a serving woman who chased children with such dexterity.

"Your brat?" he asked. Robert had felt some sympathy for the child, but it was evaporating as he thought this might be Eustace's boy.

Giselle's nose rose a few inches. "No. As a matter of fact, he's your brother."

"Come along," Giselle said. She turned on her heel, took Harold's hand, and marched up Holborn Street toward home. Harold at first tugged at her hand but she held it firmly, and said, "Don't you try anything, if you know what's good for you, young man."

It was good to have Harold's rebellion to distract her mind, for it was churning with thoughts she rather would not have. To say that she was shocked at meeting Robert was putting it mildly. She had supposed she would never see him again after he went to Normandy, although she had thought a lot about him. There had been a deep attraction which she had put aside with difficulty. But it returned so strongly at the sight of him that she could barely speak. The tug of her heart had been bad enough when he was a peasant. But now, by the laws of God and men, he was her brother, since his mother had given birth to Harold. Her feelings were sinful, and she had to be careful they did not overwhelm her and lead to a terrible mistake.

Robert dismounted and hurried to catch up with her, leading the horses. "He's my brother?" he asked, astonished.

"Oh, yes."

"How old is he?"

"Harold, tell your brother how old you are."

"He is not my brother," Harold said.

"He is so," Giselle said. "This is Robert. You've heard your mother and your sisters speak of him."

"Oh," Harold said, looking up at Robert with sudden interest. "You're the outlaw. Aren't you afraid of being arrested?"

The Outlaws

"No," Robert said with a smile. "That's all settled now, and in the past."

Giselle's heart lurched and she marched faster.

"Hey," Harold said at the quickened pace as he ran to avoid being dragged.

Robert too was caught unawares and trotted to catch up. "Do you want to ride my horse?" he asked Harold.

"Do I!" Harold's eyes got wide.

"Well, come on then." Robert boosted him into the palfrey's saddle, while Giselle watched anxiously.

Robert saw her expression and said, "She's gentle enough."

"He's never ridden before," Giselle said. But a small voice said in her head: it's about time, too. He needs to learn.

"Just don't kick her with your heels," Robert told Harold. "She might run then, and you'll fall off."

"I will not," Harold declared, clutching the high saddle pommel.

They resumed walking. Robert said, "You never told me how old you are, Harold."

"I'm four. I can shoot arrows. I never miss."

"Is that so," Robert said.

"Yes, I have my own bow. Brian made it."

Robert said with gentle sadness, "He's Lord William's son, isn't he."

She nodded, wondering how he had been able to guess the truth so readily. But it was obvious. Harold looked like a miniature version of William, so much so that it was sometimes hard for her to look at him. Something had gone wrong with her voice. She swallowed a large frog but was still unwilling to speak for fear it might come back.

"That makes you my sister," Robert said.

She thought she heard a twinge of disappointment there, as if some hope had been dashed, but she must have imagined it. She almost said "bastard sister," but she couldn't bring herself to say that either. She didn't like thinking of Harold as a bastard. Sometimes she had dreamed of him growing up to become a knight and reclaiming Hafton from Eustace and the earl. But it was just a fantasy.

Robert sounded amused now. "Fancy that."

His amusement riled her. "Don't go getting any ideas," Giselle said, and marched on ahead of him. Then she swung back and stood in his face. "And don't you say a word about it to anyone, especially Harold. No one's to know about my father. Understand?"

She was aware of how close he was, too close; their noses almost touched. The last time she had been this close to a man was when a handsome sailmaker had tried to kiss her. She had spoken sharply, more so than she had intended, but the words just came out that way by themselves, as if there was a devil on her tongue. And she expected as sharp a retort as she had given.

But Robert's eyes drooped. He looked at Harold high on his horse, having a good time and oblivious to them, and back at her.

"It's for the best," Giselle said, low so that Harold could not hear. "He doesn't know . . . he doesn't know what our father was."

"Yes," Robert said, "I suppose it's for the best."

Giselle backed up two paces and took a breath that did not ease her tension. "Come on. You need a bath."

Robert followed Giselle toward the Red Lion, trying to sort things out. Her hostility bewildered and wounded him. He had done nothing to her that warranted the instant dislike she had shown him. He had always found it hard to understand why people sometimes just never liked him, no matter what he did, sometimes without even getting to know him at all.

He couldn't take his eyes off her as she walked ahead. The sight of her slender body moving so gracefully, despite a certain steel in her backbone, made him giddy. He tried to look away. He couldn't feel like this about her. She was his

The Outlaws

sister now, and forbidden. It was sinful to have these thoughts.

He had to find a way to make peace with her because of that connection, too. He didn't know how he was going to do that, when she bridled at everything he said. He wondered if her anger was a reflection of how his mother felt. The possibility made him glum and nervous.

He had a moment for these reflections before they were upon the Red Lion. The inn was a timber-framed and plaster-covered building that sat smack on the street like its neighbors. It had two stories beneath a peaked roof, the second story jutting out a few feet over the first like the brim of a man's hat. There was a big door opening into the street, flanked by large windows whose shutters were folded down to make counters. A serving girl was visible within selling sweet cakes and ale to passersby through the open windows. The girl paused at the sight of Robert and turned away before he got a good look at her face.

Giselle sailed on without a glance left or right and turned into a gate in a high plank wall beyond the house. Robert followed, glancing back to make sure that Harold was all right. Harold was talking to himself and swinging one arm as if he held an imaginary sword.

The gate opened into a large yard with the inn on the left, a stable ahead, and a huge woodpile and an open shed on the right. Within the shed were two women beside a large kettle that simmered over a low fire. The aroma of boiling barley mash came from the pot.

Giselle marched up to the shed, and said, with a sweep of her arm, "Matilda, may I present your son, the long lost Robert." There was something mocking in the presentation, and her smile was bitter and twisted. "Sir Robert, it is, if I am any judge."

"Oh, dear God," Matilda said, hands flying to her mouth.

Robert expected to be shouted at or slapped, but instead Matilda leaped forward and threw her arms about his neck. She grasped him so hard he thought his head might pop off.

The other woman, or rather girl, stood nearby, hopping up and down, and when Matilda released him, she repeated the embrace. When she too let go, there was a third, the serving girl from the inn, whose turn it was.

"Which one are you?" Robert said when he had released the serving girl and could find his voice.

She slapped him lightly with her fingers and wiped tears from her cheeks. "I'm Agnes, you idiot."

"And I'm Alice," the other one said.

"Don't tell me you can't tell us apart," Agnes said. "We get enough of that from the neighbors."

"Well, it's been some time. When I left you were tadpoles," Robert said. "Now you're swans."

"Tadpoles don't turn into swans," Harold said.

"She has more freckles than I do," Alice said. "That's how you tell."

"Do not. You're bow-legged."

"And you've one leg shorter than the other."

"See what I have to put up with?" Matilda said. She had stopped crying.

"They look like you, mother," Robert said, a broad grin breaking out.

"Everyone says that," the girls said.

"Get me down!" Harold called, peeved at not being the center of attention.

"You hush," Alice said as she hoisted him to the ground.

"Is he really my brother?" Harold demanded.

"He is," Matilda said, smoothing Harold's hair. Then she frowned. "Why are you so dirty?"

"He's been at Cooper's," Giselle said.

Matilda's frown deepened to a thundercloud. "I told you to stay away from there. It's dangerous." She took Harold's arm to turn him for a spanking.

"She already did it!" he wailed.

"Well, now it's my turn," Matilda said.

Robert watched the spanking, wondering if his own turn would come once the glow of reunion had worn off.

373

The Outlaws

But Matilda took him by the arm and steered him toward the inn, calling for a servant to care for the horses. She planted Robert at a table by the hearth where it was warm, and the girls rushed off to fetch a trencher of spiced lamb and thick bread and sat beside him to watch him eat. Everybody, except Giselle who sat at the far end of the table, wanted to talk at once and to know everything he had done and seen, and they threw a barrage of questions at him. At last, Matilda demanded silence. "Let him eat and tell his story. You won't even let him draw a breath."

So most of it came out, the high points anyway, in a more or less orderly fashion, since story telling wasn't something that came naturally to him.

"Well, at least I don't have to worry about hiding you now," Matilda said.

"How come you two aren't married?" Robert asked the girls. "You're old enough."

The girls looked sheepish and Alice blushed.

"Mother says we're too young," Agnes said.

"Too young?" Robert said. "Why you're fifteen, if a day. Time to get you safely married before you get in trouble." He laid the purse de Borne had given him on the table before his mother. It was a bit lighter than it had been, but not by much. "That should make a fine start at a pair of dowries."

Matilda cradled the purse in her hands, astonished. "Where did you get this?"

"Services rendered," Robert said.

Then he dug into his pouch for a second purse, which he withdrew, tugged at the strings, and dumped its contents into his palm. He laid the ring, which had ridden in that purse since he had left Hafton, before Giselle.

"It's time you had that back," he said.

Giselle neither moved nor said anything. The girls gaped from her to the ring. Having the experience of the city, they could understand its value. When Robert had had it appraised, he had found it worth so much that he had been afraid to sell it. Giselle closed her fist around the ring. She rose without meeting anyone's eyes, and ran up the stairs.

"What's wrong with her?" Robert asked.

"I don't know," Matilda said. "I've never seen her act like this."

"Can I ride the horse again?" Harold piped up.

"No!" Matilda said.

"Tomorrow," Robert said.

Matilda ruffled Robert's hair as if he was Harold's age, and leaned forward and gave him a kiss on the cheek. "I'm glad you're home."

CHAPTER 3

Hafton
March 1184

Olof, the village vicar, was drunk. He didn't know it until he stood up from the banquet table. He steadied himself with his hand, and glanced around to see if anyone was watching. He wasn't often drunk in public like this, and was afraid for his dignity. He had so little of it to start with that he couldn't afford to lose any, and thus guarded what was left.

Fortunately, no one was paying him any attention, as far as he could tell, but that rankled too. He liked to think he was one of the most important people in the village, but people often didn't treat him with the respect he deserved. To most, he was another villein with a tumbledown house, a wife, and dirty faced children, just like they were.

He stepped over his bench, and wobbled through the church graveyard. His objective was the latrine pit that had been dug in the yard behind the little stone church for this occasion, the marriage of Wulfric Ploughman's youngest daughter.

As he passed around the church, a hand against its mossy stone walls for balance, the uproar of the wedding banquet faded, and a serene almost-quiet settled upon him. He wished he had another cup of ale. It was sweet, some of the best the alewife had ever made, and needed to kill the taste of that damned salted cod that never could be disguised, even by the best of cooks. Nobody ever planned a wedding during Lent! You couldn't have meat, just fish and more fish. The girl must be pregnant.

He reached the rear of the church to find he wasn't alone at the pit. Wulfric Ploughman, father of the bride, tottered at the lip, aiming with great concentration. He began to topple into the pit, but Olof saved him with a quick hand on the shoulder.

"Thanks much," Wulfric said, adjusting his drawers.

"My pleasure," Olof said.

"Who dug this pit, anyway?"

"Not sure. I think it was Angood."

"He doesn't know how to dig a proper pit. Somebody'll drown in that, mark my words," Wulfric said.

"Damned right," Olof agreed, unlimbering himself to the wind. "Ahhhh."

Wulfric started to move away, but slipped and fell hard on his behind. He seemed to be having some trouble getting back up. Olof realized that Wulfric was more drunk than he was. That shouldn't be much of a surprise. The banquet had been going on for more than three hours, and the bride and groom had already left to do what brides and grooms always did on their wedding days. They left before the serious drinking got started so the groom was not too incapacitated to fulfill his duties. A good thing too. Olof didn't think he could come to attention right now if the nominal mistress, that witch Giselle, paraded naked before him.

Olof finished his business and hauled Wulfric to his feet. "Steady there, old man," he said.

"Don't you old man me," Wulfric said. "I'm younger than you are."

"That doesn't make you young."

Wulfric laughed. "It still makes me younger than you, you old fart."

Olof did not bridle at this as he might at rough words from other men. Both almost forty, they had known each other all their lives, and had shared mud pies together when they were children and whores later when they were old enough to go to Ludlow by themselves. Wulfric was a good friend.

As they turned back toward the banquet, Wulfric said, "You'll never guess who I saw in London." He had been there two months ago, impressed as a cart driver for Earl Roger. He hadn't shut up about the journey since then, and Olof couldn't imagine what he had to say about it that everybody hadn't already heard.

"No, who?" Olof asked.

The Outlaws

"Matilda Attebrook. Remember her?"

Olof nodded. He certainly did. She had made quite an impression on the village during her brief time here, just before Lord William's death.

Wulfric said, "She's rich now. Fancy that. Owns an inn. Well, half an inn, anyway. Doing very well."

Olof shook his head. He wished he was rich, too. But he never would be. Not living here. Not as a Hafton villein.

Wulfric lowered his voice. He looked around to see if anyone was within earshot. "You'll never guess who else I saw."

"Who?"

"You got to promise not to tell, not even to your wife. Not to anyone. As sacred as a confession. All right?"

Olof nodded, puzzled and intrigued. "All right."

"I saw her!"

"What? Who?"

"Her! Her ladyship."

At first Olof thought Wulfric meant Eustace's lover, Aelfwyn. But that was ridiculous. His annoyance and bewilderment gave way to shock, though, as comprehension dawned. "You don't mean —"

"Yes, her. Our true lady." Wulfric had tears in his eyes.

The sight of the tears and the reverence in Wulfric's voice renewed Olof's sense of annoyance. He didn't go for the worship some people secretly felt for Eustace's wife, the vanished Giselle. She had been an ungovernable child and a rebellious woman who had refused to do what was expected of her. "I see," he said.

Wulfric grasped Olof's arm with one hand and waved toward the banquet with the other. "I'd not have been able to set up Emma if it weren't for her. She gave me the money for the dowry and the merchet." He wiped his eyes.

Olof tried not to look surprised. It was unheard of for someone in the gentry to pay a villein's dowry, but merchet, the fine for marrying off the manor as well. "She owns the inn too?" Olof asked.

Wulfric shook his head and grinned, although tears still tracked his face. "No, from the money she stole from him." He nodded toward the manor house: Eustace. Everybody hated Eustace. "Said that the money was stolen from the village anyway, so people should get some use out of it."

The idea one of the gentry would give money that had been squeezed from the village back to it rocked Olof. He couldn't conceive of the idea.

Wulfric patted his arm. "You won't mention a word, will you?"

"No, of course not."

"Good, good." Wulfric staggered off toward the banquet.

Olof had intended to go back himself. But instead, he wandered off to his tumbledown home, which stood close by, thinking about the witch hiding out in London.

The following day, Olof rose as early as his hangover would allow, and told his wife that he had an errand to run in Shelburgh, where he had family. But when he reached the main road south of the village, he struck out to the south on a footpath toward Harleigh manor.

He reached Harleigh about noon in a pelting rain, wet, cold and miserable, his boots sodden and chafing, his breath a pale cloud about his head.

The manor gate was open and unguarded, the yard a pond with no one in sight. He waded across, sinking above his ankles, to his further misery.

However, he found the manor hall to be as cheery as anyone had a right to expect. A big fire blazed on the hearth and the room was hot near the center, where everyone was clustered, wrapped in cloaks against the drafts.

Eustace had his feet on a stool facing the fire. His face was flushed from its proximity to the heat. He recognized Olof with surprise. "What brings you so far on a day like this?" Eustace asked.

"I have some news, my lord."

The Outlaws

"It must be important to bring you out. Fetch the man a chair and draw it close. Get warm, and tell me this news."

Olof sat as he was directed, trying to gauge Eustace's mood, which appeared to be good despite the weather.

Olof warmed his hands. "I have word of your wife."

That caused Eustace to sit up. "What word?"

Olof coughed. For some reason, his voice caught, as if it didn't want to speak. "I hear that she is in London, with Matilda Attebrook."

"Where?"

"Attebrook has an inn on Holborn Street near the River Fleet. Under the sign of the red lion. Your wife is said to be there."

"How do you know?"

"Wulfric Ploughman told me. He said he saw her there. She gave him the money to pay Emma's merchet and for the dowry."

Eustace stared into the fire. That he did not react to this news was, to Olof, more ominous than if he had cursed or flown into a rage. He said, "Thank you for bringing me this news. It is most welcome, most welcome."

"Your servant, my lord."

Neither spoke for a long time. Then Olof dared to say, "The church needs a new roof my lord. And my house is falling down around my ears. The corner posts are rotten and could give way at any time."

Eustace did not respond right away, and Olof was afraid that he had offended him. Eustace stood up, and said, "Don't worry. I'll have your house taken care of." Then he turned away and stalked from the fire calling for Reginald le Bec.

CHAPTER 4

London
March 1184

Dawn is often the best time to bag a fugitive. So Eustace and his four companions saddled up as the dawn crept across the sky above London's wall and the thin smile of a waning moon rode low over the housetops.

They had taken beds at an inn at London's Aldersgate by the north wall so as not to be seen around Newgate and alarm the quarry. Their route to Newgate and Holborn Street led by Smithfield and down dark lanes. It was a Saturday, a workday like any other, but at this hour thefew folk were about were beggars emerging from alleys where they had camped. Once they flushed a gang of ragged children crouched beneath a window, who scattered at their approach.

Eustace tested the door to the Red Lion and the gate to the yard. Both were barred.

He stood out of sight while one of his men rapped on the door. A woman stuck her head out an upstairs window and asked what they wanted.

"A morsel to start the day," Eustace's squire called out. "We've a long way to go."

"We haven't even got the fire rekindled yet," the woman grumbled.

"Just cut us off a few crusts of bread and some cold meat. We don't need much."

"All right. We'll be right down."

Eustace did not recognize the chinless woman who opened the door, but her voice gave her away as the one who had spoken from the window. The men entered the inn. Another woman was bending over the hearth in the center of the room, blowing on yesterday's embers to restart the fire. In the light from the candle on the hearth, Eustace recognized Matilda Attebrook.

Matilda straightened up. She knew him, too.

She ran toward the back stairs.

The Outlaws

Eustace took after her, and on the third step, he grabbed a handful of Matilda's gown and yanked her backwards. She fell hard on her back. One might have hoped that the impact knocked the wind out of her, but however brutal the fall, she retained enough breath to shout, "Robert! FitzWalter's here!"

Eustace bounded up the steps with le Bec right behind. He had Giselle now.

Robert was already awake before the shouting started. It wasn't unusual to hear shouting at the inn; people were always losing their tempers about one thing or another. But shouting before breakfast, before the fire was even lit, was so out of the ordinary and so frantic that he suspected trouble.

He came to his feet, and ran toward the stairs.

He made out his mother's voice shouting "FitzWalter!" as he reached the top, feeling as much as hearing the footfalls on the stairs. He collided with a body rushing up. Both of them were surprised and for a moment they held each other, as if uncertain about what to do, before Robert, reacting first, pushed the bigger man back. The fellow toppled into the mouth of the stairwell, arms wheeling, into the man behind him. The impetus of the fall drove them both back to the landing.

Candlelight from the ground floor silhouetted the figures on the landing and provided enough illumination that Robert saw a flash of silver: a sword being drawn.

His stomach turned over at the sight, and he felt naked and helpless, reinforced by the fact that he had slept with no clothes on.

Giselle emerged from her chamber, where she slept with the girls. "What's going on?"

There wasn't time to reply. The swordsman on the stairs was bounding up two at a time. Giselle had a robe on, which she was about to secure with a fabric belt. Robert pulled the belt from her hands, and turned to face the swordsman as he gained the top step and delivered a thrust.

Robert swept the sword point aside with the belt and struck the swordsman on the side of the neck with his fist. The swordsman dropped the sword and fell to his knees. Robert pushed the sword away with his foot. Giselle retrieved the sword, holding it with one hand on the blade and the other on the grip.

"What's going on?" she asked again.

"Mother said it's FitzWalter," Robert said. He took the sword from her hands. Its weight made him feel much better.

Just then the man at the top of the stairs looked up at them. Faint candlelight from below played on the side of his face. It was just strong enough for them to see who the man was.

"Well, Eustace," Giselle said, "what are you doing here?"

"I would ask you the same," Eustace said, "except I already know."

He drew back down a few steps, and Robert thought he had given up. But Eustace said to the man-shape behind him, "Get the woman. Not the ugly one — Matilda."

The companion descended to the hall. He returned with another soldier. They held Matilda between them. Eustace stepped down to the landing. He held a dagger to her face.

"If you don't come with me, Giselle," Eustace said, "I will cut off her face. And you —" he said to Robert "— should put some clothes on."

"You look funny standing there bareassed, Attebrook," le Bec said.

"He is right about that," Giselle murmured with a half smile. Louder, she said, "It will take a few minutes for me to pack my things. Can you restrain yourself that long?"

Eustace withdrew the dagger from Matilda's cheek and fingered the point. "Please don't tarry. We have a long way to go."

Brian came up to Robert. "I'll take that. You go get something on. I'll watch them."

Robert handed him the sword and stalked back to the family's chamber at the rear of the house, burning with fury.

The Outlaws

Alice and Agnes backed out of the way as Robert entered. While he pulled on his clothes, Alice said, "We've got to do something."

"But what?" Agnes said. "We can't fight. You heard what he said he'd do."

There was a pause and then both of them said at once, "The watch!"

"But we can't just shout out the window. No one will hear at this hour. We have to get out."

"How?" Alice asked.

"The window."

"It's so high."

"I'll hold a blanket and you climb down it." Both of them were afraid of heights, but it was worse for Agnes.

Alice said, "It won't reach the whole way."

"You just jump the rest. It won't be far."

Alice hesitated. "All right."

Agnes pulled the blanket off their bed and hung it out the window.

Robert, clothed now, said, "I'll hold it."

"I've got it," Agnes said. "Keep an eye on Mum, in case that bastard tries anything."

Robert nodded and went out, carrying his own sword and shield.

Alice slipped over the sill. "Don't let go," she said.

"I won't. Get going."

Alice slid more than climbed down the blanket. She felt the blanket slip, and Agnes said, "Hurry! You weigh a ton."

"Oh, shut up," Alice said.

When she reached the end of it, her feet still dangled in the air, but it wasn't so far to the ground: about as far as she was tall. She let go. The landing hurt her feet, but she had to ignore the pain. The family was in danger.

No one saw her race across the yard to the gate behind the stable and slip into the alley that ran behind this block of houses and emptied into a lane that led into Holborn Street.

Alice ran the short distance to Newgate. Dawn had not arrived, although it was light enough now to make things out, and the gate was still closed. Alice pounded on it and shouted for the watch. The tower was supposed to be full of city bailiffs, but no one responded.

A few working men, apprentices, and half a dozen carts had already lined up, waiting to get in.

One of the working men asked, "What's the fuss about?"

"Some bastard has threatened to cut off my mother's face," Alice said.

"It's a bit early for that, don't you think?" the working man said, not believing at first.

At Alice's scowl, he said, "You're serious."

"Damned right I'm serious. Where the hell is the watch when you need it?"

"Probably recovering from last night's drinking," the working man said. He turned to the others. "The little lady has a problem. Let's go see if there's anything we can do about it."

Eustace heard shouting in the street. "What's going on out there?" he asked le Bec.

Le Bec went down to the hall. When he came back, he said, "Someone's raised the hue and cry. A mob's on the way."

"Rabble," Eustace said.

"Rabble or not, there aren't enough of us to deal with them," said le Bec. "And they've the law on their side. We should go. This is hamsoken." The English word hamsoken, which meant an assault within a person's home, sounded odd dropped into the middle of a French sentence. Odd or not, it was a serious crime even for an earl's son. Not that justice couldn't be bought, but having to do so was expensive and inconvenient. And Eustace would have to explain himself to

The Outlaws

FitzWalter, which meant absorbing more contempt and insults. He couldn't bear that.

"All right," he said, hating to give up when he was this close to having Giselle in his hands.

She appeared at the top of the stairs, and would have started down if Robert hadn't put a hand on her arm. She frowned, and he said, "Help has arrived. They're leaving."

"What happened to my money?" Eustace asked, sheathing his dagger.

"What money?" Giselle asked.

"The money you stole."

"If it came from my manor I have as much right to it as you do, you thief."

Eustace's mouth worked but no reply came out. Instead, he said to Robert, "I'll have my sword back."

Robert hefted the blade, considering whether to keep it. But if returning it would help Eustace on his way, he was willing to forego the prize. So, he threw it like a spear. It struck the landing between Eustace's feet. "There you go. Be careful with it. Swords are dangerous, you know."

Eustace pulled the sword free, and said to le Bec, "Let's go." They went down to the hall.

As Robert and Giselle descended to the landing, Matilda leaned against the wall, her face in her hands.

The mob had already gathered about the door to the Red Lion when Eustace and his men emerged. They drew their swords and the mob pulled back a pace.

"That's him!" Alice said, pointing to Eustace. "He's the one!"

"Out of the way, before anyone gets hurt," Eustace said.

A shiver of indecision swept the mob. Although most of the men were armed with staves and well outnumbered Eustace and his four men, the prospect of fighting against swordsmen was not something anyone relished.

Matilda appeared at the door to the Red Lion.

"Are these fellows causing trouble?" the working man asked Matilda.

"The trouble is passed now, sir," she said. "They're leaving. We thank you for coming. It helped a great deal."

The working man nodded. If the victim of the crime was willing to let it pass, the neighborhood would not interfere. "Very well, then. Off you go, before there's further disturbance."

The crowd melted back again and made a passage toward the west.

Eustace and his men mounted their horses. He rode off without a backward look, back straight and head high.

CHAPTER 5

London
March 1184

"We ran them off good, didn't we!" Brian Attebrook gloated as they turned from the door. He was half a head taller and more muscular than Robert, who grinned at him and clapped him on the shoulder, and he hefted his sword and buckler with practiced ease. They looked so alike, those two, shocks of blond hair, innocent faces, and graceful with their weapons.

"Don't be stupid," Giselle said, irritated at their confidence. The Attebrook boys thought they could whip the world, did they? They wouldn't have stood long against Eustace's band of trained knights if there had been a fight. With a shiver, she remembered the glimmer of Eustace's sword on the stairway and the casual way he had thrust it at Robert just because he was in the way. Eustace crushed everything that opposed him.

Brian shot her a hard glance and opened his mouth to reply. He had long since got over being intimidated by her.

But his mother cut him off. "It's time you got to work, isn't it?" Matilda said.

"Right," Brian said. With a sharp look at Giselle, he pounded up the stairs to get his boots and toolbox.

Matilda, for whom business always came first, seemed to have put the incident behind her. She and her partner Margery started going about opening the inn, rekindling the fire, throwing open the shutters to the street, dispatching a maid to the baker's to fetch rolls and bread. Alice and Agnes went out and came in with a barrel of ale on a trolley.

Giselle was supposed to help, but she settled on a bench, her heart desolate. She felt Matilda throw a glance at her and expected a "Get on with it" but Matilda left her alone. Giselle would have welcomed the rebuke. The fact there was none made her feel as if she did not really belong. That hurt. She had come to think of the inn as home. It had become as comfortable and welcome as an old shirt.

The fact was, she didn't belong. She had felt twinges of that otherness from the moment Robert had returned, but she had forced those feelings from her mind. He made her uncomfortable, a walking indictment of failure. She had hoped he would go away, but it looked as though he intended to remain for a long time.

She had thought just to wait him out. But now it was clear she could not. And her presence here put their lives in danger.

"He'll be back," Giselle said to the room.

Matilda paused in front of her. "Who, dear? Eustace?"

Giselle's head bobbed.

"She's right," Robert said. He took a seat on the other side of the table. Matilda put a bowl of hard boiled eggs in front of him and he began peeling an egg. "Once he decides on something, he never gives up. He could even turn to the law."

Giselle hated to agree with him, but she nodded bitterly.

Matilda frowned. "Women run away from their husbands all the time. The law doesn't do anything about them."

"Those are ordinary women," Giselle said. "I'm just like property. I can be locked up if I don't obey him."

Matilda's face fell. "Then you'll have to go."

"The sooner the better," Giselle said.

"When?" Matilda asked.

"This morning. Right away."

Matilda looked stricken. "Where will you go?"

"My uncle in France. I should have gone there in the first place." Giselle had intended that when she fled Hafton. She had stopped at the Red Lion to pay Matilda a visit. But she had never left.

Her thoughts were interrupted by Harold, who had dropped his drawers in the yard. Alice raced out, swatted his behind, grabbed his hand, and marched him to the latrine.

Giselle nearly burst into tears.

The Outlaws

Matilda wiped her hands on her apron, a business-like gesture. She had a practical mind, and once she saw the way of things, she put misgivings aside. "You'll need money, then." Matilda headed toward the stairs and her bedroom, where she kept the strong box with the inn's receipts.

"No!" Giselle said. "I have enough." Even the Attebrooks didn't know about the buried box of pennies. She'd used up all she'd brought: the large sum she'd given to Wulfric had exhausted her reserve. She'd have to go back to get the rest now. Her Uncle Helmo would be more likely to take her in and to protect her if she had money. As much as she wanted to see Hafton again, the thought was frightening. Eustace might be there; certainly his men were. She might be caught.

Matilda looked surprised.

Giselle rose and strode toward the stairs, trying to be brave. "I'll fetch my things."

Matilda stopped her with a hand on her arm. "You can't travel alone. It isn't safe, especially for a woman."

"I'll manage," Giselle said. "There are always people on the highways." Many people chose to travel in groups against the possibility of robbers. She'd attach herself to one.

"No. Robert will go with you."

Once Matilda had made up her mind, there was no arguing with her. Their horses were saddled and loaded within the hour, and the family and servants clustered at the back gate to see them off, for Robert, who seemed to have a very suspicious mind, would not go out by the front in case Eustace had an agent watching the premises.

Giselle embraced Matilda and the girls, and strained to lift Harold up one last time. He squirmed and demanded to be put down. She kissed him on the cheek and complied. Alice seized his hand before he could run away. Giselle said goodbye to the servants and turned to Robert.

He nodded, opened the back gate, and led his horses out into the alley that ran behind the house. It was empty except for a half dozen boys playing football down the way. Giselle followed him. He helped her mount, led them through a maze of back alleys and across vacant lots that Giselle didn't even know. It was surprising that he could find his way so easily having been here but a month. In a short time, they emerged on Lyverne Lane, and she realized where she was. Giselle would have turned south toward Holborn, but Robert instead headed north toward the open country she could see at the end of the lane, which petered out in a field.

"Where are you going?" she demanded.

"Better to go around the city than through it," Robert said.

It struck Giselle that this route was more in keeping with her plans, but there was an obstacle if they were to go south, which she did not intend. "But how will we get across the river?"

"We'll go up to Westminster and cross at the ferry."

"But the ferry is more expensive than one of the city bridges."

"Eustace will not expect it. When he finds you're gone, I doubt he'll ask for you there."

"Oh."

After about three-quarters of an hour of slow riding through pastures and fields and crossing a number of streams, they came out onto Watling Street. Robert crossed the road and turned south, but Giselle turned right toward the forest that stood on a long slope ahead.

Robert reined up and called out, "That's not the way to France."

Giselle answered him without turning around, because she didn't want him to see her smile, "But it is."

"No, it's not." He sounded exasperated.

"It is for me."

He caught up with her, and slowed down to match her pace. "What do you think you're doing?"

"I have business to take care of first."

"What do you mean? What business?"

The Outlaws

"I left something in Hafton. I have to collect it first."

"You're mad. You can't afford to get within twenty miles of that place."

Giselle shrugged and said nothing.

"What did you leave that was so important?"

"When I ran away, I stole the manor's receipts. It was quite a lot of money, so much that I couldn't carry it all. So I buried it."

"Leave the money — or tell me where it is, and I'll get it for you. No sense going yourself. It's too dangerous."

"It's just as dangerous for you."

"I'm used to that sort of thing. You're not."

"Don't tell me what I'm not used to!" she shot back. "I've been in tight spots before and done well enough, thank you."

"I was only thinking of what's best for you."

"I don't need your protection, and I can decide for myself what's best for me."

She gave her horse her heels and trotted north up the road without looking back.

Stokenchurch
March 1184

They reached Stokenchurch in the evening after a ride of more than forty miles, a long way to go in a single day. There were two inns in town. The one with rooms available that did not have to be shared with another traveler was a large house at the north edge. Giselle was so grateful to dismount that she nearly cried out, except she didn't have the energy to more than grunt. Her thighs and calves were rubbed raw and her back was sore. She held onto the barn's wall to keep from falling over as the grooms trotted out to take the horses. Robert held out his arm to escort her to the inn. She hesitated, then accepted it. He was, after all, her brother, and such a courtesy from family did no harm.

The innkeeper, a stooped little man, wasn't so eager for their business. He met them in the hall, which was crowded with travelers just finishing supper. Giselle let Robert deal with him; the innkeeper would expect the man to do the talking.

She tottered out to the stable to check on the horses and to see that their packs were stored under lock and key.

When she returned, she found Robert at a corner table sitting in front of a tankard of ale, bread, and a bowl of stew. He had ordered the same for her. She slid onto the bench opposite him and broke off a piece of bread, which she dunked in the stew. The stew was a lumpy gray mess, but defied expectations by tasting good. Perhaps that was because she was so hungry she could have taken a bite out of the bowl.

She was piqued that Robert had not shown any concern about their valuables. "Everything could have been stolen while you haggled with that little man," she said.

"I knew you'd take care of it," he said and fell silent.

They had said little to each other on the long ride, but now that they were face to face across a table, the silence between them had to be filled. "How much was the room?" she asked to make conversation.

Robert grimaced. "Two farthings each."

"Each!" Giselle was scandalized. It was double the normal rate. "I could have done better."

"Rooms are dear. The town is full of people on pilgrimage to Canterbury. A very large party, it seems." He indicated the others in the hall.

"The sharps will be glad to see them," she said. The Canterbury merchants lived off the gullibility of pilgrims. She had never been there, but she had heard enough about them from others.

Robert said nothing. He stared at a spot on the wall over her shoulder, and didn't seem inclined to talk any further. He had taken to ignoring her, and it got under her skin.

She was plotting ways to get under his when she discovered she had reached the bottom of her bowl. A servant girl cleared the table. It was now dark inside and out, except

The Outlaws

for the fire on the hearth, which had burned low. A boy came in and put a clay fire cover on the coals. Giselle realized the hall was empty. Everyone had gone to bed.

She stood up. "Do you think they're trying to tell us something?"

"I suppose so."

"Show me my room, please."

Robert smiled faintly and bowed. "That way, my lady." He indicated the stairway at the rear of the hall.

Giselle swept toward the stairway. The innkeeper met them coming down and gave them his candle so they could see their way. "G'night, my lord, my lady," he said, bobbing his head.

"Good night, sir," Giselle said for them both.

As with most such large houses, the front was open clear to the ceiling to let out the smoke through a hole in the roof. The rooms on the upper story were to the rear, and her room proved to be the farthest at the back.

Giselle tipped the latch and was turning to say good night to Robert when he pushed open the door and entered the room. She was stunned speechless for a moment at this audacity and suffered a twinge of alarm. He didn't mean to do anything . . . untoward, did he? She wouldn't have imagined it of him.

He crossed the room to the bed, sat down, and began to take off his boots.

"I asked you to show me my room," Giselle said.

"This is your room." He tossed the boots into a corner. She saw they landed beside his pack, where his sword and shield stood against the wall. Then she saw her own pack in the opposite corner.

"You're not sleeping here too," she said.

"It's the only room left." Robert swung his legs around and lay on the bed with his hands behind his head. He wiggled his toes.

She stamped her foot in anger. "Get up this instant!"

"I'm not sleeping on the floor. Not while there's a good feather bed available." He patted the bed beside him. "There's plenty of room for the both of us."

"I'll not share a bed with you," Giselle said. "What will people think? I'm no harlot."

"No one will think you're a whore. I let the innkeeper think you're my wife."

That made her livid. "You had no right!"

"It's a harmless lie."

She saw there was nothing she could do. Appealing to the innkeeper would cause public embarrassment.

Seething, she said, "You'll have to turn away while I change."

"Of course." He rolled on his side and faced the wall.

She blew out the candle and kept her eyes on him while she slipped out of her dress into a linen shift in case he dared to sneak a look. But he did not move.

"You might want to close the shutters," Robert said. "It smells like horse manure in here."

It was true. The window overlooked the stable and the stench was palpable. Giselle latched the shutters and fumbled in her bags for a stick of incense. She held it out to Robert. "We need a light for this."

He rolled over to see what she wanted. Reluctantly, he stood up and took the stick.

"You can light it on the coals at the hearth," she said.

"Right," he said as if he had already thought of that and went out. "Shouldn't have blown out that candle."

"How thoughtless of me." She closed the door behind him and listened to his footfalls as he went down the corridor. Then she took the end of her belt and jammed it into the door latch. It had no lock and her belt was the only thing she had that was slender enough to fit into the slot. When she jiggled the latch, she found that, as she hoped, it would not open. She admired her handiwork with a smile, proud of her ingenuity.

Then she got under the covers.

Presently, she heard the latch.

The Outlaws

"Open the door, Giselle," Robert said.

"A married lady does not share her room, nor her bed, with a man who is not her husband."

She half feared he would make a scene himself now, but there was quiet beyond the door. She had guessed right. He would not make trouble.

"All right," he said. "At least give me a blanket. It's cold out here."

He had her there. She could let him sleep on floorboards, but it was unfair to deny him a blanket.

She threw off the covers, snatched up his blanket roll, and opened the door. She held out the roll to him. "Very well, here you go."

He took the roll and said, "They'll think we had a fight."

"I don't care what they think."

"They'll laugh at us."

"It's your fault."

"I'm used to being laughed at. Are you?"

"Go away." She tried to close the door, but his foot had got in the way.

It wasn't much of a struggle for him to push open the door, even against her best resistance. He came into the room carrying the now relighted candle and the burning incense stick, closed the door behind him, and crossed to the bed.

Giselle wanted to cry out in anger and frustration. She hated to be beaten. In the end, it was always seemed that the person who could wield the greater force was the victor. It was so unfair. But she held her tongue.

Robert put the bedroll in the middle of the bed. "There," he said. "How's that? Your half and my half. When you roll over in the middle of the night and bump something, you won't think it's me."

Giselle crossed her arms. "And what do you mean by that?" She could imagine he believed she lusted after him. All men seemed to think that if a woman just spoke to them, she wanted him.

"Nothing." He settled under the covers and rolled toward the wall. "Don't forget to blow out the candle. We don't want to burn down the house."

She seethed anew at that final barb. Of course she knew to blow out the candle. She wasn't a child or a drunk. "Be glad I don't put it out in your eye," she said.

"Then the girls could admire my eye patch," he said. "They can be quite rakish."

There was nothing she could do now but blow out the candle and climb in bed. He had turned her barb with humor, and she had no more barbs left.

She pulled the covers up to her chin, aware of the shape beside her, not just the rough canvas and wool of the bedroll, but of the heavier shape beyond. She could feel the mattress sagging under his weight and the rhythm of his breathing. I will not think of him, she said to herself. It is sinful. I will pray him away. She uttered a prayer in her mind to Saint Mary for protection and forgiveness.

Somewhere in the middle of the rather long prayer, she sank into sleep.

The Outlaws

CHAPTER 6

Hafton
March 1184

Robert timed their arrival for twilight. They waited in the woods just the other side of the crest of the hill. Robert sat with his back to a tree while Giselle wore a groove among the leaves with nervous pacing. He had no idea what she had to be so anxious about. He thought it would be easy to slip up to the shepherd's hut, dig out the chest, and be away without being spotted.

"Can we go now?" she asked when it was as dark as it was going to get for some time with a half moon overhead.

"I suppose so," Robert said, climbing to his feet.

They went up the road the last few feet to the crest of the hill, leading their horses on foot. The open field ahead swept down to the flats by the river, and beyond that there were the peaked roofs of the village strung along the street, wreathed in smoke from hearth fires. A dog barked in the village, answered by a second and then a third. A voice yelling at one of the dogs. There was a yelp and a dog fell silent, followed soon by the others. Down there, everyone should be capping the fires and retiring to bed by this time.

Robert became aware that he was heading down hill alone. Giselle had stopped and was standing in the middle of the road. Wondering why she would do that, he went back and asked, "Now, where is this hut?"

She didn't answer right away. Her shoulders were trembling and she was making a noise that sounded like choking. Robert almost pounded her on the back, the usual remedy for choking, when it realized she wasn't choking at all. She was weeping.

"What's the matter?" he asked. "We don't have time for this. If anyone's about, we could still be seen, even at this distance."

"Oh, shut up. I'll stand here if I want to."

Since Giselle knew the location of the hut and he did not, he stood there, mystified and a bit irritated at what seemed like an unnecessary delay.

"All right then. Let's get on," Giselle said.

"Time-wasting nonsense, that's what this is."

"I'll spend my time as I please, thank you very much."

"Why are you crying, for God's sake?"

She gave him a withering look which even the night couldn't conceal. "You'll never understand. You're too thick-headed."

"Not too thick-headed to understand that this isn't as easy at it seems."

"Afraid?"

"I always worry when Eustace could be about."

"No need to pee your drawers because of that. I doubt he's here."

"Keep your voice down. Voices carry at night."

"You keep *your* voice down. I wasn't the one who started this conversation, anyway."

Rather than continue down the road, Giselle crossed the ditch and started across the field to the right, her skirt brushing the tall grass.

Robert followed her with the horses. Ahead, a dull square emerged almost indistinct from the gray of the field. He realized that the whitish square was the shepherd's stone hut Giselle had spoken about earlier. There was a fenced enclosure beside the hut, and the sour odor of sheep manure and urine filled his nose. At first he thought it was empty, but rustling made him realize that the fold was full of sheep. Sheep did not occupy a fold like this unless there was a shepherd about. He stopped and his hand reached out to Giselle, but she passed out of reach around a corner of the fold. He hissed, but she did not turn around. He dropped the reins and ran to her, but she was at the door by the time he reached her.

"Don't," he whispered.

The Outlaws

"Don't what?" Giselle asked and rapped on the door. The sound of the knock seemed to echo in the night as if trying its best to reach village.

The door scraped open and a stooped figure filled the doorway.

"What the hell is it?" the figure rasped in Welsh-accented English.

"Good evening, Caradog," Giselle said.

Caradog took one step, his nose within inches of Giselle's face. "What in God's name are you doing here? Are you mad? If you excuse my tone, my lady."

"I've thought that myself," Robert said.

"Who are you?" Caradog asked, not removing his nose from Giselle's face.

"Nobody," Robert said.

"Pay no attention to him," Giselle said

Caradog's stepped back. "You're supposed to be in London."

"That," Giselle said, "was supposed to be a secret."

"Well, somehow Wulfric found out. Nothing's a secret with him. How many times a day he shits is good gossip to him. Everybody knows."

"So it seems. Eustace paid me a visit."

"And so you come back here? What, have you two made up?"

"Hardly. I left something. I've come for it."

"Now, what would old Caradog have that the lady might want?"

"Put that suspicious mind to work and I'm sure you'll figure it out. But we'll be gone by then."

"Suspicious mind, you say? Now, my lady, you know I'm a simple soul."

"Promise me that you'll forget you saw me. And keep your suspicions to yourself. Can you do that?"

"Oh, yes, my lady. I've a poor memory, and it's been getting worse. I'd forget my own name if folks weren't always saying it to my face."

Giselle gestured toward the door. "Robert, would you please? The right rear corner."

As Robert squeezed by the herdsman, Giselle asked, "And how is your family, Caradog?"

A fire burned down to embers occupied the center of the hut. It was too dark to make out anything other than that even with the illumination afforded by the moon shining through the open doorway.

Robert groped his way around to the far right corner. It was occupied by a lamb and a ewe. He prodded them, but neither wanted to move. He lifted the lamb and set it aside. It wobbled and would havee stumbled into the fire if Robert hadn't caught it. The ewe scrambled to her feet, butted Robert out of the way, and went to see about the lamb. She made such noise that Caradog ducked his head through the doorway. "What's going on in here? You be careful, hear?"

"They're all right."

"They better be, or you'll answer for it."

He scraped aside the straw covering the ground, took out his dagger, and probed the dirt. The third poke hit something solid not too far under the earth. A few more pokes suggested that it wasn't a stone, unless someone had buried a squarish one. This had to be Giselle's box. He dug with his hands, tearing part of a fingernail loose. He paused to suck the wound, wishing he had brought a shovel, but he would have looked silly riding about with one. Sparing the injured finger, he resumed digging, and in a few moments he had excavated about the box enough that he could lift it out of the hole he had created. It had a broken lid and was filled with pennies.

He filled the hole back in and spread straw upon the place where it had been.

The ewe bleated as Robert stood up. "You can have your place back," he said to her. "I'm done with it now."

The Outlaws

They were trotting as fast as any rider dared to go on a bad road in the dark when Giselle reined up.

"What's wrong?" Robert said, pulling up beside her.

"Robert," she said, "I must ask you a favor."

"Ride and ask. We shouldn't delay." He urged his horse forward, but Giselle did not follow. Robert stopped and looked back.

"I want to stay. I want Hafton back."

"Back? Don't be absurd. You can't get Hafton back."

"What if I take it and hold it against him?"

"How would you do that?"

"I'm not sure. There has to be a way."

"Perhaps an annulment should come first," he said.

"That will take years. I can't wait years. I can't bear it. I thought I could, but I can't. Not when I've seen it again after all these years. This is my home, not his, and these are my people."

Tarrying at a hut on a hillside above a village that was nothing more than a collection of vague shapes in the moonlight did not count as seeing it. "What's this favor?"

"I need you to help me."

CHAPTER 7

London
April 1184

The traveler arrived at the Red Lion as evening fell and the bailiffs walked along the street ringing their curfew bell warning everyone to get inside.

There was nothing remarkable about the traveler, although close inspection would have revealed his hardened face, broken nose, ragged hair, and the scar on his cheek, which did not fit with his clothes, the sort that might be worn by a middling merchant.

Because it was late, no one also noticed that he had not come from the west, but from the city, which was odd, since the inn never got custom from people leaving the city at this time of night; or that he carried very little in the way of baggage.

Had anyone inquired, the traveler would have lied about his business and his origins, for he was in fact a member of the Ropery Street gang, and not a merchant at all.

It was too late for supper, but the traveler made no complaint, as many late arrivals were prone to do. He paid his farthing for a place on the floor in the hall, and settled in as Matilda capped the fire and six other guests spread out their blankets on the rushes.

Matilda looked around to see that everyone was as comfortable as could be on the ground; then she checked the doors and windows a final time before retiring upstairs, taking the candle, and the last light, with her.

The hall fell into darkness. Two guests began to snore loud enough to grate the teeth. The traveler chuckled at this; he had once knifed a fellow for snoring too loudly.

The traveler had not come to sleep, however. He sat with his back to a timber, senses alert. He had work to do here that would pay perhaps the easiest shilling of his career. When he thought he had given the slumberers enough time to fall into a deep sleep, he tip-toed toward a front window. He tapped on

The Outlaws

the shutter. There was an answering tap. He went to the door and lifted the bar.

A figure slipped inside from the street. "We thought you had fallen asleep," the figure whispered.

"Not me, sir," the traveler whispered back to the knight who filled the doorway. "You can count on me, sir."

The traveler slipped into the street and the door to the inn closed, leaving the knight inside.

Reginald le Bec stood just within the doorway, alert for any sound of discovery. One of the snorers harrumphed and fell silent. Le Bec fingered his dagger just in case the fellow rose up and detected him. But the man was quiet and shortly began snoring again.

Le Bec felt his way across the hall to the hearth. There were tables and benches hereabout, and people on the floor, and he didn't want to risk stumbling over anybody or anything. The thong of the wineskin about his neck had begun to smart. He removed it as he listened for further signs of whether he had been detected.

Now that he had located the hearth, le Bec felt his way to the nearest supporting timber. He poured oil from the skin at the base of the timber, then made a trail from the timber to the hearth. He pushed aside the fire pot covering the embers and grasped a handful of straw from the floor. He held the straw to the embers. When straw blazed, he dropped it on the trail of oil.

The oil-soaked straw caught fire immediately. A line of fire swept to the foot of the timber.

Within moments, a good portion of the floor was ablaze and flames were licking up the timber. Le Bec had never been in a burning house before and he had not counted on the cloud of smoke. He could hardly breathe for it, even when he bent low and covered his mouth with the hem of his shirt. He resisted the impulse to run for the door. He was more frightened than he had ever been, yet Eustace had said he must remain long enough to ensure that no one put out the fire. That was easy for Eustace to say, since he had never been in a burning house either and had no idea what it was like.

One of the guests sat up at last, coughing and sputtering. "Fire!" he shouted.

That woke everybody up right away, and there was a scramble as all the guests, shouting and choking and spitting, gathered up their belongings and rushed for the doorway. No one thought to try to stamp out the fire, which had spread over a quarter of the floor by now with flames licking up the timber and couldn't have been tamped out anyway. All they could think of was to get out of the house.

No one noticed when le Bec joined the rush into the street.

Matilda woke up to shouting and the smell of smoke. Smoke by itself was nothing unusual. The interiors of houses always smelled of smoke. This was different. It was sharp and intense. She leaped out of bed, sniffing the air.

She got up and raced toward the stairway. There was an orange-yellow glow illuminating the landing. A gust of hot air brushed her face, followed by a cloud of smoke. Toward the front of the house smoke was coming through the cracks in the floor, where orange flames illuminated the darkness. Fear shot through her. Although panic was her first impulse, Matilda fiercely suppressed it. She couldn't afford to panic. People would die if she did not maintain control of herself. She shouted: "Everybody up! The house is on fire!"

She started to go downstairs. A guest emerged from the nearest room and grabbed her arm. "Where do you think you're going?" he screamed in her ear.

"To see how bad it is! We may be able to put it out!"
"It's an inferno down there!"
"How did it start?"
"I have no idea!"

The Outlaws

She shook free and went down. She got as far as the landing. That was enough. Through a dense pall of smoke she could see that the entire floor was burning and flames were climbing the wooden timbers of the walls. In a few moments it would catch the ceiling and spread to the upper floor, which jutted out halfway over the hall.

When she got back upstairs, people were shouting and running about. There were five upstairs guests and three laden with all their things met her at the top of the stairs, intent on escaping through the main door. Matilda pushed them back. "That way's blocked! Use the windows at the back of the house!"

She grabbed Brian "Out the window. Run for the fire watch!" She hoped that they might arrive in time to save something, but she was doubtful. The fire was spreading too quickly. She feared the entire house would go before enough people got here to fight it.

Brian looked frightened. But now that he had something useful to do, he grew determined. "Yes, Mother."

Meanwhile, Alice had begun pitching all they owned out a window into the courtyard: mattresses, clothes, stools, their only chair, combs and other odds and ends. All their goods that she could lay hands on rained into the yard.

Matilda started to look for the money box when Harold caught her attention. He stood in the middle of the hallway while people rushed every which way around him. He held onto his rag of a blanket and sucked his thumb, looking frightened. He might be four, but he was a bright boy and knew about fires. "Are we going to die, Mummy?" he asked.

"No, Harold. We'll be all right. We're not going to die."

"But the house is burning up."

"Yes, I know."

"So we could die," he said with a child's implacable logic.

"Don't worry. I won't let you die." She pulled him out of the hallway into the bedchamber.

"All right."

His trust nearly broke her heart. She had to get him out of here.

By this time, the fire had reached the upper floors of the front of the house. The heat was unbearable. Smoke poured into the room and they had to crawl on their hands and knees to breathe.

Matilda gave up any thought for the money box. Her goal now was to get the children out. She grabbed Harold and pulled him to the window. "We have to get out!" she shouted to the others "Now! The entire house is going!"

Alice quailed as she looked out the window. "But how, Mother? It's so far!"

"The same way you got out when Eustace came — hanging from a blanket."

Agnes looked scared. "Oh, God, Alice's thrown them all out!"

Alice nodded.

For an instant, Matilda almost lost her temper and slapped the girl for such thoughtlessness. But that wouldn't do any good. She said, "Then I'll have to hold you. Here, Alice, take Harold. Agnes, you first."

Leaning out the window and holding Agnes by the wrists, Matilda lowered her as far as she could. The girl's weight almost pulled Matilda out. It took all her strength. "You have to let go now."

"I'm afraid!"

"It's not that far."

But Agnes would not let go and Matilda had to pull her arms free.

Agnes landed hard on her fanny.

"Wait there," Matilda said. She ducked back into the room.

"What do we do about Harold?" Alice asked.

"The same thing."

"But he'll break a leg. He's too small to jump."

"Agnes will catch him."

The Outlaws

Harold screamed and fought her when she lifted him toward the window. He was terrified of going out the window. She couldn't calm him and there wasn't time for gentleness. It took the two of them to force him out so that each held one of his arms while he dangled below, fighting and kicking and screaming.

"Agnes!" Matilda screamed. She could feel the heat of the fire on back. It had advanced into the room behind them. Smoke was pouring out of the window above their heads.

"I'm ready! Any time!" Agnes stood below with thin arms upraised. "I've got you, Harold! I've got you!"

"Ready," Matilda said to Alice, "go!"

Harold fell on top of Agnes, knocking her to the ground.

"Now you," Matilda said.

"No. You go."

"We haven't time to argue."

"You go. I'll hold you."

"Alice, don't be a fool."

"No, mother, go!" Alice pushed Matilda to up onto the sill.

There was no time to argue. Matilda thought that if she went quickly, Alice would follow. "All right, then, but do not tarry."

Matilda slipped out the window, dangled, dropped. The impact of the landing was harder than she had anticipated.

"Hurry, Alice!" she called.

Alice stuck her head out the window. The light from the fire behind her was so strong that she was a silhouette. "We forgot Brian's tools!"

Oh, God, Matilda thought. Brian's tools were his living. They would need his income to survive. But it was too dangerous. She shouted: "Forget the tools! Get out now!"

"I see the box." Alice disappeared from the window.

She reappeared a few moments later with the tool box. She put the box on the sill with great effort, for it was very heavy. She pushed it out. Matilda danced backward to avoid it. The box shattered on impact, spilling its contents.

"Alice, hurry!" Matilda screamed.

Alice climbed to the sill. The fire writhed behind her, framed by the window like the mouth of hell itself. Horrified, Matilda saw that Alice's long hair and dress were ablaze.

Alice jumped far out to avoid the clutter below. Arms outstretched, she plunged, a falling torch trailing flames.

She hit with an audible thump and collapsed in a puddle of flame.

Matilda grabbed a blanket from a pile of their belongings laying nearby and threw it over Alice. Agnes joined her and together they smothered the fire.

When they were finished they pulled the scorched blanket away. Alice's long blonde hair was burned almost completely away. Her dress was a charred ruin that crumbled at a touch. Agnes was crying so hard she could not see. Harold was there, too, still holding his rag blanket and sucking his thumb. "Is she dead?"

"I don't know," Matilda said. She was afraid to touch Alice, afraid that she might yet be alive and that her touch would cause her suffering.

Brian appeared and knelt beside them. He was crying too. He had seen Alice's plunge from the gate.

Matilda looked up at his arrival to see that the yard and the street outside were swarming with people. The fire watch had come. They could not save the house, but they were trying to contain the blaze. In wooden cities like London, a fire in a single house could ignite the whole town and turn a minor disaster into a major one.

Alice stirred, showing them all that at least she was still alive. "Mummy," she said, "Mummy, it hurts."

"I know, sweet one. I know."

Reginald le Bec and three men-at-arms stood in the road across the street from the Red Lion. Reginald scanned the faces of everyone who emerged from the inn's gate, not an

The Outlaws

easy task now that the fire watch had arrived and the neighbors were spilling out to fight the fire.

"You and you," he said, indicating two of the men, "come with me. You," he said to the last man, "keep an eye out for her in the street in case she gets past us."

Le Bec entered the yard with a rush of neighbors bearing buckets of water. The heat was intense, the entire house a pyre. It reminded Reginald of a burning haystack he had seen once as a child which had caught fire during the night all by itself, blooming into an enormous torch. It was so hot that the firefighters could not get near it. The few who tried approached as close as they could and pitched water at the fire, a futile effort which they soon abandoned, saving their strength to make sure that the house, which stood apart from its neighbors, did not transmit the conflagration.

The fire lit up the yard like the day, and Reginald had no trouble making out the faces of everyone who was there.

He did not see Giselle anywhere.

Reginald came upon Matilda's son, Brian. He grabbed the boy by the arm.

"What the devil —" Brian snapped. Then he recognized Reginald, for they knew each other from Shelburgh. "What do you want?"

"Where's Giselle? Did she make it out? We were passing by and saw the fire."

Brian snorted. "You can tell his lordship not to worry about her. She's been gone since yesterday."

Damn! Reginald thought. It had been for nothing.

"Where did she go?" Reginald demanded.

"I'll be damned if I'll tell you," Brian said.

Reginald thought about dragging him off to a dark corner to beat an answer out of him. But with so many witnesses about, someone was sure to intervene if he tried that.

He let go of Brian and went out of the yard.

The roof of the inn collapsed and drove sparks into the sky as they struggled across the street. Embers floated over nearby buildings, to the alarm of those who had turned out to fight the fire. It meant that all the houses downwind were in jeopardy.

Four men came with an unhinged door and used it to carry Alice to the street to a neighbor's house. The neighbors cut off the tattered remains of her gown, cropped what was left of her hair, and bathed her in cool clean water. The skin on her legs and the back of her head and arms was cherry red. The damage was worst on her calves and thighs and shoulders, where the skin was coming off in spots. Although she had been in great pain at first, she soon lapsed into a daze. She vomited once, and began to sweat and her breathing became shallow and rapid. But there was no more that anyone could do for her than lay her on her stomach upon fresh linens in the master bedroom, and pray for the best.

Matilda awoke just as dawn crept through closed shutters. She sat up in alarm. She had not meant to fall asleep. She hadn't wanted Alice to die alone.

She touched Alice on the cheek. The girl's skin was still warm and she was breathing. That was a relief. Matilda said another prayer.

She turned to find Agnes curled up on the hardwood floor with Harold beside her, the pair wrapped in a blanket. She had not seen or heard them come in.

Agnes stirred and sat up, rubbing her eyes. She looked at Matilda. "Is she . . . ?"

"No. Not yet."

"She'll suffer more then."

"I am afraid so."

"It isn't fair."

"It's God's will." Matilda said, although she had definite thoughts about what had caused this disaster. She pushed those thoughts away.

411

The Outlaws

Matilda said, "Where is Brian?"

"In the hall, I think."

"What was saved before the house fell?"

"Mostly our clothes. Brian and I retrieved them. And his tools."

"Well, we won't go naked then. And he'll be able to work. That's some comfort. And the rest?" It wasn't until that moment that she remembered she had forgotten to get the money box out. It held all their savings.

"A few odds and ends."

Matilda realized she had been thinking of her own welfare. "What about the others. Did they get out?"

"Everyone. That fat man from Ely broke an ankle jumping from a window. But as far as I know, he is the only other person hurt."

"Well, thank God for that."

The problem of the money box stuck in her mind. Something needed to be done right away to recover it, if it could be found. She checked Alice's breathing. It was slow and steady. Her shoulders and neck were red and blisters were developing. But since she had lasted through the night, it didn't appear that she would die soon. If she was to go, Matilda reckoned it would be later of infection. She made a quick decision. "I'm going downstairs. Watch your sister for me, and Harold."

Matilda went across the street. The inn was a pile of smoldering rubble. What had been saved lay in a pile by the stable. A member of the watch had remained through the night guarding it against looters. She thanked him and gave him a penny for his trouble and he left.

Margery, her partner, was already there, separating her things from those of the Attebrooks.

Matilda went into the shed and came out with a rake. She walked over to the wreckage of the house and stepped over a blackened timber, covering her face with a cloth against the smoke.

"What are you doing?" Margery called in astonishment.

"Looking for something."

"You're mad," Margery called. "It could smolder for a week. Come out of there before you burn yourself."

Matilda could feel the heat from the ashes through the soles of her feet. It wouldn't be long before her shoes burned through. She realized that she would have to wait for the ruin to cool before looking for the money. She retreated to the yard.

"I suppose we can put what's here in the stable for now," Matilda said.

"That will have to do."

Matilda looked around the yard. "The shed isn't touched." There were five barrels of finished ale and three of fermenting mash in the storage shed, which sat beyond the garden at the rear of the property. Those barrels were worth something, and so was the land itself.

Staring at the remains of the house, the biggest, finest house she had ever had, she couldn't keep away the thoughts troubling her. The fire had started in the hall. She had been the last one upstairs and she had banked the fire. She thought she had been thorough, but clearly she had not. It would not be the first time that a housekeeper had forgotten to cover an ember or a twig that had cast a spark. I have killed my own child, she thought. The pain of it was beyond belief.

Margery, looking up from the pile, saw her standing there frozen. "What is it, Matilda?"

With an effort, Matilda gave her an answer. "It's nothing, nothing."

"Help put these things in the stable, then."

There was a long pause. Matilda wiped her eyes. "Surely."

413

CHAPTER 8

Gloucester
April 1184

The failure to capture Giselle smarted more than Eustace cared to admit. The Attebrook woman must know where she had gone, but with her son Robert there, it was unlikely that he could pry the secret from her.

There was nothing to do now but return to Hafton and Harleigh. Yet that seemed too much like an admission of defeat. Besides, Aelfwyn was there and she had become boring.

Gloucester was on the way, and he knew someone who lived in the city. She was not the consoling sort, but Eustace had begun having thoughts about a future beyond his wayward wife, and this woman was often on his mind. Eustace decided to stop there in the hope she was at her townhouse.

It did not do, of course, for him to knock on her door and beg admittance. So Eustace took lodgings on Eastgate across from Saint Michael's Church, and sent one of his men to Lady Judith's townhouse on Berkley Street.

She was, it turned in a stroke of fortune, in residence, and invited him around the following day.

Her house was one of the grander ones on Berkley Street. Many of the more wealthy merchants had begun rebuilding their houses in stone, and, not to be outdone by such low people, the gentry having houses in the town had begun to do the same. Hers was one of them.

Eustace stood at the door as a groom came out to take his horse, aware of the great gulf that separated him from Judith. She was rich, whereas he was merely comfortable. The fact that he was an earl's son meant nothing because he was not the heir. Yet he knew he could be charming. It had to be that. She found him amusing. That was enough for now, but he had begun wishing there could be more.

A maid escorted him through the house to the back garden. There were willows planted here about an artificial pond filled with small fish. Judith was sitting on a bench surrounded by a covey of maids. Her hair was down and one of the maids was combing it.

"You may go," Judith said to the maids as Eustace came up. She patted the bench beside her. "Sit here, my lord."

It was droll that she should address him in this way, since she was the daughter of a baron and the widow of another, while he held a single manor.

When Eustace sat but said nothing, she said, "Well, you surely didn't come here just to stare at me."

"I wouldn't mind doing just that." She was, in fact, worth looking at, although no one would ever call Judith beautiful. Striking was more the word, arresting, fascinating, bewitching. Her face was too angular and square-jawed and strong, with thick brows and intense dark eyes, for mere beauty. She possessed a cool, self-possessed manner. She was two years younger than he was, but she seemed much older. Behind that face was a sharp intelligence and a wit that she made no effort to conceal.

"Come, I get enough flattery from my suitors. I expect the truth from you."

"What suitors do you have?" he asked, alarmed. Of course, he should have expected there would be suitors. A rich widow like her was much sought after, considering the considerable lands and wealth she would bring to a marriage, which in her case included both her dower lands and those of her husband, who had died without an heir. His plan had been to seduce her ever since they were first introduced last January. Although he had tried twice already, she had not yielded.

"Do you really want to know?"

"No. I'd like to think that I am the only man in your life."

"You're not, of course. But this afternoon, we will pretend that you are."

"I can be content with an afternoon."

415

The Outlaws

"Really? Are you sure you don't want something more?"

"No. There is only one thing I want, only one thing that's been on my mind since we first met."

"Oh, my! I think you are too forward, sir. I shall have to call for a chaperone."

"That would be a mistake."

A small book lay on the bench between them. Eustace opened it. It was in Latin, a history of Rome by Livy, books six through eight — not the sort of thing one expected a woman to read. "Where did you leave off?"

Judith took the book and turned to her place. She handed it back. "You read Latin?"

"I was forced to learn it as a child. My father thought a clerical career might be the thing for me."

"And it was not?"

"Regrettably, no."

"You defied Earl Roger's will? I am astonished. I've heard he is not the sort of man you want to displease."

"It did displease him. I misbehaved at the abbey, and they sent me home."

"I'd have liked to have been there to see your reception."

"I think you can imagine it, as well as the beating that followed."

"I am sorry. Yet you seem recovered."

"In time. I don't know about him. He never forgets a grudge."

"And he has a grudge against you?"

"He had a grudge against my mother. He takes it out on me."

"What grudge could he possibly have had against your mother?"

"She left him."

"Ah. I know that sort of man very well. Their possessions are everything to them, and the slightest defiance is a personal insult. My late husband was just such a man. I have to say, it is refreshing that he is gone. Every time I pass by the ditch in which he drowned, I thank God for the freedom he left me. Yet you remain close, despite the humiliation."

"My father has no heir."

"And you think you might be it? Even with this grudge?"

"I have hope. We shall see."

Eustace looked down at Livy and began to read aloud.

He had been reading for some time when she touched his hand. "Could you use some wine?" she asked. "Your mouth must be dry from all those dusty old words."

"I wouldn't mind a drink."

Judith called to the maid who had remained at the back door for just such a summons. The maid ducked into the house and returned with a platter on which rested a pitcher and two cups. She sat the cups on the end of the bench, poured wine into the cups and handed them to Eustace and Judith before withdrawing to the house.

"I should pass by Shelburgh sometime this summer," Judith said.

"Really." He pretended disinterest.

"Yes. I will be traveling from Davensford to my manor at Hickly. It's near Warrington, you know."

Eustace nodded. Davensford was Judith's principal manor, a few miles east of Bristol, not too far from Blanche's home. Warrington was northeast of Chester. "You'll have to pay me a visit."

"Indeed. I would like to meet your wife."

Eustace smiled. "I'm sure you'll enjoy getting to know her."

"What's she like?"

"Pig-headed, like you."

Judith laughed. "Then we will get along well, I'm sure."

Eustace sipped his wine. "Will you really come?"

"Do you want me to?"

"Yes."

"As a mere guest?"

The Outlaws

"My wife is occupied with her own affairs."

"Yes, I heard about that."

Eustace suppressed a flinch. "Everyone's heard about that, haven't they?"

"Well, I shall have to see how the summer goes." Her eyes strayed to the pond, then returned to his.

A long moment passed without either of them moving. Eustace took the wine cup from her hand. Their fingers entwined. He leaned forward and kissed her on the lips. She did not draw away this time.

CHAPTER 9

Hafton
May 1184

Giselle did not have a second thought until the moment she and Robert passed over the crest of the hill and Hafton lay in full view on the flat ground below. Adamant in purpose, she had waved away every objection Robert had served up, and she had imagined, had even savored, the sense of triumph she expected at her recovery of the manor, but as they approached, followed by the two men-at-arms and five archers hired in Coventry, dread and apprehension filled her mind. Robert had been right: this could not work. It wasn't too late to back out.

She gnawed on this as they reached the first houses, and people came out to see the procession. It was just after dawn, so many people had not been up long, as it was a Sunday, the day of the week on which people slept late. They stared at her with solemn faces. People looked surprised and there was a lot of whispering about what this meant, but nobody looked glad to see her.

"They think I'm in captivity," Giselle said to Robert. "That Eustace caught me."

"That's what I'd think if I were them."

She forced a smile. "They will be glad when they learn the truth."

"I hope so."

They were through the village in no time, passing into the screen of trees on the north edge between the houses and the manor. Giselle gulped as they cleared the trees and there ahead lay her house, the roofs poking above the palisade and embankment, the little stone tower looking more covered with moss and vines than she remembered.

She wondered if anyone from the village had run before them to announce their approach. It did not look as if they had, for the gate was open, as it always was in the morning, and no one stood there to see who the visitors might be.

The Outlaws

The bailey was deserted except for Osgar, who had halted at the door to the stable. His face was thinner than it should be, made more so perhaps by his jug ears.

Giselle halted before Osgar. "Good day to you, Osgar."

"And to you, my lady," Osgar said.

"I've come home."

"I am sure our lord is rejoicing."

"He doesn't know yet. It is a surprise."

Osgar looked puzzled. "What?"

Giselle dismounted and handed him the reins. "These are my bodyguards, not Eustace's gaolors. Where are Baldwin and Eleanor?"

He gestured toward the hall. "You'll find them there, as usual."

"Please take care of our horses while we get settled. Oh, and I shall require the hand cart, the one we use for hauling firewood. There is still such a cart, isn't there?"

"Yes, m'lady. I'll have it fetched straight away."

Giselle marched across the bailey to the house. They had created enough of a commotion on their arrival that people had noticed, and faces peered at them from the windows, mouths moving in astonishment when she was recognized.

She mounted the steps two at a time, followed by Robert, and entered the hall, where Baldwin and Eleanor had risen from their seats behind the high table.

"Ahem, well," Baldwin said, clearing his throat, uncertain what to say to her, although Eleanor's severe face for once had broken into a triumphant smile. "Well, well. Where is our lord?"

Baldwin must have expected Eustace to savor this victory. Giselle stopped in front of the steward and his wife, and said, "I have no idea."

"He won't be along?" Baldwin asked, puzzled.

"Not if I can help it."

"I don't follow."

"I've come home, Baldwin, to reclaim what is mine, and Eustace be damned." A plate of sweet buns lay in front of Baldwin. Giselle took one for herself and handed the plate to Robert, who passed the plate to a man-at-arms.

"Our lord be damned?" Baldwin sputtered.

By this time, Eleanor's grin had wilted. "It means she's seizing the manor, you dolt."

Baldwin blinked. "That's, that's . . . illegal!"

"Legal or not, here I am. And you two have a quarter hour to gather your possessions and get out."

Baldwin pounded the table. Confronted with an act so out of the ordinary, all he could think to do was bluster. "This is an outrage!"

"You're wasting time," Giselle said.

"The earl won't let you get away with this," Eleanor said. "You won't be able to hold this place with that riff-raff."

"That remains to be seen," Giselle said. "Get going."

Osgar had the cart ready at the foot of the steps when the archers brought out the trunks and loose possessions belonging to Baldwin and Eleanor.

"I hate to lose the cart," Giselle said to the steward and his wife as they stood by the cart regarding it with loathing. "But you may keep it. My parting gift to you for all you've done for me."

"You're sending me off like this?" Baldwin asked. "Without even a horse?"

"You don't own one, as far as I know."

"But how will we move this thing?"

"The same as everyone else does. You pick up the traces and pull. Get going, or I'll have you whipped."

Eleanor tugged Baldwin's arm. "Come on, let's not pile one indignity upon another."

"This is against God and reason!" Baldwin shouted.

"I doubt God cares," Giselle said. "And it is perfectly reasonable."

The Outlaws

Eleanor lifted one of the traces to the cart. "Baldwin! I am not pulling this thing by myself. Quit standing there, you fat lump, and help me."

Baldwin grasped the other trace and they pulled the cart out of the bailey.

"Was that necessary?" Robert asked as they cleared the gate.

"Perhaps not all of it," Giselle said. "But it was satisfying."

CHAPTER 10

Hafton
May 1184

"He's here, sir! He's come!"

Robert came awake with the servant's hand still on his arm. He bolted to his feet, the helmet on his lap falling to the floor and rolling some distance away as the servant who had awakened him scrambled to recover it.

"It's about damned time," Robert said, for it had been more than a week since Giselle had returned to Hafton. He had expected Eustace to arrive much earlier than this, and had even been prepared for an attempt to climb the walls at night.

He clapped his helmet on his head, hung his shield from his shoulder, and ran out to the yard while trying to buckle his sword belt without tripping over the sword.

The archers were already on the walls, even those who, like him, had been dozing because of their watches during the night.

"How many?" Robert called to them as he clambered up the embankment.

"Four," one of the archers said, leaning on his bow stave as if there was no trouble.

"Four? Only four!" Robert was astonished that Eustace had brought so few. He had expected a war party. Four didn't amount even to a decent escort for someone with Eustace's pretensions.

Robert peered over the palisade. Le Bec and Eustace were on the bridge and two other knights sat on horses beyond the ditch.

"What?" Robert asked. "Forget your key?"

Eustace looked up in annoyance that changed to astonishment. "What the hell are you doing here?"

"An honest day's work. Have you come to pay a visit?"

"This is my house. I don't visit my house. I live in it."

"Giselle might have something to say about that."

"Open the damned gate."

The Outlaws

"Or what? You'll bash it in? With what? Your head?"

Eustace gritted his teeth. "I've come to talk, not to fight."

"You were always better at that, anyway. So talk."

"I've nothing to say to you that can't be said with steel. My words are for Giselle. Now let me in."

"I don't think the lady wants to see you."

"I have a proposal for her."

"What sort of proposal?"

"Open the damned gate!" Eustace shouted, losing his patience at last.

"Just for you. The rest stay outside."

Robert opened the gate a crack, sword out and ready for a sudden rush. But Eustace came through the gap alone.

"It's good to see you again," Robert said. "We've so much to reminisce about — those good times on the Continent, and all."

Eustace glared and stalked toward the house.

"Doesn't look like he remembers things with as much pleasure as you," said one of the archers who had come down to help with the gate.

"Well, he wanted to have me killed, but that didn't work out."

"If you keep this up, he'll probably try again."

"He'll probably try again anyway." Robert called up to the men on the embankment: "Keep an eye on them. I don't know about the others, but that le Bec is a snake."

Robert crossed the yard to the house, where Eustace was already mounting the stairs to where Giselle waited at the top. She stood firm with arms crossed and did not get out of the way, so Eustace stopped a couple of steps below her.

"What do you want?" she asked.

"I think the better question is, what do *you* want?"

"Baldwin and Eleanor should have made that clear."

"I'd like to hear it from you. Messages get garbled, you know."

"I'm back and I'm not leaving. And you can get off my land."

"Well, it is my land, too. The law says so."

"I don't care what the law says."

"The law has a tendency to want its way."

"Only when men with swords enforce it."

"Well, that might be possible."

"If you had that in mind, you'd be here with an army. There's no army out there. You can't afford one yourself, so you'd have to borrow one from Roger. But you haven't. Which means you don't want the earl to know."

"What matters is what we tell him about our reconciliation. Can we discuss this inside?"

"I don't think there's anything to discuss, other than the time of your departure."

"But there is."

"You've made promises before that you failed to keep. That seems to be your habit."

"I promised you a free hand at Hafton. I gave you that."

"And then you conspired to pass off another's child as mine."

"There was no promise involved in that. Besides, it was in both our interests. You'd have been the wife of an earl. Once I obtained the earldom we could have put the child aside. But your pigheaded impulsiveness ruined that."

"So what do you want to propose now?"

"A way for us to be free of each other."

"How on earth is that possible, other than by your death?"

"That is harsh, dear wife. Let me inside and I'll tell you."

Giselle had chairs positioned so they regarded each other across the hearth. There was no chair for Robert, so he stood behind her.

"Must he be privy to this?" Eustace asked.

The Outlaws

"May I introduce my steward?" Giselle asked. "Eustace, Robert Attebrook. Robert, Eustace Fitz-, FitzNothing. But I forget, you've met before. Old friends, or something like that."

"If he knows anything about how to run a manor, then I'm fit to be an archbishop!" Eustace said.

"I'll not talk to you without a witness."

"Well, no one will believe anything he says, anyway. A common man and a murderer."

"He has risen in the world, while you, it seems, have diminished. And there is the matter of a royal pardon as well, I believe. Get on with your proposal. The day is wasting, and I have so much sewing to do."

Eustace leaned his elbows on his knees and smiled. The bitterness and anger vanished and he looked boyish and handsome. "I know you want to be done with me. And to be honest, I want to be done with you. I wanted this marriage no more than you. My father forced it on both of us."

"You have a thought on how to escape from our bondage? I cannot imagine the earl would allow it."

"He won't. But he's been ill lately. Age may have finally caught up with him. We have only to wait until he dies. Then we can do as we please."

"Until he dies . . . that could be years."

"It may well be. All you have to do in the meantime is to pretend to reconcile with me."

"Would Roger believe it?"

"The appearance is more important than the reality."

Giselle sat for a long time. At last she said, "All right."

Eustace's smile broadened. "Good! Now, we must have some explanation about where you've been. It won't do for people to know you've been hiding out in a tavern."

"It's an inn."

"Tavern, inn, it's unacceptable no matter what you call it. Don't you have any regard for your reputation? We shall say that you entered a convent, a convent in East Anglia. That's so far away no one will be able to disprove it."

426

"What if Roger asks the name? Do you know of any convents in East Anglia?"

"England is full of convents. There has to be at least one in East Anglia. I shall ask after one. And you will have to visit Shelburgh with me, so that my father sees us together."

"I'm not being seen anywhere with you. Roger will just have to be satisfied with your explanation."

Eustace's mouth turned down, then rebounded to a straight line. "Finally, there is the matter of the profits of the manor. My father requires quite a bit out of Hafton. That will have to continue so we don't arouse his suspicions."

"I knew you were under-reporting your profits, and keeping what you don't remit. I doubt you've stopped that, but it will stop now. I won't have my people squeezed as they have been."

"All right. By the way, what happened to the money box?"

"What money box?"

"The one you stole."

"I don't know anything about a stolen money box. Are we done? It will be breakfast time soon, and I'd like to eat without having the occasion soiled by your company."

Robert walked Eustace to the gate. Giselle remained inside. She did not even step to a window to see her husband leave.

As one of the archers opened the gate, Eustace said, "My wife and I may have an agreement, but you are not part of it. If my father's men encounter you anywhere, your pardon has no more value than that clump of moss you use to wipe your ass."

"Thanks for the warning. I'll keep an eye out for them."

Eustace passed through the gate. Le Bec was waiting for him on the other side of the ditch with his horse. Beside him were the two knights. They'd taken their helmets off while they awaited developments.

The Outlaws

One of them was Hugh le Gros.

Robert glared at Hugh, more astonished to see him than angry he should be allied to an enemy. Hugh refused to meet his eye. Robert pointed to him. "Is he one I'll have to watch out for?"

Eustace mounted his horse. "He's not one of ours. He belongs to my friend Edward de Stokesay." He gestured toward the remaining knight. "But, yes, you'll have to watch for him just the same."

CHAPTER 11

Charingdale manor
May 1184

Eustace left Edward de Stokesay and Stokesay's retainer, le Gros, at the turn off to Harleigh. Eustace and le Bec continued on at a leisurely pace. A mile short of Harleigh, they met a rider coming the other way. Eustace recognized the man, one of FitzWalter's squires named Clarence.

"Thank God, my lord!" Clarence gasped as he reined up. "I've found you! It's the earl!"

"What about the earl?" Eustace asked. He was not used to getting breathless messengers bearing news about the earl. It meant something must have happened.

"He's taken ill," the squire said. "He had a seizure three days ago and hasn't been able to move or speak since."

"A seizure, you say?" FitzWalter was now over sixty. His health had visibly declined the last two years. He had trouble walking, his hands trembled, and he was forgetful, even when he hadn't been drinking to excess. But a seizure? Incapacitation? Eustace could not afford to have FitzWalter die just yet. He asked, "Where is he now?"

"I've just come from Charingdale. The steward said you should come at once."

"Me? He specifically sent for me?"

"If he hadn't, my lord, I'd have ridden directly to Shelburgh to fetch our lady."

Eustace's thoughts raced. His life hung on the decisions he made at this moment. He asked, "Would it be possible for you to ride more slowly to Lady Blanche? Your horse looks tired. It would be a shame to abuse him, even for such a crisis. And I'd like to have a day with my father before she arrives."

"I suppose I could, my lord."

"Good lad. Thank you."

Then it was Eustace's turn to lash his horse into a gallop as the squire turned down the track at a walk.

The Outlaws

Charingdale, one of FitzWalter's southern manors, lay in a little valley northwest of Salisbury, surrounded by its circle of outbuildings: kitchen, smithy, barns, brewery, stables, a dovecot and assorted sheds.

FitzWalter's chaplain, Gerard, greeted him on the steps of the house.

"Is he still alive?" Eustace asked.

"He is." Gerard's face was grave.

"I'll see him immediately."

Gerard hesitated.

Eustace sensed Gerard had something to add. "But what?"

"You must prepare yourself."

"For what?"

"The sight of him."

"Why?"

"He can't move his right side, and has little strength in the left. And he can't speak." Gerard shuddered. "It's disturbing. Such a strong man, brought so low."

"Where is he now?" Eustace demanded.

Gerard gestured toward the chambers on the floor above at the rear of the house. Eustace crossed the hall to the stairs, passing through the crowd of servants and hangers on who accompanied FitzWalter everywhere.

He was at the top before Gerard had caught up.

Eustace paused with his hand on the latch to FitzWalter's chamber. He had not planned for an event like this, for FitzWalter's sudden and complete incapacity. He must think of something before Blanche got here. She had always tried to undermine him. He took a deep breath and opened the door.

FitzWalter lay on the bed with the blanket pulled up to his chest. His eyes were closed. The room was decorated in Blanche's taste with rugs on the walls, carved wardrobes and chests, and a high-backed chair that faced a smoldering brazier. The exposed timbers above were painted a bright yellow with red flowers in an effort to make a drab dark room look cheerful.

Eustace leaned over FitzWalter. "My lord," he said.

FitzWalter lay as still as death. Eustace couldn't even tell if he was breathing. He was about to prod the earl when FitzWalter opened his eyes.

"My lord," Eustace said, "I came as soon as I heard."

FitzWalter's left hand stirred. He made no effort to speak.

"My lord," Eustace said, "Gerard says that you have lost your speech. Is it true?"

FitzWalter closed his eyes, and reopened them, a slower movement than a blink. This must be his way of saying yes.

So it was true. Things couldn't have happened any better than this.

"Father," he said, "I've found Giselle. She's back safe in Hafton."

He had thought FitzWalter would be glad to hear that, but the earl showed no reaction.

Eustace said, "Let me refresh myself and I will return to you."

Eustace rose and went out of the room.

"Is Richard here?" he asked, meaning FitzWalter's steward.

"No, he's gone to Winchester for another doctor who might know what to do about this affliction. The ones we've seen have done nothing."

Even better. He might not return before the following day.

"Where have they put the treasury? That must be taken in hand during his infirmity."

Gerard hesitated. The treasury, which FitzWalter took with him wherever he went, represented the earl's total wealth in hard money. Gerard said, "It's in the strong room down the hall, but I do not have the key."

"Who does?"

"My lord has a key, and Richard."

"Where's Richard's room?"

The Outlaws

Gerard pointed to a door a few feet away. Eustace pulled up the latch and went in. He could tell from the single chest against a wall that Richard's wife was not here, so he didn't have to worry about her barging in.

"Where does he keep the key?" Eustace demanded of Gerard, who stood watching in the doorway.

"I have no idea."

Eustace searched the room and found two keys hanging from a hook at the top rear of the bedpost. He wanted to laugh out loud at the discovery. Richard kept the keys to FitzWalter's fortune in an unlocked room for any thief to find.

"Out of the way," he said to Gerard, and pushed past into the hallway and stalked down the corridor to the strong room.

The big key opened the door. The smaller one was for the chest standing against the wall under the window. Eustace opened the chest just to make sure it was the right one, then closed the lid. The man who controlled the keys controlled the treasury. Right now Eustace was that man.

He stood to face Gerard. "Gerard, what will become of you when Roger dies and this distant nephew takes possession?"

"He will have his own chaplain. He will undoubtedly discharge me."

"And where will you go then?"

"I don't know. I suppose I will have to seek the good will of another lord, or return to my bishop and hope that he has a place for me." Gerard was worried at this prospect. He had enjoyed a luxurious life with the earl. Life under the bishop would be much harder.

"It would be a hard thing to lose such a good living at your age. Are you in the will?"

"Our lord plans to leave me a small bequest." There was no hiding the unhappiness in his voice. He had served FitzWalter for more than thirty years. A small bequest, which probably wouldn't last long, must be a bitter disappointment.

"Where is the will?"

"Where all the important documents are kept, in the chancellor's office at Shelburgh."

"Isn't it possible to amend wills? To add bequests you have forgotten to make or change who benefits?"

"I'm not a lawyer, but I've heard of that being done. Why?"

"The earl is obviously dying. We must do what we can to protect our positions," he said. He had to be careful now. Gerard had a reputation for incorruptibility, but resolve could fail if the stakes were high enough. "Better to be in the service of one who values you and will see to your comfort in old age."

"If only that were possible."

"I'm sure that, given your loyal attention during this crisis, he would want to leave you something substantial. He also must have mentioned to you his reservations about his will, that he entertained an intention to make me his heir."

Gerard looked distressed. "I had thought about retiring. I have always dreamed of holding a comfortable manor on which to spend my last days . . ."

"I alone can make your dream come true, my old friend," Eustace said, "but only if I secure the honor. I can't do that without your help."

Gerard kept his face an impassive mask. "I have heard him speak of your inheritance."

Eustace almost laughed for joy. "All will depend on what you say about his change of heart. You must be steadfast if there are questions." Actually, it would be better if Gerard should die. But Eustace would deal with that problem later, if the need presented itself.

"Witnesses will be needed for this codicil."

"There are plenty of witnesses downstairs."

"There is the problem of . . . your parentage."

"Bastards can inherit. It's happened before."

"But that will require the king's permission."

The Outlaws

"He will remember me from France last year. I served well there. The things the king values most are loyalty and money. He has the one, I will have the other."

"It could require quite a sum."

"I don't care what it takes."

"What if the earl regains his senses?"

"I don't think that is likely, do you?"

Gerard paused. "No, I don't suppose it is."

One of the clerks, a lesser one but with enough experience to get the phrasing right, drafted the codicil at Gerard's direction, and then an urgent errand was found for him requiring his departure for Oxford.

Eustace took the will into FitzWalter's chamber and drove out the valets so that he and FitzWalter were alone, except for Gerard who stood by the door. He sat on the edge of the bed. FitzWalter opened his eyes. He couldn't even turn his head to look at Eustace. This was much better than Eustace expected.

"I have something to read to you, father," Eustace said. "What is it, you may ask? An amendment to your will. I've learned that you have failed to provide for poor Gerard. How could you neglect that good man, after all his years of faithful service? I thought it was an injustice that needed to be corrected." He almost added: "Oh, and there's a little something in here for me, too, or, should I say, it's for my mother. She gave you so much and got so little in return. I hope you won't mind."

FitzWalter blinked and his lips moved.

"Ah, well, I know that you're tired. This won't take long."

Eustace read out the codicil, for once grateful for the years he had been forced to spend in the abbey school, since he could understand what was written, while FitzWalter could not. In the translation, somehow the part about his inheritance got left out.

"There you have it," Eustace said, when he finished.

FitzWalter blinked. It was hard to tell whether this meant anything. But his left hand also clenched and unclenched. There was something agitated about this, although why he should be upset about the handsome bequest to Gerard seemed uncharitable, but then perhaps FitzWalter didn't like Gerard much. Not willing to take any chances, Eustace took a curtain cord and bound FitzWalter's hand under the blanket.

"I think we're ready," Eustace said to Gerard. "You can fetch the witnesses."

Eustace could not fall asleep that night. He paced in his chamber to ensure that he didn't doze off and ruin everything. He had tonight to do what was necessary. Who knew what would happen tomorrow? It was possible that Blanche would appear. She was no stranger to hard riding, even as a weak woman, and this crisis called for it if any one did. When she arrived, she was sure to hear about the changed will, and he was certain she would demand to see it, and then try to undo it out of spite, if for no other reason. And there was the chance that FitzWalter might recover.

Time always drags in the dark, and he was uncertain if midnight had final arrived. He pulled open the shutters for a look at the stars, since they might tell him the time, but the sky was overcast. The house was still.

He felt his way in the dark down the corridor and past the staircase, where a floorboard creaked so that he thought it would wake the servants sleeping below on the floor of the hall.

Eustace let himself into the master bedchamber. The coals in the brazier threw a dim glow on the ceiling, but it was enough to make out FitzWalter's face when he stepped close. FitzWalter appeared to be asleep.

Now was the time. But he hesitated a moment, frozen by the enormity of what he was about to do.

Steeling himself, he reached across FitzWalter's sleeping form for the next pillow.

435

The Outlaws

Eustace thought he glimpsed glinting eyes and a face contorted in a half grimace as he put the pillow over FitzWalter's face and pressed down. For a moment, he was reminded of another time and a much smaller thrashing body. This one had no more chance than the other, and FitzWalter grew flaccid and still.

Eustace pressed for a while longer, just to be sure. When he removed the pillow, he put a shaking hand against FitzWalter's mouth and nose. FitzWalter wasn't breathing.

A feather from the pillow had got through the casing and was stuck to FitzWalter's lip. Eustace removed it. It rested on his palm without sensation. With a puff, he blew it free and watched it float to the floor.

Then he smoothed out the pillow, put it beside FitzWalter's head, and tiptoed out of the chamber.

He should have returned to his chamber, but the walls seemed to press in upon him. So he went downstairs and picked his way around the forms sleeping on the floor to the door, where he slipped into the night, and sat on the stairs. It was balmy outside. The overcast had begun to break and stars peep through.

He had what he wanted. He would be the earl and mother was avenged. But he felt no satisfaction.

From a dark place he did not know existed, from behind a door kept shut until now, a wave of emotion swept out to engulf him. He found himself shaking, tears pouring down his cheeks, wetting the hands he pressed to his face, sobbing in a soundless scream that welled out into the indifferent night.

He was sad, ever so sad. And so sorry. Oh, Father, so sorry.

CHAPTER 12

Hafton
June 1184

Giselle had never realized there was so much to do in the running of a manor until she had to superintend all the work herself — organizing the gangs cutting timber for the village priest's new house, so that they would cut in the right place and not take too much; repairing the kiln, which Eustace had allowed to fall into disrepair; ensuring that the manor had enough food to feed those enlisted to cut the demesne's hay, which would begin soon; how to replace one of the plow oxen that had fallen sick and died, a major loss to the manor since it now had five; addressing the lack of shoes that had lamed three of the horses when the village now had no smith of its own; rotting tack that needed replacing; what it would cost to put a new roof on the manor house, since the wooden shingles were rotting in spots and Wulfric predicted that the next good storm would carry off all of it. "You'll wake up one morning looking at the sky!" he had declared. It seemed that from the moment she sat down on her stool in the morning for Eanfled to comb and braid her hair, there wasn't a second when someone or something wasn't clamoring for her attention. There were moments when she regretted casting out Baldwin and Eleanor. Had they remained, they would have lightened her load.

She had so little attention left that she didn't notice for quite some time that Robert was becoming restless. She had paid off the soldiers; no sense spending money on them when she didn't need them. And, without the incentive of wages, they had packed up and departed, having put a deep dent in both her remaining savings and in the stocks in the pantry. Who knew that feeding seven men would drive an otherwise prosperous house to the brink of destitution? God help us if the king drops in, she once thought. We'd be done for in a day.

The Outlaws

Robert had not left with the hired soldiers, however, even though guarding her did not seem to be required any longer, and there was nothing to pay him. He did eat a lot, but not so much as the archers, so the cook and butler didn't complain, and the cook and his boys, in fact, enjoyed having him around for all the stories he told about life on the Continent.

He did not spend all his time loitering about the kitchen. There was a beech tree just beyond the north ditch, little more than a sapling, and in the mornings Giselle could hear him beating upon it with a wooden stave while Eanfled attended to her hair. When it first started, she asked Eanfled what all the racket was about.

"He's trying to cut down that old dead beech," Eanfled said."

"He's taking a long time to do it," Giselle replied, astonished that Robert would decide to so something so menial.

"Well, he's using a piece of wood."

"You are pulling my leg."

"No, I swear. He's beating on the trunk with a wand that Osgar made for him."

"Beating on the trunk? You can't cut down a tree like that."

"That's what I said to Osgar, my lady. But he said it was either that old trunk or he'd put up a post in the yard and beat on that. I've never seen such strange behavior. But then knights are strange, aren't they? They aren't like ordinary people."

"Ah," Giselle said, the mystery having come clear, "he is practicing fencing."

"Fencing? Trees can't fight."

"They pretend it's a man. Go watch for a while. You'll see."

"You keep me too busy to go watch a man beat on a tree, my lady, although I'm sure it's very amusing."

"Don't tell Robert that. I doubt he wants to be thought of as amusing."

"I think that you should tell him that."

"What, to stop that racket?"

"No, that he's amusing."

"I have no reason to do so."

"He might appreciate hearing something like that from you."

"That would be too forward. He's sure to get ideas, the wrong ideas. You know how men are."

"Still, how would that be wrong in this case, my lady?"

"Eanfled! Think of what you're encouraging. I'm a married woman."

"Well, it won't be the first time a married woman's looked sideways at what she shouldn't."

"Besides, there's —" Giselle almost mentioned Harold.

"What, my lady?"

"Nothing. Hurry up, now. We've a busy day ahead."

"You warned me of that yesterday, and the day before."

"And each day lived up to that promise, didn't it?"

Aside from that racket in the mornings, she had little time for Robert. She might have made some conversation at dinner, but he was seldom at dinner, often going off after beating up the beech tree in the mornings either on foot or on horseback, taking a sack of dinner with him. She had no idea where he went or what he did, although she assumed he went hunting since he often returned with deer or rabbit.

And the evenings were no better. You'd think they were a good time to relax, but then there were clothes to be mended and personal disputes among the staff to be settled. Besides, he often sat and brooded, and retired early. How do you make conversation with a man who spends his time at the hearth scowling into the fire? The lively man she had known in London had disappeared in the last few weeks.

Then on the first Sunday in June, Robert announced that he was leaving. The declaration caught Giselle by surprise, even though she had been half expecting it. There was no good reason for him to remain.

The Outlaws

"What will you do now?" she asked as they stood in the yard waiting for Osgar to fetch Robert's horses, the question sounding lame to her ears compared to what she wanted to say but could not.

Robert shrugged and smiled in the way that threatened to melt her heart. "I don't know. Return to London, I suppose. See what Mum is up to. Then I'll have to look for a position. Mum won't let me loiter around the house like you."

"Well, I would have found things for you to do, but you've hardly said two words to me since Eustace visited us."

"I would have been a distraction."

"From what?"

Robert's smile turned sad. "From what you love most." He gathered the reins and mounted his palfrey, the second horse on a lead rope. "All the best to you, Giselle. You're going to need all the luck you can get. It will take more than luck to beat Eustace. Watch out."

Giselle nodded, fearful that the lump that had taken root in her throat would make her voice sound like a frog's.

"Oh," he added. "You might want to get down to the mill. The lower stone's got a crack in it. The miller told me yesterday that it could break at any time."

Giselle had not heard of any trouble at the mill; one more thing to be worried about, one more expense, a big one, too, since mill stones cost a lot of money. "I will, thanks."

He rode out of the yard.

Giselle watched him go, feeling more alone than she had on the hillside above Hafton when she buried the money box.

About an hour after Robert left, Wulfric, who had been promoted to bailiff, came to see her just before she was about to head down to the village church for Mass. He looked worried, and Giselle wondered what could have happened now. Whatever it was, it must be serious for him to hurry here on a Sunday.

"My lady!" he cried. "Eustace is the earl!"

"What? That's not possible." They had heard that Earl FitzWalter had died, of course; news of such import couldn't fail to reach even an out-of-the-way place like Hafton, but remembering the will in the chancellor's tower at Shelburgh, Giselle expected that the distant nephew would take the honor. He would surely take little interest in Eustace's affairs and in what happened at Hafton.

"My brother came over for a visit from Shelburgh. He says the word got there last night that the king's confirmed him."

Giselle was so dazed at this that she sat down on the steps and rested her head in her hands. "Dear God, it cannot be. It cannot be."

It was bad enough to have Eustace as a husband, but as husband *and* earl, he would have such power that he could toss her aside and confiscate Hafton. Marcher earls, even the lesser ones like Eustace, had almost unbridled power. The king himself was wary of offending them.

Why, even now orders might have come to the garrison at Shelburgh to do something about her. She was defenseless if they came. The villagers couldn't be depended on to put up a fight, even if she asked them to. They'd be fighting their lord, treason in itself, but an earl besides.

"What am I going to do, Wulfric?" she asked.

Wulfric bent over her and reached out a hand to pat her shoulder, though the hand remained suspended in space. "Things'll work out, ma'am. They always have a way of doing so."

She looked up into his kindly face, wiping tears from her eyes, wondering how he could be so calm given the calamity that had just befallen them.

I could just run back to London, she thought. There's always room at the inn. She didn't want to run back there, but at that instant, she could see a convent with high walls and thick, locked doors in her future, if she had any future at all.

The Outlaws

The sound of a horse's hooves thumping on the bridge echoed through the bailey. Giselle almost jumped out of her shoes as she turned with alarm to see who it was.

Robert rode up to her and stopped.

"What are you doing here?" she asked.

"I met a fellow on the road. He was on the way to Shelburgh to pay homage to our friend."

"Eustace."

"You know then."

"I just heard."

Robert's eyes wandered to Wulfric, perceiving him to be the messenger. "Look at this. You made our lady cry."

"I- I- That wasn't my intent, sir. I just thought she'd want to know."

"No matter," Robert said, dismounting. "It makes me want to cry too, as it should anyone in the village with half a wit in his head. If you thought life was tough before, it's only going to get worse."

He grasped Giselle's arm and led her upstairs into the house.

CHAPTER 13

London
June 1184

Alice came close to death several times in the weeks following the fire. The blisters on her legs and shoulders became infected and she lapsed into a delirium. When she recovered from that, she developed difficulty breathing, wheezing through bluish lips. But she shook that off by the end of the third week. Eventually, the infection receded and the blisters dwindled, leaving scars on her legs and shoulders where the burns had been worst.

The Attebrooks and Margery lived in the stable during this time. Matilda swept a stall clean and laid down fresh straw, and the family used that as their living quarters. With summer coming and the days growing warmer, it wasn't too bad. At least it put a roof over their heads.

The Attebrooks had not been able to save any cookware, for even the kitchen had burned although it had been detached from the main house, but the neighbors made up the lack during the first few days after the fire. Women dropping by to chat often left a pan or a pot or a spoon. Matilda soon had enough to cook a meal over the fire in the shed they used for brewing ale.

No more than a day passed before Matilda started selling what remained of their ale stock, even though the rubble of the house smoldered so vigorously that people had to cover their mouths from the fumes. Although they had no building in which to sell it, she peddled it at the entrance to the yard from the back of a cart. This didn't bring in as much money as having a full blown inn but it gave them something to live on. Casting about for ways to make money in a short time, Matilda hit upon the idea of taking the ale cart down to Smithfield for the Friday horse fair, which proved to be very profitable even with the stiff license fee. It was so profitable, in fact, that Matilda wondered why she hadn't thought of doing it before.

The Outlaws

Soon Matilda was able to buy some benches and tables, which she put up in the yard, allowing people to sit down, and enough timber to build a shed to shelter them.

The oven, which stood apart from the house, was intact, and once they had enough earnings to invest in flour, yeast, meat, and honey, they were able to bake bread and cakes and little pies, which were very popular.

Everyone was busy, working from an hour before dawn to sundown. Matilda and Agnes were exhausted much of the time. But business picked up, which was a Godsend, because after the ruins of the house had cooled, Matilda hadn't been able to find the money box.

Then Margery said that she wanted to sell the land and her interest in the business.

The land had belonged to Margery's husband Odo, who choked to death one Wednesday afternoon on a platter of eel. It was the legacy of a family of wealthy farmers who had owned several plots outside the city that were close enough to the main roads that people wanted to build houses upon them. All but this one had been sold off for one reason or another or split up between sons, so that the holding had shrunk to this remaining parcel. By the time Odo came into his inheritance what wealth his branch of the family possessed had long since dissipated. In death, Odo left it by will to Margery. As a widow, the law allowed her to do with it as she pleased. Since she and Odo had not had children, there was no impediment to her disposing of it.

"You're being foolish," Matilda said. "By next spring we'll have enough to build another house. We may not even have to borrow. It won't be a grand house, I'll admit, just a hall for the customers to drink and sleep in. But we'll design it so it can be added to. In a few years, we'll have a house better than the one we lost. If you sell, what will you do?"

"I'm tired," Margery sighed, glancing about the yard and the ruins of the house, which had not yet been cleared away because they did not have the money for it. "I haven't the strength for any more of this. I just don't care about this place any more. I'm forty-eight. If I sell, I'll have enough from the land and the business to buy myself a pension."

"If retirement is your objective, sell me the land and the business on the condition that we will provide for you for the rest of your life. You can stay here without care or worry."

"No. I have my heart set on the Glastonbury Abbey. In a quiet house in the country at my childhood home."

"Have you found buyers then?"

"I've been talking to a gentleman."

"Have you reached an agreement?"

"Not yet."

"You've done this without telling me?"

"Why shouldn't I? It's my land."

"You could at least have offered me the chance to make an offer."

"This land is worth a fortune. The only smart thing Odo did in his life was hold onto it. Where are you going to get that kind of money?"

Matilda suppressed a nod. Margery was right. The plot must be worth as much as five pounds. If they hadn't lost the money box, perhaps she could have managed the purchase, but now, with the family barely scraping by, there was no possibility. Yet she wasn't willing to give up. The business they had shared had been good and provided a fine living for the family. "What do you want for your share of the business, and for the land?"

"Twelve pounds."

Matilda's mouth went dry. Twelve pounds was as much as many manors yielded in a year — an enormous sum almost beyond comprehension. She forced herself to laugh. "You can't be serious! No wonder you've had no deal from your mystery buyer."

Margery looked stubborn. "What do you think it's worth?"

"No more than two-and-a-half."

The Outlaws

"I can't live on two-and-a-half."

"What you can live on isn't the question. What matters in what the market will bear. Two-and-a-half is fair price for what we've got left."

"I've never thought you to be so cold-hearted."

"Me? You're the one who wants twelve pounds, and for what, a business that operates out of the back of a cart and a waste plot?"

"The land's on one of the most heavily traveled streets into the city. That makes it valuable."

"Tell me, what does your mystery buyer intend to do with the land?"

"Build a house on it. Rent out part, I suppose, like everybody else."

"And you think he'll pay twelve pounds? He'll have to mortgage his manor for that. What lord will be willing to put his country home at risk for a plot of dirt outside the city? We aren't even convenient to Westminster."

"Well, I hope to get close to it."

"And I suppose he's willing to bear the cost of clearing out the ruins. That's not going to be cheap."

Margery harrumphed at that and folded her arms.

"You hadn't thought of that, had you? I daresay, it's such a mess that it'll cost two pounds just to haul away the wreckage."

Margery's mouth tightened. "All right, then, ten."

"Three-and-a-half."

"I thought you were a friend, yet after all these years I find you have the heart of a thief. Nine."

"I am your friend, the only one you have left. Four."

"You come up half a pound when I've come down so generously? You cut me to the heart."

"At least I know you have a heart, while many wonder where you've put it. All right, four-and-a-half."

"They do not! Eight. I shall not come down one more pence."

"I am beginning to wonder myself about your heart. You'd leave my family to starve on the streets?"

"I rescued you when Odo died. That's evidence enough of my heart."

"I'll give you that. Five."

"Seven-and-a-half."

"Five-and-a-quarter."

"This is tedious. Why am I wasting my time when you'll never get the money, regardless of the sum?"

"You do it as a courtesy."

"Oh, very well. What does it matter, anyway. You'll never pay. Six-and-a-half and done. I'll go no lower. And if I cannot find a suitable place at the abbey, you'll provide for my support and maintenance for the rest of my life. I shall have a chamber of my own in whatever house you build, and furnishings."

Six-and-a-half pounds was still a staggering sum and more than the land and business were worth. But Matilda was desperate. "Six-and-a-half and done."

Matilda extended her hand and they shook on the deal.

Now all she had to do was find the money.

The next day, Matilda went into the city to find a moneylender. Many Christians lent money at interest, although it was illegal for them to do so. Because it was illegal, the terms were often stringent. The best deals could be made with the Jews, whose only legal occupation was the lending of money. So Matilda sought out the Jewish quarter, which lay about Jewry Street just east of Saint Paul's Cathedral.

Jewry Street was little more than an alley extending north from Cheapside. Most such alleys in the city were dark and dank from the houses jutting out over them so that they left only a ribbon of sky overhead, filled with shit and piss and garbage, muddy, with laundry hanging from ropes that stretched overhead. While Jewry Street was as dark as any other, it was clean; there was little evidence of the usual

447

The Outlaws

practice of dumping chamber pots out the window, and no piles of garbage impeded the passage. No one could do anything about the mud, of course, but at least it hadn't rained recently, so the ground was firm.

The first place that seemed open was the second house on the left. The bearded man who came to the window wore a tall, pointed hat of yellow felt which gave him a foreign appearance, but he spoke English like any other denizen of London with an accent that Matilda still sometimes found hard to follow. "Can I help you?"

"I need money," Matilda said.

The Jew smiled. "Everybody needs money."

His eyes looked Matilda over, measuring her prosperity and thus for a sense of how much she might want and her ability to pay. The Attebrooks had saved a few rags from the fire, and Matilda had borrowed her gown from the cutler's wife across the street. Yet even though it was a serviceable gown of a middling merchant family, she felt shabby.

"I need a loan," she said.

"How much?"

"Six-and-a-half pounds." Even as she said the words, she knew how impossible this sounded. No one was going to risk six-and-a-half pounds on someone like her.

Yet the money-lender's smile did not falter, nor did some sarcastic remark fall from his lips. "What for?"

"I own an inn on Holborn Street beside the Fleet. It burned recently. I need to rebuild."

"I know that place. What's it called? The Red Lion?"

"That's it."

"I am sorry about your loss. You don't need six-and-a-half pounds to rebuild an inn."

"My partner owns the land and half the business. She wants to retire. I'm trying to buy her out."

"And I suppose you intend to repay from the profits?"

Matilda nodded.

"That will take a long time. Years. The interest will be high, and the risk of default great. The profits of inns are often not very great. It is a hard business. But you know that."

"You'll have the land and the house we build on it as security."

"But we're not allowed to own land. If the courts let me take it, I'd have to sell it immediately. In such a forced sale, it's unlikely that I'll recover the value of my loan, or the cost of my lawyers. That land's not worth six-and-a-half, anyway."

"So — we can't do business?"

The money-lender shook his head. "I don't think so. I'm sorry."

"Thank you for your time. Is there anyone else here I might speak to?"

The money-lender pointed down the alley. "Isaiah's three doors down, and Jacob is across the street. You could try them, but I suspect you'll get the same answer."

Matilda indeed got the same answer from Isaiah and Jacob, and from five other lenders in the alley.

She turned the corner onto Cheapside, deep in despair, without looking where she was going, and just avoided being trampled by a team of horses pulling a wagon with barrels stacked so high that the top ones wobbled, threatening to fall and crush those rushing along the edges of the crowded street.

"Watch where the hell you're going!" snarled the driver, mounted on the left lead horse, as he jerked the team to the left, nearly sending a couple of barrels careening.

Matilda leaped back against a house, aghast at the spectacle of the wobbling barrels.

"That was a close one," a familiar voice said.

Matilda looked at the man who was also hugging the walls to avoid the wagon. She puzzled over where she knew the man and that voice, but as an innkeeper, she met so many people that it was difficult to keep them straight.

"You don't remember me, do you?"

The Outlaws

Matilda shook her head.

"Well, it's been years, and I suppose I've changed quite a bit. I'm Jean of Gloucester, or lately of Gloucester, anyway."

Comprehension dawned at last. "The wool merchant. My son worked for you."

"Yes," Jean smiled. "I expected him to fall into poverty and ruin after he left me, but somehow he seems to have done well for himself, although I cannot say how long that will last. Eustace FitzWalter's wayward wife has come out of hiding and has taken back her manor with Robert's help. All of the west is aflame at the scandal."

"I didn't know that," Matilda said. But Jean had no idea that Giselle had been hiding here, and Matilda said nothing about it, too stunned at the news that Giselle had not fled to Normandy after all.

"Yes, I like to keep up with all the news in the March. In fact, I even saw Robert last winter. He came by my house after he got back from France. I told him where to find you."

"How on earth did you know that?"

"I stayed at your inn once during one of my trips here. You didn't remember me then, either."

"I'm sorry."

"But I remembered you. You're hard to forget."

The frank and open way he stared at her almost made her blush, but then she was used to being stared at by men. "And how is your wife and family?"

"My daughter is well. My wife passed away a year ago."

"I'm sorry."

"These things happen. She was a good woman. I miss her, God rest her soul. What are you doing in Jewry Street?"

"What one normally does there, looking for a loan."

"I have a feeling that you didn't get it."

"Is it that obvious?"

"People who make loans usually look rather happier and aren't so oblivious to wagons. This must have been for your business."

"Yes."

"I heard you had some misfortune lately."

"That is a gentle way of putting it. We live in a stable and do business out of the back of a cart these days."

"But you are hoping to rebuild."

Matilda nodded, and told him of her arrangement with Margery.

Jean appraised her. "It's good that you're not willing to give up."

"What else am I going to do? I'll not have my girls become whores just for their daily bread."

Jean's gaze wandered down the street. "Perhaps there is a way I can help."

"How so?"

"I can put up the money in return for a half interest in the business and in the land."

"Why would you do that?"

"My brother died a few months ago. He ran the London side of the business. His son isn't experienced enough to handle that part of things, so I've come here to take it over. I live in a rented house. It would be nice to own the land beneath my house for a change."

"You'd live in an inn?"

"No. You'll have your inn on half the land and I'll have a house on the other half."

"I want the right to be able to buy you out."

"What, you think I'll be a bad neighbor?"

"No, and I also want you as a silent partner, without the right of control."

Jean thought for a few moments. "You are harder than I thought, certainly harder than you look. But I think we can do business."

CHAPTER 14

Hafton
June 1184

The last person Giselle expected to see again was Aelfwyn, but she rode up to the gate alone, dressed not in the blues, reds, and greens so popular with people of the landed class, but the subdued browns and blacks of the folk who toil. Aelfwyn hesitated on the bridge, as if reluctant to enter, and when she saw Giselle by the entrance to the kitchen, she waved and called, "My lady! May I come in?"

It was so much of a shock to see Aelfwyn that Giselle had to remember to shut her mouth before something flew into it. "What are you doing here, Aelfwyn?"

Aelfwyn burst into tears at the question. "I've nowhere else to go!"

Giselle crossed to the gate. "He's tossed you aside, has he?"

Aelfwyn nodded, the tears coursing down her cheeks.

"What about your father? Why not go home?"

"He won't have me back!" Aelfwyn wailed.

Giselle had heard that was true. Since she had returned and everyone had learned of her agreement with Eustace, feeling against him, suppressed by the fear of his hand, had erupted with an enthusiasm that customarily was reserved for the Welsh. Aelfwyn had made no friends for herself as Eustace's bedmate, least of all in her own family, who were quick to denounce her and perhaps made more of a show of their dislike because the special exactions and fines meted out to the villagers had not fallen as heavily on them, a matter they wanted people to forget.

"You rode all the way from Harleigh alone?" Giselle asked.

Aelfwyn nodded, sniffing and wiping her nose on her sleeve.

"I'm sorry," Giselle said, although not a particle of her commiserated with Aelfwyn.

"No, you're not."

Aelfwyn had her measure there, for in fact, Giselle was rather enjoying the other woman's misfortune; it's only right after how she treated me, Giselle thought. Then she chided herself for being uncharitable. Aelfwyn had used her good fortune to lord it over Giselle, but Eustace had used her, and tossed her aside, as Giselle had been used and was about to be tossed. The difference between them was that Giselle couldn't wait to be abandoned and had the means to support herself.

"All right, I'm not sorry."

"Please don't send me away. I don't know what I'll do."

"Spread your legs. That's what you're good at. Some man will take you in."

"It can't just be any man. You know that. I've got to be careful."

Giselle was surprised at this answer. She expected that Aelfwyn's pride wouldn't allow any admission of the fact that the one thing she did best was fall on her back for a man. "We all do. So, you expect me to put a roof over your head, and find you a decent man to wed in the bargain? That's asking more than you deserve from me."

Aelfwyn hesitated, then smiled. "Well, the roof would be nice. Until I can get settled."

"I suppose I can manage a roof, for a few days."

"Thank you so much," Aelfwyn said, crossing the bridge into the bailey.

"You'll sleep in the hall, like the rest of the servants. Supper's in an hour. I'd have someone get your things for you, but everyone's busy."

CHAPTER 15

Hafton
June 1184

Three days after her arrival, Aelfwyn sought out Eanfled, who had been avoiding her.

"Walk with me," Aelfwyn said.

"Why would I want to do that?" Eanfled asked.

"We need to talk."

"We have nothing to talk about."

"It's about your family."

"What could you possibly have to say about my family?"

"They are in danger. Perhaps you've heard."

Eanfled, who had not heard anything lately from her father or brothers, felt chilly. "No, I haven't."

"Then come. This no place to discuss the matter."

Eanfled followed Aelfwyn through the gate. They turned on the track to the river. Eanfled chewed her lip until they reached the ford. There had been something hard and sinister in Aelfwyn's tone, even though she hardly ever spoke in that way; cold condescension or sarcasm was more her style.

Aelfwyn stopped in the shade. She looked about to see if anyone was nearby. Boys often fished upstream where a curl in the river created an eddy and a hole where fish liked to congregate. No one was in view.

"What is it?" Eanfled asked. "I've work to do."

"Your father and brothers have been arrested," Aelfwyn said.

"How would you know that? I doubt you've been to Shelburgh in years, even if Eustace is earl now."

"Reginald le Bec told me."

Eanfled pursed her lips. The vague sense of unease she had felt on the way down from the manor house blossomed into full anxiety. Yet if her father and brothers had indeed been arrested, she expected one of her brother's children would have come to tell her about it. "I don't believe you."

Aelfwyn shrugged. "Believe what you wish. It's true."

"Why would they have been arrested?"

"Shorting on their weights and putting sawdust into their bread." Aelfwyn looked across the river, where a field rose up the hill. "Lead weights were found in some of their loaves."

"That's a lie. My father would never cheat like that."

"Yet he did. In loaves sold to the castle, no less."

"Why are you telling me this? I know you like gossip, but this is more than that."

"Our lord means to hang them."

"Shorting loaves isn't a hanging offense!"

"It is when you cheat the lord."

"He has no right! We are free! We have the right to the king's justice!"

"He's the lord. He can do whatever he wants."

Eanfled had never felt so cold and helpless.

"There is," Aelfwyn, "something you can do, though, to save them from the rope, and earn our lord's forgiveness."

"What?"

Aelfwyn held out a small clay pot capped with a wooden stopper. "See that Giselle drinks this."

Eanfled made no effort to take the pot. Aelfwyn grasped her hand, put the pot in her palm, closed her fingers around it, and held them closed.

"What is it?" Eanfled asked.

"I think you can guess."

"And if I don't?"

"Eustace will kill your family. And you, too."

Aelfwyn left the next morning, to everyone's surprise, since they had expected her to remain for quite a while, not that they were sad to see her go, however.

Eanfled asked Giselle if she could have the day to herself after Aelfwyn rode out the gate.

"Is something wrong?" Giselle asked. "You don't look well."

"I'm fine. I need to see my mother."

The Outlaws

"Is she sick?"

"No."

"Is anyone else in your family ill?"

"No."

Giselle had no reason to refuse this request, so she nodded. "Will you be back for supper?"

"I don't know."

"Something must be wrong. You don't want to share it with me?"

"Nothing's wrong. Thank you, my lady. I'll be going now."

Normally it took a full hour or more to walk the distance to Shelburgh, but Eanfled walked fast and made it in less time.

Most of Shelburgh, if you didn't count the castle, lay along a single street that descended from the bridge, with the remaining houses on a few narrow lanes that ran off here and there. She had to pass the lane that led to the house the Attebrooks had lived in to get to her family's house, and she thought of Robert: of mud clod fights they had after a heavy rain and how once they had all turned on the tollkeeper at the bridge and pelted him, how the tollkeeper had chased them and how she would have been caught when she fell if Robert hadn't pulled her out of the ditch they had leaped to get away; of Robert wading in when Penda and Sigbert were beating up Egfrid, a sickly boy who never stood up for himself and who was a constant target of the bigger boys; of sneaking into the lord's orchard after dark to steal apples from his trees, a terrible crime for which they were never found out; of racing stick boats in the river. Those had been good times. Most people were poor here, but didn't feel their poverty. They had enough to eat, which was what mattered most, and little to worry about other than the Welsh just to the west, the prospect of sickness or injury, the lord's bailiff, with his frequent demands for their time, and the lord's fines and rents. But everything had changed. The good times had gone, never to return, and there was nothing left of the skinny boy with the sunny smile; he was so different that his old friends wouldn't recognize him.

There were two other bakers in Shelburgh besides her father and brothers, and she smelled the scent of baking bread, thick with yeast, even as she pushed through the gate to her house. The smell, so welcome to everyone, should have been thickest here, but no smoke rose from the oven behind the house, which was alarming. Eanfled thought her mother would continue working the oven even if her father and brothers were in gaol. She could not imagine why the oven was cold.

The house was no more elaborate than anybody else's, which meant that the front door opened into a hallway that ran clear through to the back, where another doorway opened into the rear garden. The goats and sheep were kept in the room to the right, and the family lived in the room to the left, including the family of her older brother, who had got a village girl pregnant before his apprenticeship had ended. Although apprentices were not supposed to marry, because they couldn't support a family, it had been agreed that an exception should be made in this case, so Hilda had moved in. Eanfled heard the baby crying even before she reached the door.

Hilda heard Eanfled and turned her head to see who it was as she gave the child her breast.

"What are you doing here?" Hilda asked.

"I heard the news. Is it true?"

Hilda nodded. "Yesterday."

"Yesterday!" The very day that Aelfwyn had given her the news. How could she have known? "Why isn't the oven going?"

"We're not allowed to bake while they're in gaol. Lord's orders."

"Not even for ourselves?"

"No."

"How will you live?"

The Outlaws

Hilda shrugged.

"Where's Mum?"

"Gone up to the gaol. They don't feed prisoners, you know."

Eanfled nodded, remembering that was how Robert had got into the castle to free his uncle, the night Ralph the master of squires had been killed and all hell had broken loose. She sat on the stool beside Hilda and dug into her purse. She had half a shilling, all her savings. She held the coins and shards of coins out to Hilda. "You'll need this, then."

Hilda's mouth dropped open at the pile of coins, for it was a lot of money. She put the baby on their parents' bed and cupped her hands together so Eanfled could pour the pile into them. "Eanfled!"

"It will tide you through, I hope." Eanfled stood up.

"You're going?"

Eanfled nodded.

"You're not going to wait for Mum?"

"No. I've things to do. Tell her I'm sorry I missed her." It was hard for Eanfled to speak or keep a straight face, because she felt like crying, and didn't want Hilda to see. She left the house and managed to reach the street before she broke down. For her tears weren't as much for her family as for herself, and the horrible thing she had to do to save them.

Giselle began to feel sick about an hour after supper as they were sitting around the hearth while night fell and the interior of the hall grew dark. It started as a vague feeling of nausea, which came and went. At first, she was able to ignore it, but the pangs grew in intensity until a great tremor seized her and she leaned forward and threw up her supper. Thick ropes of saliva hung from her mouth to the remains of the meal in a puddle at her feet.

"Are you all right?" Robert asked, hand on her arm.

"No," she managed to say as another tremor struck and she vomited again. "What about you? Do you feel anything?"

"No," he said. He asked the servants, "Anyone else feel ill?"

Everyone shook their heads, faces anxious. Bad food could kill a person, and if one fell sick, others often followed, for everyone ate common fare out of a common pot.

She threw up twice more, now into a bowl that Eanfled held out before her. The nausea subsided a bit, but did not go away. She grasped the arm of the chair and pulled herself erect, but her legs trembled and she would have fallen if Robert had not caught her.

"Take me upstairs," she panted.

Robert helped her to her feet and half-carried her to the stairway.

"You're sure you don't feel anything?" she asked him as they climbed to the upper floor.

"Just full."

"I wonder what it was."

"Could have been a bad piece of fruit, I suppose."

Giselle nodded and leaned against him as he opened the door to her bedchamber. "Another's coming," she said, and tottered by him, falling to her hands and knees, scrambling to the chamber pot so she would not mess the floor.

When that spasm diminished, Robert lifted her to the bed while one of the maids fetched away the chamber pot and replaced it with another. Giselle expected Eanfled now to come in and help her undress, but Eanfled remained by the door, hands over her mouth, eyes horrified, then she ducked out of the room. Giselle lay back on the bed, exhausted and unable to move. Robert stood uncertainly over her for a few moments, and then touched her skirt. For a man to undress her was an unspeakable transgression. Several of the other women servants came in and shooed him out of the room so that he did no have to violate her this way.

Giselle's mouth was so full of saliva that she almost choked trying to swallow it. She was too weak now even to sit up to spit into the chamber pot. She had to grasp the side of the bed and roll to the edge.

The Outlaws

"I'm not touching her," said one of the servants who had remained in the chamber.

Another servant cuffed the woman. "I'll not hear that from you. Come on, let's get her clothes off."

One of the women emerged from Giselle's chamber, her eyes filled with worry.

"She's no better?" Robert asked.

"It's worse. I'm going for the midwife. We hope she might know what to do."

Robert couldn't stand waiting around in the hallway. He pushed open the door and entered the chamber. Neither of the two women who stood by the bedside objected to his presence now.

Giselle lay on her side, eyes open but unseeing, the pupils unnaturally large. Her breathing was fast and shallow. From time to time, her whole body shook. Threads of drool hung from her mouth which one of the women mopped up with a rag.

It seemed like hours until the village midwife arrived, but it could not have been long. A heavy woman in her forties with long gray hair and a flat nose on a wide face that gave her a frog-like appearance, she pushed Robert out of the way and knelt by the bed. She brushed Giselle's hair out of her face and wiped her mouth with one of the rags.

The midwife looked up at Robert. He asked, "What's wrong with her."

"Tell me everything that's happened."

Robert recounted the meal, sitting around the hearth drinking the last of the ale, and the sudden attack of vomiting.

"I've seen its like before," the midwife said. "Hemlock poisoning. I doubt she'll make it through the night. The next hour or so will tell."

"Hemlock poisoning?" Robert asked, bewildered. "How could that have happened?"

"No one else is ill?"

"I don't think so."

"Hemlock is often mistaken for wild carrot or parsnip. The ignorant occasionally eat the roots or the leaves. If someone in the kitchen mistakenly seasoned the food with hemlock, everyone would be sick. Because she alone is ill, it means someone poisoned her."

"You mean someone here, among us?"

"I doubt it was the fairies, lad."

"There's nothing you can do?"

"I can send for Olof. She'll need him soon."

Robert sat on a stool by Giselle's bedside waiting for her to die. Now and then, he wiped her mouth, or held her shoulder as she shuddered, often violently, her head, her arms and her legs flailing about. After an hour or so, the spasms subsided and her breathing became even more shallow, and her lips turned blue. When Robert put a finger under her nose, he felt almost nothing, a soft tickle.

"You ought to go downstairs," the midwife said. "I'll watch her. I caught her when she came into the world, I'll be there for her when she leaves it."

"No, I'll stay."

He hugged his knees and tried not to think about Giselle's ordeal, wishing that it was over and she wasn't in any more pain, for this looked like a horrible way to die. He turned his thoughts to the riddle of who had done this. The single person who wanted her dead was Eustace, since he stood to keep Hafton if she died. He would not carry out this act himself. He'd want to be kept distant from it, which meant he needed help. Aelfwyn came to mind, but she had left several days ago. It couldn't be her. Yet it was very odd that she'd come here, just to leave within days. That had to mean something. If she hadn't done the poison, she had persuaded one of the household staff to do it. He thought hard about the events of earlier in the evening, how things had gone, who had stood where, who had done what, but it was all a blur of

The Outlaws

ordinariness, an evening the same as any other. He thought back further to supper. It had been left over roast goose and leek soup, cheese, cuts of ham, and bread. The leek soup might have been poisoned, but the two of them had been served out of the same bowl, so that couldn't be it. The only thing they had not shared was the ale — no, Robert had served the both of them from the same pitcher. Afterward, they'd taken the pitcher to the hearth, where they'd finished it and asked Eanfled to bring another, which she had done. She'd been clumsy, though, when refiling their cups from the refreshed pitcher. She'd knocked over Giselle's cup and had to get another, and then almost knocked over that one too. He remembered then that she'd taken Giselle's cup to the sideboard by the door to the chapel, behind their backs, in order to fill it. Her hands had been shaking when she brought the cup back.

Robert shot to his feet.

"Had enough?" the midwife asked.

"No. I think I know who killed her."

Robert descended to the hall where everyone who slept there was still awake. They rose and gathered around him, asking whether Giselle was all right, whether she had died, and what would become of them.

"She hasn't died yet," Robert answered them. "But has anyone seen Eanfled?"

"Last I saw her," said old Burghard, directing a crooked finger toward the door, "she was on the stair outside. Grieving for our lady."

"Grieving my ass," Robert said, as he rushed across the room.

He flung open the door. A figure bathed in the light of a three-quarter moon and wrapped in a cloak sat on the top of the stairs. The figure turned, revealing a flash of white face.

Eanfled cried out and dashed down the stairs two at a time with astonishing agility, cloak flying. She sprinted toward the gate, but it was closed, of course, and afforded no escape. She could have climbed the embankment and vaulted the palisade, but for some reason, this did not occur to her, and she swerved toward the barn.

Robert could run well; he'd prided himself as a boy with being able to outrun just about anyone, and in Gloucester some drunks had even proposed to race him against a horse, which had not come off, a fortunate thing for the drunks, as they'd probably have lost their wager. But Eanfled was so quick that she beat him to the barn door and disappeared inside.

It was as dark as a sack inside even with the moon casting white light through the open doorway, and he could not make out where she had gone. But he heard her climbing the ladder to the loft, and he climbed too.

Eanfled did not stop at the deck of the loft but scrambled up a beam towards another that ran between a pair of crucks, the great curved beams that ran from the ground to the roof, forming its support. Robert panted on the loft, contemplating such a climb with dread. He was sure he would fall if he tried, and that cross beam was a good twenty feet above the ground.

"Why, Eanfled?" he asked. "Why did you do it? Who put you up to it?"

"I'm sorry!" she called back. It sounded like a sob, and then a racket of sobs stormed down from the dark above. "They made me!"

"Who made you? Come down and tell me. I won't hurt you. I just need to know."

"I know you intend to kill me. You should. I deserve it."

"Was it Aelfwyn? Eustace?"

"She said they'd kill my father and brothers if I didn't."

"I understand, Eanfled. Family comes first. But why didn't you tell us? We might have been able to do something."

"What can you do against him?"

"Well, I have some experience breaking people out of gaols." As soon as he spoke, he knew it was a mistake.

The Outlaws

"And your uncle died in the attempt. I remember that night."

And I learned from the experience, he said to himself. I could have managed it. But there was no profit in going any further along this path.

"Come down, Eanfled."

"Why? I know you loved her even more than I. And what of the rest? Would you protect me from them?"

Robert's answer was interrupted by a shadow in the doorway, and a voice that proved to be Osgar's. "My lord! She's called for you!"

"Who?" Robert asked.

"Our lady! She spoke! She's conscious, and she asked for you! The midwife said that's extraordinary! She's never seen the like before with hemlock poisoning! She think's she'll live!"

"I'll be right down," Robert said.

He was halfway down the ladder when something fluttered by and struck the ground with a terrific thump.

He stared at the crumpled thing, just visible at the edge of the moonlight.

Osgar knelt by the thing. He drew the cloak up to see what lay beneath. "Dear God in heaven!"

Giselle was sitting up against a pile of pillows when Robert reached the bedchamber. Her face was haggard, but her pupils had retracted to a more normal size and her lips were no longer blue.

He knelt by the bed since all the stools were taken and the room was crowded with everyone who lived in the house, except for Osgar, who had remained in the barn.

"Where have you been?" Giselle asked him.

"I had to make an inquiry. Sorry. Osgar says you'll live after all."

"That's what Henna claims, that I'm passed the worse of it, and she's never wrong about such things."

"Of course I'm never wrong," the midwife said. "Problem is that often times people don't follow my wise advice. Now, that you've all seen her, everyone get out and let her rest."

As everyone filed out, Henna grasped Robert's sleeve. "That includes you, too."

Robert nodded. His hand hovered over Giselle's head, then descended to her hair. He brushed it, and kissed her on the top of her head. He thought she might take offense at the familiarity, but she smiled.

"Where's Eanfled?" Giselle asked.

"She won't be coming."

"Why not?"

"I'll tell you in the morning."

The Outlaws

CHAPTER 16

London
June 1184

Jean was not the sort to waste a single day. The morning after he and Matilda consummated their purchase of the land, a work crew appeared and began clearing away the debris from the burned house. Although there was quite a lot of rubble, it took four days to cart it all away, and by the third week in June, a master carpenter had staked out the perimeters of the two houses that would occupy the plot, and masons, at his direction, had put in stones for foundation piers, since Jean intended that the buildings last longer than his life time, which they would not if the supporting beams were laid in holes in the ground.

"The expense," Matilda murmured to him as they watched the mason's apprentices and journeyman laying one course of stone upon another.

"You want to pass this on to your children, don't you?" Jean asked. "What good is a house, anyway, if it falls down in fifteen or twenty years, anyway?"

"I don't know," she replied, appalled at how much more this was likely to cost.

"We will build a higher quality establishment than you lost," Jean said. "Don't look like that. You have to spend money to make money. When we're done, we'll make it back by charging more for a bed. Now, think about how you're going to improve the food."

"Now you're telling me my food's bad! I can see that having a partner is going to be more trouble than I expected."

"You didn't learn that with Margery?"

"Clearly, you will be more trouble than Margery, especially as you have not run an inn."

"I've stayed in enough of them to know what is required."

"No, you only know what you like."

"Why isn't that enough?"

"Because you are obviously a finicky guest, not a typical one."

"We shall see," Jean said. He took her arm and steered her toward the cart that held the latest keg of ale. "Let's leave the workers alone while we have a drink. Arguing is thirsty work, after all."

"What? So you can find fault with my ale now?"

"That thought had not been on my mind, but as a partner, it is my duty to inquire into all aspects of our business. I rather relish the role of ale taster."

"I'm sure you have lots of experience in that as well. Agnes! Fetch us some cups! And what's become of Harold! Alice, you're supposed to watch him! Where's he got to?"

Throwing up a timber-framed house never took very long, and no more than a week passed before the frames were complete and the roofs were on — of tile no less, another extravagance that made Matilda faint to contemplate — and all that remained was the wattling between the timbers and the plaster that covered it. The builders completed the ground floor of the inn first, and Matilda and the children moved into it from the stable, living in the rear of what would become the hall while they opened service as a tavern in the front of the hall until the upper three floors were finished.

Jean's business kept him occupied in the city, but he managed to visit the building site at least three or four times a week. One day he turned up mounted on a fine-looking palfrey with two pack horses and a girl of about twelve or thirteen with straight brown hair, large brown eyes, and a face that was just short of being pretty.

He did not enter the inn but said to Matilda through an open window, "This is my daughter, Cicely. I'd like you to look out for her while I'm gone."

Matilda paused in mopping up spilled ale. "Where are you going?"

"I have to go to the March. My nephew has run into a problem. It seems that the new earl of Shelburgh has decided to sell this summer's wool clip to someone else."

The Outlaws

Matilda knew that this custom was a large part of Jean's business. Without it, his profits would suffer.

"You won't come in for a meat pie before you go?" she asked.

"No. I'm meeting a traveling party at Westminster. If I delay, they may leave without me."

"Well, take a pie anyway. You can eat it from the saddle. Alice! We've a visitor!" She handed a pie through the window still in its metal pan. She hated to lose the pan, but she didn't like to think of Jean going hungry.

"Will you be going up to Hafton?" she asked while Alice came out.

Jean kissed Cicely and Alice led her with one of the pack horses to the stable. Jean fetched a spoon from his belt pouch and tucked into the pie. "I may."

"Could you carry a letter for me to Robert?"

"If I can't delay for a pie, I can hardly delay for you to find a scribe." Yet he still sat on his horse spooning pie into his mouth. "I'll probably have an opportunity to see him. I'll give him your news." He scraped up the last bit of pie and handed back the pan.

"That will have to do, I suppose. Don't make too much of the fire. I don't want him to worry."

"I'll just say that you've built a new house."

Matilda smiled. "The old one had grown rather shabby. I'll try not to burn this one down while you're gone. Go with God and be safe."

"And you," Jean said. He turned his horse and headed west down Holborn.

Matilda stood at the window and watched him until he was out of sight, pleased that he looked back at least a half a dozen times before he passed out of view.

CHAPTER 17

Hafton
June 1184

Eanfled's body lay where she had fallen until the following morning. After breakfast, Wulfric and Osgar brought a cart around to put her upon it. This would seem a solitary task, but everyone in the manor except Robert and Giselle clustered around the barn door to look upon the would-be murderer, even the cooks and their boys who were hard at work preparing dinner. The crowd was silent as Wulfric and Osgar struggled with the body, which had grown stiff and was as easy to carry as an armload of untrimmed wood.

"Get back you," Wulfric snarled at the people blocking the way between door and cart, unhappy with having been given this task. "Out of the way."

A considerable amount of backing away and jostling ensued since just about the entire population of the village had assembled in the yard, starting after dawn either for word of the lady's condition or a chance to view the body of the evildoer, so that there was nowhere for anyone to go to get out of the way. They were all supposed to be working, but the events of last night had pushed even the urgent business of the fields and gardens from everyone's mind.

Wulfric and Osgar lifted the body over the side of the cart. Wulfric dropped his end as if it was a bundle of faggots. That end, Eanfled's poor head, struck the floorboards with an audible thump that caught many by surprise and elicited shudders, whether of surprise, horror, or satisfaction no one could tell, perhaps all three. For his part, Osgar laid her feet down with rather more care. He climbed into the cart and arranged Eanfled's cloak over her so no part could be seen except her ankles and feet, and a hand that refused to be concealed, the fingers curled as if reaching for something.

"What are you doing up there?" grated Wulfric. "Quit wasting time. I've a long way to go."

The Outlaws

"Not so long," Osgar said, hopping to the ground.

"Do you think she fell, or jumped?" someone in the crowd asked, a question that had been much debated throughout the night and into the morning. The matter was not trivial, since a suicide could not be buried in consecrated ground, which meant the soul could not find peace and an entrance into Heaven. But there was no consensus on the question, with strongly held opinions on either side of it that a night's debate had sharpened.

"She slipped," Osgar said for perhaps the hundredth time.

"How would you know?" someone asked, also for perhaps the hundredth time. "It's as dark as the inside of your arse in there at night. How could you tell?"

"The moon was bright last night," Osgar replied, making the same argument he had made many times before. "And that beam's narrow."

"Yeah, right," came the response, as many did not want to be convinced by facts, if there were any, and whose main opinion was that Eanfled should be cast into a pit in the forest or left for the pigs. Robert, however, had ordered that she be brought home to Shelburgh where her kin could take care of her. While people might grumble and dissent, no one was brave enough to dispute that decision where he could hear.

"Enough of this," Wulfric said, grasping the halter of the cart horse. "I'd like to get back before dinner, if it's all the same to you people."

He started toward the gate and the crowd, which had closed in around the cart, gave way with as much jostling and stumbling as before. Osgar trotted to catch up with Wulfric.

"Where do you think you're going?" Wulfric asked.

"With you."

"What for? Afraid I'll just dump her in the road?"

"I wouldn't put it past you."

"She doesn't deserve even that courtesy."

"She was forced to it. I told you."

"She could have come to one of us. She could have told us. We might have been able to do something."

"You mean Robert might have been able to do something."

Wulfric nodded. "He'd have thought of something."

"He would have." Osgar walked on without speaking until they crossed the bridge. "I'm sure he would have."

"Don't matter now," Wulfric said as they passed through the screen of trees and turned into the village.

The village was deserted, since everyone who could walk had gone up to the manor house, though from the murmuring behind them, the crowd had broken up and was heading back to work, where they should have been in the first place. The scene struck Osgar as odd and melancholy, which accentuated his feelings concerning what lay in the cart.

"What are you going to say when we get her there?" Osgar asked.

"Did she really slip?"

Osgar thought hard about his answer, as he had thought hard about what had happened in the barn last night. For he had seen Eanfled standing on the beam with her hands over her face, stifling her sobs, then topple forward, like a tree that had been cut down. There had been no misstep; there had been no step at all. But he said, "She slipped. I'm sure of it."

"All right. I'll tell them that. Damn it all. Why did this have to happen?"

The main work of June after the haying, with its pleasant nights and balmy days, was the early plowing and washing and the shearing of the sheep. The two labors coincided this year, so that, with more than eight hundred sheep on the manor by the latest accounting. It was expected to take at least three days, including the festival at the end. The manor provided food and drink on each day, and this made the event popular, expensive, and an administrative challenge, for there were many details to take care of, most of all ensuring there was enough food ready at the right times, since the lord who

The Outlaws

skimped on meals during work on manor property often found that his fleeces were not well cared for.

Giselle was still unwell, so the burden fell on Robert. Although he could wash and shear, Robert had no experience in organizing meals for one-hundred-fifty, and he had no idea what was involved. As he hurried about checking stores to decide what to serve, settling quarrels among the help, consulting Giselle who worried more than was good for her that he would bollix things up and who required frequent reports under threat that she would rise from her sickbed if the answers were not forthcoming or satisfactory, and overwatching the cooks and the village women arriving to assist who seemed to be able to manage quite well without him and who acted as if he was a bothersome intruder, he came to appreciate the labors of the quartermasters he had served with on campaign who had worked under even more trying conditions. People never gave them any credit when things went right and were quick to register complaints when even the littlest thing did not go as desired.

The washing took place on the first day in the stream between the ford and the spot where most people washed their clothes, and then the refreshed sheep, their coats white again, were driven to the wicker fold before the sheepcote, a long narrow shed that stood on flat ground northeast of the manor house. Here the ewes were separated and counted.

Wulfric gave Robert the final tally: eight-hundred-thirty-seven, three-hundred-fifteen belonging to the manor, the remainder to the villagers — all packed together, looking so fat that they might burst, spewing fleeces everywhere, a seething, bleating pond of sheep.

Sheep, of course, do not give up their fleeces just for the asking, but must be removed from their fluffy coats one at a time. An expert could have a fleece off in under ten minutes, but there were just three such experts at work, while others of lesser skill and experience toiled beside them in a race to see who could do the most, as others gathered the fleeces, and rolled and tied them in balls for placement in great linen sacks.

Some sheep objected to this treatment; others which were veterans submitted to it without apparent complaint; and those that emerged from the hands of the shearers looked different: much reduced in size since a sheep without its fleece is a rather stringy beast. Before they were let go, each sheep was marked with a painted sign on its rump which showed who owned it.

As the lady's representative, Robert could not participate in shearing without an unrecoverable loss of dignity, and, when not dithering over the details of dinner, he attempted to preside over the confusion, offering helpful encouragement, hoping that it at least appeared that he knew what he was doing. Most people did not seem to pay him much notice. Now and then he cast a glance at the manor house, where Giselle was visible at one of the windows. Once she waved and even smiled.

As the third day drew to an end and the flock was as naked as sheep could be, what had seemed a vast amount of fleece when it was on the hoof now filled two-and-a-half linen bags. They were large bags that would challenge the capacity of the average cart, to be sure, two-hundred pounds for the full ones, but still, less than three.

"It seems so little for all that work," Robert remarked to Wulfric. When he was a boy, he had not paid any attention to where the fleeces went after you cut them off. All he could think about then was the food and drink that was to come.

"Aye, so it seems. But it'll be worth fifteen pounds when we get it to market. That's a pretty penny."

"It will be welcome. That sheepcote's looking pretty dilapidated." Calling the cote dilapidated was a kindness. One long section of wall had given way, and the cote was no longer a place of confinement or shelter, but simply a roof, and an uncertain one at that, for the far corner leaned so that it looked about to fall over.

Wulfric snorted. "You're thinking of rebuilding it? As is?"
"Why?"
"Everyone's rebuilding in stone."

The Outlaws

"That's got to be expensive."

"Cost you ten pounds at least."

"Good Lord! That much?" The entire manor was lucky to take in twice that in a year.

"Last time I was in Shelburgh the bailiff was bragging about their new cote. He seemed to think that we're poor as mice here. Or would be soon." Wulfric fell silent, remembering the purpose of the trip.

"How did that go, by the way? The trip."

"Sad."

"Any word of her father and brothers?"

"FitzWalter's let them go with a heavy fine."

"It was for nothing, then."

"It appears so, sir." Wulfric spit and turned away, unwilling to discuss the matter any further. Besides, the butler had brought up a couple of kegs of ale, bags of bread and cheese, and platters of the pig slaughtered yesterday, and the crowd around them was so thick, the plowers and harriers and clodbreakers having come in to the sheep fold as well, that unless Wulfric acted fast, there would be little left for him.

Now that the hard work had passed and the fun was just beginning, Robert did not feel like sharing in any of it yet. He looked back at the manor house. Giselle was gone from the window. He wondered if she had returned to bed, or if she was strong enough now to come down to the cote.

He crossed around the edge of the embankment toward the gate. Halfway there, Giselle met him coming the other way. She had decided on her own to join the festivities, it seemed. Or he thought so at first.

For she reached him with a wide smile and announced, "Robert! A friend of yours has come calling."

Standing awkwardly behind Giselle, helmet under his mailed arm, was a friend, of sorts.

It was Fat Hugh.

"Well," Hugh said, after they stood around in silence for a moment or two, "not exactly calling."

"You looking for a place to stay, too?" Robert asked.

Hugh squinted. "I wouldn't turn my nose up at supper, if it's all the same to you. Otherwise, I suppose I'm just passing through."

"Few people pass through Hafton. You've got to go out or your way to find it."

"I wouldn't have come looking for you if it wasn't important."

"What is it? A warning? An ultimatum? We've had quite a few of those lately blowing from Eustace's direction, plus assorted calamities and disasters."

"It is, actually, a warning, anyway."

"What does FitzWalter want of us now? He's already caused enough damage."

"You know, you don't have to take that tone. I'm trying to do you a favor!"

"You're one of his men. What kind of favor could you possibly do us?"

"I'm not one of his men. I was pledged to a friend of his, Edmund de Stokesay, one of Lacy's people."

"That doesn't make you his friend?"

"I was just doing what my lord asked me to do."

"And now?"

"He's not my lord any longer."

"Sent you away, did he?"

"I left." When Robert said nothing to that, Hugh added. "Because of you. The two of you, but the lady mostly, since it's her land he covets. You, he just hates."

"You left."

"That's what I said."

"Why?"

Hugh scuffed a boot in the dirt. "Because FitzWalter and Stokesay want me to do something dishonorable."

"Murder is dishonorable."

The Outlaws

"I've said nothing about murder. Although I don't doubt that's where it would end. No, he asked Stokesay to watch the roads to Leominster and Hereford. We're to take your wool clip and any ore wagons you send that way. He wants none of your commerce to get through to market. You're to think it was just robbers. So there. I think that's worth a meal, don't you? Feed me, and I'll be on my way, and you can pretend I was never here."

CHAPTER 18

Hafton
July 1184

By royal decree, roads were supposed to be cleared for twenty yards on either side, a measure thought to deter robberies, but that law, like many others, was not much observed in the March. There were often places where the woods pushed to the margins of the highway, and ambushes could be launched on the way to Leominster, the closest market town besides Shelburgh. The road between Leominster and Hereford, the main wool market, was better maintained and more traveled. If an ambush came, it would happen on the road to Leominster.

Robert had not been down that road often enough to remember every bad spot, and even if he had, a season's growth could so change things out of all recognition that he had no confidence in his memory.

"Are they out there now?" Robert asked Hugh the morning after his arrival. The regional wool markets ran from mid-June to early July. If you couldn't sell your wool then, you might have to wait a full year to do so, and year-old wool fetched a lower price than fresh wool. So it was urgent that they not delay getting the clip to market.

"They're supposed to be. I left Stokesay the night before we were all to leave."

"And you got here the morning after. And you have no idea where they're hiding?"

"There was some discussion between le Bec and Stokesay about it, but Stokesay's not the sort to take orders from le Bec."

"What does he get out of this?"

"Stokesay? He's ambitious. He holds the manor only because of the regard the Lacys had for his father. Edward is lazy and rather stupid, if you ask me, prone to drunkenness and error. There've been rumblings that the Lacys might replace him with someone they favor more. He's looking to

The Outlaws

Eustace for advancement, especially since he's earl now. Besides, he gets to keep half your clip, and even half the clip of this little place is worth a lot of money."

"We have the finest wool in Herefordshire," Giselle said from the high table, where she had been reviewing some accounts. "Hardly any middle wool or locks. It ought to be worth a lot."

"We can't afford to have it stolen," Robert said.

"Of course not," Giselle said. "The problem is, what do we do about this Stokesay person? We haven't the money to hire guards to protect the clip."

"By the time we find such men and fetch them here, the wool markets will be closed," Robert said. "Even if they agree to take their pay after we sell the clip." He turned again to Hugh. "How many will Stokesay have with him?"

Hugh's lips moved as he counted to himself. "Eight. Three men-at-arms and five archers. Local boys, but quite good with the bow."

"Nine altogether then."

"Yes."

Robert could see the ambush in his head: the five archers shooting from behind trees where they had lain undetected, cutting down his villagers, certainly himself as he would be a prime target, then the charge of the armored men to scatter those who had survived the initial volleys. Nine determined men would be enough even if he took twenty villagers with bows and staves. But what choice did they have? They had to get the clip to market. And there was the ore to consider. It had been piling up since Giselle returned. There was money in those rocks that they desperately needed.

He stood up. "I wonder …"

"You wonder what?" Giselle asked.

"If we know where they're hiding, perhaps we can find a way around them."

Giselle put down her pen and wiped ink from her fingers. "How do you propose to find out? Ask le Bec?"

"I'll ride the Leominster road. I've a feeling I'm likely to spot them on the way."

"Only if they're stupid robbers," she said.

"Well, Hugh said Stokesay's stupid."

"Counting on the stupidity of your enemy is a good way to get killed. What if they recognize you? Stokesay saw you when he was here."

"I'll just have to take the chance."

"I don't like this plan."

"It's the plan we have, for now. Have my palfrey tacked up." Robert went past her to the stairs to fetch his gear.

Robert reached Shobdon without seeing anyone other than a man fishing on the lake east of the village.

Shobdon was small, with a dozen houses. It took no time at all to get beyond them to one of the tracks that lead to Leominster. There was a second such track a half mile or so further on.

Robert forced himself to think about matters from Stokesay's point of view. Since there were two ways to get to Leominster from Shobdon, the only certain way to catch travelers from Hafton was along the road to Shobdon. Which meant that they had to be in the woods along it and he had missed them.

He turned his horse back toward Shobdon.

The parish church was a little stone building as nondescript as a shed, the yard around it bursting with grass waist high that could have used a few sheep to keep it trimmed, and in fact, he had mistaken it for a neglected barn the first time through the village and realized it from the stone cross that peeped out of the grass. He stopped here and tied the horses to the fence around the churchyard, and went looking for the village priest.

This did not take long, as the priest was hard at work rooting out weeds from among his cabbages in the garden beside his house. He had abandoned a habit for a peasant's

The Outlaws

long blue shirt without stockings, leaving him bare-legged and barefoot in the muck, but he was recognizable as a priest from his tonsure.

The priest looked startled when Robert came up to the wicker fence around the garden, but relaxed a bit when Robert removed his helmet and pulled back his coif.

"Good morning to you," Robert said.

"And to you," the priest said, wiping the dirt from his hands on the front of his smock. "Do you require something? Directions to the manor house, perhaps?"

"My business isn't with your lord. I'm looking for someone."

"Ah, well, I doubt I can help you there. I doubt I know anyone who'd interest a gentleman of your position."

"That may be, but you might have seen them. A party of men like myself should have passed through here not more than a day ago — four men-at-arms and five archers, all mounted."

The priest pulled on his chin. "And what would your interest be in such people?"

"I'm supposed to join them."

"Truly? As I recall, you passed through from that way." The priest waved to the west.

"I went looking for them but I didn't see them. Either I missed them or they haven't arrived yet."

"Well, you missed them entirely, for they did go down the road to Shelburgh."

"When?"

"Yesterday afternoon."

"Ah, well, no wonder. Thank you kindly."

"My pleasure, I think."

Robert untied the horse and was considering what to do now when a traveling party appeared on the road to the north. Anyone coming this way was bound to be headed to Shelburgh and he thought about joining them, but rejected the idea. He'd have to return by a back way, which would take most of the day since it meant many more miles to cover, quite a few of which would be through people's fields and forests.

As he came abreast of the traveling party, he stopped in astonishment. One of their number was Jean of Gloucester, his old master. Jean was just as surprised to see him. He reined up beside Robert and said to the others, "The village well is beside the third house on the right. You can refresh the horses there. I'll be along in a moment." Jean regarded Robert with a wry smile. "How did you manage to get in so much trouble?"

"Me? Trouble? I'm not in any trouble."

"Why, man, you're infamous!"

"For what?"

"Making war on an earl! And cuckolding him in the bargain."

"He wasn't an earl when we started, and there's been no cuckolding going on. Who's saying that?"

"Why, everyone. It's the talk up and down the March. I wasn't in Gloucester half an hour before I'd heard the tale three times, each time more lurid than before."

"What rot."

"People seem to believe it. You're a hero, too, depending on who's telling the story, although I suspect your mother would be scandalized, if she knew. Which she doesn't by the way. She sends her regards, and wishes you to know that the family is doing well."

"You've seen her?"

"I've relocated my portion of the business to London. We're partners, your mother and I."

"At the inn? What happened to Margery?"

"We bought her out after the fire."

"The fire …?"

"Yes, unfortunately, the day after you left London, the inn burned to the ground. No one was hurt other than Alice, but she has recovered."

The Outlaws

Robert digested that in silence. He would have to send a letter to his mother, and contract for a return, to find out all the news about Alice. "That can't be a coincidence."

"I'm sorry? Coincidence?"

"It has to be Eustace." Robert told him about Eanfled's attempt to poison Giselle, and who was behind it.

"Those are serious accusations."

"Now that's failed, he intends to seize our wool clip when we move it to market. He has men on the road waiting for us as we stand here." Robert waved toward the Shelburgh road.

"What will you do?"

"I have to find a way to move the clip. Is there anything you can do to help? Like take it off my hands now?"

"You put me in a difficult spot. I've lost the Shelburgh business. It seems that FitzWalter has contracted to give three years to Benedotti."

Robert had heard that name before, but it took a moment to pull it out of the place which stored his memories of his time in Gloucester. "The Italian wool merchant?"

Jean nodded. "Benedotti's paid up front for all three years. For every fleece the honor can produce."

"That must have cost hundreds of pounds!"

"The Florentines have that kind of money. They're starting to make similar offers to all the large landowners. It's wreaking havoc with the markets."

"And you think you can get Eustace to change his mind?"

"I've got to try. I don't see how I can make up the lost business. If I'm to be successful, I cannot do business with you."

Robert's disappointment must have showed on his face, because Jean added, "But if you happened to turn up with your clip in Gloucester, it could easily end up in our warehouse without my knowing."

"Get the clip to Gloucester . . . I might as well try to fly it to the moon."

"Have you ever heard of a village called Bewdley?"

"No."

"It's on the Severn about thirty miles from you, where the road from Ludlow to Kidderminster crosses the river. There's a ferry, and it's a major stopping point for river traffic. Go to Bewdley, hire a boat, and ship your wool downriver to Gloucester."

The way to Bewdley wasn't clear. No one in Hafton had ever been there or to Kidderminster, so no one had more than a vague idea how to get there. The consensus was that it lay to the northeast. Reasonable people would go east to the Ludlow road, head north, and ask along the way. But direct access to the Ludlow road had been cut off if Robert's suspicions were true. So that left but one alternative — head north to Wigmore on small tracks that often were little more than footpaths before turning eastward.

Edmund de Stokesay awoke on the third morning of the ambush with a hangover and a tongue that tasted as though a goat had slept upon it. He lay under his blankets contemplating the prospect of having to get up. He did not wish to get up. He wished he could go home. The urge to pee forced him erect. It was dawn and the sun had not yet risen, so no one else was up. On campaign you posted guards to watch during the night, but this was not a campaign, so he had not felt the need for guards. No one was likely to bother him or his men, and if they did, he was certain they would be sorry.

He staggered around the remains of the fire, stubbing his toe on a root and getting his bare feet wet from the rain that had fallen yesterday and continued during the night. The rain had driven him into his tent so that he could not enjoy the fire, for the temperature had plunged from what had been a balmy day to a chilly night.

He leaned against a pine as he relieved himself, feeling miserable. He was cold, he was uncomfortable, his toes felt

The Outlaws

like icicles, and he was bored and the sun was not yet up. And, worst of all, he was out of wine. He had finished the last of it during the night. He thought he had brought enough for a week, but it had not lasted.

Apart from the week after his marriage, these had been the worst days of his life; at least, that's the way he felt right now. When he had to sit beside that miserable mouse his mother had forced upon him, he would think differently. He had the possibility of the profits from the wool clip he expected to liberate from its wrongful possessor to relieve his present dismay, but the enjoyment he obtained from these thoughts diminished as, day after day, no wool clip had appeared on the road, as promised.

In fact, they had not seen much of anyone: a traveling party of rich merchants going toward Shelburgh, fat pickings for proper robbers, and he had been tempted just for the fun of seeing the expressions on their faces when he appropriated their valuables, as he hated merchants as lying, cheating scum; a lone knight riding east, familiar looking, though Stokesay couldn't remember where he'd seen the fellow before, young but with the appearance of trouble about him; a wandering peddler, bent under the weight of his pack, from which pots and pans and other assorted things clanged together at every step, nothing worth stealing though; a few carts going to the Shelburgh market and returning in the evening; and that was about it. Oh, and a couple of boys bearing fishing poles coming back from the lake on the other side of, and just down, the road.

Around him, the camp began to stir as the sky brightened in the east. Stokesay returned to his tent, dried off his feet, put on his boots, and called to his squire to fetch him some bread and cheese and whatever ale still remained.

He ate morosely on a folding camp stool while the lookouts settled behind trees to keep watch over the road.

After the sun had risen enough to begin driving away some of the fog, one of the lookouts whispered that someone was coming from the direction of Hafton. Stokesay hefted his sword and came up beside the lookout, hoping that this was it.

But it was not, just a pair of beggars, a man and a woman, their clothes made all of patches with sacks over their shoulders.

Then Stokesay had an inspiration. He was not a man given to having inspirations, so the force of it came as a surprise and he was unable to resist. The inspiration caused him to step into the road before the beggars. The appearance of an armed man frightened the beggars, and they were about to run away, when Stokesay said, "Hold there! I mean you no harm!"

"We've nothing worth stealing," the man said, his beard so thick that Stokesay couldn't even see his lips moving.

"I can see that," Stokesay said.

"Is there a toll then?"

"There's no toll."

"Well then, what do you want, sir?" the man asked, eyeing the sword with trepidation, since Stokesay had not thought to put it back in its scabbard. "If I may be so bold as to ask?"

"I would like to hire you," Stokesay said.

"Hire us for what, sir?"

Stokesay gestured up the road, the way they had come. "There's a manor back that way by the name of Hafton. Did you stop there?"

"Don't know of any manor named Hafton, sir."

Stokesay smiled. All the better. "I will give you each a penny if you go there begging and ask about what's become of their wool clip. You can have the penny when you come back."

"Hum," the man muttered. "Why, may I ask, sir, is that a matter of interest to you?"

"You may not ask, if you want the penny, and you better not tell anyone at Hafton that you're inquiring on my behalf."

"Ah, of course." The man understood that Stokesay was up to something, but the penny was a great inducement for

The Outlaws

him to do that business and to be unconcerned with the whys and wherefores.

"Come on, Bert," the woman said, tugging at Bert's sleeve. "A whole penny. Two pennies."

Two pennies was an enormous sum for anybody. It could have been, and should have been, spent replenishing Stokesay's depleted wine stock, but the force of his inspiration had been such that he did not have any misgivings until now. But it was too late.

"We'll do it," Bert announced. "Where is Hafton, exactly?"

The beggars returned about the hour when ordinary, decent people would be sitting down to dinner, which is to say just short of noon. One of the lookouts escorted the filthy pair to Stokesay, who did not rise from his camp stool.

"I trust your journey was profitable," he said, considering whether to surrender the pennies after all. "You got something to eat and …"

"Yea, sir, we've full bellies, thanks for asking."

"And about the other?"

"Well, sir …"

Stokesay's spirits fell, for the tone suggested that they'd learned nothing and that he'd thrown away two pennies that he could ill afford. "Well, what?"

"You wouldn't mind, sir, letting us see those pennies."

So, the beggar didn't trust him. Stokesay was insulted and almost refused but something about the woman's expression made him reconsider his new impulse for thrift. He opened his purse and spilled two pennies into his palm. "There you are. See?"

"Well, then, sir, we heard that they've taken the clip north."

Stokesay was astonished and appalled. "North? North you say?"

"Yea, sir."

"Where north?"

"Wigmore's all we heard. In four carts." He added "They'll be back in a week."

A chill settled in Stokesay's stomach and ran down his limbs. "When did they go?"

"Yesterday, just before the rain."

North ... yesterday ... Wigmore. They weren't going to Wigmore, they were passing through it. It had no wool market. They had to be making for Shrewsbury, which did have such a market. They had a day's head start. Four carts. He might be able to catch them.

Stokesay leaped to his feet. "Break camp! Load up the horses!"

The men gaped at him a moment and then shot into action, realizing that their share of the plunder had, perhaps, flown away.

"Sir," Bert said, holding out his hands. "If you don't mind, before you forget."

Stokesay regarded those supplicating palms with distaste. They were dirty and the nails on the fingers were almost claws. He dropped the pennies into the palms, careful not to touch Bert. "Here you go."

"Thank you, sir. Thank you so much."

The journey to Bewdley was uneventful, which is to say it was marked only by the usual mishaps of travelers. Apart from the rain, there was a fallen tree across the track a mile out of Hafton that took more than an hour to clear; one horse threw a shoe just short of Wigmore but fortunately did not go lame, and they were able to replace the shoe at a blacksmith's in Wigmore; and a deep rut at the junction with the high road between Ludlow and Leominster caused one of the carts to tip over.

"Next thing you know," Osgar said as they righted the cart and scurried to protect its cargo from the wet, "we'll break an axle."

The Outlaws

Robert knocked on a cart railing while the others heaved that heavy wool sack back into the cart. "May your tongue fall out at such a thought."

The struggle with the overturned cart left the men exhausted, and since it was near the end of the day and everyone was miserable and damp, Robert called a halt, and they went into camp by the crossroads. At least the tents they had brought with them gave shelter from the rain, although they could not get a fire started.

With the morning came a respite from the rain, and clear skies once the fog had burned off, but that did not make the going any easier, for the road had become a strip of mud that sucked at men's feet and mired the wheels so that in spots they stuck fast, and all shoulders had to be applied to the halted cart just to get it free.

They rested at the ford of the River Teme, while Robert paced along the bank and worried about the water level. It had risen almost to the point of submerging the gravel islet in the center of the stream where a well-work path led over the hump indicating that the ford lay here, and the water in either side was without a single ripple, a bad sign. If the water was deep enough, it could float a cart and carry it away. Yet they had no choice but to press on, so he got the men up, and the carts snaked into the flood one after another.

The first cart made it across, but the second got stuck short of the islet and would not budge no matter how many shoulders they applied to it. They freed it after carrying its wool sack to the far bank and harnessing the horse from the first cart to the trapped one for extra power. After that, they carried all the contents of the carts across by hand so that none of the others got stuck.

All were soaked to the ears after this, for the river had risen to waist deep. No one was in a good mood, and they still had many miles to go. Robert had thought the journey might take two days, but it looked as though it would be at least three, and perhaps even four.

It was eight miles or more to Wigmore, and Stokesay covered the distance in just over an hour, despite the rain, the wet, and the mud. There he paused to rest the horses while the men questioned the villagers. One of the archers brought word that a small train of carts from the south been seen yesterday, and asked directions, not to Shrewsbury as expected, but eastward along a chain of lesser roads to Bewdley, one of the crossings of the Severn. Stokesay couldn't imagine why they were making for Bewdley, but then he recalled that it lay just this side of the river from Kidderminster. He wasn't sure, but perhaps there was a wool market at Kidderminster.

Summer days were long, but horses can only do so much, and the animals, unused to the pace that Stokesay set, began to tire by the tenth hour of the day, and when they reached the crossing of the River Teme, the horses were fagged. The sight of the Teme, which had risen due to the rains, dampened enthusiasm further in men who were themselves wet and exhausted, so Stokesay allowed them to make camp. While the men were putting up the tents and tending to the horses, a wagon belonging to band of players came up to the ford on the other side of the river. They had no more appetite for a crossing at this time of evening than Stokesay, and as they put up their own camp, he called across to a man who'd poised at the bank to piss in the river whether he had seen a train of four carts led by a man on a good horse on the way to Bewdley. The man called back that he had, not more than two or three hours ago.

Two or three hours, Stokesay thought with satisfaction. He would catch them tomorrow, well before they reached Bewdley.

The cart train found refuge for the night in a barn a few miles on the other side of Tenbury Wells. It was a relief to sleep with a roof over their heads on cushions of straw rather

The Outlaws

than hard, wet ground, even if the rain had stopped and the sky had cleared.

By morning, the roads had dried so that the wheels did not stick in mud, and the road was well maintained between Tenbury Wells and Bewdley, a distance a farmer told them was fifteen miles, so they made good time — better than two miles an hour. At this steady pace, Robert looked forward to reaching Bewdley in mid-morning.

The carts tended to get separated owing to the different pulling capacities of the horses, the weight of the loads, and the inattentiveness of the drivers, so that significant gaps often opened up between them. This forced Robert to keep an eye on everyone, for too much of a gap, especially in wooded areas, raised the possibility that the isolated cart could be picked off by people lurking in the forest for just such a windfall. So, he spent a good deal of time riding among the carts, making sure that they kept together.

Robert was going back to the last cart, which had fallen behind again, when he noticed a band of horsemen approaching in the distance. Bands of horsemen were not such an oddity by themselves; magnates often moved about the country on horseback and their entourages would have resembled the group. But ordinary travelers moved at a more sedate pace than the rapid trot of this band, and as the group emerged from the forest, they broke into a canter. *That* was unusual. No one had a reason to drive their horses at such a pace on this straight stretch of road in the middle of nowhere.

He had a bad feeling about it.

Robert grasped the bridle of the cart horse and urged his palfrey forward. The sudden jolt from a walk to a near gallop almost toppled the driver, who clung to a cart railing to avoid falling into the road. Robert caught up with the next cart after a few long strides. Letting go of the bridle, he surged by, waving toward a gap in the hedge ahead that gave admittance into a hay field. "Through there!" Robert called to the others. "Hurry!"

"What the hell is going on?" one of the drivers called.

"I think we're being attacked!"

"Fat chance of that," another replied, until he looked back and saw the band approaching on full out horses, and four or five number had swords drawn. "Jesus Christ in Heaven!"

As the other drivers gaped in disbelief, Osgar, driving the lead cart, and whipped his horse through the gap and into the field. "What now?" he asked as Robert halted beside him.

What now indeed? "Circle up!"

"What?" shouted one of the drivers. "Are you mad?"

"Hurry!" Robert shouted. "Before they get here!"

He jumped from his palfrey into the back of the cart holding all their provisions before it had even stopped, and began throwing down the men's bows and sacks of arrows as the carts jostled together, forming more of a square than a circle. "Get them strung! Move!"

There wasn't time for more. His shield was halfway out of its canvas bag when the enemy reached the gap in the hedge.

But now that their quarry had strung bows and arrows, they paused there and did not press what advantage they had left. They were unarmored, four men-at-arms and five archers whose own bows were still in their cases.

"I believe you're Edmund Stokesay," Robert said, tossing the canvas bag aside and drawing his sword.

"And you must be Robert Attebrook," Stokesay said. "I remember you now. You rode by us on the way to Hereford a few days ago."

"Yes, you need lessons in outlawry," Robert lied. "You stuck out like a rose in a woodpile."

"It doesn't matter now, though," Stokesay said, lips curling at the insult. "We've found you."

"And what of it?"

"Hand over the clip, and no one will get hurt."

"It's not my clip to hand over."

The Outlaws

"Well, that's the point, isn't it? Not yours to hand over, not yours to sell."

"Get on, before I have an arrow put in you."

"What, and add murder to your list of crimes? Ah, I forgot, you're already a murderer."

"But I have a pardon."

"Shoot me down, and there'll be no pardon. You're just common swine, and you got lucky the last time. I, on the other hand, am in the right here, so I've nothing to fear. And I've got you outnumbered."

"Common swine I might be, but you must know I am a desperate character. Don't push me too far."

There was more bravado in Stokesay's voice than determination, as well there might be, for his archers had begun to drift back, not liking the sight of even five bows with arrows nocked and read to fly.

Stokesay noticed their movements out of the corner of his eye. He wheeled his horse and trotted through the gap and across the road. "Come on, you snivelers!"

The attackers passed through the hedge on the other side of the road, where they dismounted and were lost from view, except to Robert, who could still see the tops of their heads.

"Do we run for it now?" Osgar asked.

"No, they'll catch us."

"What are they doing?" Hereward, one of the drivers, asked.

"Not getting ready for a picnic," Robert said. "They're putting on their armor, those who have any." He did not add that the archers in that company were stringing their own bows.

He did not have to mention the last point, for his alarm that the enemy was donning its armor sent a tremor through the carters. While they might have traded arrows with the archers from behind the cover of the wagons, they had no enthusiasm for shooting at armored men who could crouch behind their shields as they rushed. Robert could see they were within an inch of flight. He didn't blame them. No one wanted to face an armored man with a sword at close quarters, given a choice.

"Don't run yet," Robert said, pulling his gambeson and mailed shirt out of their bags and struggling to get them on. "Let's see what they do first."

"They're going to come through that gate in a dead run, that's what they're going to do!" one of the drivers declared.

"We haven't a prayer," said another.

"Robert, your honor," Osgar said, "there's a village not far off." He pointed to the east, where a pall of smoke too great to come from a single house hung over the treetops. "I think it's Bewdley."

"Take my horse," Robert said. "Ride for it. See if anyone will help. As for the rest of you, what happened to that axe?"

Robert found the axe under bags of oats meant for the horses. He tossed it to Hereward. "Cut the axles on the carts."

"That's the maddest thing I've ever heard!" Hereward exclaimed.

"Hurry. Before they come."

"My cart! My poor cart!" lamented Hereward as he swung at the first cart, chopping through the portion between the bed of the cart and a wheel.

"Keep hacking. Broken carts can be mended," Robert snapped.

The others — Bernard and his son Pim — had their bows strung and the flaps of their arrow bags open. They stood there looking as though they'd rather run than fight. Robert ordered them, "You two, one on either side of the gate."

"By the hedge?" Bernard asked.

"Exactly right. Shoot anyone in the back who comes through. But especially try to hit their leader. If you can put an arrow into him, the others will leave us alone. Everything depends on you."

"Right. And how will I know him?"

493

The Outlaws

"He'll have the best armor and he'll be doing all the talking."

Bernard did not seem convinced. "Be careful with your aim. If you shoot me," he said to Pim, "it will upset your mother."

"Just make yourself small," Pim grinned. "I can't help but miss then."

"And you do the same."

When they were in position, each about thirty yards from the gate, Robert hopped down from the provision cart so Hereward could disable that one too. At that moment, the men-at-arms, crouching behind their shields, appeared in the gate, the archers behind them.

Rather than charging, however, they stopped and gaped at the sight of the carts, leaning precariously, axles cut, nearly spilling their contents. No one noticed Bernard or Pim kneeling by the hedge, because they had not come in far enough and their attention was on Robert.

"What have you done?" Stokesay cried.

"Eustace can't have our wool and neither can you."

Stokesay stood rigid with anger. "Build me a fire!" he snapped to the men behind him.

"With what, lord?" one of the archers asked.

"With something, anything! Just get it done!"

"There's no wood."

"Goddamn it, quit making excuses. If we can't take the wool, we can at least burn it. That'll be worth something. Or do you want to come away with empty palms for all our trouble?"

The archers shuffled and began to back away. The men-at-arms at Stokesay's side also took a step backwards, but he stopped that retreat. "Not you. Hold by me."

There was a delay while the archers searched for firewood. They collected several armfuls from a nearby wood, but Robert heard one of them cursing that it was wet, which provoked more cursing from Stokesay, who seemed to think that the fact wet wood did not desire to burn was a personal insult.

While Stokesay stamped and cursed, a crowd appeared on the road, streaming toward them, with Osgar and another mounted man at the head. Stokesay stopped cursing as they came up. The mounted man had the appearance of a lord with maroon tunic and knee-high boots. The rest were villagers armed with bills, staves, and bows and arrows.

The mounted man looked across the hedge at Robert and then at Stokesay. "I am John, lord of Bewdley. What is going on here?"

"I am Edmund de Stokesay," Stokesay said. "I am trying to recover stolen wool."

"Are you, now?" John said. "The way this man tells it," he indicated Osgar, "it is the other way around. You are the robber."

"The clip belongs to my good friend, Eustace FitzWalter, earl of Shelburgh. They are taking it to market without his permission."

"That's odd. Most people want their wool at market."

"His wife sent it in defiance of his orders."

"Ah, his wife. I've heard about her." John looked at Robert. "And you must be that Attebrook fellow, the one who's cuckolded the earl. Is he Attebrook?" John asked Osgar.

"Yes, sir, that's Sir Robert."

"There's been no cuckolding," Robert said.

"There hasn't? Well, it makes a good story. And you, Stokesay, I take it you are FitzWalter's man?"

"Not exactly."

"I don't follow."

"I am his friend."

"Such a mighty earl couldn't spare a liege man for this task?"

"He asked me. As a favor. I insist that you turn these goods over to me."

"But how can I know you are telling the truth?"

The Outlaws

"You have his word!" Stokesay waved at Robert. "He's as good as admitted that he's doing the work of that evil woman."

"Hmm," John said. "Well, it is generally the law that the property of a wife, even one who dislikes her husband, and God knows, there are quite a few such women, can be disposed of by the husband. But the law is full of exceptions, too many for ordinary mortals like us to keep track of. That's what lawyers and judges are for."

"You'll not hand it over, then?"

"It is too complicated a thing for one poor man to decide in the middle of a field. I think your friend FitzWalter must take up his claim with the crown. If his wife has violated the law, she'll have to compensate him for it."

"That could take years!"

"Yes, that's an unfortunate thing about the law. And so expensive, too."

"I insist that you impound these goods, until a decision can be made."

"I think not. If I act wrongly in doing so, the wife will have a claim against me. I don't think I want to get involved in claims and counterclaims and lawsuits. It is best to let them go and have others sort out the mess."

"If you let them go, you'll be seen as an accomplice in this theft!"

"Be careful, Stokesay, not to threaten me on my own lands. I think the fact that you, a stranger, seek this property rather than FitzWalter himself, creates enough doubt to absolve me of any complicity. I am merely a humble man trying to do justice. No one will care if I am mistaken in my judgment in the end."

Stokesay's lips worked but he said no more to John, lord of Bewdley. "Let's go," he barked to his men, and they made for their horses.

John rode through the gap in the hedge now that Stokesay had cleared the way. He glanced at Bernard and Pim, arrows still nocked, and then at the carts. "You have made a mess of your carts, Sir Robert."

"I'm afraid so, my lord," Robert replied. "I'll need some help repairing them so we can be on our way."

"I'm afraid that Stokesay would object to any assistance I might give you, though I think we can find suitable wood for your axles, at cost of course. How long do you think it will take to repair them?"

"The day only, I'm sure. If we get the wood promptly."

"I'll see to it. I'd like you to be off my land straightaway."

"Thank you."

John smiled. "He's an unpleasant fellow, that Stokesay. I did not like him."

CHAPTER 19

Hafton
July 1184

Robert arrived back from Gloucester on the day of the monthly manor court. A manor court could be almost festive, since it meant a morning off work for those who cared to take it, and often the bailey of the house was full of people taking their leisure in gossip and games of wrestling, archery, and football. Eustace had not liked the fact that many people took off work and had moved the court to Sundays, despite the Olof's protests that courts were work and work was not to be done on a Sunday. ("I'm the one doing the work, and I'll bear the sin," Eustace was reported to have said.) There was general rejoicing when Giselle announced a return to Thursdays.

For those with business before the court, it meant a time for the airing of grievances and settling disputes which, while of no significance to anyone else, were matters of great moment to those involved, and often of great amusement for the observers. Today there was a dispute about boundaries in the fields, one family accusing another of moving a boundary stone a full ten feet; a complaint about a sow and her piglets getting through a garden fence and wreaking havoc with the lettuce and cabbage and peas; an accusation of spitting into the village well; complaints about a privy that was in need of burning so that the neighbors couldn't go outside without choking or their eyes watering; a dog which had crept into a house and made off with a cutlet from a pan on the fire, a problem that might not have come to the lord's attention except the dog brought the cutlet to his master, who ate it himself rather than returning it to its rightful owner, which led to a demand amounting not merely to compensation but revenge; and what to do about a lip split in a fist fight over a fishing pole that had not been returned.

When the matter of the filched cutlet came up for hearing, word spread out to the bailey, and since this case had excited popular opinion even more than the boundary stone dispute, everyone who could manage it crowded into the hall.

This created a hubbub that Robert heard from beyond the gate, and when he limped into the yard, leading a horse which was so loaded down with large canvas bags that it was impossible to ride her, none of the people clustered about the door and upon the stairs, or in one case upon a ladder at a window, gave him any mind, so consumed were they by the question whether the dog's master had sent him in after the cutlet.

Robert tied the horse to one of the posts at the foot of the stairs, and eased the canvas sacks to the ground. They were very heavy, he was very tired, and he almost dropped one.

"What's going on?" Robert asked a girl at the bottom of the stairs. She was one of the women hired to milk the ewes so they could have cheese and butter.

"Oh, your honor!" the girl said with some surprise, suppressing her irritation at the interruption. "You're back!" Her eyes wandered to his soiled, bare feet as she explained about the matter of the cutlet.

"Keep an eye on those, will you?" Robert asked, pointing to the canvas sacks. "Don't let anyone run off with them, or open them."

"Certainly, sir," the milkmaid said, not altogether happy with this assignment, since she could not now give her full attention to the cutlet controversy. "That wouldn't be —?"

"Hay, but expensive hay." There was indeed hay in the sacks. It was there to prevent the coins they contained from clanking together and attracting too much attention.

"Hay, you say," she said, not convinced.

"Yes, I know, leaving hay lying around like this is just asking for trouble, and if anyone fingers so much as a stem without my leave, I'll be very peeved. See the seals there? None should be broken."

She knelt by the bags and poked one. "It's not really just hay, is it, sir?"

499

The Outlaws

"Stop that." Robert put a finger to his lips. "Let's just pretend for now. Is Hugh about?"

The girl had to think a moment before she realized Robert meant their guest. "Inside, sir."

"I'll send him out for the sacks."

"I'll defend them with my life until he arrives."

"You'd better. If anything happens to them, your neighbors will probably skin you alive."

Robert climbed the stairs. The people upon them were so engrossed in the proceedings, which were quite loud, with a lot of shouting from the parties to the lawsuit who could not be contained once things got going, that no one paid him any mind and would not get out of the way. He tapped on one shoulder after another, slipping between the bodies, to the doorway, with an occasional "'Scuse me, sir," "pardon me," or "your pardon" to ease his passage.

Having attained the doorway, he saw that the hall was packed more densely than sheep in a sheep fold. But there was a better class of spectator here, for as soon as Robert was recognized, gasps and cries of "He's back!" went up and a lane parted for him to pass through to the high table. Even the litigants fell silent.

"You're a sight," Giselle said, looking him up and down, eyes lingering on his soiled feet. "Do you have it?"

"It's outside. Where's Hugh?"

"Here, I am!" Hugh's head appeared from behind a shoulder in the front row.

"Our money from the clip is at the foot of the stairs. Be so good as to have it fetched, will you?"

"Of course!" Hugh cried, his voice almost drowned out in the shout that went up from those in the hall, for the arrival of the money meant profits to those fortunate enough to own even a single sheep, which was most families in the manor.

"Took you long enough," Giselle said as things quieted down.

"What? You thought I might have run away with the money?"

500

"There was a rumor to that effect, but I scotched it. What happened, anyway?"

"I had to walk. It's a long way."

"Are you doing penance for something?" she asked, still gazing at his feet.

"My boots fell apart just before Hereford."

"And you didn't buy another pair?"

"I was out of money. I'd used up our expense funds by then."

"Spent it all on food and wine, and soft beds, I suppose."

"No, there were no boats at Bewdley. Only ships. They cost more than boats. Come on, now. You can at least offer me a chair. My feet are killing me."

"I daresay, I'm sure they are. Let's have a chair for Sir Robert!" Giselle said as Hugh superintended the delivery of the sacks of money, which were put on the table before her. "And court is suspended for today. We have more important business at the moment than missing cutlets."

Giselle had the accounts brought from the chapel, and based on Robert's assertion that they had received eight pence a fleece for good wool and five pence for middle wool, she counted out what was due each person on the list, and paid them off.

The usual hour for supper had come and gone before the last person received his due, and all who remained in the hall were the servants of the house. Supper was served, leftovers of swan, a soup that had once been warm but was now cold with carrots and peas floating in it, and the usual bread and cheese; and everyone ate under slanting curtains of golden light given off by a setting sun.

"I never thought I should have to have money washed," Giselle said as she finished her supper amid piles of coins and hay, which had not been removed from the table. "This money is filthy. What were you thinking, to disguise it?"

The Outlaws

"It worked well enough. I told people who showed any curiosity that it was fodder for the horse."

"And they believed you?"

"I am a believable fellow, even when I lie."

"I don't know about that. Here, let me see your feet."

"Thank you for your concern — at last." Robert swung a foot to Giselle's lap.

"Money is more important than sore feet. First things first. You walked all the way from Hereford like this?"

"If you're worried that I'll soil your gown, they're all scabbed up now. It wasn't too bad till the end. But English roads have more stones in them than most people appreciate. I think I stepped on every one in my path."

Giselle returned Robert's foot to the floor. "We'll need to do something about these. Gangrene might set in otherwise. Hugh! Help Robert to his chamber, if you will. Heloise, I'll need warm water — warm you hear, better than what the cook called soup tonight, and fresh linens."

"Yes, my lady," Heloise said and rushed for the kitchen, the main place for heating water.

Having had the chance to sit down, it was now harder than Robert expected to stand and walk, and he did need Hugh's support.

Hugh deposited Robert onto his bed and stood back, uncertain what to do now, but ready for any further orders that came his way.

Heloise entered with a basin of water and linens over a forearm. She put the basin on the floor and gave the linens to Giselle, who came in after her.

"All right, then," Giselle said. "I think he can manage on his own." She eyed Heloise and Hugh.

"All right, then," Hugh said, in echo. "I wonder if there's any ale left?" He went out. Heloise followed and shut the door.

Giselle regarded Robert with crossed arms. "The last person I saw as dirty as this was a beggar at Broad Gate in Ludlow."

"It's hard to stay clean when sleeping in barns and in the woods."

"I can see that. I doubt you've even so much as washed your face since you left, what, almost three weeks now!"

"I did so, at least twice."

"Huh. Well, let me have those feet."

She knelt, dipped an end to the linen cloth in the water, and grasped one of his feet. "They are worse than I thought. I'm surprised you can even walk." She applied the linen to the bottom of his foot with more vigor than seemed called for by the amount of dirt upon it.

"Ow! Not so rough," Robert said.

"Be quiet!" Even though he'd tried to jerk the foot out of her grasp, she held it firmly, and continued to rub. "It's no less than you deserve."

"What are you talking about?"

"After the way you worried me so! After so much time, I was certain you'd been killed along the way. Carrying so much money through the country, alone, it's a miracle you're here at all."

"I was careful, more so than you are being with my poor foot."

"Damn your poor foot. Hold still, I said." Giselle continued to rub, moving to the top. She set the foot down and took up the other, to which she gave the same treatment. "You could have rented another horse, you know, and spared yourself the delay and the suffering."

"I told you, I ran out of money."

"You could have used our share."

"Our share?"

Giselle looked up at him now, her hair, which had come loose from its braid and shielded her face from view, parted, and he saw that there were tears in her eyes, and her lips were trembling. "A slip of the tongue," she said.

The Outlaws

"Of course," he said, dropping to his knees before her. Robert brushed her cheek with his fingers. He expected her to draw away, but she remained still.

"Don't," she said. "It's wrong."

"I know. Harold," he said, pushing her hair behind an ear so it could not conceal her face or get wet. Because his mother had had a child by her father, custom and the church reckoned them to be brother and sister.

"Not to mention I still have a husband."

"It would not do to give truth to the rumors, either, I suppose."

"No, it wouldn't."

Yet he leaned forward, while she sat like a rock. A tear slipped down her cheek. He kissed her, as if brushing the petal of a flower. She did not move at first, but then she kissed him back.

After a long time, they drew apart.

"I've longed to do that," Robert said.

Giselle glanced toward the shut door. It should have been left open. She brushed his coat. "When you clean up, you can again."

CHAPTER 20

Shelburgh castle
July 1184

A letter arrived for Eustace FitzWalter about midmorning on the last day of July, borne by a cleric on his way to the priory in the Radnor Forest just to the west. It was not unusual for Eustace to get letters; he might receive two or three a week, most of them from correspondents in Winchester, London, or the king's court, who kept him informed of developments, for it was easy to lose track of events isolated in the March, and now as a major figure in the kingdom, he could not afford to be out of touch. Thinking it was just such a routine letter, the steward, Richard d'Evry, almost gave it to one of the castle's clerks. But after he paid off the messenger and arranged for him to be fed, he happened to glance at the seal. *This* letter the lord would want to see right away, so he took it himself to Eustace, who was training a hawk in the fields outside the castle.

He had to pass Reginald le Bec. Le Bec was sitting on a stump watching Eustace, and rose at the sound of d'Evry's approach.

"He doesn't want to be bothered," le Bec said.

"He'll want to be bothered by this," d'Evry said.

"By what?" Then le Bec spotted the letter in d'Evry's hand "By that? I'll give it to him." Le Bec positioned himself so that d'Evry would have to step around him, and he started to do so, but le Bec moved so as to remain between the steward and the lord.

Le Bec was a tall man and muscular, exuding cocky menace, and d'Evry was well acquainted with his propensity for violence. He remembered the days when le Bec's idea of good sport was to set dogs and cats afire just to see them squirm. D'Evry had not liked him as a boy and now feared him as a man, since he had Eustace's trust, God knew why.

"All right then," d'Evry said, handing over the letter.

The Outlaws

"That's a good fellow." Le Bec tucked the letter under an arm, but before crossing the field to Eustace, he paused to pee, half turned away from d'Evry so that the steward had to back up to avoid being splashed. Le Bec put himself back into his clothes and said, "Ah, nothing like a good piss, except maybe a good fuck."

"A man can't get enough of either one," d'Evry said, although most men, including him, got plenty of one and never enough of the other.

"Your sweetheart's written you again," le Bec said.

Eustace's scowl vanished, replaced by an expectant smile as he took the letter. He enjoyed Judith's letters. She had a way with words that made it seem that she was there, speaking to him, unlike most letters, which were stilted and formal, and in Latin. He held out his arm so that the hawk could step from his wrist to le Bec's, who grimaced as the bird's talons penetrated the fabric of his coat.

Eustace broke the seal. As he read, his smile wilted.

"What's wrong?" le Bec asked.

"Gloucester's been approached by another suitor." Often, widows like Judith were allowed to choose their next husbands, but legally, she was the ward of the Duke of Gloucester who had the right to approve any such marriage, and he was powerful enough to make considerable trouble if she did so without his consent. Eustace planned on making an arrangement once he was free of his wife, but as yet Giselle was still an obstacle because she had refused to die. "She says that the suitor has offered a manor worth thirty pounds for her hand. She thinks she might be able to persuade the Duke to postpone a decision, but no more than three or four months."

"How're you going to better an offer like that? You already owe as much to the king for the honor. And that doesn't take into account the bitch that stands in your way."

"I know."

"I've told you before, we should just ride over there, twenty of us or so, and settle things."

"And I've told you before that I cannot have her death laid at my doorstep. She holds Hafton from the king. Her father was his friend and loyal servant. The king may not take lightly to accusations that I'm responsible for her murder. I've got a long way to go before I pay what I owe for the honor. He could easily change his mind."

"I guess you'll have to look for another sweetheart then."

"No. I'll have to go through with an annulment after all."

"Pity to lose the manor."

"It is, but I don't see how it can be helped at this point."

"This Judith is going to be an expensive wife. I hope she turns out to be worth it."

Eustace tapped his palm with the parchment. "She will. She comes well endowed. I should have done this in the first place. Now haste will cost me more. But perhaps not Hafton. Perhaps in the end I'll find a way to keep it."

CHAPTER 21

Hafton
August 1184

"My lady!" Osgar gasped, bursting into the hall, out of breath. "You've a visitor!"

Giselle turned from the doorway to the pantry, where she had been superintending a rearrangement of its contents. She took in Osgar's gasping and wheezing as he stumbled into the middle of the hall, puzzled that the appearance of a visitor would generate such alarm. "What visitor?"

"Le Bec!"

"Reginald le Bec?" Her heart hammered as she imagined horsemen flooding into the bailey. She was on the verge of dashing for the old tower that stood against the house, a defense built more than a century ago against the Welsh. "How could you call that man simply a visitor?"

"He's waiting at the bridge. Alone."

"Why is he doing that?"

"He said he wants to talk. To you."

"Go fetch Robert."

"Yes, my lady." Osgar turned toward the door, but stopped after a few steps. "Where can I find him?"

"He said he was going to the sheepcote."

"Very good, my lady."

"And hurry."

Osgar ran out the door.

When Osgar reached the sheepcote and gasped out his message, the few words that made any sense to Robert were "Le Bec," "our lady," and "the house."

"He's here?" Robert asked.

Osgar nodded, hands on his knees.

"How many?"

Osgar held up a single finger.

Robert glanced at Wulfric, disbelieving what he had just been told. He couldn't imagine le Bec coming alone. Robert had left his weapons in the house and he felt naked with just a dagger. An old shepherd's staff leaned against the door frame of the cot. He snatched up the staff and sprinted for the gate.

He came around the curve of the embankment and slowed to a walk when he saw le Bec upon the bridge sitting on his horse. Although he carried a sword, he was not armored. No one else was in view.

Le Bec regarded Robert with a bored expression. "Taken up tending sheep, have you, Attebrook? It's what you ought to be doing, rather than pretending to be what you aren't."

"What are you doing here?"

"I've come to talk to Giselle."

"What could you possibly have to say to her?"

"That's for her ears, not yours, you useless piece of shit. Now go tell her I need to speak with her. How many times do I have to ask people around here? Bunch of idiots!"

Robert suppressed the impulse to reply to the insult by knocking le Bec off his horse. Something was up, something that had to be important. So without a further word, he strode through the gate and across the bailey to the house, where Giselle was watching from a window.

"What does he want?" Giselle asked.

"He wants to speak to you. He wouldn't tell me why."

"I'll be right down."

She appeared in the doorway with a sword in each hand, Robert's and her father's, each still in their scabbards. She gave Robert his sword and they crossed the bailey to the gate.

"Watch you don't hurt yourself with that," le Bec, eying the sword in Giselle's hand.

"You know that my father taught me how to use it well enough to deal with shit like you," Giselle said.

"My lady, how unlady like," le Bec said, dismounting. "I am shocked."

"We ought to kill you where you stand for what he's done."

The Outlaws

"He? Eustace? How could he possibly have offended you?"

"You know. He sent Aelfwyn here to poison me."

Le Bec spread his hands. "She may have put that out to shift the blame, but it was her idea and her plan alone."

"I cannot believe that."

"She wanted to be mistress of Hafton. She thought she might accomplish that with your death. You have, after all, been a bit of trouble to our lord."

"A farfetched idea."

"Nonetheless, I swear to you it's true."

"Your oaths have no value. And there's the matter of the wool clip."

"Ah, that Stokesay. We heard about that. A greedy fellow, with many debts."

"I hardly think he would have got the idea on his own, you bastard."

"Well, I suppose we could spend the rest of the day insulting each other, but we have some business to discuss. Business that will benefit the both of us."

"I cannot imagine what that might be."

"Hear me out, at least."

"My patience for you wore thin a long time ago."

"And I am such an amiable fellow, too. You wish to be relieved of your marriage. Our lord, unfortunately, needs money — urgently."

"What for?"

"He owes the king quite a sum for the earldom. A substantial payment is due at the Michaelmas accounting. We are rather short of funds."

"So?"

"If you petition for an annulment on the grounds of coercion, our lord will not contest the allegations, provided that you pay him ten pounds sterling."

Giselle laughed. "You mean that all I have to do to send him into poverty and ruin is to refuse this offer?"

"We'll find the funds from some other source, squeeze the tenants till they drip blood, something like that. But it will take longer, and the delay might anger the king. None of us wants that. He's frightful when he's angry. Even Eustace is afraid of him, although he won't let on."

"I suppose he wants payment up front."

"No. We understand that you are too untrusting for that. We'll simply need to see that you have the money at the time the petition is heard. You can pay after it is granted."

"These things usually take time. It's unlikely the petition would be granted before Michaelmas. That's less than two months away."

"Oh, we think it will. Our lawyers advise that uncontested petitions are often granted right away, especially if there is a bequest to the diocese."

"And who would have to make that gift?"

"You, of course. We have hardly any cash to spare. We're already drinking English wine. Terrible stuff. Chalky. But much cheaper than Gascon."

"My heart goes out to you in your privation."

"You are most kind. What do you say?"

Giselle glanced at Robert, her lips a tight line. The price for her freedom was stiff, since they had no idea what the gift to the diocese would cost. "What do you think, Robert?"

"I don't trust them. But this may be your best chance."

"All right, then," she said. "We'll do it."

"Excellent," le Bec said. "We will bear the cost of drafting the petition and have it filed in your name. You'll save on the cost of lawyers, at least."

"I am underwhelmed by your generosity."

Le Bec bowed. "Thank you, my lady, for your courtesy." He mounted his horse. "See you soon in Hereford. And you, Attebrook, don't you have sheep to attend to?"

"I'll see the petition before it's filed, and I'll arrange to have it filed myself!" Giselle called to his back.

"As you wish!" le Bec replied without turning around. "Just be sure you ask for the bishop himself to hear the case!"

The Outlaws

A summons arrived in mid-August directing Giselle to present herself before the bishop of Hereford on Tuesday, September 4.

She rode down with Robert and Hugh, fretting at what she would have to do once they reached Hereford. She had never borrowed more than pocket money in her life, and the thought of the vast sum they would need to set her free was stunning — almost the entire revenue of Hafton for a whole, including next year's woolclip. The twenty-mile ride could not go quickly enough for her and her anxiety got worse when passed through the Eign Gate on the northwest of Hereford.

The last time they had been here, to engage a lawyer of the church court, or proctor as they were called to distinguish them from the lawmen who appeared in the king's court, he had directed them to an inexpensive inn on Behynderthewall Lane.

They took rooms at the same inn and went round to the money-lender's house, whom the proctor had recommended as the best source of ready funds in town.

It was a grand house on Jews Street near the wall, five stories tall, each stacked upon the one below like ill-fitting boxes and the whole seeming to lean out so far over the street that it threatened to topple over.

Giselle stopped at the door.

"What's the matter?" Robert asked.

"I cannot breathe," she said. "I cannot. It's so much. What if we cannot pay on time? Can he really take the manor?"

"It's the only way. You'll not get the money otherwise. And without the money, you'll never be free from Eustace."

"I know. I just cannot do it."

"We'll find a way to pay it back. We will. With scrimping and saving."

"Scrimping and saving. You learned that from your mother."

"She is good at it."

Giselle took his hand and drew a deep breath, then another and after that one more. She closed her eyes.

"Let us go in and do what must be done," she said.

They entered the house hand in hand.

The proctor called at the inn after they returned. He sat with Giselle and Robert — Hugh was upstairs guarding the money boxes — in the common room not far from the hearth that blazed in the middle of the floor, but just far enough away that they did not get much warmth from it.

The proctor's name was Raimond, and he was a small man so thin that a good sneeze might knock him over. In ordinary clothes, just a fur-lined blue coat, yellow stockings, and a gold medallion on a chain round his neck denoting his profession, he seemed more meager a man that he had appeared to them when wearing his judicial robes. He had a face that was grave, as befitted a lawyer, for it was no good for clients to think a lawyer given to frivolity, but he was even more grave than they had last seen him as he sank to the bench opposite them.

"I've some news. A change of plan," Raimond said, accepting a pewter tankard of wine from a serving girl, not noticing that both Robert and Giselle's tankards held less expensive ale.

"He's changed his mind," Giselle said.

"Who?" Raimond asked, confused.

"Eustace," Giselle said.

"Oh, no. Not that I know of anyway, and I'd have heard of that straightaway. His proctor and I are good friends. We bowl together every Sunday after church. No, it's the bishop. He has unexpectedly left town. Some sudden business in the country, I'm not sure what. It was all so quick."

"So we made the journey for nothing?" Giselle asked.

"I don't think so. The bishop has referred your case to a judge of the consistory court. He will hear the matter in the

The Outlaws

bishop's place. However, the first hearing cannot take place for another four days."

"Four days," Giselle repeated. "It's bad enough that I have to pay a settlement rather than the other way around, and a gift to the diocese besides. Now I have to bear the expense of five nights in town? I am not made of money. Pretty soon what we have will run out."

"Speaking of the gift, how much to do you have?" Raimond asked.

"Two-hundred shillings," Robert said. "The amount you specified."

Raimond looked at Robert for the first time. "I said two-hundred? I don't remember that. Well, his honor had hoped for more. But in a matter like this, involving people of such stature, I suppose it will have to do."

"We told you before that's all we could afford to borrow."

"Well, I thought, you know, that you might be able to be more generous." Raimond tossed back the rest of his wine. He wiped a dribble from his chin with his palm.

"If the bishop expects more, it might diminish what we have available for your fee," Robert said.

"Oh, dear. We don't want that."

"The bishop's absence won't delay things, will it?" Robert asked.

"No, it shouldn't. I rather suspect that he's done this to avoid embarrassment. He solemnized the lady's marriage, after all. It makes him look bad if he has to annul it now. You can understand that, can't you? He doesn't want to appear having been a fool. Don't worry, my lady, I shall ask for an immediate decision. Since the earl will not contest the allegation, I expect his proctor will also seek an immediate ruling. At least, he's told me he will."

Raimond stood up, his wine gone and with no one in sight willing to replenish the cup. "I'll check with the judge the day before the hearing to ensure it's going forward as planned. My boy will come round and let you know."

Raimond's boy, who was in his thirties and one of his clerks, came by the following day. He stood behind Robert, who was bent over a backgammon board across from Hugh, and cleared his throat. "Ahmmmm," he intoned. "Ahmmmm." Perhaps he intended to sound discrete, but instead he gave the impression of choking on something. When neither Robert nor Hugh looked up to see what he wanted, he said, "Your honors, my lord has asked me to come by on a matter of urgent business."

"What is that disturbance?" Robert asked Hugh as his fingers hovered over a piece.

"A tall person with the biggest jaw I have ever seen," Hugh said.

"Is he armed?"

"Doesn't appear to be."

"Does he look dangerous?"

"Only to himself."

"He's not from Eustace then." Robert turned now and, just to dispel all doubt, asked, "You're not from the Earl Eustace FitzWalter, are you?"

"Goodness, no," the clerk said. "I serve Raimond of Winchester. I am his clerk."

"The lawyer," Robert said, almost as alarmed now by the clerk's appearance as if Reginald le Bec had popped out of the ground behind him. "It's not been moved up, has it? The hearing?"

"Oh, no, I'm afraid not. But there is a matter of business affecting the hearing that my master has asked me to take care of."

Robert could not imagine what that might be, but he said, "All right, then. What is it?"

"The, ahmmm, gift. My master has sent me around to collect it."

"You? All by yourself?"

"Well, yes."

515

The Outlaws

"You do know what this gift is, don't you?"

The clerk glanced left and right and lowered his voice, a difficult task as it was a rather loud voice. "A bit of money, sir."

"More money than you're likely to earn in half a lifetime, and you're going to just carry it away? All by yourself?"

"Those were my instructions. I'm to take it to the bishop's palace and deliver it to Marc de Poitu."

"I don't know a Marc de Poitu. Why is he getting our money?"

"He is the clerk to our judge."

"I assume you know this Marc."

"Of course."

"He can be trusted with such a fortune?"

"Since he must account to Father Theophile for the whole amount, he had better be."

"And who is Father Theophile?"

"Our learned judge."

"We can't just deliver it to him on the hearing day?"

The clerk looked scandalized. "Most certainly not! It would look like a payment! It is the clerk's task, among other things, to accept gifts given to the church by litigants appearing before the court. To avoid the appearance of impropriety, you see."

"I had not considered that."

"The judges are most sensitive creatures. Especially to suggestions that they have been compromised."

"Aren't they?"

"Aren't they what?"

"Compromised."

"Most definitely not. It is a sacred thing to give gifts to the church. How could that compromise a judge?"

"I must be a simpleton. I have no idea." Robert dropped the backgammon piece and stood up. "We'll carry it for you. I'd like to meet this Marc. And you're liable to hurt yourself carrying it by yourself. Not to mention the attention you're likely to attract, and I'm thinking of the unsavory kind."

"It isn't that far to the bishop's palace. Nothing untoward is likely to happen between here and there. And it is broad daylight."

"Nevertheless, we will take it there."

Giselle's book settled to her lap. "You're not leaving me alone here!"

Robert knelt down and felt under the bed for the smaller chest. They kept the money under the bed rather than in the inn's locked storage room, where many people put their valuables, because there was so much money that they didn't trust the innkeeper or his boys not to pilfer the contents. Under the bed was a poor place to put the chests, since the inn had a common room upstairs filled with beds separated by curtains, but it was out of sight. "We won't be long."

Giselle stood up. "I'm going. Hugh can stay." They took turns sitting with the money as if it was a sick child. "I'm tired of being cooped up here."

Robert dragged out the smaller chest. Sixty shillings didn't take up that much space, but it still weighed quite a lot, and he didn't relish carrying it to the bishop's palace. He had no idea how far that might be.

"I don't mind," Hugh offered.

"Of course you don't," Robert said, "since now I'll be the one to carry it."

"You weren't thinking of making me carry it? Me, a Gascon knight?"

"You're not a knight yet."

"Well, almost a knight. Son of a knight. That ought to count for something."

"Remain here and guard our fortune from all the dangers that threaten it and you may be made a knight for your courage."

"And who's going to do that?" Hugh asked.

Robert pointed to Giselle. "She can't give you land or money, but she can give you honor."

The Outlaws

"English women can make knights?" Although Hugh had been in England for several years and even had a decent command of the common language, but with a heavy accent that often made him hard to understand, there was still much about English life that was a mystery to him.

"Truly," Robert said, although he had never heard of such a thing.

"Well, as I said, I don't mind." Hugh stepped to the window, which overlooked the inn's yard. "It smells like shit. That privy desperately needs burning. But somehow, I shall manage."

Giselle handed Hugh the book. "This will help distract you from the odor."

"You can balance it on your head," Robert said to Hugh, and added for Giselle's benefit, "He can't read."

"Reading is not expected of knights," Hugh said, occupying the chair that Giselle had used.

"If you can't read, how will you ever know that you're being cheated by your steward?" Giselle asked.

"My steward wouldn't dare," Hugh said. "If I had a steward."

"Yes, you are too fiercesome," Robert said as he lifted the chest to his shoulder and went out.

Giselle remembered enough about Hereford to realize that when the clerk turned right out of the door to the inn that the route they would take went by Earl Roger's — now Eustace's — townhouse on Brode Street.

"Not that way," she insisted.

"It is the quickest, my lady," the clerk said.

"The less distance I have to carry this, the better," Robert said.

"It's longer only by a few steps. You can survive those." Giselle turned about and headed back to the corner behind her. "I'm not going that way."

Robert looked at the clerk and shrugged. Then he followed her.

"His townhouse lies along the way. I might see him," Giselle said as he caught up. "I don't want to see him."

"You have to at the hearing."

"That's different. It can't be helped." She did not add that the townhouse held very bad memories that she had tried hard to suppress, and she worried that the sight of it might bring them back.

At the corner, Giselle marched left. The street here was broad enough for two carts to pass each other. Quite a few carts must have taken the opportunity, because the dirt was quite chewed up and had dried hard so that the dips and ridges carved by them made walking difficult.

"This was not a good idea," Robert said, after he had stumbled.

"It wouldn't have been any better on Brode Street," Giselle said without turning around.

In many towns, shops dealing in a particular thing often clustered together so that there was a draper's lane, a butcher's row, or a grocer's alley. But here, the shops seemed varied. She passed a draper's, a cutler, two taverns, another inn, a bakery that smelled of fresh bread and made her mouth water, a stable whose odor of horse canceled out the bakery, and a pot and pottery shop that had a copper pot on display that brought her up short. It was unusual to find a copper pot, and it even had handles.

Robert, following closely and paying more attention to his feet that the commerce, almost bumped into her. "What now?"

"I like that pot," she said.

"It looks expensive."

"It probably is," Giselle said, resuming her march. "Another day, perhaps, when we have money. It's going to be a hard winter once I pay *him* off." She couldn't bring herself to say Eustace's name. She had not realized how much hate

The Outlaws

she had inside. Only now that she was almost free did she sense it.

"Well, if things get really strapped, we can always borrow enough to see us through."

"Do you really want to do that?"

"No. Not unless we have to. Debt should be avoided like a fever."

"Then why bring it up?"

"Just a thought. Just in case."

Giselle knocked on a corner post of the pot shop. "Let's hope it doesn't come to that."

It was almost a relief to reach the end of the street because of the sights and smells of all the things that she couldn't have. She paused at the corner, and asked the clerk, "Left, isn't it?" although she was certain that was the way, as the red stone towers of the cathedral loomed above the tops of the houses in that direction.

"Yes, my lady," the clerk said. "Left it is."

Giselle was about to step out in the direction of the cathedral when a figure emerging from a church to the right caught her eye. The church had been built in the middle of the street, or perhaps the street had emerged around it, and carts passed on either side. The figure, that of a woman, paused to restrain two boys from rushing into the street as a four-horse wagon drove close by and might have run them down. When the wagon passed, she released the boys and started in Giselle's direction.

"What is it now?" Robert asked. "More pots?"

"No," she said. "Someone I recognize."

"Not Reggie, is it?" He said this lightly, however, as Reginald le Bec was nowhere in view.

"Not le Bec. Someone I knew in Shelburgh."

"So we're stopping for a chat?"

"Yes. If that box is too much of a strain, put it down."

"My poor back thanks you."

"Your poor back is welcome."

Giselle's impulse had been merely civil, since it was rude not to speak to people you knew on the street, and her hatred of Eustace did not extend to everyone at Shelburgh.

But when the woman caught sight of her, she withdrew to the other side of the street, and seemed intent on passing by without stopping or acknowledging Giselle's presence, as though she was a leper.

"Clarimond!" Giselle called out, more sharply than she intended, and advanced across the street, dodging a cart towing a bull as she did so.

Clarimond looked frightened. But she halted and called, "Boys! Wait!"

"You're not even going to say hello?" Giselle asked.

"I can't be seen talking to you," Clarimond said.

"For God's sake, why?"

"You're an enemy now."

"What are you talking about?"

"He means to destroy you."

"What? How?"

"I can't tell you. I don't know. He and le Bec, they plot about it all the time. They've even sought to draw my husband into it."

That well might be, since Clarimond's husband was the deputy castellan. Giselle said, "But he's about to be free of me. I don't see how that fits into such a plan."

"I don't know either, but you know how they are. They never forget a slight or willingly give up something they have." Clarimond's eyes fixed on the ground and her hand went to her throat.

Then Giselle noticed the pin that secured her cloak. Giselle reached out to it, but Clarimond drew back.

"Where did you get that pin?" Giselle asked.

"My husband gave it to me, why?"

"I've seen its like before." Giselle did not say where, but it had been her father's, the pin he wore the night he died and which was not found with his body. "Do you know where he got it?"

The Outlaws

"He won it at dice from le Bec."

From the instant she spotted the pin, she had felt as if she wasn't living in her own body. But now she felt a spasm of pain so intense that she almost bent over. "Le Bec!"

"Yes. What is it? Are you all right?"

"I'm fine."

"I have to go. Please! I can't be suspected of having given anything away."

Giselle grasped her arm. "I will give you anything you ask for the clasp."

"Why?"

"My father had one just like it. I wish it to remember him by it."

"My husband will notice its absence."

"Tell him it was lost. Tell him anything. Please, this is very important to me."

Clarimond withdrew her arm, and Giselle thought she would refuse. But Clarimond nodded and named a price that would exhaust what funds they had left to spare.

"Please pay Lady Clarimond, Robert," Giselle said.

Clarimond collected her handful of coins, then the boys, who had taken to playing in the dirt, and hurried off toward Brode Street.

CHAPTER 22

Hereford
September 1184

The day of the hearing dawned clear and chilly, hinting at the autumn just around the corner, the sky blue with wispy clouds scudding to the east. It had rained again during the night and the passage of carts and wagons had not yet turned the sodden dirt into mud, but the ruts and potholes from previous churnings were filled with puddles, so that Giselle, Robert, and Hugh kept as close as they could to the buildings to avoid stepping into any of them; more than a few looked formidable enough to swallow a person, or even a wagon.

The hearing was not set to take place until the third hour of the day, but they got to the bishop's palace early, since Giselle wanted to watch how other cases were conducted in case there was something useful to be learned. But the doors to the chambers to which they were directed by a caretaker were locked, and Robert reported, when he put his eye to the crack between the double doors, that no one seemed to be there.

Robert and Hugh set down the money chest, and Giselle used it for a seat while Hugh went off to find out what was going on. He returned with word that court would start at the third hour sharp.

Giselle's stomach was growling at it often did just before dinner time when a clerk came along and unlocked the doors to let them in.

"Stay on this side of the bar," the bailiff said, indicating the wooden barrier that separated a long table at the far end of the hall from the remainder of the vast space.

"Are there no other cases today?" Giselle asked.

"Only one," the bailiff said in a tone that suggested being required to answer a question was an imposition. He hurried away before anyone could aim any others in his direction.

"I wonder if it's our case," Robert mused as the bailiff vanished through the doorway.

The Outlaws

"It had better be," Giselle said. "I've already spent enough on it."

They did not have long to wait among the echoes before the two proctors strolled through the doorway in their black robes and four cornered hats, followed by half a dozen clerks each.

"Ah, good, you're here," Raimond said as he reached them. He bent down by the chest. "It is locked? Do you mind if I take a look?"

He had already taken a look once, but Giselle understood that the look wasn't for him. She nodded, and Raimond flipped up the lid. "Are you satisfied?" he asked the other proctor.

"It's all there?"

"Of course it's all there," Giselle said.

"His lordship wanted it counted," the proctor said.

"He can count it himself after we're done."

The proctor smiled. "Living up to your reputation, I see, my lady."

"And what reputation is that?"

"Quarrelsome."

"You'd be quarrelsome, too, if you had to put up with him."

"Hmm," the proctor said. He went through the barrier followed by his clerks.

"We're the only case?" Giselle asked Raimond as he too went through the gap in the barrier.

"A special setting," Raimond said. "For the earl."

"That's thoughtful."

"Well, he is an important man."

It was some time before Eustace showed up, and he brought a great entourage that filled up the hall, big as it was. They were noisy, almost boisterous, as if this was a feast rather than a solemn judicial occasion. Even the pair of judicial clerks who came in with parchments, ink pots, and quills, and a cushion for the single high-backed chair behind the table made no effort to calm down the crowd.

A few other people not part of that entourage tried to enter with them, but a pair of bailiffs pushed them out and barred the door.

Eustace stood on the far side of the hall from Giselle and acted as if she weren't there. A striking woman stood at his side; not beautiful, but arresting nonetheless, with an angular face and brooding eyes, and a chilly, almost regal bearing, except when she and Eustace put their heads together and exchanged words; then the chilliness dissipated as she smiled with clear pleasure. Giselle at first wanted to think that the woman was just common whore like Aelfwyn, but there was something about her bearing and her fine gown and fox-lined cloak, the delicate weaving of her silken wimple, and the rings upon her fingers, including a large red-stoned one on a thumb that could have been a ruby, that suggested she was a woman of high quality, higher than her own. Once the woman caught Giselle's eye and they measured each other. The woman smiled, but it was not in friendship. It was dismissive, and a challenge.

At last, the head judicial clerk called for order, and announced that court was now in session. He spoke court French, which most of Eustace's followers couldn't understand, but the importance of the moment was obvious to them, and they quieted down.

The judge entered the hall and sat in the high-backed chair. "Call the next case," he said also in court French, as if he didn't know what it was.

"The matter of FitzWalter versus FitzWalter," the clerk bellowed rather more loudly than he needed to be heard by those in the hall.

"You may proceed, counsel," the judge said to Raimond.

Raimond stepped forward and unfurled a long parchment.

The petition had been written in Latin rather than court French or English. She did not listen closely, for she knew the gist of it: that she had been coerced into the marriage by the former Earl Roger by beatings and threats while a tender ward in his care. She had wanted something put in about Eustace's

The Outlaws

beatings and threats, but Raimond had refused to agree to that. "It will only anger him," Raimond had said. "You don't want that. You need his cooperation." She had reluctantly agreed.

When Raimond finished, the judge said to Eustace's proctor, "How does the respondent plead?"

"The respondent does not contest the allegations," the proctor said. "In fact, he wishes to add that he himself was coersed. Earl Roger threatened him with a loss of inheritance if he did not agree to the marriage."

"No contest then?" the judge said.

"No contest, your honor," the proctor said.

"One wonders why the earl would want his only son to marry such a . . . low woman, of such ill character, too," the judge said. "It makes no sense. But a marriage is a sacrament that cannot easily be put aside."

There was a long pause, as if the judge was struggling over what to do now, although five pounds of encouragement should have put him to no struggle at all, unless it was in how to spend the money.

Just when Giselle thought he might get up and leave, the judge announced, "I declare this marriage to be void *ab initio* for lack of consent. You may both go hence without day."

The judge rose and stalked out of the room with a swirl of red and white robe, leaving a clerk behind to scribble an account of the proceedings and the ruling on a court scroll.

Eustace turned to leave, the regal woman at his side. He still did not look at Giselle, but then why should he? She was flotsam in his wake. But the woman glanced back at her, a triumphant smile on her face as she linked her arm with Eustace's. There was something possessive about that gesture. Eustace had never allowed Aelfwyn to act like that. She was more than a concubine.

Giselle trembled as a pair of Eustace's retainers, one of them Henry, Clarimond's husband, collected the chest at her feet. She had the sudden feeling that she had been had. He had needed this annulment as much, or more, than she had; yet he tricked her into paying dearly for it.

"I've been a fool," she said.

"What?" Robert asked. He had missed the signs thrown off by the regal woman and did not understand.

"Never mind. Take me home."

They turned left on Pipewell Street after leaving the bishop's palace to avoid mingling with the back end of Eustace's entourage, and headed toward the bridge rather than away from it, which was the proper route back to the inn. The narrow street turned left then right before emptying into Bridge Street, and it wasn't until they reached there that Giselle realized whom she had not seen in court.

"Le Bec wasn't there," she said, stopping dead in the road.

"No, he wasn't," Robert said. "That's odd. Eustace never goes anywhere without him."

Giselle wasn't concerned about the oddness of it. She was overcome with fury that she had set aside during her concern about whether Eustace would live up to his agreement over the annulment. But it flooded back now so strongly that she shook with it.

"If I were a man, I'd kill him," Giselle said.

"If I were Le Bec, I'd still watch out," Robert said. "You're frightening when you're mad."

"Don't patronize me."

"I was stating a fact."

"I can't do anything about him. He killed my father and there's nothing I can do about it."

"No, there probably isn't."

"You could, though."

"What, lie in wait in the forest and shoot him in the back? He's surrounded by retainers. There's no way to get to him."

"I could acuse him at the next assize."

The Outlaws

"To what purpose? Eustace will only hire a champion to fight for him, even assuming le Bec picks trial by combat. Besides, any accusation will compromise Clarimond. She's your only witness connecting le Bec with the pin."

"And he will just say he bought it somewhere, or someone gave it to him," Hugh said behind them.

Giselle and Robert both stopped and looked at him.

"That's true," Robert said. "You have no proof. You don't even know if it was really him."

"It has to be," Giselle said.

"Believing it doesn't make it so."

"Will you find out the truth?"

"Why would I do that?"

"Because we're family."

"That's an odd thing for you to bring up since we've spent so much time pretending it wasn't so."

"You'd do it if you were my husband."

"I would. But I'm not."

"But you could be. If you want to."

"Do you want that?"

"Yes."

"Despite our impediment?" Robert asked.

"What impediment?" Hugh asked.

"It's nothing," Robert said.

"I wish that were true," Giselle said.

"What impediment?" Hugh asked again.

"Pay no attention to that," Robert said. Locking eyes with Giselle, he said, "Then I marry you."

"And I marry you," Giselle said.

Robert said to Hugh, "You're our witness."

"That's it?" Hugh asked. "That's all it takes?"

"In England, yes," Robert said. "All you have to do is say the words."

"I thought you needed a priest."

"Not to make a marriage, although it helps."

"Well, we have to go by St. Nicholas'." Hugh gestured to the top of Bridge Street where the red bulk of St. Nicholas' church could be seen almost as if blocking the road. "Don't you think it would be prudent to stop there anyway? Since you're in such a hurry?"

Giselle linked her arm with Robert's. "I think we should take that advice, my husband."

"As you wish, wife."

CHAPTER 23

Hereford
September 1184

It did not occur to Robert until they returned to the inn from St. Nicholas' church that he was lord of Hafton now. The realization came after they had the horses saddled, when he cupped his hands to help Giselle mount her mare, and she put her hand on his shoulder and said, "Thank you, my lord." For a moment, he thought she must be speaking to someone else, and he almost looked around to see what high person had suddenly approached. But there was no one else in the stable but Giselle and Hugh.

"My pleasure, my lady," he said. In a stroke, he had gone from being a poor nobody to being landed gentry. He had dreamed of having his own land, but the ambition had seemed so far out of his reach that he had never taken the possibility seriously. Now it had happened. A lord and a husband all at once. It made him dizzy.

Robert glanced at Hugh, who was fiddling with a girth. Hugh's horse was one of those that liked to bloat up upon being saddled, and Hugh didn't want to have to stop later and tighten the girth. "Hurry up, there. I thought you knew how to saddle a horse."

"I know well enough, m'lord," Hugh said with a large grin, as if calling Robert a lord was a joke. "It's just the horse doesn't like to be saddled."

Robert grasped the horse's bridle and shook a finger at it. "I order you to cooperate."

"That's not helping," Hugh said, grunting as he heaved on the girth strap.

"The dumb horse doesn't know how important I am now," Robert said with a grin of his own.

"What kind of lord are you if you can't make a horse obey?"

"Clearly I have a lot to learn about lordship," Robert said.

"That's true," Giselle said.

"I'm sure you'll correct me when I'm wrong."

"You can count on that."

"You've never been shy about it in the past. I can't see any reason why that would change." He looked up at her and touched her calf, an intimate public gesture that he had never allowed himself before. She removed his hat and brushed his hair.

"Come on," she said, returning his hat to his head, "it's getting late. It'll be dark before we get back."

Hafton
September 1184

It was dark by the time they reached the top of the hill overlooking the village. They were tired and sore and ready to be home, even though it was a mere twenty miles from Hereford, and Robert felt the relief he always got at the last leg of any journey, when the prospect of a warm meal, sweet ale, and a good bed lay just ahead.

The first inkling Robert had that something was amiss was the large number of fires twinkling in the distance. They had the appearance of campfires, but they could not be that. Why would people in the village have lit campfires?

Giselle noticed them, too, and stirred in the saddle. "That's odd."

"The fires?"

"Yes. I wonder what's going on."

By the time they reached the big oak where people took shelter during breaks from work, it was apparent that something was very wrong.

"The houses," Giselle said. "Where are all the houses?"

For the peaked roofs that should have been visible against the night stars and the light of a rising, almost-full moon were not there, and the smell of smoke hung in the air, thick and choking, and worse than usual.

Giselle urged her mare to a trot. Robert hurried to catch up, full of dread. He suspected now what awaited them. He

The Outlaws

had seen such things before in France. He had not wanted to contemplate anything of the sort happening here.

When they reached where the first houses had stood, they saw nothing left but burned-out shells, a few timbers standing where the houses had been. Some of the ruins were still burning, although they were piles of ash, and these were among the fires they had seen from the hill. Others were, in fact, campfires lit in the yards.

People came out to the road and followed them as they rode toward the church and the village well.

They stopped at the wide spot around the well. Giselle sat with a hand over her mouth while a crowd gathered around, drawn by the whispered announcement that she had returned.

"Are we quit of him at last?" someone called from the back of the crowd.

Giselle choked up and could not answer.

Robert answered for her. "If you mean the earl, yes. She's free of him. But I'm afraid to say that you've only exchanged one lord for another."

"Whose the new lord?" another called.

"Me."

"How's that?" a third voice asked out of the dark.

"I've married our lady."

"Not wasting any time getting his hands on the manor, is he," someone muttered loud enough for Robert to hear. "Not that it'll do him any good now."

Pride and position required that he address such disrespect, but Robert ignored it. He saw Wulfric Ploughman, the bailiff, at the rear of the crowd, distinguishable by his height and the rag bandage about his head. Robert beckoned him to come forward. "What happened, Wulfric?"

"It was the Welsh, sir," Wulfric said in a far more respectful tone that Robert had heard from anyone else yet. The others seemed angry, as if this terrible misfortune was somehow his fault.

"Last night!" someone yelled.

"They've taken everything!" a woman called out. "Even my pots!"

"We've been stripped bare," a man said. "Harvest gone, our animals driven off."

"Even the sheep?" Robert asked.

"Yeah," Wulfric said. "There's hardly any that got away. Though we still have our pigs. The oxen for the plough teams are missing as well."

"Can't get through the winter eating just pig!" a voice said out of the dark. "There aren't enough of them for all of us!"

"They even burned your barn," Wulfric said.

"The manor barn?"

Wulfric nodded. "Many of us sought refuge at the manor house, so many that they dared not to attack it, but they shot fire arrows over the walls. We managed to put out those that struck the house, but we couldn't save the barn."

"Was anyone killed?" Robert asked.

"Four," Wulfric said. "John the hayward, Howard Makepeese, and Richard Tailor. There was one other, a woman, Kate the fish wife. We found her cut down on her doorstep. And two girls are missing, Horsa's daughter and Fred the tanner's."

Giselle has listened to this report with a stricken face. "You'll need houses," she said, finding her voice.

"We need something to eat!" someone called. "They even trampled the gardens! We've nothing but bark and old shoes!"

"We can't do anything about that now," she replied. "But we can allow you the liberty of the forest so you can rebuild your homes." She glanced at Robert, as if his permission was an afterthought. "If my lord concurs."

Robert nodded. "You can start rebuilding tomorrow. And then we'll think about what to do about your stomachs."

The Outlaws

CHAPTER 24

Hafton
September 1184

A wedding day was supposed to be filled with celebration, but supper that night was a sad affair of hard cheese, harder bread, and cold sausage.

Not even the household staff's gripping description of their heroics in resisting the attack lifted Robert's or Giselle's spirits. One bit turned out to be true: two sons of the goatherd had been up at the top of the tower (where they were not allowed) when the Welsh came, and after the three or four arrows shot at the house stuck to the wooden shingles, they had shimmied down a rope to the rooftop and put out the fires at great risk of falling off. As this incident had been witnessed by everyone in the yard, there was no denying that it was true.

When the story came out, the goatherd, a villein, apologized for the fact the boys were playing in the tower.

"We were not playing!" one of the boys protested. "We were hunting rats!" As if rat-catching, a useful occupation, might excuse their trespass.

"Nonsense!" their mother Hannah said. "I know you! I've told you to stay out of there!"

"Never mind that, Hannah," Robert said. "If they hadn't been there, we wouldn't have a house now." He dug into his purse, and counted out ten silver pennies, just about the last of his savings. "Here's five pence for each of you, for your bravery, boys. Just stay out of the tower from now on."

Hannah fell to her knees before the high table, babbling her thanks as Robert poured the money into her hands.

By the time everyone had had a chance to brag about the brave things they had done, it was very late. Those of the staff who were not waiting on the high table brought out their pallets and laid them about the hall, while Robert, Giselle, and Hugh finished their supper.

Robert tapped his portion of the bread on the table. It made the same sound as if he had struck the table with a stone. "Have we no flour left?" he asked the cook who stood by with an ale pitcher, on guard for the appearance of an empty cup.

"We've two sacks, m'lord," Cook said.

"That's quite a bit," Robert mused. Each sack held about thirty pounds of milled flour. "But no one baked bread today?"

"We thought we should save what we have," Cook said. "And I thought the smell of fresh bread might bother those who could not have any."

"And they burned the mill as well?" Robert asked.

"Gone, a heap of rubble. No one's looking forward to grinding what we saved by hand. Although we could always take it to Shelburgh."

"I'll not pay Eustace for my bread," Giselle said. "I've paid him more than enough already."

"Then there's always Leominster," Cook said.

"That's too far away," Giselle said. "We need to do something about the mill."

"The stones broke in the fire, my lady," Cook said "Even if we rebuilt we'll need new stones."

"Those cost a lot of money," Robert said.

"Money we don't have," Giselle said.

"Even with stones," Robert said, "there's hardly enough grain to see us through the winter, let alone the people in the village."

"There's nothing we can do about them," Giselle said.

Robert was shocked, although he shouldn't have been. Even in famines, the gentry didn't go hungry; they kept what they had for themselves and gave no thought to the people under them. "Yes, there is. We can feed them."

"Feed them? I've never heard of such a thing. Why?"

"It is an obligation."

She said nothing that. Robert went on, "You've never been hungry."

The Outlaws

"I have so! On the way to London, I had nothing. Well, almost nothing."

"Then you should remember how it was. I remember going to bed hungry. It's a terrible thing. And if we don't feed them, people will run away rather than starve. You won't even be able to hold the villeins. By spring there will be no one to work the manor."

"How do you propose to do this?"

"I'm not sure. We have some money left."

"Not enough for that."

"We have the forest. We could cut more trees and sell the timber. We could see if we can make the mine productive again."

"I suppose."

"We need to take a long view. We'll need to replace the oxen for the plough teams, the millstones, and buy a ram and ewes to rebuild the flock. It might even be worth going a little deeper into debt."

"Dear God! You will ruin us!"

"We'll have a few tight years ahead, but in the end, we'll set things back the way they were. I don't see any other way."

Giselle was quiet for a long time, as her fingers played with her own chunk of hard bread. "I don't like it."

"In the meantime," Robert said, "there's something we should do?"

"What?" Giselle asked.

"Take the flour in one of those sacks and bake a few loaves for the villagers."

"You are mad, truly mad."

"We've fences to mend and the mill to rebuild. It will be payment for that."

Giselle put her palms on the table. "I don't know which is worse, Eustace's fury or your charity."

"My charity will pay returns in the end."

"We shall have to hope so. I cannot afford another annulment."

CHAPTER 25

Hafton
September 1184

Now that the decision was made to plunge the manor further into debt, Robert spent several days nerving himself up to it.

On the morning he intended to set out, he came out of the house after breakfast. His eyes fell on Osgar exercising one of his palfreys on a leading rein, running him in circles, after having saddled the other palfrey and Hugh's horse.

Hugh was waiting on the steps with Wulfric and Odo. "What's a good riding horse worth, Wulfric?" Robert asked.

Wulfric sucked on his front teeth considering the matter. "Five pounds? Six? Somewhere thereabout."

"How many oxen can we get for five pounds?"

"That's more than enough for several plow teams."

"With money to spare."

"Indeed."

"Isn't tomorrow the feast of Saint Matthew?"

"It is," Odo said.

"I see your point," Wulfric said.

"What point?" Hugh asked.

"Yes," Giselle said, emerging from the house. "What point."

"We're going to Ludlow," Robert said. "Not Hereford."

"Ludlow?" Giselle asked. "I didn't think there were any moneylenders in Ludlow."

"I'm sure there are one or two," Robert said.

"But will they have enough to spare for us?"

"I think they might."

"You think that the presence of the fair will make it easier to borrow?" she asked. The Ludlow harvest fair started on the day of the feast of Saint Matthew.

"Could be," Robert said. "We shall see."

"Safe journey, my dear," she said, not convinced.

"Do you want to come?"

The Outlaws

"No. I think not. It will revive an unpleasant memory."

Robert kissed her and descended to the yard.

He held out his hand to Osgar. "I'll take that rope."

Robert waved to Giselle as they crossed the bridge. She waved back, frowning, wondering why he had decided at the last moment to take the second palfrey.

Robert had never been to the Ludlow harvest fair, although it was impossible in this country not to come across people who had attended it. So he had some idea what to expect — crowded inns, the only place to stay the north pasture, where the castle bailiff rented plots for the pitching of a tent. At least it should cost less than an inn. A bed, even one with just a straw mattress, was preferable to sleeping on the ground. But in their present financial condition, he would be lucky to afford the plot for the tent.

In the event, the cost was less than Robert expected, a farthing a night for the two of them. They pitched their tent next to a broad oak so big around that four men's outstretched arms could just encompass its girth, and some of its limbs sagged so low that they could be used as seats or, as in one case, a fence for hanging laundry. There must have been at least a dozen families camping without tents beneath the tree, and the bailiff was emphatic that no one could build a fire under it or anywhere near it, which included Robert and Hugh.

"I'll not have any of you burning down my lord's oak," the bailiff declared as if he had never delivered this message before, although from the indifferent reception it received from the people camped under the tree, he had probably repeated it at every opportunity. "It's worth more than all of you put together." He wagged a finger at them. "No fires!"

The few dwellers under the oak had horses to pull their carts, and they had arranged those carts to form a paddock for the horses. They allowed Robert and Hugh use of the paddock at no charge, if one of them devoted an hour of the day to watch the paddock against thieves. Robert volunteered Hugh.

"I am not a horse ward," Hugh said. "We should pay some boy to do it."

"With what? I've got enough for food, and that's about it."

"Well, you should at least take a turn. Share the misery."

"What misery? You just sit in that cart with a sword at your feet. Guarding things requires hardly any real work."

"I suppose. I'd feel better if you'd fetch me a pitcher of ale. Look there! There's a fellow carrying a barrel on his back. Here, you!"

The man carrying the barrel came over and deposited it on the tail of a wagon. "Thirsty, are you?"

"He is," Robert said. "We'll take a pitcher." He rummaged in their pack for their pitcher and held it while the ale-seller turned the tap to fill it.

"That smells like right good ale," Hugh said, trying hard to sound English.

"Made yesterday. Best in town."

"Best in this field, anyway."

"You sure you don't want any?" the ale-seller asked Robert.

"I've got work to do."

"That never stopped no one before," the ale-seller said.

"He's religious," Hugh said. "Doesn't drink before supper."

"I've never heard of anyone doing that."

"It's a strange vow, I'll give you that." Hugh took a long pull on the pitcher, since Robert had neglected to furnish him with a cup. He licked his lips. "Not as bad as one of those hairshirts, though."

"I wouldn't know about that. Never tried one." The ale-seller put his arms through the straps attached to the barrel and made off in search of more customers.

"What business do you have, really?" Hugh asked, examining the inside of the pitcher.

The Outlaws

"It's best to climb down before you have to pee," Robert said, as he turned toward the town.

The next morning, Robert led the palfrey out of the paddock of carts and up the slope into town. During his inquiries yesterday, he had been told that he needed to go to the bull ring on Old Street. He and Hugh fell in behind a cart laden with a dismantled stall and baskets of apples and peaches on its way to High Street, where the main activity of the fair took place. They passed through a narrow opening in the town embankment that was more a sally port than a proper gate. Most times, such ports were unmanned since only locals used them. But today a pair of wardens stood just inside ready to take the toll charged for entry into the town, since this was the quicker way to reach High Street than going west to Corve Gate.

Just inside the gate stood a large timber house across from an orchard behind a brownstone fence.

"Rich draper lives here," the farmer said to them as they passed it. "And there," he pointed to a neighboring edifice, "the priests live."

Robert wondered why that was worth pointing out until he realized that just ahead was the stubby tower of the parish church, Saint Laurence's, set off from the rest of the town by a brownstone fence.

They reached the head of the lane, and to the right in the broad street that stretched all the way to the gates of the castle, and saw the fair was already in progress: a riot of stalls with awnings of every color imaginable, interspersed with tables and benches and upon them pottery, combs, cutlery, jewelry, carpets and tapestries, cookware and pots, cabbages, leeks, onions, mushrooms, leather goods, pewter platters and bowls and cups — so much stuff in one place that the mind could not take it all in at once.

"Go ahead," Hugh said. "Let's have a look."

"No," Robert said. "I've got to find the bull ring."

"That way," the farmer said, turning the corner. "Just keep going toward Galdeford Gate. You can't miss it." He trudged on muttering to his boy, "Our space had better not be taken, after what I've paid for it."

"Galdeford Gate," Hugh repeated.

"As if we know where that is."

"Well, it's somewhere that way."

The street to the left narrowed so that it was a challenge for two horses to pass at the same time, and thank God no cart came along, otherwise they'd never have got through. The shops belonged to drapers, mercers, and grocers, and the smell of wool and the stench of tallow from a lone candlemaker.

They were soon through the defile and into a more open street, and there ahead dominating the open expanse had to be the bull ring. It was several fenced off rings, not all of them containing cattle. There was a ring for them, of course, but also one for sheep, one for pigs, one for goats, and a low wicker one for chickens which were making a great racket, when one of the people by the fence tossed them a handful of grain, producing a scramble in which feathers fluttered into the air. There was even one for dogs, although it was only large enough for one dog at a time, and he kept jumping out to perform tricks for which the spectators were expected to put coins in his master's hat. A man on stilts came up through the crowd, and the dog raced around the stilts yipping and yowling until the stilt walker wavered and fell over, crying out in alarm and wheeling his arms. This produced more coins for the hat than any of the ordinary tricks.

"No ring for horses," Robert said. He had been sure there would be one. People always came to fairs to buy horses.

"You're making a mistake," Hugh said. "You can't sell him."

"Better the horse than take a loan."

"It will be a long time before you can afford to replace him."

"I'll make do."

The Outlaws

They stood by the bull ring for the rest of the day without anyone showing more than polite interest in the horse. There was quite a bit of haggling over the cows, bulls, and oxen, and more for the goats, sheep, and pigs so that by sundown, the populations of the pens had declined. Even the chickens grew weary as the sun settled below the roof tops and the streets fell into shadow. The owner of the dancing trick dog had long since collected his wages and disappeared with the stilt walker into the tavern across the way, where someone was singing a song about a naked woman.

Robert was on the point of giving up when a group of men emerged from the defile leading to Castle Street, led by a florid man whose nose had been knocked askew like a nail that had been mishammered. He had to be the leader, since he was the best dressed, with an embroidered hat, squirrel-lined collar and cuffs on a coat that hung to his knees, and red-and-yellow checked stockings just visible above high boots. He also wore the medallion of the undersheriff on a chain round his neck. One of the group pointed out Robert and they came toward him.

The man with the medallion planted himself before Robert, hands on his hips as he surveyed the stallion. "This is your horse?" he asked without any attempt at an introduction.

"He is, your honor."

"He's for sale, then?"

"That's my intention."

"Where did you get him?"

"He was a gift from a friend."

"An expensive gift. You swear you came by him legally?"

"I'll swear to that if I need to."

The undersheriff pondered that answer. He seemed satisfied. "How much do you want for him?"

"Eight pounds."

The undersheriff laughed. "He's not worth eight."

"He was bred in Spain."

"That may be, but I'll not pay eight." The undersheriff went through the motions of inspecting the horse, running his hands over the horse, examining the hooves, and peering at his teeth. "I'll pay you two."

"That's robbery. Seven pounds nine shillings."

"Dear God, man, you sound like a grocer. Three. It is a waste of money even at that price."

Robert appeared to think hard about this offer, and then said, as if in great pain, "I suppose I could let him go at Seven pounds three."

"You look to me like a man who is desperate for money. I am a generous man and mindful of the misfortunes that can befall even the best of men. So, I will come to three pounds four shillings."

"I can see you are most generous, but your perception that I am desperate is mistaken. Seven."

When the undersheriff hesitated, Robert added, "It's getting late. I can see that I've tried your charity and good humor, and reached its limit. We'll just have to come back tomorrow and see what fortune we have."

The undersheriff continued to think, foot tapping. "All right then, I'll come to Four. I cannot go any higher. If that will not do for you, you shall have to gamble on fortune."

Robert, however, worried that tomorrow would be worse than today. "Five pounds ten shillings then, but you hurt me sorely, sir."

The undersheriff's foot stopped tapping and he smiled. "Bring him around to the castle then, and I'll see that you get your money."

"Who should I ask after?"

"My name is Gilbert Braz de Fer," de Fer said as if he expected Robert to know who he was.

"Of course."

"And you are?"

"Robin of Bristol."

"Good evening, then, Robin of Bristol." De Fer turned about and strode off, trailed by his deputies.

The Outlaws

"Why did you give him a false name?" Hugh asked when they were far enough away they could not hear.

"I know who he is now."

"You do?"

"I'm surprised you don't, seeing as you were so close to Eustace FitzWalter. The Braz de Fers hold land from him. I have a feeling that he would not want to buy anything from me if he knew who I really am."

Hugh clapped Robert on the shoulder. "I suspect you're right about that. Come on. Let's go get our money before he finds out."

"Our money?"

"Well, I helped guard him. That's got to be worth something."

The fair was breaking up for the evening when Robert and Hugh led the horse into High Street. The vendors were packing their goods away in either the bottom of the guild hall or temporary sheds erected for that purpose which would be locked for the night.

About halfway down the street, they passed a wicker enclosure holding perhaps a dozen sheep. Robert paid no mind to this, since it was so common a sight that it held no significance. But Hugh tugged at his sleeve. "Look there."

"Where?"

"Those sheep. Those marks. They look like ours."

At least three of the ewes in the enclosure had painted symbols on their rumps. Robert stopped dead. "They are."

"What are they doing here?"

"Come for the fair, like us."

A boy with a dog by his feet was about to open the enclosure. He paused when Robert came up. "Can I be of service, sir?"

"Where did you get those sheep, the ones with the painted marks?" Robert asked.

"My father bought them."

"From whom?"

"A fellow from south of here. I'm not sure, exactly. But father knows."

"Where is your father?"

"Over there." The boy pointed toward the guildhall, where a tall, thin man leaned on a staff in conversation with some of the town bailiffs. "Dad! This gentleman wants a word with you!"

The man with the staff crossed the street. "What is it, sirs?"

"I want to know where you got those sheep. Our entire flock was stolen a short time ago, and those are our marks."

"I didn't steal them! I bought them fair!"

"I'm not suggesting that you stole them. I want to know whom you bought them from."

The man ignored the question, so horrified of the possibility that he might be accused of theft. "I swear! I had no part in any theft."

"All you have to do is tell me where they came from."

"I got them from a fellow named Fulbert. From Shelburgh, he was."

"Shelburgh." Robert couldn't believe what he had just heard. "You're certain?"

"As certain as I'm standing here, sir."

"Fulbert was his name, you say?" Robert didn't know anyone from Shelburgh named Fulbert, but he had been away a long time. While people in the village didn't change much, the garrison of the castle often turned over.

"Yeah."

"Where did you buy them?"

"Leintwardine. I don't live far from there."

"Leintwardine? What's a Shelburgh man doing selling sheep there?"

"You know, I wondered about that. Seemed odd."

"But the price was so good, you didn't ask questions."

The man with the staff scuffed a toe in the dirt and looked away toward the castle.

The Outlaws

"I'll give you double what you paid for them," Robert said. "Those three there, the ones with the marks."

CHAPTER 26

Hafton
October 1184

Oxen walk no faster than snails, so it took two full days to return to Hafton. Robert would not have minded this, except for the fact that the carts he had hired to carry back seed grain and what they would eat through the winter charged by the day.

In a way it was a good thing that the oxen were so slow, because the thirty ewes and the ram Robert had also bought to rebuild the flock were little faster, and, having no dog to police them, they tended to wander, which caused one delay after another as Robert and Hugh had to collect the wayward sheep and usher them in the right direction.

The track led past the mine, where a few people still lived, eeking out a living from what bits of iron still seemed to remain, and a couple of boys ran ahead from there to announce their arrival. By the time they crossed the ford, Wulfric Ploughman and several other men were waiting to receive them. Two men directed the sheep into the sheep fold, while the cart train crept along into the bailey.

Robert saw that in their absence a good bit of the debris from the barn had been cleared away, and a temporary shed had been thrown up opposite where the barn had stood. At least there was a place prepared to protect the grain from the wet.

There was also a temporary pen, its sides rickety and in danger of falling down, for the oxen. Wulfric took charge of them and, after ushering them into their new home, examined each one, as if he doubted Robert's ability to buy a decent ox. He seemed to be satisfied, however, because he voiced no complaint or pointed out any shortcoming in any of the animals.

Giselle came out as the carters and some of the household servants were unloading the sacks of grain into the shed. She appraised the oxen. But when she looked over the carts and

The Outlaws

noticed something missing, she asked, "What happened to your other horse?"

"Sold."

"You didn't!"

"He's just a useless mouth to feed."

"Oh, Robert. I'm so sorry. I never meant for you to do that."

"I can always buy another." But it would be years before they had recovered enough from the raid to have the cash in hand for such an extravagant purchase. "We need to get the plowing underway without delay. It will be too late soon for sowing winter wheat," he said, changing the subject, he had regrets he'd rather not share.

It was hard to tell if Giselle sensed that regret, but she plunged into a discussion of her latest plans for the manor, which involved which tracts of forest to fell for timber.

"That is a good plan," Robert said as they walked toward the house. "There's something more you should know."

"Oh?"

"In Ludlow, we found three of our stolen sheep."

"Our sheep? You're certain?"

"They had our marks. I've brought them back if you'd like to have a look."

"The Welsh are going to the Ludlow fair?" Giselle asked, astonished.

"Not the Welsh. They were sold by one of Eustace's men."

"What is one of Eustace's men doing with our sheep?"

"I'd like to know that too."

"You don't think he bought them from the Welsh?"

"It's possible, but I have the feeling that he didn't." He told her what he had learned from the shepherd at Ludlow.

Her face darkened. "It does not seem possible. No one will be believe it if we accuse him."

"I know. Not without solid proof. And even then, it may come to nothing."

"I'll not give up on this that easily. We could go to law."

"There is that. But you've seen how easily judges can be bought. The first thing we have to do is find out who this Fulbert is and see what he has to say."

"You're not thinking of riding over there yourself?"

"No, I'll send Wulfric. He has more cousins in Shelburgh that anyone we know. One of them is bound to know something useful."

It took a day for Wulfric to carry out his errand. He was back by supper time, and owing to the urgency of his mission and the eagerness with which Robert and Giselle awaited his report, he stayed for supper.

"Well?" Robert asked as Wulfric chewed on a mouthful of herring.

Wulfric swallowed, not willing to be hurried. He put his fingers in the bowl of herring, but removed them at the expressions on Robert's and Giselle's faces. He almost wiped his hand on the table cloth, but then he seemed to remember that at least in this house that was impolite.

"There's a Fulbert in Shelburgh, all right," Wulfric said. "Your guess was correct that he's one of the garrison, a sergeant, in fact."

"A sergeant?" Robert asked. "What's a sergeant doing selling sheep in Leintwardine?" A sergeant was an armored soldier a step below a knight. While usually from a more humble background, few would stoop to something so menial as the selling of sheep if they had the choice.

"I've no idea. Nor did my kin. They thought it as odd as you."

"You didn't have a chance to lay eyes on this Fulbert or speak with him, did you?"

"I did ask after him, but he's been gone for a month. Somewhere in the Radnor forest. The priory, I heard. Him and a dozen others, apparently."

"That many . . ." Robert mused.

"The secret barn," Giselle said.

The Outlaws

"The what?"

"He has a secret barn in the Radnor forest, just as he had here."

"We can't be sure of that unless we go look for ourselves."

"Which is exactly what you must do."

CHAPTER 27

**The Welsh March
October 1184**

Robert had heard of the priory in the Radnor forest, of course. You couldn't have lived in Shelburgh and not be aware of it, as it had been endowed by Lady Blanche. But beyond the fact that it lay about five miles west of Shelburgh in the deep woods of a wild and perilous land which did not seem suitable for an English priory, he knew nothing about it, or even where it was. Someone in Shelburgh was certain to know, but he couldn't ride in there asking for directions without losing his head.

The only place where Robert thought he could safely ask for directions was in Wales itself, so he took Hugh and the shepherd Caradog with him, one for comfort and companionship, and the other to ask questions.

They by-passed FitzWalter lands by riding along the south branch of the Lugg and cutting cross country to Radnor village.

Robert and Hugh waited outside the village while Caradog went to make inquiries about the priory's location.

It wasn't long before Caradog returned. Robert tossed him a strip of dried beef. "So? Where is it?"

"That way." Caradog waved toward the north.

"That is not helpful."

"Don't worry. We'll find it. There's one thing they told me I think you'd like to know. Seems a Welsh raiding party passed by here last month. They had quite a bit of plunder."

"Our raiders?"

"It would seem so."

"Did anyone say where they came from?" Robert asked.

"The Ithon valley."

"The Ithon?" Robert repeated, never having heard of it.

"It's a river to the west not more than seven, eight miles or so. A fellow named Iowerth claims he's the lord of it."

The Outlaws

The way to the priory from Radnor village was not an hour's ride away, although they almost missed the turn, a track through a forest that was so overgrown that it would have given trouble to most carts.

The forest gave way to cleared fields spreading across flat ground surrounded by wooded hills. The priory was visible about a quarter mile off as a collection of wooden buildings.

They crossed the fields before the priory at a rapid trot. The priory layout was like that at most such places: church on the north side, a line of buildings to the south of it comprising storerooms, refectory, dormitories, chapter house, and chapel that would surround an open square within. Outside this complex were a large barn, a sheepfold, chicken coop, smithy, a few other assorted sheds and buildings, and a collection of houses where priory servants and dependents made their homes.

A monk who had spotted their approach crossed from the barn.

"Sirs," the monk asked, "may I ask your business?"

"We're just passing through," Robert said. "Could you spare some water for the horses and perhaps a bit of ale for us?"

"I think that can be managed," the monk said. "If you'll follow me, the well is this way."

He turned toward the passageway into the cloister. Robert and Caradog followed him with the three horses. Hugh waited until they had passed from sight, then headed toward the sheepfold.

The monk stopped at the well, which stood in the middle of the cloister. Caradog worked the crank to raise a bucket which he put on the ground for the horses.

"This way, sir, if you wish a spot of ale," the monk said, crossing to a low timber building that had to be the refectory. The shutters were open, and Robert heard voiced coming from within it. Monks were supposed to observe the rule of silence, as least as far as he knew, so there should be no talking, even at meals. When he got close enough, he saw that one table, the source of the noise, held a half dozen rough looking men who had to be soldiers. He thought he recognized some of them. He spun about and headed quickly back to the well, hoping that he had not been seen.

"I say, sir!" the monk said when he realized he was no longer being followed.

"I've changed my mind about the ale," Robert said, collecting his and Hugh's horse. "We'll be going now, thank you."

The monk looked perplexed at this sudden change of mind, but he was not one to urge ale on a fellow who had lost interest. So, having much else to do, he went about his other business.

Outside the cloister, Robert met Hugh coming from the sheepfold.

Hugh nodded as they came together.

"How many?" Robert asked, taking the nod as a sign Hugh had spotted some of the stolen sheep.

"I counted at least thirty with our marks."

"There are soldiers in the refectory. I don't think anyone recognized me, but let's get out of here before somebody thinks to take a close look."

"What are soldiers doing in the refectory?" Hugh said as they mounted.

"Guarding the plunder I would imagine."

"What now? Summon the sheriff?"

"No, I think I will have a talk with this fellow Iowerth first."

The Outlaws

CHAPTER 28

The Welsh March
October 1184

The Welsh land to the west was called Powys. It was one of several such regions yet unconquered by the English, not that they hadn't tried. It had been much larger once, stretching eastward farther than Shrewsbury. Now it was a smaller place of hills, steep valleys, roads that were often little more than pack trails, and swift streams.

The people of this land were a fractious people, difficult and ungovernable, whose principle enjoyment was a love of fighting. When they weren't fighting the English, they attacked each other. Summer often saw petty, regional wars between one prince or another, and if the princes were too preoccupied for battle, the Welsh were happy to attack their neighbors just over the hill.

Robert had heard every rumor about the Welsh while growing up, and so he was reluctant to ride into the Ithon Valley and knock on Iowerth's door by himself. He felt he needed more clout than he had to offer himself. He thought hard about how to make his approach, and resolved that he best way was an indirect route, which called for the services of the prince of Powys. The problem now was where to find the prince. The prince's principle residence was a place called Mathrafal, but where that place lay Robert had no idea.

They stopped at Radnor village on the way back, but the people there could no more say where Mathrafal was any more than they knew the way to Rome: north, they said, beyond Montgomery somewhere.

He had to look elsewhere for guidance, and the closest place that sprang to mind was the fortress at Wigmore, the seat of the Mortimer family about six miles to the north of Hafton. The Mortimers had been fighting the Welsh for generations. They would know.

The village of Wigmore lay at a crossroad, one road running north-to-south and the other heading east where the blacksmith's house stood, arriving at Ludlow and other points after many twists and turns.

The Mortimers' castle sat on the slope of a steep ridge to the west of the crossroads, beyond a little stone church that was covered in moss and ivy and looked as though it had been there forever. Someone had strung their laundry from a rope tied to posts set up in the little yard between the church and the street, and a crow standing guard over the laundry watched Robert from atop the clothes line as he, upon his palfrey, ambled up the narrow road to the castle.

The castle itself, when it came into view, proved to be not much different than most other castles in England, apart from its awkward position on the downward slope of the ridge. It was built in wood, and consisted of the usual towering motte capped with a wooden watchtower high up toward the top of the ridge, and two baileys, the smaller upper one appearing to be stuffed with thatch-covered buildings behind a steep embankment and palisade that was roofed over for almost its entire length, and a larger one enclosed by a much more modest embankment and palisade on the flatter ground below.

No guard met Robert at the gate to the lower bailey, and once he was through, he saw that a good portion of the open ground within it was given over to a garden beyond the cluster of houses, a barn, and a small chapel by the gate, and a massive woodpile lay stretched beside the road for at least forty yards. No one challenged him as he made his way toward the upper bailey, where a wooden bridge ran over a deep ditch to a great square gate tower, although a pair of cats upon the woodpile kept a close watch.

A bored guard just within the gate rose from his stool as the clumps of Robert's horse upon the drawbridge gave away his approach.

"Good morning, sir," the guard said. "Do you mind if I ask you your business?"

The Outlaws

"I'd like to see the castellan, or constable, or whatever you call him."

The guard seemed of a mind to ask why, but said, "You'll find Sir Louis in the hall. It's that building there." He pointed to a three-story house to the right, smack against the embankment, its timbers painted a dignified black and the plaster between them a gleaming white.

"Of course it is," Robert said. "Can't miss it."

"Well, some have managed to," the guard said, "but it was dark and they were very drunk."

"Not you, though, I'm sure," Robert said with a grin.

"Certainly not."

Robert tied the palfrey to a post by the door and went into the hall.

Sir Louis was taller than Robert with a wide nose, a pockmarked face, and what looked like a perpetual scowl. He was in conversation with five carpenters about whether to tear down one of the towers which was infected with rot, or only to repair the damaged portions. Robert had to wait for more than an hour while this discussion went on.

Louis motioned Robert to approach. "And you are?"

"Robert Attebrook of Hafton."

Louis' scowl gave way to a smile. "Ah, FitzWalter's cockold."

"The lady waited until her annulment, if it's all the same to you, and I've married her."

"So we heard. And about your misfortune. The Welsh burned you out." He seemed genuinely concerned about the raid. "The earl was much incensed when he learned of it. Breach of the treaty and all that. We're glad that they didn't come here, but there's still the possibility."

For a moment, Robert thought Louis meant Eustace, but then he realized that the reference was to Earl Roger Mortimer. "What treaty?"

"Why, the one between the king and Owain ap Cyfeiliog. They've pledged perpetual peace between our peoples, although forever always seems to be a shorter time than one

556

would expect where such matters are concerned. The earl has written to the king about it, and the other troubles we've been having with the Welsh. He doesn't wish to be connected with any of it in — his unfortunate troubles over Cadwallon ap Madog, you know."

"I don't follow."

"Where have you been these past few years? Living in a hole in the ground?"

"I've been on the Continent."

"Ah, I forget. You're that carpenter's boy who killed FitzWalter's friend, and ran off."

"I've been pardoned."

"Pardons have been flying around like snowflakes these last few years. Seems anyone can get one, even carpenter's boys. The earl has his own as well. Makes you two members of the same club, I suppose, although I would hesitate to say that to the earl."

"What's his for? Rebellion?"

"Don't be impertinent. He was accused of killing Cadwallon when he was on safe passage to answer for breaching the last peace treaty."

"Cadwallon? I don't think I know the name, or the story."

"How could that be? It was a great scandal in the March. You'd have to be deaf and blind not to know of it"

"As I said, I've been out of the country for the past few years."

"Ah, well, certainly you should have heard something of it. But someone else will have to tell you the story. I will say that Cadwallon was a thorn in our side for a long time. He was once prince you know, but fortunately no longer. We thought that with him out of the way, we could expand westward." Louis sighed. "That's not possible at the moment, given the treaty, and the fact that the king's sharp eye is fixed on us, watching for every possible infraction. The king would love to see the earl hanged. What is it you want anyway? You didn't come here to pass the time."

The Outlaws

"I need a guide to Mathrafal. I thought you might be able to suggest one."

"Why?"

"I want to speak to Owain ap Cyfeiliog."

"To find out who's responsible for your misfortune?"

"That is my intent, but I'd rather that it did not get about."

"Could you wait a moment?" Louis said to a passing servant: "Please tell the earl a matter requires his attention in the hall." He faced Robert again. "I suppose you can have a seat if you like while you wait."

Earl Roger Mortimer was a broad-shouldered man whose graceful movements gave the impression of physical power. He was eight or nine years older than Robert, and youth still showed on his face, which was framed by curling brown hair.

He examined Robert more with curiosity than the disdain of his steward. "So, you are our new neighbor."

"I shall do my best to be a good one, m'lord."

"You've made Eustace unhappy. There's something to be said for that. What I can't make out is why the Welsh came to your house rather than ravaging Shelburgh. Seems odd — a richer village right there on the road, while you're tucked back in the woods where hardly anyone can find you."

"We have wondered that too, m'lord," Robert said. "Perhaps they were afraid of his retribution. Us?" he shrugged. "We haven't the power to take action against anybody."

"No, you're all alone and friendless, it seems. Yet how would the Welsh know that? The annulment was only a short time ago." He leaned forward. "You do need friends, Sir Robert. You've made Eustace your enemy by taking his wife. Even if he didn't want her, he will see it as an insult that you've snatched her up so quickly, especially with all the rumors."

"He was my enemy before."

Mortimer nodded. "I had forgotten about that. An old grievance. I suppose one should only expect that Eustace will take it up now. Since he's earl he must carry on with it, or seem weak, I suppose. You've only made things worse for yourself by marrying the Lady Giselle. So you will need friends, with such a dangerous man so close. I can help you with that."

"You can?" Robert said, sensing what was coming.

"No need to look so worried. I wasn't going to ask if you were interested in my protection, or fealty, or anything like that. But I am prepared to be your friend."

"I would like that," Robert said carefully, because befriending a great lord as ambitious as Mortimer could carry a high and unexpected price.

"Good. Because it seems to me that we can help each other. I understand that you want to speak to Owain."

"Yes, m'lord."

"You think he might know who was behind the raid on your lands?"

"I thought he might. I can't see how you could keep something like that a secret."

"Nor do I. Word gets out about such things eventually, and it's a ruler's job to know if his subjects are stirring things up, unless he's the one behind the stirring. I've already written the king about it, hoping that he will act, but he's more interested in peace in the March, so I doubt anything will come of your misfortune." Mortimer spread his hands, palms up. "In truth, the king loves peace because he wants to keep us from acquiring new lands. He fears that we might come to rival him. Peace keeps us in our place, small and tractable. Even humble."

Robert wondered who "us" was, then realized Mortimer was talking about all the Marcher earls.

"Of course," Mortimer went on, "if we had proof that this raid was no chance affair or the product of brigands, but a matter of state, who knows what opportunities, might arise?"

"And if I can find no such proof?"

The Outlaws

Mortimer shrugged. "The facts are what the facts are. But if proof of Owain's complicity can be found, winter's sting will not be so sharp for Hafton. Also, there are lands to the west, ready for the taking. A suitable portion could be yours. Who knows? You have only one manor now. Think of what it would be like to lord over several."

Mortimer provided a guide named Rhun. He was short and thin, with black hair hanging to his eyebrows and beard framing watchful eyes that darted about. When introduced to Robert, he spoke in little more than grunts, which seemed to be all he could manage in English.

As a consequence, they said little to each other during the ride, which took them through Knighton, Clun, and Bishop's Castle, where they spent the night before venturing northwest toward Montgomery, which guarded a ford of the Severn and marked the end of English land.

Robert would have preferred a more talkative companion, since conversation helped pass the time. But he had a lot to think about. Mortimer had not asked him outright to lie about whether Owain ap Cyfeiliog was behind the raid, but the earl had implied that he should do so, and had offered a considerable incentive for him to trim the truth. It was a great temptation to have the chance to get his hands on the sort of wealth that could be his if he acquired new lands. The question nagged him all the way.

Montgomery was just another motte-and-bailey castle indistinguishable from any other of its kind, the embankment capped with a palisade that was roofed over for almost its entire length, the bailey small and packed with timber buildings so that there was little open space other than the small patch just within the gate.

The gate ward asked their business, as he would any other stranger, but Robert was in a foul mood, and snapped, "I'll take it up with your lord."

"He may not want to take it up with you," the guard said.

"He will. I've come on behalf of Roger Mortimer."

"Have you, now?" the guard asked. "All by yourself?"

"Enough questions. Where is de Bollers?"

"Can't say as I know, exactly. He doesn't tell me where he's going."

"Thanks. You've been most helpful." Robert handed the reins of his horse to Rhun. "I'll be right back." Rhun nodded and grinned in his idiot's way so that Robert wasn't sure he even understood. Robert left the horse in Rhun's care and entered the hall, which lay across the open space before the gate.

The lord of Montgomery, Robert de Bollers, was not in the hall, but servants more respectful of people claiming to be the emissary of an earl gave Robert a seat and found him a cup of ale, wine being in short supply this deep in the March.

De Bollers came in from a doorway opening toward the motte. He was in his mid-forties, a vigorous looking man with graying brown hair and hands that seemed a bit over large.

Robert stood at his approach. "My lord."

"They said your name was Attebrook," de Bollers said.

"I am."

"And you've come from Mortimer?"

"He's sent me to speak to Owain ap Cylfeiliog."

"Ah. Do you mind if I ask why?"

"There has been raiding in the south. Mortimer wants to know who's behind it."

"Raiding?" De Bollers looked alarmed. It was his business to guard the ford below the castle against just such incursions.

"A manor was burned."

"God Lord!" He rubbed those big hands together. "It's been quiet here. We had a pack train in from the west just a day ago — not a whisper of trouble. And they'd have said something. They're the talkative sort. What can I do for you?"

"I was hoping if you could tell me if Owain is at Mathrafal."

"There's no telling for certain, but I would expect so this time of year."

561

The Outlaws

"The next question is how to get there."

De Bollers smiled. "You don't know?"

"I've a guide who claims he can find it. But he speaks hardly any English, and I'm not sure I trust him."

"It's not far, but it can be hard to find. There are few real roads in Wales, just footpaths, mostly. It's easy to take the wrong one."

"I was afraid of that."

"I can't spare anyone for a guide right now, if that's what you're looking for, but I'll have one of my people speak to your fellow. We'll find out if he knows what he's up to."

"I would appreciate it."

"Meanwhile, you might as well make yourself comfortable. While it's probably no more than fifteen miles as the crow flies, it will take you a day to reach Mathrafal. It's too late to start for it now."

Rhun led the way across the ford of the Severn after dawn the following day, which was marked by a path that descended into the stream where white water churned over stones upon the bottom. It was dead quiet, the only sound made by the splashing of the horses and moisture dripping from the trees.

Rhun picked up a trot when his horse reached the bank, as if he was in a hurry to get away from the water, and Robert had to canter to catch up with him.

"What's the hurry?" Robert asked as they slowed down, not expecting an answer. One of Bollers' sergeants, a Welshman himself, had told him at supper that Rhun could speak English as well as anyone and knew his way about Wales from one end to the other. "He just doesn't like to talk much," the sergeant had said.

"Never liked that place," Rhun said, surprising Robert, as these were the most words he had spoken since they left Wigmore. "I had a brother who drowned here."

"I'm sorry."

"He was drunk. Fell off his horse, the idiot."

"I'm still sorry."

"No, you're not. You don't give a shit."

"So Wales loosens your tongue?"

"The air's better here. There's less stink than in England."

"Does Mortimer know you hate the English?"

"What Welshman doesn't? Anyway, he pays me."

"How far to Mathrafal?"

"We can be there by noon if we don't tarry."

"Why hurry? It's a pleasant country."

Rhun nodded. "That's why you English fancy it so much. Except for the mountains. Life's hard there, but the English fancy everything they can't have. So I expect you'll want that too."

"Isn't that the way of things? If you can't defend what you have, others will take it from you. Not even the Church has been able to change that."

Rhun nodded. "That's so. If you want to be free, you have to fight for it."

At long last, they rounded the shoulder of a hill and there, on the downslope, stood a motte-and-bailey castle to the right of the road, a river visible through the trees beyond it, and a village clustered on the flat ground to the north.

"Mathrafal," Rhun said as they turned off the road toward the gate.

"It's about time," Robert said, standing in his stirrups to ease his aching bottom.

"What? Didn't think I could find it?"

"I had begun to wonder."

Rhun spat into the dirt as they stopped before the gate, which stood open but was blocked by two spearmen. Another couple of heads appeared at one of the windows in the gate tower. One of the men above called what had to be a challenge, which Rhun answered, lips curling as if at a bad smell. The answer must have been satisfactory, because the spearmen stood aside to admit them into the bailey.

The Outlaws

Robert looked around with interest. He had not had any idea that the Welsh built castles, same as the English, but on reflection, there was no reason why they shouldn't. Any lord who wanted to be taken seriously had to have one. The bailey was a lopsided square, the walls consisting of the usual embankment and palisade, roofed over against the elements with the walk open at the back. This time of day there were no wardens upon them, giving the impression of a castle not expecting trouble. The bailey was packed with the usual half-timber buildings, the wood unpainted and the plaster green with moss. None were more than one-story, except for what had to be a barn. The motte on the northern side of the bailey was also not as imposing as you might find in an English castle, only about twenty feet high. The tower upon it, however, was new, the wood still yellow. A red and yellow banner hung in the dead air from a pole on the roof, which capped the tower like a pointed bishop's hat.

One of the men in the gate tower had climbed down the ladder and met them as grooms came from the stable take the horses. The fellow stood with hands on hips, the furrow between his black brows made even more prominent by his frown. "What's an English knight doing all alone in the land of the Cymru?" he asked in good English.

"Well, I am not alone. There is Rhun here, although from his lack of conversation I could as well have been. Not quite what one hopes for in a guide and a translator."

"I know Rhun," the man replied. "A poor choice for a translator."

"Let's leave off poor Rhun. He was good enough to get me here in one piece. My name is Attebrook, Robert Attebrook. I'd like to see Prince Owain, if that's not too much trouble. And you are?"

The man's lips pressed into a flat line. He did not seem disposed to surrender his name, so Rhun said, "His name is Maredudd."

"I did not give you permission to speak," Maredudd snapped.

"You don't have the authority to give me orders," Rhun snapped back.

"Men from Gwynedd do what they are told in our lands, if they know what's good for them."

Rhun reached for the axe in his belt. Maredudd grasped his sword.

They were both drawing their weapons when Robert stepped between them.

The Outlaws

CHAPTER 29

Mathrafal, Powys
October 1184

One of the spearmen from the gate ran up and helped Robert keep Rhun and Maredudd apart. There was a great deal of posturing and shouting, most of it in Welsh, before either of them quieted down, and Maredudd stalked into the hall, which stood at the foot of the motte.

"Bastard," Rhun spat at Maredudd's back as the door closed.

"Easy," Robert said. "I need a favor from them. I won't get it if you make them angry."

"I don't give a fuck if they're angry."

"If I tell Mortimer that you were not helpful, I doubt he'll give you the rest of your fee."

A Welsh word shot from Rhun's mouth with such force that it had to be a curse.

"All right, then," Robert said. "Glad that's settled."

He entered the hall.

A servant collected their weapons at the door, just as at an English hall, and left them to themselves. No one was about. There was nothing for Robert and Rhun to do but to wait for Owain to put in an appearance, yet the day wained without any sight of him.

Supper time arrived, and the hall began to fill up. Servants put Robert and Rhun at one of the lower tables and they were getting seated when a man who had to be Owain came in from a rear door and took his place at the largest chair behind the high table.

He was in his forties, with a square, broad jaw, a black moustache flecked with white, dark glittering eyes, a high pale forehead beneath a receding hairline of white-salted black hair, and easy grace.

"That's Owain ap Cyfeiliog," Rhun said, confirming the guess.

"Thank you, Rhun. I'm glad to see you're done with your tantrum."

Rhun grunted.

"And in future, you'll speak politely to me. No curses in Welsh, or any other language."

Rhun grinned. "They do sound good in Welsh, though, don't they?"

"There is a certain music to them, but I'd prefer you directed them to others."

"I lost my temper is all. Maredudd does that to a man."

Robert eyed the high table where Maredudd was speaking into Owain's ear. He wondered what they were talking about. "Perhaps he would be more pleasant if you made a similar effort. No doubt after our cheerful encounter he's up there poisoning Owain's mind against me."

"Maredudd is the sort who thinks first of his own advantage, and how to get the best of you. You could do worse for a friend than old Rhun."

"Since you are the only one about, you'll have to do." Robert broke the loaf in half which a servant had placed before him and gave one part to Rhun. "The question is how and when to approach Owain. I'm not sure of the protocol for accosting Welsh princes. I doubt it's as easy as walking up and saying 'How do you do? Mind if I have moment of your time?'"

"Don't trouble your head with questions like that. He'll send for you. Maredudd was supposed to find out your business at the gate, but crafty Rhun stopped his questions. He's a canny one, that Rhun is." He tapped his temple with a finger while biting a large gouge out of the bread. "It wasn't all anger and bitterness."

Robert didn't believe the last claim for a moment. "Yes, I am sure you are, probably more than is good for you."

"What do you mean by that?"

"Never mind. And would you finish chewing your bread before you speak next time? You're getting bits of it on yourself."

567

The Outlaws

After supper, the servants took down the tables, except for the high one, and left the benches, which people moved closer to the four hearths that smoldered at intervals down the center of the long hall. The fires had burned down, but now servants brought in thin splits of wood which they heaped on the fires, and soon there were blazes throwing sparks toward the rafters and casting off orange light that made the spare hall, which lacked the tapestries or painted wood you'd see in most English halls, seem almost cheerful. But then a warm fire on a chilly autumn night was always a comfort to be savored.

A band of wandering jongleurs had somehow found their way to Mathrafal, along with at least two pack trains, the members of which applauded at the suggestion of music, and the singers brought out their harps, flutes, and drums to entertain those within the hall. One of their number was an acrobat, and he capered about, and rolled and twisted and walked on his hands until he grew too tired to do so.

When the singers had exhausted their repertoire, or perhaps the prince's patience, the audience was subjected to a poet. The performance was in Welsh so Robert couldn't understand more than a word here and there. People about the hall threw glances in his direction now and then, and there was some sniggering that appeared to be at his expense. Rhun offered to translate, but Robert declined. Poetry made in another language lost its flavor in translation to the point that it was humdrum and dull. This poetry sounded like song and was pleasant enough even without any idea what was being said. But Rhun persisted, "Sure you don't want to hear? It's about battles."

"And the Welsh are fighting bravely and winning every one, I would think."

"Well, that's true."

"Then I don't need to hear."

It was late by the time the poet ran out of verse, and many people had already begun to retire to the corners as servants brought in canvas pallets filled with straw.

Fearing that Owain was about to retire himself, Robert slipped through the crowd to the prince, who had his head together with Maredudd. They saw him stop before them but neither acknowledged his presence. Robert waited until Owain glanced at him again. "My lord, may I have a word?"

"Who are you?" Owain asked in English as fine as if he had been born and raised in Shropshire. His expression said that the intrusion was a bother.

"Robert Attebrook, my lord."

"Can't it wait until morning?"

"It could. But it concerns the peace in the March."

Owain drew back in his chair, hands on his thighs. "What about the peace in the March?"

"It was broken a couple of weeks ago."

"And you speak of this to me . . . why?"

"Raiders from somewhere west of Shelburgh came to my manor. They burned it and carried off the harvest and all our livestock."

"And you think I had something to do with it?"

"Some would like to think so."

"Like Mortimer."

"Yes."

"Where is your manor?"

"Three miles east of Shelburgh."

"So you hold from FitzWalter, or Mortimer, then?"

"No, my wife holds straight from the king."

"Your wife." He smiled. "You're the cockolder we've heard so much about. FitzWalter's put her aside, has he?"

"It was a mutual parting."

"You didn't waste any time snapping her up. Well, it is lovely gossip, but we were speaking about the peace. Do you know who was responsible?"

"No, m'lord. That's why I've come to you."

The Outlaws

"So, you don't accuse me of complicity, merely of knowledge. Which amounts to the same thing."

"A prince should know what happens in his lands. If not now, then eventually."

"And if I do not now, I am a poor excuse for a prince."

"I don't mean to imply that either."

"Either way we turn, you make me look wanting."

"That is not my intent. It's only to find out who was responsible and to recover some of the plunder."

"One may be easier to accomplish than the other."

"Well, the raiders took two girls. I'd like to get them back, at least. My information is that the raiders came from the Ithon valley."

"And why should I help you in this endeavor?"

"Because you want to keep the peace in the March. You don't want to be seen as the one who broke it. The king's peace is the only thing keeping FitzWalter and Mortimer out of your lands. Mortimer itches for proof of your complicity. He asked me to find it."

Owain's fingers drummed on the arm of his chair. "But you are not Mortimer's tool, then?"

"No, but my guide is. I suspect he will report everything he sees and hears here."

"I know what Rhun is."

"There is one other thing."

"Oh?"

"Someone on our side of the March played a part in the raid. I need proof of who that was."

"And you know."

"I think I do."

"Not Mortimer."

"Not Mortimer."

"Your wife's former husband, perhaps?"

"He bears grudges and has a long memory. Now he has one against us both."

"And you are small and on your own. A bad spot to be in. Mortimer could help you, yet you do not do his bidding."

"I cannot bring myself to lie."

"Yet duplicity is what makes English lords rich." Owain chuckled. "You shall always be a poor man, if that's your tack." He slapped the arms of the chair. "Maredudd!"

"My lord!" Maredudd answered in Welsh, eyes on Robert, and not in a friendly way.

Owain spoke in English, for Robert's benefit. "Would you be so kind as to ride down to Iowerth' hold tomorrow and see what he's been up to lately?"

"Certainly," Maredudd answered again in Welsh.

"Well, then," Owain said to Robert, "that is is the best I can do. We shall have to see what comes of it. Now, if you will excuse me, I have other business and it is quite late."

The Outlaws

CHAPTER 30

Hafton
October 1184

Giselle and Hugh went out to the south field on the fourth day after Robert's departure to check on the progress of the plowing. Of all the tasks that had to be done before winter, this was the most critical, for it determined whether they would starve come spring. Although Robert had returned from Ludlow with oxen for two plow teams, they had lost more than a week of plow time, and two teams weren't sufficient to cover enough land for the winter wheat. November was close at hand and then the first frosts came, which killed seedlings that were not hardy. At Hugh's urging, Giselle had delved into the money afforded by the sale of the horse and rented two more teams.

"They are making good progress," Hugh remarked as they paused by the big oak at the roadside. "As well as can be expected."

"I suppose," Giselle said, arms crossed, feeling less optimistic than Hugh, who never seemed to be dismayed by anything. For her part, she worried about everything, and that meant a lot of worry, almost every waking minute. "They could go faster, don't you think?"

"Oxen have only two speeds," Hugh said. "Standing still and plodding. You'll not get more than that out of them."

"I've known horses like that," Giselle said. "I had one when I was a girl. Get people started on the harrowing and sowing on the strips that have been plowed. We don't have time to waste until the whole thing's done."

"As you say, my lady," Hugh said. He smiled as he gazed around. He had fallen into the role of steward, which he seemed to relish. He liked seeing things grow and tending to them.

Giselle glanced back at the village. Three-quarters of the houses had already been rebuilt. Plowing didn't take everyone, although that would change when the sowing began because a good many hands were needed to keep the crows from the seeds. But for now, people were throwing up more than a house a day. By tomorrow, the day after at the latest, all the houses would be finished except for the thatching, which took more time since it had to be done by people with experience, and there were only two of those in the village, and not enough straw to go around.

"They'll be done with the houses soon," she said.

"I expect so, and then on to the sowing."

"Then I'd like them to throw up our barn."

"Hmm. Everyone?"

"We're feeding them, and providing seed grain. They owe us that. They've agreed."

"I'll put it to Wulfric, then."

"And after that, more lumbering. We'll sell what we cut after the barn's done."

"If it doesn't get stolen on the road."

"We'll take it to Wigmore, Ludlow even. The northern roads will be safe."

"I wouldn't be so generous as to call them all roads. I've seen them, you know."

"They will have to do. I've been thinking about the mine, as well."

"What about it?"

"I wondered if it wasn't possible to reopen it."

"I thought it was played out."

"It won't hurt to have someone look at it again."

"That will cost money."

"As long as people are eating the grain I've bought, they can pay for it with labor. I am not a charity machine. We cannot afford loafers. We all have to work for our bread. When we're beyond this crisis and making money again, I'll think about wages."

They were turning back to the village when Hugh put his hand on Giselle's arm. She almost jerked away at the familiarity, not sure whether to be alarmed and offended.

573

The Outlaws

"Look there," Hugh said, glancing back to the top of the hill to the south. "We have a visitor."

A figure on horseback was visible descending the hill. He did not seem to be in a great hurry to get down the hill, but when he saw they were waiting for him, he took up a trot. The horse alone was enough to tell anyone that this was a person with some means, and his clothing gave more away, although not that well off: well-stitched boots, iron spurs rather than silver, green stockings, a blue coat over a red shirt, a floppy felt hat, and a sword and buckler at his belt. Well off he might be, but he was someone's minor functionary, and a young one at that, no more than seventeen or eighteen.

"Are you Robert Attebrook, sir?" the fellow asked, directing his question to Hugh.

"No, I am his friend and companion, Hugh Fontaine. And you are?"

"Neville de Waltham."

"And what can we do for you?" Hugh asked.

"I'm looking for the mistress of this place."

"That would be this lady here," Hugh said indicating Giselle.

Waltham looked surprised for a moment, since Giselle was dressed in a simple brown wool gown, not the sort of thing the lady of a manor ordinarily wore, but this was a working day when she was out and about and she didn't want her better clothes soiled; they were hard to keep clean. "I am sorry, my lady."

"I see no reason you should be. Are you hungry? Tired? We've had a misfortune here lately so there isn't much we can spare to make you comfortable, but we can surely try."

"That would be much appreciated, my lady. But more important than my comfort is my message. My lady has asked I deliver it without delay."

"Your lady?"

"The Lady Blanche."

"Ah," Giselle murmured, perplexed. She could not imagine why the dead Earl Roger's widow would send her a message. They had nothing to say to each other. "And that is, then?"

"My lady has fallen ill and has taken to her bed. She fears she will not rise from it."

"I am sorry," Giselle said.

"She asks that you come — immediately, without delay."

"I am rather busy here."

"She understands. She knows about your misfortune. She has something to tell you. Something you will want to hear."

"And you have no idea what it is? You can't just tell me now?"

"No, my lady. It is a well kept secret, and a dark one, if I am any judge. All I know is that it has to do with your father. That's all my lady would say. But you must hurry if you wish to hear it."

The Outlaws

CHAPTER 31

Powys, Wales
October 1184

Maredudd was no more talkative than Rhun, and barely spoke to Robert as they rode south.

At a ford where Maredudd paused to take a piss, Robert said as they were remounting, "I get the feeling you don't like being sent on this task."

"We should be fighting the English rather than helping them."

"You're a friend of Iowerth's then?"

Maredudd grunted. "Hardly. He's a lying, thieving prick."

"But he fights us. You must approve of that."

"Raiding is hardly fighting, but you can't blame a man for that. A good raid can make a man wealthy. And he's got his position to keep up. He calls himself lord of the Ithon valley from Saint Padarn's church to Saint David's. It's not a great patch of land, nor fertile, good for sheep mostly. But he can call up forty men at least. More than we have here. So we've got be careful how we approach him."

"It's there, just ahead," Maredudd said, a day later. He gestured toward an old ringwork in the distance. Across the way, beyond brown fields where a few sheep wandered, was the fortress, an embankment crowned by a graying palisade. "That thing's been here since before the Romans. If I'm any judge, someone used it to guard one of the passes to the west. It was unoccupied until Iowerth moved in twenty years ago."

"There is one thing, before we go in," Robert said.

"What's that?"

"If we find my goods and recover them, I will give you half, and the other half to Owain, if you pry from Iowerth who put him up to the raid."

"Iowerth doesn't need anyone to put him to a raid."

"He was put up to this one."

Maredudd's eyes narrowed. "We best hurry. We're wasting time."

The gate, which faced to the northeast, was open and unguarded, except for a single spearman on the wallwalk. The guard called a challenge. Maredudd answered it with a wave as they rode across the bridge. The man on the wall disappeared, and they saw him next racing across the bailey to a hall on the other side.

Half a dozen men armed with spears and shields spilled out of the hall as the riders arrayed themselves in a semicircle before the doorway.

Robert could not follow what happened next because it was all in Welsh. The exchange between Maredudd and a thin man started out amiably enough, although the politeness seemed exaggerated. Finally, there were some sharp words, a few curses that Robert understood, and then the thin man, who had to be Iowerth called to the house, where faces lined the open windows.

The upshot of the argument turned out to be over whether Iowerth would let his hall be searched. He gave in and five Mathrafal men went inside. The door opened and the two missing girls stepped into the light.

"They were in the cellar with the cheese," one of the Welsh sergeants said.

Iowerth spoke again.

"He says that he bought them at Llandrindod Wells," Maredudd said. "He wants to know what you'll pay to get them back."

"Three feet of German steel was my thought."

Maredudd chuckled, and translated Robert's reply for Iowerth, who scowled.

"I suppose he denies the raid," Robert said.

"Of course he denies it. Wouldn't you?"

"And you believe him?"

577

The Outlaws

"I wasn't born yesterday. We'll have a look around. Your cattle were marked, weren't they?"

"Yes, of course." Robert knelt and drew the manor's mark in the dirt, a vertical stroke with two slanting lines through the middle. "And the sheep as well, though only with paint."

"They will be harder then." Maredudd spoke to several of the men-at-arms, who remounted and trotted out of the gate, which was now guarded by four Mathrafal men. Robert had a glimpse of a crowd on the bridge, some of them armed, but they made no effort to get inside when the new guards opened the gate for the six riders and then closed it again.

"Where are they going?" Robert asked

"Iowerth probably doesn't have any of the livestock here," Maredudd said. "They'll be in folds about the manor if they're anywhere. While we're waiting, let's see what these girls have to say."

The girls had little to say at first, but once they were surrounded by Mathrafal men with Robert's presence to give them courage, they started talking. It proved hard to quiet them down, and they directed loud abuse at the people within the hall. "They treat their dogs better than they treated us," Emma said bitterly. She pulled up her shirt so that Robert could see her legs, which were marked with weals where she had been whipped. "Can you make them pay for that, m'lord?"

"I'd like to, but I doubt it. It must be enough to get you back safe."

As the girls ran out of insults to shout at Iowerth's people, some quiet returned to the yard. Maredudd said, "Well, there's no doubt who's responsible for their presence in our fair country. I don't think we need to find the sheep or cattle, although I'd still be glad to see them."

"You have work to do before any of them belongs to you," Robert said.

"We shall see."

While attention had been riveted on the girls, Iowerth had edged for the doorway of the hall and slipped inside. The first inkling the men in the yard had of this was the thud of the bar being shoved into place.

"You may have to content yourself with getting the girls back," Maredudd said.

"You'll not take him?"

"I'll have to burn down the hall to do that, and I hesitate to go that far."

"What good is a prince who cannot enforce his will?" Robert spat.

"Princes cannot always to as they wish," Maredudd said.

But he went to the door and knocked. "Iowerth!"

A voice answered from within the house speaking rapid Welsh.

Maredudd glanced back at Robert. He shouted again, this time in English, "Iowerth! Come to the door so we can talk!"

There was a long pause, then the door opened a crack. The same thin man could be seen in the crack. He spoke in Welsh, but Maredudd cut him off in mid-sentence.

"Speak English," he said.

"Why? It's the language of dogs," Iowerth said, nonetheless in English.

"So that my guest can understand."

"Him?" Iowerth asked looking over Maredudd's shoulder at Robert.

"The very same. Now be polite. It's the least you can do after burning the poor man's house."

"I make no excuses for what I've done."

"No one's asking for an apology. The fellow is so gracious that he has not even suggested such a thing."

"What do you want? What does he want?"

"Information."

Iowerth snorted.

"We have a deal for you," Maredudd said. "If you tell us what we want to hear, I do not burn your house and you get to keep a quarter of what you stole."

The Outlaws

"What about them?" Iowerth gestured at the two girls. "Are they part of the bargain?"

"Of the cattle and sheep," Maredudd said.

Iowerth considered this proposition for a few moments. "What do you want to know?"

Maredudd turned to Robert. "It's your turn now. Ask your question."

"How did you come to raid my manor?" Robert asked. "Who put you up to it?"

"You can't already figure that out?" Iowerth sneered. "It was your neighbor, FitzWalter."

Maredudd tapped his thigh with his whip. "All right, then. You have what you wanted."

"You're not going to arrest him?" Robert asked. "He broke the peace!"

"That's not part of the deal."

"What are you going to do with the other three quarters?" Iowerth asked. "Return it to that English scum?"

"No," Maredudd said. "It belongs to Prince Owain now. He'll decide what we do with it."

CHAPTER 32

Hartscombe, Gloucestershire
October 1184

Giselle, Hugh, and Burghard arrived at Hartscombe on a cold afternoon. The rain which had plagued them almost from the hour they had set out from Hafton had let up, and was now a nuisance rather than a misery.

The village lay off any main road a good two hour ride east and south of Gloucester and had been hard to find. They had made two wrong turns during the day because of bad directions, and although they had started in the morning thinking they had plenty of time, it was nearly dark.

Now that they had reached Hartscombe, Giselle did not see anything to recommend it as the favorite dwelling place of an earl's wife. She had expected something more grand and prosperous, with a castle glowering over the village as a mark of the power and prestige of the ruling family. This was as small and plain as Hafton, huddled around its little stone church which, like Hafton's, looked as though it had been here since the time of the pagan gods.

Now that they were here, they still had to find the manor house. From where they stood, at a crossroad before the church, one track leading east and the other south in the direction of wooded hills, there was no indication of where it might lie, and with the rain there was no one about.

"You may as well inquire, Burghard," Giselle said. "I do not enjoy lingering in this wet."

"Yes, my lady," the old groom said without enthusiasm. He dismounted and slopped through the muck and the puddles to one of the houses that sat across the road from the church, where he knocked on the door.

Giselle fretted then that perhaps she should have asked Hugh to go for directions. Asking directions from this or that peasant was something that was beneath a knight when there was a servant about, and she had been afraid after their last argument to ask him to perform this chore. So it fell to

The Outlaws

Burghard. But he was getting old and his memory did not seem to be as strong as it used to, and she suspected that he had been responsible for their wrong turns. Yet it had to be easier to find a manor house in its village than a little village lost in the vast English countryside.

Hugh looked at her sourly. "It's not too late to change your mind."

Giselle sighed, her breath producing a jet of steam. Their last argument . . . that's how she had thought of it. But in truth, it had not stopped. "I've made up my mind."

"It's a trap."

"You've been saying that since we started out. I've heard nothing more from you for two whole days."

"He's clever. You of all people should know that."

"He's clever and ruthless, yes."

"Then why in God's name are you going ahead with this mad plan?"

"Now that Blanche is a widow, I don't see what hold he could have over her. Or why she would cooperate."

"You have no idea what deal they might have made. The summons might not even have come from her at all."

"I have to know."

Burghard squelched back from the house. He pointed down the track leading east from the church. "That way, my lady. About a quarter mile, they say."

"That far," Giselle murmured. She wanted this journey to be over more than she had ever wanted anything. She ached from the ride, but there was more. She had been having cramps, as if her period was about to come, but it had not. Her breasts were sore and swollen. Last night, when she had examined them in the candlelight, her nipples seemed to be darker than usual. The other symptoms she had been able to explain away, but not the darkened nipples. That was a sign she had frequently heard about from other women. She was pregnant. It could be nothing else. She had expected to feel joy at this prospect, but with all the misfortunes and uncertainty that hung over them, it seemed like just another burden. She wished Robert were here. She wanted that smile of his. She wanted to be cheered up. She wanted to be free from anxiety and dread.

Without thinking about what she was doing, she slid off her horse. She landed in a puddle with a splash and scampered out of it.

"What are you doing?" Hugh asked.

"You go," she said. "You go and see if she's there and if there is any sign of danger. Burghard and I will wait here." She brushed moisture from the hollows in the stone of the low wall around the churchyard and sat down. It felt good to sit on something other than a horse. "Try not to get killed."

"I'm good at that," Hugh said, not much mollified with this decision.

"Yes," she said regretting what had been meant as a jest. "So Robert has said. I'm sorry, Hugh. Just come back quickly, before I melt from this rain."

Hugh returned in half an hour, which Giselle spent watching raindrops spatter the puddle and shivering. The woolen cloak repelled water but had begun to soak through.

He dismounted and sat on the fence beside her. Rain dripped from his hat and droplets had collected in his beard. He wiped his face as much from fatigue as from the wet.

"Not there?" Giselle asked.

"Oh, she's there."

"You saw with your own eyes?"

"They let me look in on her."

"Do you still think it's a trap?"

"If it's a trap, it is not well laid. There are only two retainers and a steward. The steward's a twig of a man. The retainers look rough, but I don't think they'll be trouble. At least not to us."

"No one else? You're sure?"

"I looked in the stable. There aren't enough horses and tack for more than that."

The Outlaws

So she had been right. She smiled, unable to resist a little jab. "They could be hiding in the barn. Did you check that?"

"No one hides in barns."

"Some people do," Giselle said, remembering the story Robert had told her about how he had broken his uncle out of Earl Roger's gaol. She stood up. "Let's go. You need to dry out. You look as miserable as a wet cat."

They dismounted at the foot the stairs, and climbed toward the doorway, leaving Burghard to take care of the horses.

Giselle nearly slipped on the wet wood and might have fallen had Hugh not caught her arm.

Hugh knocked on the door and a woman admitted them into a hall where a fire was burning high in the raised stone hearth at the center of the hall.

"Ah," said a small man with a narrow mustache that looked like someone had smeared ash on his face. "You're back. We wondered where you had gone. Who is that?"

"The Lady Giselle Attebrook," Hugh said.

"The Lady Giselle?" the small man asked, puzzled.

"If you're wondering whether I am Eustace's former wife, then you can top fretting," Giselle said, advancing toward the fire as if she owned a place there, and a servant hastened to remove her sodden cloak. "I am."

"We had heard . . ."

"What have you heard?"

"That our lord has put you aside."

"I have been fortunate in that regard. He was a dreadful husband. I have found a much better one."

"So," the small man said, as if all his conversation had been used up, or perhaps he was so surprised at these developments that he had no idea what to do. Then he thought of something to fill the silence. "I am Maurice FitzPoyntz, the steward here."

584

It seemed clear that he had no idea what she was doing here. If Blanche had really issued a summons, he did not know about it. That was curious, because it was not something that ordinarily would have escaped his attention. The thought made her choose her words with more care than she otherwise might have done and to spice them with lies. "I have come to pay a visit to Lady Blanche. I have no love lost for my former husband, but Blanche and I were close once. I have need of her advice."

"Ah, well, you are too late, I'm afraid."

"Too late? How could I be too late? Is she gone?"

"Oh, she lives, but she is desperately ill."

"Ill how?"

"The physicians are not sure. We've had the best from Gloucester, but they are stumped."

"She can't be seen? She's contagious?" Everyone had a horror of infections and fevers because no one knew how they spread from one person to another, and they were often fatal. A person could be perfectly fine one day and then cold as stone the next. But Giselle was certain that Blanche's illness was something more than that, some lingering thing that dragged death out so that you saw it coming from far away and had plenty of time for dread.

"Ah, no, I don't believe so. But she cannot speak. She can barely open her eyes. It would be too much of a strain for her to entertain visitors, I think. The last one taxed her horribly."

"But you are not a physician. You are merely a caretaker."

FitzPoyntz's lips compressed to a thin line at the insult. While stewards were basically caretakers, they did not like to think of themselves as such, especially since stewards were almost always drawn from the gentry. "No, madam, I am not a physician."

"Then I will see her straightaway. If she is as ill as you contend, there is not a moment to waste."

The Outlaws

Even if Giselle was a disgraced former wife, she still stood higher on the ladder of rank that FitzPoyntz, so he was not in a position to refuse her demand once she had put her desire so plainly. Only physical restraint would deter her, and FitzPoyntz was not ready to take such a step. Reluctantly, he escorted her to the foot of the stairs leading to the chambers above one end of the hall. Giselle thought he would leave her there to find her way, or perhaps delegate that menial task to a servant. But FitzPoyntz mounted with her, Hugh close behind, the two burly retainers that Hugh had warned her about remaining at the foot of the stairway where they crossed their arms and leaned against the handrails.

FitzPoyntz stopped at one of the doors a few steps down the hallway. He opened it without knocking and stood aside for Giselle, but cut in front of Hugh to enter right after her.

It was almost as dark as night time, with the shutters closed against the rain which still pelted the roof overhead. The room held very little. Two trunks stood against one wall. A table with a wash basin occupied the space under the window. The walls were not painted, nor did they have any rugs hanging from them, as was often the case in the rooms of the better off. The largest feature was the bed, which occupied half of the available space. The posts were carved in the shape of armored knights, not the sort of thing one expected to find in a woman's bedchamber. The curtains were not drawn as was often the case with an occupied bed. A shape was visible under the blankets which had to be Lady Blanche. The shape did not move at the commotion they made at their entry. Giselle worried that she had indeed arrived too late after all.

"As you can see, madam," FitzPoyntz said, "my lady is quite incapacitated."

Giselle strode to the bed and sat upon the edge. She felt Blanche's face. It was warm and dry, but not flaming with fever as she had expected.

Then Blanche opened her eyes — just a crack. There was recognition in those eyes, even half hidden by the gloom. Blanche's lips moved. Her tongue licked her lips. The fingertips of one hand brushed Giselle's thigh. She seemed about to say something. Giselle leaned forward, ear against Blanche's mouth. Blanche whispered, "Get him out of here."

Giselle said, "Leave us, please."

"Madam," FitzPoyntz remonstrated, "I must be near in case there is a crisis."

"I can handle crises well enough. I've weathered enough of them. Leave. I will speak to her alone. Our business is women's talk. Her, too." Giselle just now noticed a woman sitting unobtrusively in a corner.

"But the nurse is a woman. Surely her ears will not be offended by women's talk. Besides, she is only a servant."

"Get out. Hugh, please see that Master Maurice and this nurse find something else to do."

Hugh stepped to FitzPoyntz's side. "Your honor."

Hugh was not a tall man but he topped FitzPoyntz by a full head, and his glower made it clear that if he did not go peaceably Hugh would help him find his way. FitzPoyntz stalked out. The nurse followed. Hugh shut the door. He put his ear against it, then padded across to Giselle, where he said in a soft voice, "They're still there."

"Listening through the keyhole, no doubt."

"I almost expect those two downstairs to break through at any moment."

Giselle chuckled without humor. "They seem more like gaolors than servants. The whole place smacks of a gaol, a comfortable gaol, but a gaol. I wonder what's going on."

Hugh nodded. "Things are not right."

"That nurse isn't meant to be here in case of a crisis. She's to keep watch."

"But for what purpose?"

"I suspect our lady will tell us."

Blanche's eyes were fully open and more life showed in them than Giselle had expected, although the rest of her looked on the brink of death. Blanche's cheeks were sunken

The Outlaws

and even in the dimness her skin appeared like brittle parchment. She wasn't yet forty but she could have been a hard sixty.

"He found you," Blanche said.

"Who?"

"My cousin. A good boy. One of the few of my kin that Eustace hasn't charmed or bought. I never saw that he could be so dangerous. I've been a fool. Help me up." Blanche struggled to sit up.

"Are you sure?"

"I am strong enough, stronger than they suspect, although I don't know for how much longer. So we best get our business over while we can. Dear Lord I am so parched!"

"Hugh, would you be so good as to fetch something for Lady Blanche?"

"Certainly." Hugh went to the door. He flung it open with more force than necessary, startling the nurse, who was on her knees, ear to the keyhole. "Do something really useful. Bring some wine."

"We haven't any, sir," the nurse said.

"What do you mean, you haven't any? Who ever heard of a house without wine?"

"It was taken away, sir, along with many other things."

"By whom?"

"Our lord, sir."

"What lord is that? I understood that this land belongs to Lady Blanche."

"By the order of the earl, sir. While our lady has been sick."

"That is a strange order. Bring ale, then. Hurry up now, we're tired of waiting."

"Yessir." The nurse curtseyed and hurried down the hall. They heard her footsteps on the stairway and the murmur of voices questioning her below, probably wondering why she had abandoned her post at the door.

Hugh almost came back in the chamber and shut the door, but Giselle held out a hand for him to remain where he was.

Blanche's head sank back to the pillow. "Who is that? That isn't your husband, is it?"

"No, he is a friend."

"Is he good at keeping secrets?"

"I believe so. I trust him with my life."

"You better be able to. Your life's in more jeopardy than mine."

"So I've learned. He tried to have me poisoned."

"Only tried?"

Giselle nodded.

"You're more lucky than I."

"What do you mean?"

"You can't think that this is some random sickness." Blanche waved a hand at her face.

Before she could say any more, the nurse returned with a tray supporting three mugs. Hugh let her in the chamber but barred the way for the retainer who had followed her. There was a moment when it looked as though the retainer might try to force his way in, but he changed his mind and made do with pressing his nose close to Hugh's and shrugging his shoulders in a menacing way.

The nurse put the tray on the table under the window sill. She handed one mug to Blanche and one to Giselle.

"You can go," Giselle said.

"Yes, my lady," the nurse said.

"Thank you, Hugh," Giselle said when the nurse was gone. "You can shut the door now, if you please."

Blanche handed Giselle her mug. "Pour it out the window. I'll have yours if you don't mind."

"You think it's poisoned?"

"I rather doubt they'd try now, with you here, since they don't want anyone to know what they're up to, but I still don't trust them."

"Are you sure? It smells sour."

The Outlaws

"Going bad, is it? Hides the taste of the poison better than fresh. I'll take it anyway. I'm so thirsty that I could drink puddle water."

Blanche sat up again, took the mug, and downed the contents in a series of great, indelicate gulps. She gave the mug back to Giselle. "I'll have that too."

By "that too" she meant the mug on the tray. Giselle went to the window. She poured out the mug meant for Blanche over the sill, wetting her hand from the rain before she could close the shutters. Then she returned with the remaining mug, which Blanche emptied with as much enthusiasm as she had the first one.

"I've been fooling them," Blanche said. "Once I suspected, I've not been drinking anything. It's been almost six days."

"Why is he doing this to you?"

"Why? Why does he do anything? He wants my manors."

"But don't you have heirs? That cousin, surely."

"Think, girl. What trumps an heir?"

"A will?"

"Exactly."

"But you've made no provision for him. I'm sure of it."

"Of course I haven't. He'll make provision for himself, like he did with the earldom."

"I don't follow."

"You don't think that Roger voluntarily named Eustace his heir do you?"

"He forged the will?"

"Of course he forged it. Just as he'll forge mine. Probably got it done already."

"But what proof do you have?"

"Proof? I don't need proof. I know Eustace too well. It was far too suspicious when Roger died unexpectedly and this new will suddenly popped up. Roger never thought Eustace was man enough to be earl. He'd never have made out a will in Eustace's favor."

"I never understood why Roger thought so little of him."

"Roger thought he was weak and lazy, a constant disappointment. It sprang from something that happened between them long ago, but he was wrong on both counts. I tried to tell him, but he wouldn't listen to anyone once he'd made his mind up about something. You were around him enough to know that too."

Giselle nodded, remembering. "About this secret."

"You can have the secret once you've paid for it."

"What do you mean?"

"You have to get me out of here. If I remain, I'll die. You're the only one who can." Blanche's head sank back to the pillow. "There's no one else left I can call on."

Giselle had a cot brought into Blanche's chamber and took over the nursing duties. Over the next couple of days, she emerged from time to time to issue ever more pessimistic reports about Blanche's condition: that she could not keep her food down, that she was weaker, that she could not speak, and eventually that she opened her eyes for no one and did not respond to speech or prodding. The bit about the food had proven to be the hardest thing to make convincing. Giselle had vomited her meals in the chamber pot in Blanche's place. That had been unpleasant.

One would expect that FitzPoyntz should find these reports distressing, and although he put up a show of sympathy that might have fooled most people, the retainers standing in the shadows gave the game away, for they could not conceal their relief that this task would soon be over. No doubt they had a substantial reward coming.

On the evening of the third day, Giselle came down as supper was concluding. She took a chair beside FitzPoyntz before the hearth. He looked at her inquisitively, but she was silent, staring into the fire.

The Outlaws

"You had better fetch the priest," Giselle told him at last with as much sadness as she could convincingly pretend. "I don't think she is going to make it through the night."

"You're certain?"

"She has no strength left."

Perhaps it might have been Giselle's imagination, but a smile seemed to flicker upon FitzPoyntz's lips. He said, "I'll have him summoned from the village right away."

"You'll need a carpenter, too."

"Ah, yes, for the coffin."

"And I'll need linen for the shroud. Do you have any?"

"We have. Will you need assistance?"

"No. I'd like to do it myself. She was my friend, you know. In fact, almost a mother to me."

"I understand."

Giselle suppressed a smile. "Is there any supper left? I'm starving." Her throat and mouth were raw from throwing up, but she could not mention that. She was glad that was over.

"Herbert!" FitzPoyntz called to a servant. "Bring something for the lady."

"At once, my lord."

Giselle almost wolfed down the meal when it came, since it was the first good food she had had in days that she was allowed to keep. She put aside the bowl of peas and beef when it had been swept clean and the last of the bread was gone.

"Where are you going?" FitzPoyntz asked.

"I don't want her to die alone."

The priest arrived within half an hour. One glance at Blanche's graying face and thready breathing, and he wasted no further time administering last rights.

"Is there a place for her in the churchyard?" Giselle asked the priest.

"There is room," he said.

"She is a great lady," Giselle said.

"So I understand."

"I will have a stone put up for her so she will not be forgotten. It is a shame that she has to die friendless like this."

"But you are here."

"So I am. That was good fortune."

Giselle spent the night alone with Blanche, and in the morning she emerged and announced that Blanche had died.

To FitzPoyntz, she said, "I will need that linen now, and you had better summon your carpenter, if you haven't already."

"That's taken care of," FitzPoyntz murmured.

Giselle wondered if there hadn't been a coffin waiting in the barn for many days before she had arrived. "You are a credit to your mistress."

"Did she," FitzPoyntz ventured, "have any last words?"

"She never spoke," Giselle said, and turned away.

Giselle prepared the body for burial alone, rejecting repeated offers of help from FitzPoyntz and the servants. "She was my mistress and like a mother to me. I will do her this last service myself."

When she had sewn up the shroud, she allowed Hugh and Burghard to bring in the coffin.

The two men lifted Blanche from the bed and gently placed her in the wooden box, the groom at her feet and Hugh at her shoulders. FitzPoyntz watched from the doorway.

"Put the top on to keep off the rain," Giselle said.

"Shall I nail it, my lady?" the carpenter asked.

Giselle hesitated a fraction of a moment, thinking fast. "Yes. Go ahead."

"You're not suggesting we bury her now," FitzPoyntz said. "You can't dig a grave in weather like this. They'd as well

The Outlaws

dig soup." While it had been dry for a few days, rain had come again.

"Quite right," Giselle said. "But we can at least let her lie these final hours in the village church, until her grave is ready for her."

"I was thinking of the barn. Just until the rain clears. Then we can take her down to the village."

Giselle was horrified. "You would let your mistress lie dead in a barn?"

FitzPoyntz backed away from that suggestion. "Well, why not here, then?"

"I wish to use the bed tonight rather than a pallet on the floor, and I don't want to share the room with a corpse, if you don't mind. You know how unlucky that is. And I will not have her lying in the hall or in the undercroft. So it will be the church, which is the best place anyway. I will take her there. Hugh and my groom will help me. That way, you won't have to get your head wet. Just fetch us a cart."

FitzPoyntz followed the procession of cart and riders to the village.

He even followed Giselle and the coffin into the church and watched it set before the altar. Giselle, Hugh and the Burghard knelt to pray. When it appeared they meant to pray a long time, or rather that Giselle meant to do so with the others keeping her company, he withdrew.

As soon as he had shut the door, Giselle flew there and put her eye to a crack at the door jam. She could see FitzPoyntz mount his horse and head up the lane to the manor house.

She drew a deep breath, then let it out. "God, I thought he would never leave."

Taking a candle from the stand by the door, she marched across the bay of the small stone church to the coffin. She bent over and drew the dagger she always carried with her since the day she had run away from Hafton. She pried at one of the nails with the tip of the dagger. She wished now she had told the carpenter not to nail the lid shut. "Damn," she said.

"What is it, my lady?" Hugh asked, mystified.

"How are we going to get these nails out? I hadn't thought of that."

"Nails out? Good God, what for?"

"Never mind what for. We have to get them out, and quickly."

Hugh considered the problem. "There should be a smith here. He'll have pliers."

"Well, someone run and fetch them."

Hugh nodded to Burghard, who ran off on the errand.

Burghard was gone for a long time before he returned with a set of big black pliers that the smith used to hold hot iron.

Shaking his head, Burghard worked the nails free.

When they had the top off, Giselle slit the linen shroud with her dagger.

She took the cool face in her hands. "My lady, wake up. We're away."

Blanche's corpse drew a shallow breath, then she opened her eyes and blinked. "Oh, my," Blanche whispered.

Hugh staggered back, horrified.

Burghard fell to his knees with a cry, crossed himself and began to mumble prayers so fast no one could make out the words.

"Stop that, all of you!" Giselle commanded.

"But she was dead!" Hugh said, almost a wail.

"No, she wasn't. Now help me get her out of this thing or she will be soon."

Hugh recovered enough to lift Blanche out of the coffin and steadied her on her feet. Giselle wrapped her in the blanket from the coffin, and the two of them half carried her

The Outlaws

to a back corner of the church where the older woman slumped to the ground.

"Thank you, my dear," Blanche murmured.

"What is this secret you spoke of?" Giselle asked.

"Can't you wait until I catch my breath? It's quite simple. I know who killed your father."

"How could you possibly know that?"

"Because it was Eustace."

The shock of hearing this was so great that Giselle could not speak for some time. "You were in on his plan."

"No, it was his alone."

"Then how do you know of it? Did he confess?"

"He's not the confessing sort. He gave himself away, not to everyone, mind you, but those whose eyes were open could see the evidence of his guilt. Isn't it time that we were off, don't you think? I'd like to be as far away from this place by nightfall as I can get. We can talk more on the way, if that's your wont."

CHAPTER 33

Gloucester
November 1184

When he stood alone in his bed chamber, dressed for his wedding, Eustace FitzWalter was overwhelmed with trepidation and doubt. Most women were stupid and weak, easily controlled with a little flattery and charm, or simple brute force. Judith, however, was neither stupid nor weak nor easily controlled. She did whatever she wanted, and did not seem concerned about the consequences. After Eustace's experience with Giselle, he knew only too well the trouble that could come from an uncompliant wife. A voice in his head urged him to back away now while he still could. He hadn't said the words yet, nor paid Gloucester or the king for the privilege of her hand. Yet he felt powerless to resist what was about to happen. It wasn't her money, although he wanted that, needed it desperately, in fact. It was this mad attraction he had for her — mad because he knew that marriage was too important a business to leave to the whims of passion.

"I am a fool," he said aloud. "An utter fool."

Someone knocked at the door, four quick raps with a pause before the fifth. Le Bec entered. "The horses are ready."

"All right," Eustace said with as much indifference as he could muster. "Let's go then."

Down in the yard of the townhouse, his wedding companions were already mounted and waiting for him. Le Bec held his horse's head and his stirrup as he mounted. Eustace wheeled the horse and let him prance to show off a bit, then trotted out of the gate into Blackfriar's Lane.

The procession, preceded by the heralds, entered Southgate Street and turned north. Eustace's destination was Saint Aldate's Church, a small parish church by the north gate. He would have preferred Saint Peter's Cathedral, but Judith's family supported Saint Aldate's and she wanted the wedding to take place there.

The Outlaws

Shortly, they passed the stocks, where some boys were throwing apples at an old man and woman locked up side by side. The boys scattered as the wedding party approached. A few of them made obscene gestures and a couple of others called out insults. Eustace hated people like that, but they were like gnats and not worth bothering with unless you could catch one.

An apple sailed by his head, and he turned to see which of the brats had thrown it, but they had all disappeared down alleyways as Eustace's men-at-arms stirred at this sign of disrespect.

He considered having a word with the town bailiff. With a small purse as an incentive, the bailiff could send someone round to the brats' hiding place to administer a beating or two.

But the sight of something else drove that thought from his mind as he passed the mouth of Southgate market, a square off Southgate Street across from the All Saint's Church, where some of the more minor grain merchants did business.

"Did you see them?" Eustace asked le Bec.
"See who?"
"Back there. In the market."
"Uh, no."
"It was Giselle and that fellow Hugh le Gros."
"You sure your eyes aren't playing tricks?"
"My eyes aren't playing tricks. I saw them."
"That's strange."
"I'll say it's strange. It's a long way from Hafton. I wonder what they're doing here." Eustace pondered for a moment. "I want you to have someone find out."
"What for?"
Eustace repressed a sigh. "Because I want to know. That should be enough."
"Right."
"Good then."

He reached the market cross at the intersection with Eastgate Street. Traffic gave way as he continued on to Saint Aldate's and his appointment with destiny.

Being an earl meant having to live up to people's expectations, even if one didn't have the money. So Eustace's wedding party was as lavish as borrowed funds could make it. There were two hundred guests from western and southern England, including quite a few Marcher earls such as the FitzAllans, the Mortimers, and the FitzRoberts from Chester, not to mention the multitude of gentry from his and his new wife's lands who had come to pay their respects to the bridal couple and curry as much favor as the few moments with them permitted. Consequently, Eustace spent a lot of time talking to people he would rather not have spoken with, and too little time currying favor from his neighbors, who were bigger and more powerful men than he was, some even with the king's ear. He had to be concerned about Mortimer, whose lands abutted his own and who was a man of uncommon ambition. While most of that ambition was directed westward, he could not be trusted not to rouse a dispute with a neighbor when the Welsh were quiet.

The affair went on past sundown and the ringing of the curfew, but the magnates felt that curfews didn't apply to them, and the wine was still flowing at midnight. The bride and groom should have retired long ago to consummate their marriage, normally done under the eyes of the groom's relatives to ensure that the bride was a virgin, and allowed the festivities to carry on in their absence. But since both had been married before, no one thought this little ritual of any importance. So they were still in the hall when the last of the guests finally left.

Judith had at last turned to him with a cocked eyebrow, and asked, "Are you still in the mood, husband?" when le Bec appeared. Eustace had not seen much of him during the evening and he was impatient with the interruption.

The Outlaws

"You said you wanted to know," le Bec said.

"Know what?"

"Why Giselle and that fellow le Gros were here."

"Oh, that. Can't it wait until morning?"

"What's this, husband?" Judith asked. Her tone sounded bored and amused, but she was so good at dissembling that Eustace was not always sure of her true feelings. "Why this interest in your former wife?"

"It's not what you think, dear."

"What is it, then?"

"She and I have scores to settle, and that new husband of hers."

"You forget. I've heard your complaints more than I care to remember. If this must take priority . . ."

"Of course. Later, Reggie."

Eustace linked arms with Judith and they turned to the stairway.

"They'll be gone in the morning," le Bec said, keeping pace.

"What of it?" Eustace asked.

"If we're going to do anything, we've got to do it tonight."

"Take care of it then, will you?"

Judith stopped abruptly. "What is going on, Reggie?"

"They've bought a pair of mill stones."

"Mill stones?"

"The ones she had were shattered in the fire."

"The fire? Oh, that unfortunate Welsh raid you spoke about. I suppose that means they'll be carting them back to Hafton. Such a long way." She looked sharply at Eustace. "Mishaps could happen, couldn't they."

Only then did Eustace remember telling her about Stokesay's attempt to intercept the wool clip. He wondered what else he had told her. Infatuation makes the lips grow careless. "Yes, they could."

"You'd like to see that happen, wouldn't you, my dear."

"Yet I should know nothing about it."

"Of course not. Reggie, you know what to do," Judith said.

"I wonder where she got the money for that?" Eustace asked. "Mill stones are expensive."

"I expect she had enough left over from the note," le Bec said

"Note?" Judith asked.

"Yes," Eustace said, "she took out a large note to fund our annulment."

"You made her pay for it?" Judith sounded surprised, but amused.

"It seemed the right thing to do."

"A note," Judith said, brows coming together in thought. "They've given a note. You know, notes can be bought."

"For what purpose?" Eustace asked.

"Creditors have great power over debtors. They can be imprisoned if they do not pay. Their property can be seized, even sold."

"It would be a pity if that happened," Eustace said.

"Clearly," Judith said. "They are such good neighbors. Thank you, Reggie. You've done well. Now be off. You've a lot to do tomorrow. Bring us word of your success."

CHAPTER 34

On the road
November 1184

Le Bec held Stokesay in contempt until he had to try the same play himself. Intercepting any old prize that came down the road was easy. Catching a particular one turned out to be another thing altogether. There were several roads that Giselle Attebrook could take from Gloucester. He could not know in advance which one she would choose. And in the end, he almost missed her, for she left the town in a way he had not anticipated.

Le Bec's plan was to follow Giselle's carts at a discrete distance, then ride around them across country before springing the ambush. But the scout he had sent to follow her from the stone merchant's warehouse by the quay brought word that she had not gone by cart after all. She had taken a ship up the Severn.

"She's bought passage to Worcester," the scout said, ready to bolt in case le Bec got angry with the bearer of the news.

"Worcester! Why is she going to Worcester?" le Bec shouted.

"I don't know," the scout said. "Why would anyone go there?"

"It's not worth the spit on a rock," le Bec fumed. But then it occurred to him why. They had to cart the stones to Hafton. It was cheaper to carry it by ship to Worcester and then cart them from there to Hafton, than to cart them all the way from Gloucester.

Le Bec received this intelligence in a mushy meadow just across the Severn bridge, where he and his fellows were hiding behind a small copse of trees. His first impulse was to curse and go back to the townhouse. But cold dread with a whiff of panic replaced that impulse. Eustace would probably forgive the lapse. He invariably forgave le Bec for his lapses, real or perceived, and in le Bec's mind they were more perceived than not. But he wasn't sure about the new wife, Judith. She was altogether different than that girl, Giselle, who had been hardly more than a child. Giselle had been easy to frighten. He had no hope of frightening Judith, and indeed, she frightened him. If she wanted him punished, Eustace would do it, too, even if it was unfair.

He ran to the western foot of the bridge and looked down into the sluggish brown water as if he expected to see Giselle gliding up river. But the only boats in view were one disappearing round a bend to the north, and another tied to a tree at the shore just above the bridge, stepping its mast so it could pass under to the town quay.

He thought furiously. It was thirty odd miles by road to Worcester, and longer by the winding Severn. Horses could travel much faster than boats — five or six miles an hour to a boat's two, under oars, because that's how the boats got upstream. Men rowed them. He could get there before her.

And there was but one way out of Worcester if you wanted to go to Hafton.

He would catch her there.

He ran back to the men, feet squelching in the muck. "Mount up, boys! We've a hard ride ahead!"

There was no warning.

One instant the road ahead was empty, curving off to the right, dim and spooky.

Then three men stepped out of the woods about thirty yards ahead.

They carried strung bows and nocked arrows. There was no mistaking who they were and what they wanted.

"It's outlaws!" Giselle breathed. She allowed herself a moment of despair, then shook it off as quickly as it came. She could not afford the luxury of the distraction.

The wagon's driver, a boy of about fifteen, looked frightened. "What should I do?"

603

The Outlaws

"Stop. Don't resist them. They'll only kill us if we do." She glanced over her shoulder, certain that these men were not alone. She saw immediately that she was right. Other men had appeared at the rear of the wagon behind her. The driver of the wagon following hers deserted his seat for the woods.

Giselle wished now that Hugh was here. But after allowing Blanche a brief period of recovery, he had taken her to London for safekeeping at the Red Lion in London.

Giselle stood up in the cart and prepared to get down.

One robber drew his bow string to his cheek, aiming at her belly. There's no reason to do that, she thought. We aren't fighting back.

Another outlaw hissed, "Do it! Do it!"

She had never been this close to death before, had never stared down the business end of a nocked arrow, and for a moment, her resolve to be hard melted away. Her legs turned to lead. She couldn't move. All she could do was think: why are they doing this?

The boy also realized they meant to kill her, and just as the outlaw loosed the arrow, he pushed her off the cart.

The arrow hissed through the space she had occupied and glanced off the mill stone behind her, rattling branches as it vanished.

She landed hard on her hands and knees.

The boy vaulted out of the cart and landed at her side. "Mistress," he gasped, "we must run!"

She nodded, scrambled to her feet, and they ran into the woods.

There were shouts behind her and the sound of running feet on dry leaves. Two arrows flew by, one burying itself in the turf and the second careering off a tree trunk ahead, turning end over end.

She gathered her skirts higher and tried to run even faster. She felt slow, sluggish. As a child, she had been able to outrun everyone in the village, including the boys. Perhaps her pregnancy had changed her body. She was able to keep up with the boy only with great effort.

Branches whipped her face and clawed at her clothes, threatening to pull her off her feet, so that she began to fear them almost as much as the men pursuing her. Why were they still coming? Why hadn't they given up? Didn't they have what they wanted?

It must be the money. She still had the money.

She should just throw the purse to the ground and they would go for that and forget about her.

But she didn't want to give it up. Every penny was so dear.

They came to a ravine. At the bottom lay a stream. She and the boy slid down the bank, splashed across and began climbing the opposite side.

There was a shout behind them. Giselle glanced over her shoulder as she reached for a projecting root, and saw that there were four outlaws who had given chase. One drew an arrow from the bag on his hip. Before he could nock it, she pulled a loose stone from the bank and threw it as hard as she could. It flew at the the outlaw's face. He had to duck to avoid being hit and dropped the arrow.

It gave her enough time to gain the top of the bank.

The outlaws jumped off the bank and splashed across the stream.

Giselle ran on, chest burning from the exertion.

They were not going to give up. She was very afraid. She couldn't outrun them, it was clear to her now. They would catch her in time, take the money, and kill her just for the sport of it and for making them chase her.

Then she and the boy burst into a clearing in the forest, a small assart with a peasant's hut on the far side, surrounded by its wattle fence, pigs rooting in the stubble of a field beside it. More than a half dozen dirty faces turned in their direction as they stumbled across to the hut: a woman and her six children, who ranged in age from about twelve to a swaddled baby.

"Help us!" Giselle gasped with what little breath remained to her. "Please help us!"

The Outlaws

The question on their faces was answered by the appearance of the outlaws.

"They mean to kill me!" Giselle cried.

The woman looked from Giselle to the four outlaws, who were advancing across the clearing toward her.

Giselle turned to face them. She was too spent now to run any farther. If they meant to kill her, at least they must do it before witnesses, if they dared.

The boy remained with her, and when she glanced at him, she saw the fear on his face. He too knew that death was advancing toward them across the clearing.

"Go," she said, "Find the lord of this place and bring help."

"Lady . . ." he stammered.

"Go!"

He turned and ran into the woods.

Giselle meant to face death squarely, and she reached to the small of her back for her dagger. She held it in front of her in the low guard as her father had taught her, gasping for breath.

She regained some calm, and her vision began to clear. She saw to her astonishment that one of the outlaws was not an outlaw at all. It was Reginald le Bec, dressed in rags to look like an outlaw.

"You!" she spat. "Where did you get that silver broach? The one you lost at dice to Henry?"

"I don't know anything about a silver broach," he said, and kicked the knife out of her hand. Giselle scrambled for it, but he caught her by the hair, jerked her off her feet, and pulled her head back, exposing her neck.

He stood over her and drew his dagger. From the savage smile on his face, she knew he meant him to cut her throat.

"Hold there!" the peasant woman shouted. "Use that blade and it'll be the end of you."

Giselle saw the peasant woman and the oldest boy in the windows of the hut. The woman held a crowbow and the boy a hunting bow.

Four men to a woman and a boy were good odds from the outlaws' perspective, but the woman and the boy had the advantage of the house as a fortress. Le Bec spat. "Keep a steady finger there, grandmother," he said. "I'll stay the blade."

"I've got my eye on you," the woman replied. "And don't think you can carry her off, either. I know what boys like you want, and it ain't all about money."

Reginald dug into Giselle's pouch and came out with the purse. He straightened up and said, "Good day to you, grandmother. We have what we wanted."

"Good. Then get off my land."

CHAPTER 35

Hafton
November 1184

Giselle wiped her sopping face and turned from the washbasin, where she had scrubbed off the dirt from her journey. "You haven't heard what I said. It was Eustace. He killed my father. It wasn't le Bec after all."

"Well, there always had been the possibility that le Bec's possession of the broach had an innocent explanation," Robert said, more stunned about the fact of Giselle's pregnancy than what she had learned from Blanche. He had expected fatherhood as a matter of course, eventually. He just had not expected it to come so quickly, and in the middle of all their troubles, too. "But we need to be careful. Blanche's word is not proof. And what she saw is thin evidence in any case."

"What, you're a lawyer now? It is proof enough for me."

"If we are to accuse him, the evidence must be firm. And even then it may not matter. When were you planning on doing this? At the next assize?" Robert asked, referring to the periodic courts held by the circuit-riding crown justices who heard pleas involving crimes against the crown. "It will be easy for a man of his stature to avoid answering a plea brought there. He could delay things for years until people finally forgot about the matter."

"I will accuse him before the king. He will have to answer then. I have that right, don't I?"

"Yes, and because it involves your father you may get a more sympathetic hearing. But the king must be careful how he disposes of matters affecting Marcher earls. I learned that much in Limousin. Justice is pliable where they are concerned."

"It will not be pliable for me."

"You think so? Maybe," he hastened to add at her furious expression, "but then what? He'll not stand for trial before a jury like an ordinary man. He'll demand trial by combat. He has that right, no matter what your proof, and Eustace won't fight himself. He'll use a champion, the best money can buy. Who will fight for us?"

The answer to that was obvious. They could not afford a champion, so it would have to be Robert. He would do it if she asked him to. But hired champions made their livings fighting judicial duels, and they were very good. He was merely adequate with a sword; he had no illusions about that. He watched her struggle with the question, wondering how far her desire for vengeance would push her.

"What can I do?" she asked.

"Sometimes you just have to bear the loss."

"I cannot!"

"I know. It is a terrible weight."

"What do you know about how I feel?"

"You forget. My father was murdered as well. Nobody knows who did it. I have wondered every day since."

She was quiet a long moment. "I had forgotten. I'm sorry."

He went on, "You may not have to bear the pain, unavenged, though. We will find a way to ruin him."

November yielded to December, when the first snow of the season arrived, leaving a blanket of white on the ground and a dusting on the roofs, fences, and branches of the trees. It looked pretty from the shelter and relative warmth of the manor house windows, but everyone in Hafton greeted the snow with trepidation. Winter was never a time people looked forward to, since it meant discomfort, wet and cold, nasty drafts, and hunger toward the end. And this year, there was so little to go around that everyone expected to be starving by February, perhaps even before then.

For the manor-born, December was less dreary a month than it was for everyone else. During the twelve days of Christmas, there were feasts at the houses in the neighborhood, each house giving one on a separate day so

The Outlaws

that manor folk trooped from one house to another to enjoy them all. There would be no feasts for Robert and Giselle, however. Since they could not afford a feast of their own, they could not in good conscience attend any of the others.

Corn was in short supply after sowing the winter wheat. They had no mill yet, of course, and with the new millstones lost, there was no likelihood of rebuilding any time soon. The suggestion was made at the November manor court to take a month's supply to Wigmore for grinding, but faint-hearts pointed out the vulnerability of the carts on the way to unpleasant people from Shelburgh. So village folk kept at grinding their own grain between flat stones, cursing at the effort and the waste.

Robert used the cold spell to have more wood cut in the forest on the other side of the river. Within a week, while it was still cold, they had a dozen carts loaded with lumber.

"What are you going to do with it?" Giselle asked him as they walked to what was left of the hidden barn. Even this out-of-the-way place had felt the torches of the Welsh raiders.

"I've arranged to sell it at Leominster," Robert said. "We can't afford to carry it any farther. We'll buy some corn, enough I hope to see everyone through the winter. After that we'll cut more and keep the money to repay the loan. I hate to think of how much we'll have to clear to pay it back. But then, I suppose we can use the cleared land for planting."

"We should get on the road before the weather breaks."

"We?"

"I don't like being cooped up here any more than you do."

"I thought that Hafton was all you cared about."

"Not all." She took his hand. "It would be nice at least to look in the shops, even if we can't buy anything. It would be nice to have more candles. We're almost out."

"Candles," he said. "You'd like some candles."

"Scented ones. You can buy them in London, you know. I've not seen any in Leominster or Hereford yet, though."

"I'll write my mother and ask her to send some."

"We couldn't afford the letter."

"That's true."

They gazed at the ruins of the hidden barn for a time. A few charred timbers projecting above the white carpet were not made any more cheerful by their own dusting of snow.

Presently, they turned toward home, where a warm supper awaited and a roaring fire.

They had some good fortune in the fact the snow was not deep enough to hinder cart travel, since they had to take the roundabout route: the straight road, more or less, ran about ten miles through Shobdon, whose lord held from Eustace FitzWalter, and so was an enemy. This way, which took them to the north toward Wigmore then east of Shobdon by Mortimer's Cross, was a good fifteen miles, a long way to travel on any day, and a hardship in winter. As fully laden carts move slowly, it was midafternoon before they reached the town, even though they started just after dawn.

The late arrival didn't matter as much as it would if the town market was the reason for the journey. But Wulfric had been sent ahead the week before to find a buyer, and they took it to that man's warehouse on the Hereford Road just beyond the town's ditch and wall.

Robert left Hugh to supervise the unloading, while he and Giselle wandered back into town so she could visit the shops and torture herself over the things that she could not buy.

Even with the snow and cold, the shopkeepers had their shutters down, and as they walked along High Street, Giselle had a good view of the wares for sale — rolls of woolen and linen fabric; gloves of every size and color from yellow to red to blue, short ones that reached to the wrist and others that stretched to the elbow, many with elaborate stitching; caps and hats for which the town was famous, some round, some pointed, some with broad brims to keep off the sun in summer yet were of a material that could not be mistaken for a peasant's ordinary wear.

The Outlaws

Giselle lingered at one glover's window. She sighed and took a step forward for a better view. Robert told her if she took another step or tarried a moment longer, he would carry her bodily away. She laughed at that. It was a happy moment amid all the troubles.

"Next year," he said as they turned toward Burgess Street. "It will be better next year."

"It will be. I'm sure of it. Eustace will be gone. We'll be safe then."

At the intersection of Burgess and Church Street, which led east to the priory, stood the Angry Cat Inn, where they planned to stay the night. It was the best inn in town, and Giselle had made Robert promise that they would not have to sleep in a barn, like the men from the village who had driven the carts.

"I wonder why they call it the Angry Cat?" Robert mused as they approached the doorway. "It's an odd name for an inn."

"I heard that the original owner had a cat that sat in ambush on a rafter just inside the door, and it would leap on people's heads."

"It's a wonder no one killed it."

"It was too quick and crafty."

They were within ten feet of the door when four men spilled out into the street. The four were carrying swords in their hands, and just now began to belt them on. As in many towns, it was forbidden to carry swords, but Leominster was so small it had few bailiffs to enforce the ordinance. However, innkeepers were on the spot and eager to remove the tools that sometimes led to riot and disorder, so they collected swords at the door. Robert and Giselle would have just got out of the way, except one of the men was Reginald le Bec.

Robert's mouth went dry. He gripped the scabbard of his own sword with the left hand, easing the blade out an inch with his thumb in preparation for a quick draw. He was about to grasp the handle with the other hand when Giselle spat, "Bastard!" and stepped forward. Her fists were balled and for

612

an appalling instant he thought she meant to strike le Bec. He grabbed her shoulder and pulled her back.

If le Bec was surprised to see them, he covered it. "That's no way to greet a neighbor."

"You thief!" Giselle cried.

"You need to restrain your wife, Attebrook. People die over words like that."

"Perhaps you deserve to," Robert said.

"We were such good friends as boys. Look what's become of us. At each other's throats at every opportunity."

"We were never friends."

"What is it, Attebrook? You want trouble here? Now?"

"It's as good a place to settle our differences as any."

"In the street, like beggars? I don't think so. But wait! You'll be a beggar soon, in any case." Le Bec circled away from them, hand on the grip of his sword, yet giving every indication that he did not intend to draw it.

"What is that supposed to mean?" Giselle asked.

"It means that Eustace has your measure. He's bought your note. When you can't pay next summer, we'll take the manor. You can go door to door and beg for your supper then. Or scuttle back to that hovel in London where we found you."

"You won't fight then?" Robert asked.

"With you? You're just a cotter's boy with airs. Your words don't sting. I cannot hear them. Besides, Eustace won't like it if I deprive him of the pleasure of your ruin. You two go on. Have a good day. You won't have many more."

Giselle sat with her elbows on the table, face in her hands. Robert could still see her eyes through her fingers, and they were frightened. Around them was the low hum of conversation in the Angry Cat as supper was laid on the tables for the evening's guests.

"That's that then," she said, her voice muffled by her palms.

613

The Outlaws

"That's what?" he asked.

"The end. Even if we kill Eustace, his heir can take the manor."

"The only reason we will have trouble paying is because of his interference."

"What are you saying?"

"It's obviously his plan to prevent repayment. If we can't earn enough by summer, we could always take out another loan to cover that one. We'll be longer in debt, but at least we will still have the manor. There is one thing, though."

"What?"

"You must have no part in the accusations."

"Why not?"

"You forget. The loser in trial by combat is convicted as a perjurer if he isn't killed outright. The penalties for that should fall on me. Not on you. Since the manor is your dower, it cannot be confiscated."

"What do they do to perjurers?"

"If they have no property, they cut off their noses for a start. Anyway, I've never fancied the one I have so it will be a small loss."

PART 6
1185

The Outlaws

CHAPTER 1

Ludlow
January 1185

The king's descent upon a place was never a cause for celebration. The king did not travel alone, of course. He was always accompanied by a great entourage of followers, noble and gentry, who had servants of their own, not to mention the uncountable number who served the king, which included chaplains, pages, a steward or four, secretaries, waiters, surgeons and physicians, grooms for the horses which outnumbered the people, waiters, carvers and servers, musicians, kitchen staff, and drivers for the many carts and wagons that now so cluttered the town's streets that passage could hardly be had on some of the lesser ones. And all of them expected to be bedded and fed at the host's expense. They could suck an estate dry of its surplus in a matter of days, leaving little to get through a winter.

The Earl de Lacy, being quick to seek his best advantage, pushed some of the host's responsibilities onto the town. Since he owned every square inch of it, there was nothing the burghers could do, although they did their best to recover their costs by raising prices on everything in sight.

All this bother was made worse by the fact that a council had been called at Ludlow to address the recent disorder in the March and the breach of the king's peace. Fortunately for the town, those who came for the conference had to pay their own way, which relieved the burghers of a good bit of the burden imposed by the visit of the court itself.

But it meant that the town was so bursting that not a bed was to be found within the town, and many people resorted to sleeping in tents as they did for the autumn fair. In fact, it was rather like a fair, with festivities in High Street every day and impromptu, unlicensed markets springing up like mushrooms as country people took advantage to sell whatever they could. The town bailiffs were busy from morning to night patrolling for these illegal markets and exacting fines whenever they could catch one at work. Oddly, they had considerable trouble doing so, although in the evenings many bailiffs could be found in the town's better inns drinking more than they could usually afford.

The Attebrooks might have missed this great event even though it was just up the road from Hafton, isolated as they were with unfriendly neighbors all about, had it not been for a rider who delivered a writ ordering Robert to attend.

There was more to the writ than what was on the parchment, and in compliance with the messenger's instructions, Robert and Giselle did not arrive until the day before the conference. This left them no choice but to put up a tent on the field to the north of the castle, but the rider had instructed them to do this rather than stay in the town, as well as not to lift any banner or colors that would draw attention to them, and for Robert to keep the canvas cover on his shield, which might also have identified him.

Although it was middle January, a week of warm weather had melted the snow so that crusty patches remained, and the ground was sodden and squelched at every step, with puddles everywhere in the brown grass. No wood could be had from anywhere that wasn't wet as well so they had no fire for cooking or comfort. This was miserable enough, but shortly after they arrived, clouds slid in from the west and it began to drizzle, cold and stinging to the cheeks.

They had one tent for themselves and Burghard and Osgar, and with the bad weather there was nothing to do but huddle inside on folding stools with blankets wrapped about them.

As the light began to fade, Giselle cracked the tent flap. "It's almost sundown. Time to get going."

"Osgar," Robert said, rising and giving his blanket to Giselle.

"Where are we going, exactly, my lord?"

The Outlaws

"I explained that already, an inn in Bell Lane. That's the first right down Broad Street from the High Street."

"And we're meeting whom, exactly?" Osgar stood up.

"I don't know. Just make sure there's a feather in your cap. He's supposed to know us by that. You haven't lost it, have you?"

"No, it's around here somewhere."

A few minutes were lost searching for the feather, which had been mislaid among the piles of blankets and pallets of straw they had brought along so they wouldn't have to sleep on the ground.

The feather had been almost snapped in half, and the end drooped. Osgar stuck the feather in his hat band. "How do I look?"

"Like an idiot," Burghard said.

"I wasn't asking your opinion."

"Sounded like you were. And you have it anyway. Now get on and find out what the lord wants. The sooner we're out of here, the better." Burghard hugged his blanket about his shoulders against the draft that rushed in at Robert's and Osgar's departure. "Lord, what I wouldn't give for a decent barn right now."

"And a decent meal," Giselle said, settling down to await their return. She glanced at the tent flap. "I wish Hugh would hurry."

"This weather will slow him down, my lady," Burghard said. "Wet roads are slow roads."

"And he has a long way to come."

Bell Lane was in the shadow of late afternoon by the time Robert and Osgar reached it. Robert had never been down it and had no familiarity with the lane other than the off-hand glances he had given it as he passed its mouth on other business. He did not have any idea what the inn looked like. Fortunately, it advertised itself with a sign, a turtle sitting on a bundle of grapes. Otherwise, they might have missed it, since it looked no different from any other house.

They wiped the mud off their feet on the threshold and went in. A fire burned so hot on the hearth in the middle of the floor that they could feel the heat as soon as they entered. The inn's servants were just clearing off the remains of supper, and there was quite a lot of that since the tables and benches were packed with guests. There seemed to be no vacant benches anywhere. Robert stood near the fire wondering what to do now when a well dressed fellow in a green coat touched his elbow. "This way, sir, if you don't mind."

Green Coat conducted them to a corner, where a lean man in a crimson coat and yellow stockings occupied a small table all to himself. Not one but two candles stood upon the table in puddles of wax for lack of candle holders. Between the candles lay an inkpot and a pile of parchment sheets covered with writing. The quill belonging to the inkpot rested between the long fingers of the lean man occupying the table. He had the air of a lawyer, an impression reinforced by a glance at the writing on the parchment. He was working on a part headed "Quid sit magna asissa," which Robert, whose Latin was rudimentary, at least understood to mean, "The nature of the grand assize," which was a gathering where the king himself decided legal cases.

The lean man looked at Osgar. "That is the saddest feather I have ever seen." The remark did not seem to require a response, and Osgar kept prudently silent. The lean man turned his attention to Robert. "You must be Attebrook. Please, have a seat."

Robert settled on a stool on the other side of the table. "And you are?"

"My name is Hubert Walter. I am secretary to my lord Ranulf de Glanvill."

"The chief justicar?"

The Outlaws

"You've heard of him even here?" Walter seemed amused. He had kindly eyes that were well suited for amusement, almost as if that was their natural light.

"We know that much, at least. You are rather too important yourself to deal with the likes of me."

"But you are rather important yourself, at the moment."

"How could that be so?"

"You have an important part to play in tomorrow's mummery."

"Mummery?"

"Well, the majestic procedure of the law is not exactly that, but we must be sure that certain things occur as his grace wishes them to do."

"I don't follow."

"Look, my dear fellow, this is not just some random visit by the king. He is here for a purpose. Mortimer, FitzWalter, and several of the other Marcher earls have appealed to the king to reconsider the peace. They have been making a great deal of the troubles in the March, exaggerating the ordinary theft of cattle and such into a cause for war. The king does not wish there to be a war, and it is your part to help ensure this does not occur."

"What am I supposed to do? Disavow what happened to my property?"

"Not at all. In fact, we are quite interested in your testimony, in particular what was said at this Iowerth's hold. There are, however, some who may not wish the king to hear it, and who may be keen to prevent you from appearing at court when the council is convened. So we are making certain arrangements to see that you get there untroubled, and remain unnoticed until the proper time. I will tell you what those are in a moment." Walter sat quiet for a few seconds gazing at a spot beyond Robert's shoulder. "You are not the ideal witness, I have to say that."

"Why not?"

"Your conflicts with FitzWalter provide fodder for accusations of interest. I've heard all the stories, how you grew up on FitzWalter land, how you broke your uncle out of Earl Roger's gaol, how you killed his cousin, and so on. And then there is the problem of your wife."

"What about my wife?"

"Why, she is FitzWalter's cast off."

"She is glad to be that."

"So I've heard. So many have said, just as many have said you were dipping into the jar before she was set free."

"A lie. People will say anything."

"Oh, they will, and the worse they can say about someone the more they enjoy it. In any event, is there anything else I should know about your tortured relations with FitzWalter that I have not mentioned?"

Robert pondered whether to say anything more. "There is the murder of Giselle's father."

"Sir William? What about it?"

"We have evidence that FitzWalter was behind it."

"Dear me, what could you possibly know?"

"William was found with an arrow in him. Lady Blanche said that it was an arrow belonging to FitzWalter. She said he fetched the arrow at night from his tent the night Sir William was killed."

"Hmmm," Walter muttered, his lips pursed as he considered this evidence. "And I suppose you mean to accuse him?"

"Yes."

He spoke sternly. "You are not to appeal against FitzWalter for this murder you contend he committed."

"I cannot let it lie," Robert said. "It may be nothing to you, but it is no small matter for us."

"Oh, please believe me, homicide is a direct offense to the crown and we never view it as a small matter. You are free to make your appeal against FitzWalter before the next assize. Just not now."

"That's not till the autumn!" After the note was due. God knew what other plans Eustace had to prevent any effort to repay the note.

621

The Outlaws

"It will have to wait. These are your orders. Your testimony must appear to be as free from prejudice as possible. But we don't need to add to your considerable pile of grievances yet. It is already known there is ill feeling between you, your wife, and FitzWalter, and it must appear that his ill will exceeds yours and you are but its innocent victims. I assume you are innocent, correct?"

"We have done nothing to merit his attentions but occupy ground he wishes to take for his own."

"Ah, just so. Be sure you repeat that statement tomorrow with that exact tone of righteous indignation. As for the other, the king does not want the well poisoned any more than is already publicly known, for it will empower those who would claim you are a liar. You understand this, do you not?"

"I am not sure I do."

"Well, whether you understand the king's motives is not important. What is important is that you understand what is required of you. Do I have your promise you will do as expected?" The amusement had gone from Walter's eyes, replaced by a steely purpose.

"You do, my lord."

"Thank you. That is good." Walter blew out the candles and gathered the parchments into a neat stack. Green Coat hastened to his side with a leather pouch and slid the stack into it. "Now as to our arrangements for tomorrow . . ."

The following morning, Robert and Giselle presented themselves at Ludlow castle's main gate. They wore their poorest cloaks with the hoods pulled up to conceal their faces, a gesture that could not be taken for a ruse since it was cold enough to bring a sting to their faces.

Green Coat was there waiting for them. Without a word, he slid down into the castle's ditch and led them around toward the river. The ditch ended where the ground fell steeply toward the river. A mill sat on the riverbank below them, its wheel creaking loudly enough for them to hear. A miller's boy was unloading a cart at the door. He paused to look at them as they turned the corner. There was no ditch because of the steepness of the hill, but they crept along under the outer bailey's embankment and palisade.

"Get back to work!" Green Coat shouted at the boy, as if he didn't want that attention. It did no good, for the boy continued to stare.

"That's telling him," Robert said.

"Lazy good for nothing."

"Where are we going?"

"Sally port. Just ahead." Although Robert merited a "sir" from the likes of Green Coat, his proximity to the justicar's secretary must have made him feel immunized from common courtesies.

The embankment and palisade which enclosed the castle's great outer bailey ran into a square corner tower and stone wall.

They stumbled along until they reached a copse of sapling hawthorns beneath another tower where the wall turned back toward the town. Around the bases of the trees grew a profusion of dog rose. There, visible only when you were up close, was what appeared to be a cave. But it proved to be a doorway secured by rusted iron bars. A soldier stood behind the iron bars. He spat through them. "What the hell took you so long? You get lost?"

"Unlock the damn door," Green Coat said.

"If I don't you'll tell your mum?" the soldier asked. But he fumbled with a set of keys and unlocked a heavy padlock and swung the barrier open with a great squeak.

"Need to do something about that. You can probably hear it for miles," Robert said.

"I expect so, your honor," the soldier said, standing aside so Robert and Giselle could enter. "But it ain't my job. Now if you just go straight ahead, minding your heads, because the passage is a bit low in spots."

The passage was lined with stone, musty and smelling of damp. The ceiling was slightly arched, as if designed to

The Outlaws

accommodate one's head, but uneven so that if he hadn't minded the warning, he might have bumped his head on the low points. He evaded them because he ran his hand along the ceiling, and said "Mind the bump" to Giselle when he came to one.

The passage ended at a ladder. They climbed the ladder and emerged in the ground floor of the tower. It was dark here, the only light from narrow windows intended to provide shooting for archers in the event of an attack. They could see enough to tell that the place was filled with sacks and barrels, with a ladder leading to the upper floors.

Green Coat climbed up beside them. "If you would step toward the door, your honor. Hoods up now, so you won't be recognized."

The door opened into the inner bailey, which was packed with people. These were lesser folk, prestigious enough to merit admission into the inner bailey, but not so high that they deserved the comfort of the hall. Knights and their families, they milled about among barrels of ale and bonfires lighted to provide some warmth.

"This way," Green Coat said. He led them through the crowd to the hall, a tall timber building roofed with slate that stood just to the left of the tower. It too was jammed with people, but these were earls and barons and their families. Among this profusion of furs and elaborate embroideries, of yellows, blues, and reds, of feathered hats and silks, Robert felt dowdy and plain, as indeed he was. Giselle must have felt the same from the uncomfortable look on her face.

Green Coat escorted them to a corner as far away as possible from the high table at the opposite end of the hall, where the top of the king's head was just visible. At least, Robert thought it was the king's head from the reddish hair streaked with gray.

"Stay here until your name is called," Green Coat said. "You're to talk to no one." He turned away and disappeared into the crowd.

"Some secret," Giselle said, trying not to make eye contact with the questioning glances that were cast their way now and then. "I wonder if he's here already."

"He must be," Robert said.

"And we can't say anything."

"Only what we've been told to say."

"I hate this."

"What choice do we have?"

"None, I suppose. But I can still hate it."

Robert expected that since the point of the king's visit was to investigate breaches of the peace in the March that he would get right to business. But he was wrong. The king spent the morning entertaining pleas and deciding cases in much lesser disputes, mainly about the ownership of this bit of land or that, or about encroachments and boundaries. It was dull business, although King Henry seemed to enjoy it, and it consumed the entire morning.

There was a break for dinner just short of noon. Green Coat ushered Robert and Giselle outside, since they were not important enough to be invited to dine with the king in the hall, and they had to make do with buns and a bit of ham bought from a vendor in the yard.

As things dragged on, it was hard to remain unnoticed, at least for Giselle, who had friends among those admitted to the inner bailey, and she was recognized several times despite the disguise of the cheap cloak. This required her to engage in conversation, for it would have been impolite and even insulting not to do so. She was in one such conversation with a childhood friend from Cleobury Mortimer and over the other girl's shoulder she spotted Lady Blanche, with Hugh behind her, emerging from the gate tower into the inner bailey.

"A moment, Lucy, if you don't mind," Giselle said. She turned to Robert. "Lady Blanche is here. You best have a word with her. Let her know the plan has changed."

The Outlaws

"The plan?" Lucy asked. "What plan?"

"Ah, supper plans, my dear," Giselle said without hesitation. "I am entertaining my former mother-in-law this evening."

"I am surprised you still get along with her," Lucy said as Robert slid through the crowd to intercept Blanche.

"Lady Blanche," Robert said as he stopped before her.

"Ah," she replied. "I suspect you are Robert Attebrook."

"Guilty, my lady."

"As you are guilty of so much, from what I've heard over the years."

"That probably depends on whom you're talking to."

"Well, neither Roger nor Eustace had much good to say about you. Your crime rankled more than you know. The pardon did nothing to relieve the sting."

"Eustace hasn't forgotten it?"

"How can he? It was against the family. The fellow you killed was Roger's cousin, or has that slipped your memory? Such things are never forgotten. You know that. After all, you have your own such grievance."

"About that — we've been ordered not to bring up the matter of William's murder."

"Who gave you such an order?"

"Someone close to the king. Apparently his grace thinks it will be a distraction from some other plan he has in mind."

"That is a disappointment."

"More than you know."

"I know well enough, don't doubt that. So I came all the way from London and put myself in jeopardy for nothing?"

"I'm afraid so."

"A pity not to profit from it." She took a deep breath. "Well, then, at least get me something to eat. I'm famished."

After dinner, Green Coat retrieved Robert and Giselle, and escorted them to their corner in the hall. The king took up legal cases again, but these were such minor things that those far away from the high table paid no attention, and the hum of conversation drowned out what was going on. After a couple of hours of standing around, Giselle asked, "Can you find me something to sit on? My back is killing me."

"Not your feet?"

"Those as well."

Robert crept along the walls looking for a free stool or chair, but there were none in sight. He had worked his way to the front of the crowd, and would have gone farther, but Eustace FitzWalter and a woman who must be his wife were there. Robert was about the slink away when Eustace bent over and spoke to another woman. With a start, he saw it was Blanche. Eustace and Blanche locked eyes for a moment. Then she caught sight of Robert staring at her. Her eyes returned to Eustace, and she nodded. She gave no sign she had spotted Robert, and Eustace did not look behind him.

"No spare benches?" Giselle asked when Robert returned.

"None I could find. But I saw Blanche talking to Eustace."

"What about?"

"I wasn't close enough to hear."

"A pity. It gives me a bad feeling."

"Why?"

"She hated Eustace. What could she possibly have to say to him?"

"Ha, ha, you thought I was dead, but I'm not?"

"Did she look like she was doing that?"

"No. They seemed rather friendly, actually."

"Something is going on."

"What, do you think she intends to give the game away?"

"There's nothing to give away at this point. The king himself has ordered us to keep silent."

"Well, about the raid."

"I never mentioned our suspicions to her about that."

"We'll just have to wait and see, I suppose."

The Outlaws

"I'm done waiting on my feet. Damn the appearances." Giselle sat down against the wall. "I'd just like to get this over with, before things have a chance to get worse than they already are."

There was a lull while the king left the chamber with several of his ministers. When he returned he plucked an apple from a bowl on the table and took a bite out of it. He swallowed and said, "Call the next case."

The clerk opened his mouth to speak but Blanche FitzWalter called out from the front row, "My lord king! Will you hear my plea?"

There was a time for hearing pleas, and this was not it. But King Henry lowered his apple while raising a hand to the clerk to be silent. He squinted at Blanche with the look of a man whose eyes were not as good as they used to be. "Lady Blanche, I heard that you had passed away. The tale was wrong, apparently."

Blanche stepped away from the crowd. "As you can see my lord, I am well. I had been ill, but I am mended now."

"I am pleased to hear that. You have a plea? Can't it wait? We still have a long list of matters to get through today."

"I have come a long way to see you, your grace. I beg your indulgence."

"Very well. What is it you wish?"

Blanche took a deep breath and turned. She pointed at Eustace. "I appeal against Eustace FitzWalter for imprisoning me against my will and despoiling my estate for his own purposes."

Quiet settled on the hall at this accusation. While it didn't quite have the excitement of a murder charge, it was novel enough against a day of boundary disputes, squabbles over inheritances, and the occasional assault to fix the audience's attention.

Henry seemed taken aback at the charge. "I see. Well, then, Earl Eustace, I see you there hiding behind your wife. What do you answer?"

Eustace stepped up beside Blanche. The top of her head came no higher than his armpit which gave the impression he towered over her. "I deny the charge, my lord, and I demand wager of battle."

"Battle? You want to fight your step-mother?"

The crowd laughed and even Eustace smiled.

"She is a match for me, but due to her recent illness I am sure she will appoint a champion," Eustace said.

"That would be prudent," Henry said. "All right then, this is moving rather fast. Next month all right with you? I will appoint a marshal to oversee the matter."

"I ask that you be the judge, my lord," Eustace said. "I have the right to be tried before the king on any charge, and I wish it to be so now."

Henry nodded with obvious reluctance. "That is your right."

"And I wish the matter to be settled immediately. I do not want my name blackened or made the subject of mocking songs."

"No one likes to be the subject of mocking songs, although it seems to be something no one of prominence can avoid. I can even think of a few unflattering verses myself about locking up a step-mother." Henry was about to add something else, but William Marshal approached and whispered in his ear. Henry was heard to mutter "Damn!" Marshal withdrew. Henry looked again at Eustace.

"Well, then," Henry said, "I suppose we can accommodate you tomorrow morning after all, if it doesn't rain — that is, if Lady Blanche has a champion in mind already."

"I have, my lord," Blanche said.

"And who will that be?"

"Sir Robert Attebrook."

The Outlaws

"Sir Robert Attebrook," Henry repeated slowly. The name hung in the air. He looked very displeased.

"You've heard of him, my lord?" Eustace asked.

"Heard of him? I don't think so."

"He married my former wife, Giselle, formerly Giselle de Hafton. Without your permission."

"Ah. He did? Can he be fetched here in time for tomorrow?"

"I'm told that he's here already," Eustace said.

"Oh. Is he? Bring Sir Robert here." Henry shot a hard look at Ranulf de Glanvill, who passed it on to Hubert Walter, who in turn threw it at Green Coat, who hurried to Robert and Giselle's corner.

Robert, who had heard the charge and the exchange, was just pulling Giselle to her feet when Green Coat reached them.

"You're wanted by the king," Green Coat said.

"Now we know what's up," Robert said to Giselle.

"But where does it lead?" she asked.

"Attebrook," Henry said, leaning against the table with crossed arms, "you heard the charges?"

"Yes, your grace."

"So you know that Lady Blanche wishes to name you her champion. Have you discussed this with her?"

"No, your grace. It comes as much of a surprise to me as it does to you."

"I find that hard to believe. Do you accept this appointment?"

Robert felt Giselle's fingers dig into his arm. He looked down at her. She nodded.

"I will accept, your grace," Robert said. "On the condition that Eustace represents himself."

"I will accept, but on a condition of my own," Eustace said.

"And that is?" Henry asked.

"That we fight with knightly arms, not those silly square shields and clubs."

"Is that acceptable to you, Attebrook?"

"It is."

"Is tomorrow too much of a burden for you?" Henry asked. There was something in the way the king spoke that suggested he might welcome a delay.

But Robert said, "No, your grace. Tomorrow is fine."

Henry sighed. "Very well then. Tomorrow morning it will be."

CHAPTER 2

Ludlow
January 1185

They hardly spoke when Robert lay down beside her that night. He kissed her and said "Goodnight." Then he lay on his back with his hands crossed on his chest.

She sneaked a look at his face. She wished he would take her in his arms, but he didn't move. She turned on her side and was about to reach for him when he stood up. At first, she thought he was just headed for the chamber pot, but then he began to get dressed.

"Where are you going?" she asked.

"The paddock."

"What for?"

"To check on the horse. He doesn't know me well enough."

Since Robert had no warhorse of his own, he had to borrow Hugh's. Giselle didn't know much about warhorses, other than they were frightfully expensive and difficult to manage. But she knew enough that horses and riders were a team and should be accustomed to working together. It was a dangerous thing to ride a strange horse in a fight. Still, this sounded like a thin excuse.

He went out.

Giselle lay in bed a long time before she fell asleep.

Giselle awoke to the sound of a church bell ringing the hour of Prime. The sun was just rising. There was fog among the tents pitched in the field. It was so thick that she could not see more than thirty feet. Robert had his shirt off despite the cold and was washing himself in a bowl on a folding table.

She got up to help him towel off. "You'll catch your death from this cold," she said.

He smiled at that — a distracted thing, but at least a smile. Then she helped him put his shirt back on.

They went outside for a simple breakfast consisting of bread and weak ale. Many people were already up. Some just stood around and watched. Others offered encouragement and good luck.

When they were done eating, Hugh helped Robert arm. First came the gambeson, the padded garment worn under the byrnie. Hugh fumbled with the ties securing the front of the heavy coat as if his fingers were sausages.

"I was a better squire than you are," Robert said. "At this rate, I won't be ready until noon."

"My fingers are cold," Hugh said. "They don't work when it's cold."

"What will people think, if I'm late?"

"We'll tell them you were up all night drinking and carousing."

Giselle watched from her seat on a stool as Hugh held the mail byrnie so Robert could slip it over his head. She wished this were not happening. She wasn't fooled by these jibes. She sensed now why he had slept so little during the night. He was afraid. He didn't speak of it; he didn't show it. But it was there. He didn't think he could win against Eustace. She had wanted this moment with all her heart, and now that it had arrived, she wished she were elsewhere, for the prospect of revenge that had seemed so certain now felt remote. It had been a mistake to push Robert to this point, but it was too late to turn back.

When Robert had the byrnie settled in place, Giselle brought over Robert's sword. She fastened the belt around his waist.

"From the look of you," she said, "if I were Eustace I'd run and hide."

"I am a fierce one, aren't I?" Robert said. He cradled his helmet under his arm as Hugh draped the shield's strap around his shoulders so that the shield hung on his back. "Let's go frighten Eustace, then, shall we?"

633

The Outlaws

A wall of people surrounded the tent and campsite so closely that some were in danger of being pushed into the fire. They were people of all sorts, lesser gentry such as themselves, and ordinary people who could not afford accommodations in the town. They quieted down at the sight of Robert. Osgar and Burghard had polished the mail shirt in a leather bag filled with sand last evening so that it shined like silver, and even in the gray light he seemed to glow.

"We'll need to get through there," Robert said, pointing to the paddock on other side of the tree.

The crowd parted to make an aisle. Robert, Hugh, and Giselle slipped through to the paddock, where Osgar waited with the horse and Burghard held their lances. Osgar handed Robert the reins. "Give him hell, sir."

"That is my intention."

Robert led the way up the slope toward the town with Hugh and the lances just behind him and Giselle at his side, her hand on the horse's bridle.

"Watch out," Robert said to her. "He bites."

"He will not dare bite me."

Nonetheless, Giselle let go of the bridle. She linked arms with Robert.

It seemed such a long way up that slope to town, made longer and more difficult by the fact her feet were heavy with dread. Yet in no time at all, they were at the small gate leading through the town's embankment and palisade to College Lane. Gate wards were waiting for them, and they opened the gate so Robert and Giselle passed down the narrow street, by the church, to High Street.

High Street itself was blocked by a crowd. Small boys in the back of it alerted their elders to Robert's approach and everyone turned for a look at him. The clamor was so great that Giselle wanted to cover her ears. Robert had to put his lips to her ear so he could be heard. "There should be a platform for the king. They should have a chair for you there."

She looked into his face. She searched his eyes for any sign of the fear she had felt earlier, but he seemed calm, even smiling slightly. She wanted to fling her arms around his neck and hug him close. But she merely nodded. "God be with you."

"With us," he said.

She turned away with Osgar leading the way as the crowd slipped apart to create a pathway for her to the open space in the center of High Street. There, down by the guild hall, was the platform, its new wood yellow and bright. She marched toward it, head up.

The market occupying High Street yesterday had been swept away so that the wide street was roped off for the combatants. While the king was to be the judge, William Marshal was his deputy, and he had deputies of his own. They were identified by a white ribbon tied around their arms and by quarterstaffs. Two of them met Robert and positioned him and his horse at the east end of High Street.

Now came the hardest part, the waiting. Robert was always most nervous before the contest. Once it got started, he would be too busy for fear. But until then, he had to hold himself carefully so the people straining at the ropes and filling the windows of the houses lining the street could not see his knees shaking. It was easier to conceal the shaking if he kept moving, so he paced back and forth before the horse, swinging his arms and trying to look as dangerous and as eager for the fight as possible. "Let's just get this over with," Robert muttered to himself.

"What?" Hugh asked. "Did you say something?"

"I said, where the devil is Eustace?"

"Getting his hair done, I would imagine. He shows as much interest in his appearance as a woman."

"If only he fought like one," Robert said.

"Once you get him off his horse, you'll stand a better chance."

635

The Outlaws

"And how am I going to do that?"

"Look, he's going to want to spear you as if this was a joust. It's what they all do — all that riding at the quintain and the stories they tell each other about knocking people off horses. It's all they think of to do, at first, anyway. You need to be unpredictable. Find a way to get past the point and grapple with him."

"Get past the point . . . easier said than done."

"You know what to do, or you should. You're my star pupil. Don't shame me now."

"I'm your only pupil."

"That makes it all the more important."

"I'll give you a story to tell over the hearth on a cold night, don't worry."

"See that you do. I want to take some credit for your success. If I can't have money, at least I can be famous. Ah, there now. He's come."

At the other end of the street, there was a commotion in the crowd, and Eustace stepped into the clearing, recognizable by his height and long black hair.

"Do you see le Bec?" Hugh asked. "I don't see him."

"Probably off torturing someone. Now we only have to wait for the king."

A half hour passed before the king appeared. He mounted the steps and took a seat on the high-backed chair in the center of the platform. Giselle and Blanche occupied a bench to his left, and Eustace's wife Judith sat to the king's right, an empty chair away. Robert wondered who the empty chair was for.

The king held the baton signifying he was the judge, but William Marshal would perform the actual work. He signaled from the edge of the platform to the heralds beside the combatants.

"You may mount up now, sir," said the herald by Robert.

"Watch you don't fall off the horse," Hugh said as he handed Robert his shield and the lance.

"I remember that lesson."

Marshal waived to the fighters to come forward to the platform. They approached at the walk, their lances on their shoulders.

"My lord earl," Marshal said, "the king asks that you reconsider, and submit to trial by jury."

"I think not," Eustace said without looking at Robert.

"It is your right," Marshal said. "The king has also stipulated one rule. You are not to strike the horses. He sees no reason why they should be harmed. Understood?"

"That would be unsporting," Eustace said.

"Do you agree, Sir Robert?" Marshal asked.

Robert's plan had been to kill Eustace's horse at the outset, forcing the fight to continue on foot. Now that possibility had been snatched away. He did his best to conceal his dismay. "Of course. My friend will be glad to hear this rule. It's a borrowed horse."

"Lose yours playing dice?" Eustace asked.

Marshal looked sharply at Robert as it to send a warning about whatever reply he might be considering.

"What happened to my horse is none of your business," Robert said.

"Do I detect a touch of fear, Attebrook?"

"No, a touch of dislike."

"Only a touch?"

"Gentlemen," Marshal cut in, "enough. Return to your places."

Hugh held the bridle to keep the horse in place until the signal came to start. Robert's nervousness, meanwhile, had risen to the point that he could barely breathe, and he panted to keep from passing out.

The Outlaws

Marshal stepped to the edge of the platform and dropped a white handkerchief. Hugh released the bridle and stepped away. He said something that was lost as the crowd roared.

Robert squeezed the horse, asking for a walk, careful to keep his lance vertical. The stallion stepped out almost in a prance.

Eustace also came on at first at a walk, but picked up a canter.

Robert asked for a canter, mindful to keep it slow and collected. A gallop might increase the force of the impact, but it threw off the aim. Being a good lancer took many years of practice, which he did not have.

Somewhere about the second or third stride, Robert's nervousness evaporated. All he saw was Eustace drawing closer and all he thought about was Eustace's lance and his own.

Eustace edged to Robert's right. Had there been room, Robert would have gone right as well to keep Eustace on his left, but there was not and Eustace succeeded in getting on Robert's unshielded side.

They were close now, and Eustace's lance came down, aiming at Robert's head.

Robert brought his own point down, also aiming at the head, as both men twisted in the saddle and brought their shields over the pommels of their horses to cover their right as much as they could.

At the last instant, Robert dipped his point and brought his lance around from one side of Eustace's lance to the other, and bore down on Eustace's lance pole, deflecting the point from Robert's face yet able himself to thrust home.

Eustace ducked behind his shield. Robert's point glanced off, and they were beyond each other, wheeling for another pass.

As they approached again, Eustace kept his lance shaft vertical, and as Robert dropped his lance and took aim, Eustace brought his right hand to his chest so that the pole angled over his left shoulder. Robert knew what was coming and shifted his lance from his right armpit to his left just as Eustace attempted to bat down Robert's lance. Eustace missed and they passed each other again.

Robert changed leads and came sharply left, driving at almost a gallop, hoping to catch Eustace by surprise. He couched the lance into his right armpit, and braced himself against the cantle for the impact.

The lance head stuck in Eustace's shield. The pole bent, then snapped so violently that Robert felt as though he had been hit in the ribs with a bat.

The stallion carried Robert by Eustace and almost into the crowd, but the horse skidded to a halt that Robert was unprepared for, as spectators ducked and scrambled away from a possible trampling. Robert swayed in the saddle and almost fell. He spared a moment to feel embarrassed about his horsemanship, but it was a moment he really could not afford to waste. For Eustace had wheeled again and was bearing down on him: straight for him rather than off to the side as a sensible person would do, as if he intended a collision. It was mad, riding full tilt one horse into another, yet he bore down — and at Robert's unshielded right side.

Robert ducked over the pommel, wishing himself smaller as if he might shrink out of danger by sheer desire, feeling fear for the first time since the fight started, and spurred the stallion mercilessly. The stallion reacted with a great bound that took them out of the way of the collision at the last instant, and Eustace now had his own awkward moment against the ropes as his horse skidded to a stop while more of the crowd scattered, the lance point coming perilously close to a woman holding a child, before it swayed away as Eustace jerked the horse's head hard around.

Robert slowed his stallion to a canter as he rode away across the plain of High Street. He halted just beyond the king's platform and drew his sword.

There was a pause as Eustace worked the broken shaft of Robert's lance free from his shield. A patch of daylight

The Outlaws

showed through the panels: the head had gone all the way through and left a sizeable hole.

Eustace fixed his eyes on Robert. His lips moved as if he was talking to himself. It looked like he said, "Let's get this over with." His horse broke into a walk, and then a slow canter.

With time to think, fear paralyzed Robert. He had used up every trick he knew for the lance. None of them had worked. He doubted that what little he knew about fighting sword against lance would work either. Eustace would know those tricks and be ready for them. He needed something different, something unexpected. Then it came to him, a trick he had learned for fighting on foot. It was a crazy thing to do, but it was all he could think of in the moments available to him.

He walked his horse toward Eustace, edging it rightward with leg pressure to keep Eustace on his left. As Eustace drew near, he swung his shield onto his back, and turned away as if intending to run. He squeezed with his calves for a canter from the stallion, leaning well forward.

There was not that much room to run. The castle gates and the end of High Street were only a hundred yards away. Before Robert knew it he was almost there. He slowed the stallion to turn sharply left and glanced about as if in desperately seeking some escape. Eustace lowered his lance as he came in for the kill. He sneered as he sensed triumph just moments away.

Robert dropped his reins and parried the thrust with his sword in the hanging guard, hand high, the blade sloped before his face, catching Eustace's lance with his left hand. He gripped the shaft as the stallion carried him away, tearing the lance from Eustace's grasp.

Wheeling again to face his enemy, Robert called, "You've lost your spear, Eustace! What will you do?"

"I don't need that toothpick to finish you," Eustace said.

"Well, I don't want it. You can have it back!" Robert threw the spear, not expecting it to do any harm, which it didn't, for Eustace warded it off with his shield.

There was almost a pause now as they went to swords. They circled each other, trying to deny the other his right unshielded right side while gaining it for themselves, so there was a great deal of wheeling and riding in circles without a blow being struck, for simply beating on the shield brought no advantage and put the sword hand at risk of being cut off.

Superior horsemanship told in the end. Eustace got to Robert's right without surrendering his own. He threw a series of blows from behind his shield that Robert could only parry as best he could with his sword as he tried to back the stallion and turn him.

But Eustace prevented any escape by driving his horse's head over the neck of Robert's so that they were almost locked together; at the same time delivering a thrust at Robert's face, which he avoided by ducking behind his shield.

For a moment, Robert could not see Eustace, who took advantage by shoving hard against Robert with his own shield.

The shield blow knocked Robert off his horse, and he landed heavily on his back. Stars streaked across his vision. His lungs burned and when he tried to breathe, nothing worked. He had the impression of the stallion trotting away. He was glad he had not been stepped on. But then, as he started to sit up, Eustace urged his horse forward. With shock Robert realized Eustace intended to trample him.

Robert brought his shield across his chest just as Eutace's warhorse trod upon him. The full weight of the horse bore down on him, smashing him into the dirt, driving out what little breath remained to him.

As if that was not bad enough, Eustace yanked the reins. The horse reared and came down again on Robert's shield. The boards shattered with a crack.

The horse reared again. With Robert's last bit of strength, his shield arm shouting with pain, he rolled out of the way.

Somehow, he found himself on his feet, the shards of his shield dangling from his arm, which he clutched to his chest. Robert pointed his sword at Eustace, the only thing he could

The Outlaws

think of to keep him away, not that it would do much good in the end.

He fought for breath, backing away, while Eustace followed at a confident walk, a smile of triumph on his face.

Then Robert heard the crowd. They were booing. He thought at first it was for him. But he realized they were booing Eustace. They did not like what he had done with the horse.

The same understanding finally came to Eustace, too. He looked around at the faces in the crowd, at first perplexed, but then with a scowl. He dismounted.

Eustace stepped forward and lay on with one sweeping blow after another.

Robert could do nothing but parry as best he could and back away from Eustace's advance, for he had neither the strength nor the opportunity to reply with a blow of his own, since Eustace, well protected by his shield, presented no target.

Backing away was never a good idea, for you never knew what obstacles lay behind you. It was clearly Eustace's plan to wear him down and hope that he fell under the rain of blows or tripped on one of the many ruts in the street.

Yet Robert inched back with just enough care that he did not fall.

After some time at this and perhaps sensing the end in the increasing weakness of Robert's parties, Eustace threw his shield aside and lay on two-handed.

These blows were even more powerful and Robert could barely set them aside. Several clouts broke down his parry and pounded off his helmet.

On the last such blow, he staggered and the point of his sword fell to the ground.

It must have appeared to everyone that he was finished, for the crowd fell silent.

Eustace must have thought so, too, since he paused to gather his strength for the final blow. He lifted his sword above his head. The sword came down as he stepped forward, his face a grimace of effort.

Yet some strength still remained to Robert. He brought his sword up and grasped the blade with his left hand, heedless of the pain, to take the blow on the high shield parry. The blades clashed as Robert pushed Eustace's sword to the right and he hooked Eustace on the neck with the point of his own to throw Eustace on his back.

Robert collapsed on top of Eustace. The chin strap of his helmet had broken and it flopped forward on his head. He grasped the helmet by the brim and began to beat Eustace on the face with it.

Eustace clutched Robert about the waist and pressed his head to Robert's chest to avoid the battering.

Robert felt Eustace fumbling with his grip. Then Eustace found Robert's dagger, drew it, and stabbed Robert in the side. It felt at first like being poked with a stick, while the rings of the byrnie held. He tried to catch Eustace's hand, but missed as Eustace stabbed again. This time, the rings parted, and the dagger penetrated the byrnie and the padded gambeson beneath it — and Robert's side.

Robert gasped at the pain and bent over. Eustace stabbed once more, but this time, by some miracle, Robert caught his hand, tore the dagger from his fist, and tossed it away.

But it was over.

Pressing the wound with his elbow, Robert slouched over Eustace, who pushed him off and stood up, blood dripped from his nose and one eye already beginning to swell shut. Eustace tottered over to his sword, and picked it up.

Dully, unable to resist, Robert gazed up at Eustace. A few snowflakes settled on his face. He closed his eyes, too spent to keep them open even for the end.

The king waved to Marshal, who jumped from the platform and ran to the two fighters. He put his staff between them.

The Outlaws

"What the hell is this?" Eustace snarled. "Get out of my way."

"The king has rendered his judgment," Marshal said. "Your innocence of the charge is established. The combat is over."

"But I haven't killed him yet."

"And you will not. Back away, I said."

"It was to the death."

"There was no such arrangement."

Eustace's mouth twitched. He threw down the sword and stalked away.

CHAPTER 3

Ludlow
January 1185

Someone important arrived on the following day. Giselle heard the commotion in the yard, and looked out the narrow window of the chamber in the gate tower that had been given to them. A flood of men was emerging from the gate beneath her. At their head was a tall man with salt and pepper hair cut in the style of the Welsh, as if a bowl had been placed on his head and the ends of his locks clipped up to the rim.

At first, she had no idea who this was, but when Henry himself came out of the hall and embraced this new arrival as an old and dear friend, she knew he had to be important.

"I think Owain has come," she said, turning from the window.

"It's about damn time," Robert croaked, for he found it hard to speak.

Giselle peeled back the dressing covering the wound. It reeked of piss and mustard. She suspected the odor was meant more to cover the smell of rot rather than to ward off the corruption that made most wounds deadly. At least there were no signs of infection yet. She had been checking every hour to make sure.

"Should I make my will?" Robert asked.

"Why, are you expecting to die?"

"Just in case."

"You haven't anything worth mentioning to give to anyone. I wouldn't bother."

"Well, there is my armor and weapons."

"I shall save if for our son."

"If we're having a son."

"Our daughter's husband, then. As a wedding gift."

"This conversation has left me so cheered up. Why don't you go see what's happening below?"

"You want to be rid of me?"

645

The Outlaws

"I'm sure it's boring to watch me mend, or waste away, whatever is happening. Why don't you find out what the king and Owain are up to?"

"I suppose I should. I am not wanted here, apparently."

She came back an hour later with not one cleric, but two. The senior one, Hubert Walter, had a fine collection of rings set with red and green stones to compliment his brown habit. The other, a gray little man, labored to carry a folding writing table and stool.

Walter looked around for a place to sit while the other one set up the writing table and arranged parchment, quills, and ink pot upon it.

"Do you mind, my lady, if I use that?" Walter pointed to the other stool in the room. "My old legs, my poor feet. Standing is such a trial now in my old age. If you don't mind, of course."

"No. It's not my stool anyway."

"Ah, well, naturally, it belongs to the actual inhabitant of this chamber. One of the guard sergeants I suppose?"

This was an accurate guess, since the chamber occupied a corner of the gate tower on a floor where much of the castle guard slept. The sergeant had been moved into the common room beyond the door to make way for Robert.

Walter settled onto the stool and patted Robert's hand. "A close run thing yesterday, wasn't it."

"I'd have killed him if the king hadn't stopped the fight," Robert said.

"I'm sure you would have in the end. It was a good fight. Everyone is still talking about it. It provided more excitement than this little town has seen in many a year. Are you strong enough to speak now?"

"Strong enough."

"Good. The king in his wisdom asked me to take your deposition. He's worried you might die before you have a chance to give your testimony."

"Then we should not delay. I might expire at any moment. At least my wife seems to think so."

"Taking good care of you, is she?"

"Better than he deserves," Giselle said.

"Marital bliss, such a wonderful thing to behold. All right then, let's get on with it. Jasper, are you ready?"

Jasper, the little man with the quills, nodded. "Ready, sir. Just make sure he talks slowly."

"You heard that, sir?" Walter asked Robert. "Speak slowly and clearly so Jasper here can catch every word. His ears are so full of wax that sometimes he misses things. Do you swear before God that everything you are about to say is the truth?"

Robert nodded.

"Good. As I understand the matter, after your manor was attacked, you journeyed into the land of the Welsh . . ."

Robert was so exhausted by the end that his voice had fallen to such a whisper that Jasper had to prompt him to speak more loudly or repeat what he had said.

At last, however, Walter had what he needed, and he motioned for Jasper to put away his ink pot, quills, and parchments.

After Jasper withdrew, Walter paused at the door to the guardroom. "It is a pity," he said to Giselle, "that your husband is our only real witness, and now we are deprived of his voice. Such testimony has so little impact when read aloud by others. His grace is very displeased at how things have turned out."

"What do you mean?" Giselle asked. "Iowerth is not here?"

"No, I am afraid to say that he declined not one but two invitations to pay a role in our pageant. Feared for his life. Imagine that."

"So the only person able to speak of his confession is Robert?"

"That is the case."

The Outlaws

As Walter turned to go, she put a hand on his arm. "My lord! There may be another — no, two others who may be of use."

"Indeed?"

"My husband found evidence that Eustace kept a portion of the plunder for himself. He hid it at the Saint Augustine priory in the Radnor forest. Summon the prior. He can testify about this."

"And the other?"

"He is named Grelli. He lives in Shelburgh. He was at the priory with several members of the Shelburgh garrison."

"Fetching them will take time, assuming they can be found," Walter said almost to himself. "Thank you, my lady. I shall see what can be done with that little scrap."

It was put out the next morning that King Henry had taken sick, so the conference was postponed until he felt better. But after a day, whatever ailment struck him had run its course. So the conference which had excited so much interest at last convened. The remaining Marcher earls had finally come in, and there were so many other important people whose main business seemed to be following the king around that the great hall was hardly big enough for all of them, and when Giselle tried to get in, the guards at the door turned her away. She asked the guard to send word to Hubert Walter that she was waiting outside and wished to attend. The guard came back with instructions that she was to remain in the yard and wait until she was summoned. That stung. Her fate was to be decided and she wasn't allowed to hear how it might be done. She lingered at the windows, but there was too much noise to make out what the principals were saying and doing, although there was quite a lot of shouting now and them.

The conference broke up before the dinner hour, signaled by a flood of people leaving the hall who were not invited to dine with the king. Tables for these lesser folk had been set up in the yard, and they milled about, fetching ale for themselves and taking places as a large crew of servants brought in carts with tubs of soup and long boards with piles of roasted birds, along with baskets of fresh-baked rolls.

Giselle asked one of the servants to gather food for her and Robert, which she planned to eat in the tower chamber, when Eustace stalked out of the hall, followed by Judith.

He looked furious. He caught sight of her, but his eyes slid away.

She was about to head for the gate tower when Hubert Walter found her. "My lady, the king would like a word with you before dinner."

"Me?"

"Indeed."

Giselle could not imagine why the king wanted to speak to her. She was sure it meant nothing good, and the words she wanted to say stuck in her throat. She coughed, and said to a pair of the servants, "Please take this to my husband. He is confined to bed in the sergeant's chamber of the gate tower, the first floor."

To Walter, she said, "Well, then, my lord, where is the king?"

Walter opened the door to a chamber off the hall and closed it after Giselle. She looked around the chamber a moment to collect herself: tapestries of hunting scenes on the walls, a fire in a hearth of its own at the center, a long table pushed against a wall, and three chairs. Only one chair had an occupant, King Henry, who balanced a wine cup on his thigh. He was not alone. Blanche stood before him, a tight expression on her face.

Giselle advanced across the chamber. "My lord king, I am told you sent for me."

"I did. I have some questions to ask you."

"I am at your disposal, your grace."

Henry smiled. "I wish that were so of all my subjects, but many are so . . . fractious." He did not invite Giselle to sit, but

The Outlaws

turned his gaze to Blanche then back to Giselle. "Lady Giselle, I am troubled that your husband fought FitzWalter. I had given instructions that he should keep out of the way and not attract attention to himself."

"I had heard that, your grace."

"Yet he did not obey."

"I do not believe he had a choice."

"Well, that is curious. Why, of all people, would Lady Blanche choose your husband as her champion? I understood that your family and the FitzWalters were enemies."

"I suppose because we provided her aid in a time of trouble."

"So she says. Tell me, did she make this accusation with your foreknowledge?"

"No, your grace."

"And you had no intimation that she intended to name your husband as her champion?"

"No, your grace."

"Such things are usually arranged beforehand."

"This was not."

"Very well." Henry looked again at Blanche. "As for you, my lady, why Robert Attebrook? Such an unlikely champion, if you ask me. There are many better men in England. It's almost as if you sought to lose your case."

Blanche breathed heavily. "Eustace asked me to propose him."

Henry's eyebrows shot up. This was clearly not an answer he had expected. "Eustace did!"

Blanche nodded. "He had me held prisoner — all my charges were truth, even if God did not grant me the judgment. And Eustace threatened to take me again and kill me this time."

"A threat you took seriously, despite your new friends?"

"You have no idea what he's like, what he's capable of, to what lengths he will go to get what he wants. He murdered her father and —"

"— Lady Giselle's father?"

"I was here in Ludlow with my lord and Eustace attending the fair. Roger and Eustace had gone to a bear baiting, which was to occur in the evening just after sundown. An hour after sunset, I went out to conduct a toilet. I saw him return, go into his tent and leave shortly after with a bow and arrows. I recall being surprised that he had them because I had seen no sign he had included them in his baggage. He went back in the direction of the town. It was dark and he did not see me, but I could tell it was him. I was awake when he returned perhaps half an hour later." She added, "I wanted to see what he was up to."

"And what did you see?" Henry asked.

"He did not have the bow and arrows when he returned. In the morning, as you have heard, William was found dead, shot with an arrow in the field near the camp. The arrow was one of those Eustace took with him."

"So you have shown that he had the opportunity and the means," Henry said. "This is all very well, but why would Eustace kill William? A man always has a reason for murder, even if it is not one we all understand."

"His reason is clear enough to those who understand him. William's death was necessary so that Roger could secure the Giselle's wardship. Eustace's object was to convince my lord husband to force the girl into marriage with him. Roger fancied bringing her land into the family — you may recall that the manor once belonged to the FitzWalters and had been lost by sale to raise money for a crusade. Roger yearned to get it back, and he needed a patrimony to give to his bastard, since both then believed I could bear him children who might survive."

"You indict Roger in this as well?" Henry was surprised.

"No. I do not believe that late husband played any part in the murder. I can only tell you that he fancied the land. Eustace wanted to please him by giving Roger a means to recover it. He saw an opportunity with William out of the way, and took it. I was there when Eustace presented the

The Outlaws

scheme to secure the wardship and the marriage. It was his idea, and his alone."

"That is a very bold charge, my lady," Henry said.

"There is more."

"Good Heavens!"

"I believe he killed Earl Roger and forged the will naming him as heir."

"What proof do you have of that?"

"Roger was dissatisfied with Eustace. He always had been. The boy was a disappointment to him in many ways. Roger would never have named him heir."

"So you think. Perhaps he had a change of heart at the end. Men often do when death approaches."

"He could have. But I do not believe it. Roger still had hopes for another child if not with me, then Roger would have found another wife. He was not the sort to be balked when he wanted something, and he yearned for a legitimate heir. The facts are plain. Eustace made an unexpected journey to see Roger. Then Roger died while he was there, and this will was suddenly found. There is too much coincidence."

"Coincidence is not proof."

"No, but it is sufficient to warrant an inquiry, and distrust and caution."

"Caution?"

"Eustace is ambitious. There is no telling how far that ambition stretches, or whom he might destroy to satisfy it."

"Are you suggesting Eustace is a threat to me?"

"I don't know, your grace. But I would not trust him. He may not be one of the greater earls yet, but he is young and could well grow. Look at how he conspired to destroy Hafton. Look at how he colluded with Mortimer to use that raid as an excuse to make war on the Welsh so he could expand to the west."

"Of course you say these things because you have a grudge against him."

"I have a grudge, I admit, and it is well founded. Ask Giselle. She freed me from my prison."

"Yet you give me little to go on."

"My word is not enough?"

"Your word counts a great deal. But I wish there was more."

"There is a witness, I think."

"To this murder of William?"

"No, to the forging of the will, at least. And to Roger's last days. A cleric in minor orders who came into sudden and unexpected wealth, a little man named Gerard, who was even mentioned in the codicil. He did not deserve such fortune, and it was a great puzzle for those of us close enough to Roger to care about such things."

"Where is this Gerard now?"

"He has a little manor of his own south of Shelburgh."

Henry stroked the edge of his mouth with a fingertip. "Say nothing about this conversation."

"I am good at keeping secrets, your grace."

"So it appears. You have kept these for years, until it suits your advantage."

"If I have been silent, it is from prudence, and fear for my life."

Henry fixed his eyes on Giselle with such intensity that she could not repress a shiver. "And I mean you too."

"What will you do, your grace?" Giselle asked.

"You will know when I decide to do it."

Henry rose and went to a window. With his back to them, it was clear they were dismissed.

The Outlaws

CHAPTER 4

Ludlow
January 1185

King Henry tarried in chambers for most of the afternoon, consulting with one advisor after another. Every time the door opened and someone went in or came out, a buzz would erupt among those waiting in the hall as people strove to give meaning to each little event, even if all of it was rank speculation. It did not pass beneath notice that the king spent a good deal of that time alone with William Marshal. And when the sheriff of Herefordshire joined the two of them at the end, tension swept the hall, for these things had to be significant, though of what no one could be sure. There were, however, quite a few people convinced that they had the answer.

Giselle stood among all the gadflies, yet was apart from them, since Hubert Walter had told her to remain inside now. Few tried to engage her in conversation owing to the fact she was the wife of the defeated champion. That was just as well, since she was not in the mood to speak with anyone.

Just when Giselle was about to leave the hall to take the weight off her aching feet, the sheriff emerged and left the hall in a hurry. Shortly afterward, Marshal came out, followed by the king.

The heralds at the ends of the high table called for order, and the chatter that filled the hall subsided.

"I have reached a judgment," King Henry said. "Earl Eustace FitzWalter, please step forward."

Eustace stepped into the clear space below the table. Giselle was too far back in the crowd to see over the heads in front of her, so she could not see his face.

"My lord earl," Henry said, "you stand accused of wasting the manor of Hafton and of complicity in manslaughter in the deaths committed there. Of this, I adjudge you guilty."

The king continued to speak, but shouts from the crowd drowned out his words. The heralds again called for order to quiet the crowd.

"However, it is also clear to me," the king went on when he could be heard again, "that your purpose went beyond a grievance you have with your neighbor. While what occurred at Hafton was an offense against the crown, what you tried to make of it was far more serious. It was, in my judgment, treason."

If the shouts before had been loud, these there thunderous. It was much harder and took longer this time to settle down the crowd, and as the shouting tapered off, Eustace called, "How is private war treason?"

"It is treason because you sought to disturb my peace here in the March, to use it for your own purposes, to expand your own power at my expense."

"You've not given me a chance to answer to that!"

"But I have. These proceedings have been about only that very thing. That should have been plain to you from the beginning."

While the king and Eustace had been speaking, the sheriff returned with a dozen armed men, who made their way forward, but people were so fixed on the interchange between king and earl that their passage escaped the notice of everyone except those who had to give way to let them by.

The armed men arranged themselves behind Eustace, cutting him off from any support he might receive from his men and his friends.

Eustace looked behind as the armed men closed up, shock and surprise on his face.

"Therefore," the king said, "I order that you be placed under arrest while I determine your fate. Sheriff, if you will escort the earl to his new lodgings . . ."

The Outlaws

CHAPTER 5

Ludlow
January 1185

Hubert Walter came to Giselle as King Henry retired again to the solar and the crowd began flooding into the bailey now that the conference was over.

"What is it now?" she asked him, alarmed at his approach, since every time he had appeared to her nothing good had come of it.

"It seems you are summoned again," he said, not unkindly. "I wonder if the king hasn't taken a liking to you."

"If his manner at my last audience was any indication, I would think not."

"You cannot always tell his mind by how he acts. He would make a good mummer, you know. Don't tell anyone I said that."

Walter held the door for her, but this time instead of leaving her alone with King Henry, he followed her. There was another, older man in the chamber as well.

"My lord Chancellor Glanvill," Walter said by way of introduction. "You may know of him, but I don't think you have met."

"My lady," Glanvill said in a gravely voice as Giselle made her reverence to the king who was leaning by a window looking out at the bailey.

Henry came over and took a seat. He gestured to an empty chair next to him. "You may sit."

This sounded like a command rather than a courtesy, so Giselle settled onto the chair. It did not seem likely that Henry would pronounce some dreadful fate after asking her to sit. Yet his face was grave. The two witnesses, for that is what they had to be, were equally grave. So something serious was afoot.

"Now that I have found Eustace guilty, there is the question of what to do about your loss. I am thinking of awarding you one of his manors in compensation. Do you have one in mind that suits you?"

Giselle mind froze. The question caught her by surprise.

Henry smiled at her stammering. "It cannot be Shelburgh, though. You'll have to pick another."

Feeling the heat of a blush, Giselle said the first thing that came to mind after Shelburgh. "Harleigh. There is a place called Harleigh not far from us."

Henry nodded. "You shall have Harleigh, then."

"Thank you, your grace!" She could not believe this good fortune. A whole manor! It meant wealth and prosperity beyond all expectation — and a solution to the threat of the note.

"There is something I will require of you, however," Henry said.

At this "however," the blush left Giselle's face. She did not have much experience with regal "howevers," but she expected that they entailed a lot of strings and much suffering.

"Yes, your grace?"

"There is this troublesome matter of your marriage. I cannot have wards running around marrying anybody they choose without permission. Particularly my wards, which is what you were once you quit yourself of your marriage to the earl."

"I know I have transgressed against you, your grace."

"And didn't waste any time at it, if the stories are true!" Henry slapped the arm of the chair with a smile. "It is refreshing when someone readily admits a mistake. You have no idea how hard I often have to work to pry the truth out of people. What shall I do about it?"

"You will take back this manor?"

"No, I think not. I shall fine you half the profits for half the year. Does that do justice, do you think?"

"I don't believe your grace needs my satisfaction to render this judgment."

"No, I don't. But it pleases me to have it. And if it pleases you, you may go now."

The Outlaws

CHAPTER 6

Ludlow Castle
January 1185

Giselle touched Robert's forehead lightly so as not to wake him. He felt warm, which was a cause for worry, since it could mean the onset of fever.

She was about to pull up the blanket to have another look at the wound. She'd looked at it an hour ago, just as the sun set, and it had seemed fine then. But fevers were mysterious things. The wound could have got corrupted in that short a time for all she knew, and if it had, she did not have much time left with Robert, for he would surely die.

A knock interrupted Giselle as her fingers reached the hem. She let the blanket settle back, and groped her way across the dark room to the door.

William Marshal stood in the doorway when she opened it, his blunt features partly in shadow of light cast by oil lamps burning in the guard room. "Good evening, my lady. May I come in?"

"Of course, my lord."

"You've been sitting here in the dark?"

"We can't afford candles."

"Some can be spared for you. In any case, I need to have a look at him. He hasn't died yet, has he?"

"Not yet."

Marshal called to the guard room for a candle, but all they had to spare was another oil lamp, which gave off a thread of black smoke and an evil odor. He held the lamp on his palm and pulled the blanket back to inspect Robert's wound.

"How does it look?" Robert asked.

"I've seen worse. I'm afraid you're likely to live."

"I hope my wife will be relieved."

"I'm tired of you laying around demanding to be nursed," Giselle said as lightheartedly as she could manage.

"She's in a hurry to be home," Robert said.

"Well, it will be a week yet before you can attempt that."

"Quit making excuses for him," Giselle said, relieved that Marshal expected Robert to recover. A man like Marshal must have seen a multitude of wounds and could tell the bad ones from the good.

"There is a matter we need to discuss," Marshal said. "The king has decided that Eustace shall forfeit his lands to the crown. I will be appointed custodian of those lands, but I have many interests that will prevent me from the day-to-day management of the honor. I will need a deputy."

"You weren't thinking of asking Giselle?" Robert said.

"Not quite, although I don't doubt she would enjoy the task. No, it's you I have in mind. When you've recovered, of course."

Robert licked his lips. "I'm to be steward of Shelburgh, then?"

"I'm not sure that's the right title. You'll be a bit above the ordinary steward. But we'll find a title ponderous enough for you. The bigger the title the more important the man."

"Baron would be nice."

"I don't think we can manage that. Are you in for it? It will mean a lot of work and long absences from home."

Robert glanced at Giselle. She nodded. He said, "Yes, my lord."

"Good lad."

"This won't be announced until day after tomorrow. Can't pass sentences on a Sunday, you know. So keep it quiet."

"You've no reason to worry about us."

"That's why I'm here."

Reginald le Bec nearly jumped out of his skin at the bang of the shutters opening at a window in the gate tower. When he looked up, he could see the ghostly shape of a face in the dark frame. It looked to be a woman, so he relaxed and turned away.

The Outlaws

Le Bec and the two men-at-arms with him crossed the inner bailey from the chapel, where they had been hiding to the small tower just to the west of the tower gate. He paused at the well, which stood before the doorway. The bailey was quiet, not even the sound of the watches' feet scraping on the wall walk. The door was unlocked and unguarded. This was expected. The upper floors were being used as a barracks for part of the king's retinue. No one checked on their comings and goings.

The ground floor of this tower, like all the others in the castle, was a storeroom, filled with bags and kegs. Beyond them in a far corner was a pit where prisoners were kept. Le Bec had even seen it once years ago when he and Eustace had visited the castle as boys. He remembered it to be covered over with a locked trap door. Ordinarily, the authorities trusted to the lock and did not require a guard. But the prisoner in the pit was deemed too important to rely upon the lock alone, and le Bec's intelligence was that there was a guard. A guard who had the key.

He wished he had a light, but that might attract attention or alert the guard, for no one had any business approaching the pit during the night. He felt his way along the sacks and barrels, the musty odor of oats, a faint tang of onions, in his nose. He stepped slowly as if he was stalking deer, even though the ground underfoot was bare earth. Halfway around he heard the guard snort. He froze. The guard began to snore. Sweet dreams, asshole, he thought, but not without relief. He waited a few minutes, then edged the last few feet until he and the others were standing over a cot.

"Take him," le Bec said to the others.

The two men-at-arms seized the guard's arms while le Bec clapped a hand over the guard's mouth should he be inclined to call out.

He put the point of his dagger to the man's chin. "Quiet. Quit your struggling. Do you know what this is?"

The guard nodded.

"Good. Where's the key?"

"In me pouch," the guard said.

"If you want to see the morning, you'll make no disturbance."

The guard nodded as le Bec rummaged in the man's belt pouch for the key. When he had it, he straightened up. "Tie and gag him."

While the men-at-arms worked with the ropes and the gag, le Bec unlocked the trap door and pulled it up. "Eustace, off your ass. It's time to go."

"Took you long enough," Eustace said from down there in the dark. The ladder shook as he climbed. He emerged from the pit.

"Well, we had to finish our supper first. Some things are more important than others."

"What are you going to do with him?" Eustace asked, meaning the guard, whom the men-at-arms now held trussed and gagged between them.

"Well, I suggested that we cut his throat, but a certain someone ordered me not to."

"You mean . . ." Eustace said. He almost uttered Judith's name, but caught himself.

"Right. Said we should put him in the pit in your place."

"Very well. Let's not tarry then."

"Down he goes, lads. Don't break his neck."

The guard squirmed at the thought they intended to toss him into the hole. His expectations were dashed when the men-at-arms heaved him over one of their shoulders, and that man climbed down the ladder.

"There you go," le Bec said. "Nice and easy."

"Hurry up," Eustace said.

After the man-at-arms had climbed back out of the pit, le Bec said into the hole, "Try to get a good night's sleep."

He closed and locked the door. "With luck, they won't notice you're gone till well after breakfast."

"Now what?" Eustace asked.

"Now we get you over the wall."

"I know that. But how?"

The Outlaws

"Come on. You'll see."

Le Bec led Eustace into the bailey. He paused again at the well to listen and look to see if there was any sign they had been discovered. It was quiet, except for the wind. Still no sign of the night watch. He had been told to expect two men on the walls, the usual number on the night watch. In this cold, the watch often spent as much time as they could get away with sheltering in a tower. There was no reason to think this night would be any different.

The wall walk was accessible by stairways within the tower, but there was a wooden stairs across the bailey behind the chapel. Rather than cut straight across the bailey, le Bec walked slowly to the gate tower, then skirted along it to the timber building beside it which served as the inner stable.

They climbed the wooden stairs, stepping lightly should any one of them decide to creak.

Now came the worst part, the journey along the wall walk. They would be exposed here, and movement along the walk would excite far more suspicion than movement below, and there was a half moon in the sky that cast down a brilliant light. Le Bec had wanted to wait until the moon had set, but Judith had insisted that he free Eustace as early as possible so that he could be as far away as a good horse allowed when his disappearance was discovered. Le Bec felt confident enough to argue with just about anyone, Eustace included, but Judith scared him. So he had given in to this part of the plan, even though he did not like it.

Fortunately, however, the night was cloudy so that the moonlight shone intermittently as clouds passed overhead. Le Bec waited for such a cloud, then hurried to the north wall. There he headed to the west tower, which held the sally tunnel. He could have liked to use that tunnel, but there had been no time to steal the key.

This part of the wall walk lay behind the peak of the great hall so that they could only be seen by someone who happened along. A long length of rope had been concealed in the tower. One of the men-at-arms retrieved it. Le Bec lashed the rope himself to one of the crenellations, not trusting anyone to get the knot right.

"That should do it," le Bec said. "Down you go, old boy. Be sure you use only the strand on the right. Pull on the left one and it's a long fall."

"A horse knot, eh?" Eustace asked. "Clever."

Le Bec nodded. He'd tied the rope off using the same sort of slip knot used to tether a horse to a post. One end held securely; the dangling one had only to be given a gentle pull and the knot released.

Eustace did not seem concerned about the danger. He clambered to the gap between the crenellations and climbed down the rope.

Le Bec almost claimed the second place out of nervousness, but he ushered the two others through the gap.

When they were down, he climbed down himself, worried all the while that the knot might release by itself. But it held and he reached bottom.

Le Bec gave the left end a tug. The knot fell apart and the rope slithered down, landing at his feet with more noise than he would have liked. The men-at-arms coiled the rope.

"Where to?" Eustace whispered.

"There are horses waiting for us by the bridge."

Le Bec led the group around the tower and they descended the steep cliff that overlooked the River Teme to the bridge by the mill. They crept by the mill and crossed the bridge. The horses were waiting for them in a copse of trees at the foot of the bridge.

"A good plan," Eustace said as they mounted. "Did you think of it?"

"You can thank your wife," le Bec said. "It was her idea. The only thing that no one's figured out is what comes now."

"I'll think of something," Eustace said as they rode into the night away from Ludlow.

The Outlaws

CHAPTER 7

Shelburgh
February 1185

It was over a month before Robert felt well enough to make the short journey with Hugh to Shelburgh on the back of a horse.

Rather than travel the main road, Robert took a trail that was little more than a footpath that ran along the north side of the Lugg. This was Mortimer land, and he felt safe here, even though he was supposed to have nothing to worry about from the people in FitzWalter territory.

The track hit the road to Wigmore about a half mile from the river, and he headed down toward Shelburgh at an easy walk. He did not yet feel up to the battering of a trot.

The bridge itself over the Lugg was unchanged, but there were four houses now on this side of it.

At the bridge, the toll collector emerged from his shelter. It was lame Tom, looking older and more careworn. Tom tugged at his woolen cap. "Good morning to you, sir. We've been expecting you."

"My lord Marshal has been here, I presume?"

"Yessir. Came right after Earl Eustace's arrest. Left shortly after. Sad times these are, sad times."

"You miss the earl?"

"People don't like disruption, sir. You ought to know that. We like things to be steady like. New lords, that always means trouble for the little folk."

"I won't be changing things much."

"That's good to hear. Not even," Tom ventured with trepidation, "to settle the scores you left behind?"

"People are worried about that?"

"A little. They didn't always treat your family right, especially at the end."

"No need to worry about that. It's in the past."

"Good to hear, my lord. Good to hear. Lord! Who'd have ever thought I'd be calling you that!"

"Sticks a bit in the mouth, doesn't it."

"Oh, no, sir. It suits my tongue right fine."

Robert glanced at the river, which was frozen over, the ice covered with snow, but marked here and there where the village boys and girls had been playing upon it as he had done when he was young. "It's cold here. I'll have a blanket sent to you."

"Why, thank you, sir!"

The castle had changed out of all recognition from what he remembered. It was at the same place, of course, just west of the village, but its wooden palisade had been replaced by a fine stone wall which was coated in white-washed lime so that it seemed almost to be made of snow, and there was a grand stone tower on the top of the motte, round and squat with a peaked wooden roof.

The guard at the gate asked Robert's name before he would admit him, but hastened to do so at the answer. One of the tower guards ran across to the hall to fetch the steward.

A man Robert did not know clad in red, yellow, and a fur-lined cloak approached in a hurry as he and Hugh dismounted at the stable.

"My lord!" the fellow said. "I hope your journey was uneventful."

"As uneventful as a short three miles can make it. Who are you?"

"I am Beavis de Hindal. I am the steward here."

"What happened to Richard d'Evry?"

"He retired some years ago."

"And Earl William let you remain?"

"He said my continued employment would be up to you."

"Well, then, as long as you keep me happy and the honor profitable for the king, you'll stay employed."

"Very good, sir. This way, sir, if you please." Hindal gestured toward the hall. "If you had only sent word of your coming we would have prepared a better welcome for you."

The Outlaws

Robert did not move. He pointed toward one of the towers, the third from the gate, which Giselle had described to him. "Is that the clerk's tower?"

"It is indeed," Hindal answered, puzzled at the question.

Robert took off toward it with Hindal jogging to catch up.

"What are you doing, if I may ask?" Hindal panted.

"I want to see the accounts and correspondence."

"Now? First thing?"

"Yes."

"Yourself? You did not bring a clerk?"

"I'll use yours if I need assistance."

"Very good, sir," Hindal said, although it was clear he did not think it was very good. It was so out of the ordinary for any lord to hasten to the accounts rather than to retire to the comfort of the hall and its supply of wine and food, that something bad surely must be afoot.

They reached the tower and went in. Robert was no more than three or four stairs up when there was the thunder of footfalls above and two boys raced into view. Robert recognized them as the two children of the deputy castellan, whom he had seen with their mother in Hereford at the time of Giselle's annulment. The boys halted their headlong rush at the sight of him and continued at a much slower pace when he got out of their way.

The boy's mother looked down from above. "Dear Lord! Boys! Mind your manners!"

But it was too late for such warnings as they had already gone by and raced out of the tower.

"I'm sorry, my lord," the mother called down. "Please forgive them."

"Nothing to forgive," Robert said as he reached the first floor where Giselle said the clerk kept the honor's important documents.

Robert went into the clerk's chamber. The clerk was in residence, although not at copying anything. He was reading a book by the window. He shot to his feet at Robert's entrance.

"Our lord's deputy," Hindal said by way of introduction to the startled clerk.

"Good day, sir," the clerk said.

"It is." Although in truth it was cold and blustery. Robert looked around. The table was piled with parchments and there were several chests along the wall. "Are those locked?"

"The chests?" the clerk asked. "Yes."

"Unlock them. Then you can go. Remain within earshot in case I call."

The clerk unlocked the chests and, with a backward glance, left the chamber.

"You can go too," Robert said to Hindal.

"My lord," Hindal extemporized.

"Remember what I said about keeping me happy. It makes me happy to be alone. Run along and see that my friend Hugh gets enough to eat. That will be challenge enough for you, I'm sure. He has the appetite of three men."

"As you wish, sir." Hindal shut the door behind him.

Robert found the note at the bottom of the third chest he searched. He spread it out on the table and weighted down the ends so they wouldn't curl up. He read it over again several times, hating every word that was written on the parchment.

His plan had been to burn the note without anyone looking on. But now he hesitated to carry out that plan. He had not remembered until this moment that the note was no longer Eustace's property — it was property of the king. If he burned the note, he was destroying the king's property and depriving the king of income that was his. As much as he wanted to, he could not easily do it.

He stood over the note for some time, at war over what to do. Ever since he was a child, his mother had expected him to do whatever was necessary to protect the family. Yet now to do that he must commit treason.

Then it was as if he heard a voice speaking in his head, "You are the lord now. You can decide when to call in the note."

The Outlaws

Of course. He did not have to call in the note when it was due this autumn. He, as the lord's representative and deputy, could grant whatever extensions he liked. It would be repaid, just not until next year. It was not the right thing to do, but it would save the manor.

Robert rolled up the note, returned it to the chest, and went down to the yard.

Robert did not go to see the old house for a week. It took that long to get through all the accounts by himself so that he would have an unfiltered understanding of the honor's financial condition. He was not good with figures, but by the end he concluded that Hindal was skimming money from the revenues of the lesser manors. It surprised him that Marshal did not discover this during his visit. The earl surely had clerks who were quicker with numbers than he was.

He had Hindal arrested and ejected his family. No sooner had the family passed through the gate when Robert called for one of the grooms to bring him a shovel.

"What do you need a shovel for?" Hugh asked.

"What does anyone need a shovel for? To dig for something."

"Wouldn't that be undignified — in your situation, I mean?"

"Right. That's why you're going to do it."

"Me? Have you no concern for my position? It isn't as great as yours but it is high enough to be above the use of shovels."

"No one's going to see." The groom ran up with the shovel. Robert passed it to Hugh. "Come on."

Hugh's pout, however, forced Robert to have pity on him for what he felt as a humiliation. He took the shovel from Hugh and tossed it back to the groom. "Bring this along, if you please."

They went into the village. Robert saw a great many people that he recognized despite the passage of years. And they no doubt recognized him, but no one waved or offered any hint of enthusiasm at his presence.

They reached the little lane just before the bridge over the brook, and turned down it. Within moments they came to the fourth house on the left. It was no longer the last one on the lane. Another had been built just beyond it, where a pair of dogs roamed in the yard and the remains of the garden, watching Robert through the fence in case he came their way.

Robert stood in the lane and regarded the house. Like lame Tom, it was older and more careworn. The thatch was disheveled, like a man's hair after a long sleep, and plaster had fallen off in places to reveal the wicker and mud underneath. It was time to tear it down and build anew.

"What are we doing here?" Hugh asked.

"Paying a visit."

"You know these people?"

"No. I know the house, though. I used to live here."

"In that?" Hugh sounded shocked.

"The very same. We were happy here once, despite the look of it. Most of the time and until the end, anyway."

"And everyone in the village knows this?"

"That I lived here? Of course they know."

Someone in the house had sounded the alarm, and the housewife was waiting warily in the doorway as Robert pushed through the gate and crossed the yard.

"Mind the pig, sir," the housewife called as she came out with a switch to drive off the house pig which had trotted around the house to investigate the intruder.

"I'd like to borrow your house for a while, if you don't mind," Robert said, glad that she had persuaded the pig to return to the other side of the house. Nothing was more fearful than a sow who felt threatened.

"Whatever the lord commands. Children! Out of the house! Now!"

Three little girls ran out and clustered about the wife's skirts.

The Outlaws

"Thank you, good wife. We won't be long. Gentlemen, shall we?"

The people who lived in the house now were more impoverished than the Attebrooks had been, and the house was even more sparsely furnished: a table, two benches, one stool and a set of shelves against a wall. There was not even a bed as there had been. Instead, canvas mattresses stuffed with grass were stored in the loft.

The bed had sat in the far corner. Robert probed the ground with his sword where it once stood. After a few moments, the point struck something solid. It did not feel like a stone or a root.

"Dig here," he said.

The groom set to work with the shovel, and it wasn't long before he had uncovered a small chest about a foot long and half a foot wide. He heaved it out of the hole.

"It's heavy," the groom gasped in surprise.

"I should hope so," Robert said. He lifted the lid. The chest was full of silver pennies.

"Good Lord!" Hugh exclaimed. "Buried treasure! How did you know to find it here?"

"It is mother's savings. She buried it under the bed."

"That looks like quite a bit of money for a poor family."

"Mother was careful." Robert scooped a handful of pennies from the hoard and shut the lid. "Bring it along, will you? I'll take that shovel off your hands."

Robert went out to the yard where the wife was waiting, curiosity on her face. He handed her the pennies. "For your trouble."

"My lord! What?" She had a right to be surprised and astonished. Lords did not ordinarily throw money at peasants for a few moments alone in their houses.

"It should be enough to get you a new house."

EPILOGUE

February 1185

Just after dawn, a ship pulled away from the beach at Pembroke in the far west of southern Wales. She was small, no more than forty feet long, a Norse-style cargo vessel called a knorr very much like the longships that had terrorized the coasts of England and Ireland at one time, but broader-beamed. She had a crew of six, four pulling on the oars to bring her out into the bay. The captain, a young fellow no more than twenty-five with a wispy blond beard, a big red nose and eyes bloodshot from too much drinking the night before, leaned on the steering oar. He shouted to the man at the mast to be ready to raise the sail.

She carried two passengers, who sat on the deck beside the captain. The journey had hardly begun and already the passengers looked miserable, wrapped in their cloaks against the stiffening breeze that had churned the waters of the bay into a vigorous chop.

They were half a mile from the beach and Eustace had begun to regret his decision. He could see it was going to be a rough passage, as he watched the tower of Pembroke castle shrinking in the distance. He had taken this ship because the fare was cheap and the captain, a Dane from Ireland, was not the sort to ask questions. And she had been easy to board while avoiding the customs officials whose duty it was to check on all passengers leaving English land. All he and Reginald had had to do was throw on a worn old cloak and woolen cap, and act like members of the crew. He hadn't even had to bribe anyone.

This was good, since he hadn't much money. Judith had sent him a purse, but he needed to conserve the money to rent horses when he reached Cherbourg.

His heart lifted when he thought of her. She had surprised him. He had thought that she would discard him when she learned he had been deprived of his lands and position. But instead, she had sent the purse and a letter saying that she

671

The Outlaws

would meet him in Normandy, where she had cousins who would be willing to take them in. Apparently he had misjudged her. Perhaps even that flinty heart of hers was capable of love.

After their reunion in Caen, he had decided that they would go to Poitou and attach themselves to Duke Richard's court.

He had seen Henry's face, pasty and pale and drawn, and had realized the man did not have long to live. Henry must be well past fifty now anyway, an age when most men died. So Richard would be king soon. Perhaps not this year, perhaps not the next. But soon. And he was sure that Richard had taken a liking to him when Eustace had been campaigning in France. That, and a well-crafted story of injustice and an offer to serve without reservation should lay the groundwork for the recovery of everything in time. He had only to be diligent in service, outwardly humble and patient. He could be all that. He had done it before.

Once he recovered his earldom, he would be free to take vengeance on those who had harmed him.

Within an hour and a half of leaving Pembroke, the ship passed between Ann's Head and Sheep Island at the broad mouth of the bay.

The water grew even rougher here, for this was the sea.

Eustace found he could no longer hold back the turmoil in his belly. It erupted despite of his greatest efforts. He stood up, leaned over the side of the ship, and threw up.

He reflected miserably that it was a long way to France.

August 1185

Giselle went into labor on the afternoon of the last Thursday in August. Matilda, who had come out from London to be midwife to her first grandchild, recognized the signs right away and sent a messenger to Shelburgh to fetch Robert.

Robert and Hugh left within half an hour of the messenger's arrival, and rode through a night black and dreary from a heavy rain that drenched them on the way.

Robert burst into the hall to see Jean, his daughter Cicely, and Alice still up and warming their feet at the hearth. "Put another log on there, old man," Robert said. "We're soaking and need to warm up."

"It is cold for August, isn't it," said Jean.

"Is it over yet?"

"I rather think that it's just started. First labors usually take longer."

"Until they get the hang of it, eh?" Robert said settling into a chair.

"Don't be stupid," Alice said. "It has nothing to do with practice."

"How would you know? You've never had a child."

"Agnes and I were there when mother had Harold. She gave birth on a blanket in an alley with only us to help her, so shut up about it. It's nothing to joke about."

Robert looked at Jean for support, but Jean was studying the fire. "I suppose I shall then."

Robert caught Hugh's expression. He was watching Alice with undisguised surprise, probably that anyone would speak to Robert in that fashion and get away with it, and . . . fascination despite the scars from the fire that could be seen on her neck. He had not met Alice before. She, Jean, and Cicely had come out from London after Matilda, leaving Agnes in charge of the inn and of Harold. Hugh did not know any of them other than by name, when Robert had spoken about them, which wasn't often.

"I'm forgetting my manners," Robert said. "Hugh, that monster with the sharp tongue is my sister, Alice. She has a twin just as venomous. Alice, this is my friend, Hugh."

"How do you do," Alice said without much interest.

"I am pleased to meet you," Hugh said in a voice that squeaked rather out of the ordinary.

"You're French," Alice said.

The Outlaws

"Gascon."

"The same thing."

"It is not," Hugh said.

"Well, you're a foreigner anyway."

Robert grinned. "See what I mean? Alice, I know it's hard, but try being nice to Hugh."

"I suppose," Alice said.

"Yes, he may not be handsome, but he's going to be the steward of Harleigh, which will make him a person of means as well as a valiant knight."

"Your other manor?"

"That's the only other manor we have."

"What is this about not handsome?" Hugh asked. "I'm better looking than you are."

"He's right about that," Alice said.

"And," Robert said, "that will make him as good as an Englishmen, even if he doesn't talk like one."

"May I get you some wine?" Hugh asked with exaggerated courtesy.

"My lord, I should be so honored," Alice replied with the same exaggeration.

"My pleasure." Hugh waved to a servant. "Wine for the lady."

"I'm not actually a lady," Alice said after they were done laughing at what obviously was meant to be Robert's expense.

"From where I sit, you are," Hugh said.

Cicely looked over her father's head at Robert with arched eyebrows and shook her head, as if to say "Oh, nonsense!"

"If I have a daughter like Alice," Robert said to Jean, "I'll probably throttle her."

"No, you won't," Jean said.

"You'll be cursed with sons who disappoint you, who don't respect you, and who don't do what you say," Alice said, sipping her wine.

"I hope not." Robert returned his stare to the fire, thinking of Earl Roger FitzWalter and his relationship with

Eustace. That's how that one had turned out, and it had led to murder if Lady Blanche was right.

The conversation faded then, as the hour had grown late. After a time, Alice went to the cupboard for something, since the servants had been given leave to go to bed. Hugh went over to her. They were together, whispering in the dark, for quite a while before they returned to seats across the fire.

Sometime during the middle of the night, with the rain and wind rattling the shutters, Matilda came downstairs to the hall. She woke Robert with a touch on the arm. "Would you like to see him?"

Robert sat up, groggy. "Him?"

"Yes. Him."

"It's a boy?"

"That's what 'him' usually means. Couldn't you hear? He has the lungs of a bear. No girl could shout like that."

"I didn't hear anything."

"Come along."

"And Giselle? How is she?"

"Tired, but fine."

Alice and Cicely had awakened at this little commotion and followed Robert upstairs. He was about to object to Cicely's entry into the birthing room, but Alice said, "You can't keep Cicely out. She's our sister now."

"What?"

"You are thick. Mother's married Jean."

"No one told me that."

"Mother sent a letter about it. You didn't get it?"

"No."

"Well, it's true. Don't stand there with your mouth open blocking the doorway. We've a baby to attend to."

"Pray that I don't get in your way, then."

"Exactly right for once."

The girls went first into the room. Robert asked Matilda, "This is true?"

The Outlaws

"You find fault with it?"

"No, it's just a surprise."

"Get in there. Your son and your wife are waiting."

He came up to the cradle where the baby lay already swaddled. Alice took one of Robert's arms and Cicely the other.

"He looks a little squashed," Robert said. "And wrinkled."

"They all look a bit like that," Matilda said. "You did too, but you turned out all right. So will he."

"I'd like to hold him again," Giselle said. She was propped up on pillows, looking tired in the candlelight. "Now that he's washed and swaddled."

Alice scooped the baby from the crib and handed him to Giselle.

"What will we call him?" Robert asked as he sat on the bed beside her. They had tossed around several names but had not decided on one. Now they had to do so, since the baby needed to be christened first thing in the morning.

"William," Giselle said. "There needs to be a William in Hafton. The manor has been too long without one."

Printed in Great Britain
by Amazon.co.uk, Ltd.,
Marston Gate.